THE LIAR'S KNOT

By M. A. Carrick

ROOK & ROSE

The Mask of Mirrors
The Liar's Knot

THE LIAR'S KNOT

ROOK & ROSE:
BOOK TWO

M. A. CARRICK

orbitbooks.net

Copyright © 2021 by Bryn Neuenschwander and Alyc Helms
Excerpt from *Rook & Rose: Book Three* copyright © 2021 by Bryn Neuenschwander and Alyc Helms

Cover design by Lauren Panepinto
Cover illustration by Nekro
Cover copyright © 2021 by Hachette Book Group, Inc.
Map by Tim Paul
Author photograph by John Scalzi

Orbit
Hachette Book Group
1290 Avenue of the Americas
New York, NY 10104
orbitbooks.net

First Edition: December 2021
Simultaneously published in Great Britain by Orbit

Orbit is an imprint of Hachette Book Group.
The Orbit name and logo are trademarks of Little, Brown Book Group Limited.

The publisher is not responsible for websites (or their content) that are not owned by the publisher.

The Hachette Speakers Bureau provides a wide range of authors for speaking events. To find out more, go to www.hachettespeakersbureau.com or call (866) 376-6591.

Library of Congress Cataloging-in-Publication Data
Names: Carrick, M. A., author.
Title: The liar's knot / M.A. Carrick.
Description: First edition. | New York, NY : Orbit, 2021. | Series: Rook & rose ; book 2
Identifiers: LCCN 2021016583 | ISBN 9780316539715 (trade paperback) |
    ISBN 9780316539708 (ebook) | ISBN 9780316539722
Subjects: GSAFD: Fantasy fiction.
Classification: LCC PS3603.A77443 L53 2021 | DDC 813/.6—dc23
LC record available at https://lccn.loc.gov/2021016583

ISBNs: 9780316539715 (trade paperback), 9780316539708 (ebook)

Printed in the United States of America

LSC-C

Printing 2, 2023

For Kyle and Adrienne, who let us take over the den

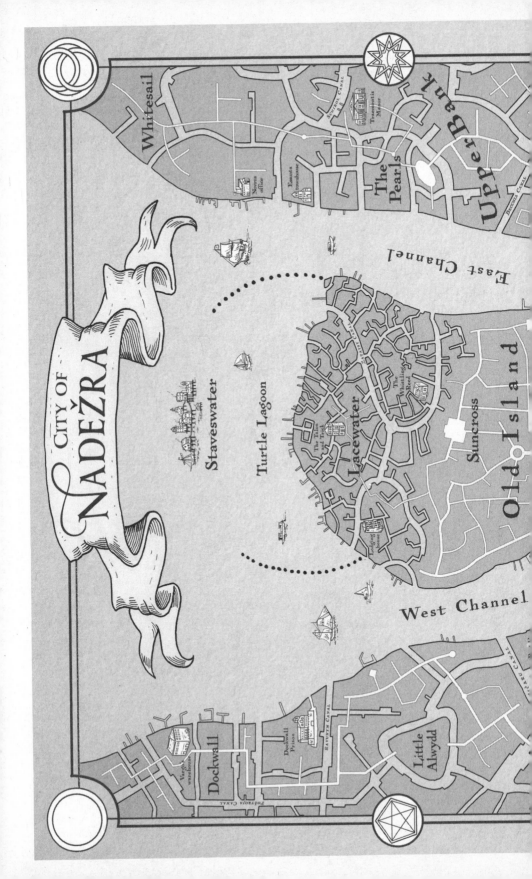

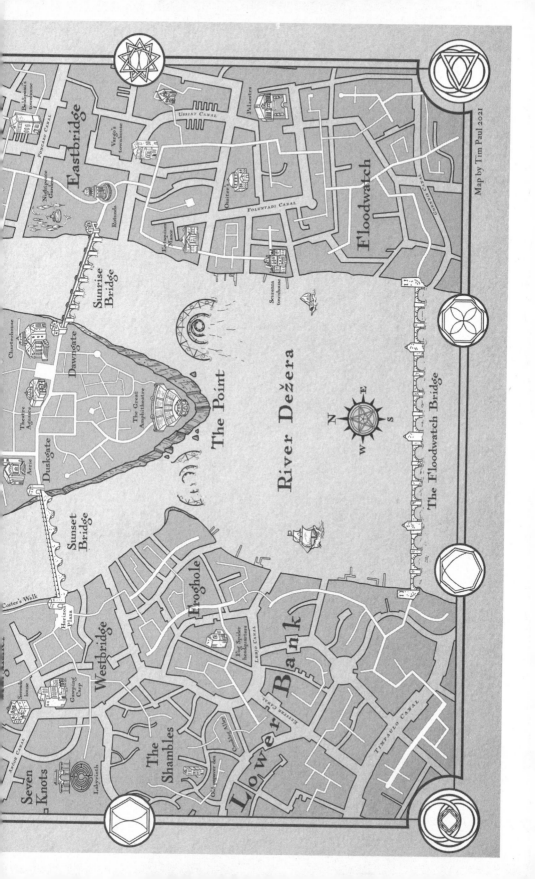

Dramatis Personae

Ren—aka Renata Viraudax, aka Arenza Lenskaya, a con artist

NOBILITY

House Acrenix

Eret Ghiscolo Acrenix—head of House Acrenix, Caerulet in the Cinquerat
Carinci Acrenix—his stepmother
Sibiliat Acrenix—his daughter and heir
Fadrin Acrenix—a cousin

House Coscanum

Faella Coscanum—sister of the head of house
Marvisal Coscanum—her grandniece
Bondiro Coscanum—her grandnephew

House Destaelio

Era Cibrial Destaelio—head of House Destaelio, Prasinet in the Cinquerat
Eutracce Destaelio—one of her many daughters

House Extaquium

Eret Sureggio Extaquium—head of House Extaquium
Parma Extaquium—a cousin

House Fintenus

Egliadas Fintenus—a cousin
Nencoral Fintenus—a cousin

House Indestor (disbanded)

Eret Mettore Indestor—former head of House Indestor, former Caerulet in the Cinquerat (deceased)
Mezzan Indestor—his son and heir
Breccone Simendis Indestris—married in from House Simendis (deceased)
Meppe Indestor—a cousin

House Novrus

Era Sostira Novrus—head of House Novrus, Argentet in the Cinquerat
Benvanna Ecchino Novri—her latest wife
Iascat Novrus—her adopted heir

House Quientis

Eret Scaperto Quientis—head of House Quientis, Fulvet in the Cinquerat

House Simendis

Eret Utrinzi Simendis—head of House Simendis, Iridet in the Cinquerat

House Traementis

Era Donaia Traementis—head of House Traementis
Leato Traementis—her son (deceased)
Giuna Traementis—her daughter
Letilia Traementis—her former sister-in-law, originally called Lecilla
Colbrin—a servant
Suilis Felsi—a servant

House Vargo

Eret Derossi Vargo—crime lord and upstart nobleman
Master Peabody—an unusual spider

DELTA GENTRY

Tanaquis Fienola—an astrologer and inscriptor working for Iridet
Agniet Cercel—a commander in the Vigil
Ludoghi Kaineto—a lieutenant in the Vigil
Facosse Dimiterro—high commander of the Vigil
Rimbon Beldipassi—a rising success
Quaniet Scurezza—head of her house
Idaglio Minzialli—a wealthy gentleman
Orrucio Amananto—a ubiquitous gentleman

THE STADNEM ANDUSKE

Koszar Yureski Andrejek—former leader of the Stadnem Anduske
Ustimir Hraleski Branek—his rival and new leader
Idusza Nadjulskaya Polojny—loyal to Andrejek
Ardaš Orsolski Ljunan—loyal to Andrejek
Šidjin Drumaskaya Gulavka—loyal to Branek
Dmatsos Krasnoski Očelen—loyal to Branek
Tserdev Krasnoskaya Očelen—his sister, head of the Crimson Eyes knot

VRASZENIANS

Grey Serrado—a captain in the Vigil
Kolya (Jakoslav) Serrado—Grey's brother (deceased)
Alinka Serrado—Kolya's widow, an herbalist
Yvieny and Jagyi—their children
Dalisva Mladoskaya Korzetsu—granddaughter of the Kiraly clan leader
Mevieny Plemaskaya Straveši—a blinded szorsa of the Dvornik
Ivrina Lenskaya—Ren's mother, an outcast (deceased)

THE STREET

Nikory—one of Vargo's lieutenants
Pavlin Ranieri—a constable in the Vigil
Arkady Bones—boss of the biggest knot in the Shambles
Dvaran—keeper of the Gawping Carp
Oksana Ryvček—a duelist
Fontimi—an actor known for playing the Rook
Tess—Ren's sister
Sedge—Ren's brother
Ondrakja—former leader of the Fingers, also called Gammer Lindworm
    (deceased)

FOREIGNERS

Diomen—a Seterin inscriptor
Kaius Sifigno—aka Kaius Rex, aka the Tyrant, conqueror of Nadežra
    (deceased)
Varuni—sent to safeguard an investment in Vargo

The Rook—an outlaw

A Note on Pronunciation

Vraszenian uses a few special characters in its spelling: *č* is pronounced like *ch* in "chair," *š* like *sh* in "ship," and *ž* like the *z* in "azure." The combination *sz* is pronounced like the *s* in "soft," and *j* has the sound of *y*.

Liganti names and terms have the vowels of Italian or Spanish: a = ah, e = eh, i = ee, o = oh, u = oo. The letters *c* and *g* change before *e* and *i*, so Cercel = cher-CHELL and Giuna = JOO-nah; *ch* and *gh* are used to keep them unchanged, so Ghiscolo = gee-SCO-loh.

Seterin names share the same vowels as Liganti, but *c* and *g* are always hard, and the *ae* vowel combination sounds like the English word "eye."

The Story So Far

**(Or, this is their past, the good and the ill of it,
and that which is neither...)**

Five years after poisoning her gang leader, Ondrakja, and fleeing
Nadežra, the half-Vraszenian con artist Ren returned with her
adopted sister, Tess, in tow. Their plan was simple: Ren would masquerade as a relative of the noble but declining House Traementis.
Once adopted and inscribed into their register, she and Tess could
skim enough wealth to set themselves up for life.

But none of it went as planned. Ren found herself caught
between the Traementis leader, Donaia; the Vraszenian Vigil captain Grey Serrado; the crime lord turned respectable businessman
Derossi Vargo; and the Rook, a vigilante who opposes the nobility.
To win acceptance with the Traementis, she had to gain them a new
charter to replace the broken numinat responsible for cleansing the
West Channel of the River Dežera—a magical structure destroyed
through Traementis corruption some years before.

Polluted water was only one of Nadežra's problems, though. A
sudden rash of street children dying from an inability to sleep led
Grey to stories of "Gammer Lindworm," a monster from Vraszenian folklore, while Vargo uncovered evidence of a new drug called
ash, which gave its users nightmarish visions with the power to kill.
On an evening later dubbed the Night of Hells, someone poisoned
the city's leadership and visiting Vraszenian dignitaries with ash—
and Ren along with them. But instead of giving horrible visions,
it pulled them all into the shifting realm called Ažerais's Dream.
Together with Donaia's son, Leato, Ren attempted to escape...but
they encountered Vraszenian creatures called zlyzen, and a twisted

hag Ren recognized as Ondrakja. Although the Rook pulled Ren from the dream into safety, ending the nightmare, the zlyzen tore Leato apart.

In the aftermath, Ren found herself incapable of sleep. With her con threatening to unravel around her, an unlikely set of allies came together to save her life. Vargo ultimately journeyed into Ažerais's Dream to bring back the missing part of Ren's spirit, restoring her ability to sleep. Because the Rook had discovered her con during her sleeplessness, Ren speculated that Vargo might be the vigilante and had saved her to protect her secret. She also learned that Leato's death was no accident: The decline of House Traementis was due to a long-standing curse—one that had somehow managed to strike Ren as well. Although the astrologer Tanaquis Fienola was able to remove the curse, its source remained unknown.

Ren, Grey, and Vargo realized that Ondrakja had survived the poisoning and become Gammer Lindworm, and that she was creating ash by letting the zlyzen feed on children's dreams. Before they could capture her, an agent of Mettore Indestor, Nadežra's military leader, sparked a riot among the restless Vraszenians of the Lower Bank. Quelling it caused a schism among the Stadnem Anduske, a group of Vraszenian radicals, which left their leader, Andrejek, near death.

But even the riot was only a cover for Mettore's true plan. Working in partnership with Gammer Lindworm, he planned to use ash to destroy the Wellspring of Ažerais, the holy site of the Vraszenian people, and then to blame it on the Anduske. While Vargo dismantled the magical numinat around the wellspring and the Rook fought Mettore, Ažerais's Dream transformed Ren into a masked heroine, the Black Rose, and she confronted Gammer Lindworm. Betraying Ondrakja a second time, Ren turned the zlyzen against their mistress.

For Mettore's crimes, House Indestor was disbanded. For his assistance in saving the city, Vargo was elevated to nobility. The events at the wellspring had proved to Ren that he was not the Rook…and worse, she discovered he had betrayed her. Vargo was secretly working with another nobleman, Ghiscolo Acrenix, and he'd sold her out to Mettore on the Night of Hells. Realizing that Vargo had also killed Grey's brother, Kolya, Ren vowed revenge.

As did the Rook. For the man who wears the hood...is Grey Serrado.

THE LIAR'S KNOT

Prologue

Three kinds of business ran out of the Attravi dyeworks in Frog-hole. There was the legitimate kind that stank of urine and starch, overseen by workers with faces steamed red and rough from the dye vats. There was the illegal kind that took advantage of the stench and proximity to the fouled West Channel to smuggle aža, saltpeter, papaver, and other illicit goods into Nadežra.

Then there was the business that came with no questions asked.

Vargo learned about the third sort the afternoon a foreign-sounding cuff came to the dyeworks.

His head was shaved bald like a plague victim, but he dressed as fine as any man from the Pearls, in a velvet coat dyed a plum so dark it could have been mistaken for black. The gaze that fell on Vargo when he darted forward at the foreman's snap was like a fen vulture's: dark and void of emotion. "This isn't your usual boy."

"Jaršin came down with the shivers. En't getting back up again," the foreman said, scowling at the rudeness of Vargo's predecessor, dying like that. "This one's solid, though. Running three months and he en't filched or scarpered yet."

Not that the foreman knew, anyway. Vargo stood straight and did his best to look trustworthy.

"I see." That black gaze narrowed at him. "How old are you?"

"Near eleven," Vargo said. It wasn't quite a lie; for many rookery kids, guessing took the place of knowing.

"Good enough." The man handed Vargo a tightly wrapped bundle, the strings webbing it sealed with wax, and a letter tucked under the bindings. "Eastbridge, along the Pomcaro Canal, number seventy-one. It's from Balmana and Schiamori. You're not to leave until he's tried it on, understand?"

No, but who could suss out the strange demands of cuffs? Easier to just nod. So Vargo did, and the cuff left, and the foreman sent Vargo off to the Upper Bank.

And if Vargo made a stop on the way, wasn't anyone going to be the wiser.

Even before he'd started running contraband for the dyeworks, Vargo knew the uses of steam—one of many secrets shared among the runners of Nadežra. Like reading. If delivering a message could only hook you a mill, knowing its contents might earn you a decira. Someday, someone at the top of the heap was going to realize the untapped potential of the runner network, and there wouldn't be a secret in Nadežra that was safe.

But for now, Vargo only cared about the secret of the day. Hunched in his squat on the roof of a dumpling shop, he held the letter next to a vent and waited for the steam to soften the sealing wax enough to peel it open.

"Who do you think that was, Peabody?" he asked the bottle tucked away in an inner pocket of his coat. He'd lifted it from a merchant last month, hoping for some zrel to warm him against the spring rains. Instead he got a baby king peacock spider no bigger than a pea, living in a little glass world of twigs and moss. Better than zrel in the long run, even if Vargo was the one doing the warming.

The spider couldn't answer, of course, and the letter didn't explain much more: thus-and-such merchant wanted some cuff's custom, and please accept this token blah blah. Vargo sealed it back up and went to work on the strings of the package.

A bit of wiggling got him a corner of midnight velvet, with onyx and smoke-dark topaz worked into the embroidery. Before he'd slipped into Jaršin's old job at the dyeworks, Vargo had run packages for a laundry in the Shambles. Before that, it was a tailor in

Westbridge. If they had anything in common, it was that customers rarely noticed a few loose gems . . . and if they did, it wasn't the messenger who took the blame.

"You'll be dining on the finest grubs in Nadežra tonight," Vargo told Peabody. Drawing his thumb knife, he carefully snipped the edge of the embroidery, taking his cut of Nadežra's wealth.

"Where did you say this comes from?"

The townhouse Vargo stood in was like nothing he'd ever seen. Books lining every wall, a desk messy with scribbled-on papers, and spiraling around the slate floor, enough prismatium to keep Vargo in porridge and dumplings until the day he died.

The cuff seemed surprised to be receiving anything, and baffled at Vargo's insistence on waiting for a response. "Balmana and Schiamori," Vargo repeated.

"And you're an . . . apprentice there?"

At the cuff's skeptical look, Vargo stood taller. His trousers were well-darned, his coat shapeless and oversized. Nobody with sense would mistake him for a tailor's apprentice. "Hope to be, altan," he said, doing his best to scrub the rookery stain from his accent.

It must have worked, because the cuff nodded absently and said, "There is no shadow so deep, nor ignorance so embedded, nor sin so great that it cannot be revealed and redeemed by the Lumen's light. But one should strive to improve oneself in *this* life."

His yammering faded as he snipped the last of the cords and midnight velvet spilled out of the package. Vargo had only seen a corner; the whole was like the starlit Dežera on a summer night, flowing through the cuff's gloved hands. Almost made Vargo wish he *was* apprentice to a craftsman who could make something so beautiful.

He wished even more that he could punch the critical frown off the cuff's face. "You should inform your potential masters that cloaks of this cut haven't been in fashion for at least a decade." The man lifted it to the light to get a better look at the embroidery. "And their attempt at numinatrian figures are muddled and ill-informed. These lines here—completely unnecessary."

Ass. Vargo pasted a stupid look on his face. "En't supposed to leave until you try it on."

The cuff glared as if a dirty look was enough to push his unwanted visitor out the door. He sighed when Vargo stood firm as the Point. "Very well."

Swinging the cloak around like a Vraszenian veil dancer, he settled it on his shoulders and fumbled with the two halves of the smooth enameled clasp before clicking it into place. The light caught the scatter of gems as the cloak settled, flashing and winking at Vargo like a fall of meteors. "Now will you—"

His words choked off. Coughing, the man clawed at the collar like someone had stepped on the trailing hem. His chalk-pale face darkened to a sickly purple as he dropped to one knee. The gems burned like stars.

"What did you do?" the cuff rasped. He caught Vargo's wrist before Vargo could bolt, his grip surprisingly strong for someone who lived among books. "Get it off. Get it off me!"

Vargo did his best. But the clasp seemed fused together, burning his fingers when he tried to pry it open. "Maybe if we cut it off?" he said. Panic beat in his throat. *He'd* done this. *He'd* mucked up some numinat in the embroidery, and now the man was going to kiss Ninat good night.

"Cut off what, my head?" the man snarled.

"No, the cloak!" When Vargo wedged his thumb knife into the collar, though, the velvet held like woven steel. The only thing he cut was the skin of the cuff's throat.

The cloak wasn't strangling the man, not if he could still breathe enough to berate Vargo. But something was badly wrong; the plum bruising his cheeks was burning into grey ash by the moment. Something dangerous and desperate bled into the man's eyes. "I have an idea—I'll need your help. Open your shirt."

Any other time, Vargo would have told him to shove his glove up his own ass, but fear and guilt drove him to comply.

Snatching a pen and inkpot from his desk, the man said, "Hold still." His hand trembled as he inked a numinat onto the skin of Vargo's chest.

"How's this gonna help?"

"Don't distract me." The man lurched over to a mirror and repeated the process on himself. Then, slopping ink onto a tiny chop, the cuff pressed it to the center of the figures: first his own, then Vargo's.

Pain erupted through Vargo from the hot core of the numinat. The smell of flesh burning singed his nose. Someone caught him before he crashed into the ground, dragging him toward the prismatium spiral laid into the floor. He blinked up at the cuff, whose ashy pallor had broken into a flush. Sweat shone on his brow. "I promise, this is only temporary. I just need you to share the burden of the effects until..."

He trailed off as he moved about, the ominously twinkling cloak still sweeping behind him. Now the whole floor was his canvas, chalked with an increasingly complex web of lines. Vargo tried to move, tried to watch, but he kept fading in and out of consciousness. When he reached for the brand burning on his chest, his hand bumped against something hard in his coat. The flask, with Peabody inside. Vargo clutched it tight to the burn, wishing the cool glass could leach away the pain.

Finally the man lurched to a halt and knelt, chalk in hand, straining to reach the outer circle so he could close it without moving from his place.

Primordial agony engulfed Vargo. Worse than any burn, than any cut; it felt like the flask had shattered, driving shards of glass into his heart. His vision went black. Vargo screamed. *He's killing me. He's killing me to save himself.*

And then the world was gone.

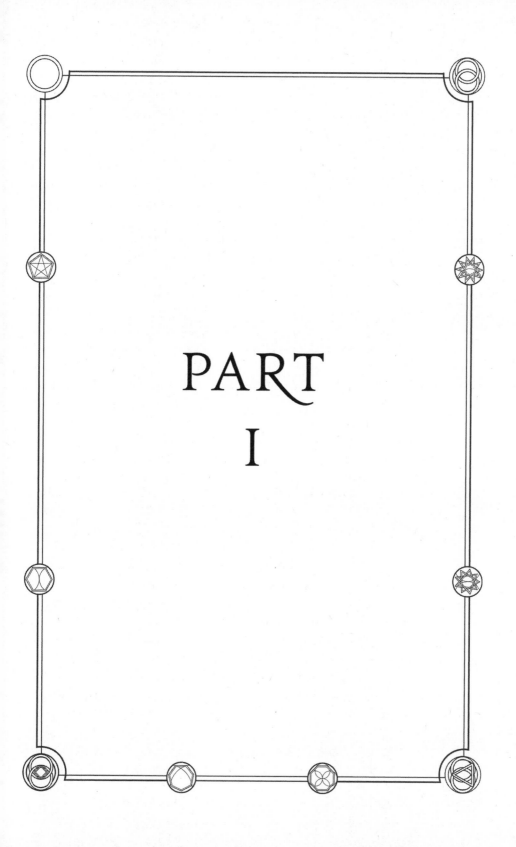

PART

I

1

The Face of Gold

Tricatium, the Pearls: Fellun 15

The precise elegance of a numinat reflected an orderly cosmos: one where each person and thing had their place, and the relationships between them could be measured to perfection.

Donaia Traementis knew all too well that order was often nothing more than a mask over chaos. The long scroll of the Traementis family register connected names with the lines of marriage, adoption, and descent...and far too many of those names were overlaid with the Ninat of death. For past generations it was only natural, but the truncated limbs of Donaia's family tree gave mute testimony to the curse that had haunted House Traementis in recent years.

A curse now lifted, thanks to the name Tanaquis Fienola was inscribing into the register.

Three women stood around Tanaquis as she wrote: Donaia; her daughter, Giuna; and Renata Viraudax—soon to be Renata Viraudax Traementatis. Ordinarily a registry inscription would draw a crowd of observers and well-wishers to ring the participants. Instead, the Tricatium echoed around the small cluster that had gathered, all empty benches and soaring arches of polished oak that gleamed like satin and smelled of linseed oil.

Scaperto Quientis was there as Fulvet, the Cinquerat seat that oversaw civic matters like adoptions. Utrinzi Simendis, who held the religious Iridet seat, had emerged from his usual seclusion to oversee the inscription itself. A handful of trusted servants had come in the place of family members. And the friends of House Traementis, all two of them: Sibiliat Acrenix and Derossi Vargo.

Donaia's house had done a fine job of alienating half of Nadežra, long before the curse began reaping them like grain.

A final sweep of Tanaquis's compass inscribed the closing circle around the newest register entry. "It needs only your mark, Alta Renata. One moment—"

Renata rocked back on her heels to stop her forward momentum as Tanaquis stepped out of the silver circle embedded into the floor and set the closing arc in place. Like a sluice opening, the power of the Lumen coursed through the figure, the warm welcome of honey in tea.

"There." Tanaquis dusted her hands, though for this numinat she'd used no chalk. "Now you may sign."

Renata glanced at the register, then at Giuna and Donaia. Once, she had hesitated to accept Donaia's offer of adoption. Once, Donaia had hesitated to offer. Now she nodded, and Renata stepped forward and signed the register with economical flourish.

And so she became family, as Leato had so earnestly wished.

Donaia hid her trembling hands under the apron of her surcoat, a tight ball of grief pressing into her stomach. Not even a month since her son had died, and so much had changed. Some of it for the better, yes... but all of it brittle and colorless now that her sweet boy's light had returned to the Lumen.

He would want this to be a bright occasion, though—a rare moment of growth and celebration, a new dawn for their house. "Welcome to the family," Donaia said to Renata as Tanaquis deactivated the circle and retrieved her quill. Giuna was already flinging herself at her new cousin with unseemly enthusiasm. Clasping her hands tight to keep from doing the same, Donaia asked, "About the rest... Are you certain?"

"It's only until next fall, when Giuna comes of age," Renata said over her new cousin's shoulder. "I should be asking you and Giuna—are you *sure* I'm not treading on toes by doing this?"

"As far as I'm concerned, you're welcome to remain heir," Giuna said softly.

Before Donaia could think of a way to scold her without embarrassing Renata, Scaperto Quientis interrupted. "Ninat willing, this precaution won't be necessary," he said, setting a sheaf of pages down on the podium abandoned by Tanaquis. "I hope to cross wits and disagree on civic matters with you for many more years, Era Traementis."

Donaia smoothed her skirts and joined him at the podium. By all rights she ought to resent Eret Quientis; his family had taken the Fulvet seat from hers when the Traementis fall began. But he never ground their faces in it—he'd even granted them their first new charter in years—and he'd worked with Renata to stop the riots during Veiled Waters the previous month.

She accepted the pen from him and smiled. "I'd rather work together, if you don't mind."

As she signed her name to the legal documents, Quientis said softly, "Once your heir is settled in . . . I know House Traementis sold its villa in the bay. Should you need a respite, you're welcome to the use of ours."

Her grief would haunt her no matter where she went, but Donaia had to admit it might help to leave Traementis Manor for a time. "Thank you," she said, equally softly. "I'll bear that in mind."

Then she stepped away so Renata could sign as well, finishing the paperwork. Tanaquis stood nearby, tugging her gloves back on. "Congratulations," she said to Donaia. "An auspicious day for such matters, and now that your curse is gone—"

"Not here," Donaia hissed. Vargo and Sibiliat both were waiting at a distance, but not so far that a keen ear couldn't catch whispers in the echoing Tricatium. Even the scratch of Renata's pen nib seemed loud.

Tanaquis pretended to smooth the ever-straying wisps of her dark hair. "I only meant to say that Traementis's fortunes should be on the rise. I'm happy for you."

Donaia caught her hand—the glove ink stained, as always—and gave it a squeeze. "Thank you. You've been a true friend to our house."

Better than some. Sibiliat was kind enough to Giuna, but even House Acrenix, legendary for their friendships and alliances across Nadežra, had been less than eager to help the Traementis during their decline. And Vargo…

The man slid up to them, smooth as a river eel and faintly resembling one with his scarred throat and his coat of river-green caprash wool. The gaudy spider pin on his lapel was no complement to the ensemble, but Donaia wasn't going to be the one to tell him. When he spoke, the polished courtesy of his baritone voice held no trace of his Lower Bank origins. "My congratulations as well, Era Traementis. I can't imagine how hard these weeks have been for you, but I hope you can take some comfort in Alta Renata. She is a treasure."

"Thank you, Eret Vargo," Donaia said, her diction almost as clipped as Renata's. His presence rankled, a reminder that he was now her equal, in legal status, if in nothing else. No ennoblement would ever erase what he was.

A fact that didn't seem to bother Renata. She joined them with a smile and a Seterin-style curtsy for Vargo, thanking him for attending. Vargo lifted her gloved hand from her shoulder and said, "I'm only sorry that you've refused all my attempts to arrange a celebration. Now I'll have to devise some other ruse to lure you from your duties."

"*My* duties?" The lingering touch of his hand brought color to Renata's cheeks and snapping amusement to her eyes. "I believe you're the one now in charge of a noble house—with no one to assist you."

"But much less business to conduct than House Traementis. I think it comes out even."

That, Donaia knew, was a bald-faced lie. Though it would be interesting to see how quickly the city's nobility closed ranks against the upstart who had somehow wormed his way in among them.

His flirtatious manner worried her. Renata was still a stranger to Nadežra; she didn't understand what kind of man Vargo was.

She trusted him, and so far their partnership had been useful... but Donaia would have to ensure that relationship remained one of business only.

"I'm surprised you aren't already neck-deep in applications from people wishing to be inscribed into your house register, Eret Vargo," Donaia said. "I fear my desk might collapse under the weight of them. Though of course, Traementis can afford to be discerning."

"Your house has always had that reputation," Vargo said with a mocking bow. "And your first adoption has set quite a high bar."

It was a skillful knife thrust, a subtle gibe at the old Traementis habit of insularity and a reminder that he'd seen the value of Renata before anyone else did, all neatly wrapped up in a single package. Donaia was glad when Scaperto approached and handed her the leather folder containing the formal adoption and heirship papers, held shut with a loop around the stacked triangles of the Fulvet seal.

Scaperto looked no more friendly to Vargo as he said, "This isn't the time or place for it, but we need to speak soon about your plans for the river-numinat charter."

"Of course," Vargo said smoothly. "Is tomorrow too soon? I'm eager to get started while the weather is warm and the winds are fair."

And the fox has gone a-courting. Donaia pressed her lips against the third line of the old delta farmer's saying and took Renata's arm to lead her out before Vargo could claim it.

He might have extended the first hand, but now she was Donaia's to protect.

The Aerie, Duskgate, Old Island: Fellun 15

Grey Serrado strode up the wide steps of quartzite and granite that rose from Vigil Plaza to the Aerie. He was back in his blue-and-tan dress vigils, the double-lined steel hexagram of his rank once more pinned to his collar. It was almost like the upheavals of the last few months had never happened... if one didn't look too closely.

That was Nadežra. Built on the shifting shoals of a river delta, the city lacked the feeling of permanence that grounded the inland cities of Vraszan. Like the dreams and the river it was named for, Nadežra changed while the mind was elsewhere.

But some places anchored the city, as surely as the Old Island stood against the river, splitting it into the East and West Channels. The amphitheatre built atop the Point; the Charterhouse, where Nadežra's laws were made.

And the Aerie, where those laws were—occasionally, when it benefited the powerful—enforced.

The Aerie's shadow fell over Vraszenians more often in threat than protection, but Grey had joined the Vigil hoping that something that couldn't be broken from the outside might be shifted from the inside. The crisis during Veiled Waters had damaged that naive hope, but the changes since then had breathed new life into it.

He'd dressed that morning intending to witness Renata Viraudax's inscription into House Traementis—an adoption he was still conflicted about, for reasons he couldn't share with Donaia. But then a messenger arrived at his door, instructing him to report to the high commander's office at sixth sun. Any other captain might wonder if such an invitation hinted at a promotion, especially after the service Grey had rendered in evacuating the Great Amphitheatre during Veiled Waters. But Grey knew there was no world in which a Vraszenian would be promoted past captain.

He smoothed down his waistcoat and entered the Aerie. His timing was flawless; the bells of the city rang out the noon hour as he presented himself to the lieutenant working the desk outside High Commander Dimiterro's office. "Captain Grey Serrado, reporting as ordered."

The old secretary was gone, swept away with the previous high commander. Grey recognized this one by sight but not name. The man nodded, without the barely veiled contempt many of the Vigil's lieutenants directed at its only Vraszenian captain. "The high commander will be with you—"

The heavy door of the office swung open. "—now," the lieutenant finished, without missing a beat.

"Serrado." Commander Cercel gave Grey a once-over as though worried he might have worn his patrol slops to meet their superior. He must have passed muster, because all she said was "Come in."

The first thing he noticed when he entered the high commander's office was that the shelves full of bottles of alcohol were gone, as were the Ghusai carpet and the smell of old wine soaked into it from years of abuse. The second was that Dimiterro wasn't alone. The man seated to one side of his desk wore not the uniform of a hawk, but the finely tailored silk coat of a nobleman, its glacial shade harmonizing elegantly with the darker blue of the Vigil hangings.

Grey snapped his heels together and bowed to his new high commander, then pivoted and bowed a second time. "Your Mercy."

He eyed Eret Ghiscolo Acrenix warily, recalculating the possible purpose of this meeting. The man might be Liganti and a nobleman, but unlike his predecessor as Caerulet, he had no reputation for loathing Vraszenians. So what did he want with Grey?

Acrenix waved him to stand at rest. "Captain Serrado, welcome. As I understand it, we have you to thank for the salvation of the Great Amphitheatre."

And the people who were in it. But Grey had long practice in keeping such thoughts behind his teeth.

"The lack of public commendation for your efforts is unfortunate, but unavoidable, I fear," Acrenix said. To his credit, his regret seemed genuine. "The mood in the city is extremely delicate right now. The plan to destroy the amphitheatre and the wellspring may have started with Mettore Indestor, but there's a great deal of negative sentiment against Vraszenians for their role in it, and in the riots. You deserve *something*, though. While I can't take official action as Caerulet, I can send a reward to you from my private coffers. A bonus for hazardous duty."

"I don't need a reward for doing my job." The reply was as automatic as it was brusque. Only when he noticed Cercel's wince did Grey soften it with a nod and a soft "Your Mercy."

"An admirable sentiment," Acrenix said. "The Vigil could use more people like you. But a reward isn't a bribe for doing your job; it's a reminder to myself not to take such efforts for granted. So for my sake, if not your own."

More people like Grey? That wasn't merely a different tune from Mettore Indestor's; it was being played on an entirely new instrument.

Cercel cleared her throat, and Grey realized his startlement had left them hanging in silence for too long. Nor had it given him any time to think of a way to refuse. Besides, the Masks knew he could use the money. Ancient callings might make for good stories, but they didn't pay well.

Bowing again, Grey said, "Thank you, Your Mercy."

"Don't thank me too much," Acrenix said dryly. "I'm afraid the true reward for competence is more work. You see, while Mettore Indestor may have manipulated the Stadnem Anduske into attempting to blow up the Great Amphitheatre...the fact remains that they *did* try, and they're free to try again."

These were dangerous shoals, given some of Grey's recent activities. "Though they've left Nadežra, the ziemetse share Your Mercy's concerns. Their envoy is making every effort to find the perpetrators."

"And will this envoy turn those perpetrators over to us? Or will they face the justice of the clan elders, as Mettore Indestor did?" Dimiterro's harsh tone said well enough what he thought of that.

Acrenix held up one hand. "Those were extraordinary circumstances, but we can't deny the ziemetse's decision to execute him was both earned...and useful." His wry smile faded as he turned to Grey. "Convenient as it was, though, that sort of justice isn't something we should allow to continue. Which is why I asked to speak with you. Your familiarity with the situation on the Lower Bank is particularly needed just now."

Ah, there it was. The expectation that Grey would be their pet Vraszenian.

Aren't you? His inner voice in that moment sounded very

much like Koszar Andrejek, the leader—or former leader—of the Anduske. Andrejek, who could barely move after the beating he'd taken from his people when he gave the order to stop the amphitheatre attack.

Grey kept his tone neutral. "You want me to hunt down the leaders of the Stadnem Anduske."

"This setback won't stop them for long," Acrenix said. "Easier to prevent them from doing something worse while they're fractured and scattered."

Fractured. Was it possible Acrenix knew that Andrejek no longer had control of his people? Even Grey had to admit the group posed a greater threat without Andrejek's idealism to leaven them. People who would cut knot and beat their leader because he showed a minimum of sense wouldn't confine themselves to printing broadsheets of dissident rhetoric.

Leaning forward to make sure he had Grey's attention, Acrenix went on. "I'm not looking for scapegoats to string up in Suncross. It may satisfy a few people's bloodlust to have someone to blame, but in the long run, it does nothing to root out the problem. The high commander suggested you could be trusted *not* to grab the first Vraszenian you hear cursing the Cinquerat over a cup of zrel."

That suggestion had to have come from Cercel; Dimiterro was too new to know anything about Grey beyond his blood. And as much as Grey hated the idea of being treated like the Vigil's pet Vraszenian, he was grateful to his commander for using him to protect the people who were just living their lives. Most of the Liganti and Nadežran officers wouldn't care. He was surprised—and surprised to be gratified—that Acrenix seemed to.

But also puzzled. Because while Caerulet might hold the charter for the Vigil, that charter restricted how directly the seat could be involved in its running. Mettore had toyed with those restrictions like a game of dreamweaver's nest. Was Ghiscolo no better?

"I'm assigned to Kingfisher," Grey said. "The Anduske could be anywhere. As for additional assignments, I take my orders from my commanding officers." He nodded at Cercel and Dimiterro in turn.

Cercel's flat look said Grey would pay for that bit of obstinance later, but Dimiterro nodded as though that was the only proper response. "Well spoken."

Acrenix said, "Indeed. But in this case, I'm afraid I've been unclear. I've granted a new charter for a special force, the Ordo Apis, to address the issue of insurgents within Nadežra. They won't be limited to any particular district, and they'll answer directly to me. I'd like you to join in a command position. Given your experience, I think you'd be well-suited to help with this mission."

The implications chilled him. The Vigil was flawed, with a tendency toward inefficiency, corruption, and abuses of power, but there were checks against that: good people within the Vigil who cared about their mandate, and Fulvet's judges to prevent people disappearing onto penal ships without due process.

Perhaps that was what Acrenix wanted in asking Grey to join— in a command position, even. Grey could be such a check.

Or you can be the mask they hide behind.

Much depended on Ghiscolo himself. Until recently, no member of House Acrenix had ever held a seat in the Cinquerat. His rise might have been a new shift in the hidden structure of Nadežra... or the culmination of something already there.

Regardless of the answer, the offer was impossible. Even if Grey trusted the intent of this charter, he couldn't turn around and hunt the people he'd already helped hide. His conscience wouldn't stand for it.

And he could never work directly for a nobleman. The mask *Grey* hid behind wouldn't stand for it.

Grey bowed his head. "I'm honored by your trust, Your Mercy, and grateful for the opportunity. I'd like some time to think about it. I have other responsibilities—"

"You mean your vendetta against the Rook?" Glancing at Cercel, Acrenix impatiently tapped his fingers on the arm of his chair. "Your commander assures me you haven't made improper use of Vigil resources to pursue it."

"That isn't what I meant, no. Though I do want the man who

murdered my brother to pay." Let Ghiscolo think that the anger burning in Grey's response was meant for the Rook.

Studying him with a gaze as intent as any hawk, Acrenix eventually nodded. "Understandable. I would want the same." He stood, signaling an end to the unexpected meeting. "I hope you'll still consider joining the Ordo Apis. Let your commander know your decision. I'll be collecting a roster of candidates at the end of the week."

With a nod to Dimiterro, he left. Grey trailed Cercel out of the office. She waited until they were alone in the hallway to say, "I suppose I'm not surprised, but I *am* glad you decided to stay on. Don't tell the others, but you're my best captain."

After the tension of that meeting, Grey was relieved to see she knew him well enough to know he'd already made his decision. "I thought I was your biggest headache."

She flicked his hexagram pin. "You really want to remind me of that right now, Serrado? We're having a moment."

"My mistake."

His smile faded as Cercel walked away. Grey's hooded friend had wondered for decades whether the Acrenix were touched by the corruption that threaded through Nadežra, but had never found any proof.

Grey wanted to believe in the possibility that they weren't. That for the first time, he was serving under an honest power.

But he knew better than to trust it.

Isla Prišta, Westbridge: Fellun 15

Although Renata was prepared for the knock, it still made her tense.

She forced herself to wait, sitting quietly in her damaged parlour, while Tess answered the door. The patchwork light slipping between the boards Sedge had nailed across the broken windows fell on a room mostly stripped of its elegance: the looters had taken all the small valuables, everything easily carried, and even some things that weren't. The couch Renata perched on was the only piece of furniture left in the room. Her erstwhile landlord had tracked down a few of the stolen items, but the shady markets of the Lower Bank were glutted from the riots two weeks ago. Even Derossi Vargo's web couldn't catch everything she'd lost—especially when three-quarters of the things she'd listed for him didn't exist.

Tess curtsied in the doorway. "Alta Giuna is here to see you."

"Thank you, Tess." Renata rose and smoothed the front of her loose surcoat, as if it were the fine silk she'd been wearing for the adoption earlier that morning, instead of plain tabinet. Half the pretense of her con might have fallen into dust, but the other half had to keep standing.

Giuna had changed into her usual shapeless and dull clothes, fitting for the day's work, and had her golden curls pinned up and covered with a cotton kerch. The nervous twisting of her fingers in her skirts and the press of her lips as she entered the parlour were new. They'd had little chance to speak in private after Giuna learned the truth of Renata's finances, and no chance at all after Giuna had forgiven her.

Her gaze flitted around the ruined parlour, from the boarded windows to the bare mantel to the broken remains of glass Tess had swept into the corner. "I thought Westbridge was supposed to be safe," she murmured. "Or did Indestor's people do this when they abducted you?"

"The riots." Renata allowed herself a bitter laugh. "They must have been terribly disappointed when they realized how little there was to take."

"Oh." After a silent moment of shifting foot to foot and looking anywhere but at Renata, Giuna lifted her chin and straightened her shoulders. "About that. I...here." She held out a wrapped bundle of fabric.

Renata knew, even as she accepted the bundle, what Giuna had given her. The weight and shape were familiar, and brought an unexpected hitch to her breath.

But she had to unwrap it, even as she silently damned Giuna for catching her off guard. The fabric made a soft nest in her hand.

Tucked into its heart was the blue glass bauble she'd bought for Giuna at the Autumn Gloria, five months and a lifetime ago.

"I thought, since you...lost...the one you bought for yourself, you might accept this one as..." Giuna's babbling ended in a soft exhalation. "As an apology."

"You have nothing to apologize for," Renata said, cradling the glass sculpture in both hands. "That falls to me instead." And to Sibiliat Acrenix, who hired someone to break into her townhouse while Renata lay unconscious in Traementis Manor, exposing the secret of her poverty.

"Then shall we strike palms and call it even? Otherwise, we'll be arguing all day over who owes an apology to whom, and I don't want you spending another night under this roof." Giuna nodded at the boarded windows. "It's not safe."

No, it isn't. But not for the reasons Giuna thought.

After they touched palms, Renata took her supposed cousin's hand in her own. *True cousin, now—at least as the Liganti count such things.* Her voice dry with irony, she said, "Shall I give you the tour?"

Ren's skin pricked as she took her new cousin into the service rooms, buried in a half cellar with only narrow windows near the ceiling for light. This was her true home, the place where she and Tess had launched this con. The one place in Nadežra where she could be herself: not Alta Renata Viraudax Traementatis, nor even Arenza Lenskaya, the Vraszenian pattern-reader who came closer to the truth of who she was, but *Ren.* A river rat born and raised in the Lacewater slums, trained in the arts of lying and thieving after her mother died.

But Giuna knew nothing of that. All she knew was that Renata had entered their lives hoping to live off the wealth of House Traementis.

Giuna wrapped her hands around her elbows, standing awkwardly in the middle of the kitchen. "You should have told us at the start. We would have done *something* to help. Well, perhaps not Mother; she still hates Letilia. But I would have. And...and Leato."

Ren had been in this kitchen with him, in the shifting realm of

Ažerais's Dream. Just before she led him up to the Point—and to his death.

It was easier not to think about that, to do what needed to be done without dwelling on the why. But then she would catch sight of the ripples—Donaia's hands trembling before she hid them in her surcoat, Giuna's breath hitching before saying her brother's name—and guilt dragged at her like a drowning tide.

If only she'd turned away when she encountered him in the nightmare. If only she hadn't invited him to join her at the Charterhouse. If only she hadn't returned to Nadežra in the first place. If, if, if...

Sensing the spiral of Ren's thoughts as only a sister could, Tess snatched a well-scribbled sheet of paper off the kitchen table. "We should get to work," she said briskly. "Master—I mean Eret Vargo's agent will be here to take the keys at first earth, and we've a lot to do. Alta Giuna, you're on candle duty. Make certain you spatter and scrape at least three layers. Alta Renata, you're on floor scuffing and window smudging. I'll start dusting."

She passed Giuna three candles, each a different shade of pale beeswax. Renata was handed a bag of shoes—not just the fine ones she wore, but men's boots and servants' brogues, picked up cheaply from a secondhand vendor because they lacked mates. Tess said, "When Sedge gets here, he'll help me shift the furniture and rugs. Any questions?"

Giuna's startled look flickered between them. She'd witnessed the close relationship between mistress and maid, but this was the first time she'd seen Tess take charge. In fact, apart from using the correct title and name, Tess seemed to have forgotten herself, talking more to Ren than to Renata.

Ren hated doing it, especially in the kitchen that had been their refuge, but she had to step in before Tess slipped up more. She put a quelling note in her voice as she said, "Very well, Tess. Shall we, Giuna?"

Flushing at the reprimand, Tess lowered her eyes and bobbed a curtsy before trailing them back up to the main floor.

For the next hour, the house echoed with more sound than it had heard since the looters broke in. So far as Vargo knew, Renata had been using the entire house she rented from him. When she left, it needed to look like that was true—hence the dripped wax, the bootprints, the marks on the windows, and other small signs of use. She was strangely grateful for the riots, which gave her the perfect excuse for having so few possessions to carry out. Nobody had been paying attention when she moved in, but Alta Renata was well-known enough now that her few paltry crates would have seemed suspicious.

Giuna was helping her heave the mattress up to the bedroom when Sedge's rough voice came from below.

"Perhaps we could let your footman take over?" Giuna asked, out of breath and blotting sweat from her brow with her sleeve. Her gaze snagged on her bare hand. "Oh, my gloves!" She darted across the entry hall and snatched them from a sideboard, yanking them on before she could be caught half-dressed—leaving Renata halfway up the stairs, clutching at the top of the mattress to keep it from sliding back down.

The weight lessened before her grip failed. "I got you, alta. Fine lady like you en't supposed to do this sort of thing."

With Giuna safely obscured by the mattress and Sedge, Ren was free to give him an ironic look. He'd said that kind of thing sometimes when they were Fingers together, children in Ondrakja's gang, faking the manners of fancy cuffs. Now she *was* a fine lady—by law and by lie.

"With one hand, Master Sedge?" she asked, arching a brow at the wrist Ondrakja had snapped, bound with an imbued brace of Tess's making. "I think this 'fine lady' is at least as useful as you are."

He grimaced at her, and together they got the mattress up into the bedroom. Sounds from downstairs told Ren that Tess had Giuna busy for the moment, so she risked asking in a low voice, "Any luck with Vargo?"

"If by luck you mean he en't put anyone on me yet, then I'm swimming in Quarat's own blessings." Sedge rested his corner of the mattress on the floor, rubbing the pale stripe around his wrist where his knot bracelet had been. The one cut after Sedge chose to protect Ren over his own boss. "Nobody will talk to me for fear it'll get back to Vargo. Even if I somehow crawl back in, I'll just be saddled with scut work. Only way I'm getting close enough to know Vargo's business is if I save his Lig-spitted ass. *Again.*"

Ren was tempted to arrange a chance. The scabs and bruises from the beating the Fog Spiders had given Sedge were mostly healed by now, but she couldn't look at their remnants without feeling cold anger. Vargo's people had hurt her brother, and she wanted to hurt them back.

The best way she could do that, though, was by getting Sedge into a position where he could keep an eye on Vargo. And by smiling at the man as if she still trusted him, the way he'd lured her into doing before. Only then could she figure out his true game...and how to destroy it.

"I know that look." Sedge lifted his end high enough to make her stumble. "That look gets me in trouble."

"I've gotten you in enough trouble," Ren murmured, heaving the mattress onto the frame. Not just with Vargo, but long before that.

Sedge's light touch to the inside of her wrist stopped her from shoving the mattress into place. The skin there bore a faint scar: the mark of their kinship, sworn with blood in the Vraszenian way. Sedge had a scar to match, and so did Tess. His grip was loose, his tug gentle enough for her to resist if she wanted.

She let herself be folded in his arms, trusting that Tess would make enough noise to warn them if Giuna came up the stairs. "Got me out of just as much," Sedge said, his voice even rougher than usual. "Weren't you that got me severed and beat. That was my choice, and I already told you I'd choose it again. So stop dragging it around. Fine lady like you shouldn't carry that weight—might sprain something."

It made Ren laugh a little, as Sedge intended. A moment later Giuna did come up the stairs, and together they finished their work on the house, and Renata went off to Traementis Manor and a fine lady's life.

Isla Traementis, the Pearls: Fellun 15

Donaia hadn't given Renata the set of chambers normally allotted to the heir. Those had been Leato's, and Renata would have refused them if Donaia had offered. Instead she was in a suite intended for an honored guest—back when the Traementis could afford guests.

Once she would have taken that as a calculated insult on Donaia's part. But she understood: They were the nicest rooms Traementis Manor had to offer after the heir's suite and Donaia's own, the bedding and window dressings of silver and teal silk faille, the walls paneled in pale birch over numinata meant to keep the room temperate year-round. And she didn't mind being on the guest side of the manor, away from Donaia and Giuna.

Her new quarters even had a bath. And not just a hip bath, but a tub big enough for her whole body, in a special tiled chamber off her bedroom. Never in her life had Ren been fully immersed in clean water. She found the sensation both luxurious and profoundly strange, as if she suddenly knew what it felt like to be a tea flower.

Tess chattered on about servant gossip as she mopped out the tub where Renata had first scrubbed down, Liganti style, before stepping into the soaking tub. The heated water was easing the dull ache in Ren's lower back. She almost slopped some of it out of the tub when she realized she could finally afford something that had seemed wildly out of reach before: a contraceptive numinat, which would also suppress her monthly courses.

She swallowed that thought before it could come out of her mouth. Not just because she'd been about to speak in her Vraszenian accent, but because the servants would be shocked to learn that the supposedly wealthy Alta Renata didn't already have a contraceptive charm pierced into her navel.

"—and Suilis says to him, 'You should be a skiffer instead of a footman, as obsessed as you are with your pole.' Fair robbed him of all his breath for bragging."

Tess's giggle faded into silence when Renata didn't respond in kind. Setting mop and toweling aside, she sank onto the bathing stool in a puff of skirts. "You're that quiet this evening. I thought you'd be happy. Or leastwise relieved it's all over."

"The riots and the troubles with Indestor? Yes, certainly." She answered in her Seterin accent, and held Tess's gaze when their eyes met. With one dripping hand she gestured toward the door. Servants came in and out of nobles' chambers all the time. There was no reason one would be in her bedroom now, but the walls in this old manor were thin. She couldn't take that risk—couldn't relax into herself on the assumption that nobody would see or hear.

Part of what made Tess such a bad liar was that her skin was always striving to match her hair; every emotion flushed more red to her freckled cheeks. She covered them now, then her mouth, as though she could catch the words that had already gushed forth. She stumbled to her feet and into a quick servant's bob. "Begging your pardon, alta. Here's me going on and disrupting your quiet."

Then she sat again and spoke in a barely audible voice. "What do you want to do? We can't keep at this all the time. Even odds which of us will snap first."

It wouldn't be Ren. It *couldn't* be Ren. She was legally a noblewoman now, and therefore couldn't be tried for the crime of impersonating a noble...but that didn't mean she couldn't suffer other consequences if the truth came out. For at least the next five months, she was bound by numinatria and her word to be a Traementis. A role she'd have to play at all times, waking and sleeping.

Even with Tess.

That realization tangled her voice, so that her whisper came out in a dreadful mixture of accents, neither Seterin nor Vraszenian. "Tess...you wanted a dressmaker's shop. You can have one now. There's no need for you to be trapped here."

The look Tess gave her was almost as fierce as one of her

tongue-blistering curses. "Well, there's me out five mills, for clearly you're the one whose wits went a-begging. As though I'd leave you a fox among the hounds that you thought were chickens." She grimaced at her tangled metaphor. "Besides, I'll have more success if you lend out my services to a few people. Cuffs pay as much for exclusivity as they do for quality. I'm more worried about you."

"I'll be fine," Ren said, now securely in Renata's accent. If Tess could make the best of this, how could Ren be the one to complain?

Such confidence was harder to maintain after Tess bundled her out of the tub and left her to sleep. The bed was too soft, and too empty; for months she'd slept on a pallet in front of the kitchen fire, with her sister only a breath away. But now Tess was in the servants' quarters, and Ren was alone—except for her nightmares.

Gammer Lindworm. Mettore Indestor. The horrifying days of her sleeplessness, when dream and waking life had twisted into one. The Night of Hells, her mother burning, the clan animals hunting her through the streets. Ash writhing through her blood and bone.

The zlyzen, tearing into Leato, over and over again.

Ren woke tangled in sweat-soaked sheets, but this time there was no Tess to brush the damp hair from her face and murmur something reassuring in sleepy, impenetrable Ganllechyn dialect. Clawing her way out of the covers, Ren curled into a huddle with her back against the headboard, knees up to protect her belly as though the zlyzen might reach out from nightmare to claw her in the waking world.

During the day, she could do her best to forget Leato's death. But every night she relived it: the zlyzen's hunger, his screams.

Her helplessness to save him.

"I'm trying," she whispered to the darkness, scraping away tears. "I'm trying to help them." It was the least she owed his family for abandoning him to save her own life.

A creak and groan came in response. The house settling, she told herself, but her gaze raked the shadows for any twisted, burnt-bone forms lurking there.

Lay a red thread around your bed. But Renata Viraudax Traementatis couldn't indulge in Vraszenian superstition.

The suite of rooms had a balcony, overlooking a side garden. A neglected garden these days—no doubt Donaia would see to that eventually. For now, it suited Ren just fine; all she cared about was fresh air.

When she pulled the curtains aside to open the balcony doors, though, she froze.

A small corner of white projected between them. With careful fingers she pulled it through, unfolding it to find...a blank scrap of paper.

That seemed very improbable.

Rich cuffs lit their houses with numinatrian stones that didn't risk burning the place down. But there was incense to sweeten the air, and a tiny numinat that set aflame whatever was placed inside it; Ren used that to light a stick of incense, then passed the paper over the fire until its hidden message manifested like a brown ghost.

R,

Thanks to "the boss of the biggest knot in the Shambles," the Black Rose's popularity has eclipsed even my own among Vraszenian audiences. The ziemetse wish to speak to her about matters I think would interest you.

Many titles have been attributed to me over the years, but I never expected to add "messenger boy" to the list. Perhaps you can find a different go-between to make arrangements. Arkady Bones seems resourceful and <u>very</u> enthusiastic.

Your servant,
R.

Ren slid down the wall with a breathless laugh. She hadn't realized the fame of the "Black Rose" had spread so far. Or that the Rook would stoop to leaving a message wedged into her balcony doors—not after how they'd parted. *Your servant*, indeed.

The Black Rose had been an emergency measure, a disguise

pulled from Ažerais's Dream to get her past Grey Serrado at the amphitheatre. She hadn't expected that guise to gain a name, much less notoriety.

She hadn't expected the mask to remain in her hand when the leather petals of armor had faded.

It was tucked into the back of a top shelf in her wardrobe. Ren had to stand on a chair to retrieve it: a piece of rose-patterned lace, cut along the edges of petals and buds. She climbed down and let it slide through her fingers, hesitating.

Then she lifted it to her face.

Black material flowed over her body, just as it had before: silk and leather, layered like petals, gloves and boots and all. Not an illusion; it was solid and real. A gift from Ažerais—one she was apparently meant to keep.

To *use*.

"Fine," Ren whispered in the darkness. "I guess we're doing this."

2

Lark Aloft

After the death of Kaius Sifigno, the Tyrant of Nadežra, the Cinquerat had torn down his palace and built a park on the grounds, intending it to be an exclusive precinct for the leaders of the city to disport themselves. Over the years its exclusivity had declined, along with its reputation, and the Gardens of Peaceful Night became Nightpeace Gardens.

Territory Ren had worked more than once in her days as a Finger. It was the perfect hunting ground for anyone who could fake wealth and gentility enough to pass scrutiny.

With spring well underway, the paths Giuna guided her down were bordered with a restrained riot of color, the landscaping cultivated with as much care as Tess gave to her sewing. It was a maze of small islets, the larger ones boasting tiled plazas for dancing and duels, the smaller holding jugglers, tumblers, patterners, and puppet shows. Arbors and pergolas winding with climbing honeysuckle and sweet pea provided aromatic shelter from the sun during the day and shadows for evening trysts—not all of them between the city's elites. Nadežra's night-pieces took their name from the gardens where many of them plied their trade.

Renata wondered if the gardens were especially busy tonight, or if it was only crowded in their vicinity. No sooner had she and Giuna set slipper onto the first dance plaza than they were accosted by people she'd only met in passing—mostly delta gentry, but also some from noble houses. The sort of people whose names were so close to the margins of their family registers, they were in danger of falling off the edge.

"Is your arm still attached?" Giuna asked as Renata fled the dance square and the clutch of the enthusiastic seventh son of a rice merchant. "I'm not certain about my toes."

Giuna wore the delicate pink-and-gold ensemble that Tess had made for the doomed Coscanum-Indestor betrothal, while Renata's underdress and surcoat were layered river greens. Together, they looked like wildflowers springing from the reeds—catching the eye of many, and making a splendid advertisement for the rise of House Traementis.

"I think Mede Galbiondi might turn his family millstones himself," Renata said, only half in jest. She rotated her aching shoulder and pressed her fingers into the muscle to massage out the strain.

"It almost makes you miss Parma, doesn't it?" Giuna used the excuse of reclaiming her wine from Tess to avoid another hopeful applicant's gaze. "Too bad she and Bondiro have been permanently banned."

"What mischief earned *that*? I thought... What's the saying? 'All is forgiven at Nightpeace.'"

"Except sabotaging the place, trying to get House Cleoter's charter revoked." Giuna's grin was impish against the rim of her glass. "I believe a barrel of honey was involved. And several sacks of chicken feathers. And for some reason, a weather vane."

Renata paused, trying to figure out what that might have been for. Then she shook her head and sipped from the cup Tess handed her. Chrysanthemum wine, chilled and very welcome. "I'm beginning to feel as if I should have just rented one of the booths and set up a sign saying 'Here Be Marriage Bait.'"

"Better you than me," Giuna murmured, her gaze catching on something in the crowd of dancers that made her cheeks turn pinker than they already were. Before Renata could follow to its source, a different source of blushes distracted her.

"Oh happy glass, with your lips upon it. Oh happy glass, your fingers caressing its curves. Oh happy glass, filled with sweet wine. And yet even the happiest glass is empty come morning—so goes life and love."

Oksana Ryvček sauntered up, recognizable despite the shadows of her grey leather fox mask, the skirts of her silver crepe coat swaying with her hips. She clinked her glass against Renata's. "I know, I know. Keep to the dueling grounds, not the stage. But I'll wager it was better poetry than whatever they've dragged your ears with." She waved at the dance plaza.

The rich depths of Ryvček's Vraszenian accent were oddly comforting. As was the fencing master's next comment: "Let me know if anyone needs to be taught a lesson."

"Bad poetry isn't worth dueling over," Renata said.

"And you a Seterin noblewoman," Ryvček scoffed. "Careful; you'll get a reputation for being sensible."

The warning pricked like a knife under her ribs, a reminder that a liar was never safe. "I'd only hate to waste your talents on something so trivial."

"Mistress Ryvček enjoys keeping her blade warm." That came from the direction Giuna had been looking. The white-feathered egret mask approaching belonged to Sibiliat Acrenix, with Marvisal Coscanum, masked in gold iris, following several reluctant steps behind.

"Alta Sibiliat. Alta Marvisal." Renata offered them both a cautious curtsy.

She got none in return. "Must we be so formal? You're dear Giuna's cousin now, after all. You must call me Sibiliat, and I will call you Renata."

Was that an overture of peace? Sibiliat had resented Renata when she first "arrived" in Nadežra, as a threat to her own social prominence. Perhaps now that Sibiliat's father finally held a seat in the Cinquerat, she felt secure in her position—secure enough not to share her discovery of Renata's financial straits with anyone beyond Giuna.

Then again, Ghiscolo Acrenix had conspired with Vargo to get that seat...and Renata had been a tool in their schemes. How much did his daughter know about that?

It would be easier for a friend to find out. Renata smiled and said, "You're too kind, Sibiliat."

After a pause long enough to be uncomfortable, Sibiliat's elbow knocked Marvisal's. "Alta Renata," Marvisal began, before her thin lips pressed together at the formality of the address. She took a breath, her willow-thin frame straightening with resolve. "While I can't hope for the friendship you have with Giuna and Sibiliat, I would like to assure you that I hold no ill will against you for your role in Mezzan's downfall and the dissolution of my betrothal." Another elbow, and a flinch. "And I hope that you will not hold his crimes against me."

"Of course not," Renata said warmly. "You were as much a victim as any of us."

Arrant nonsense, but the show of sympathy was necessary. Marvisal relaxed, and the conversation turned to the pleasures and perils of Nightpeace Gardens. They were closed during the winter months, so Sibiliat justifiably believed Renata had never seen them before.

When Ryvček cleared her throat, Renata assumed the duelist was preparing to excuse herself. But no: Ryvček was alerting her to the approach of an unfamiliar man with a tortoiseshell mask gripped tight in his hands. He stopped just far enough away to be awkward and offered a stiff bow. "Alta Renata. Please excuse the interruption. My name is—"

"You," Marvisal hissed, eyes narrowing. "You have Quinat's own hubris, showing yourself here."

Sibiliat caught Marvisal's wrist before she could raise a hand against the man. "I remember you," Sibiliat said. "You transferred Caerulet's records to my father. Meppe, yes? Formerly Indestor?"

"Er. Yes. But don't hold that against me?" Meppe's voice

quavered in a nervous chuckle that died under Marvisal's glare. "Right. Sorry. I just...I'm not very good with words. Books, those I'm good with. Should have written a letter instead."

That last was muttered low enough that Renata suspected she wasn't meant to hear. His awkwardness supplanted her reflexive hostility with curiosity. "What do you want?"

"I know it's presumptuous." His tense laugh scraped like a dry pen nib across paper. "Given what Mettore did. But—well—your house is recruiting—"

"And you think she'll adopt *you*?" Marvisal spat at his feet. "I'm amazed Meda Capenni even let you in here. Nightpeace Gardens truly have fallen, when a kinless man can walk their paths."

Meppe hunched in like the tortoise who'd given its shell for his mask. Twinges of sympathy and suspicion warred within Renata. House Indestor had been large enough that surely most of them knew nothing of Mettore's plans...but this was Nadežra. Its foundations were built of lies as much as stone.

"Capenni's net might need mending after a long winter," Ryvček said, passing her wine to Giuna and shaking out her freed hands. "Bigger fish than this guppy seem to have slipped through."

"Marvisal!" Mezzan's shout would have carried across the dance plaza; from only six paces, it was unnecessarily loud. He waved a bottle for her attention, oblivious to everyone else. " 'Visal, I hoped you'd come tonight. Your brother can't stop me from seeing you here."

The people nearby cleared space as though preparing to watch a fire-eater or a juggling act. Or perhaps it was just from the fumes, Renata thought as Mezzan stumbled closer; the bottle's contents seemed to have gone as much down his chin as his throat. His shirt was stained with days of sweat and drink, his waistcoat unbuttoned. The thick, steel-blue velvet of his coat was better suited to winter than late spring, and one sleeve was torn as though he'd been dragged. His gloves were nowhere to be seen.

"Oh, Tyrant's pisspot. I thought you said he'd left the city," Sibiliat said, pulling Marvisal to safety as Mezzan swayed closer.

"I said Bondiro *dumped* him outside the city," Marvisal hissed. "Clearly, he found his way back."

And had run into some hazards along the way. Reddened lumps adorned Mezzan's face and hands; they appeared to be bee stings. He said, "You'll help me, 'Visal, won't you? Egliadas slammed the door in my face. Like I'm some kind of—" His gaze slewed sideways and landed on Renata. "Traitor!"

The bottle shattered on the tile as Mezzan dropped it in favor of his sword. Meppe-formerly-Indestor stepped forward, mask half-raised like a shield, trying to placate his ex-cousin—but that only made matters worse. "You're crawling at that foreigner's heels now?" Mezzan snarled, his blade's point rising unsteadily to Meppe's nose. "I'll deal with you after I've cut her face to ribbons." He swerved and lunged at Renata.

Like a conjuror's trick, Ryvček appeared in his path. With one hand—and an expression that said she regretted having to touch him even that much—she seized Mezzan's wrist and twisted it until his sword dropped from his fingers. She caught it in her other hand and swept it to the side, well out of his reach. "I believe it's illegal for you to carry a blade nowadays. But when has the law stopped your kind?" With a nod to Renata, she said, "If you would..."

Renata took the sword from her, resisting the urge to turn its edge upon Mezzan. After all, there were better ways to hurt him.

Pitching her voice to carry, she said, "Send your petition to House Traementis, Master Meppe. I will give it due consideration."

Mezzan spat curses until Ryvček wrenched his arm harder. "Are those...bee stings?" she said, studying him. "Those aren't from the Rook. Though I hear he gave you about half the thrashing you deserve, after your house was dissolved. Come; I'm sure we can find a Vigil officer to give you the other half." Even with Mezzan in a joint lock, she managed to bow to the quartet of noblewomen. "Alta Renata, that's a fine sword. Vicadrius, I believe. Bring it to my house next Tsapekny, at fifth sun; you should learn how to use it properly."

With that, she headed off, forcing Mezzan ahead of her, leaving Renata with a bared blade and a crowd of gossiping onlookers.

And the other three altas, one of whom stood with hunched shoulders and arms wrapped around her middle, as if she regretted having set foot outside tonight.

Sibiliat pulled Giuna close enough to press a kiss to her temple. In a soft voice, she said, "I'd hoped to steal you away from your admirers, little bird, but..." She nodded at the miserable Marvisal.

"I can come with you," Giuna blurted, then touched Renata's wrist in apology. "You don't need me, do you, cousin?"

"I'll be fine. You go." When Giuna hesitated, Renata added, "I'll see what I can do to disperse the gossip."

She'd made the offer to reassure Giuna, but it was Marvisal who turned to her with too-pale cheeks and said, with a quaver in her voice, "Thank you."

When the altas were gone, Renata sent Tess to have the sword delivered back to Traementis Manor. Then she called for the musicians, who had stopped playing, to strike up a gratzet—one of the only dances she'd properly learned—and flirted aggressively with every one of her changing partners until nobody was talking about Mezzan anymore.

Fortunately, before any of those partners could try to press what they thought was an advantage, she caught sight of Tanaquis at the edge of the floor. Using that as an excuse to escape, Renata dragged the other woman off.

"I hope you don't mind," she said. "You may have wanted to dance, yourself."

"The figures are interesting," Tanaquis said. "There are theories about performing numinatria, walking the lines instead of inscribing them. But I don't think the gratzet holds any power." Her magpie mask sat on her forehead as though she'd pushed it up and then forgotten it was there. The stylized black feathers blended with her dark hair and brushed the skin of her pale cheeks as she studied Renata. "You were surprisingly kind to poor Meppe."

"Mostly to needle Mezzan," Renata admitted. "Donaia will never adopt him. Still, it does no harm to look at his proposal. And we *do* need people."

Tanaquis's grey eyes were thoughtful. "Back from the brink of death, yes. I'll be very interested to see what the new House Traementis looks like. Whether its...old ways carry over, or whether you take on an entirely fresh character."

"I'm only relieved we have the chance now." Renata drew Tanaquis onto a nearby bridge, a tiny, decorative thing that would mostly serve to keep anyone else from standing close enough to overhear. "With everything that's been going on, I haven't had a chance to speak with you about the curse. It troubles me that we still don't know where it came from. Indestor was our most obvious foe, but there's no sign that they were behind it—which means we may have another enemy out there." Possibly even a szorsa. Pattern had uncovered the existence of the curse; pattern might have laid it in the first place.

Tanaquis bit her lip, oddly hesitant for a woman whose tongue was usually only checked by the swift intervention of others. "About that...I'd like to invite you to an event on the solstice. But I can't say where. Or why. You would just need to trust me without asking questions. And you may not say anything to anyone else. Not even Donaia."

Renata didn't bother to control her rising eyebrows. "If you can't say where, I'm going to have a difficult time attending."

"Oh! Yes." Fishing in the pocket under her surcoat, Tanaquis pulled out a circle of soft cotton with precise blackwork crossing it in the lines of a decagram Illi numinat—one without a focus. "Pin this to your shoulder and wait in Traementis Plaza at tenth sun on the solstice. Someone will escort you."

Renata accepted the numinat and smoothed it in her palm. This had all the marks of a secret society. But why would Tanaquis be involved with such a thing? "This has to do with the curse?"

"After a fashion," Tanaquis said. "I'm intrigued by what you've shown me regarding pattern, and very much want to know more. But we can't have a proper conversation if my own tongue is leashed." She clicked it as if impatient to cast off its restraints.

Against her better judgment, Renata was intrigued. Tanaquis

knew a great deal about numinatria, but almost nothing about pattern; their previous conversations had made that clear. And so far as Ren knew, pattern and numinatria had nothing whatsoever to do with each other.

But everything she knew had come from her mother. There might be more out there to learn.

She tucked the cloth away, into the bodice of her surcoat where a pickpocket wouldn't get it. "Thank you."

Her laugh ominous, Tanaquis said, "Wait until you know what you're thanking me for."

Nightpeace Gardens, Eastbridge: Fellun 29

Holding Mezzan's blade like a rotting eel carcass she was taking out to trash, Tess wandered the crowds in search of one of the off-duty hawks House Cleoter paid to keep the gardens' peace. She couldn't very well take the blade back to Isla Traementis herself, nor pay a common runner to do it. But hawks were required to serve if a noble requested it.

She did her best to ignore the curious glances cast her way. Freckled Ganllechyn girls in servants' greys-and-whites brandishing fancy blades weren't something folk saw often outside one of Mallort's tales, but Tess straightened her spine and marched along as though she were the Maid of Mavourneen herself.

It kept the cuffs and their ilk from stopping her but didn't do twaddle for helping her find a hawk. "Always circling when you're wanting some peace; not a feather to be found when you need one," she grumbled, a moment before spotting a flash of blue and tan. "Ha!"

Her triumph lasted only as long as it took to circle a knot of portly gentlemen betting on the number of moths drawn by the light of a bridge lamp. A light that also very nicely limned the honey-dark cheeks and needle-fine features of the last hawk—or person—Tess wanted to see.

Pavlin Ranieri. She hadn't clapped eyes on him since the day of the Lower Bank riots. She'd been half hoping that luck would stay with her and she'd never have to see his lying face again...but the Kind Ladies had a sense of humor that was anything but funny.

Tess spun on her heel to escape—and promptly brought fate upon herself when she ran face-first into the back seam of a gentleman's coat.

"Here now, you made me lose count!" He grabbed her shoulder, ignoring her apologies and attempts to squeeze past him. His breath stank of sour wine. "I don't give an osprey's arse if you're sorry, girl. You know what we had riding on this?"

"Going to have to start the count all over," said one of the other men, earning a groan from the entire lot.

"Foul!" said a third. "It'll have changed since Beldipassi took the bill. We'll have to give every man's mark back to him."

"You're just saying that 'cause you've already lost!"

"Now, now," said the gentleman holding the betting billet. "I'm certain we can—"

"See the trouble you've made?" Tess's captor shook her hard enough to rattle her head on her neck. "And what's this? What's a rust-head doing walking around with a duelist's prick?"

"Is there a problem here, mede?" asked a soft, pleasant voice that Tess knew too well. She let her eyes slide closed and prayed the Crone would make her trip and fall on the blade that had tossed her into this tangle.

At least the drunken man released her. "I'll say there is. This girl's a thief. Faked a stumble to pick our pockets, and no telling who she stole that sword from. Probably wears that uniform so she can move about without notice."

Tess could feel everyone's eyes upon her, Pavlin's most of all. She opened her mouth to argue, then shut it just as quickly. Men like this didn't care for any truth but their own.

"I see," Pavlin said. "Thank you for catching her. You have the Vigil's gratitude. With your leave, I'll deal with it from here."

Taking Mezzan's sword in one hand and Tess's elbow in the

other, Pavlin led her off. Behind them, the gentlemen busied themselves with congratulating each other for putting a stop to such a menace, and commenting on how much more diligent the Vigil had become now that Ghiscolo Acrenix was Caerulet.

No sooner were they over the bridge and onto the next islet than Tess yanked her arm from Pavlin's grasp, hard enough to wrench her shoulder. "They're lying. I wouldn't put a hand into one of their pockets for an entire bale of byssus."

"I know."

"And that's Mezzan Indestor's sword. He attacked my alta—"

"Is she all right?" Pavlin touched Tess's shoulder, and she winced at the contact. At his concern for Renata. At the reminder that he'd only ever paid court to Tess so he could spy on her sister.

"She's unharmed. Oksana Ryvček was there to deal with him. My alta sent me to deal with the sword, so there you have it." Tess hugged her middle to keep a bitter laugh from escaping. "Please see it's delivered to Traementis Manor, as a service to the house. I'll be on my way."

"Tess, I'm sorry." His words caught her as she turned to go. Against her will, she glanced back at him, and wasn't *that* a mistake. He was so beautiful, with his dark eyes warmed to gold by the lamps and lashes spiked with tears. And her so shallow that all it took was a pretty face and a bit of remorse to make her want to forgive him.

Anger—at him, at herself—sharpened her tongue. "Sorry you spied on us, or that you were caught at it?"

"I'm sorry that I used you to do it. And that I kept visiting after the captain said I should stop."

You were told to stop? Tess wanted to scoff, but hope was a curse disguised as a blessing. Burying her fingers under her surcoat before they could give her away with their trembling, Tess asked, "Why did you?"

Pavlin's hands tightened on the sword. "I was worried. I knew things were harder than you let on, and I wanted to help."

That explained the baskets of bread...but not the kindness, nor the kissing. And Tess found she didn't want to know. Whether he'd been lying about that or not, she had secrets to keep—her own and Ren's. She couldn't afford to forgive him, even if she wanted to.

Hands clenched in her underskirts to give herself resolve, she said, "So, it was pity. Well, I thank you for it, but I've no need of it anymore. My alta's a Traementis now, and we've all the bread we could want."

Turning away again, she hurried back toward where she'd left Renata waiting. And if she thought sadly of the spice cakes Pavlin used to bring that were her favorites, the ones she'd never taste again...she had only herself to blame.

Nightpeace Gardens, Eastbridge: Fellun 29

Though she was the gate that determined who could enter Nightpeace, Meda Tiama Capenni rarely danced in her own gardens. So when she approached Vargo with one hand extended in invitation, he knew she wanted something.

But she was a gentlewoman, which meant they were halfway through the dance before she shifted from pleasantries to business. "I hear you're the man to speak with about Isarnah parrots."

An earthwise woman, Tiama was taller than him, especially in her heeled shoes; Vargo had to tilt his head to glance up at her. "For your gardens, I presume. Be warned—they're loud creatures."

"And amusing, if they're taught to say the right things." She was leading for this dance and spun him out and back so that the full, weighted skirts of his coat swirled very satisfyingly. As a child Vargo hadn't given a shit about clothes beyond what he could get from the costermongers for a stolen coat or surcoat, but he'd long ago admitted that Alsius was right; there was pleasure in being well-dressed. Power, too.

The same went for having useful connections. Tiama Capenni might be a gentlewoman, but that didn't mean she was a law-abiding citizen. And Vargo happened to know that Mažylo—the leader of the Night Moths, the knot that controlled crime in Nightpeace

Gardens—was Tiama's husband in all but register. Above water or below, she found a way to profit from everything that happened here.

"I think I can provide," Vargo said as they came back together. Parrots weren't among his usual commodities, but Varuni claimed to have a whole menagerie of them back home; she'd know what to recommend. "It'll take a while, but you should have them before the gardens close for the winter."

"I knew I could rely on you." The dance came to a close; she exchanged a curtsy for his bow, and then they parted.

Leaving him at inconveniently loose ends. He got a good survey of the backs of everyone's coats and surcoats as people turned away from him, and he kept his expression steady behind his mask of beaded net. Less than a month, and the novelty of the Lower Bank crime lord turned nobleman had already worn off. While the lower ranks of the city saw opportunity in his elevation, their superiors had identified him as a threat—and correctly so, Vargo reflected, tamping down on a smirk. He was here mostly to show the snubs didn't bother him. He knew where his path forward lay.

He was thinking of leaving when he turned a corner and almost walked straight into Ghiscolo Acrenix and one of Cibrial Destaelio's four thousand daughters.

There was no way to dodge a conversation, nor time for Alsius to take cover under his collar. *Brace yourself,* he warned the spider, and stepped up to the pair as though he'd been invited to join them.

The Destaelio woman made a face like she'd just been fed a live eel, but she couldn't raise a fuss when Ghiscolo welcomed Vargo with a smile. "Eret Vargo. Eutracce here was just commenting on how the gardens have declined this year. What are your thoughts?"

"Oh, I'm certain Eret Vargo isn't familiar enough with gardening to have an opinion," Eutracce said.

He gave her a benign smile. "Quite right, alta. Charter or not, when sun hours turn over to earth, I'm just a merchant."

"A merchant." Eutracce's mouth soured further. Her mother held the Prasinet seat, which oversaw Nadežra's finances, banking, and trade. As a smuggler, Vargo had only ever been one of a swarm of irritating river gnats to her. Now that he'd been ennobled, Her Charity Cibrial Destaelio would do one of two things: swat him, or strike a deal. He was hoping for the latter.

Ghiscolo chuckled. "Such modesty, Eret Vargo. Nadežra's power has always been founded on trade. The right mercantile connections can be as valuable as holding a critical mountain pass."

Like, say, the connections that allowed Vargo to bring Isarnah goods through Nadežra while dodging Prasinet's punitive tariffs. Those had been imposed fifty years ago, after Isarn backed a Vraszenian rebellion...but Cibrial might profit handsomely if she lifted them.

That was helpful of him, Vargo thought as Eutracce's mouth shifted from sour to thoughtful.

::Yes, he's always been good at that.::

Until Ghiscolo became Caerulet, House Acrenix's status had derived entirely from their ability to play the game: a useful alliance here, a well-timed withdrawal of support there. The latter always with a show of regret, so that no stain of treachery marred their reputation.

In truth, they were as dirty as Vargo. Just better able to hide it.

Ghiscolo's comment meant that instead of excusing herself from the conversation, Eutracce stayed and asked probing questions about Vargo's business, which he deflected with pleasant responses that revealed nothing. Partway through this, he caught Ghiscolo watching him with a faint, puzzled frown. When Vargo raised a questioning brow, though, Ghiscolo shook his head. "Only noting the cut of your coat. Did Alta Renata's maid tailor that for you?"

Vargo smoothed a hand down the textured surface of his waistcoat, avoiding Alsius masquerading as a pin. The fabric was an Arthaburi import he hadn't yet released even to Tess. "No, though I recommend her services—assuming you can get them. I hear she's quite busy."

"Perhaps a friend of the alta's might put in a good word for me," Ghiscolo said, smiling.

Vargo doubted Ghiscolo's thoughts had been tied up in tailoring, but their conversation ended with him no more enlightened. And any useful guesses were driven from his head when he saw Iascat Novrus standing, quiet and watchful, at the center of a boisterous group of young cuffs. Scowling, Vargo ducked across a bridge to the next islet before he could be spotted in return.

::Are you certain? He looks lonely,:: Alsius noted as he crept to hide under Vargo's collar points. ::I could make myself scarce.::

He was a tense little lump after that encounter with Ghiscolo. Normally Vargo didn't bring him anywhere near the man, and he wished he could have avoided it tonight. As for Iascat... *Rumor has it that Sostira's threatened to disinherit him. I don't know if that's because of our assignations, but he can't afford a public encounter with someone like me.* If Vargo was going to burn his asset in House Novrus, he would do it for some better reason than idle chitchat in Nightpeace Gardens.

His change of direction was an auspicious one, because it took him toward a familiar figure standing on a toy bridge, beautifully attired in layers of watered silk. Alsius noticed, too, but his thoughts went in a different direction. ::There's that Fienola woman! She has an admirable mind. You should arrange a meeting to discuss the river numinat.::

Vargo had barely noticed Tanaquis Fienola standing in Renata's shadow. They had their heads close together as if conspiring—and then, with a movement that was probably supposed to be furtive but only drew more attention to itself, Fienola handed over a familiar-looking scrap of cloth.

Well, isn't that interesting. Not surprising; Renata had done a splendid job of making herself a desirable commodity in Nadežra. Vargo had been the first to see it, but now any number of people wanted to invest in her, for a variety of purposes.

::Interesting on both counts,:: Alsius said. ::And also useful. Even more reason to ask Fienola—::

Yes, yes. The last thing Vargo needed was a mental voice prompting him like an actor who'd forgotten his lines. He reached under his collar and scooped out Peabody, depositing him atop a nearby topiary. *There's Silvain Fiangiolli by the acrobats. Make yourself useful and find out why he's so intent on flirting with that Essunta girl? The last thing we need is those families managing a truce.* Ignoring Alsius's grumbles, Vargo straightened his waistcoat and approached the two women.

"I see Tess spared no time diving into the fabrics I sent," he said after paying a proper salute to both Renata and Tanaquis. He kept hold of Renata's hand, turning it in his to draw her closer. "I was right. The green suits you."

"You have an unexpected eye for such things." Renata surveyed his own ensemble, a velveteen as dark as pomegranates with swirls burned out to show the black currant silk underneath. Its thread-of-gold embroidery at cuffs and hem could only be smuggled out of Ganllech. This was part of their dance: They both knew they looked good, and both did it to invite the admiration of others. Displaying that admiration was a discreet form of applause.

He did so enjoy interacting with someone who appreciated his skill at playing the game, rather than spitting on him for it.

Releasing Renata's hand, he said, "Meda Fienola—before I forget. I'd like to speak to you at some point about my plans for the West Channel numinat. The timing of such endeavors is important, and I'm not astrologer enough to chart it out."

Tanaquis brightened. "Yes! Not tonight, though. I'll send you an invitation. And perhaps you'll indulge me in a few questions about your other numinatrian endeavors."

She might have been talking about the amphitheatre numinat, or the ones he'd dismantled during the riots—including the one inflaming the crowd's anger. But her gaze was fixed on Vargo's chest, as if it could bore past coat, waistcoat, and shirt to the numinat burned over his heart.

Showing her that mark might have been a mistake, but at the time he had no other way to convince her to send him into the realm of mind after Renata. Vargo fought to keep his expression unruffled. "Of course." *Right after the Dežera freezes over.*

"I'd love to be a part of that conversation," Renata said. "Since the charter is in Traementis hands, after all."

It was an odd relic of their past circumstances that Vargo, a fellow noble, was administering someone else's charter. That wasn't the reason Tanaquis tapped her lips, though. "Yes, she should join us. I presume you're not intending to give your own life to imbue the numinat, Vargo. But possibly Renata can supply what you need."

"I beg your pardon?"

Renata's reply could have cut steel. Tanaquis's brows rose, while Vargo's heart thudded in sudden shock. "Oh, not by *dying*," Tanaquis said. "I meant with pattern."

"Pattern?" Vargo glanced at Renata. Her cosmetics couldn't quite hide the blush that stained her cheeks. Interesting. He knew she'd sought out that patterner, and maybe put too much faith in the cards, but this was something else. Something novel enough to stir Tanaquis's boundless curiosity. He let his voice drop, dark and teasing. "Have you been hiding a secret, Alta Renata?"

"Hardly a secret," she said with a thin laugh. "A—well, I thought it was a silly game. Except after the Night of Hells..." She dismissed that with a shake of her head. "A story for later. But, Tanaquis, I'm afraid I don't have my cards any longer. Mettore's kidnappers took them from me, and I haven't seen them since."

"I might be able to find them," Vargo said. "Eret Acrenix holds the charter for storing possessions confiscated from criminals— Well, held it, since it's supposed to be separate from Caerulet's office. I don't know if he's transferred it yet."

He spoke on reflex, covering for the completely different thoughts now racing through his head. Was this why he'd seen pattern cards in the realm of mind when he went after Renata's spirit? He'd assumed it was simply because of the place's connection to Ažerais, but her comment about the Night of Hells suggested it was more personal than that.

He'd have to tread carefully, though. If Renata discovered he'd sold her out to Mettore that night, everything he'd built with her would come tearing apart like the broken West Channel numinat.

Tanaquis's eyes were fever-bright with the possibilities. "I think it would be useful. Since the realm of mind appears to be the same as Ažerais's Dream, and the dream is connected to the wellspring, and the wellspring can act as a focus and be affected by numinatria, it only stands to reason that pattern and numinatria might be more deeply connected than anyone has ever surmised."

No denying Alsius's admiration of her mind was warranted. They had their own hypothesis about how to make the river numinat work—but it was only a hypothesis, untested so far. He would sleep easier if he had a second possibility to hand. "You think pattern can be used to augment the focus?"

"I've done it before," Tanaquis said blithely. Then she bit her lip and shot Renata a guilty look.

A boom overhead forestalled any reply to that. Vargo looked up to see a firework blooming in the sky—a regular occurrence in the summer months. He hoped the Lacewater knots were doing their work to make sure no wandering sparks set the tenements alight. The river might still be in full flood, but the weather was dry, and the Old Island could all too easily burn.

Around him everyone was laughing and clapping in delight, but from Renata there came a sound of dismay. He turned to ask whether she didn't like fireworks, and found her mourning a torn spot on her hem. "I stepped on it," she said ruefully.

Her maid came swooping in like a sartorial hawk. "Oh dear. I knew I should have taken that up a finger higher. Follow me, alta, and we'll have you set to rights before the skies go dark again."

Vargo watched her go, two fingers drumming against his thigh. He'd never followed up on his thought from months ago, of having one of his Seterin contacts look into what had brought such an elegant noblewoman to Nadežra.

Maybe it was time he did.

Nightpeace Gardens, Eastbridge: Fellun 29

The skin shock of fear stayed with Ren as Tess hurried her away. Bad enough having to smile at Vargo as if she didn't know what he'd done—but *damn* Tanaquis for bringing pattern up in front of him. Forcing Renata to stumble her way through a clumsy lie, because Vargo had seen her mother's deck when she met him as Arenza, and he was too good of a gambler for her to trust he wouldn't recognize the hand-painted cards if he saw them again.

Have you been hiding a secret, Alta Renata?

She couldn't let herself think about that right now. She had somewhere else, and someone else, to be.

"Well, that worked," Tess said, examining her skirt. A tearaway hem wasn't a trick they could use too often—otherwise Alta Renata's clumsiness would become the talk of the Upper Bank—but it was effective.

Near the northern edge of the gardens, they slipped into the shadows of an enormous tree. Arranging the meeting the ziemetse requested had taken a good deal of finagling, and this was the best Ren could manage: a rendezvous in a back corner of Nightpeace Gardens, where any combination of flashy clothes, a glittering mask, or a slipped bribe could gain Tiama Capenni's permission to pass through the gates.

While Tess pulled the jade ribbon from Renata's hair, loosing a simple braid, Ren reached into a pocket no lightfinger would find and drew out the mask of rose-patterned lace.

Her disguise cascaded over her like water, covering the surcoat and underdress of her Liganti-style clothing, leaving her in a tight-fitting coat and breeches. Experimentally, Ren reached for her kissing-comfits, and wasn't surprised to find she couldn't touch them. For all she knew, her ordinary clothing had gone...somewhere else.

Tess sucked in a quiet gasp, trailing her fingers over the leather petals flowing down Ren's arm. "Not a stitch or seam to be found. How does that even work?"

"A blessing from Ažerais?" Ren said, but it was no more than a guess.

Shaking her head, Tess flicked her hands in a shooing motion. "Never you mind about my curiosity. Go and come back, before people start wondering where Alta Renata went off to."

A quick glance around showed Ren no one nearby. Taking a deep breath, she stepped out and headed for the meeting point.

She didn't try to hide, exactly; that was too likely to draw attention if she failed. But in dark clothing, at night, in a place like the gardens, it was easy to take paths that kept her from coming too close to anyone. Despite the tension curling in her gut, a smile tugged at her lips. Was this what it felt like to be the Rook?

As she neared the northern boundary of the gardens, the path was empty of anyone save a few pity-rustlers. Their presence was explained when a lump of a shadow atop the bridge rail jumped down.

"See? Told you she'd show." Arkady Bones had all the swagger of a man grown, packaged in the body of a spindle-thin girl. She gave Ren a cocksure bow and then nodded to the gaggle of waiting pity-rustlers. "Tell the others to keep the hawks and the moths away."

After they vanished, she flicked a hand at two shadows sitting in the lee of the bridge. "Go on, then. En't nobody gonna listen in."

As Ren passed her, one of the shadows rose from the bench and moved into the dim light. "Except you, Ča Bones."

Perversely, the fact that Ren was already on edge kept her from twitching. The representative the ziemetse had sent was the granddaughter of the former Kiraly clan leader—someone she'd met twice before. Once in the nightmare, and once at the Seven Knots labyrinth, where fear had sent Ren bolting from a friendly gesture.

"Don't mind me." Arkady levered herself back onto the bridge post, feet dangling and boots thumping against the support. "Usually my silence is for sale, but tonight it's free. I keep the Black Rose's secrets." She winked at Ren.

The Kiraly woman paused. When Ren made no objection to Arkady staying, she nodded in acceptance. "Thank you for coming, Lady Rose. I am Dalisva Mladoskaya Korzetsu of the Kiraly. I wish to thank you again for all that you did to save the wellspring, and for sending that Liganti worm Mettore Indestor to us for justice."

There was limited space in Ren's vocal range where she could sound natural. As Renata she spoke on the higher end, and with a

Seterin accent; as Arenza she went low and Vraszenian. Now she pitched her voice toward the middle, and made her vowels purely Nadežran. *If I have to invent a fourth persona, I'll be out of cards.* "Mere thanks wouldn't have required a meeting. What makes the ziemetse interested in me?"

Arkady snorted. "Bet they want you to do something for them."

Dalisva shot her an irritated look, but didn't refute it. To Ren she said, "You are the Rose of Ažerais, sent to us in a desperate time. Yes—we have need of your aid. Will you help?"

"That depends on what you're looking for."

"The Stadnem Anduske," Dalisva said. "You were at the amphitheatre during Veiled Waters—but know you what happened before that?" When Ren didn't respond, she went on. "Their old leader, Andrejek, planned the bombing. But from the Cinquerat he took a pardon, in exchange for calling it off. He cut his knot, and for that treachery his lieutenant Branek tried to kill him."

Ren bit down on the urge to say, *That's not what happened.* A Cinquerat pardon? Snow in Nadežra was more likely. Andrejek backed down because Grey convinced him the whole thing was playing into Mettore's hands.

But it was Renata who'd been involved in that, not the Black Rose. "What exactly do you want *me* to do about that?"

"Have you no wish to help Vraszenians? Andrejek has long been wanted by the ziemetse, but Branek...he was Andrejek's attack dog, held on a tight leash. Now that leash has slipped. He believes violence is the only way to break the Cinquerat's hold, and he will not flinch from hurting ordinary people. Already his allies in the Stretsko knots attack the businesses of those on the Lower Bank with too much Liganti blood."

The inconvenience of a mask was that it hid small responses like an arched eyebrow. "First you speak of me helping Vraszenians, and then you worry about people with Liganti ancestry. What do you actually want?"

Dalisva wore no mask, and her passion blazed like a torch. "With Branek leading them, the Anduske will wind up only hurting

Vraszenians, by provoking the Cinquerat to tighten their grip. But his hold over the Anduske is not yet secure. If you could capture some of his key supporters and deliver those people to us—even Branek himself—"

They had a high opinion of the Black Rose, if they thought she could pull that off. But Ren couldn't disagree with their concerns. While House Traementis hadn't yet suffered any losses on the Lower Bank, that was mostly because their reduced state had left them without much to attack. The nobles were muttering about needing to restore control down there after the riots...and the kind of control they had in mind never meant anything good for Vraszenians.

"I have a list," Dalisva said, drawing it from a pocket of her shawl and holding it out. "If the ones named here were removed, the rest would be able to do little more than shake their fists."

Ren eyed the paper, not reaching for it. "Removed."

"She means killed," Arkady helpfully supplied from her perch.

Dalisva kept her chin lifted and shoulders straight. "Their fate is for Ažerais to set and pattern to guide. But the ziemetse are wise enough to avoid creating martyrs."

Smart politics. If the clan leaders didn't have some skill at that, the delicate balance between Liganti-controlled Nadežra and the rest of Vraszan would have collapsed long ago. Which was, of course, what people like this Branek wanted.

But none of that was Ren's business. After Veiled Waters she'd lost track of Idusza Polojny, her friend in the Anduske, and she couldn't afford to spend time being Arenza Lenskaya when she had to be Renata Viraudax Traementis every waking minute. Nor could she worry about Vraszenian politics when she was busy making amends to House Traementis, for a debt whose magnitude they didn't even know.

"Please," Dalisva said, desperation creeping in. "You are the one Ažerais chose. You were conceived—"

She cut herself off, but not soon enough. Ren's gaze shot to Arkady, whose hands flew up in a warding gesture. "I en't said nothing!"

From the shadow still sitting in the lee of the bridge came a soft, weary voice. "Only those born of Ažerais can destroy the children of Ažerais. And only those born of Ažerais can save the children of Ažerais."

Words Ren had heard in the nightmare, when she stood before the twisted echoes of the Charterhouse statues. A szorsa had spoken them—the one who stood for the dead Ižranyi clan in the Ceremony of the Accords.

It would look the opposite of dignified and mysterious if the Black Rose fled from an old, blind woman. Ren forced herself to stand as Dalisva retreated to help the szorsa make her way forward. A strip of embroidered cloth covered the pits where her eyes had been, before something in the nightmare tore them out.

"Forgive us," the szorsa murmured. "I am Mevieny Plemaskaya Straveši of the Dvornik. We mean no threat to you or your secrets, Lady Rose."

Ren's words came out far steadier than she felt. "How did you know?"

Dalisva sighed. "In the nightmare, a Vraszenian woman told Szorsa Mevieny that 'all of us' by that wine were poisoned. But she was no part of our delegation. Nor was she the Cinquerat's servant, or they would not have needed to hunt her. A woman conceived during the Great Dream appears on that terrible night...and then, when Mettore Indestor attempts to use one such to destroy the Wellspring of Ažerais, the Black Rose appears to defend it. Connecting the two was a guess, but—"

"Not a guess," Mevieny said. "Blind I may be, but the cards speak to me still."

They didn't know everything. Only that the Black Rose was the woman they'd met before. If Arkady truly had kept her mouth shut, they didn't even know her name was Ren.

It was still enough to send spiders crawling up Ren's spine. *My secrets are not safe.*

Mevieny said, "Ažerais has blessed you, Lady Rose. Once at your birth, and again when you became her servant. For what purpose wear you that mask, if not to help her children?"

I'm wearing it because you asked for this meeting. Were it not for the Rook's message, she might have left it to gather dust in her wardrobe forever.

No—that was a lie. And the disguise had come again when she put it on. As if Ažerais truly did have a purpose for her, beyond saving the wellspring.

Was that wishful thinking? A thread of Vraszenian meaning for her to cling to in her new Liganti life, like the rope the Rook had used to draw her out of the pit. An excuse to involve herself in that world again, to be someone other than Alta Renata all the time. To feel like she wasn't a slip-knot.

Wishful thinking or not, the possibility brought an ache into her throat.

Wordlessly, Dalisva held out the list of names. Ren accepted the list between the tips of two gloved fingers and—*why not*—made it vanish up her sleeve. "I make no promises...but I'll see what I can do."

The Friendly Fist

Upper and Lower Bank: Fellun 36

When Vargo's invitation arrived at the manor, Ren almost refused it. Living as Renata was exhausting enough without having to pretend she still harbored warm feelings for the man. But unless she got Sedge back into his circle, the only way for her to learn anything was to maintain the fiction of their friendship, so she gritted her teeth and forced herself to pen an acceptance.

She was pulling on her gloves and considering whether it was worth overheating under a veil to protect her skin from darkening in the sun when the door to Donaia's study opened.

"Thank you, Captain," Donaia said. Her voice was constantly rough, scraped raw by the sorrow she tried to hide when she wasn't alone. "Perhaps I'm being overly cautious, but after everything—"

"Think nothing of it, Era Traementis." Grey Serrado gave Donaia one of those heel-clicking bows that made him seem even more stiff and unyielding than his fellow hawks. "The Vigil is happy to serve, and I'm used to following in Alta Renata's wake."

"My wake?" Renata echoed, hoping it didn't sound as wary as she felt.

Brushing invisible lint from Renata's sleeve, Donaia said, "I've asked Captain Serrado to act as your escort to Froghole."

He nodded. "Not all of the Lower Bank is as safe as Westbridge, and you aren't accustomed to rough areas." One hand rose to the hilt of his sword.

Renata wanted to refuse. Except that Donaia, who'd managed to project a facade of confidence even in the worst days of House Traementis's decline, kept touching Renata and Giuna both as though they might disappear in an eyeblink. After Renata's part in Leato's death, the least she could do for Donaia was accept an escort.

Besides, she wasn't doing anything Serrado shouldn't see. And her nightmares about him kicking in her door had mostly faded, in favor of horrific visions of the zlyzen. Gloves settled, Renata said, "Very well, Captain—let us go see what Eret Vargo has found."

They didn't talk much on the trip across the river, until their skiff approached a wharf swarming with activity. Half a dozen people were in the water itself, their heads bobbing above the brown wavelets, while Vargo watched from above. In his loosely tailored coat of tan suede, he could almost pass for one of the laborers—except they'd all shed coats and surcoats to work in their shirtsleeves.

"I didn't realize it would take this much effort to retrieve a chunk of prismatium," Renata said, shielding her eyes from the sun as their skiff drew up to the landing stair.

The water must have carried her voice to Vargo. "When it's the size of a horse cart and buried in mud, it does. The divers have dug out as much as they can." He motioned at the swimmers. "Once they attach the cables, the crane will haul it out the rest of the way."

It spoke to both her opinion of Vargo's cleverness and her worry about his cunning that she wondered if he'd somehow arranged this discovery. That such a large piece of the broken numinat could have somehow escaped the old salvage efforts, even buried in mud, seemed unlikely. But what would Vargo gain from planting a fake fragment in the riverbed?

She had no choice but to accept his hand to steady her as she left the skiff for the weed-slicked surface of the landing. "Will this make your work easier? Having such a large piece?" That ignorance, she had to neither hide nor fake; no one expected Alta Renata to be an inscriptor.

Of course, they didn't expect it of a Lower Bank crime lord, either. Vargo said, "We won't know that until I see it. But if I can study a full cross section rather than the glimpses offered by the few fragments that escaped reuse..." Vargo let the conclusion drift as Serrado stepped off the skiff after Renata. "Captain."

"Eret."

"Come to make certain we aren't attacked by river pirates?"

Serrado met Vargo's mockery with his usual mask of stoic courtesy. "If necessary. Why, have you done something to offend the Stretsko?"

Renata hid her wince. Before Vargo's rise, the most powerful gangs on the Lower Bank had been dominated by Vraszenians from the Stretsko clan. They hadn't appreciated the competition, and she doubted they were any happier about their erstwhile rival now counting himself among the nobility.

Perhaps I can make use of that. Stretsko also made up a large percentage of the Stadnem Anduske, and in the wake of Veiled Waters, those groups were getting more tangled than ever before. Several of the names on Dalisva Korzetsu's list were related to some of Vargo's biggest enemies.

The only problem with that fight was she didn't want *either* side to win.

Vargo led her up to the dry ground of the embankment, with Serrado following at a polite distance. Ropes stretched up from the water's surface, leading through the crane to a team of horses hitched and waiting in a narrow alley. Renata tried not to shudder as a diver surfaced. The high waters of the Dežera in flood had washed away a goodly portion of the filth that clogged the West Channel, but that still didn't make the prospect of swimming in it inviting.

The diver's signal was taken up by a woman at the base of the crane, then by the teamster handling the horses. He started them walking, the ropes creaking as they pulled taut.

Vargo leaned close to be heard above the noise. Even over

the river's stink, she could smell the sandalwood and clove of his perfume and the leather of his coat. "I promise this will be more interesting once—"

A crack like thunder cut across the creaking of the ropes, followed by a groan and rumble as the crane shook. Spooked by the noise and the sudden lack of resistance, the horses slipped the teamster's lead and lurched forward. Renata was distantly aware of a hawk's blue and tan as Serrado lunged for the traces, but the flash of shadow to sun to shadow again disoriented her.

Only when she heard the screams did she realize the shade she now stood in was cast by the crane falling toward her.

Vargo dove for safety. Ren went the other way, rolling frantically through the muck, not sure how far would be far enough—until the cobbles shook beneath her, and something crashed across her legs.

She waited, arms curled over her head, not daring to move, until the only sound left was the thunder of her pulse and the shouting beyond. Then she looked up to find a small beam pinning her legs, a much larger one where she'd been standing, Serrado running one soothing hand down a horse's neck, and Vargo climbing to his feet on the far side of the chaos. He stripped off his ruined coat with a snarl.

Handing the leads off to the shaken teamster, Serrado rushed to lift away the beam pinning Ren and help her stand. "Alta, are you hurt?" His hands hovered at his sides, as though he dearly wished to check her for injuries, but didn't dare.

She gingerly felt her own legs through the layers of her skirts, wincing at the tenderness across her shins. "Bruised, I suspect, but nothing worse."

"No thanks to him." Leaving her to set herself to rights, Serrado strode around the wreckage to Vargo. This time, the hands he held in check were balled into fists. "Eret Vargo—"

Scowling, Vargo waved Serrado off. "I'm fine as well, Captain. No need to concern yourself."

A less controlled man might have shoved him. "What concerns me, *Eret* Vargo, is that you thought only for your own safety and not that of the woman at your side."

Vargo met Serrado's glare, his brow furrowed in what seemed to be honest confusion. "I don't know what you think I could have done. And she's fine now anyway, so what does it matter? I'd expect you to be more concerned about what caused this to happen in the first place." He kicked one of the splintered crane supports.

What does it matter? That was the true face of the man who'd sold her to Mettore Indestor on the Night of Hells—and helped her afterward, true, but Ren knew the stories from Sedge. Vargo had a habit of putting people into trouble and then getting them out of it, so they would owe him a debt.

She only half attended to the rest of the conversation, Vargo remembering that he had the right now to call on the Vigil to investigate, Serrado agreeing through gritted teeth. She was too busy wondering whether the crane had been meant to kill Vargo, her, or both of them.

Then something else took the entirety of her attention.

It happened as Serrado was sending a runner to the Aerie and Vargo was arranging a watch on the river so nobody would steal the numinat fragment before he could build another crane. A flicker of gaudy color scurried across a crate; Vargo absently held one hand out so his spider, Master Peabody, could climb up his arm.

And the voice she'd heard that day in the Charterhouse said, ::What happened here?::

Vargo's lips were pressed into a thin, angry line. Yet she still heard him, an unspoken growl she had to strain to pick out. ::An *accident*. One of the outriggers for the crane just bolted—but not before I saw the Stretsko knot under her sleeve.:: "Fucking rats."

That last curse was out loud, she realized, as Vargo slapped the dirt from his gloves and glared at the wreckage of the crane. His shifting gaze swept over her, and she busied herself straightening her own clothes. As if she hadn't just heard the conversation between him and his coconspirator—who was, somehow, inexplicably, in the body of a spider.

Peabody's many eyes glittered from the shadows of Vargo's collar. ::Rats, indeed. I came to tell you that Premyk has made up his mind. He'll be handing the aža payout to Tserdev tonight, behind the Seven Knots labyrinth.::

Ren's heart stumbled in its pace. While she'd never heard of Premyk, Tserdev Krasnoskaya Očelen was the head of the Crimson Eyes, the main Stretsko gang controlling Seven Knots. She wasn't on Dalisva's list... but her brother Dmatsos was. He'd been leading a lot of the attacks on Liganti-run businesses. And rumor said he'd gone to ground with his sister—if only anybody could locate Tserdev's lair.

::The hell he will.:: The ice of Vargo's mental voice belied the bland smile he directed at Renata. ::Aža is *my* business. Keep watching the Odd Alley den, and I'll gather people for the labyrinth. We'll show Premyk what happens to anyone who tries to cut knot for the Stretsko.::

Now Ren knew when and where to find Tserdev. And through her, possibly Dmatsos.

All I have to do is dodge two knots ... and Vargo himself.

Froghole, Lower Bank: Fellun 36

Grey chewed on the inside of his lip, watching his runner pick her way across the fallen beams blocking the river stair. He should begin investigating what was clearly no accident... but that would mean leaving Renata here, when Donaia had asked him to protect her.

She stood with aristocratic poise amid the wreckage, as if she hadn't just nearly been crushed. It must have rattled her, though, because her hands were clenched in the soiled front panel of her surcoat and her gaze, fixed on Vargo, betrayed the tension within. Vargo paid her no mind; he was too busy giving orders to his own people. *A pity that crane didn't land on him.*

Except that would have robbed Grey of his revenge. He meant to see Vargo pay for what he'd done, blowing up the Fiangiolli warehouse and taking Grey's brother, Kolya, with it. What form that vengeance would take was a question he wrestled with day and night... but a beam crushing him flat wasn't it. Whether Vargo fell to a duelist's sword or an executioner's ax, Grey would be the one who made it happen.

He wrenched his gaze away and saw one of Vargo's fists jerk his chin for the man's stone-faced Isarnah bodyguard to follow him into the shadows of the alley.

Grey had been taking every opportunity to spy on Vargo's business. With a swift glance around, he eased behind a stack of crates, close enough to hear their hurried conversation.

"Boss is calling a strike on the Odd Alley Gang tonight," the fist said. "Wants you to put together a hit team."

"He thinks Premyk's behind this?"

A thud, as of a wall being kicked. "Naw, Premyk's a britch-pissing coward who finally decided to cut knot for the Crimson Eyes. But you ask me, this is the sort of thing Tserdev would order. She en't never been happy that Vargo took the aža trade. The Eyes want it back."

A pause. "We'll need more than just the Fog Spiders."

"Makes you miss Sedge, hey?"

The thunk that followed was bare flesh on wood. "Fuck Sedge. If I see him again, I'll skin him for parchment. Tell Vargo I'll handle it, but he's staying home."

"I en't telling Vargo where he can and can't go."

"Who's the britch-pissing coward now?"

Grey slid away before the two broke apart, his mind whirling.

A gang war was the Vigil's business. A noble using his strength against the people of the streets was the Rook's business. And Vargo was a noble now.

Hang his Vigil duty. Grey fell into step behind as Vargo offered Renata his arm and led her away. The man didn't care who he got killed, so long as he achieved his own goals. And Grey owed it to Donaia and Leato to make certain the heir to House Traementis didn't get caught in that man's schemes.

Renata ignored Grey with the studied indifference of the noble-woman she pretended to be. All her attention was on Vargo, in a pretense of friendliness—at least, Grey thought it was pretense.

She wouldn't have told the Rook about Vargo's involvement in Kolya's death if she had any real liking for the man.

Vargo, however, cast an annoyed look over his shoulder. "There's no call to accompany us when you're needed here to investigate, Captain. I can see to the alta's well-being."

Like you did when the crane fell? Grey's voice sounded cold to his ears as he said, "It will take some time for my squad to arrive. I can be spared until then. Unless you mean to leave the alta standing around while you find a replacement coat suitable to be seen in the Pearls."

Renata's soft cough could have been interpreted a dozen ways, but Grey suspected it was meant to hide a laugh. He adopted a concerned frown. "Especially when she might be taking sick."

It was a testament to Vargo's own self-control that he didn't visibly pull back from Renata. His fear of disease wasn't nearly as secret as he probably wished. "Alta Renata, I'd be happy to offer you the services of my phys—"

His words cut off as a quartet of young men rounded the corner up ahead. They nudged each other when they spotted Vargo, smirking like they'd found the trouble they were seeking.

Younger members of the delta houses tended to wear incongruous accessories, the better to flaunt the wealth and reach of their families' trading endeavors. Grey recognized the gold-shot scarves of silken caprash wool that marked these four as Essunta. And thanks to a mercenary charter, they all wore swords at their belts.

They'd been Indestor's clients. After the fall of their patron's house, the Essunta had no reason to love Derossi Vargo.

The man in the lead was Meda Essunta's younger son, Gaetaro. He approached closer than manners allowed, as though Vargo would be intimidated by a bit of posturing. "Why, *Eret* Vargo," he drawled with exaggerated surprise. "Fancy finding *you* on the Lower Bank."

Looking for a fight, it seemed. It galled to be in a position where Grey had to protect Vargo, but Renata was here, and couldn't be carrying more than a hidden knife or two. Setting a hand on his sword, Grey moved to Vargo's other side, hoping the reminder of Vigil presence—and the new Caerulet's patronage—would be enough to make the Essunta boys rethink their grudge.

"Mede Essunta." Vargo's smile was as pleasant as sunlight. "I see you've dislodged your mouth from your mother's teat. Too bad you didn't suckle any wit from her while you were there."

Djek.

Gaetaro's hand went for his sword. Grey made to step forward, but Renata beat him to it, interposing herself between Vargo and the Essunta. "Come now," she said, her Seterin accent a crisp rebuke. "It befits the stature of neither of your houses to brawl like commoners in the street."

"He *is* a commoner," Gaetaro snarled.

"Not any longer," Renata said. "And that means there's a proper way to settle this matter."

Grey's teeth were set hard against each other; it helped keep the sudden laugh inside. He wasn't the only one to hear the echo, either. Vargo drawled, "Alta Renata. You're remarkably fond of volunteering other people for duels."

"Assuming he knows Uniat from a night-piece's hole," Gaetaro spat.

"I'm familiar with both in their contexts," Vargo said with a smile that was half bedroom and all innuendo. "But if I get confused, I'll poke you a few times to remember the difference."

He might be a nobleman now, but he carried no sword, which meant he would need a champion. Grey was trying to figure out how to word his flat refusal when Vargo lifted his walking stick. It had always seemed like a tasteless affectation...but with a twist of the handle, Vargo drew forth a blade. It was thinner than Essunta's but finely made.

Grey's eyes narrowed. Vargo had been carrying that stick for at least a year. But Grey couldn't retroactively arrest him for that. *More's the pity.*

"First blood," Renata said, stepping back as Gaetaro drew his sword. "Conduct yourselves with honor."

What are the chances, Grey thought. It was only a question of who would cheat first.

Within the first pass, he knew that Vargo was either hiding his skill or not actually a very good swordsman. He fought like a man with a really long knife. It was painful to watch, in both style and form—but also because Vargo wasn't aiming to score a point. He was trying to tear into his opponent's softer bits to make him bleed.

Which meant that sooner or later, he was going to lose. And either Vargo preferred to lose dirty rather than clean, or his river rat instincts overwhelmed his pretense at civility.

He'd gotten in too close to make good use of the longer blade. Hooking Gaetaro's foot from beneath him might have been borderline legal—easy to pass that off as simple footwork—but Vargo kicked the man's knee out instead.

Grey had just enough time to swear again before the rest of the Essunta quartet howled in.

If Renata hadn't been there, he would have been tempted to leave Vargo to his fate. But she was, and right now, he was an officer of the Vigil. One who would have to answer some very awkward questions if he hurt a pack of delta gentry. Grey aimed to disarm instead, twisting one blade free with a binding parry, getting the second in an arm lock, but that left the third—

It left the third on the ground, with his sword in Alta Renata's hand. She panted and brushed her hair from her face like she could smooth her genteel mask back into place.

Vargo was in no position to notice. Gaetaro had backed him against a wall, with the point of his blade at Vargo's throat. "Cheating means you lose," Gaetaro snarled. "But here's a mark to make it clear." A quick flash, and Vargo's cheekbone bled.

The retaliation was swift: Vargo seized Gaetaro by the ears and slammed his own skull into the man's nose.

Four delta gentry and the head of a noble house arrested in one go, Grey thought in mixed fury, amusement, and resignation as he flung away the two Essunta swords he'd collected and waded back in. *I can't wait to see Cercel's face.*

Seven Knots, Lower Bank: Fellun 36

This fucking day, Vargo thought sourly as he waited with Varuni and Nikory in an alley behind the Seven Knots labyrinth.

It hadn't taken long for him to get out of the Aerie. That tight-assed Captain Serrado must have known the arrest wouldn't stick; he'd just leapt at the chance to inflict a bell's worth of embarrassment on Vargo before his inevitable release. But on the heels of that farce of a duel with Gaetaro Essunta, and *that* coming on the heels of the crane sabotage . . .

He was almost glad his business tonight was dealing with Premyk. Vargo was in a mood to make people bleed.

Even at this hour, Seven Knots was never really quiet. There were always babes yowling the tenements awake, dogs snuffling in the street for scraps, laborers and skiffers and laundresses making their way between work and home. When a plaza went silent, it was a sure bet that something unpleasant was about to happen—and people around here knew better than to be present when it did.

Premyk waited alone in the plaza. Vargo had sent Nikory and a few others to round him up well in advance of this meeting, giving him plenty of time to stew. The greedy ass had decided to throw his lot and two months of aža profits in with the Stretsko knots. By the time Vargo arrived, Premyk had convinced himself he was doomed to die on the spot . . . which just showed again that he didn't understand his boss.

Retribution would come later.

For now, Premyk was staked out in the plaza as bait, flanked by two of Vargo's people. Tserdev would come to take the traitor's oath and payment, and Vargo would be waiting to take *her*.

He couldn't leave this sort of maneuver to his people, no matter how much Vargo would have preferred to spend the sweltering summer night at home under the cooling effects of a numinat and a slab of cold meat for the lump throbbing on his forehead. The scars on his back were beginning to itch under the layers of sweaty brocade. He was losing the fight against the urge to scratch himself bloody in search of relief when Varuni stiffened beside him.

On the far side of the plaza, an older man with iron-grey braids, one ratted into the long tail of the Stretsko, emerged from the shadows.

"Foolish to be out this late, when even Ažerais lies dreaming," he said in Vraszenian.

After a moment of silence and a surreptitious prod from one of his guards, Premyk blurted, "But Ažerais looks out for fools and children. And w-we are her children."

The Stretsko man gave a low, two-toned whistle that sounded like the call of a dreamweaver bird. After several tense moments, two others entered the plaza, boots clomping and shoulders hunched under the weight of a covered sedan chair.

"Wh-what's this?" Premyk's voice wavered as the bearers set it down. "Tserdev was supposed to take my knot oath herself. That was the arrangement."

"The boss isn't stupid, to walk out in the open," the Stretsko man said. "Half this district wants her netted. Hawks leave the chairs alone." He approached Premyk, pulling out a braided cord knobbed on two ends with small beads. At this distance and in the dark, Vargo couldn't tell the colors, but he'd wager they were crimson. He knew a knot bracelet when he saw one.

"Go on," said the man, holding out the cord for Premyk to take. "Say your words, show your loyalty, and then Tserdev will respond in kind."

Premyk edged back like the man was holding out a snake. Only the presence of the guards at his back kept him in place. "I . . ."

"Is there a problem?" The Stretsko's voice was silk-soft and sure, like he already knew the answer.

Enough of this theatre. Vargo stepped out of the shadowed alleyway. "It seems there is," he said, approaching the sedan chair. The bearers only managed half a shout each before they slumped into choke holds from Varuni and Nikory. "Premyk's proven he has all the loyalty of a cat in heat. I thought I might save your boss the trouble of being betrayed the same way he's betrayed me."

"En't no loyalty to be had with cuffs. Not to them, not from them," the Stretsko man said, shifting into Liganti. He turned to Premyk, as though he had no concern for Vargo's approach or the fact that he was outnumbered at least five to one. "You should have kept that in mind before betraying the Crimson Eyes, slip-knot."

"I didn't have a choice!" Premyk wailed. "He didn't give me a choice!"

"There's always a choice," the man said, drawing a knife. Vargo tensed—but instead of turning the blade on any of them, the Stretsko sliced the cord he was holding in half before casting it into Premyk's face, followed by a glob of spit.

He was disarmed and on the ground a moment later, held kneeling by Premyk's guards. Vargo pressed the tip of his cane to the man's sternum. "That was both dramatic and unnecessary." Then he raised his voice to address the sedan chair and its occupant. "Tserdev, why don't you come out of there before I have my people drag you out."

The chuckle that answered him was too low to be Tserdev's. Vargo had the sinking realization that the Masks were laughing at him, a moment before the chair door opened...and, like a black bird spreading its wings, the Rook stepped out.

Vargo choked twice on his incredulous laugh at the sight of the famous vigilante ducking under the chair's lintel: first because he thought it was some trick of Tserdev's, then because he knew it wasn't. No ordinary hood cast such impenetrable shadows.

"This fucking day," he muttered, lifting his cane from the Stretsko's chest, though he wasn't stupid enough to draw the sword hidden inside. Vargo was no duelist; he'd had proof enough of that this morning. He couldn't slap down a delta pup with his blade, much less a master like the Rook.

But maybe it didn't need to come to swords. He dredged up a careless smile. "This is a surprise and an honor. To what do I owe the pleasure? The Rook doesn't usually trouble himself with knot business." A few twitches of his fingers silently ordered Varuni and the others to be ready in case his bullshitting failed.

"Knots tangling are usually no business of mine, no," the Rook said. His voice was resonant and unplaceable. Vargo kept his gaze on the shadow where a face should be, but there were no clues to be had. *I hate not knowing who I'm dealing with.*

Except he knew enough. Nadežra's legendary outlaw, who usually only troubled himself with—

"Nobles," the Rook said, "are a different matter."

Fuck. All the time Vargo had spent calculating the costs and benefits of gaining a title, and he'd never considered this.

We have a small problem, old man, he thought to the spider he'd sent out to play backup sentry.

::More than one, I fear, and rather large. The Stretsko brought more than just the Rook. They've got our people surrounded.::

Double fuck. That left Vargo with Varuni, Nikory, and the two fists set to keep Premyk in line . . . against the *Rook.*

Vargo stalled for time. "If I'd known you were so keen to meet, I'd have thrown a ball in your honor and spared you having to deal with Tserdev." He took a slow step back, two, and the Rook followed.

"Making me compete with all the others who want a piece of you?" The Rook's blade whispered free of its sheath. "I preferred a more intimate setting for our first dance."

"Lucky me," Vargo said, keeping his voice falsely light. "But as flattered as I am by the attention, I fear I must decline."

At his signal, Varuni's hidden chain whip coiled around the Rook's ankle and yanked him off balance.

And Vargo fled.

Orostin had bribed the caretaker to leave the back door to the labyrinth unbolted. At least that part of the operation hadn't gone cocked; it swung open easily, and Vargo bolted it behind him. The Rook would have to scale the wall to come after him—after fighting through the mess outside.

But that was the only thing to go right. Not a moment later, three Stretsko appeared by the gate at the front of the labyrinth.

Vargo crouched, choking up on his cane. Unlike born nobles and their duelists, he didn't have to follow any rules besides the main one: survive.

The Stretsko eyed the cane warily as they crossed the looping path of the labyrinth toward him. That gave Vargo the distraction he needed to palm a knife with his other hand and flick it into the leftmost rat. He aimed for the gut and got the arm instead, but it was enough to slow the man down as the other two charged.

He wielded his cane like a stick at first, trying to bull his way through. When one of the Stretsko was stupid enough to make a grab for it, Vargo twisted the sword free and cut a deep gash along her forearm. But with three on one, he didn't have enough room to make good use of the long blade, and then one of the rats locked his arm behind him and—

::Vargo, watch out! There's someone else here!::

A black shadow leapt from the roof, hooking a Stretsko rat and dragging him to the ground. *The muck-fucking Rook*, Vargo thought furiously—but it wasn't.

The newcomer was too slender, her form obviously feminine where the Rook's was swathed into ambiguity by coat and hood. Overlapping leather plates layered like black petals down her chest and arms. Her dark hair was pinned to her head in a swirl of Vraszenian braids, and a mask of rose-tatted black lace broke the upper part of her face into an obfuscating pattern.

"I know you," he said, frozen by the realization. "You were at the amphitheatre."

She'd been one of the people fighting the zlyzen across the lines of the great numinat melting the line between waking and dream. He'd set people to find out more about her, and gotten only children's tales and wild gossip in return. "You're—"

A Stretsko arm tightened around his throat before he could say *the Black Rose*. "Fuck off," a rough voice snarled in Vargo's ear, while the man's other hand hovered ready with a knife.

"What disrespect, using such language in Ažerais's sanctuary." Her voice didn't have the unplaceable quality of the Rook's. It was melodiously Nadežran, with a thin veil of amusement over cold disapproval. "Wasn't Indestor's desecration enough? Or will you commit murder right here on the sacred path?"

She has a point, Vargo wanted to say, but he hadn't survived this long by turning smartass when a man had a knife at his throat.

::Maybe he's afraid of spiders—::

Maybe let's not test that theory? Vargo thought back before Alsius decided to play hero.

"Ažerais don't give three blinks for the likes of this one. Kinless, gutless, *and* a cuff. That's three times worthless," the Stretsko holding Vargo snarled. But his voice and knife wavered as though the Black Rose's words had struck home.

"Shed blood here, and it is *you* who becomes worthless. If he is meant to pay, pattern will bring him to you again."

The brawl outside couldn't be over, but inside the labyrinth, everything was quiet. The Stretsko at the Rose's feet crawled to her friend with the knife in his arm. Helping him stand, she muttered to the one holding Vargo, "Kill him and you bring all his knots down on us. Tserdev has no wish for open war, not yet. Let's go."

"Him first," the Black Rose said, nodding at Vargo. "Then you."

Vargo had a thousand questions—but he also had a self-preservation streak as wide and deep as the Dežera. And questions could be answered by other means, once he was out of this rats' nest. He slipped away when his captor's arm loosened, only pausing when he was at the entrance to the temple. "You have my thanks, Lady Rose."

Come on, Alsius. Time to go. Plunking a forro into the stone offering box, Vargo saluted them all with his cane.

Then he got the fuck out of Seven Knots.

Seven Knots, Lower Bank: Fellun 36

The old man sweeping the floor had sensibly vanished. Once Vargo had time to escape, Ren let the Stretsko leave. Alone, she blew out a long, slow breath.

One that stopped short when a familiar voice said, "You let Vargo get away. You *helped* him get away."

Dust rose where the Rook landed on the edge of the labyrinth, but little sound accompanied it. Only his words, low and steady as a duelist's blade. Although his sword was sheathed as he circled around the path toward her, that meant little with the Rook.

And she'd just set herself against him.

When she'd made her plan to eavesdrop on Vargo's confrontation with Tserdev, she hadn't expected it to be shot awry by the Rook. But one chance lost was another gained: If Vargo believed the Black Rose was willing to aid him, he might try to make use of her.

Assuming the Rook didn't strike her down for getting in his way.

Ren held up her empty hands in a gesture of peace and spoke in the Black Rose's voice. "You don't kill. Do you want other people doing it for you? Not as justice, but one knot tearing another apart? In a labyrinth, no less." He might not care about that, though. There was no hint that he was Vraszenian, apart from knowing the language. She'd even once thought he could be Leato.

"You could have stopped them without letting him go. But it seems you have other loyalties." The Rook stepped closer—close enough to attack, if he chose. "I thought you knew what he was. I thought you were different. But I suppose I was wrong about you, *Lady* Rose."

The stress on that title was a warning in its own right. He knew who she was. Ren. Arenza. Alta Renata.

Nobles are a different matter, he'd told Vargo. And while her nobility had been a lie before, her recent adoption had made it truth.

"I know what he is," she said, letting her fury creep into her voice. "What I don't know is his real aim. He trusts . . . my other self, but she's not in a position to see everything he's doing. If he trusts the Black Rose, too, I get a view into what he does when he *isn't* playing at noble life."

The hood cocked to one side. "So that was your plan? Why you *happen* to be here tonight? So you can earn Eret Vargo's trust?" It sounded faintly mocking, but some of the cold anger had left his voice.

She grimaced. "No, I was going to follow Tserdev back to her lair. The ziemetse want to have words with her brother Dmatsos. By the way, thanks for sinking my plans."

A moment passed in silence, followed by a noise that sounded like... Was he *laughing* at her?

"It seems we sank each other's plans," he said. "Shall we call it a draw, and agree to warn each other in the future?"

His words seemed friendly enough. But Ren couldn't let herself forget: Whoever was under that hood knew her secret. Knew she was a con artist, not Letilia's daughter. And becoming a noblewoman had put her among his enemies, just like Vargo. He'd promised not to use the truth against her... but that was before her adoption. If those two things came into conflict, which would prove stronger?

If only she knew *his* identity. That would be leverage enough to keep her safe. But in the absence of that, she'd have to try another tactic.

"I think we can do better than that," Ren said. "When I told you Vargo was responsible for Kolya Serrado's death, you said you work alone. But..." She hesitated, artfully, emphasizing it to make sure her uncertainty wasn't hidden by her mask.

He'd gone still. "But what?" he asked, all trace of laughter gone.

"I patterned you," she said, letting the words out in a rush. "It didn't tell me who you are under there, only confirmed things people already guess at. That you aren't the first Rook. That it's passed from person to person. But it also showed me—"

This time the hesitation wasn't calculated. She could see the tension building in his body, calling forth the same in her own. She should never have started talking—except that he needed to know what she'd seen. Her voice slipped toward Vraszenian cadences, if not its sounds. "I know not what the Rook was created for, not specifically. To fight some kind of poison in this city. But the cards told me you have a chance now to do something about that—something more than what the Rooks before you have done. A chance to end it. Or..."

He knew enough about pattern to guess at her meaning. "Or a chance to fail."

Forever. If the Rook missed this chance, then whatever he fought against—a corruption that went deeper than the nobility—would win. "I don't want that to happen," Ren said, and she didn't have to fake the tremor in her voice. That reading had shaken her to the bone. "I want to help you stop it. And I bet you anything it has something to do with Derossi Vargo."

"Vargo." He turned away from her, and for a moment she thought he might slam his fist into one of the pillars. Instead he leaned against it, the empty shadow of his hood staring at the writhing facade of Šen Kryzet. The Mask of Worms: the same card she'd seen in her patterning of him. "That's a bet I wouldn't take," he said softly. "Nobody rises to power that quickly without something backing them. Not in this city."

Then the hood turned toward her. "Nobody."

Did he suspect *her*? Of what? "The only person backing me is Tess. If she is your corruption, then I have a great many questions."

He huffed, suspicion draining out of his shoulders and back. "Yes, I've spent the better part of two centuries fighting against the terror that is Ganllechyn seamstresses."

"You haven't seen what she's like when sewing. The terror is more real than you think." Her reply seemed to come out on its own, carried by the relief of that tension passing. *What do I call him?* "Rook" seemed too direct. It was a title, not a name. She opted for no name at all. "I can help you. With Vargo, and with—whatever it is you're fighting."

That was a less-than-subtle invitation for him to explain, but he didn't take the bait. "In return for what?"

She hadn't thought that far. Normally she would have had the whole thing planned: offers and counteroffers, points of concession and demand. This time her only thought had been to help. But how plausible would that be, coming from her?

"Revenge," she said at last. "Vargo...he made me trust him. I thought I could read him, and he used that to make me believe he saw me as a friend. Not a tool to further his schemes. I want him to pay for that."

"It seems Eret Vargo has many debts coming due. I'll keep your offer in mind—and endeavor not to get on your bad side." The Rook backed away and unbolted the rear door of the labyrinth. "If you have need of me, you can leave a message on your balcony. Sleep well, Lady Rose."

And with a nod, he vanished.

The Face of Weaving

Kingfisher, Lower Bank: Colbrilun 13

Almost two weeks after the debacle in Seven Knots, the Faces finally looked kindly upon Ren.

Dalisva Korzetsu's list didn't just name Branek and his key supporters, the ones who had backed the amphitheatre bombing. It also named Idusza Polojny, the channel through which Mezzan Indestor had provoked that bombing in the first place, as well as the person who'd belatedly tried to stop it: Koszar Andrejek.

Ren knew the former leader of the Anduske had been badly injured in the schism. Some of the rumors said he was dead, and certainly no one had seen him since Veiled Waters. But if he'd lived, his allies might have sought treatment for him, so Ren—as Arenza—was scouring the bonesetters and herbalists of the Lower Bank.

After opening far too many mussels, she finally found a pearl. "I know not if it's the one you seek," an old Meszaros gammer told her, "but I saw a fellow around that time taken to Alinka. Beat up, he was, and bad. Those with him, not much better."

"Where can I find Alinka?" Arenza asked, and received directions to a tenement in a part of Kingfisher hard by the border of Seven Knots.

It was one of the buildings that used to house a wealthy

Vraszenian family in the days before the Tyrant's conquest, two stories tall and built around a courtyard. Now it was carved up into many smaller dwellings, usually with shops or workrooms on the ground floor and sleeping rooms above. Ren had lived in a similar place as a child, and her throat tightened at the memory.

Especially since there was a child outside the door she sought, playing with dolls on the cracked flagstones of the courtyard.

Bloodthirsty play, from the speech one doll was making to the others. "—won't let these Liganti pigs treat our city like a sty," the girl declaimed. Her toy was a strange study in contrasts, with a beautifully carved face and wooden limbs and hair of braided burgundy silk, but wearing a stained patchwork coat of rags and tattered ribbons. "To the river we will drive them, and stand on their shoulders till they drown in their own muck! On rooftops we will dry their bloated bodies, and burn them in the fens! We will not rest until the clans hold Nadežra once more! Who stands with me?"

The girl gave a whispered roar for the crowd's response. If the clothes and hair hadn't given it away, the speech would have. The doll was meant to be Elsivin the Red, born a son of the Kiraly, later becoming a szorsa. Like some who chose the path of the rimaše, her interest in pattern reading was lackluster at best. But she'd been a dedicated revolutionary, determined to take back Ažerais's holy city. Fifty years had passed since her revolt failed, but Vraszenians still paid the price in increased tariffs, while Elsivin's name was still honored in whispers. And apparently, in children's stoop games.

Ren's confidence in her lead solidified. The child had learned to play at sedition from someone; this might well be a Stadnem Anduske safe house.

The girl looked up as Arenza approached. Her sun-streaked hair was coming out of its two braids, and her clothes were patched and dusty. "Are you looking for my mama?" she asked, squinting into the sun.

"If your mama is Alinka, yes."

"MAMA!"

Arenza wouldn't have been surprised to see that bellow blow the

front door off its hinges. Instead, after the pigeons squawked and settled, the door opened to reveal a careworn young woman. Her hair
was kept out of her face by a practical crown braid, and both strands
of the marriage token braided into it were the grey of the Kiraly raccoon. When she saw Arenza, she hurriedly wiped her hands clean
on the frayed panel sash that decorated her skirt. "Can I help you?"

"I'm Arenza Lenskaya Tsverin," Ren said in Vraszenian. "I seek
some friends of mine, and I heard that to you they might have come
for healing."

The curiosity in the woman's expression closed into guarded caution. She glanced past Arenza, searching the courtyard—not busy,
but by no means empty. Untying a cord from her sash, she tugged a
toddler out from his hiding place in her skirts. "Yvieny, keep watch
over your brother," she instructed, tying the cord around the girl's
wrist. "And wander not from the stoop. It'll be supper soon."

Ignoring the girl's grumbles, Alinka gestured Arenza into the
workshop and closed the door. The lamplit interior seemed doubly
dim after the brightness outside. Ren smelled the herbs before her
eyes adjusted to see them, a mix of floral and medicinal, fresh and
pungent, one step off from the incense and resin that had scented her
childhood home.

The counter running along the back of the room had been transformed into an herbalist's workbench, but hanging alongside the
curtain that veiled the stairs going up to the sleeping rooms were
coils of cording in every color of the dreamweaver. Finished knots
dangled from a beam: the tight budded rose of Ažerais for good luck,
the seven-lobed wagon knot for longevity, the simpler triple clover-
leaf for family. The table dominating the center was long instead of
round, better to lay sick clients on than patterns, but the pot kept
warm by the hearth steamed with the starchy scent of cooked rice,
and the chairs around it were padded with thickly embroidered
pillows.

It felt like home. Simultaneously a soft embrace, and a knife of
grief between the ribs.

Alinka didn't move farther into the room. Likely she'd only let

Arenza in to keep their conversation secret from her children and anyone who might be loitering in the courtyard. "A healer should not speak of her patients to strangers," she said. "Who are your friends?"

If this were a Stadnem Anduske safe house, Arenza would have been asked for a password. "Idusza Nadjulskaya Polojny is my friend, but Koszar Yureski Andrejek is the one who needed help. I have for them a warning." She straightened her shawl, drawing Alinka's attention. It was the fine shawl the Rook had given her, and while the hidden knives were no use here, the embroidery was.

Alinka's eyes widened when she recognized it as a pattern-er's shawl. Immediately she stepped back, hand to heart as though Arenza were an honored guest. "You are Idusza's szorsa friend! Apologies for my rudeness. It is only . . . not all who ask after friends are truly friends. Will you take some tea?"

"Thank you, yes." There were shoes by the door, and Alinka was wearing slippers; that and her liquid accent marked her as not from Nadežra. A southerner, with the customs and speech patterns of a true Vraszenian, born and raised away from Liganti influence. It made Ren feel out of place as she surreptitiously wiped her boot soles and stepped across to the table. "I understand your caution. I've searched since the terrible business during Veiled Waters, but they have hidden themselves well."

"Yet pattern brought you here. You are as gifted as Idusza claimed."

Play my skill up, or down? "Pattern, and a good deal of searching," Arenza said with a laugh. "I hope you can shorten my quest."

Alinka had busied herself with brewing the tea. It wasn't just hospitality; she was hiding trembling hands. "Koszar was badly injured, and then infection set in. Several days he lay here, before they could move him. I know not where they took him after that."

The tea she brewed was soothing, fragrant with chamomile and mint, as though Alinka could tell Ren had been living the lives of three people with the hours of only one. But the steaming cup thunked a little too hard onto the table. *You know exactly where he is,*

Arenza thought, blowing across the surface of the tea. Alinka was right to be cautious, though. Any woman with the right kind of shawl could claim to be Idusza's szorsa friend. "Have you some way to send them a message?"

Alinka brightened. "Certainly!"

"I would be grateful." The mug had a small crack on the far rim. The room was cozy and clean as such places went, but Alinka's clothing was patched like her daughter's, and there wasn't a lot of food on the shelves. Once upon a time it would have looked ordinary to Ren...before her adoption into House Traementis.

The same impulse that made her offer to aid the Rook drove the words out of her without thinking: "I can pay for your help."

"What? No, no." Alinka waved her hands in front of her. "To reunite friends, I'll take no money—and doubly not when helping a szorsa. This city has not changed me so much that I forget to honor those blessed by Ažerais."

It had been a clumsy offer, more Liganti than Vraszenian. With outsiders they haggled, but among themselves, debts took a different form. Arenza said, "Then let me thank you with a pattern."

Delight bloomed in Alinka's expression. But as Arenza reached for her deck, Yvieny's voice pierced the walls again—this time in a shriek of delight—and a moment later, the door opened.

To reveal Captain Grey Serrado.

In rumpled clothes that were neither his dress vigils nor his patrol slops. He had the toddler balanced on one hip, a basket overflowing with greens on the other, and a shrieking Yvieny riding his leg as he dragged them all through the doorway.

"Mama! Mama! I got honey stones, see?" Yvieny released her grip to hold up a cone of hard, sticky candy.

Serrado set down the basket, freeing a hand to tousle the little girl's hair into even wilder tangles. In Vraszenian he said, "Scold me not, Alinka. I know you wish her to..."

His words faded as he caught sight of Arenza sitting at the table. Ren hoped desperately that her face wasn't showing what she felt: the free-fall horror of realizing exactly what she'd stumbled into.

Grey Serrado had worked with Idusza to stop the bombing. Of course he'd helped the wounded Koszar afterward.

I'm sitting in his house. And Alinka is his wife.

Kingfisher, Lower Bank: Colbrilun 13

"You…have a client." Grey's words thudded like cobbles, inelegant and stupid. Yvieny had warned him that someone was with Alinka; he'd been braced for anybody other than the woman in front of him. *She found me. She found us. How the hell did she figure out the Rook's secret?*

He diverted his attention to Jagyi, who had seized his ear and was tugging like it would detach if pulled hard enough. Hopefully, that would cover for his flinch on seeing Ren—Arenza—sitting blithely at Alinka's table. He had to get her out of here before she said anything she shouldn't…but first, he had to act like everything was normal, so Alinka's suspicions wouldn't be aroused.

What was normal in this situation? "I meant not to interrupt—"

"You interrupt nothing." Alinka sorted through the basket he'd brought. "And a dinner of rice alone would be bland. Watercress. Taro. No lotus root?"

"There was none to be had." He shifted to keep Arenza in his peripheral vision while pretending to listen to Alinka's scolding. Her gaze was on her tea, chin tucked low to hide her face. As though *she* was afraid he'd recognize *her*.

Relief and doubt warred within him. If she was hiding, she didn't realize he knew she was Ren, and Renata. Which meant she had not, in fact, unmasked him as the Rook.

Except Grey had seen firsthand how good of a liar she was.

He was chasing his own tail, the usual mental divisions that kept his life separate from the Rook's falling apart like cheap paper in rain. He hadn't yet figured out what to do when Alinka took Jagyi from him, saying, "Let go of your uncle's ear, bibi," and Arenza's gaze came up in startlement. It flicked briefly to Alinka's marriage knot, then to Grey's hair, too short to hold a braid, before skittering away. He nearly laughed. *She thought Alinka was my wife.*

Then a shadow passed across her expression as she tied the threads together. Grey was a northerner, Alinka southern, so they couldn't be born to the same family. That meant Alinka must be Kolya's widow.

Normally Grey was able to juggle these kinds of situations like a master street performer. But it was too much, with too little warning: the collision of what he knew, what Ren knew, their assorted identities and secrets. He needed space to think it all through, without her watching; he couldn't trust his own mask right now.

Since he couldn't throw Arenza out, Grey took the vegetables from Alinka instead. "I'll deal with this. You should see to your client."

"Actually, I am *her* client," Alinka said. "She offered to pattern me—"

The chair scraped across the floor as Arenza stood up. "My apologies; I just remembered I have not the time today. And you are busy besides. But I will come back, if I may. And you will pass the message to Idusza...?"

She was looking for *Idusza*? True, they'd met during the riots—but no, that had been Renata, not Arenza. Did she know Koszar was upstairs, still bedridden from his wounds? What in eleven hells was going on?

That chin tucked down, hiding her face. He'd seen that posture before...in the pretty young patterner he ran off a street corner months ago. And Idusza had sought Grey out because an unnamed szorsa told her to.

He'd assumed he'd discovered all of Ren's games. *More fool me.*

Ordinarily Alinka would have pressed a guest to stay for dinner, but with the dangerous secret just above their heads, she offered only assurances and farewells as Arenza departed. Once the intruder was gone, she pulled on gloves to clean the taro root and said, "I know you distrust szorsas, but that one has Ažerais's gift. How else to explain how she found us?"

Grey feared the explanation had nothing to do with Ažerais. Ren was resourceful, and no matter how careful he'd been, someone could have noticed Andrejek's midnight arrival. "We cannot keep him here," he said, gaze straying to the stairway.

"Ask me not to move a man so injured. When his eyes focus and his speech stops slurring, then I'll consider it." Kneeling, she gathered Yvieny into a hug and kissed her daughter's thistle-wild hair. "You did so well, alča. Keeping watch and keeping secret. Can you continue doing that for Mama?"

More interested now in her honey stones than in the stranger upstairs that mostly slept, Yvieny mumbled agreement around sticky fingers. Alinka met Grey's eyes. "And can you take a message to my patient's friends? Perhaps a szorsa can help them where we cannot."

"I will," Grey said, giving Alinka a kiss on the brow and calling out a farewell to Yvie and Jagyi.

He was halfway out the door before Alinka realized he was leaving. "I meant not for you to go now—"

"Best not to wait, and I still have a pile of Vigil paperwork to get through. Wait not for me. Likely I will sleep in my office again."

Grey closed the door on her objections, worn thin after over a year of living on top of each other. After his brother's death, Alinka had needed support, and Grey couldn't afford to pay for both his rented room and this place. But neither could he risk her or the children catching him sneaking out at night. Dodging his fellow hawks was easier.

It wasn't the Aerie he headed to, though, nor Idusza. After the Black Rose's warning in Seven Knots, and knowing Indestor had chosen Ren for his ritual because she'd been conceived during the Great Dream, Grey was inclined to agree that she had uncanny insight and luck. Was this the first time a szorsa—a true one, blessed with the gift—had ever patterned the Rook? Had the hood really been enough to hide him from the eyes of a goddess? What if Ren took it into her head to pattern *Grey*?

He cut through Kingfisher with rapid strides, toward the

townhouse of the person who knew the Rook the best...because she used to be him.

Kingfisher, Lower Bank: Colbrilun 13

Ryvček's silver-shot hair was damp with sweat, and she hadn't bothered putting down her practice sword before opening her door. "Szerado. You look like a zlyzen is on your heels."

"Don't joke about that," he muttered, sliding past her into the entryway.

"Would you like to come in? No, worry not; I was sitting idle when you arrived." She shut the door behind him and headed for the back of the narrow townhouse. "Whatever it is, you can talk while I practice. Though why I bother when every two days some idiot hires me, the Masks alone can say. Has everyone forgotten how to settle grievances without steel?"

The back room was Ryvček's training space. She might be one of the top duelists in Nadežra, but only fools thought that meant she didn't have to practice anymore. In addition to teaching her students, she spent at least two hours a day here, stretching, drilling footwork, lunging at the wall until the paneling cracked and had to be replaced again. The eyebrow she arched at him asked silently whether he was as diligent, and Grey hid a guilty wince. Most of his "practice" took the form of either Vigil or Rook business.

He slouched against the wall, well out of reach from his former teacher's sword. "Two weeks ago, I escorted Alta Renata on a trip to the Lower Bank. That night, the Rook ran into the Black Rose in Seven Knots. And just now, Arenza Lenskaya was having tea with Alinka. In her *house*."

Ryvček's blade thudded into the wall a good three inches above the usual mark.

She retreated from her lunge and stared at him. "She knows?"

"I'm not sure." That steady gaze made him feel like a new student who'd never touched a blade. Ryvček had worn the hood for over twenty years before she'd passed it on to him, less than two years ago; compared to her, he was as green as spring grass. "She had plausible reasons for being in all three places, and today she rushed out like she was afraid of being recognized herself. But in Seven Knots, she told the Rook she'd patterned him. And she knew things we don't talk about."

The stillness of Ryvček's body was that of a swordswoman, preparing to strike. "You wondered about her success. Think you that she knows these things because of pattern? Or because she has one of the medallions?"

The possibility had crossed his mind before. "The Traementis started falling to ruin when Letilia left. And started improving when Renata returned. A medallion might explain the shift."

He didn't want to contemplate it. Ren had been an ally to him and the Rook both; if it weren't for her help, Veiled Waters would have ended very differently. The thought that she might hold a piece of the Tyrant's corruption—the same corruption the Rook fought against—made Grey feel sick.

For once, talking about pattern was preferable. "As for the reading...she *is* born of Ažerais. I don't think she's a charlatan."

"Unlike all the others?"

Grey met Ryvček's smirk with a glower. "Perhaps." She knew a little of his life before coming to Nadežra, and why he disliked frauds. But his teacher was good at putting boundaries between the past and the present; she didn't really understand why bygones might still scar him now.

Ryvček resumed her lunges, the point of her sword beating a steady rhythm against her wall, undoubtedly to the annoyance of her neighbor. "Then what will you do?"

He'd come to her because he didn't *know*. But while Ryvček tolerated him asking for occasional advice, in the end, she was no longer the Rook. She'd walked away from it—something very few of their predecessors had managed.

Grey scrubbed at his face. "She knows there's a poison lacing through this city. She offered to help. I didn't find a medallion when

I searched her townhouse after the Night of Hells, but I could have missed it. If she does have one, it's possible she doesn't know what it is. Which means she might actually work with me." Maybe that was what her reading meant: the chance to finally break through a wall that had stood for two hundred years.

Even if it was a slim chance, it made his answer clear. "I think I need to risk getting closer. If she trusts the Rook, maybe she'll tell him something."

Ryvček paused again, this time in thought. "You were concerned that she cannot defend herself—not as a noble should. I have begun training her. A chance it might offer me, to learn something useful." Familiar amusement flared in her smile. "If nothing else, I'll have a few afternoons of getting sweaty and close with a lovely young woman."

His teacher had always been good at surprising a laugh from him. "I almost wish I could watch. She might not be much with a sword, but when it comes to verbal sparring, I think you'll find you've met your match." He grinned. "Especially if she drops the Renata act and fights dirty."

Ryvček's dark eyes twinkled as though she would like nothing better. Then they dimmed. "And if she starts to see through *your* act?"

It wasn't the first time someone had gotten close to discovering the Rook's identity. Grey had centuries of ways to deal with it that he could draw upon. And he might not like szorsas, but he knew how they worked—not the ones with the true gift. The charlatans.

He said, "Then I'll give her a better performance to distract her."

Isla Traementis, the Pearls: Colbrilun 14

Too many nights awake and days sleeping had thrown off Donaia's old habits. Exhaustion dragged her eyelids down as she sat with Tanaquis and Renata in the salon, abetted by the afternoon sunlight dancing on dust motes and Meatball draped heavy in her lap. And the gentle burr of Tanaquis's voice as she went over the astrological charts of the petitioners for adoption...

Donaia jerked her head up from its dip, dragging herself back to Tanaquis's words. "I can't recommend her. Bad fortune from now until Ninat claims her. Nencoral Fintenus, on the other hand..." Tanaquis shuffled one chart off onto an empty chair co-opted for that purpose and presented the next one. "Very promising. Prime in Quarat True with an Alter in Tricat, and both Paumillis and Corillis full at her birth. I wouldn't be surprised if House Fintenus counteroffered in a bid to keep her."

"I've no interest in getting mired in a bidding war," Donaia said, pinching her brow in an attempt to ward off sleep. "House Traementis is established enough that people should fight to join us."

She felt guilty for asking Renata to sit in on this meeting. The girl was run ragged these days, handling their Charterhouse business; Donaia ought to hire another advocate to take some of the burden off her. Another advocate wouldn't have Renata's style, though, her gift for reading people's moods, her ability to lure people into believing her foreign origins made her an easy mark.

But when it came to evaluating candidates for adoption, Donaia knew the waters best. She couldn't hand this task off to Renata. At the same time, she was strongly considering taking Scaperto up on his offer of time away, in his bay villa—which would mean leaving Renata in charge of the house. The girl would need to know who she was dealing with. Her and Giuna both; after all, whomever they adopted would be their new cousins.

"It needn't be a bidding war," Renata mused. "I've met Nencoral a few times. I suspect we could offer her some...nonmonetary benefits. After all, she wouldn't have applied if she were happy in House Fintenus."

That was the other reason to have Renata here. She looked at these people and saw potential. All Donaia could see were flaws.

She didn't *want* new family. She wanted the family she'd had. The family she'd lost.

Donaia pressed one hand against her belly. Last night she'd

dreamed she was bearing, and in the way of dreams, it had been both her pregnancy with Leato, and a new child coming. Only when she went into labor, she gave birth to one of those hideous monsters that had killed him. A zlyzen.

Renata and Tanaquis kept talking, moving from chart to chart. Donaia was so glad to see a friendship growing between those two. Renata had plenty of friends in Nadežra, but sometimes she wondered if the girl felt at all close to any of them. Superficial entertainments were no substitute for a true bond. She'd learned that all too sharply when House Traementis's false friends had fallen away.

"Would *you* consider it?" she asked.

The question popped out without her thinking, and cut through the conversation like an imbued knife. Tanaquis blinked. "Consider what? Adopting Algetto myself? I don't think he'd accept demotion to gentry status. And House Fienola, all one of me, has even less to offer him than House Traementis used to."

Renata shifted in her chair, and Tanaquis blinked again. "I suppose that sounded bad. Don't worry. I don't *mind* being the last; everything dies eventually."

"No, I meant—" Donaia struggled for a more polite phrasing, recalled that it was Tanaquis she was speaking to, and cast delicacy aside. "If we offered to adopt you. Would you join House Traementis?"

Renata's lips parted on a soft "ah," her hazel eyes darkening as she ran social calculations at the speed Tanaquis could run astrological ones. But it wasn't Renata's approval Donaia wanted. If she was going to open her house and her register, let at least one of the new entrants be an old friend.

"Hmm. Ninat does lead to Illi. The death of the old makes way for the birth of the new," Tanaquis mused, oblivious to Donaia's shiver at the mention of death and birth together. "My chart should be acceptable. And you're no longer cursed. You have more than enough room at Traementis Manor for more people…but my observatory is set up just how I like it."

Tucking a stray wisp behind her ear, Tanaquis gave Donaia the same look Meatball had when he didn't understand a command. "I see no significant flaws—but also no profit to you."

"Not everything is about profit," Renata said.

Donaia's emphatic gesture at her niece took the place of the words welling up in her throat, crowding too close to get out. As Tanaquis's brow furrowed, her grey eyes shifting back and forth between the two of them, the knot untied itself enough for Donaia to say, "You're a friend. And you'll stay a friend regardless of whether you accept the offer—but I want the chance to choose *one* person for something other than mercenary reasons."

"Oh. I hadn't considered that aspect." After a moment's more hesitation, Tanaquis reached over and awkwardly covered Donaia's hand where it rested on Meatball's ruff. "It's a kind offer. I should consider what the consequences for us both might be, and I'll need to cast more charts...but I will think about it."

Splinter Alley, the Shambles: Colbrilun 17

Vargo didn't know the Shambles as well as some of Nadežra's other slums. It was a rabbit's warren of stalls and squats and seedy shops servicing the merchants and mercenaries who traveled the Dawn and Dusk Roads, everyone squeezed between the Cinquerat's taxes and the local fire crews. The only organized activity that made any profit in the Shambles was the off-book brothels fronted by papaver dens, and that was one business that Vargo did his best to stay out of.

The brothels, and the children caught in them.

Vargo might not know the Shambles well, but he knew not to walk its streets in his usual finery. He'd forced himself into the unwashed coat and shirt of one of Nikory's crew—his skin itching at the inevitability of lice—and he'd donned a cheap mask despite the urge to take his disease-preventing one instead. The Shambles was no place for Eret Vargo.

Even with those precautions, he drew the notice of the beggars and pickpockets working the spaces between stalls. The knot of art-fully hollow-eyed waifs that flocked around him looked hungry, but not for food. Pity-rustling must be more lucrative than he remem-bered, if they depended on makeup and dirt smudges to ply their trade.

"How long has she been in operation?" Vargo asked Nikory, who flanked him opposite a frowning Varuni. Since the events at the amphitheatre, he hadn't been allowed to take a shit without her standing sentry. He might have been touched, if he didn't know she was just protecting her family's investment. They relied on him to get their goods past the tariffs.

"Started hearing her name about two years back," Nikory mur-mured, his split tongue flickering out to wet his lips as he eyed the children. They'd swelled in numbers, which might have been more threatening if any of them came higher than Vargo's elbow. Even so, Varuni's chain whip clinked as she studied the gathering crowd.

Vargo side-eyed Nikory. "And you didn't tell me about her because...?"

"She was an eleven-year-old brat!" Nikory's voice went high with incredulity. "We was supposed to take that seriously?"

I was eleven.

::And definitely a brat.:: Vargo hadn't expected the reply, and he flinched. He hadn't meant to think that loud enough for Alsius to hear.

He flicked his collar, where the spider had hidden himself away. *Takes one to know one, old man.*

Smiling at the mental sputters that followed, Vargo stopped before a run-down building not much different than all the others lining the narrow, winding alleyway. A plank hanging from one corner was carved with a crude, four-petaled flower, smoke curl-ing lazily up from its center. The vermilion paint had long worn away, remnants of it clinging only in the deepest grain of the wood, like veins of heart's blood. Tarry soot blackened the window on the inside, but Vargo spied the twitch of a curtain parting and then fall-ing back into place.

At his nod, Nikory rapped on the door.

The speed and efficiency with which they were let in, searched, and divested of the few weapons they'd brought was impressive. Varuni was allowed to keep her chain, but only after her look promised pain for the large boy who'd tried to take it from her.

Vargo wasn't worried. Over two years, Arkady Bones had risen to become the biggest—and youngest—knot leader in the Shambles. Hurting Derossi Vargo, leader of half the knots on the Lower Bank, would be stupid; this girl had proven she was anything but.

Once the door crew was satisfied that Vargo and his people posed no danger to their boss, a guide led them through a main room packed with nests of blankets. Some of those were occupied by multiple children snuggled together for comfort. From beyond a curtain-veiled doorway came the meaty aroma of steamed dumplings.

But their guide led them past that, up a curving flight of stairs to the balcony that ringed the main floor. There sat Arkady Bones, in a recessed alcove that gave her a view of most of the room. Her high-backed chair was too big for her spindle-thin frame: a tyrant in miniature, surveying her domain.

Her knife-cut hair stuck out in jagged points from under a bright red cap. A patched coat hung over the back of her chair; both of her bare arms were bound from wrist to elbow with thin, braided cords. The same cords worn on the wrist of every child he'd seen since entering the Shambles, in an array of colors as diverse and clashing as Master Peabody's abdomen.

Had she sworn individual knot bonds with every child in her crew? Vargo marveled at the madness.

"Eret Vargo," she said, as overly solemn as an actress cast in a role too large for her skill.

Keeping his smirk at bay, Vargo bowed with a hand over his heart, equally solemn. "Mistress Bones."

A tense moment passed. Then the girl grinned, sharp as a dagger, and twisted on her throne. She kicked her legs over one arm and leaned back against the other. "You en't looking half bad for a cuff whose back was shredded worse'n a night-piece's skirts. I figured you for Ninat's pyre after Veiled Waters. Glad to see you're upright enough for fucking."

"...Thank you," Vargo said, nonplussed. In the back of his mind, he heard laughter. *Alsius?*

::Don't mind me, my boy. Just feeling nostalgic.::

Fuck you.

"How'd you do it?" Boots thunking to the floor, Arkady leaned forward, sharp gaze searching Vargo like she could see under his borrowed coat. "They say you're some chalk-eating inscriptor. You use a numinat to save your ass? You got scars? Can I see 'em?"

This time, the snicker was out loud, and it came from Varuni. Arkady had managed to crack that impenetrable facade? She *was* dangerous.

"Yes, I am. No, I didn't. Yes, I do. No, you may not," Vargo said sternly—only realizing after the words were out that he was acting as Alsius had in their early days. Which was probably a mistake.

Definitely a mistake. "Guess we know where you stick your chalk when you en't using it," Arkady muttered.

Vargo snorted and matched her insolent expression. "My edge and my compass fit up there, too."

Grin returning, Arkady asked, "And your self?"

"A man can but try."

Arkady cackled. "Butt try!" Her laughter launched a wave of giggles from the children ringing the balcony. Vargo could almost feel Varuni rolling her eyes, and he knew Alsius was doing the same—all eight of them.

The tension broke with the laughter. Arkady grabbed a round pear from a bowl at her elbow, then tossed one to Vargo as well. "Guess we should stop shitting about and talk business. I en't stupid. You want to take my crew, and nothing I can do to keep it from happening. But you try doing it by force—" She held up both arms, voice descending into a hiss. "And I will 'but try' to fuck you with your own cock for every one of these you make bleed."

Before Vargo could find words, Arkady smiled again. He was

beginning to realize that all her smiles were knives. "Or we can do this peaceful-like. You leave my people alone, and maybe we can work something out. I don't come cheap, but I'm worth more to you here in the Shambles than floating belly down in the West Channel."

Covering his surprise with one hand, Vargo tapped his lip and pretended to consider. "I believe you might be."

::Vargo, we didn't come for this.::

No reason we can't use it. He had no interest in taking over Arkady's tangle of knots—but she didn't know that.

"We can work out the details later," Vargo said, glance traveling over their audience. Stick-thin legs dangled from every space along the balcony ring, wide-eyed faces pressed into every gap between the rails. He suspected Arkady would make him pay well for her cooperation, but that was always more profitable in the long run than bleeding a new knot dry. "In private. But as a gesture of good-will, I have a question and a favor to ask."

Arkady crossed her arms, chin lifting as though she feared what he wanted but wasn't going to let it cow her. "Sure. En't this an old papaver den? First toke comes free."

She needn't have worried. Vargo's request was as soothing and easy as poppy smoke. "I understand you're friendly with the Black Rose. I want to know what you know about her. And I want you to pass on a message."

Westbridge and Kingfisher, Lower Bank: Colbrilun 18

There was an ostretta, the Laughing Crow, where Arenza had said she would look for messages—and it was there that she found word from Idusza, four days after she accidentally walked into the Serrado house.

The reply was unwritten, just a verbal message from the bartender: "The bridge south of where you two met. Noon tomorrow. And she says to be careful."

Luckily, Ren knew how to be careful.

A small laundry stood at the foot of the bridge, adding its steam to the heat of early summer. Arenza wasn't surprised when Idusza popped out and beckoned her inside. But she had to applaud the ingenuity of the plan; Idusza led her past the women churning the washing tubs with their heavy wooden paddles, to the hatch where they dumped wastewater. It jutted out over the canal, and by the simple expedient of hanging upside down out the hatch until a splinterboat went by, Idusza was able to arrange for a ride.

"For weeks I've searched," Arenza said as the skiffer began poling them up the canal, away from the river. "I thought—"

Idusza waved her to silence. So Arenza waited while the boat took them deeper into the Lower Bank, finally depositing them at a canal stair in Kingfisher. Only when they were off the boat did Idusza say, "Was that necessary? Who can tell. I know only that I wouldn't want to learn the hard way that I should have been more careful."

"I feared you were dead," Arenza admitted, covertly studying the other woman. Idusza had always been a hard bite in a deceptively soft wrapping, but now that softness looked tired and worn around the edges. The braid that had once curved around her head to drape over her shoulder had become a simple straight plait, as if there was no point in doing anything prettier. "It was the cards only that gave me hope. The last place I expected to find word of you was in the house of a hawk."

"You're no more surprised than we were to be there. But Szerado is Kiraly, and those gutter cats are never without their masks. I think his might be made of feathers rather than fur. He defied even the ziemetse to help us."

Feathers rather than fur. Ren was so used to seeing him as a hawk...and as a slip-knot, currying favor with the Liganti rather than holding fast with his own people. But he'd protected them after the Night of Hells, and defied Mettore Indestor to rescue people from the amphitheatre. It couldn't be easy, standing between two worlds like that.

She glanced around and realized she recognized the neighborhood. "Masks have mercy. Tell me you are not living *in that hawk's house.*"

The smile Idusza flashed in return was too tight for real humor. "The last place any would look for us. But no—only Koszar is there. And that only because he cannot yet walk well enough to leave. He dislikes putting the children in such danger."

Ren didn't like it any better, and she could hardly imagine the Serrados did, either. She silently followed Idusza back to the courtyard house, but this time not to the front door. Idusza led her around to the back entrance, and knocked in a specific pattern before opening it.

Alinka rushed to meet them, hands twisting when she saw Arenza. "My apologies, szorsa, for not trusting you before. But—"

Arenza waved the apology away. "But you must be cautious. I fault you not. Why bring me here, Idusza? Anything this healer has not done for Andrejek, I am unlikely to do." She hoped Idusza didn't expect the kind of miraculous—and wholly staged—changes she'd once wrought in Sedge.

The answering scowl said it wasn't healing Idusza had in mind. "Koszar asked you here for your insight. But I will let him tell you. If he is awake?" That last was directed at Alinka, who nodded and gestured them to the staircase.

In all her dealings with Idusza, Arenza had never met Koszar Andrejek. The man waiting in the room upstairs was younger than she expected, though made older by the thin face and lank hair of a recovering invalid. Despite his splinted leg, he made as if to rise and greet her, only to be pushed gently down by the man at his side. That one she recognized: Ardaš Orsolski Ljunan, whom she'd met when she advised Idusza on how to steal Fulvet's saltpeter. His name, like Andrejek's and Idusza's, was on Dalisva's list.

She had no intention of handing them over. If Ažerais truly had created the Black Rose for a purpose, it wasn't to fight people like these.

Biting down on obvious pain, Andrejek said, "Szorsa Arenza. I

am Koszar Yureski Andrejek of the Anoškin. Thank you for coming. Few enough friends I have these days; it is a relief to count you
among them."

"What happened?" Arenza asked, not hiding her concern. "The
tales I have heard—"

By way of answer, he unbuttoned the collar of his shirt with his
good hand and dragged it open, revealing a complex piece of knotwork around his throat. "Inspect it if you wish. You will find stains,
faded colors. My knot I have worn without pause since I was twelve;
those of my predecessors, since I was nineteen. The cut charm
Branek displayed was a fake."

"Then you were still tied in when they attacked you?" Arenza
whispered, fingers clenching in her skirts like they had the day
Ondrakja lurched at Ren with fever-poisoned fury. "*They* were still
tied in? When they tried to *kill* you?"

Idusza snarled another curse. "Branek should have his name
stripped from him, and be called Zevriz from now until death."

Her condemnation sent a trickle of cold sweat down Ren's back.
On the streets, a knot oath was only as strong as the people who
took and kept it, but the threads led back to older Vraszenian tra-
ditions of clan and kureč. Bad enough to be cast out, as her mother
had been...but to be called Zevriz—to lose one's name entirely—
was the worst condemnation possible. Such a person was cursed to
receive neither food, nor drink, nor shelter from anyone, until the
day they died.

She hadn't believed what Dalisva said about a Cinquerat pardon,
but Andrejek might have cut his knot when he realized those he led
would no longer follow him. Instead he'd been betrayed, and blas-
phemously so.

The way Ren had betrayed Ondrakja.

Unaware of her bleak thoughts, Andrejek gestured at a truckle
bed piled with colorful patchwork blankets—no doubt where the
children slept. "You came seeking us, but it is we who need your
guidance, if Ažerais will bless us with a pattern."

It was the least she could do for him. Ren had read some of the seditious pamphlets the Anduske printed in secret, and she'd heard Idusza's tales about their leader. She didn't agree with everything Andrejek argued for, but he was somebody she would enjoy debating. He seemed like the kind of man who would listen to contrasting views and consider them before making a decision.

Now the organization he'd led was in the hands of Branek. Even if Ren was a hypocrite for condemning anyone's blasphemy, she had no problems with condemning Branek's other actions. The other day a family of Liganti glassblowers had tried to adopt a Vraszenian orphan, but a group of Anduske had stolen the child away, leaving the would-be parents bleeding and half-conscious.

She hadn't brought a bowl for the offerings, and Andrejek didn't have any coin on him. Idusza passed him a few centiras, then took them back when he injudiciously tried to lean over and lay them on the truckle bed. She put them next to Arenza's knee as Andrejek said, "I cannot leave the Anduske in Branek's hands. How am I to win back my people, though, when so few will even listen to me now? Perhaps your cards can say."

Arenza had healthy confidence in her skills as a pattern-reader, but Koszar might be asking for more than she could provide. Nevertheless, she gave the cards an honest shuffle, praying one by one to the ancestors of the clans, and Ižranyi last of all. *If only the Ižranyi could fix this* . . . She doubted they could have. But in the centuries since their clan was wiped out in the destruction of Fiavla, people had taken to speaking of them as if they'd had miraculous powers. The Ižranyi could have stopped the Tyrant. The Ižranyi could have won back Nadežra. The Ižranyi could have healed all the rifts that separated the clans and the kretse, mending the tears that kept Vraszan divided and weak.

"This is your past, the good and the ill of it, and that which is neither." Her breath huffed out at the first card. "The Face of Stars: You have been a very fortunate man, favored by Ir Entrelke."

Andrejek grunted, trying and failing to find a comfortable position on the bed. "Not *always* fortunate."

"No one is," she agreed, touching the card in the veiled position.

Four Petals Fall, the card of nature. The flower it depicted was beautiful, but already fading, and its dropping petals were as white as snow. "Some disaster in your past...in the mountains?" She knew he came from one of the trading kretse, which traveled the Dawn and Dusk Roads. It was a hard life, and full of danger. "You lost many people to nature's wrath."

"A rockfall." The grief that shadowed his voice was old enough not to bleed, but the scar remained. "Two of us survived. The other never walked again."

Bereft of a kureč, he'd come to Nadežra. Much like Ren's mother had. To Nadežra, and the Anduske—represented by The Mask of Mirrors at the center of the line. Secrets and lies. Trying not to choke on the irony, Arenza said, "And so you entered a life full of deception. But some lies are necessary. Force of arms has failed to take Nadežra back, more than once; perhaps more-subtle means might succeed." *Someday.*

For his present, the good was Three Hands Join, and she exchanged a wry smile with Andrejek. The card of aid needed no explanation, when he lay hidden in Alinka Serrado's house. The other two were a matched pair, The Face of Light in the middle, and the eyeless shape of The Mask of Nothing on the left. The two aspects of Gria Ežil Dmivro: Gria Ežil representing rationality and the future, and Gria Dmivro, madness and lack of control.

"Branek?" Andrejek asked, nodding at The Mask of Nothing. Then he grimaced. "Apologies, szorsa. I should not presume."

She sighed. "You are not wrong, though. He believes that bold action alone will suffice—that if he shows his strength, others will rally to it. Blind faith, as the Mask itself is blind. But it means not only him." She tapped The Face of Light. "This is the crux for you, and your whole pattern. Against Branek you burn to act...but you must have patience. Now is not the time for action, and not only because your body is still weak. If you wish to defeat him, you must be careful, and you must plan."

Even as she spoke, she knew it would frustrate him. For one brief flash, Andrejek reminded her of Donaia: not a parent, but someone who cared deeply for the people under his care. Not being able to help them would be torture.

Sure enough, he said, "Plan for what? And *with* what? You see here the extent of what Three Hands Join has brought me." He gestured at the two people with him, the family downstairs that courted danger by hiding him.

Her mind was beginning to work, pulling together the threads, both in the cards and beyond them. "Of the Black Rose I'm sure you've heard—that she saved the wellspring. But have you heard the more recent tales?"

Idusza made a small, enlightened noise. "They say for Branek's allies she's been causing trouble."

"It seems she has no love for those who would slaughter for the cause. Be patient, and let her do her work. Your enemies she will weaken for you." Not that she'd managed any significant successes yet...but Ren had some thoughts about how to make that happen. And if it bought Andrejek time to plan, so much the better.

"Once I can move—" Andrejek growled in frustration. "Always I must wait for that. But perhaps, szorsa, you can guide me to this Rose."

The last thing Ren needed was to meet him in both personas. But had she expected him to say anything else? Rather than answer, she turned over the top line. The good of his future was The Mask of Hollows; the ill, The Mask of Ravens; that which was neither, Storm Against Stone. "Six Faces and Masks," she murmured, glancing down at the rest of the pattern. "The deities have taken a strong interest in you, Ča Andrejek."

"Koszar," he said. "And I would make offerings to them if I could walk a labyrinth. But tell me—what do they say?"

The Mask of Ravens was hatred and war. "Divisions run deep, within the Anduske, within Naděžra, within Vraszan. This is where Branek would lead us...but not only him. By your own actions you might go there, if your heart is fed too strongly by revenge. Focus not on taking down Branek—though that may happen—but on bringing the Anduske back to your side."

Idusza muttered a soft curse. "As if that will be easy."

"I never said it would be. Many forces stand in the way of that." Arenza shivered, looking at Storm Against Stone. During the Night of Hells, in the pattern laid out by the dream of her mother, that had been the central card. An unstoppable force, a tempest howling around the Charterhouse—and Mevieny, the blinded szorsa, had been desperate for Ren not to give into it. "This is not simply a problem for the Anduske, or even for Vraszenians. Nadežra itself struggles. For you to succeed..." She was losing herself in the pattern, trying to feel what lay hidden in its threads. "Other things must change. Things beyond your control."

Koszar smacked one hand against the bed. "Mean you that I cannot succeed? But I have a good fate as well. The Mask of Hollows—what must I lose?"

The starving mien of that card did represent loss... but not only that. "Revealed, this says your strength will be in those who have little. Ča Andrejek—Koszar—"

She hesitated. It was one thing to carry out a short-touch con on the street, or even to pass herself off as a Seterin noblewoman to Nadežra's elite. This was harder. Ren had always thought of herself as Vraszenian, but spending time with people like these only reminded her of how much she *wasn't*. She needed makeup to hide her mixed blood, practice to make her Vraszenian speech fluent again. They welcomed her because they thought she was one of them.

And that was one of their problems.

Softly, she said, "To the people of Nadežra, the Anduske are Vraszenians, fighting for Vraszenians. And that is not wrong. But how many here trace their ancestors to more than one land? Those people suffer also under the Cinquerat's control. The poor laborers, the knots on the streets... How often have you considered that they, too, might be your allies?"

Her thoughts had been on the politics of Nadežra, not on planting any specific idea in their heads. But by the brief conversation Idusza, Koszar, and Ardaš had, all in nods and headshakes and eyebrow twitches, she'd struck an unexpected chord.

One that resolved into a sigh from Koszar. To his allies he muttered, "That one can hardly be called 'one who has little'—but very well." He turned his attention back to Arenza. "Vargo. He had people looking for you some months ago. Rumor says he found you, and yet you walked away unharmed."

"You think to ally with *him*?"

"Not if you advise against it," Andrejek said. "We seek your wisdom in this."

Her fingers curled around the deck. The logic made sense: Branek and many of those who followed him were Stretsko, and kin of those same Stretsko were causing Vargo problems up and down the Lower Bank. Hadn't she herself pursued Tserdev Očelen in the hopes of finding Dmatsos? Common enemies had created stranger allies.

Once she wouldn't have hesitated to tell Koszar to work with Vargo. Now...

Now, I can use this.

At least she had a cover for her knowledge of him. "I laid his pattern when we met. He is a dangerous ally; to bind yourself in his web risks becoming his prey. But above all, he desires benefit for himself. Show him there is profit in alliance, and with you he may work."

Possibilities were starting to take shape in her mind. She let a little of her distaste show and added, "A man like him wants assurances up front, though. Likely you will need to give him some aid unasked before he'll consider your words."

Given the state of Koszar's tiny faction, she wasn't at all sure they could offer much. But Idusza brightened immediately. "Tserdev Krasnoskaya Očelen of the Crimson Eyes plans a strike against Vargo's home, on the night of the solstice. We had word of this from one who remains loyal to us, hiding among the traitors. Would a warning persuade him?"

"It might," Arenza said, concealing her satisfaction. "I can take word of this on your behalf, if you wish."

She wasn't stupid enough to walk up to Vargo again as Arenza...

but she didn't have to. *Only way I'm getting close enough to know Vargo's business is if I save his Lig-spitted ass*—that was what Sedge had said. While this wasn't quite saving Vargo's life, it might be enough to get Sedge's foot in the door.

With a final prayer, she swept up her cards and tucked them away. "What else can you tell me of Ča Očelen's plans?"

5

The Peacock's Web

Upper and Lower Bank: Summer Solstice

The Traementis kitchens were usually bustling at noon, but with Altas Renata and Giuna out for the day and Era Traementis taking nothing but broth and bread in her room, Colbrin had declared a similarly spare meal for the servants. Nobody complained, as half the staff had been given the night and the next morning off and would be gorging themselves on solstice festival fare, celebrating the New Year. The other half were still recovering from their freedom the night before.

But they'd gathered at the changing of shifts to exchange gossip. Sitting in the chair she'd claimed, Tess sipped her broth and let the liquid and the company warm her. In Nadežra or in Ganllech, in Westbridge or the Pearls, the kitchen was the heart of every home.

Her cheer cooled like a hearth banked as she thought of Westbridge. Uncomfortable as it had been, at least there Tess could be with her sister.

"What's that frown for?" asked Suilis, poking a plump finger at the furrow between Tess's brows. The Nadežran girl had been hired to see to Donaia and Giuna after the Traementis fortunes improved. She was round, cheerful, and a comfort to have in the house, with them both being so new.

Also terribly nosy and much too observant. Tess had to constantly remind herself to be on guard. She shook off her frown and gave Suilis a happy smile. "Only thinking of the crowds."

"Worried you won't find a quiet corner to share with your sweetheart? You're off to see him tonight, right?"

Tess's grip on her bowl tightened. She'd almost managed to forget about Pavlin and their meeting at Nightpeace Gardens last month. She'd only shared the details with Ren. How did Suilis know? "I—I don't have a—"

"Come off it, now. Sure, he may look like he crawled out of the rookeries, but what's a rough face to a sweet disposition?" Suilis sighed in happy jealousy. "And those shoulders..."

Panic sputtering, Tess said, "*Sedge?*" Suilis knew Ren was sending Tess to see him?

Then the rest of Suilis's words hit her. *Sweetheart. Sweet disposition. Shoulders.* Tess stifled a groan with the last sip of broth. What had she been thinking, to leave that gossip unchecked? And yet, it was safer than any of the truths Tess daren't tell. She *was* off to see Sedge; this would keep anyone from questioning why.

She dredged up a grin. "He does have nice shoulders." Like Ren always said: Speak the truth and let others fill in the lie.

Suilis giggled and leaned close. "Hope you've got a contraceptive numinat," she whispered, patting Tess's stomach where the slight bump of her new navel ring was hidden under layers of skirts. "That one could father children with a look."

He's my brother, *you*—Groaning, Tess pressed her brow to her empty bowl and prayed to the Maiden to save her from Suilis's curiosity.

Thankfully, Colbrin gave them their leave soon after, even passing out paper masks and pouches of coin as New Year's gifts. House Traementis was still frugal by noble standards, but Donaia had insisted—without any prompting from Renata—that the staff who remained loyal through their impoverishment should enjoy their new enrichment. She said they were "family as much as anyone in the register." A nice sentiment, if laughable from a woman who never emptied her own chamber pot.

Avoiding speculative looks and knowing grins from the other servants, Tess headed for Westbridge and the ostretta that had become her meeting spot with Sedge since their reunion.

Sedge was already waiting outside when she arrived, but so was what seemed like every other resident of the district. And no few of them seemed to be trying their luck with him, his broad shoulders attracting almost as much interest as his scars and scowl warned off.

His frown cleared when he spotted Tess fighting the current of the crowd. He mouthed a question she couldn't hear, but she knew well enough to guess he was asking after Ren. Rather than shout their business over the noise, she gestured for him to follow her. Even if they could squeeze into the ostretta, their usual alcove would be taken.

Sedge was very useful for bulling his way through crowds. Wrapping a long arm around her shoulders, he forged a path for them both, in search of someplace quiet and safe.

Ironically, they ended up sitting on the retaining wall of the canal behind the townhouse where Ren and Tess had squatted for almost a year. The damage had been repaired, but the windows were dark. "I suppose they've not found a new tenant," Tess mused, eating fried river oysters off a skewer. She accepted the elderflower wine Sedge passed her and took a swig from the bottle. It chased the oily weight of the oyster with the sweet warmth of a summer rain.

He waved the bottle away when she offered it back, then sprawled along the wall with his head resting on her thigh. "Wouldn't know. En't like Vargo or the Spiders are sharing their secrets with me no more." He scratched at the pale stripe on his wrist.

Setting the bottle aside, Tess tangled her fingers in his hair, nails scraping his scalp. "I wish it were easy to be sorry. But after what he did to Ren, and thinking about those zlyzen attacking her at the amphitheatre—"

"I don't regret it." Pressing into her hand, Sedge sighed. "Well, I do. But I wouldn't choose different if I had to again."

His words doubled the weight of what Ren had asked her to do. Tess was that tempted to drown it with another swig of wine.

To forget everything and drag Sedge back to the solstice revels for some dancing and more oysters...but it wasn't her choice to make. It was his.

"What if there were a way to get back in grace with Vargo?"

Sedge's snort was louder than her soft question. "I left him to get shredded by the zlyzen. Not even Ren's tongue is silver enough to buy his forgiveness for that."

"Not her tongue, no. But the news she got from the Stadnem Anduske, maybe."

Sedge caught her wrist and pulled her hand from his hair, sitting up. "What news?" And then, because they all knew each other too well: "What game is Ren running now?"

Tess passed along their sister's explanations. That Vargo's ennoblement had sparked a war among the Lower Bank gangs, and he was losing people. That the ousted leader of the Anduske was looking for an ally, and hoped he might find one in Vargo. That tonight the Stretsko were going to use the solstice revels to attack Vargo in his own home in Eastbridge.

Sedge's jaw tightened. "And if I take this to Vargo, Ren's hoping he'll welcome me back into the Spiders. So I can spy on him for her."

Put like that, it sounded cold. Especially when Ren had sent Tess to make the request rather than do it herself. Tess opened her mouth to assure Sedge that wasn't the case, but he pressed three fingers to her lips.

"It's fine. Makes sense. He's up to something, and we need to know what. And maybe if I'm there, I can protect the other Fog Spiders from whatever he's up to. My oaths were to them anyways, not Vargo."

"You'll do it, then?" She let Sedge help her down off the wall, only stumbling a little when the ground rolled beneath her feet. Maybe broth and an oyster skewer weren't enough cushion for the amount of wine she'd drunk.

Sedge glanced at the sky, cloudless and blue, the sun making its slow way toward the horizon. "Better do it now if they're coming tonight. You'll be all right alone?"

Tess nodded and pushed him ahead of her. "I can see to myself." Her cheeks were warm, and she was feeling bold. She waved Sedge off one way, then pulled down her mask and set off in the other direction with a determined step and a half-full bottle of elderflower wine.

It was the New Year, a time for new beginnings. And time for her to prove to Nadežra and to herself that she didn't need a false sweetheart to find true happiness.

Isla Traementis, the Pearls: Summer Solstice

Gazing out over the streams of gaily dressed delta gentry and merchants swirling through the streets and plazas of the Pearls, Ren thought, *Never let it be said this city passes up a chance to celebrate.*

The chill fogs of Veiled Waters had vanished like a dream. In the Vraszenian calendar, which followed the moons, the New Year had come and gone. But why have one festival when the people of Nadežra could have two? In the solar Seterin calendar, these five days around the solstice were the turning point of the year: a moment outside of time, cutting the month of Colbrilun in half. And while Donaia claimed it was supposed to be an occasion for contemplation and austerity, Ren had never seen any sign of that.

Instead the streets filled with stalls selling food, flowers, trinkets, and more. The masks people wore were paper or lightweight fabric sculpted by wire, made for burning when the five intercalary days were over. Everyone strolled arm in arm, disputes laid aside until time resumed its usual pace—at least in theory. She'd already seen a petty shoving match on one of the bridges that led off the Isla Traementis, when a wandering seller of lemon ice refused to step aside for a man with a cart of honey-drizzled rice balls. The heat was making everyone irritable.

And it was making Renata impatient. *Wait in Traementis Plaza,* Tanaquis had said. She wore the stitched numinat on her sleeve, as instructed, and the nearest clock tower had rung out tenth sun nearly a bell ago, but there was no sign of anything happening.

"Rose of Ažerais, alta?"

The question made Renata jump. Was this what Tanaquis had told her to wait for?

No. It was an ordinary flower seller, one of a thousand crisscrossing the city hawking the beautiful violet roses named for Ažerais. They bloomed in the aftermath of Veiled Waters, and Ren would have loved to buy one. What stayed her hand wasn't a lack of money; it was the ever-present awareness that she had to remain in persona all the time now. Renata could buy the flower seller's whole cart... but the Vraszenian tradition was a reminder Ren's heart couldn't afford.

"No, thank you," she said, and resolutely turned away as the flower seller moved on.

The next person to approach her was a man, judging by his build, and gentry or better, judging by the fine goldenrod fabric of his coat. He wore a full mask—a blank face with only shadowed eyes staring out and a narrow slit cutting across the lips, entirely out of keeping with the style of the festival.

"Are you the one I'm waiting for?" Renata asked.

By way of answer, he held out another mask. This one, like his, was shaped like a full face of plain white—but mute and blind. It had no holes cut for the mouth or the eyes.

Her pulse quickened. "You—want me to put that on?"

His hand didn't waver.

Tanaquis invited you to this. She isn't the sort to play games. Tanaquis, who said this might help with uncovering the origins of the Traementis curse.

Trying not to show her apprehension, Renata accepted the mask and slid it over her head.

The man took her hand and led her forward at a slow pace. Ren's breath came hot and damp against the inside of the mask; she was almost glad the lack of eyeholes meant he couldn't see her fear. She hated this already, with every bone in her body—walking blind, trusting a total stranger to guide her. Then she heard the slosh of water, and the hands guided her down into a splinter-boat; she fumbled for the nearest bench, found it, and sat. A moment later the boat rocked into motion.

You're not in the box. Mettore is dead.

Clutching the edge of the bench so hard her knuckles ached, Ren prayed that Tanaquis would not steer her wrong.

Floodwatch, Upper Bank: Summer Solstice

Even hearing the sounds of celebration from the Upper and Lower Banks made Giuna feel guilty, as if she were betraying Leato by not sitting at home with her grief.

Your life shouldn't stop for me, minnow. She could imagine his voice as if he sat next to her, and she swallowed down the lump in her throat. *Especially not when the family needs you.* Donaia was at home, and Renata was busy with Meda Fienola; someone had to take care of house business.

"Thank you again," she said to Sibiliat as the skiffer poled them upriver toward Floodwatch. "For all your help." House Traementis's social dealings had been curtailed for too long; they benefited greatly from Sibiliat's evaluation of their adoption candidates. She'd even offered to accompany Giuna today, using the excuse of the solstice to visit some of those candidates and see how they interacted with their current families.

The way Sibiliat draped herself over Giuna from behind, her magnolia perfume warming the air between them, made Giuna feel eight kinds of awkward at once. Was Sibiliat truly serious about her flirtation? Or was this simply a game for her, a pleasant diversion not meant to last?

"Help like this is what House Acrenix is for," Sibiliat answered, her breath tickling Giuna's ear. "We're everybody's friend."

"Everybody's friend but Renata's," Giuna said, before she could stop herself.

Sibiliat drew back, taking her warmth and smile with her. There was a facade of amity between those two, but Giuna could always hear the barbs underneath each comment. Sibiliat hadn't forgiven the deception over Renata's finances...or the way Renata had displaced her as the center of young noble life.

Giuna expected a catty response. Instead, Sibiliat's reply was barely audible over the rush of the river and the noise of the celebrations. "You're right. And I'm sorry." Her half-sun mask ended at her cheekbones; it didn't hide the press of her lips. "I just still worry that there's more to your cousin's story than she admits. That she may not have your best interests at heart."

"Don't judge what you don't understand," Giuna said firmly. "Renata may not show her true face to the world, but that's just her way of being strong. She blames herself for Leato's death, and *she* nearly died when she couldn't sleep after the Night of Hells. And she kept us all brave when we found out about the curse."

She was grasping at any argument to soften Sibiliat's suspicion, and only realized what she'd said when Sibiliat's attention sharpened. "Curse? What curse?"

Giuna clapped her hands over her mouth as though that could catch the words already escaped. But perhaps knowing what they'd been through together would help Sibiliat understand why Giuna had forgiven Renata for misleading them.

Lowering her hands and voice, Giuna said, "It's what took Leato. And every cousin in our register since before I was born. It would have taken Mother and me as well, if Renata hadn't put a stop to it."

Sibiliat's eyes went wide. "Renata? I didn't think she had any skill with numinatria. How—"

"I...shouldn't speak of it." Giuna straightened her gloves, avoiding Sibiliat's gaze. She'd already said more than Renata or her mother would be comfortable with.

After a moment, Sibiliat reached out and took one of those hands in her own. "Never mind. It's enough that you're safe now."

"Don't tell," Giuna said, scrambling to undo the damage from her loose tongue. "If anyone hears of this, they'll scorch parchment rather than let themselves be inscribed into our register. Our reputation can't take that blow right now."

Sibiliat delivered a swift kiss to her gloved fingertips, then released her hand. "Of course not. If the curse was as old as you say... Doesn't your mother always say Letilia took the Traementis luck with her when she left? Perhaps Renata brought it back."

Giuna shivered as the heavy shadow of the Floodwatch Bridge fell over the skiff. The collapse of the previous bridge happened before Letilia left. Had the curse taken hold of them even then? Or was it just the result of her grandfather's grasping ways?

Tucking Giuna at her side as though the summer night carried a chill, Sibiliat said, "I'll try to be... not kinder. She'd mistrust that, and I couldn't manage it anyway. But I'll do my best to find an equilibrium. For you."

"Why do I feel like I just did Renata a grave disservice?" Giuna asked dryly, and fought a pleased smile when Sibiliat laughed.

They disembarked on the Upper Bank side of Floodwatch and made their way to the Scurezza townhouse. Giuna was arriving early—the house parties wouldn't truly get going until full dark—but her list of targets tonight was long enough to require a head start.

The Scurezza footman bowed in greeting. "The family are still at dinner, but Meda Scurezza is expecting you. If you'll follow me?"

Giuna straightened her mask of iridescent green hummingswift feathers and trailed after the footman as he led them toward the dining room. He opened the door with another bow—and the scene inside froze them all where they stood.

Members of the Scurezza family lay twisted in their chairs or sprawled across the table. The stench of vomit and worse billowed out, and dishes had been knocked onto the rug. Coevis, the cousin who'd applied to join House Traementis, was nearest the door. She had fallen from her chair and lay open-eyed on the floor.

No one moved except Meda Quaniet Scurezza.

She sat at the head of the table, one manicured hand gathering small brown nuts from a dish. The crunch of her teeth on them was the only sound in the world.

Quaniet drew in a strained, rasping breath, but the smile she directed at Giuna was serene. "Now they'll never leave. We'll be a family forever."

Giuna's mask tumbled from her head as she clamped her hands over her mouth, trying to keep everything inside. She didn't realize she'd bolted until she was on the front step, heaving the contents of her stomach into the street. A moment later Sibiliat was there, her hand rubbing soothing circles into Giuna's back. She'd removed her gloves, and used the soft cotton of one to dab the sweat from Giuna's brow and the bile from her lips.

"Little bird," Sibiliat said, her voice full of horror. "I'm—I don't even know what to say."

"Hawks," Giuna whispered. "We need to call the hawks."

"I sent the footman. Will you be all right if I leave you here?"

Giuna nodded like a puppet, and the warmth on her back went away. Only as the sweat chilled to ice did she wonder why Sibiliat had gone back inside.

Maybe some of them are still alive.

She forced herself to her feet. Sibiliat might seem sharp and hard, but it was the hardness of glass. It could be chipped. Even shattered. Giuna couldn't leave Sibiliat to face that nightmare alone.

Back inside the room of death, Quaniet had slumped forward, a few nuts still clutched in her limp hand. At first Giuna thought Sibiliat had gone somewhere else. But then she saw her friend crawling out from under the dining room table with something in her palm. A smooth violet circle, like a numinatrian focus, though it wasn't etched with any divine sigil that Giuna could see. The rug, as in many fashionable dining rooms, was woven with a Noctat numinat, to heighten the pleasures of eating and drinking.

Sibiliat saw her in the doorway and pocketed the focus. Giuna's discarded mask dangled from her wrist. Grimly, she said, "I think Quaniet wanted to make sure everyone would eat their dessert."

The bowls of nuts. One for every diner, most of them empty.

"Careful!" Giuna yelped as Sibiliat tipped a few into her clean glove.

"I am. One of our apothecaries should be able to say if these were the cause." As she headed for the door, Sibiliat's shoe came down with a wet, squelching sound in the puddle of vomit and blood next to Coevis's head. She staggered to one side, clapping one hand over her mouth. Through her fingers, she moaned, "Oh Lumen—"

The glass was cracking. Giuna helped Sibiliat back to the street, where all the household staff had fled and a crowd was gathering, and sacrificed her own gloves to tend to Sibiliat's delayed reaction.

Now Meda Scurezza's words sank in. Giuna whispered, "She wanted them to stay a family. Coevis talking about joining us..." Tears burned in her eyes. "Is this *our fault*?"

Sibiliat gripped her hand, strong enough to ache. "*No*, little bird. This—this wasn't normal. Quaniet went mad. Anyone who blames you for that will face me in a duel."

It didn't make the sickness go away. But Giuna held on to Sibiliat's bare fingers until the hawks came.

Froghole, Lower Bank: Summer Solstice

With Tess's warnings driving his pace, Sedge skiff-hopped up the river to the Fog Spiders' den in Froghole. He chafed the bare spot on his wrist where his knot bracelet used to sit, still paler than the rest of his skin after years of being hidden from the sun. Vulnerable, just like him.

Now Ren's got me walking into the center of the web. But he couldn't blame her. He was the one who'd chosen blood bonds over knot oaths. And Vargo hadn't had him killed for it, which not many bosses would grant.

That gave Sedge hope that Vargo might listen to the warning, rather than having him beaten away from the door.

Of course, first he had to get *past* the door. Which got off to a good start when it opened to reveal Lurets. "Hey," Sedge said, keeping his voice low. Lurets was as friendly a face as he could hope for, but others in the building wouldn't be as soft. "Nikory in? Got news Vargo'll want to hear."

He didn't keep his voice low enough. Or maybe there were some street kids keeping watch, and they'd warned the Spiders he was coming. Sedge's hope shriveled—along with his balls—when Lurets unceremoniously vanished from the doorway to be replaced by Varuni.

She'd been even more pissed than Nikory when Sedge brought Vargo back shredded and near dead during Veiled Waters—blaming herself for not being at Vargo's back; blaming Sedge for not guarding it like she would've. Her face now was polished teak, smoothed of all expression. She eyed him like she was planning how to make one of her chain whips out of his spine.

But Sedge was in it and couldn't back out, so he rolled his shoulders, prepared for a fight. "Hey, Varuni. Brought some news for Vargo's ears."

"I don't think there's anything he wants to hear from you."

"Why don't you let him be the judge of that," Sedge said, knowing it for another mistake as soon as the words were out. You didn't get past Varuni by slamming yourself against her.

He couldn't do this his way. Faces help him, he had to do this Ren's way.

Sedge let his shoulders slump, let the belligerence drain off. Let a little of his loneliness show. He might be here for complicated reasons, but at the core of it was a truth. "Look, I en't stupid. I know it's asking for a beating or worse to show my face. You think I'd be here if it wasn't important?"

Varuni knew Sedge. Some people would be stupid enough to come back and beg, but he wasn't one of them. She studied him for a long moment, then hauled him inside and slammed the door. It wasn't a welcome; it was her not wanting Vargo's business shouted out on the street. "Give your news to me. I'll decide whether he needs to hear it." *Or whether you need a swim in the nearest canal*, the set of her jaw said.

It wasn't good enough, but with time running short, it would have to be. "Remember that patterner I brought for Vargo? Turns out she's with the Stadnem Anduske—the ones who tried to call off the bombing. That Andrejek fellow. And she gave me a warning to pass on."

Varuni shifted. Interested, but not entirely hooked. "Why you?"

"Because she thinks I'm still with Vargo. Andrejek says he din't cut his knot, and he wants an alliance against the oath-breaking bastards who claim he did—bastards who're in with the Stretsko gangs. The szorsa sent me to tell Vargo that they're planning an attack on him. Tonight."

Ren was running a hell of a risk, having him name Arenza as his source. Sedge still felt like he'd eaten bad dumplings when he remembered taking Ren to see Vargo—Ren, half-insane with lack of sleep, and trying to lie to Vargo's face. She'd survived... but she'd also made Vargo interested in her, and now Sedge was reminding him she existed. If the payoff was getting Sedge back into Vargo's good graces, though—well, he *hoped* it would be worth it.

Varuni's skeptical gaze swept toward the inner door that led to the rest of the building. It was closed, but there would be people listening on the far side. "Here? Let them try."

"Not here. His townhouse."

That just made her raise the other brow. "And how do they plan on getting enough people there to do any damage? Caerulet's got hawks on the Sunrise Bridge, keeping the riffraff out."

"The skiffers. Half of them are rats, after all. And en't Vargo's place just off the main canal? Easy enough to pole in and away without stirring up the hawks." Sedge leaned forward, daring to catch her wrist. Surprisingly, she let him. "At least tell Vargo. I don't think the Stretsko plan on killing him, but they won't hold back if they get a chance, neither."

The tension in her arm told him to let go before he regretted it. But the anger wasn't directed at him.

"Lurets!"

Varuni's bellow knocked Sedge back a step, just in case she was calling Lurets to drive him off, rather than dirtying her own boot. When the inner door swung open, though, Varuni began giving a clipped series of commands—the kinds of orders Sedge used to take, not that long ago. Muster fists to watch the house on the Isla Čaprila, get various crews watching the river landings near Stretsko home turf. Fetch a couple of pigeons that had been trained to fly to a coop on Vargo's roof, so the people there would have warning when the Stretsko moved.

Sedge heard what she *didn't* say. At no point did she tell anybody to take word to Vargo. Which meant Vargo was busy somewhere else—alone.

No wonder Varuni was pissed.

Sedge stayed where he was, keeping clear of the people hopping to follow Varuni's orders, but the den wasn't a place for someone with nothing to do. And it was hard, knowing that he used to have a role in this well-ordered bustle. Harder still when some of his fellow Fog Spiders cast him unreadable looks, making him feel even more the outsider.

He reached for the door before the tightness in his chest made him do something stupid. Like offer to help. Or cry.

Varuni's harsh voice nailed him in place. "The fuck you think you're going?"

His skin pricked, and he couldn't say if it was fear or relief. Sedge thumbed at the door. "Just figured I'd keep out of your way."

"Drop this on us and then scurry off? Not likely. If you did this to distract us, I want you where I can find you."

Fuck. Now his fate hung on the quality of Ren's information. And while Sedge trusted his sister, that didn't extend to the Stadnem Anduske or the Stretsko.

Let's hope all these preparations don't send them into their holes, he thought, and followed Varuni to meet his fate.

Isla Čaprila, Eastbridge: Summer Solstice

Night in Eastbridge was a bright affair, especially during the festive intercalary days when the plazas thronged with those who had wealth enough to be bored, but not enough to own one of the villas out in the bay. The crowds were restless; the patrolling hawks were kept busy putting down minor arguments before they could become brawls.

But the brighter the night, the darker the shadows. The Rook hid in one of those, under a domed cupola where a pair of dreamweavers had made their nest. Quiet enough to leave them undisturbed... and to avoid notice from Vargo's fists, gathering along the canal backing his townhouse. The birds only roused when several skiffs bumped up to the wall and dislodged a score of people proudly displaying the red-knotted wristbands of the Stretsko.

The ensuing scuffle was brutal, but too far from the noisy plazas to attract official notice. Vargo's second-in-command led the defense, lashing about with that chained menace of hers with a fury that made the Rook's ankle and wrist twinge in sympathy.

The fight along the canal made an excellent distraction, just as Ren had suggested. It would have been nice if she'd given him more advance warning... but to be fair, he didn't check her balcony for notes on a nightly basis, either. If they were going to work together, he might need to change that.

And give her more opportunities to catch you?

That was both the Rook and Grey's own natural wariness talking. Setting that debate aside for later, he jumped across the small gap between houses, then jimmied an upper window open while dangling over the edge of the roof. A bit of oil helped it open quietly.

Or so he'd hoped—but a high whistle rose up when the pane slid along its track. A flick of his knife broke the lines of the numinat painted on the inside of the sill and left the Rook with a stinging hand from the shock of power improperly disrupted. A glance down at the brawl confirmed that they were too busy pummeling each other to have heard it. The Rook slipped through the window and closed it softly behind him.

He remained where he was, surveying the room before taking another step. It was a remarkably well-stocked library, but not one designed for comfort; the close-packed shelves left no room for a chair. A quick scan showed him countless works on numinatria, astrology, mathematics, trade, but no obvious traps lying in wait.

If I were Derossi Vargo, where would I keep the source of my power?

Through an adjoining door he found Vargo's study and made

quick work of the desk and shelves. He glanced into the room beyond—a bedroom decked out in luxuriant decadence—and checked the thickness of the separating wall to confirm that there wasn't a secret compartment hidden between. A spot of clashing color among the pillows drew his attention, but it was only Vargo's pet spider running loose.

Jerking back, he shut the door. The venom of a king peacock was supposed to be remarkably painful. And while the Rook could deal with pain, a bite from a spider that oversized would be a pure distillation of agony.

He committed to a more thorough search of the study, not bothering to hide his visit—why waste the time when he'd already broken the window numinat? Let Vargo think the Stretsko got in. The desk locks eventually yielded to his picks, but a quick perusal of the papers produced nothing incriminating, and a knock on the backs and bases of the drawers proved them solid.

Most of the study was given over to an open space inlaid with a blank spira aurea of rainbow prismatium. The slate flooring was dusty with chalk residue, and showed no sign of hidden spaces beneath. Inscription tools filled the cabinets along the wall: a silver basin and ewer for ritual cleansing, a bucket of broken colored chalks, compasses and calipers as small as the Rook's finger and as long as his leg, waxy chops and blank plugs for foci. Organized clutter that spoke of frequent use.

The dwindling sounds of fighting reminded him that his time was finite. Only centuries of enduring failure kept him from kicking over one of the cabinets in frustration. Coming here had been a slim hope built on an even slimmer one: that Vargo's rise was due to supernatural influence, and that he kept the source of that influence somewhere obvious enough to find in a mere bell of searching.

There were ten medallions in Nadežra—ten sources of power, of the poison that tainted everyone who touched them. In two hundred years, the Rook had been lucky to stumble across one every few decades. Never for long, and never with any success at destroying them. He'd hoped that with Vargo, he'd finally found the key.

If so, the man knew better than to keep that key here.

The Rook was backing toward the open window, sweeping his gaze over the room one last time, when something odd caught his eye.

Everything in Vargo's study was beautiful, to be sure, but it all had a use. From the thick curtains to the numinatrian tools to the books on the shelves, there was nothing that didn't have function as well as form. No art on the walls, no quirky Dusk Road oddities gathering memories and dust.

So why would a man so obviously impatient with useless things keep a plinth in the corner with a plaster bust of some Seterin philosopher?

One shattered head later, the Rook found the storebox hidden in the top of the plinth.

Anything this carefully concealed would be protected. He spied the numinat buried amid the carvings before he opened the box. The memories that lingered in the hood weren't enough to make him a master inscriptor, but it was easy enough to guess at this figure's purpose; it would torch the contents of the box if not properly disabled.

But the first Rook had known enough inscription to embed it into every piece of the costume. Most simple numinata could be disabled simply by removing the focus. And Grey knew enough woodworking from Kolya to make a chisel of his knife.

Preparing for another sparking backlash, he wedged the point of his blade in place and hammered at the pommel, chipping off the top layer of wood at the middle of the numinat. Something sizzled along his arms, leaving behind the odor of scorched hair—but the magical protection was gone.

The lock was more complex than the ones on the desk. It was also more delicate, though; easy enough to wiggle the point of his knife into the seam between lid and box and force-pry the thing open.

Heat flashed, followed by the smell of burning paper. He threw the contents to the floor, racing to stomp out the flames before everything useful was destroyed.

Lifting the blackened remains of the box, he found the faint inlay of a second numinat on the inside. One that would have been deactivated if he'd used a pick or a key to turn the lock, rather than brute force.

Points for persistence, the Rook thought sourly. He should have known Vargo wouldn't trust anything important to just two layers of protection.

But Ir Entrelke hadn't entirely abandoned him. The shell of the box had smothered the flames better than his boots, leaving a few browned remnants of the papers inside. He lifted them carefully. The outside pages were too blackened to read, but the inside ones had only browned at the edges.

The writing was in neat lines and columns, like it had come from a ledger. A ledger of *what,* the Rook hadn't the first clue. But there were family names. Locations. A few shorthand notes.

> *Nespisci & Lucovic, Suncross, Apilun 206, bar fight to bread riots*
>
> *Isla Ejče, Fellun 207—Cyprilun 210, Omorre Richerso (money-lender, backed by Attravi)*
>
> *Skiffer strikes—Colbrilun 207, Canilun 208, Similun 208, Equilun 209*
>
> *Siren's Folly, Suilun 209, mutiny*
>
> *Silvain Fiangiolli & Elessni Essunta, Similun 210—fucking (blackmail?)*
>
> *Yariček (Cut Ears), Apilun 210, broke knot oath, turned evidence to Caerulet (remnants gathered in)*
>
> *Scurezza, Fellun 211, breaking betrothal contracts*

There were other notes—names and dates and places too fragmented to make any sense out of—but the implication was clear enough. Vargo's interests went well beyond any feud between Indestor and Novrus, and his reach went far beyond the Lower Bank gangs. Hundreds had died in the bread riots. And people still spoke in whispers about the atrocities committed by the crew of the *Siren's Folly.*

What other chaos had Vargo been causing—and reaping the benefits of? What other plans of his were now in ashes on his study floor?

And what was his ultimate aim?

Carefully, the Rook tucked the burned pages away in the hopes he could fill the spaces between the fragments later. Giving the room a final glance, he saw the spider had squeezed in somehow; it was on the desk, hiding ineffectively behind the inkstand.

The Rook briefly considered crushing it, but refrained. The spider was innocent.

Its master was not.

Bay of Vraszan: Summer Solstice

Focusing on what clues she could gather helped keep Ren's panic at bay. From the Pearls the splinter-boat had moved into broader waters—the East Channel—then downriver, because they didn't pass through the cleansing numinat. The sounds of the festival faded behind them. When the boat stopped, she thought they'd arrived. But hands, more than one pair, transferred her instead to another boat, this one larger. Canvas flapped in the wind, marking this vessel as a sailboat.

The panic clutched tight again. *They can't be selling me into slavery. I'm the Traementis heir now. Even if they know I'm an imposter, they can't simply make me disappear.*

The pitch and roll of the boat increased, giving Ren something new to distract her: nausea. It had wrung her out like a rag the whole way from Nadežra to Ganllech, when she and Tess fled; it had been no kinder on the journey back. The breath-damp air inside her mask threatened to choke her. Ren wrapped her hands around her elbows, gripping hard enough to bruise, and prayed that Tanaquis was right, that this was worth it, that it would be over soon. *Masks have mercy, let it be over soon.*

A flurry of activity was presumably the boat coming to shore.

They hadn't gone that far—one of the islands in the bay? A noble villa, maybe. Ren almost didn't care; she was just grateful for solid ground under her feet again, and a hand guiding her up a path and into a building.

The air inside was cool and dry—unusual in summer, but Renata had visited enough nobles' houses at this point to recognize the feel of a numinat at work. Fresh incense cut through the stagnant air inside her mask, helping to settle her stomach. She tried to gauge from the murmur of voices and the shuffle of feet how big the room was, how many people were in it, but the blind mask and the unknown surroundings were too disorienting, like she was both too close and too far away to know anything.

A touch at the center of her back almost made her reach for the knives hidden in a shawl she wasn't wearing.

"You're doing well." Tanaquis's voice, low but encouraging. "I know this is unnerving, but it's a necessary first rite. It will be over soon."

First rite. Whether Tanaquis meant it to be or not, that was a clue. For one absurd moment, Ren wondered if nobles swore knot bonds like common river rats, but no—this would be something else. Still, it was familiar enough to steady her breathing and her wits. She was Renata, heir to House Traementis, and needed to behave accordingly.

Tanaquis's hand guided her a short distance, then pressed on her shoulder until she knelt. The floor beneath her was unpadded stone. Small sounds told of other people nearby: How many? Renata couldn't suppress a flinch when Tanaquis took hold of her wrists and wrapped a cord around them. Not an effective binding—she could easily get out of it if she had to—but she hated this blindness, hated having to *trust.*

With a brief squeeze to Renata's shoulder, Tanaquis brushed past her. From a short distance to Renata's left came a man's voice, familiar, but she couldn't put a name to it. "What are—" Someone must have done something, because he didn't finish the question.

A tense silence fell. The incense, which had seemed so light at first, began to tickle her nose. She breathed slowly and carefully, and even that seemed too loud.

Then someone else spoke. Not anyone she'd ever heard; she would have remembered this voice. Seterin in its accent, resonant and deep, like the tolling of a huge, brazen bell.

"When we see, we do not know."

Three voices answered. Tanaquis was one; Renata struggled to identify the other two. "So we close our eyes."

"When we ask, we do not learn."

"So we close our mouths."

"When we reach, we do not grasp."

"So we bind our hands."

"Ignorance is the path to enlightenment."

There was no sound of footsteps. Without warning, a heavy hand landed upon Renata's head, and she jerked at the touch. "First postulant. Do you swear to keep our secrets, to speak to no one of what we do, to protect the mysteries of our sect, upon pain of eternal blindness?"

Fuck you. Her throat was too tight for the words to come out, which was probably a good thing. The rational part of her knew this was theatre, a rite designed to evoke exactly the tension winding her tight. But after everything she'd been through...

Tanaquis had brought her to this so she could find answers about the curse and learn more about pattern. She wouldn't have done that without good reason.

And besides, Ren had already broken one sacred oath in her life, when she killed Ondrakja. *Twice.* This one held far less meaning for her, and if she found herself in a position where she had to break it, she already knew what she would do.

"I swear."

The hand left her head. "Second postulant. Do you swear..."

It was the man who'd started to speak before. He sounded more eager as he swore; did he know more than she did?

The third voice took no effort at all to identify, a baritone she knew all too well. "I swear," Derossi Vargo said.

What is he *doing here?*

"You have taken ignorance into you and made it your own," the deep, Seterin voice said. "You have passed the first gate and begun your journey down the path of the Illius Praeteri."

Villa Extaquium, Bay of Vraszan: Summer Solstice

The crash of a gong shattered the air, and light blinded Renata as Tanaquis pulled off her mask.

She and the others knelt in a small, bare room with no windows, likely in the cellar of a house. Before them stood a pale Seterin man, tall and strongly built, his head shaved and his eyes cast in shadow by the lights above. "Greetings," he said to the three of them. "I am Diomen, your guide."

Renata blinked away stars while Tanaquis unbound her hands and drew her to her feet. "There," Tanaquis said briskly. "First step done—I'm afraid there's more to go, but I think that one's the worst, don't you?"

"Tanaquis." Her name was a warning, but an amused one, and it came from Ghiscolo Acrenix. Renata wasn't surprised at all to see him at Vargo's side, as Tanaquis was at hers. The Illius Praeteri: She'd heard that name from him before, in the conversation she'd spied on after he was raised as Caerulet. When he offered to invite Vargo into their ranks.

What is this?

The final postulant proved to be Rimbon Beldipassi, the delta gentleman who owned the exhibition of curiosities she and Leato had visited back in Pavnilun, before everything went wrong. His sponsor was Sureggio, the head of House Extaquium. Beldipassi chafed his wrists and looked nervously at Diomen, who stood as unmoving as a statue. "Eret Diomen? Or altan?"

"I bear the title of Pontifex here, and need no other."

Somehow, he made that sound chilling. Beldipassi said, "Pontifex, then. What is this? Eret Extaquium hasn't told me anything."

"Nor should he." Diomen still hadn't shifted, standing with his hands concealed in the opposite sleeves. His stillness was an effective trick, Renata had to admit; it gave him an otherworldly air. "The man at the beginning of his journey cannot see the end. But as you progress, more will be revealed. The three of you have been chosen, not only by your sponsors, but by far greater forces. It is my task to lead you along the path that will reveal the fullness of the blessings you bear."

He moved at last, lifting one hand to gesture toward the door. "Go now. Celebrate the first of your achievements. I will see you again."

Renata fought the urge to glance over her shoulder as Sureggio led them upstairs. It would only make her look nervous and uncertain, and anyway, she was confident that such a glance would only show her the Pontifex, hands once more hidden, watching them go. He was too good at this theatricality to ruin it by moving so soon.

Sureggio led them through a cellar and up into what was clearly his bay villa. Over his shoulder, he said, "I insisted we hold the first initiation here so I could offer you refreshments afterward."

Like his manor in the city, his villa was sumptuously decorated to the point of excess—and Renata didn't think it was the heat that explained why the servant who brought them a basin of cool water and a stack of napkins was wearing only a loincloth.

Ghiscolo dampened a napkin and gave it to Renata, smiling. "I still remember how I sweated underneath my mask for my first rite, and that took place in late winter."

"Thank you, Your Mercy."

"Ghiscolo," he said. "One of the charms of the Illius Praeteri is that we don't stand upon rank during our gatherings."

Vargo helped himself to a napkin. "Outside it, on the other hand..."

"We all swear to keep the secrets of the order," Ghiscolo said. "Including who is a member. It would be something of a giveaway if we shed the courtesies outside our rituals."

Vargo unbuttoned his collar so he could mop his neck. There

had been a time—it seemed like years ago—when Renata had felt so comfortable around him that she'd even considered taking the irrevocable step of revealing her true identity. Now everything had to be calculated, weighed for what would seem natural. Renata had shown an attraction to him before; he might wonder at its absence. She let her gaze linger for a moment on the open throat of his shirt, where the scar stood out more lividly than usual, before flicking away.

Only to catch Sureggio Extaquium doing the same thing, far more openly.

She wished they were anywhere other than his villa. Hedonism was one thing; the rumors of the excesses he enjoyed out here in the bay were far darker. Slavery was illegal in Nadežra...but Mettore Indestor had once spoken of selling her to Sureggio.

"Speaking of secrets," Vargo said. A soft ring echoed as he tipped a glass of chilled wine against Tanaquis's. "You should take more care in the future. I saw you pass the invitation to Renata at Nightpeace Gardens."

He gave Renata what he must have thought was a charming smile. "I knew what was to come, so I didn't think you needed a warning. Forgive me?"

Ghiscolo said something, but Ren couldn't hear it through the roaring in her mind. She fought the desire to smash her glass into his jaw.

Someday, you will scream for what you've done. And I will enjoy watching.

Her smile was more than a mask to cover the urge to rip his throat back open. It was a weapon: a way to manipulate him, as he'd manipulated her. "Surprises lose their savor if you see them coming."

Rimbon Beldipassi joined them, round cheeks flushed and shining. "How did you know, Mas—er...Eret...no. Uh...Derossi?"

Vargo's smile tightened. "I pay attention."

Renata sipped her wine. For once it wasn't Extaquium's own pressing, thankfully, but she still contrived to look ill, putting one hand against her stomach and setting the glass aside. "Forgive me. I'm afraid the trip out here left me feeling unwell, and I could use some fresh air. Which way to the nearest balcony?"

"I'll show you," Tanaquis said.

It was warmer out on the balcony, almost muggy without the cooling numinata. Nadežra was a misty yellow glow in the distance, and on the other side was the black rush of the sea. Tanaquis led Renata to a circle of chaises, their padded benches exuding the salty-sweet aroma of seawater and beach pea.

"I *am* sorry for the discomfort," she said, settling at Renata's side and pressing a cool hand to her brow and cheek. "Usually we hold our activities closer to the city, but it's always like this when Sureggio decides to sponsor someone. Some members of the Illius Praeteri are more interested in style than they are in the substance."

"You indicated this might help with the curse," Renata said, keeping her voice low. "Well, I've joined your society. What now?"

Tanaquis hesitated, casting a glance over her shoulder. She actually looked nervous, as though she thought someone might be listening in. "You've *started* the process of joining. There are three Gates of Initiation, of which this is the first. You'll need to go through two more before you're a full member of the Praeteri—and before I'm allowed to talk freely."

Very few things leashed Tanaquis's tongue. She wasn't the sort to be impressed by Diomen's theatrics; if he intimidated her, then there must be more to him than mere showmanship.

Pointing that out wouldn't do any good, and neither would pressing her to speak. Renata said, "Is there *anything* you can tell me about the Illius Praeteri? That name..." She let the question dangle, hoping Tanaquis's pedantic impulses would rescue her. A Seterin noblewoman ought to be able to translate that phrase in her sleep.

Sure enough, Tanaquis wrinkled her nose. "I know. Awful, isn't it? I'm honestly surprised the Pontifex puts up with such mangled Old Seterin. It's meant to indicate something like 'those who go beyond Illi.' We deal with... some of the deeper secrets of numinatria. Among other things."

Renata wondered what those "other things" were. Tanaquis clearly found them tedious, which meant they weren't intellectual in nature. The trappings of ritual, perhaps; Renata knew enough to recognize the term *pontifex* as meaning "bridge builder," but more generally, "high priest." She sighed. "I see. Am I allowed to know who's a member?"

"You will, but not yet."

"What about past members? Mettore Indestor?"

"No. I think Ghiscolo was concerned he might try to shut us down, or take us over. But the Praeteri are mostly from delta families and smaller noble houses. The Cinquerat has enough power in this city; seat holders aren't allowed to be sponsored in." Tanaquis huffed in annoyance, her breath stirring the hair at Renata's cheek. "Honestly, Ghiscolo's elevation has caused quite a fuss. We've spent more time arguing about that than anything interesting. Sponsoring Vargo might be his last act as a member."

That left Renata with another unanswered question, one she couldn't share with Tanaquis.

If he wasn't a member, how had Mettore discovered that she was conceived during the Great Dream?

The Praeteri had seemed like a potential lead. Mettore hated Vraszenians; he would never visit a patterner. And Ren had never told Ondrakja—though Ondrakja might have guessed. That was the most likely explanation.

I just wish everyone who could answer that question weren't dead.

"You told me this first step was the worst," she said. "What are the others?"

"I won't be your sponsor for those, though I'll get you through them as fast as I can. Other members will lead you through the second and third gates—I know several who are eager. For the second, you'll know who it is when they give you this signal." She interlaced her fingers, tucking them inside her palms with only the forefingers extended. "After that, you must submit to whatever orders they give you, no matter how absurd they seem."

"*Any* orders?" Renata didn't bother hiding her alarm. "What if they tell me to do something against House Traementis?" *Or against Tess.* Delta gentry and minor nobles: They would see a mere servant as a natural playing piece in their games.

Tanaquis looked thoughtful. "I suppose that's possible, depending on your sponsor...Oh, don't worry," she said, catching Renata's growing unease. "'Possible' isn't the same as 'likely.' I get to pick your next sponsor; I won't choose someone who hates you. The orders are usually more embarrassing than anything else." She hesitated, looking like she might say something more, then brushed it away. "I won't pretend there aren't challenges farther down the road of initiation—but it's up to each member how far they want to go."

How far did Renata want to go? For its own sake, not very. She had no particular interest in numinatria and could guess at the other sorts of things these cuffs got up to in their secret rituals. But she was desperate to discover how the Traementis had gotten cursed—including how she had been caught up in it, when she wasn't related to the family at all.

And she wanted to know what Vargo was up to. He hadn't spoken to his spider spirit tonight that she could tell, but with more opportunities to observe, she might learn something.

"Thank you for the warning," she said, thinking bitterly of Vargo's words a little while ago. "I breathe more easily when I know what's coming."

PART

II

The Mask of Night

East Channel, River Dežera: Colbrilun 29

To look at the pleasure barge easing slowly up the East Channel, oars churning against the river's current, Nadežra was a world where no one went hungry, no one lived in fear, and certainly no one ever committed mass murder.

The horrors of the Scurezza slaughter had been good for a week or so of gossip, but the Vigil was keeping its collective mouth shut tight about the details—including what Quaniet had said to Giuna. With no fresh news about who killed them or why, the Upper Bank had soon moved on. Aided and abetted by Sibiliat, who had paid for today's revelry out of her own pocket.

But not for her own sake. No, this was a celebration of Renata's twenty-third natal day.

A canopy sheltered the revelers from the summer sun, while bottles of wine rested in buckets chilled by numinata. The musicians playing in the stern could scarcely be heard over the chatter of the guests. Nobles and delta gentry all, and skewing heavily toward the young, unattached set—men and women who might hope to win a place in House Traementis, Renata's bed, or both.

So far as Ren could tell, the process of adopting new members into House Traementis bore more resemblance to competition over charter administration rights than anything she recognized as familial. Her would-be cousins submitted applications and gifts, and were weighed more on the assets, skills, and connections they would bring to the house than on any personal feeling. Not that the latter was irrelevant—Donaia was still hoping for Tanaquis's acceptance, and Giuna drowned the hopes of Diambetta Terdenzi by quoting some of the choicer insults she'd flung in the past—but with the Traementis ranks and coffers so depleted, they couldn't afford to support anyone who wouldn't bring much benefit with them. Vraszenians seeking to insult the Liganti often said they bought and sold their relatives, and now Ren had a box seat from which to watch the horse fair go.

Not everyone was angling for her bed or her register, of course. At Renata's suggestion, there were a few guests closer to Giuna's age, and Benvanna Novri had for some reason insisted on accompanying Iascat...but on the whole, this party might as well have flown the sign she'd jested about at Nightpeace Gardens: *Here Be Marriage Bait.*

The most awkward thing was, she suspected Sibiliat was trying to be helpful. Ever since the New Year, her erstwhile rival had been distinctly friendlier. Because of Renata's newfound connection with her father, through the Illius Praeteri? An attempt to comfort Giuna after the horror they'd stumbled upon that night? Or some other reason?

Of course, even Sibiliat's friendship carried an edge. She'd led the social world of Nadežra's young cuffs before Renata came, and today she seemed eager to make Renata prove her right to that role...or lose it.

Part of Renata wanted to let her have it. No—part of *Ren.* Even as she met Sibiliat's challenges and answered with some of her own, even as she laughed and flirted with the guests, she felt hollow. None of these people were really her friends. They gave her gifts, but they'd turn on her like sharks if they knew the truth. Even the occasion was a lie: This wasn't her birthday at all, and she wasn't twenty-three.

Ahead rose the shimmering arcs of the cleansing numinat that spanned the East Channel. The silver of the containing circle curved like a bridge of spun sugar over the prismatium spiral that held the figures themselves. Her guests took it for granted, and the clean water it brought them; they didn't even look up as the barge passed through the spira aurea. They were too busy listening to Bondiro Coscanum mock the absent Giarron Quientatis for trying to adopt an entire orphanage—an impractical move even for a man as kind-hearted as he was reputed to be.

Renata intervened before the mockery could get too cruel, then drifted along the barge to make sure Giuna was doing all right. Her cousin was playing hexboard with Orrucio Amananto, and seemed happy enough.

"More wine?" Sibiliat appeared at Renata's elbow. She hadn't quite gone so far as to propose a drinking contest, but she seemed disappointed that Renata kept declining refills. "I'm sorry there's no aža. Magistrate Rapprecco has been cracking down on the illicit trade."

"It's too hot for alcohol," Renata said, cooling herself with a fan that wafted citron with each pass. "How do you endure the heat?" She should get back under the canopy . . . except too many people lay in wait there.

Sibiliat smirked. "If you think this is hot, wait until Lepilun."

She made even that sound competitive. Hoping to blunt it, Renata said, "Thank you for arranging this. I'll admit, I wasn't intending to have any kind of party—it seems too soon." A year would have been too soon. They were all toasting her as the heir to House Traementis, but every time she heard that phrase, all she could see was Leato left behind at the bottom of the empty wellspring.

Sibiliat leaned in and murmured, "Oh, it is. But you also have to keep up appearances, don't you? House Traementis is recovering. People need to see that. If Donaia can't do it, you must."

It sounded like genuine advice. And Sibiliat wasn't wrong. Donaia was handling as much business as she could, but her mourning left her no will to face the social side of Nadežra's politics. Whether this was Ren's idea of a good time or not, she owed House Traementis her best effort.

You used to dream of this. But every dream has both a Face and a Mask.

The barge made its slow way upriver, past the Point, which split the Dežera, to where the heavily built-up islets began to give way to more open space, houses interspersed with vegetable gardens and goats. Up ahead lay the heavy stone bridge at Floodwatch. The party's mood grew more raucous as they neared it; some of Renata's suitors started taking dares, competing with each other to impress her.

When the barge moored on the far side of the bridge so one of the servants could go buy fresh berries, those dares wound up sending Iascat Novrus over the rail to chisel off the river mussels encrusting the embankment. He'd shed his shirt to avoid ruining it, and by the time he slopped back on deck, his pale shoulders were already turning pink. Everyone retreated a step to avoid being splattered as he tossed a large, encrusted clump of mussels onto the deck. "Get to shucking," Iascat said, examining the scrapes lining both of his hands. "There better be a pearl in one of those, or I'll have injured myself for nothing. Fintenus, if I lose a hand to infection, I'm telling my aunt it's your fault."

"What, you want us *both* to lose a hand?"

For the first time that day, Ren felt a touch of real pleasure. She and Tess and Sedge used to duck Ondrakja's eye every so often and make the walk up to Floodwatch for fresh mussels. Now she readily joined the others in claiming shells and whatever sharp implements could be found to pry them open. But her guests tossed theirs aside with disappointed mutters, meat and all, when each one proved to be empty.

Her annoyance at their waste almost made her stab her thumb as she opened another shell. The bitten-off curse turned into a gasp as she saw the contents. "I found one!"

She held up the pearl like a trophy in her filthy glove, stained with river water and grit. "That means good luck," Parma told her, clapping.

Benvanna's voice rose above the congratulations and good-natured grousing. "So the Vraszenians say...but only if you eat the mussel you found the pearl in. Raw."

The congratulations turned to hoots and cheers, chanting for her to eat it. Benvanna was wrong about having to eat the mussel; the actual tradition said she was supposed to keep the shell in her purse, to attract more wealth. But Renata wouldn't know that—and she would think eating a raw mussel was disgusting, especially above the cleansing numinat. Giuna was protesting, not that anyone paid her any heed.

Benvanna gave her a sharp-edged smile and propped her chin atop her forefingers, tucking the rest of her fingers between her palms. "Come on, Renata. Eat up."

Renata almost dropped the pearl as she recognized the hand gesture. *Benvanna* was her sponsor for the second gate? Tanaquis had promised to pick someone who didn't hate her.

But it explained Benvanna's presence today. And regardless of what they thought of each other, for Renata to continue her initiation into the Praeteri, she had to follow any order her sponsor gave. At least this one didn't bother her nearly as much as Benvanna probably expected.

She struck a pose, raising the mussel with a brave flourish—then slurped it right down. "Mmmm," she said, dabbing her lips with exaggerated delicacy. "Not bad."

She grinned cheekily at Benvanna while the barge erupted in drunken cheers. The other woman gave her an unreadable smile in return. Satisfaction? Or annoyance that Renata hadn't been more put off by the mussel?

Renata didn't get a chance to ask. As she palmed the mussel shell and tucked it into her pocket, a Galbiondi man whose name she didn't remember said, "Hey—aren't we near the Scurezza house? Little Giuna, didn't you and Sibiliat find them? Let's have the tale firsthand!"

The laughter fell to dead silence. In that hush, Renata heard the strangled sound Giuna made. Her cousin wavered, hands rising to her mouth—then broke and fled.

Sibiliat followed immediately. Renata didn't. Instead she pinned the Galbiondi with a cold gaze. Then she went to the rail, stripped off one stained glove, and put her fingers to her mouth for a piercing whistle. The skiffers near the river stair began poling toward her, racing to see who could get there first.

Renata pulled a decira out of her purse and pressed it into the Galbiondi's palm. "For your passage home."

Then she went after Giuna.

She found her cousin with Sibiliat at the stern. The musicians were taking a break; no one was nearby to hear. Sibiliat was stroking Giuna's back, murmuring softly in her ear.

Only when Renata saw her cousin did she realize what her knee-jerk response had been. *Defend Giuna.* The same way Ren had once defended a copper-headed Ganllechyn girl who'd just joined the Fingers.

When it came to comforting, though, she was out of her depth. This had always been Tess's strength, not Ren's—but Tess wasn't there. "I'm so sorry," she said awkwardly. "I should have thought... We should have gone downriver instead."

"It's all right," Giuna whispered, though it clearly wasn't. "Of course they're talking about it. Everybody wants to know what happened."

Renata wondered what would eventually come of that. High Commander Dimiterro knew the truth, but since the culprit was already dead, Ghiscolo had seen no benefit in sharing what Giuna and Sibiliat had seen and heard. If the Upper Bank knew Quaniet Scurezza had killed her entire family because Coevis had applied to House Traementis, the gossip would be all about the return of the Traementis's ill luck. It was a stigma they couldn't afford.

Renata glanced at the skiff now headed downriver, with the Galbiondi man aboard. "Do you want to go back to the manor? I'll come with you. I've had enough of this heat."

That made Giuna straighten and wipe her cheeks. "No. No, we can't show weakness like that. And I don't want to ruin your special day."

The only thing special about the day was how much of a masquerade the whole thing was. But Giuna was right about maintaining the show. As Sibiliat had been earlier.

Renata hugged her cousin. Then she drew in a deep breath and settled her mask back into place. If people expected the ruling star of the social scene, then she would give them that.

Striding back toward the bow, she stripped off her other glove and flung the ruined fabric into the water. "More wine!" she commanded, and the party floated on.

Whitesail, Upper Bank: Colbrilun 30

In some ways Tanaquis lived the life Renata had pretended to in the Westbridge townhouse. She had no footman and kept only one maid, a taciturn woman named Zlatsa whose chief recommendation was that she took all of Tanaquis's oddities in stride. There was no cook; whether Tanaquis realized it or not, her food came from nearby stalls and ostrettas, when she remembered to request a hot meal at all. If rooms went days without being dusted—or even months—she didn't mind, so long as her workshop remained clean. Many of the things others would rely on servants for were instead done with numinatria, or not done at all.

Which was why Renata arrived for her meeting with Tess in tow and a hamper of food. Tess made quick work of dusting the relevant bits of the parlour, then laid out plates, glasses, wine, pastries, and Liganti-style sandwiches with cheese and ham. Much to Ren's surprise, she'd found that she quite liked cheese, as long as it wasn't the type that stank like it was rotting.

"Thank you, Tess," she said when that was done. "You may go. I'll have Zlatsa bring the hamper back later."

It was both a relief and a wrench to send her away. Ren had seen almost nothing of Tess lately, except in the mornings when she woke—after far too little sleep, and that little bit disturbed by nightmares of zlyzen.

The only upside was that Tess had more liberty to pursue her own work. She was in high demand as a dressmaker now. Soon Tess would have enough to reach *her* dream: a shop of her own. Then she could be free of the lies that bound Ren tight.

None of which they had discussed. There wasn't any opportunity . . . and it was a conversation Ren dreaded having.

For now, Tess left with a curtsy and a worried pinch between her brows, and Renata settled in to wait for Tanaquis.

But her plan to arrive early so that she and Tanaquis could discuss private matters ran aground on the rocks of Vargo's punctuality and their hostess's absentmindedness. "I'll remind her you're here. Again," Zlatsa said with a long-suffering sigh after she led Vargo in.

"Renata." Vargo took both her hands in greeting before she could occupy them with tea. "Is that a bit of color in your cheeks? Summer suits you."

Summer plagued her. In addition to her usual imbued cosmetics, she had to invest in creams to shield her skin from the sun's kiss. Renata tugged out of his grip on the pretext of covering her cheeks. "I'm afraid I spent more time out on the river than was wise."

"Your natal day, yes? I'm sorry to have missed it." He followed her to the mismatched couch and chair—selected for comfort rather than style, Renata suspected. When she took the chair, hoping for some distance, he flipped back the crisp poplin skirts of his mulberry coat and settled on the footstool at her side. "Though I suppose I wouldn't have been welcome among your guests."

Before Renata had to offer an insincere apology for leaving him out, Tanaquis wandered into the parlour, nose pressed close to a scroll. She seemed startled to find them there. "Is it noon already? Next time, don't depend on my maid. Come up and announce yourselves. She's always interrupting me, so I've learned to ignore her." Tanaquis marked her place in the scroll with a clip and perched on the edge of a chair, studying the repast as though she'd never seen food. "Did she do this?"

"No, I arranged it, as I imagine we'll be working for quite some time." Renata poured coffee for them all and took faint pleasure in seeing Vargo's smile grow fixed as he took it. Apparently he liked coffee no better than she did.

Tanaquis, by contrast, drank it black and with evident pleasure. "Did you serenade Carinci Acrenix at the Rotunda yet, Vargo?"

"This morning," he said. "If you have any other pointless orders for me, can you make them less inconvenient to my schedule?"

She frowned at him. "But the inconvenience is the point. If it's easy, then it misses the purpose. 'Submission is the door to freedom.'"

So Tanaquis was the one ordering Vargo around for the second gate of the Praeteri. Renata had assumed they were forbidden to talk about it, but Tanaquis turned to her and said, "Though it isn't supposed to be *too* dreadful. Has Benvanna asked you to do anything that goes too far?"

"Not at all." Renata hesitated, weighing what she should say in front of Vargo. Likely he knew already; Sostira had hardly been subtle about showing her interest in Renata, and Benvanna couldn't be subtle about her jealousy if she tried. "I'm merely surprised. You promised you wouldn't choose an enemy."

"I didn't." Tanaquis paused in her dismantling of one of the sandwiches, apparently so she could eat each element separately. "I thought you were on good terms with House Novrus."

"That's hardly the same thing."

Tanaquis nodded as if to say she understood, while her expression made it clear she never would—and didn't care. "Well, I think you've both done enough to count as having passed the trial. I'll talk to the Pontifex and arrange the second initiation. One more challenge after that, and you'll be properly in."

"I was surprised to hear a Seterin voice at the first ceremony," Renata said before Vargo could speak up. "Has the Pontifex been in Nadežra long?"

Tanaquis's reluctance to break the secrecy of the Praeteri apparently didn't extend to discussing their leader. "Sixteen years or so. Would you consider that long?"

"Compared to me, at least." Renata forced herself to sip the coffee. "What brought him to Nadežra, of all places?"

::Money.::

At the intrusion of the spirit's voice, Renata spilled coffee into her saucer. While she mopped that up, Tanaquis said, "I believe it had to do with the law passed against mystery cults back in your homeland. Too many of them were being used as breeding grounds for political coups."

::No one in Nadežra would *dream* of staging a coup.::

That sardonic response was in Vargo's mental voice, and got a chuckle from his spirit. But Vargo sounded only impatient when he said, "As interesting as the Pontifex's history may be, could we get to the actual purpose of the meeting?"

"Yes, certainly." Tanaquis patted her pockets and glanced around before finally discovering her scroll under the table. "I've drawn up a few charts for you. Early Similun is much too soon, but there are other possibilities. If you're expecting to make a cleansing numinat work on that scale simply by timing your efforts to the stars, though, I'm afraid you'll be disappointed."

Vargo set down his coffee like a man determined to "forget" it was there and passed over a leatherbound folder much like the one he'd given to Renata so many months ago. "The details of my plans are with Fulvet's office and the Traementis, but I made you a copy as well. In the absence of a skilled inscriptor willing to give their life to imbue the working…" He and Tanaquis exchanged ironic smiles. "The fragment I fished out of the river turned out to be layered, as I suspected. I don't think it was a simple matter of passing the water through multiple numinata, each of a more reasonably achieved scale and sustainable level—but it supports my theory that an approach of that sort could work. Better than what we have now, anyway."

"Hmm. Inefficient, expensive," Tanaquis muttered, tossing aside the pages until she got to the design sketches for the numinat. "Inelegant."

::I beg your pardon?!:: the spirit squawked. ::I spent years devising this plan!::

::What happened to 'Oh, I like that girl; excellent chalking'?::

"It's the only feasible route open to us," Vargo said, as though there weren't an incensed spider grumbling at him. "Or that's my best prospect, anyway. Though after Veiled Waters, I'm wondering if there might be an alternative—given what I saw of the numinat in the Great Amphitheatre."

"You don't propose to use the wellspring?" Renata was astonished that she could keep her voice steady.

::It's an idea . . . ::

"No." Vargo might have been answering both her and the spirit. "But it does prove that numinata can be powered by sources other than ordinary foci. Perhaps even by the Lumen itself—without the limitations imposed by foci."

Tanaquis lit up. "Yes! I'd previously discounted pattern as mere superstition, but Renata's proven it can have actual metaphysical validity. Not in the rational, predictable fashion of astrology, though. It's more . . . intuitive, you might say. Or unreliable."

::*Now* what's inefficient and inelegant?::

Renata tensed to keep from glaring at Vargo—or rather, at the rose-hued shadows of his collar, where she could just see the spider lurking. Tanaquis, oblivious, was still talking. "That doesn't mean it isn't possible to connect the two, though. There are sixty cards in a pattern deck, which divides neatly into ten groups of six, following the calendrical division of months and weeks in the year, leaving out the intercalary period. Renata, if you were to associate each card with one of the numina, how would you sort them?"

"I wouldn't," she said, gathering her scattered attention. "They aren't organized that way—and there used to be more than sixty, you know."

The speculation in Tanaquis's eyes brightened. "There were? How many? Perhaps we don't have to discount the five intercalary days after all."

I shouldn't have said that. Improvising, Renata said, "I've been reading up on pattern—what little I can find that isn't written in Vraszenian, at least." She made a mental note to buy such books. Surely some had to exist. "One of them said there used to be seven more cards, one for each of the clans. They've fallen out of use, but still."

It dammed the flow of Tanaquis's enthusiasm. "Seven. Drat."

Vargo drummed his fingers against his knee. "You mentioned this at Nightpeace. Using pattern to augment a focus, I believe?"

In a minor miracle, Tanaquis hesitated and looked at Renata, rather than immediately spilling the whole tale of the curse. But Renata had already spilled that tale herself, back when she thought she could trust Vargo. She said, "The spiritual affliction I told you about, the one affecting House Traementis. Tanaquis was, thank the Lumen, able to lift it from us. And yes, she used cards in the numinat."

The discussion that followed was too abstruse for Renata to follow, but that was fine. It gave her the freedom to focus instead on Vargo, watching his reactions, listening to the brief comments his spirit interjected.

That comment about a coup... was *that* Vargo's aim? She wanted to laugh it off—if Elsivin the Red's rebellion failed, Vargo with his knots was unlikely to succeed—but not long ago she would have laughed off the idea of Vargo becoming a noble.

She had no love for most of the Cinquerat, but the idea of *him* ruling over the city was no better.

In her distraction, Renata failed to steer the conversation into safer waters. She was startled when Vargo turned to her. "You read pattern?" The scar through his brow flexed into view as he arched it.

"If a few experiments deserve that name," she said, hoping her tense laugh sounded like embarrassment. "I find it intriguing, but there was only so much I could learn in Seteris."

"Another fortunate reason for you to come to Nadežra," Tanaquis said. "I'm so eager to learn more."

The ringing for seventh sun echoed faintly from the street. Vargo eyed the slant of light gilding the dust in the air and grimaced. "As am I, but I can't be late for my appointment with Meda Fienola's boss. Not when it's taken me three weeks to *get* that appointment." He straightened his coat with an aggrieved tug. "Some clerk in His Worship's office has apparently decided now is a good time to revive an old rule that all requests must be made within the hour of seventh sun—to honor Sebat—and filed in triplicate. With *brown* ink, mind you, not blue. I'd assume they're stonewalling me specifically, but I'm not the only one having problems."

Renata would have enjoyed his frustration more if she didn't share it. "I had a petition rejected because apparently when the clerk said I had three days to file, he meant down to the bell."

"Exactly. And unless someone has a better proposal than mine, I need to get started on transmuting prismatium for the numinat."

"Yes, you'll need rather a lot of it," Tanaquis said, her fingers drifting across the spread of pages that had overtaken the table. "For that alone, you have my sincere support in finding some other method. Creating prismatium is *so dull*."

::Dull? What does she mean, dull? The Great Work is the highest form of . . . ::

Renata could at least take comfort that Vargo departed on a tide of telepathic pique. She hid her amusement with a frown as the door to the parlour closed, leaving her alone with Tanaquis.

"Something troubles you?" Tanaquis asked in a rare moment of observation, looking up from restacking and bundling the designs.

Now it was Renata's turn to hesitate. Of anyone in Nadežra, Tanaquis was the most likely to be able to answer her questions. But asking them would require her to thread her way through a very delicate maze.

"Ever since my sleeplessness," she began, then wiped that away with a stroke of her hand. "No, I think . . . ever since Vargo rescued me from the realm of mind. I've been noticing something . . . odd." It hadn't actually begun until the amphitheatre, when she strengthened the thread that connected her to Vargo, but Tanaquis didn't need to know that.

Tanaquis's nod prompted her. "I've been hearing a voice," Renata admitted. "Around Vargo. I think it's a spirit of some kind, speaking to him. And he answers it."

"A spirit?" It was almost unnerving, how Tanaquis watched her without blinking. "What does it say? How does he answer it? Aloud?"

"No, I—I think I'm hearing his thoughts. But not all of them; only the ones he sends in reply. It happened a few times just now, while Vargo was here. The spirit seems to know a great deal about numinatria."

"Fascinating." Tanaquis sipped her coffee, not seeming to mind that her cup had gone stone cold. "I wonder if it has anything to do with the numinat on his chest. You've seen it, yes? Though I imagine you were preoccupied with other concerns."

Something about the way she said that... "We aren't lovers, Tanaquis. But I caught a glimpse of it on the Night of Hells." Through the body paint that had nearly been the most opaque part of his costume. The flash of heat that went through her at the memory was chased by a cold touch of anger. "When did *you* see it?"

"He showed it to me—Ah, right; you were not of sound mind at the time. Why do you think I let him go into the realm of mind after your spirit? It's some sort of anchor or binding numinat, so I thought him less likely to become lost. Beyond that, however, it's like nothing I've ever seen before. I'd dearly love to take a tracing of it."

Half the people in Renata's life would have meant that as innuendo. Tanaquis's interest, though, was purely intellectual. It helped distract from the memory of dancing with Vargo that night—the paint on his skin, the interest in his kohl-smudged eyes. "You think that numinat binds him to the spirit?"

"It's the most likely answer. Could you sketch what you recall of it?" Before Renata could protest, charcoal and a mostly blank sheet of paper were thrust into her hands.

It was months ago, eclipsed not just by the paints covering the mark but by the other events of that night, and Renata was no artist. She drew a dubious, lopsided circle, then attempted to fill in some lines. "But how did he do it? And why?"

"If this spirit is as knowledgeable about numinatria as you claim, there's your why right there. I'd wondered how Eret Vargo managed to learn so much, given his background. How amazing it must be, to have a conduit of cosmic wisdom at your disposal! As to the how... That's even more of a mystery, if he managed it without any guidance." She wrinkled her nose at Renata's sketch. "You can stop. That isn't the least bit useful."

"I'm afraid I was always hopeless at even basic inscription."

Tanaquis didn't appear to find that suspicious. She patted Renata's hand absently as she took the charcoal away. "You have pattern instead. A whole realm of the cosmos I never gave much thought to before! So short-sighted, attempting to destroy the wellspring. There's much to be learned here—from you and Vargo both."

Westbridge, Lower Bank: Colbrilun 33

In the Vraszenian calendar, the holiday of Six Candles was a time of nonviolence, out of respect for the memory of the dead Ižranyi. People flocked to the river to float reed votive boats down the Dežera, then visited the nearest labyrinth to make offerings to Čel Tmekra, the deity of death, that the lost spirits of that clan might someday find their way to Ažerais's Dream.

Ren hadn't celebrated Six Candles properly since her mother died. And she wouldn't this year, either—because she was busy helping Koszar and Idusza shift to the new refuge she'd found for them.

In a normal year, it would have been an ideal time to move someone who didn't want to be seen. The streets and bridges away from the river were relatively quiet, with fewer eyes to note a man who still couldn't walk without support. But with all the tensions in this city, it wasn't a normal year.

"More of Branek's knot-traitors," Idusza hissed in Arenza's ear, nails digging into her arm as they both peered past the corner of an ostretta. The squad of armed fists lounging in the plaza were the third they'd run afoul of since Arenza, Serrado, and Idusza sneaked the hooded and limping Koszar out of Alinka's courtyard tenement. "They have Gria Dmivro's own courage, to still wear that cord on their wrists. But if they catch us, we'll be wearing a red smile at our necks."

She kept her voice low, but Koszar heard her. He pushed himself painfully off the wall and said, "We must go back, and try at night."

At night there would be more Vigil patrols. They'd been keeping a close watch on the Lower Bank since the riots, and especially since Branek had begun inciting trouble. Arenza said, "More danger to go back now than to press forward."

"I can distract them somehow," Serrado whispered. "Long enough for the three of you to sneak past."

Koszar shook his head. "They'll know you for a hawk, and one I've worked with before."

"Will they know me?" Arenza asked. The silent look Idusza and Koszar exchanged spoke louder than words. "I thought not. I will distract them."

Serrado's hand on her arm stopped her as she pulled her shawl tight. His hand narrowly missed landing on one of the knives hidden in it—though she supposed he would hardly wonder why she went armed, given the situation. "You don't have to," he said, his voice rough.

"This was my idea," she said. Not just moving Koszar today; the refuge itself. She'd arranged it through some of Renata's resources, hiding the connections seven layers deep. "On me it lies to keep you all safe."

She drew away before anyone could say more and strode out into the square.

Szorsas weren't priests, but at certain times of the year—the Night of Bells, Veiled Waters, Six Candles—they stood for the voices of the dead Ižranyi. Rather than softening her footfalls as she had before, Arenza let her bootheels strike the cobbles with authoritative force. In strident Vraszenian, she demanded, "You scoundrels! Why sit you here, idle and drinking, on this sacred day? You should be at the river, at the labyrinth, praying for those whose spirits are lost even to the dream! Is this how the Ižranyi are remembered now by our people in Nadežra? Truly, I weep for our holy city, when such disrespect profanes the day of mourning!"

Several of the fists jerked upright at her words, as if their own mothers were scolding them. The leader was made of sterner stuff, though. He spat onto the cobbles. "Fine words from one wandering around idle herself."

He was still sitting, leaning back on a stool. One swipe of Arenza's foot took it out from under him, dumping him on his ass. "I remember the Ižranyi by making certain others forget them not!"

One of the fists knuckled her brow. Giving Arenza a jerky little bow, she said, "Szorsa, we mean no disrespect. Those chalk-faces blasphemed already on Veiled Waters; what if they cause more trouble today? Our orders are to keep everything under control."

Gesturing at the silent plaza, Arenza demanded, "See you anyone who might cause trouble? No? Of course not, because trouble follows our people, and all our people are at the river or the labyrinth. As you should be. Come, I will show you the way, since you seem to have forgotten *our* ways."

Not even a szorsa's haranguing would move Branek's fists from their post, but she hadn't expected it. She'd achieved enough to distract them, though. When the respectful woman promised she'd visit the river before dusk, then spend the night in prayer with her family, Arenza accepted that as sufficient victory and left.

Looping around to the far side of the plaza was much easier when she wasn't trying to hide an injured man. She met the others along a back canal that threaded between townhouses, just as they were climbing out of it. The summer's dry weather had drained the channel down to mud, which clung to the bottom of Andrejek's cloak and spattered Serrado's and Idusza's boots.

"Ažerais blessed me with the more pleasant route," Arenza said, holding the end of her shawl to her nose at the pungent scent.

"Or punished us for our sacrilege," Idusza said, smiling wryly. "The three of us weren't even the target of your ire, and yet my feet itched to take me to the river, just to escape it."

"You serve the ancestors more than they do," Arenza assured her. "Come, let us move on."

They made it to the half basement she'd rented on the Uča

Drošnel without any further difficulties, and none too soon. Koszar sank down onto the cot with a muffled sound of pain, and Serrado produced a flask of something Alinka had brewed before they left. Koszar drank it while Idusza settled their few belongings and twitched the ragged curtain shut over the high window that looked out onto the pavement.

"We'll leave you to rest," Serrado said, accepting the empty flask back.

But when Arenza turned to follow him, Idusza caught her sleeve. "Szorsa—Arenza—if you would spare us just a moment more?"

After the door closed behind Serrado, Koszar pushed himself upright, groaning. "Your words to Branek's people...It may have been a ruse, but the words you spoke were true. Too much time in this city robs us of the memory of who we are, and what is important: the ties we have to the past, and to each other."

Reaching into his pocket, he took out a length of braided cord, purple and white and black. White for Anoškin, Arenza surmised; that was Koszar's clan. Purple for the dead Ižranyi; the Stadnem Anduske were the "faithful children of the dreamweaver." Black evoked the koszenie, the shawls on which Vraszenians recorded their ancestry.

Then she stopped thinking about the individual strands and realized what he was holding.

"Idusza has said you are alone here. For one of our people, that is no fit state." Koszar smoothed the knot bracelet over his knee. "Many times I have thought of inviting you to join us. But I was cautious before—cautious of the wrong things, it turned out. Now I am weak, and all but alone. This is not the act of a leader to a recruit, but rather of a friend to a friend."

A quiet huff from Idusza. "I know it must feel like embroidering what has already been sewn—you have helped us so much already—but we would tie ourselves to you. If you will tie yourself to us?"

Bitterness flooded Ren's mouth as she stared at the braided strands of the charm, unable to even blink. Twice she'd tied herself into a knot, and twice she'd betrayed it: six years ago when she poisoned Ondrakja, and again during Veiled Waters when she begged Ondrakja to take her back, then turned the zlyzen against her. *I'm a murderer and a knot-cutting traitor. Just like Branek.* They would never invite her to swear if they knew.

They didn't see that, though. They only saw Arenza, the pattern-reader newly come to Nadežra. Just like the Traementis, they had grown attached to a mask.

In a knot, there were supposed to be no grudges between members. No debts. And no secrets. It wasn't a spiritual compulsion, and even faithful knot members sometimes bent the oath a little...but hiding the truth about herself would go well beyond a small bend. Either she'd have to tell them everything—Renata, the Black Rose, the lies she'd told to gain their trust, all her masks and the half-Vraszenian outcast behind them—or the oath would be broken the moment she swore it.

The silence had stretched out long enough that they could tell something was wrong. "We will not ask for you to risk yourself against Branek," Idusza assured her. "You are a szorsa, not a fist. Your gift must be protected."

I don't deserve your protection. Nor their trust. Ren wasn't worthy of a knot bond, just as she hadn't been worthy of a life among her mother's kin. She wasn't Vraszenian enough for that.

Only Vraszenian enough for it to hurt.

Disappointing the hope in their eyes cut deep, but not as deep as the alternative. "It isn't that," Arenza said heavily. "I..." She should have some clever excuse, but the weight had crushed all agility from her mind. "I cannot."

Awkward silence followed, as Idusza stared at the flagstone floor, and Andrejek tucked the bracelet away.

"If you cannot, you cannot. Forgive us if we presumed too far," he said. Arenza was braced for suspicion—for anger—but he only sounded sad. And tired. "If you wish not to risk yourself further by helping us, then we understand."

"It is not that!" The words burst out of her, startling them both. She dragged her voice down with an effort. "I will still help you."

She *had* to help them. If she couldn't be their knot-mate, she could be the Black Rose, the thorn in their enemy's heel.

But she couldn't say that to them. Weakly, she said, "I—I am still your friend. If I have not offended you too much."

Idusza's laugh was too loud for the small room. Bright like the thin line of sunlight streaming through a gap in the curtain, and with the same hard edge. "Think you it takes so little to offend us? Of course we are friends. But we should not keep you any longer. As you reminded all of us, it is Six Candles. Since we cannot visit river or labyrinth, we can only light our candles here in the dark."

"Perhaps you can take our respects to them for us," Koszar said. Gently, but it was a dismissal all the same.

She had nowhere to go but back to Traementis Manor, and the life of a cuff. "I will," Ren promised, and hated herself for the lie.

Westbridge and Kingfisher, Lower Bank: Colbrilun 33

Grey told himself it was because of Branek's fists on the streets that he loitered outside the new safe house, waiting for Arenza Lenskaya. It was a lie, but one that made him feel slightly less awkward.

When she finally came out, only a few moments after he'd left, he was glad he'd stayed.

She didn't look upset. Instead her face was a stone mask, her gaze fixed straight ahead without any of the lively wariness she'd shown on the way here. Which meant he was probably right about why Idusza had asked her to stay...and right in his guess about how she would respond. He didn't know the full story of how she'd ceased to be one of Ondrakja's Fingers, but he'd caught some of the words that passed between them that night in the Great Amphitheatre.

It seemed she held that bond sacred enough to despise herself for breaking it.

Having Koszar under his roof had forced him to interact with Arenza more often than was wise, and interacting with her had made it hard not to empathize right now. "Walk back with me?" he asked softly. She nodded once, a sharp jerk, and fell into step with him.

Twilight was beginning to fall as they threaded the lanes between the river and the plazas where Branek's fists still loitered. Apart from a mumbled apology when their elbows bumped or their fingers brushed, neither of them spoke. With nothing to hide—*Well,* he thought wryly, *no Anduske fugitives*—they didn't need to worry about avoiding notice from the Stretsko making themselves a visible and threatening presence on the streets.

Until they came to the edges of Kingfisher, and her step began to drag.

"I should..." She made a feeble gesture in the opposite direction from the way to Alinka's house. He'd never pressed Arenza on where she lived, but he suspected Ren had a lie prepared if he did.

He should let her go. Every moment he spent with her was another opportunity for her to untangle his web of deception. But sending her back to Renata's life—tonight of all nights, when she'd refused a gesture of trust from her friends—it felt wrong. Grey reached out when she started to turn away, hand hovering just short of touch.

"You could spend the evening with us. It's Six Candles. Isn't it less lonely, to remember what has been lost together?"

She ducked her chin, but not before he saw the flicker of reaction, like he'd gut-punched her. He hadn't expected the offer to hit so hard, and he was still trying to find a graceful way to apologize when she whispered, "Yes. Thank you. I—I will."

They went from the thickening gloom of the streets to the bright comfort of the house, from painful silence to the bustle and chaos of a kitchen with two small children underfoot. Alinka was predictably delighted to have a szorsa as their guest, and just as predictably refused the proffered help; instead Grey got assigned to vegetable-chopping duty and a report on how the transfer had gone, while Arenza told fables of the clan animals to Yvie and Jagyi. The latter chewed on a wooden block, listening raptly, while the former ricocheted around, one moment a fox, the next a noble horse.

Eventually the chaos resolved into a meal and a table cleared for the dishes. Grey wound up with Arenza at his right hand, and Yvieny beyond her. "Wish you to lead the prayers?" Alinka asked her.

Arenza shook her head. "No, this is your family and your home. Please."

Six precious beeswax candles went onto the table, carefully wedged between the bowls. "Ažerais, mother of us all, hear our prayers."

Grey closed his eyes as Alinka began the recitation. The substance of her version was the same as the one he'd grown up with, a recounting of how the Ižranyi had died: the eleven nights and days of horror that swept through Vraszan, as every person who bore that clan name fell into madness, tearing themselves and those around them apart. The city of Fiavla, their main stronghold, was a haunted wasteland to this day. No one knew how the terrifying power of a Primordial had come to be unleashed upon them; they only knew that one of those demonic forces, older and wilder than the gods themselves, had destroyed the seventh clan.

But Alinka's approach to that subject was different, and he preferred the way she told it. The version repeated around his childhood table, before Kolya returned from his carpentry apprenticeship to take Grey away, had dwelt heavily on the possible causes of the disaster: the wrongs some unknown person must have perpetrated, to bring such calamity down on their entire clan; the ill luck some people were simply born with, bringing death in their wake, striking everyone else while leaving them unscathed. Always told with meaningful looks that weighed on Grey despite his tightly clasped hands and determinedly bowed head, wishing, wishing, *wishing* the meal would end.

A soft touch on his arm dragged him back to the present. Alinka, holding up a beeswax candle, new-bought and taller than the remnants from years past. Compassion furrowed her brow. She knew, without ever being told directly, why Grey and Kolya lived in Nadežra with no clan or kureč beyond each other.

He fumbled with the flint, striking several times before the spark caught and the flame burned for the Ižranyi.

Once it had flared and settled, Alinka touched the wick to each of the six stubs to light them. A prayer for the souls of the Ižranyi, lost even to Ažerais's Dream; a hope that someday they would find peace. A promise that their lineage would be kept alive in the other clans, through those who bore their blood. No one had ever attempted to reconstitute the Ižranyi—not after that incomprehensible tragedy—but their memory would never be forgotten.

When the prayer finished, she blew out the seventh candle.

It made for a subdued meal under the flickering of the six remaining lights, and he almost regretted inviting Arenza to join them. But despite the somber mood, the tension gradually eased out of her shoulders. How often did she get to do things like this? Not often, he suspected. He'd seen her at the Seven Knots labyrinth when his clan gathered to mourn their dead ziemič—a loose thread that let him follow her back to the Westbridge townhouse, unraveling her deception at last—but he didn't think she made a regular habit of visiting such places. Alta Renata was a busy woman. So was the Black Rose; he'd heard tales of her interfering with Branek's attempts to consolidate the Anduske under his control. Neither left much time for her to be an ordinary Vraszenian.

Maybe she needed that.

When Alinka carried the sleeping Jagyi upstairs, Arenza helped Grey clear the table of dishes. "We'll wash them later," he said quietly, nodding toward Yvieny dozing next to her empty bowl.

"Thank you," Arenza said. "You were right. This was a good way to spend this evening."

Her gaze flickered toward the door as Alinka came downstairs to collect the sleepily protesting Yvieny. She ought to leave; he ought to let her go.

"The evening isn't over yet."

He ought *not* to have said that.

Her eyebrow ticked upward. "Are you suggesting something, Captain Serrado?"

That tone . . . The hint of playfulness in it sounded like something she would have said to the Rook. His sense of humor had slipped free during the preparations for dinner, jesting comments at odds with the stoic facade of Captain Grey Serrado. Had they sounded too much like what the Rook might say? Did she know—or at least suspect?

Either way, she'd handed him a perfect opening. A false hole in his defense that he could use to lure his opponent in for the disarm. And as much as Grey hated to end this gentle night with a trick, he couldn't pass up the chance to deflect any suspicions she might have.

He sent up a silent prayer that the deities would forgive him for interfering with a szorsa's cards. The Masks might curse him for it anyway . . . but they'd already cursed him, long ago.

"What better night than Six Candles to seek a szorsa's insight?" He dug into his pocket and laid a centira on the table. The standard prayer was bitter with irony on his tongue. "May I see the Face and not the Mask."

Kingfisher, Lower Bank: Colbrilun 33

Ren stared at the coin, then at Serrado. Her visits to this house had made it all too clear that he didn't like szorsas. So why was he now asking her to pattern him?

Not asking—challenging. His bland expression seemed to question whether she had the confidence to accept. And that made her straighten up, take out her deck, and shuffle with all the flair of which she was capable.

But she didn't want to seem too much like a streetside performer, either. They often skipped the prayers to the ancestors, so she made a point of including them—only to get a sardonic look in response, as if he could tell she was trying to be more authentic. By the time she passed the deck to him for the last shuffle and cut, she had to glance away to escape the weight of those blue eyes. She muttered the final prayer to Ižranyi with her gaze fixed on the extinguished candle, and didn't look up until he handed the cards back.

"This is your past, the good and the ill of it, and that which is neither."

The Ember Adamant, Wings in Silk, and Sword in Hand. The first and third from the woven thread; the second from the spinning. She touched the first card. "Like your sister, you are not from Nadežra. But people helped you when you came here. A debt you have repaid many times over, I think."

"The story of every Vraszenian who comes to this city." His voice was deeper when he spoke their language, with a pleasant burr at odds with his unimpressed tone.

"Not all of them Vraszenian," she added, even though she shouldn't. She knew that as Renata, from things Donaia and Giuna had said, not from the cards. She pointed to Sword in Hand. "This debt you have repaid partly through your duties in the Vigil. Unusual, one of our people rising so far...but I think you see it as a challenge."

"Most 'true' Vraszenians call me a slip-knot for that."

She'd called him that before, in her own thoughts. Not anymore, though; not since she'd seen him with his family, and with the Anduske. He was more Vraszenian than she was. "Wings in Silk. Transformation. To be in this city, you have changed—a necessary change, but one that comes with a price. And with regret." She frowned at the card, then at him. "But this is no simple matter of cutting your hair. You have in other ways changed, I think. Just as the Vigil is not the only cause you have taken up. The Anduske, for one." Also vengeance for his murdered brother. Perhaps other things as well. There were more layers to Grey Serrado than she used to believe.

He crossed his arms, a defensive gesture. "I have a lot of causes to pick from. And a lot of regrets."

His brother's death lay like an open wound between them. She'd never told him that Vargo was responsible. She *couldn't*; if Serrado knew, nothing would stop him from going after Kolya's killer. And there was only one way that could end.

She took refuge in the next line of cards, and a soft breath huffed from her at the sight. "All from the spinning thread; that is a strong sign." For the good, Aža's Call—straightforward enough. "Slipknot others may call you, but there is a difference between the mask you wear and the face beneath it. You keep up appearances because it is necessary...but beneath that, you pursue your dream."

What dream, though? Neither logic nor the other two cards told her. Lark Aloft and The Mask of Nothing...three from the same thread ought to be significant, but she couldn't tease out their meaning. "You seem not the sort of man for rash action or blind assumptions, neither for good nor for ill. But perhaps this has to do with Lark Aloft—have you had a recent message? Bad news from some quarter that into foolishness might provoke you?"

His shoulders relaxed, arms resting on the table as he leaned over the spread to give her a teasing look. "Besides right now? I think we need to finish the reading before we can determine that. Is it foolish to purchase protection charms?"

She fought the urge to make a rude gesture. His own sister by marriage crafted such things, at this very table; she doubted he scorned the charms themselves. But hawking them was too often the hallmark of a charlatan, who would first scare the client and then offer to avert their doom, promising more protection than a mere piece of knotwork could provide. Ren's mother, Ivrina, had despised that practice.

Hopefully the future line would give her something solid enough to prove her skills once and for all. "This is your future, the good and the ill of it, and—"

The words died in her throat, strangling tighter with each card she turned over. Labyrinth's Heart. The Mask of Bones. Sleeping Waters. All from the cut thread, and this time there was no mistaking their meaning. It writhed through her like the touch of ash, warping the world into nightmare.

She tried to speak, but nothing would come. Her breath rasped in her ears, too shallow, too fast, and her pulse beat like a dying moth in her throat. She couldn't even reach out to turn the cards back over, to hide their meaning from her view. Pain spiked up her fingers as her nails scraped the table's edge, seeking something, *any-thing* to steady her.

She found it in Grey's hands, lifting her own before she gouged splinters under her nails. The teasing smile had vanished into wide-eyed concern. "Szorsa? Arenza. *Breathe.* It's all right. Whatever you see, they're only cards."

"They are—*wrong*," she whispered, forcing the words out. "I have nothing to sell you, I'm not playing a trick—this is bad. Not simply bad meaning, but something worse." As if someone had cursed him.

Grey's voice remained steady. "But they hold the solutions to the problems they show, yes? We won't know until we read them." He released her hands and tapped the cards in succession. She couldn't hold back a flinch as his fingers touched each one. "Labyrinth's Heart. Calm, patience, stillness. That's nothing to fear. The Mask of Bones in the ill position is . . . well, it's death. But other kinds of end-ings, too. Unhappy ones, in this case. Sleeping Waters simply means that some sort of place is important."

He knew the cards well for someone who scorned them . . . but there was a difference between knowing and interpreting. "No. Yes, but no. The Mask of Bones—this is not the alternative to Laby-rinth's Heart, choose stillness or choose death. It will come either way. Different deaths; you cannot avoid them all."

"My death?"

His voice was neutral, controlled. Ren shook her head. "I—I don't think so. Not the death of your body, at least. And the still-ness . . ." It was like the pattern Ivrina had laid in the nightmare, where even the good cards were warped to malevolence. "You must choose which action not to take. 'Both' is not possible. Whatever you do not do . . ."

Someone would die for it. She couldn't make herself say it, but his nod acknowledged the meaning in her silence. "And Sleeping Waters? Is it a place I should go, or somewhere I should avoid?"

The card depicted the Old Island, the Point rising up from the river. At its top, the Wellspring of Ažerais, which he'd helped protect from the bombing. But it didn't mean that place specifically, not again—and yet, not *not* there. "There is a place you must go, a place you will be. But—" Her vision blurred, doubling. "You will not be there. You will and you will not. It all depends on what you choose."

Tears burned at the edges of her eyes. "This is all wrong," she whispered again, more to herself than to him.

But he heard. Grey exhaled noisily, his bare fingers sliding along the edge of Labyrinth's Heart. "You're not the first patterner to tell me that."

He tried to keep the words light, but she could hear the weight of old resentment dragging it down. "Pattern is not fixed," she said fiercely, seizing his hand. "Whatever has gone wrong can be mended."

For a silent instant he sat, his hand in her grip, his gaze meeting hers. What she saw there wasn't doubt; he didn't *disbelieve* in pattern. The wound he carried was of a different sort.

Then the window closed and his hand pulled away. "Perhaps. But the only mending I'll be doing tonight is my socks." He dug out another two centiras and set them on either side of the cards. "For the Face and the Mask...and an apology to you. I should not have asked you to do this."

Money for her, when she was Alta Renata and he was struggling to keep his brother's family fed. "I—would like to help. If I may."

The stairs creaked under the soft shuffle of Alinka's slippers. "I'm sorry I took so long. Help with what?"

She stopped at the base of the stairs, blinking in astonishment at the cards laid on the table, the coins set on either side. Ren swept them up, cards and coins alike, before Alinka could study them.

It didn't hide what had happened, though, and Alinka's jaw sagged. "You let her pattern for you?"

"I asked," Grey said mildly.

She turned her astonished look on Arenza, now tinged with concern. "Tell me he insulted you not."

"Alinka! I have better manners than that." His aggrieved look showed no hint of what had gone before, that bitter resignation to a twisted fate. Idusza was right: The Kiraly were never without their masks.

And Ren needed to protect her own. "I've stayed far too long," Arenza said. The people in her other life would be wondering where she'd vanished to.

Alinka frowned at the darkness showing through the window. "You will be safe going home? Perhaps Grey should—"

"I would not trouble the captain," Arenza said, heading off Alinka's suggestion. "He has mending to do."

"And here I thought you were offering to help with that," he murmured, amused, as he held the door open for her.

It was a friendlier comment than she was used to hearing from him. The warmth of it stayed with her as she headed for the clothing she'd stashed under the eaves of a nearby house—until she remembered it was Arenza Lenskaya he was being friendly to.

If he ever found out the truth, that would change faster than she could blink.

7

Sleeping Waters

Froghole, Lower Bank: Colbrilun 35

This time Sedge went to see Vargo by invitation. Not a fancy invitation like the ones Ren was buried under these days; just Lurets scuffing cobbles outside Sedge's Shambles boarding house until his landlady came up and told him to make the visitor shoo before she called the hawks.

They didn't say nothing on the walk toward the river. Not even complaints about the stinking summer miasma rising thick from the West Channel debris caught and rotting on Froghole's bend. Just pulled their collars up over their noses until they passed the threshold and into a building kept cool and sweet-smelling by Vargo's numinata.

Not that Vargo came by Froghole much these days, but the Fog Spiders still reaped some benefits from being the first knot he took over. Magic air freshening was one. Being the unofficial Charterhouse for Vargo's business was another.

Several of the Spiders were lounging around, cleaning weapons or fingernails or each other's pockets in games of sixes. But there were also others: Blackrabbit Drifters, Roundabout Boys, and Moon Harpies; the new boss of the Odd Alley Gang after Premyk was fool enough to turn knot-traitor; even what was left of the Cut Ears from

Lacewater, who took refuge with Vargo after *their* knot-traitor boss sold them out to Caerulet. Sedge spotted the colors of every knot that ever tangled with Vargo and lost.

He met them all, stare for stare, as Nikory took over and led Sedge across the room. No chance of fighting them off if Vargo decided he wanted Sedge bloody, but leastwise he could make them think he wasn't britch-pissing scared of it. Only once they'd entered the back office did Sedge release a shaky breath and let his fists unclench.

Too soon, maybe. The smaller room felt even more crowded than the outer floor, the leaders of all those knots circled around like a damned Vigil inquisition. Vargo sat at the center behind his desk, Varuni at one shoulder, that spider of his perched on the other. He was the only one smiling in a sea of scowls.

Maybe it was the smile, maybe the blatant display of power. Maybe Sedge was sick of knowing he was fucked no matter what he did, and it made him crusty. He spoke before Vargo could set the tone. "Knew you all missed me, but I didn't expect a big welcome back. You gonna crack out the chrysanthemum wine, too?"

"Got a taste for that among the Stretsko, did you?"

Vargo's response—soft as silk and sharp as a knife—rocked Sedge back on his heels. "The fuck? I warned you *against* them."

"And while my people were conveniently occupied with their assault, the Rook broke into my house."

This time he went back a full step. "The f—I missed a chance to see the *Rook*?"

It was a damn fool response to an accusation of treachery, the kind of thing a kid half his age might say. But the twitch of Vargo's lip told Sedge he might just have saved his own neck. There was no faking that kind of surprise, not unless you were as good a liar as Ren.

Ren. Sedge doubted it was an accident the Rook had shown up during the fight. But she hadn't told him...and this moment was the reason why.

Which meant his best option was to continue with honesty.

Or as much honesty as he could offer. "Whatever." Sedge slumped, his gaze dropping to the desk. Surly and resentful. "You think what you want, but I just brought you the message from the Anduske. I din't have nothing to do with the Stretsko. I en't no knot-traitor."

"The wounds I took at the amphitheatre say otherwise."

"Fuck you!" Sedge slammed his fists on the desk to keep from slamming them into Vargo's face. Everyone in the room shifted closer, ready to stop Sedge if he was stupid enough to attack.

But Sedge didn't need fists to take Vargo down. Just the truth.

Through his teeth, he growled, "I thought it was more important, stopping folks from frying you every time they stepped on the numinat. Maybe I chose wrong; I en't no inscriptor. But even if I did, my oaths are to Nikory and the Fog Spiders. You want to tell me how I broke them? Or maybe you want me to explain to everyone how I *didn't*."

Vargo's eyes went flat. "Out," he said to the room at large. "Varuni, Nikory, stay. And you." His gaze didn't move from Sedge's.

The other knot leaders obeyed without a sound. By the time the door shut, Sedge had plenty of time to consider whether that might not have been the brightest thing he'd ever done.

But fuck it—that bare spot on his wrist *hurt*, worse than the lingering ache from the broken bone. Knot members didn't have to wear their charms all the time, but fists like Sedge usually did, because they wanted people to know who they fought for. Getting cut out when he hadn't done anything wrong... That heartless bastard weren't sworn to nobody. He didn't understand loyalty.

Nikory did, though. They hadn't ever been friends; knot leaders couldn't afford friends among their followers. But they'd had a bond. Nikory cared. Sedge suspected he was the reason that beating hadn't left any permanent injuries.

He didn't look happy about his mercy now that Vargo's river-cold glare was turned on him. Nikory muttered, "I've never said nothing about us leaders not being sworn to you. Not to my fists. Not to anyone."

Your secrets are my secrets. Nikory might have cut him out, but that didn't make Sedge a knot-traitor. And he wasn't going to let Vargo trip him into becoming one. "I didn't actually know," he said, backing Nikory's lie. "Not for sure. Until just now."

Real bright, making Vargo think Nikory had just spilled one of his secrets by accident. But it worked, at least for the moment, because the man changed topics abruptly. "You think one warning is enough to get you back in?"

At least this was firmer footing. "I think you might want what the Stadnem Anduske are offering. And you don't have the time or patience to risk blowing it, getting them to trust someone else as your go-between."

"Hmmm." Vargo ran his thumb across his scarred knuckles. His mouth remained still, but Sedge recognized that look. It was the one Vargo got when he was having a conversation with himself.

Or with that spirit Ren said was riding along in the spider.

When Vargo glanced at Nikory, the leader of the Fog Spiders nodded without hesitation. "You'll set up a meeting," Vargo told Sedge. "Someplace away from the Stretsko. If the Rook shows up to *that*, I'll carve your eyes out and give them to Varuni for sling stones."

I'll make sure Ren knows. Sedge saluted like he used to, before he could think better of it. Vargo's mouth soured, but all he said was "Also, I want to talk to that patterner again. Lenskaya."

Arenza Lenskaya was supposed to have vanished for good. According to Tess, though, she'd gone back to Grey Serrado's house to pattern the hawk's sister. *Ren better stop that, or she's gonna wind up in front of Vargo again.* "I'll see what I can do."

Vargo left soon after that, taking his spider spirit and a tight-lipped Varuni with him. Which left Sedge alone with Nikory for the first time since his ousting.

"Din't mean to get you in trouble," Sedge said, not certain if an apology meant anything when he'd done it anyway.

But Nikory just shrugged. "At least you distracted him into thinking *he* gave it away."

Sedge shifted from foot to foot. Then the words burst out of him: "The Rook really broke into his house? You *gotta* tell me about that."

Nikory barked a laugh, slapped him on the shoulder, and said, "Let's go get a drink."

Kingfisher and Westbridge: Similun 18

For months after Kolya's death, Grey had avoided returning to the Gawping Carp, until Leato's need dragged him back there. Too many memories seasoned into the knotted wood of the bar and tables; too many stories spilled alongside zrel and ale and elderflower wine. He hadn't wanted to salt that happy ground with tears.

But it felt right to return after Leato's death, sitting alone at a table with two empty chairs for his ghosts, two empty cups leaving more in the bottle to slosh into his own. He felt older than his years, lonelier now that both his brother and the friend who was almost one had gone ahead of him. And since Leato was Liganti, there wasn't even the hope that they might meet again. Memory was the only piece of his soul Grey could still touch.

"Better to mourn bad deals and empty pockets," one of the old gaffers had told Grey on his last visit, replacing the cup in his hand with cards for their eternal game of nytsa. "Leaves your heart open for new friends to come in."

Those men had loved and lost more in their lifetimes than Grey could fathom. Their advice made him laugh and ponder the possibility of dragging Donaia to Kingfisher—for both their sakes. Did she even know the rules for nytsa? Had her slipper ever touched land on this side of the Sunset Bridge?

He'd carved an hour free and was idly embroidering the notion of abducting her for an afternoon when he ducked through the threshold of the Carp and found the taproom a shambles: tables and chairs overturned, bottles smashed, and the air thick with eye-watering fumes. There was no sign of the old gaffers and other regulars. Only Dvaran, broom in hand and doing his one-armed best to clean up the mess.

Grey hurried forward to help him right a table. By the time it was on its legs, he'd slipped fully into his hawk's feathers. "What happened here?" he asked, guiding Dvaran to a seat and pouring him a drink from one of the few unbroken bottles. The Gawping Carp wasn't the sort of place where brawls broke out, but the mess was too extensive for a robbery. It almost looked like a protection hit...but Dvaran paid his dues to the local knot, and Grey wasn't the sort of Vigil officer to let his constables indulge in side business.

Mopping his brow with the rag usually kept for the bar, Dvaran leaned heavily on his stump and surveyed the damage with a resigned gaze. "Some new knot aiming to take Moon Harpy territory? These wore armbands instead of braids. Black and yellow, like they was wasps." He tugged on his pinned sleeve. "They said they was looking for Anduske. Took all the old gaffers. Questioning, they said."

Grey's fury chilled at Dvaran's report. Not thieves or gangs. Not even Vigil violence. He hoped this wasn't what he feared. "Where did they say they were taking them?"

"Didn't." Dvaran hefted himself to his feet and dragged his broom with him. "But a few of them said they were going to check a tip in Westbridge."

That was enough to put Grey into motion, out the door and only a few streets over to the canal that marked the boundary between Kingfisher and Westbridge. Fishing his captain's hexagram from his pocket, he pinned it to his coat.

It was almost a shameful relief when he heard shouts and the sound of breaking wood, because those noises *weren't* coming from where he feared. Whether it had been their initial target or not, Dvaran's attackers were at a sedan chair workshop, and one of them was systematically splintering the sides of the nearly finished chairs with his boot.

A man Grey recognized all too well.

"Mezzan!" he snapped, swallowing the name that tried to follow. Not Indestor anymore, not since their house register was burned. Touching his pin, Grey said, "By the authority of the Vigil, I arrest you for—"

"For nothing," Mezzan said. His arrogant sneer was back as if it had never left, and he turned insolently to display a black-and-yellow armband. "I'm a member of the Ordo Apis, carrying out my duty."

The Ordo Apis—that was Caerulet's "special force" for dealing with the Anduske, the one Grey had declined to join. Why the hell would a kinless man like Mezzan be accepted into the ranks of the stingers, after the way House Indestor fell?

A familiar, cynical knot tightened in Grey's chest. *You know why.* All those genial, reasonable words Ghiscolo Acrenix spoke that day in the Aerie had been a lie. This was just more of the same brutality, in different hands.

And maybe for the same reason. Acrenix had taken over Mettore Indestor's seat in the Cinquerat. *Maybe he's taken something else, too. Maybe Mezzan used it to buy a new beginning for himself.*

That was a question to chew on later, with his hooded friend. Right now, his duty was to the Vigil. "Does carrying out your duty require—"

"What are *you* doing here, Serrado?" Lud Kaineto appeared from inside the workshop. His haughty face matched his tone, and he took obvious delight in not having to call Grey "Captain" any longer. "You've got no grounds to interfere with us. Your district is Kingfisher. Surely even somebody like you is smart enough to see we're in Westbridge."

Somebody like you. Kaineto's hands might be gloved, but his words weren't. He'd loathed serving under a Vraszenian captain, seeing it as an unforgivable insult to his status as a gentleman. Grey had briefly thought he'd shed a headache when Kaineto left the Vigil for the Ordo Apis. Instead it had only removed the man's leash.

Keeping his voice level, Grey said, "You damaged a lot of property in Kingfisher. I'm following up."

Kaineto clapped Mezzan on the shoulder, grinning. "Got a tip that some Anduske might be there. We had to make sure they weren't hiding."

Grey's jaw ached as he bit down on his response. Getting into a pissing contest with Kaineto wouldn't do any good—not when something else demanded his attention much more urgently.

"I'll be having words with Commander Cercel about this," he said.

Kaineto laughed derisively. "Sure, go hide behind her pin. Yours isn't worth its steel."

That bit deeper than it should have. But Grey had years of practice in swallowing his fury; he only turned without bowing and strode away.

As soon as he was out of sight, he took measures to make sure nobody was following him. He knew the rooftops of this area nearly as well as its streets, and that gave him a more direct route to his destination. He only dropped to the ground at the Uča Drošnel, slipping his hexagram pin back into his pocket. After one last check to ensure there were no watching eyes, he knocked on the door of a half basement. "Six bees on a pin."

Ardaš Ljunan was the one who cracked the door, knife in hand. He lowered it when he saw Grey, and swung the door wider in silent welcome.

Idusza rose as he entered. Instead of the usual greeting, Grey said, "Don't go outside today. The Ordo Apis are hunting Anduske in Westbridge, and you can't risk them seeing you."

Andrejek was lying on the narrow bed, rubbing one of Alinka's ointments into his healing leg. He sat up abruptly. "Do we need to move?"

Grey shook his head. "That just makes it more likely they'll catch you. I think this place is safe for now—though we'll need to see if we can find you another hideout later." He said it as if he had anywhere to send them. Ryvček would have choice words for him if he asked her to shelter Andrejek. And he didn't know how Ren had set this one up, except that he suspected the answer involved Alta Renata.

He transferred his attention to Idusza, who had picked up a cudgel as if she expected someone to come through the door any moment. "Mezzan is one of them."

Her grip tightened on the cudgel. She'd clung hard to the belief that her lover truly sided with the Anduske; after that broke, her fury had been frightening. But Idusza was disciplined enough not to seek revenge when it would put her knot at risk.

Grey couldn't do it for her, either. But he could keep the Anduske safe, at least for today.

"I'll make sure they don't head this way," he said, turning back to the door.

The bed was close enough to the door for Andrejek to lean out and catch Grey's arm in a surprisingly strong grip. "May you see the Face and not the Mask."

"And you," Grey said, and headed back in the direction of the sedan chair workshop.

The stingers were still there, shouting at the woodwright. Grey's hands tightened into fists, helpless to stop them. He'd learned in his early days as a constable that intervening would only incite further bullying—a lesson that almost made him quit before he'd even begun. Only the hope that someday he could command enough power to shield others kept him going.

What power he had was useless here. The Ordo Apis was not answerable to the Vigil.

One hand slid into his coat and touched the concealed pocket there. Grey Serrado couldn't do much to stop the Ordo Apis...but the Rook had always been like red meat to the hawks.

Time to see if he was as useful a distraction for wasps.

Owl's Fields, Upper Bank: Similun 28

The ritual of the second initiation was thankfully brief. It took place on the outskirts of Nadežra, in a pavilion among the gardens that supplied Nadežra with fresh produce, and Renata wondered if that was Benvanna's suggestion. The woman's final act of domination had been to bring her by sedan chair to the livery stables on the edges of Whitesail, where noble houses kept the horses for their carriages, and travelers or hunters rented mounts for going outside the city. House Traementis hadn't yet bought new riding horses, and Benvanna no doubt believed that ordering Renata to walk while she rode behind on her gelding was absolute torture.

The heat was bad enough to make it unpleasant, certainly. But given that Ren had never sat on a horse in her life, walking was preferable to the alternative.

The second gate proved to be that of submission, as the first had been of ignorance. When the initiation ceremony was over, servants arrived to serve chilled peaches and wine. Vargo shucked formality along with his sleeveless summer coat; his loose shirt hung limp from the heat. Benvanna fanned herself, complaining of the heat; even Tanaquis had loosened the side lacing of her surcoat. The only one who seemed unconcerned was Sibiliat, and Renata wondered why she was there.

Hoping to avoid Diomen, Renata stepped outside for a breath of fresh air and contemplated whether she could simply flee down the lane. Sixteen years out of Seteris or no, the Pontifex was better equipped than most to catch her out in a lie.

Before she made up her mind, he cornered her in the leafy shade of a pea trellis. Hoping to steer the conversation onto a safe footing, she spoke before he could. "Mede Beldipassi couldn't join us today?"

"He has not yet passed his second trial," Diomen said coolly. "Apparently his various businesses keep him quite occupied. If he lacks even the dedication to submit at this stage, I question whether he will advance very far."

Renata sighed ruefully. "Well, that is his reputation. Always beginning things; rarely finishing them. But perhaps—"

"I understand you grew up in Endacium," Diomen said, cutting her off. He plucked a pod from the trellis and snapped it. Instead of sucking out the peas inside, though, he examined each before letting it fall to the ground uneaten. "I gave a lecture once at the great agora there. It saddens me that no such centers exist here."

"There's the Rotunda," she said, shaking her head when he offered her a pod.

Diomen's deep voice was well-suited to scorn. "Hardly a center of learning. And Iridet spares only minimal effort to see to the education of the people. When we speak of the gateway of ignorance, it should not be so literal." The richness of his laugh was an invitation to relax, but his next words sharpened the edge she balanced on. "Who saw to your schooling? As I recall, House Viraudax holds learning in high esteem."

"A private tutor. I was often sick as a child, so my education was more...irregular than most."

"And yet by Quinat's grace, you have blossomed into health. Do not worry. You carry a blessing from the Lumen; as Pontifex, it is my duty to make certain that blessing reaches its full potential. I would be pleased to tutor you privately, and fill any gaps left in your knowledge."

With anyone else, she would have read uncomfortable innuendo into his offer. With Diomen, the discomfort was of an entirely different flavor. "That's very generous, Pontifex," Renata said. "At present I'm afraid I'm busy and then some with House Traementis's business. But perhaps at some more leisurely point in the future." *Right after the moons sink into the sea.*

Before Diomen could press, she smiled and turned back to the chairs set to take advantage of the breezes sweeping inland off the ocean. Two servants had propped the flaps of the pavilion up on poles to create a shade break, and were passing out cups of lemon-flavored ice on trays etched with frosted lines of numinata.

Vargo rose as she approached, offering his seat to Renata. Once again, the spider seemed not to be with him; she'd heard no silent conversations, and his wilted collar couldn't have hidden a fly. Was there a reason Vargo came to these events alone?

"You seem flushed," he murmured, passing her his kerchief.

"Who wouldn't be, in this heat? Sometimes I regret leaving Seteris."

Sibiliat left off sucking ice from her spoon to say, "I imagine they regret letting you go. But their loss is our gain. Wouldn't you agree, Derossi?"

"Vargo." His smile matched Sibiliat's for sweetness. "But that's the only point I disagree on."

"Can we conclude business?" Tanaquis said, pressing her reddening cheeks. "I'd rather not spend tomorrow shedding like Illi's serpent."

All eyes went expectantly to Diomen. Renata wondered if his robe was imbued for coolness; he seemed unaffected by the heat. Sliding his hands into the opposite sleeves, he said, "In order to pass the third gate, you must prove your determination to join our ranks as a full member of the Illius Praeteri. There are no orders to obey now; the choice of proof is yours. Choose carefully, though: You must satisfy the judgment of your sponsors."

With a poisonously sweet smile, Sibiliat waved her closed fan for Renata to come stand in front of her chair, while Benvanna did the same with Vargo. Renata bit down on a curse. *Tanaquis's choice of sponsors for me is getting worse and worse.*

Benvanna spoke first. "Derossi Vargo. How deep does your wish to join us run? How will you show me your zeal?"

"I haven't already shown it?" he asked, smirking at Sibiliat.

Benvanna looked confused, but Renata could read his hidden meaning: his deal with Ghiscolo to take out Mettore Indestor. Had that all been aimed not at a noble title—or not only—but at *this*? Was access to the Praeteri his true goal all along?

Sibiliat gave him a tiny smile and a shake of her head. "You were ignorant before, remember?"

Like hell he was.

Vargo pressed his lips tight and turned back to Benvanna. "Then how's this. I understand House Cassiones has just opened a new sickhouse attached to the Quinatium in Dockwall. I'll offer my services as an inscriptor there for a day, to help improve their imbued medicines. Is that sufficient?"

"A mere day?" Benvanna scoffed. "To do something you already have skill with?"

Vargo's expression darkened. "I don't think you understand how much I dislike sickness."

Sedge had spoken more than once about Vargo's horror of disease. Renata cleared her throat and said, "I know it isn't my place to judge whether his offer suffices, but I can vouch for his sincerity. If the test here is to prove our zeal by doing something we'd very much prefer not to, then this would certainly qualify." *And I certainly don't mind the idea of him suffering a bit.*

Benvanna gave Renata a look like she was still sucking on her lemon ice, but then waved a hand and addressed Diomen. "If *she* says it's so, it must be true. I'll accept this as proof of Vargo's dedication."

"And what will you offer as proof, Renata?" Sibiliat asked, carving small arcs in the air with her fan. "Fair warning—I'm not as easily convinced as Benvanna."

An elegant noblewoman like Renata might go slumming for entertainment, but never for real work. "I can't be useful at a hospital like Vargo, but I presume Nadežra has orphanages. I will—"

"No," Sibiliat said before Renata could even finish the offer. "Try again."

She'd proposed her action too readily. This time Renata bit her lip, pretending to think, before she said, "You must have heard that I didn't fare well on my way to the first initiation. Being out on open water nauseates me. House Traementis lacks a villa now, but—"

Sibiliat stood, putting herself at eye level. "Do better," she snapped, tapping Renata's shoulder with the fan. "Or I'll assume you don't actually want to join the Praeteri."

I don't. Except that Vargo did, and she had to know why. And Tanaquis hovered just at the edge of Renata's peripheral vision, jittering with impatience or nerves. Tanaquis, who didn't dare break the secrecy of the Praeteri but thought their secrets were important enough to suffer through all the theatrical preliminaries.

Sibiliat was looking for real fear, real dread. Renata could try to fake that—but if she failed, she might hamstring herself. Ondrakja had always taught her, though, that the truth was a better weapon than any lie.

The swift wetting of her lips was a nervous reflex, allowed

through rather than suppressed. "I can't swim," Renata said, her voice trembling. "So I will jump in the river."

The vicious curve of Sibiliat's smile said she'd finally cut deep enough. "I suggest the Floodwatch Bridge," she said sweetly. "After all, you *are* a Traementis."

The Great Amphitheatre, the Point: Similun 31

Vargo's attention was divided like a fraying thread. This way the Praeteri; that way the river numinat; and, doing its best to tear the whole thread to pieces, the Stretsko. Tserdev's fists had started patrolling Seven Knots, hassling or even attacking any Liganti-looking person who wandered in there alone, and the Vigil's answering crackdown was undercutting several of Vargo's businesses. Then an ambush while he was busy in Dockwall left half his Moon Harpies bleeding in the streets of Kingfisher.

Now here he was, legs burning as he finished the long climb up the Point and entered the Great Amphitheatre. *Would have been nice if we could have arranged this meeting somewhere more convenient.*

The last time he'd been in there, the amphitheatre had glowed with the light of the great, twisted numinat that dragged the Wellspring of Ažerais from dream into reality. In comparison, the brightness of Paumillis and Corillis both waxing toward full was as reassuring as daylight... but the memory of what he'd gone through here made the scarred skin of his back crawl.

No monstrous zlyzen lurked in the emptiness, though. The stands echoed back the rush of the Dežera, the call of nesting dreamweaver birds, and, distantly, the hollow bells of the city chiming sixth earth. Midnight.

::I don't like this,:: Alsius grumbled.

"You and Varuni both." It had taken a lot of convincing for her to let him enter the amphitheatre alone, especially after Sedge's failure to protect him last time. She compromised by waiting a shout away, both of them knowing that even that might be too far if this went sour.

Vargo prayed for Quarat's luck that it wouldn't go sour.

Arkady had sworn—once he paid her enough to pry the advice out of her jaws—that Vargo had to meet the Black Rose alone and in the Great Amphitheatre, because she was Ažerais's servant. If he'd had any other route to contacting the masked woman, he might have told the little extortionist where to shove it.

But he had a Vraszenian problem; only made sense to turn to a Vraszenian solution.

Keep the interruptions to a minimum, Vargo said mentally as he tried and failed to resist smoothing his coat of wine-dark errandi silk, stitched with lace roses in honor of his hoped-for guest. *I'll need to think.*

::I always do,:: Alsius said. And then, ::She's here.::

The way Arkady talked, the Black Rose should have risen up out of the stage where it covered the site of the wellspring. Instead she lounged against the back wall, arms crossed and one boot hooked across to rest on its toe. She must have come from backstage, but neither he nor Alsius had seen her enter. He had to grant that it was effective theatre.

"Come to thank me for Seven Knots?" she asked, her voice carrying like that of an actress.

Alsius had spent years drumming into his head that good manners were an effective tool. "Among other things, yes. Thank you. For Seven Knots, and my life." He swept an arm to encompass the stage where he'd come too close to becoming a corpse. "If I didn't know better, I'd think your Lady had taken a liking to me."

"But you do know better?"

As if he had the favor of anything divine. "I think your Lady cares for the peace and well-being of her city."

"You did help save this place. And bled more than a little in the process. Not exactly what your reputation would lead anyone to expect."

Vargo shrugged one shoulder. "Only those who aren't paying attention. The loss of the wellspring would have destabilized Nadežra rather badly. That's bad for my business. And stopping it has gained me quite a bit. Blood's not a pretty coin to pay, but everyone has some to spare."

::You more than most.::

"So it seems," the Black Rose said, almost as though she'd heard Alsius's snarky comment. A silence fell, and he fought the urge to break it. He couldn't read anything past her rose-patterned mask, not at this distance. "You often find multiple ways to profit, don't you?"

"Life's too short to do only one thing at a time," he said dryly.

Arkady claimed the Black Rose was immortal, but since no one had heard of such a person before Veiled Waters, he doubted that. "I asked to meet with you because I think we might have overlapping goals. You know it was the Stretsko who tried to bomb this place. And they didn't much care how many Vraszenians would be here when it blew."

"They did try to steer people to the Charterhouse instead," the Rose said.

::Interesting that she knows that,:: Alsius murmured. ::Since it happened before she supposedly "manifested.":::

Vargo spread his hands. "But when that failed, they went ahead anyway."

She uncrossed herself and strolled across the stage, hands linked behind her back. Who had made her disguise, and where had they gotten the materials? *Alsius, can you recognize anything of what she's wearing?*

::You'd have to get closer for me to see.::

Not much chance of that. The Rose stopped and pivoted to face him, well out of reach. "Your pitch might be more plausible if the cousins of those Stretsko weren't causing you trouble all over the city. But as it stands, I think you're trying to recruit me to take care of your personal enemies for you."

He matched her posture, hands folded behind, leaning in, and raised it with a smile. Charm: another tool Alsius had taught him to use. "Life's too short to do only one thing at a time."

::Noble business, knot business, numinat business, Alta Renata, the Praeteri... Why do two things when you can do seven?::

Vargo continued as though he didn't have a peacock spider providing sardonic commentary. "It's true, Tserdev and some of the other knots I'm struggling with have tied themselves to Branek's Anduske." It was a weird form of flattery: They'd begun copying his model of organization. Or at least what they thought was his model, each knot leader swearing an oath to a central boss. "If you want to focus on the original core of the Anduske, that's fine by me. I'm only saying that if Ažerais *does* want revenge, I'd be happy to facilitate."

"Justice," the Rose said. "Not revenge."

Justice is revenge in formal dress, he thought, but he conceded the point with a bow. She was nibbling at the hook, which meant he'd baited it correctly. "The Ordo Apis is after Branek and the Anduske, too. But if you'd prefer them delivered to Vraszenian authorities instead, I have no objection. Don't much care where they go, as long as it's away."

::Downriver, the Depths...::

Vargo pretended to smooth his collar, jabbing his thumb into the spider hiding inside. *You're bloodthirsty tonight.*

::I don't like this place. We almost died here. And we don't have time to go through such nonsense again.::

Yes. No time for dying. Do you mind if I finish, then?

::Very well.:: Alsius hunched deeper, sulking, while Vargo tried to find the dangling end of his conversation with the Rose.

"I'm not alone in this," he told her. "The old leadership of the Anduske—the ones who decided *not* to blow up the amphitheatre—they've reached out to me."

She cocked her head at Vargo. "You would help them?"

Why did he get the impression that pleased her? Whatever the reason, he could use it. "I think Nadežra's better off with someone in charge of the Anduske who doesn't want the canals running with blood. And I think you agree." He hadn't heard any tales to suggest she was hunting Andrejek. "But one woman—or whatever you are—can only do so much. If we work together, we could do a lot more."

She stopped and studied him, her expression unreadable behind the black lace. Then: "Do you know where Šidjin Drumaskaya Gulavka is hiding?"

And hooked. "She's in Staveswater, my people tell me, under the protection of her uncle." Staveswater, the biggest Stretsko stronghold in all of Nadežra. And Gulavka was one of Branek's highest lieutenants...as well as the person bringing most of the non-Anduske knots under his control. "You may be Ažerais's agent in the waking world, but I don't recommend going in there alone. You'll need help."

He didn't say, *my help.* If she went another route, he'd lose out on this bid for alliance...but he'd learn something useful from that refusal.

Her jaw didn't tighten; she gave off no sign of frustration or struggle with her thoughts. She merely said, "Give me a few days. I'll let Arkady Bones know."

Vargo glanced ostentatiously around. "If she's not watching us already."

"Oh, she isn't."

He huffed a laugh. "You sure? How much did you pay her to stay away?"

The Rose, heading for the stage's exit, paused to cast a mocking smile over her shoulder at him. "Nothing. She doesn't charge her friends."

The Great Amphitheatre, the Point: Similun 31

Ren hid backstage until she heard the receding sound of Vargo's footsteps. Once the amphitheatre was silent, she climbed one of the covered side staircases meant to give performers access to the stands, then surveyed the ranks of benches from above.

Of course she saw nothing. Ren called out, "I hope that was useful."

"Are you going to work with him?"

The voice came not from in front of her, but from behind—and above. Ren turned and saw a shadow detach itself from the weathered stone at the top of the amphitheatre.

She sighed. "To be honest, I don't have a lot of choice. I can't get Gulavka on my own. But if she's pulled out of the fabric, Branek will have a harder time consolidating the Lower Bank knots under his control." Not to mention it might stop some of the violence. Gulavka had led an attack on the Quaratium in Westbridge the previous week, killing two and injuring nine. The new leader of the Anduske was hardly the only one with a taste for blood. "The ziemetse may *think* I'm some legendary hero, but—well." Her mouth quirked. "We can't all be the Rook."

The wind lifted the skirts of his coat as he jumped down to her level, landing silent as a cat. The hood didn't so much as ripple. "I'm not certain it's wise to strengthen his position, even if there are benefits. In fact, I'm positive it isn't. He's a master at manipulating events to fall out in his favor." A grim note entered his voice. "More than I ever credited."

"Oh, believe me—I'm wary. Unless you want to branch out from targeting the nobility and their schemes, though, I need *someone* to help me in Staveswater."

"I have full respect for your wariness. But I found something troubling when I searched his house." Reaching into his coat, the Rook pulled out a fold of paper. "That's a copy of what I could salvage. Most of the original caught fire in his office."

She'd heard him angry before, when he'd confronted her in her own kitchen. This was new, though: He sounded pissed at *himself.* Ren took the paper and skimmed it, her eyebrows climbing. "I suspect he killed the Scurezza, too," the Rook said.

"No, he couldn't have. Quaniet was still alive when Giuna and Sibiliat got there; she confessed to poisoning them all. But the rest..." She folded the paper. "How could he be behind all of this?"

"That's what I need to find out."

Ren glanced up at him. "Have you heard of the Illius Praeteri?"

His anger transformed into a contemptuous scoff. "Rich cuffs playing at a mystery cult so they can feel superior even to their own kind. They've been around for over a decade; I look into them periodically. It's business as usual, dressed up in special robes."

"Vargo's been recruited to join them. As have I." She sat down on one of the benches, folding her legs tailor-style. "I'm going along with it as a way to keep an eye on him. But I think he knew about the Praeteri even before he joined. And Ghiscolo—"

The hood turned so rapidly, an ordinary garment would have shifted to show a hint of face. "What about Ghiscolo?"

"Vargo's working with him," Ren said, eyeing the Rook warily. *Why did* that *get his attention?* "I heard them talking, after you and I met in the Charterhouse. Vargo made a deal with him: a noble title in exchange for bringing down Indestor. And, not so coincidentally, opening up a seat in the Cinquerat."

The Rook's voice sank to a growl, and his gloves creaked as they curled into fists. "So much for thinking the Vigil might improve."

Ren tried not to stare as he paced. The strength of his reaction to that... The Vigil had been hunting the Rook since he began. And under Mettore, their corruption and greed had been a major target of the Rook's efforts.

But his reaction sounded more personal. Like the last of a dear hope was bleeding out.

Out of the corner of her eye, she watched his stride, measured his height against the amphitheatre's back wall. Grey Serrado was hunting the Rook; everyone knew that... but everyone knowing a thing didn't make it true.

Could the Rook be hiding within the Vigil itself?

The pattern she'd laid for Serrado hadn't turned up any hint of it. Only that hideous future line, something poisoning his fate. But maybe the forces that protected the Rook's identity had blocked her reading. Meanwhile, the Rook had been pursuing Kolya Serrado's killer for the last year, while Kolya's brother supposedly hunted *him*.

It was a tenuous thread at best. Besides, she'd been wrong before about who was under that hood. She didn't want the humiliation of being wrong again.

He still hadn't spoken. Ren was loath to break the silence—but there was more she hadn't said. "Acrenix is only half of it, though. Maybe less than half."

The Rook pivoted like a man facing a new opponent. Ren said, "Vargo has some kind of spirit bound to him."

"I assume you don't know this because he told you?" Before she could answer, he muttered, "Though I should know better. People tend to tell you things."

She bit down on the urge to say, *So tell me who you are.* "They're connected, mind to mind. I think the spirit is contained in that spider of his, Master Peabody." She gazed down at the empty floor, where Vargo had stood. "I've been trying to find out what it could be. Some kind of ghost? It talks like a person—like a Nadežran, in fact, and one familiar with numinatria. Vargo called him Alsius."

"I should have crushed that thing when I had the chance," the Rook said in disgust. At her raised brow, he added, "The spider was at the house when I visited. It was watching me the entire time. How is it you can hear them?"

"When we fought here...I saw connections between people. A strong one between Vargo and this spirit, and another between me and Vargo. I..."

She trailed off, trying to think how to describe what she'd done. "I strengthened it," she said at last. "To get him to finish erasing the numinat. But I think that's why I can hear them now."

"And Vargo doesn't know?"

"If he did, I doubt I would be talking to you now."

Hipping up onto the balustrade, the Rook propped a boot on the wall and looked out at the amphitheatre. She saw more than heard his sigh, in the movement of his shoulders. "So Vargo has a spirit that can keep watch for him but can't stop intruders. And he hasn't bothered to improve the protections at his house, which says there's nothing there that needs it."

He sounded like he was thinking out loud. Ren stayed silent, waiting to see what he would let slip. "Would be nice if I could drop that bodyguard of his in a dark hole for a few bells," the Rook said, rubbing absently at his calf, as though remembering Varuni's chain whip. "Vargo strikes me as the sort to think there's no safer place in the world than his own pocket."

Ren had once been a very skilled pickpocket—but she might as well go ahead and cut off her own hand now, rather than try that on Vargo. "If you could catch him alone...that would be useful?"

Even in good light, she could never see more than the edge of a smile within the Rook's hood. With the moons silhouetted behind him, she couldn't even see that much. But she read a hint of amusement in the tilt of his head. "The Black Rose has a plan?"

"Not the Black Rose," Ren said, the idea taking shape in her mind. "Alta Renata."

Isla Traementis, the Pearls: Similun 34

The Rook had patience. Those who wore the hood had worked toward eradicating Kaius Rex's corrupting influence from Nadežra for two hundred years. And yet as he crouched above an open window at Traementis Manor, listening to the nobles inside discussing inanities over hand after hand of cards, it felt like an interminable wait.

But his patience paid off. Alta Renata's crisp Seterin voice asked her cousin to go down to the kitchens for spiced chocolate. Her instructions were *very* precise, and the lilt in her request implied Giuna could—in fact, should—take her time. The half-suppressed giggle in the reply promised Renata would have all the time she might want alone with Eret Vargo.

The door clicked shut. The Rook slipped down, one booted toe nudging the window open wider so he could balance on the sill. A gauzy curtain softened the interior of the upstairs salon where the card game had been set up, until the silvered tip of the Rook's rapier lifted it aside. Vargo's back was to the window, and Renata...

Renata looked like she was enjoying something immensely, and the Rook suspected it wasn't Vargo's company. He crept into the room, silent as the slide of the curtain over his shoulder.

"Not that your new cousin isn't charming company," Vargo said as he shuffled the cards. "But I'd hoped we might have at least *some* time alone."

The Rook lived for invitations like that. His blade whispered along Vargo's ear. "Too bad you won't get any," the Rook whispered into the other.

Vargo went utterly still. The sword's edge rested just a breath away from his throat; any sudden movement on his part would add a scar to match the one on the other side. Across from him, Renata sat frozen, back pressed hard against her chair, looking for all the world like a noblewoman caught off guard by a vigilante who hated her kind.

A flash of color scuttled to the other side of Vargo's collar. Scooping it up, the Rook flung it out the window and into the night. Vargo jerked as though he'd been struck, and the Rook said, "I don't like spiders."

"We're not much fond of birds," Vargo managed, with the ghost of his usual sardonic edge.

The man's sword cane was leaning against the arm of his chair; that followed the spider out the window. Then the Rook circled around, blade at the ready, until he had both Vargo and Renata within reach of a lunge.

His gaze flicked down to her gloves, set aside so she might more easily handle the cards. "I seem to have a knack for catching the alta when she's undone."

"It takes more than a scrap of fabric to undo me," she said coolly.

He couldn't resist saying, "That sounds like a challenge. What *would* it take to fluster you?"

One fine eyebrow arched. She must pencil them thicker when she was Arenza; he would look, the next time they met in that guise. In a cool voice, she said, "I thought the Rook specialized in flustering nobles. Surely you don't need *my* instruction."

"Less a challenge, then . . . and more an invitation to experiment?"

"Should I give you two a moment?" Vargo drawled.

So much for pleasant distractions. "Not necessary," the Rook said, his voice hardening. "It's you I came for. You ran off before we could finish our conversation."

Vargo smirked. "I thought it was a dance."

The Rook's cold, eternal anger at the nobility flared up with the heat of Grey's hatred for his brother's killer. "It's neither," he spat. "And it isn't a game. You have something. I've come to take it from you."

"This 'something'... Is it what you were searching for when you broke into my house?" Vargo leaned back in his chair, balancing it on the rear legs. "Or is it something more ephemeral, like my life?"

Neither Grey nor the Rook was stupid enough to believe that throwing away the cane had left Vargo unarmed. But a man with a knife was at a serious disadvantage against one with a sword. It would be easy: a single lunge, and Kolya would be avenged.

Or would he? Vargo had survived some appalling wounds at the amphitheatre—survived, and recovered with unnatural speed.

Either way, the desire to kill was Grey's, not the Rook's. *This is what the medallions do*, he thought. *House Taspernum, House Adrexa, House Contorio... all destroyed, because someone else craved their power.*

That wasn't Grey's reason. But still: He'd sworn not to cross that line. "If I were here to kill you, you'd be dead. Stand up."

Jaw clenched, Vargo stood and endured the rough pat-down the Rook gave him. Two knives and a sap went onto the table, scattering the abandoned cards, while Renata sat watching in tense silence.

Then, sword re-sheathed, the Rook started a second, more thorough pat-down. Arms, legs, front, back; his gloves ghosted over every part of Vargo in search of the one piece that might unlock the whole puzzle. Assuming it was on Vargo. Assuming that was the reason for his sudden rise to power. The Rook lingered over the small lump at Vargo's navel until the man winced and muttered, "If you want a contraceptive numinat, you can get them at the Sebatium."

The Rook shoved him away. Frustrated. Disgusted. But not ready to give up.

"Strip."

"*What* now?"

A muffled sound came from Renata, too. The Rook couldn't spare attention for her. "You're a clever man. I assume you're good at hiding things. And having gone to all the trouble of tracking you here, I'm not going to quit before I'm sure."

When Vargo didn't move or respond, the Rook's hand crept toward the hilt of his blade.

"What are you going to do—cut my clothes off of me?" Vargo's voice was careless, but his body was tense.

Steel whispered a hand's breadth free in reply.

"Fine," Vargo growled. "Put that back. I like this coat; I won't have you making ribbons of it."

The coat was pomegranate dark, swirls burned into the velvet, and too closely tailored for him to easily remove it himself. The Rook was tempted to slash it off just to destroy something precious to Vargo. Instead, he nodded at Renata. "Help him." She edged past, as if wary of the Rook, to pull the coat from Vargo's shoulders, then retreated with the fabric draped over one arm.

With insolent slowness, Vargo untied his cravat, held it up, and dropped it like a flag of surrender. Next came the buttons at his wrists and neck, then his waistcoat. A tease, but not a sexual one. Vargo's kohl-shadowed glare promised vicious retribution.

His resentment was a mere spark compared to the bonfire that drove the Rook. "I'm growing impatient," he snapped.

Vargo's smile was sharp as the Rook's blade. "I'm worth the wait."

And then the door opened. The Rook had one frozen instant of seeing the mixed alarm and annoyance on Renata's face before he heard a high-pitched shriek.

Giuna Traementis. Leato's little sister, whose departure from the room had been his cue to enter—and who, by Renata's expression, should not have returned anywhere near this fast. Behind her, red-faced and reaching as though she'd tried to stop her, was Renata's maid, Tess.

Djek! For an instant he was Grey Serrado, broken from his focus on his goal.

Then calculation took over again. "Be silent. Shut the door." Her scream would bring the household, but the Rook still had a few moments to see this through. Vargo would bleed if cut from his clothes, but it wouldn't kill him. The Rook turned, some half-formed jest on his tongue about having an audience, but...

Giuna, white-faced and trembling like a bird as she pressed close under Renata's protective arm. Giuna, whom he'd held just so after he brought her the news of Leato's death.

Alta Giuna. She was a noble. He didn't have time to coddle her tender sensibilities.

But neither did Grey have the stomach for frightening her. He backed toward the window, less graceful than he might have been as his conscience struggled against the purpose to which he'd pledged himself. He might be letting his best chance slip through his fingers—

—or there might be nothing there to find.

"It seems luck is with the house tonight," he said to Vargo. The curtain fluttered down from its rings when he yanked it aside with too much force. "We'll meet again, Eret Vargo."

"When we do, perhaps I'll force *you* to remove something, Master Rook."

Better men than you have failed.

Shouts were building inside the house. He was out of time. Cursing his ill fortune, the Rook swung up a trellis to the rooftop and escaped.

The Mask of Ravens

Floodwatch, Upper Bank: Lepilun 6

Somehow the Floodwatch Bridge had seemed less imposing to Renata when it was looming over her barge than when she stood atop it, waiting for Sibiliat Acrenix.

The Dežera's flood had long since subsided, leaving the water a very long way down. Its channel ran deeper here than around the Old Island, where its waters divided in half; in hindsight, she was glad Sibiliat's pettiness had made the woman suggest this spot. People had broken their legs jumping or falling from the Sunrise and Sunset Bridges, because the water was too shallow to slow them much before they hit the mud below. At high tide, this should be safe enough.

She'd gone to Tanaquis for swimming tips in preparation for her third Praeteri trial, the two of them splashing in the shoulder-deep canal behind the house in Whitesail. Only now was it clear to Renata just how different this situation was. How unprepared *she* was.

"News! News!" A scrawny boy with a stack of broadsheets tucked under one arm waved a copy in the air. "Scurezza killers found! Buy a copy, learn all about it!"

Found? Quaniet killed her family; Giuna's account had made that clear. Chill with foreboding, Renata fished out a centira and took one of his broadsheets.

A moment later she crumpled the cheap paper in her fist, grinding her teeth to hold back a Vraszenian curse.

A sedan chair stopped at the eastern end of the bridge, amid the agricultural bustle of the nearby bean market. The bearers weren't ordinary hirelings; they wore swords at their hips and House Acrenix's emblem of a snake twisted into a double loop. They stood at attention as Sibiliat disembarked, brushed her surcoat clean of imaginary dust, and set out toward the center of the bridge.

Renata shouldn't care, but—"What's the meaning of this?" she demanded of Sibiliat, brandishing the ruined broadsheet. "Blaming the *cook*? And saying the Anduske put him up to it?"

Sibiliat didn't even have the grace to look surprised. "It's astonishing how fast word spreads," she mused. Delicately pinching the edges of the paper to avoid staining her gloves with the ink, she spread it enough to let her peer at the text. "Yes, this has the right of it."

"It's a lie," Renata snapped.

"The right *story*," Sibiliat clarified, letting the river wind take the paper. "One that everyone will believe—after all, the Anduske were ready to commit murder at the amphitheatre. And Father already has the Ordo Apis hunting them for their other crimes; what's one more?"

Ren's anger was like one of the Vigil's attack dogs, fighting the chain that held it back. *One more crime* was another reason for common Nadežrans to fear Vraszenians, another reason to consider them all cold-blooded criminals. Branek and his ilk might deserve to hang for some of the things they'd done . . . but they hadn't done *this* thing, and they weren't the only ones who would bear the consequences of that accusation.

Some hint of fury must have leaked through despite her best efforts, because Sibiliat aborted her move to lay a hand on Renata's shoulder. "Honestly, you should be thanking me. Father and I did this for *you*—for the Traementis. People were beginning to talk about the lack of answers. With a clear target to blame, no one will think to lay Quaniet's actions at the feet of your house. You don't want them saying all the Scurezza died because Coevis thought about leaving them, do you?"

Ren almost slapped her. On another day, under other circumstances, she might have had better self-control. But she'd been standing here for two bells, waiting to jump off a Mask-damned bridge, and there was a tiny part of her that admired the economic elegance of the lie.

In that moment, she hated herself more than she hated Sibiliat.

The other woman sighed. "Well, it's done, and I don't care if you're grateful or not. This isn't what we're here for, is it? You'd best get to it."

"Fine," Ren snapped—and without letting herself think twice, she climbed the rail and leapt.

She'd worn trousers instead of an underdress, and she'd meant to bundle the front and back skirts of her surcoat around her waist before she jumped, but in her haste, she'd forgotten. The linen flew up and blinded her, so the impact of the water came as a shock. And then the river was closing over her head, and she was sinking.

Ren flailed, the wet fabric of her surcoat tangling everywhere like weeds. Her jaw ached as she clamped down on the urge to scream. This was fucking stupidity—no Mask-damned cult was worth this! She was going to drown for Sibiliat's petty cruelty, for cuffs and their idiotic rituals—she was going to leave Tess and Sedge alone—

Panic clawed at her throat, choking the air from her lungs. Her whole body jerked with the urge to drag in a breath. Not yet. Light above her glowed like Ažerais's wellspring, calling her to safety. All she had to do was reach it.

But she wasn't only in the river. And if the wellspring was the light above, it was also the darkness below, dragging her down into the nightmare that had overtaken everyone on the Night of Hells. She was drowning in that dream again, trapped in a canal, nothing to cling to, nobody to help pull her out.

Ren fought to keep her eyes open, to keep her focus on the light. The water swirled with shadows like the liquid movement of the zlyzen. They waited for her down here, in the river; they waited everywhere her fears lurked. In the water. In the Depths. In Ondrakja's malice, the tightrope walk of her masquerade, the fire that had burned her childhood to ash.

In her dreams. Haunting her night after night. She thrashed, struggling to escape the river like she struggled every night to escape those nightmares.

Her head broke the surface. Like a bladder filled with air, she'd floated through no skill of her own. And there was the skiff she'd paid for, almost close enough to hit her; the skiffer reached down and hauled her out of the water, and Ren lay in a trembling puddle in the bottom of the boat, not even able to lift herself to a seat.

Fuck Sibiliat, and fuck all cuffs. Fuck Tanaquis for bringing her into the Praeteri.

And while she was at it, fuck herself for ever having agreed to this nonsense.

Isla Traementis, the Pearls: Lepilun 6

The afternoon shadows lengthened across Donaia's study as Giuna paced, skirting the dozing hulk of Meatball by the hearth. Her mother rarely used the study these days, and the imbued barrier of the door ensured that servant ears were less likely to hear what went on inside.

Like Giuna yelling at her cousin for being a damned fool.

The glow had dimmed to twilight gloom and Giuna had worked up a good head of fury by the time Colbrin appeared and ushered Renata inside. Her dusky rose surcoat and underdress were clean and dry, but the remnants of her madcap adventure could be seen in the rumpled wave of her half-dried hair.

The moment the door closed, Giuna snapped, "What in Lumen's light do you think you were doing, jumping into the Dežera on a dare?" Meatball startled awake, and Renata stepped back. "I know you're the heir now, but that doesn't mean you need to mimic Leato in *all* aspects."

"Mimic—" Renata's expression flickered with familiar pain at Leato's name. "I don't understand what you mean."

"You *jumped off a bridge*! You could have gotten yourself killed!"

Orrucio Amananto had brought the news, the last link in a flower chain of gossip racing across Nadežra. Had Renata thought no one would hear? Judging by the look on her face, yes. She said, "I didn't do it on a lark; I had reasons. And I took precautions. I know it was risky—that House Traementis needs me as heir for a few months longer, but—"

"Who gives a wet leech about that? You're *family*. If you'd been hurt, if you drowned, I..." The salt of tears stung the back of Giuna's tongue. "I know your mother let you go your own way, but it's different now. We care about you. And that means that you can't just go jumping off bridges or—or diving under falling cranes!"

That wasn't how the accident in Froghole had gone, but if Renata quibbled, Giuna was going to throw something at her. Instead, her cousin just stared at her with a look like—

Like the last thing she'd expected was for *that* to be the reason for Giuna's concern.

"Giuna..." Renata passed one hand over her eyes, looking weary. Or maybe hiding that flash of vulnerability. She took a deep breath and said, "Thank you. You're right; I—I'm not accustomed to taking that into account. To taking *you* into account, in that fashion. And I'm sorry for worrying you. If it's any comfort, I truly would not have done it without good reason."

Even faced with that weariness, Giuna wasn't quite ready to be mollified. Crossing her arms, she demanded, "What reason? What could possibly require you to endanger yourself like that?"

Renata's laugh was brief and unamused. "Ask Tanaquis. There's...I'm not supposed to talk about it, but I'll say this much. There's a secret society she's invited me to join, because she has things *she* can't talk about except with other members. Things she believes will shed light on the Traementis curse. The bridge was part of the initiation for this society. I just pray the Lumen will make it worthwhile."

Of course Renata was trying to help. That was what she did, ever since Leato died. She tried to make up for a loss she saw as her fault.

She didn't understand that being Traementis meant there was no debt to repay.

Laying a hand on her cousin's arm, Giuna said, "I know you want to help, but *please* don't risk yourself like that again. Nothing is worth losing you. I know Mother would agree."

After a brief hesitation, Renata laid her hand over Giuna's. "There's something else you should know. Eret Acrenix has constructed a story blaming the Stadnem Anduske for the Scurezza murders."

It doused Giuna in cold like she was the one who'd jumped into the river. "But...it was Quaniet. She confessed as much when she died. Sibiliat *heard* her. Why would they blame the Vraszenians?"

"Because they can." Renata's words were bitter as gall, and she drew a sharp breath in their wake. In a softer tone, she said, "The Vigil and the Ordo Apis are already hunting the Anduske leaders anyway. This allows them to wrap up the investigation without letting it be known that Quaniet killed her whole family rather than let House Traementis adopt her cousin. He's sparing us the scandal."

Just like he'd done when he suppressed news of Quaniet's confession in the first place. If people knew the truth, it *would* cast a shadow over House Traementis. After so many years of decline, it wouldn't take much to convince people they were still ill-starred.

And it would be so easy to let the lie stand. Quaniet was dead. The Anduske were criminals anyway. House Traementis was still vulnerable.

Easy—but wrong.

Giuna shook her head hard enough to pull a tress down from its pins. "It isn't true, though. And if people think Vraszenians were behind this, who knows who might get hurt? We have to say something." Her gaze flicked up to Renata's. "Don't we?"

A tiny, shameful part of Giuna half feared Renata would disagree. She was foreign born, and sometimes too pragmatic for comfort. Would she care about Vraszenians being blamed?

Her cousin's eyes blazed like the Lumen. "We do," Renata said, in a hard voice Giuna had never heard from her before. "And we will."

Staveswater: Lepilun 8

Staveswater was the forgotten part of Nadežra. People *looked* at it all the time, whenever they had business with the shipping downriver, or gazed past the masts crowding Turtle Lagoon to the buildings beyond. Though "buildings" might be more a courtesy term than anything else: Staveswater was a hodgepodge of boats and rafts and rickety houses on stilts joined by planks and rope bridges until it hung together in something like a district. When people spoke of Nadežra's regions, they named the Upper Bank, the Lower Bank, and the Old Island—never Staveswater. It was a relic, a poor and close-packed reminder of what the delta had looked like before Nadežra sank stone foundations into the mud and built itself up into a city.

It was the main bastion of the Stretsko clan, and the fists of their various knots kept close watch on the bridges that led from the rest of Staveswater to the area they controlled.

Ren had taken extra care with her makeup this time, painting herself to look not just old, but like a specific old woman. At night, with slow Paumillis's full face veiled by thick clouds, it was enough to pass. The guards nodded as she creaked her way across one of the connecting bridges with a snail-bag of mending and piecework; one even stepped forward to help her shrug it higher on her back.

Once past them, she tottered her way onward, through the cramped shantytown, until she reached a gap in the structure. In between flowed the waters of the Dežera; across the gap, a set of add-ons clung to a central building like barnacles to a ship. There, gratefully, she put the bag down and pulled its mouth open.

Arkady had insisted she was "too famous" to just walk in like the rest of her beggar pack had done over the last few days. Now she wiggled out of the bag while Ren slung a clawed, padded hook across the gap, trailing a coil of lightweight rope behind it. Once that was secure, a line of small children bearing lumpy, squirming bags emerged from nearby hiding places and began to monkey across.

By the time the first of them touched down in the Stretsko headquarters, Ren had moved onward. Conveniently, she didn't even have to scrub off the old woman's guise; all she had to do was slide the lace mask down, and the Black Rose's costume formed itself around her.

If Renata was a burden she couldn't put down and Arenza was a reminder of the life she'd never had, the Black Rose was her refuge from all that. Ren knew better than to put much stock in what Dalisva and Mevieny had said about her being chosen; believing too strongly in divine favor was the kind of thing that got a person killed. But putting on the mask made her feel strong, and sometimes, even the illusion of that was enough. The Black Rose wasn't an orphan, wasn't a traitor, wasn't someone without a place to belong. She had a purpose.

She was going to yank a thread out of the middle of Branek's tapestry and see how much of it unraveled.

If the Stretsko fists were any good, any kind of dramatic move would get her stabbed first, questioned later. Ren found her solution in an unoccupied chair wedged into one corner of a small, uneven platform where three shanties came together. *When drama won't do, be casual.* She picked up a piece of cord and looped it around her fingers to play dreamweaver's nest until three chatting Stretsko came around the corner.

Then she smiled at them, friendly but sharp. "Evening. I trust you've heard of me? I'm here to talk to Prazode."

Their reactions were exactly as she'd hoped: startled and wary, but not immediately violent. The rumors about the Black Rose's connection to Ažerais kept the fists respectful—though it didn't stop them from patting her down for weapons while one of their group went to warn the others. Only when a hand brushed too close to the lace shielding her eyes did she pull back. "You may *not* see the face. Only the mask."

When they were satisfied she was unarmed, they led her onward. Crossing the single rope bridge that led to the home nest, Ren saw no sign of Arkady or the others. The wind had picked up, which was all to the good; its rush would cover any sounds they might make.

Inside, the Stretsko had mustered an impressive number of fists to receive her, but the usual swagger was tempered by uncertainty. She even saw a couple of people touch their brows in respect.

Prazode, their leader, showed no such courtesy. He sat in a comfortable chair on the far side of the room, with a one-eyed woman at his side; that would be Šidjin Gulavka. Rumor said she was trying to persuade her uncle to swear himself and his knot to Branek, the way Tserdev had done. If she managed that, others would follow, until Branek controlled almost every Stretsko knot.

Ren's gaze slid to Prazode's other side, and her breath caught. She'd missed her chance to follow Tserdev in Seven Knots...but here was Tserdev's brother Dmatsos. His hawk-like nose and light eyes were well-described in Dalisva's list.

If she could grab both Gulavka *and* Dmatsos...

"So you're the Black Rose we've heard so much about." Prazode was a heavyset man with a balding pate, a full beard, and a gleam to his eye that said he was no fool despite his wide smile. "Whom we all have to thank for saving our wellspring."

At an indecipherable grumble from Gulavka, the amusement left his face and voice. "*All* of us—which is why I will listen to what you have to say. But I should warn you that listening is all I agree to. My niece and I may disagree in our philosophies, but..." He shrugged. "Family is family." Many of the people watching bore more than a little resemblance to Prazode. Large family was a blessing for Vraszenians, but especially for the Stretsko. Family was wealth, strength, power, and posterity.

Ren had to choose her words carefully. "I come to speak not of philosophy, but of sacrilege. Šidjin Gulavka endangered the Wellspring of Ažerais—the holiest site in all of Vraszan, the gift through which our goddess's blessings flow. She must answer for that."

"You're a tool of that kinless bastard Vargo," Dmatsos spat. "I heard how in Seven Knots you rescued him."

She turned a cool gaze upon him. "You mean how I prevented another sacrilege—murder on the sacred path. My concern is with those who blaspheme against Ažerais and her children, not the struggles of Nadežra's streets." She returned her attention to Prazode. "Surrender Ča Gulavka and Ča Očelen to me, and I'll see to it that the ziemetse judge them fairly."

"What fairness have the ziemetse?" Gulavka asked. Not angry like Dmatsos—sad. Betrayed. "They live upriver and visit Nadežra once a year to get drunk on sacred aža with their Liganti masters. They care nothing for the city or our people here. They have forgotten us, as they forget—"

"Enough. You will not disrespect our elders." Prazode waited until Gulavka clamped her lips and nodded in grudging agreement. Then he turned his gaze on Ren. "And you. What power have you over the ziemetse, that you can influence their judgment? I think you make claims you cannot support, Lady Rose."

"It is not my power or influence that matters, but that of Ažerais."

Dmatsos stood, throwing his pipe to the floor. "Then tell Ažerais to come and claim us!" he snarled.

Ren never expected Prazode to agree to turn over his niece— but that had never been the point of coming here. And while she could stall all night, Dmatsos's challenge proved too good an opening to refuse.

Spreading her hands as though the matter were beyond her control, she said, "Perhaps you will heed your ancestor instead."

On those words, a shrieking rain of rats descended—and one spitting-mad tomcat.

Shouts burst from the Stretsko as the rats fell from the ceiling. Many hit the floor, righting themselves to scurry around in a panicked daze, but some caught themselves mid-fall, flailing claws hooking into braids and clothes and sometimes skin. Ren, out of the immediate scuffle, stifled a laugh as the cat added to the chaos. There were too many rats for one lone tom to handle; she stepped out of the cat's path as he streaked for the door.

And waited, as the Stretsko tore the rats from their hair and coats and set them down with the care only their clan would show.

And waited, as the rats leaked out through gaps in the walls and the floor or climbed back to the ceiling and the smoke hole through which Arkady had dumped them.

And waited.

Anytime now, Vargo.

Any. Fucking. Time.

She didn't know what had gone wrong, but the chaos was dying down, and Prazode's attention was back on her. Extemporizing, she spread her arms. "Do you doubt me now? The Children of the Rat are known for their strong bonds—but those bonds are to *all* Vraszenians. Even now, you are with the ziemetse woven into a single fabric. And of all clans, the Stretsko should understand that you must find common ground on which to stand...or all of you will fall."

Ren felt no divine presence. She hadn't even planned her words, much less their timing.

But no sooner had the word "fall" left her mouth than the floor splintered into kindling.

Not the whole thing. Just the center of it, an area about three paces across. Enough to drop a double handful of Stretsko into the water, and some of the rats with them.

But a clever rat had more than one way out of his hole. Prazode whirled up from his seat and kicked something behind it, and the back wall swung down with a heavy crash, reaching across to the shack on the far side of the water. He wasted no time in bolting, Gulavka and Dmatsos right behind him.

Ren swore. A running leap got her enough of a grip on an overhead beam to sling herself across the gap, avoiding the remaining fists in the room. The wall had taken damage in the transition to its new life as a bridge, and it bowed ominously beneath her feet as she sprinted across. But it held long enough for her to reach the far side.

Up ahead, the trio had split. Prazode, Ren ignored; he wasn't the one she'd come for. But Gulavka and Dmatsos ran down different walkways, and she couldn't follow them both.

Gulavka was the cake. Dmatsos was the frosting. She went after Gulavka.

Unfortunately, the Stretsko woman was fast on her feet, and she knew the warren of Staveswater far better than Ren did. Gulavka dodged around a corner; if she got properly out of sight, Ren would never find her. She put on a burst of speed—

As she skidded around the corner, she heard a crash and a grunt of pain.

Gulavka was sprawled flat on the walkway. Ren knelt on her back before she could rise, and bound her hands with the cord from the dreamweaver's nest, looping it so the woman couldn't just wriggle free. Gulavka opened her mouth to shout, but Ren grabbed a rag and wadded it into her mouth to muffle her.

"That's what you get for fucking up Veiled Waters!" Arkady sprang up onto the walkway next to Ren. She twirled the skiffer pole she'd used to trip Gulavka, nearly braining Ren with it. "Did you see the cat? That was my idea. Wish I could have seen it."

Glancing back the way she'd come, Ren made another snap decision: to trust that Arkady was as competent as she boasted. "The cat was perfect. Can you get this one to the skiff?"

"She won't go nowhere we don't want her to. Hey, Blinky—you know how to play sedan chair?" A sharp whistle brought several of Arkady's kids sliding down from the rooftops, while Arkady sat on Gulavka and directed the kids to carry them both.

With her focus no longer fixed on Gulavka, Ren heard the

shouts echoing through Staveswater. Vargo was taking advantage of the whole situation to lead a strike against the river pirates who'd been cutting into his smuggling business, and from the sound of it, the fighting was fierce.

But the Black Rose wasn't here to help a Lower Bank crime lord take down his enemies.

Coming and going from Renata's balcony had put her back in climbing trim. Ren swarmed up the side of a shack and arrived on the roof to find the cloud cover thinning out, Paumillis's light breaking through to illuminate the scene. A swift glance around oriented her: If she'd followed Gulavka *this* way, then Dmatsos would be...

On the rooftops himself, trying to skirt the chaos below.

Ren sprinted after him. The roofs were no more solid than the fallen wall had been; their moldy shingles and boards bent beneath her feet, threatening to send her back down to what passed for ground level. Dmatsos heard her coming and jinked left, changing course for some unseen target.

No you don't, Ren thought, grim and exhilarated all at once. Compared with bureaucracy and Praeteri rituals and her life of constant lies, there was something pure about this. She felt like her feet had wings as she closed the gap between them.

Then Dmatsos put his foot right through into someone's house, sinking up to the thigh. By the time he wrenched his leg free, Ren was close enough to bring him down with a flying tackle.

Down—and *down*. They rolled off the edge of the roof and hit the walkway below, Dmatsos cushioning Ren's fall, as much as he could cushion anything when the boards ripped free of their nails at the impact. She let go of him to clutch desperately at the remaining planks, the sluggish waters of Staveswater flowing just below the toes of her boots.

She almost lost her grip at the feel of a hand on her calf, another on her ass. Ren didn't have time to be offended before she heard Varuni's dispassionate command: "Drop."

With Varuni's strength guiding her, the boat barely dipped when Ren touched down. Dmatsos didn't receive the same gentle treatment; Varuni hauled him out of the water by his collar and tossed him to the center of the boat, where two of Vargo's fists bound him with ropes. At the far edge, a third man pulled them into hiding under the walkways.

Which left them one short of the crew who *should* have been there. "Where's Vargo?"

Varuni's mouth hardened. "Problem with the numinat. Had to set it off manually. We're going to pick him up now." Her gaze flicked back at one of the fists—the one who'd been responsible for making certain the inscribed raft drifted into place to blow the floor out of the headquarters. "You certain you don't want to swim for it, Ublits? He'll *probably* forgive you. If he doesn't catch cold."

"Too late," Ublits said with the resignation of a dead man. In the shadows ahead, a pale blot was splashing toward them, kicking up spray with every stroke. Unlike Ren, it seemed Vargo could swim.

He caught hold of the boat's edge, then Varuni's hand, and used them to roll into the bottom with a slop and a groan. His trousers were black with river water, his coat and waistcoat discarded who knew where. The fine cambric of his shirt was all but transparent, plastered to his skin. Through it, Ren could see the blurred lines of his strange tattoo.

"I get so much as a sniffle, you're all burning in the Ninatium," Vargo growled. After another heavy breath, he pushed himself up to his feet, then looked down at Dmatsos with a puzzled frown. "That doesn't look like Gulavka. Got too many eyes, for one thing."

"The Stretsko were so generous, they gave me two," Ren said lightly. "Our friends have the other."

"Mind leaving me the spare?" Vargo nudged Dmatsos with a stockinged toe. His boots must have gone the way of his other clothes. "You've still got Gulavka to satisfy the ziemetse, and I can think of several ways to make use of this one."

When she didn't immediately answer, Vargo glanced up. "I don't plan to kill him. But his presence as my guest would make the Lower Bank a lot more peaceful."

Your hostage, you mean. She had no doubt he *would* kill Dmatsos, if he thought that would be more productive. Sedge had made that clear, long before Ren saw for herself what Vargo was really like.

She wanted to refuse. The ziemetse had asked for Dmatsos as well as his sister; giving Vargo a prisoner of his own had never been part of their deal. But Ren was in a boat full of Vargo's people, heading upriver as fast as the oarsmen could row, and she didn't think he had enough reverence for the Black Rose to bow to her demands.

Still, she couldn't show weakness, either. She met Vargo's gaze steadily. "Call it a loan. I'll want him back later . . . or a favor in return."

Vargo's smile curved like a sickle. "I could get to like us doing each other favors, Lady Rose."

It was too close to the words he'd spoken to Alta Renata. But a shout saved her from having to smile back at him: Arkady and her crew, working three to an oar to row a stolen boat free from Staveswater. Arkady herself was sitting on top of Gulavka, and she waved with the arm that wasn't holding a familiar tomcat. "Where do you want this one delivered?"

Temple of the Illius Praeteri: Lepilun 9

Diomen's resonant voice was impressive even in a pavilion. In the subterranean chamber where Renata now knelt, it echoed like the voice of the Lumen itself.

"We stand, a few scattered sparks against the darkness of ignorance—but gathered, our light is stronger."

There was no light for Renata, thanks to the blindfold she wore. Tanaquis had placed it on her in Suncross; their journey after that had gone into a building and then into a tunnel. But not the Depths—the lack of damp and mold told her that. They must be somewhere higher in the Point, somewhere between the river and the amphitheatre above.

"Today, two more flames join the light of the Illius Praeteri. We shine where the Lumen cannot and bring that new light into the world. When we see, we do not know."

"Ignorance is the path to enlightenment." The chamber echoed with the reverent response of dozens of voices.

"When we ask, we do not learn." A hand brushed over Renata's head, untying the knot of her blindfold.

"Submission is the door to freedom," the crowd responded.

The silk fell away, and she blinked against the brightness of the light.

"When we reach, we do not grasp."

"Dedication is the key to mastery."

"Sister Renata Viraudax Traementatis. Brother Derossi Vargo. You have passed through the Gates of Initiation; welcome to the ranks of the Illius Praeteri." Diomen took their hands and drew them to their feet.

Around them stood several dozen people in plain, undyed silk robes. Parma Extaquium and Bondiro Coscanum, Sibiliat Acrenix and Benvanna Novri. Tanaquis and Ghiscolo, of course, and Sureggio Extaquium. But others, too: She saw members of Essunta and Fiangiolli both, Attravi and Elpiscio, Lud Kaineto—even Toneo Pattumo, Renata's former banker. At least half of the delta houses were represented, maybe more. *I had no idea the Praeteri extended so far*, Renata thought, chilled by the sight.

The space they stood in was lofty stone, the light reflecting off burnished gold surfaces and dark marble veined with sparkling quartz. Nearby stood an enormous podium, with a scroll spread across its top. "A register?" Vargo said, clearly surprised.

Diomen folded his hands into his sleeves. "We address each other as 'brother' and 'sister' not merely as a matter of equality beneath the Lumen, but as a reminder of our bond. While this is not quite the same as a family register, it serves to join us together. Today you were able to enter this place only because you were escorted by others. Once your names are inscribed, you will be able to pass on your own through the warded passage that leads here."

Renata used the excuse of straightening her surcoat's skirt to hide her twitch of surprise. She knew the passage Diomen referred to; it was legendary among those who used the tunnels of the Depths. Some unknown magic prevented anyone from passing through.

But she had the distinct impression that the Praeteri hadn't existed in Nadežra until Diomen's arrival sixteen years ago—and the warded tunnel long predated that.

Vargo was busy examining the register, his scarred brow arched. As he added his name, Renata said, "This is extraordinary. I had no idea you'd carved out an entire temple within the Point—and warded it against intruders, no less."

"Oh, we didn't build it," Tanaquis said. "This temple dates back to Kaius Rex, or perhaps earlier. He mostly used this place for point-less orgies and the like, but we aspire to more."

Parma snickered. "Our orgies have *points.*"

She sounded like she meant it literally. But Renata trusted Tan-aquis wouldn't have put her through this for something merely car-nal. While she took Vargo's place at the podium, Diomen said, "The Gate of Desire may draw you the most strongly, Sister Parma, but our new members may choose a different path. Sister Renata, Brother Vargo, many challenges yet lie ahead: the four Gates of Revelation, and beyond them, the Gates of the Great Mysteries. To pass them all can be the work of a lifetime."

Then he raised his voice, making good use of the hall's echo-ing power. "But today we celebrate our newest brother and sister. Come—let us feast."

The food and drink waiting in an adjoining chamber were a dis-play of such excessive abundance that Renata knew Sureggio was responsible before he even claimed credit. Mingling and making small talk, she soon realized that for most of the members this was little more than another way to forge connections with their fel-low gentry and nobles, spicing their deals with the pleasure of doing so under the cloak of secrecy and ritual. "Making your way to the Great Mysteries takes *effort*," Bondiro told Renata, in a tone that left no doubt as to his low opinion of that. "We don't know exactly how many have gone that far, but it's only a few. Tanaquis, Ghiscolo—"

"Breccone," Parma said. "Though I suppose he doesn't count, now that he's dead. Cousin Sureggio has, too. But they can't talk about it—Sureggio tried once, and he got the *worst* headache. It didn't go away until he made penance to the Pontifex."

Renata was doing her best to avoid Sureggio, whose gaze lingered on her as much as on Vargo. He slipped up to her side in a damp cloud of cloying perfume when she was perusing the dishes, though, and stood so close his bony elbow kept brushing hers. "Try the stuffed dreamweaver," he said, gesturing at a half-dismembered bird lying amid a scatter of iridescent feathers. The open cavity of its chest was filled with pickled eggs. "The sauce is divine."

Dreamweaver. It was a common accusation from Vraszenians, that the nobility feasted on their sacred bird. Of course Extaquium, whose tables groaned under every exotic delicacy money could buy, would do exactly that.

"Excuse me," Renata said, her voice tight, and escaped into the less crowded confines of the temple's main hall.

Where had Tanaquis vanished to? Now that Renata had become a full member of the Praeteri, Tanaquis had better be able to speak freely about whatever it was she thought might be useful. If Renata had to get all the way through to these so-called Great Mysteries first, she might quit right now.

But before she could go in search of Tanaquis, Vargo caught her.

"I'll admit," he said, coming up to her side, "your presence makes this whole process more pleasurable. I've hardly seen you since our card game was so rudely interrupted. I hope you don't blame me for what happened."

She'd been avoiding him, but she could hardly admit it. "I've only been busy with Traementis business. I'm trying to reach a point where Donaia can take some time away; His Grace has offered her the use of his villa." She didn't see any members of House Quientis among the cultists. Scaperto himself would be barred due to his position in the Cinquerat, and perhaps all his registered kin were too sensible for this nonsense.

Vargo's voice lowered to an intimate, flirtatious note. "At the risk of being the fish calling the duck wet, you might do with some time away yourself. Care to come by my townhouse on your way home tonight? My wine is better, and we could compare notes somewhere without an audience."

"Notes on the wine? Or this?" She gestured around at the Tyrant's former temple.

"This—and what comes next. I suspect you're no more here for the food than I am. Perhaps we can discuss that . . . and how we could help each other."

How you could use me, you mean. She knew that look. To Vargo she was nothing more than a valuable tool, and now he'd found another place to employ her.

His gaze flicked to something past her shoulder, and Renata turned to greet that distraction like salvation—only to realize it was like reaching for a rope in dreams and finding a snake.

"Sister Renata," Ghiscolo said. "I hope you don't mind me addressing you with such familiarity."

She made her tone light. "Why would I, Brother Ghiscolo?"

"That unfortunate affair with the Scurezza family. I was shocked to hear yesterday that your cousin has announced the full tale of what she saw—despite the consequences to House Traementis. Consequences I was hoping to shield you from."

It was true that quite a few letters had arrived at the manor soon after, withdrawing petitions for adoption. But there were still enough that the Traementis could afford to be choosy, and Tanaquis had decided to accept, which put a genuine smile on Donaia's face when she heard. "Anyone who would hold Meda Scurezza's insanity against *us*, Brother Ghiscolo, is no one we would want in House Traementis."

His expression was affable and a little hurt. "Still, you might have warned me."

Giving you a chance to talk us out of it? Before she could force an insincere apology through her teeth, he added, "Sister Quaniet was one of ours. We were also hoping to protect her reputation."

A soft breath came from Vargo. Renata said, "Her reputation

hardly matters now, with every Scurezza dead at her hand. I applaud your zeal for pursuing the Anduske, Brother Ghiscolo—but I think their own crimes are enough to hang them."

One hand rose to his heart, fiddling with a shirt button in an uncharacteristic show of agitation. The reply, however, came not from Ghiscolo, but from behind Renata's shoulder. "You show an admirable desire for justice, Sister Renata."

She hoped her step back looked like she was welcoming Diomen into their circle, rather than escaping the trap of being surrounded by three men she trusted no further than an arm's reach. "Pontifex."

"My congratulations to you and Brother Vargo both on progressing so quickly through the Gates of Initiation." He didn't smile, but something like satisfaction glittered in his eyes. "Your success only reinforces my belief that you both carry a great blessing. Perhaps you will join the select few who can attain the Gates of the Great Mysteries."

"You judge me more highly than I deserve," Renata murmured. She wasn't getting anywhere near another damned gate if she could help it. But right now, to get away from Vargo and Ghiscolo... "I would love to receive more instruction, though. Perhaps you could give me a tour of this temple?"

Vargo drew breath to say something, but Diomen beat him to it. "It would be my pleasure, Sister Renata." She took his arm as if he had offered it, and they left the two conspirators behind.

"This temple long predates the Conqueror," Diomen said as they began a circuit of the main hall. "Or the Tyrant, as Kaius Sifigno is more often called here. I confess I do not know its precise age. A Tricat numinat can be used to weigh such things, but only by comparison: older than one thing, younger than another."

"I wasn't aware of that." Which was true, but also an invitation for him to expand more.

Diomen fixed his unnerving gaze on Renata. "The inscriptor's art has many subtleties the layperson does not understand. Were you born in Canilun?"

"Colbrilun. The twenty-ninth."

A faint line marred the skin between his brows. He brought his hands down in mirrored arcs, marking a circle, then stared into his cupped palms at the base. "What I sense must not be due to birth, but some other resonance with Tricat. Something connected with your family, perhaps—something that has stained them."

"The late Sister Quaniet—"

"I speak not of recent politics." Diomen's voice cut her off like a knife. "This is a spiritual stain of long-standing origin. It is gone, but traces linger, like a ghost."

His behavior might have chilled her more if she hadn't manipulated other people the same way. "Tanaquis has spoken to you."

"A skeptic." Diomen lifted his hands as though he could do nothing about her doubt. "I have not spoken with Sister Tanaquis about you, other than to express surprise when she nominated you for initiation. She has never sponsored a candidate before." A pleased smile did nothing to soften the sharpness of his gaze. "But your reaction tells me I am right."

He would be a fool to lie about his source, given that she could verify it with Tanaquis easily enough. Vargo? She *had* made the mistake of telling him about the curse. It would mean he'd had contact with Diomen, outside the organized rituals of the gates—but that seemed all too plausible.

Renata folded her hands. "Tanaquis invited me because she thought your work here might shed light on...call it an affliction, on House Traementis. It's gone now, but we still aren't certain where it came from. If you have insights to offer, I'd be glad to hear them."

He studied her with unblinking eyes that reminded her of a fen vulture waiting for its prey to die. Then he said, "I am merely a conduit for the Lumen—as are we all. I have no insights. But I know how you might seek them...if you believe yourself ready."

I'm certainly ready to see what you're up to. She hid satisfaction and apprehension both as she nodded.

He led her through the archway to a small, nondescript room, whose walls bore more signs of destruction. The floor was unmarred, though, save for a numinat: a circle containing only a many-sided figure and a five-pointed star, oddly twisted upon itself.

Diomen said, "We all learn meditative worship as children, but only in its simplest form: the quieting of the mind, the cleansing of the soul. This numinat is designed for more. Someone has wronged you and your house. Here, you may attune yourself to the energy of that action...and in so doing, perhaps trace it."

Renata didn't bother hiding her surprise and skepticism. She was hardly an expert inscriptor, but that didn't sound much like the numinatria she knew. Diomen took no offense; he merely set a smooth plug of amber glass into the numinat's focal point. "Stand within, and meditate as if you were in a temple."

She obeyed cautiously, though the blank surface of the focus was puzzling. "I see no god named here. You mentioned Tricat; should I direct my thoughts to that numen?" Amber was Tricat's color.

"Direct them to those who have harmed you—whether you know their faces or not."

Diomen's smile was anything but reassuring. But this must be why Tanaquis had brought her to the Praeteri: to uncover the origins of the curse, through some different form of numinatria. She would have felt better with Tanaquis present...but if this brought her answers now, she might be spared having to return.

Renata stood within the star and clasped her hands while Diomen activated the numinat.

Then she waited. If she'd been the Seterin noblewoman he assumed, meditation might have been easier. Her only previous attempt had been after days without sleep, after the living nightmare, the zlyzen, Leato screaming as she left him behind...

"Think back to this stain upon your family." Diomen's voice was like a burr, irritating instead of soothing. "When did you first know of it?"

"After the Night of Hells," she admitted, swallowing down the hollow ache in her heart. "Leato said something before he...died."

Before Mettore Indestor's schemes killed him. And Ondrakja, poisoning them all with ash. And Vargo, who'd sent her there. And herself. "Tanaquis later confirmed that the curse affected all the members of House Traementis." Dragging them down into what they considered poverty. Ludicrous, compared to what she'd lived through—but the deaths they'd suffered were nothing to laugh at. *If I'd detected the curse sooner, would Leato be alive?*

"The Traementis have made many enemies over the years. Who might have cursed you?"

She thought at once of Letilia, who had always looked down on her—a maid prettier than her mistress—and taken enjoyment in making Ren's life miserable. Would she have been petty enough to curse Ren after she and Tess fled?

Easily. "Letilia," Renata spat, remembering too late that she shouldn't call her that. "My mother." Her tone twisted the word into a parody of itself. But could Letilia—vapid, vain, and self-involved—wield enough power to bring down an entire house? Wasn't that the purview of the divine? Like whatever force it was that Ren had sensed in Ažerais's Dream, the furious storm that raged against the stone of the goddess's presence.

Ažerais was different from the other deities. She had no Face and Mask duality; she was simply herself. But what if that wasn't true? What if what Ren had sensed *was* her Mask—the malevolent, wrathful side of her power? Maybe centuries of Liganti oppression had warped her, their amphitheatre sitting atop her sacred wellspring, Vraszenians forced to pay for the right to visit it. And this temple beneath it, where spoiled cuffs played games of power.

None of this had anything to do with the curse she was supposed to be thinking about. But Ren didn't trust herself right now to answer Diomen in Renata's accent.

Yet he kept asking questions. "Where do your thoughts take you? Toward justice? Toward vengeance? What tool lies ready to hand, that you might employ in righting this wrong?" Prodding her off balance instead of letting her collect herself, until she wanted to snap at him to *shut up already.*

She'd been this angry while sleepless after the Night of Hells, but only because she was exhausted beyond all reason. She ought to be in control of herself now. She tried to shape an answer for him, but the only things that came to mind were Ren's answers, not Renata's. Renata's life was good. She had the comforts of wealth and the rank to protect her from Nadežra's brutality. It was *Ren* who saw all the things wrong with it, *Ren* who lost almost everything.

The acidic rage burned under the mask of her cosmetics, under the mantle of Renata's clothes, until she was ready to throw it all off and burn the world down.

"Ah, this is where you've gone off to." Vargo sauntered in, his manner casual—but his wary gaze slid from Renata to Diomen. "I apologize for interrupting, Pontifex, but Renata and I have plans this evening."

Lies. He'd asked, but she'd never agreed to accompany him home.

Vargo. Now *there* was a target Renata could be angry at.

"You presume too much, *Eret* Vargo," she snapped, letting her fury hone her Seterin accent to a razor edge. "And I hardly think I'm likely to accept another invitation from your hand, given where the last one sent me."

He stepped back as though struck. "I . . . see," he said, gaze dropping to the numinat she stood in. But clearly he didn't see, because he extended a hand. "Maybe you should come with me."

"You are interrupting a ritual, Brother Vargo," Diomen said, frowning with disapproval. "Sister Renata is approaching the first of the revelations. She must complete her journey."

Vargo ignored him. "Renata, you look a little flushed. Why don't we get you some wine?"

Her hands clenched so hard her nails cut into her palms. "Did you know he intended to poison me? Maybe you provided him with that ash—after all, you *are* the aža trade in this city. All for a mercenary charter; well, that's fitting. You'll sell yourself to anyone who will pay, won't you? You'll whore and you'll kill, like you killed Kolya Serrado." The only reason she was able to laugh was because she knew it would cut. "Was Leato's death also part of the plan? Or merely an unexpected benefit? You failed to get one Traementis heir into your bed; now you have a new one to chase."

The room was small. There was nowhere for Vargo to retreat from her accusations, but his back pressed against the stone wall as if he could melt into it. Away from her.

"How long have you known?" he asked, voice rough like it had been stripped.

"That you're a liar and a manipulator? Not nearly long enough." She spat at his feet. "Would you believe, I was ready to trust you? Well played, *Eret* Vargo. You had me convinced that you were better than you seemed—but I know now you're just another river rat clawing your way out of the sewer. And I will see to it that you drown in the shit that birthed you."

Her voice was so distorted with fury, she didn't even know what accent she was using anymore. When Vargo lunged forward, she recoiled to strike him, but he trapped her wrist in a bruising grip and twisted her arm until she had no choice but to stagger out of the numinat. He dragged her past Diomen, out of the room, and into the nearly empty hall. The scattering of people who were out there turned to stare as Vargo stumbled to a halt.

"Thank you for your honesty. It seems we can both stop pretending." His voice shook, composure hanging together by threads as frayed as a cut knot. Releasing her wrist, Vargo strode toward the exit, his parting words loud enough for the few present to hear. "That's the last favor I do for you."

She choked on her reply, not even sure what it would have been. The fury that had possessed her was draining away, leaving her cold with horror.

What have I done? She'd just destroyed every shred of trust she'd wrung from Vargo. A stupid move, ruinous to everything she'd tried to build—but she hadn't been able to hold back. Ren prided herself on self-control, on her ability to maintain her mask no matter the provocation; now she'd thrown that away. And she didn't even know why.

People were staring. She should go back to Diomen, demand

answers for *what in the hell had just happened*...but she didn't trust herself anywhere near that conversation. She didn't trust herself near anyone at the moment.

Praying that Vargo had started moving faster as soon as he was in the tunnel, Ren fled.

Eastbridge, Upper Bank: Lepilun 9

Vargo slammed through the front door of his townhouse and up the stairs to his study, ignoring Varuni's startled grunt and Alsius's welcoming chatter. Renata's words rang louder than the clock tower bells, counterpoint to the drumbeat of blood inside his skull.

Not the accusations about what he'd done; those were true and fair and nothing he hadn't flayed himself with in the dark hours when Alsius's voice fell silent. Yes, he'd used people to get where he was. Didn't everyone? Yes, he'd fucked up—trading Renata to Mettore, the deaths of Kolya Serrado and Leato Traementis, more sins she'd never know about, going all the way back to Alsius's death.

I didn't know and *It was a mistake* didn't undo any of it. All he could do was harden himself and move on. Like he'd done before.

No, what shook him were her other words. However much he tried to shrug them off, they ate away at his foundations, relentless as the Dežera. He'd thought she wasn't like the other cuffs. She made it seem like she saw Vargo for himself, for what he could do rather than where he came from. He'd thought that, despite their different backgrounds, they shared a similar outlook. That beyond using each other, they were—could be—friends.

Tonight was supposed to be when he told her the whole story. What the Illius Praeteri were, what they'd done, why she needed to be careful.

At least she'd revealed her true feelings before he made *that* mistake. Shoving his worthlessness in his face, like she was so much fucking better.

Isn't she?

Chalk hit the paneled wall with a pitiful puff of dust. Vargo wanted to throw something better, but the only thing in his study that might have done was that stupid bust of Mirscellis, and the Rook had already stolen that satisfaction.

The urge to laugh tangled with his fury and despair, dragging him to the floor. The Rook. The only person in this city who *shouldn't* have a reason to despise Vargo. Maybe he should hunt down that kinless bastard and tell him they were after the *same fucking thing.*

Fuck the nobility: a sentiment Vargo heartily agreed with. *And now I'm one of them, so fuck me, too.*

He scrubbed his face, the soft kid of his gloves a reminder of everything he wasn't. The hot shock of humiliation was fading, leaving behind the silence of a cold, familiar resentment. Someone was pounding on his study door. Varuni, demanding to know what had happened. And just out of reach, a spot of chalk-dulled color bounced anxiously.

::Vargo? Is everything...all right?::

Varuni, who only guarded his ass because her people had paid so much for it. Alsius, who'd spent sixteen years shaping Vargo into his tool.

Just another river rat clawing your way out of the sewer. Renata, who'd been born with every privilege and didn't have the first fucking clue who he was, where he'd come from, or why he'd done what he'd done. Alike? They were *nothing* alike. And he was glad of it.

"Fuck you," he growled. At her. At all the cuffs who thought Vargo good enough to use but not to respect. Rising, he tore off his gloves and sent them flying in the direction of the broken chalk. To shut everyone up, he snarled, "I'm fine!"

The pounding stopped. Alsius didn't. ::What happened? Where's Renata? I thought you were going to tell her tonight? Did something go wrong with the initiation? Was Diomen there?:: He scuttled after Vargo and sprang onto the desk. Ignoring him, Vargo pulled out paper and yanked the cap from his inkwell. ::Did he do something?::

"Not to me." Later, Vargo would sit down and tell Alsius what he'd seen, and they would discuss the implications and their next move.

But he couldn't go back to being a tool just yet. He needed...

Vargo dashed off a quick invitation, devoid of names so it couldn't be used against him later. Ignoring Alsius's questions, he stripped bare and threw on something that wouldn't be out of place in the Froghole slums. Something fitting for Derossi Vargo, biggest knot boss in the whole damned city, and to Ninat's hell with what any cuff thought of him.

He left his gloves on the floor of his study and slammed down the stairs, startling Varuni into a facial expression. "Get me a message runner and a sedan chair."

::Vargo, please.:: Peabody scuttled along the wall, following Vargo as he paced. ::If something happened with Renata—::

"Fuck Renata." He didn't care what she thought of him.

::I only meant...::

Vargo stepped outside and shut the door so Alsius couldn't follow. *Unless you want to listen to me nailing a cuff into a wall, I suggest you stay home.*

Alsius wisely fell silent.

When the chair arrived, Vargo handed the note to the runner. "Take this to Iascat Novrus. Tell him he's got till midnight if he's interested. Otherwise, don't bother."

The boy reached for the note, but Vargo didn't let go. "Wait."

Something in the nipper-cheeked runner's expression reminded Vargo uncomfortably of the boy he'd been—and of Iascat. The soft smile when he tried to call Vargo by the only first name he knew, and the bruised look when he forced Vargo to admit their fucking was just a way to get at Sostira's trove of information. Maybe one day Iascat would become like the rest of them... but aside from Renata, he was the only other person who looked at Vargo like he had value beyond his utility. It was a lie; they both knew it—but Vargo wasn't feeling quite vindictive enough to rip down the rest of Iascat's illusions just because he was pissed. Time and this fucking city would do it soon enough.

"On second thought," he said, "take it to Fadrin Acrenix."

Vargo would be the one nailed to the wall, but that felt right. He'd spent his entire life getting screwed by cuffs. What was one more night?

The Face of Balance

It took half a bell of pounding on Tanaquis's front door to wake Zlatsa. She blinked sleepily at Renata and said, with a lack of tact worthy of her mistress, "Do you know what time it is?"

"First sun. Yes. I need to speak with Tanaquis."

"Meda Fienola was out late last night. She hasn't risen yet."

I know she was out late. I was there.

Ren had spent the whole night pacing the streets, first heading back to Isla Traementis, then veering away when she realized she didn't dare go back yet. The fury that had possessed her faded over time, but it left fear in its wake. She didn't understand what had happened, and the only person who might explain it to her was Tanaquis.

She couldn't even tell whether it was the numinat's lingering effect or just natural consequence that she wanted to grab Zlatsa by the shoulders and shake her. "I wouldn't be here if it weren't an emergency. Wake her. Now."

Zlatsa brought her into the parlour and left her there for what seemed like an hour, though only one bell chimed. Finally, the stairs creaked again, and the maid appeared in the doorway. "You're to go up to her workshop."

The attic skylights flooded the room with early-morning light, gilding the shelves of books, reflecting too sharply off Tanaquis's telescope and the lapis-blue star chart enameled into one wall. Tanaquis sat in one of the overstuffed chairs, yawning. "Renata. You should have stayed last night; I wanted to talk to you. Now that—"

"*What was that?*" Renata's voice trembled: with exhaustion, with fear, with residual anger. "What did Diomen do to me?"

Tanaquis squinted blearily at her. Sleep still crusted the corners of her eyes. "The Pontifex? He did nothing. It was the eisar."

"The *what?*"

"It's what I wanted to talk to you about—the reason I brought you into the Praeteri. Now I can. Why don't you sit down?"

She must be looking truly distraught if Tanaquis was showing such concern. Renata's feet ached from too much time walking in fashionable shoes; she sank into a chair and wrapped her arms around her body.

Tanaquis sighed, rubbing her eyes clear. "You mustn't tell anyone what I'm about to share with you. Parts of it are supposed to be secrets held only by those who achieve the Great Mysteries—in fact, we take measures to make sure no one has a loose tongue. I've eased those bonds on myself, but if the Pontifex finds out, I suspect he will *not* be pleased."

"I can keep secrets," Renata said through her teeth. "Talk."

She forced herself to be patient, because she recognized the signs of Tanaquis sorting her thoughts into an order other people could comprehend. Finally Tanaquis said, "I told you the Illius Praeteri deal with the deeper secrets of numinatria. When most people think about channeling energy, they stop at the obvious things: light, sound, heat, and so forth. Life energy, for fertility or contraception or execution. That sort of thing.

"But there are more subtle types of energy. You recall how I sent Vargo into the realm of mind, when you were sleepless? Mirscellis's experiments with—"

Renata's palm slapped hard against the table, hard enough to rattle the books atop it. "I don't give a damn about Mirscellis. What happened to me didn't have anything to do with the realm of mind."

Tanaquis brushed a wisp of hair out of her face, unaffected by the outburst. "Quite right. No, last night Diomen led you to the Gate of Rage, and what you experienced there was the influence of eisar. They're a type of spirit, without physical form or individuality, an emanation of..." She trailed off, as if weighing how much scholarly explanation Renata would tolerate. If so, she read correctly that the answer was *not much*. "They're the energy of—feelings, I suppose you could say. Emotions."

"That numinat was controlling my *mind*?"

"Not controlling, no! Eisar have no power to force you to feel anything. They can only touch and amplify what's already there."

If Tanaquis meant that to be comforting, she failed utterly. Revulsion coiled in Ren's gut. Her life depended on her self-control; if that broke, she could ruin everything. Not only for herself, but for Tess, Sedge, the Traementis—everyone she cared about.

Tanaquis was still talking, trying to put out the fire with more words. "Emotional energies—the eisar—are *meant* to flow through us. It isn't good for them to be blocked, for the channels to be closed off. The point of the Praeteri rituals is to free them, so they can reach their natural end. Don't you feel better, having released that anger?"

Not in the slightest. Not with the damage it had done.

But in the moment...

Months of holding her tongue, biting down on all the truths she wanted to fling in Vargo's face. Forcing herself to smile at him as if all the warmth and trust he'd coaxed from her weren't rotting inside her heart. It had felt freeing to throw that burden away at last—if only she didn't have to live with the consequences.

"Diomen should have warned me," Renata said, her voice shaking again. "Not sprung it on me as a surprise."

"That was unconventional," Tanaquis admitted. "The Gates of Initiation require a certain degree of secrecy; ignorance, submission, and zeal can only really be tested by keeping you in the dark. But now that you've passed through the initiations, you should have been instructed before exploring the revelations. The Pontifex has mentioned a blessing he believes you carry; perhaps that spurred him to act more precipitously."

"He was more concerned with what has *stained* me. I can only assume you told him about the curse."

Renata was watching closely as she said it. Either Tanaquis was as good a liar as Vargo, or her surprise was genuine. "Not me. He spoke to you about that? How interesting. What did he say?"

Her head ached. Pressing cold fingers into her eyes, she said, "Tanaquis. You promised me this would help with finding the source of the curse—but so far, all it's done is make things worse."

"I'm sorry." Tanaquis's hands tugged her own down, hot against the chill of Renata's skin. She chafed them to bring some warmth. "I can only stretch the bindings I'm under so far. The Pontifex believes that if we give knowledge too freely, then initiates would feel they've gotten all they needed from the Praeteri. He doesn't want to lose your involvement in our society. But what I wanted to tell you is that I believe the Traementis curse was driven by eisar."

The eisar. Emotional energies. Like anger? Diomen had told her to focus on that, on her desire for vengeance against those who had wronged the Traementis. But even so . . . "How could that be?"

"How much do you know about how the various members of House Traementis died?" It seemed to be a rhetorical question, because Tanaquis kept talking. "Between you and me, quite a few of them brought about their own ends. Oh, not on purpose—they didn't seek death—but take Donaia's husband, Gianco. He ruined himself through his addiction to aža. With others it was carrying their greed too far, or unwise choice of lovers. All hells of their own making. That can't be caused by everyday numinatria, nor through imbuing. I am *very* curious to know if it can be done with pattern. But eisar numinata can affect the mind, making people act in certain ways. Destructive ones, even."

Ren scraped through her memories, trying to think if anything in her past felt like the rage that had overtaken her the night before. There was nothing that strong or immediate—it would have been impossible to overlook that—but perhaps something that had been slower, more subtle?

Diomen had spoken about the Gate of Desire; that must be one of the types of eisar. Hadn't it been her own desires that carried her into this situation? The decision to infiltrate House Traementis, the risks she'd taken to make that happen. Had all of that been due to the eisar? Not creating the urge, just feeding the hunger already in her heart?

But that still didn't explain *how* she'd become cursed. Tanaquis had chalked it up to blood—but Ren didn't have a blood connection to the family. No connection at all, until she was inscribed into their register.

She couldn't tell Tanaquis that part. "Assuming the curse was caused by eisar...does that mean one of the Praeteri cursed us?"

Tanaquis's brows rose, as if the possibility had never occurred to her. "We're not the only people to practice this kind of thing; there are similar sects elsewhere, primarily in the north. But in Nadežra— yes, I suppose it's logical for you to suspect them." Curiosity flared bright in her gaze. "I've been trying to figure out where pattern fits into all of this, how it can be reconciled with the order of the cosmos. And how it manages to interact with eisar—as clearly it *can*, given that you detected the curse with your cards, and your cards helped with its removal."

Renata stifled a sigh. Tanaquis would never let go of her belief that someday she would find a way to slot pattern into her well-organized universe. "I don't know. Pattern is a thing of intuition, revealing the connections between people—which is how I assume it worked to lift the curse—but there's no emotion involved. It's just... patterns." She lifted her hands, unable to give words to something she just *knew*.

Before Tanaquis could irritate her with another attempt to subsume pattern into the paradigm she knew, Renata added, "Regardless, I can't try now. I don't have a deck with me, nor the concentration to use one." She needed to sleep—and needed to tell Donaia and Giuna that she'd fallen out with Vargo. What would that mean for their partnership on the river numinat? When it came to business obligations, the law didn't care if they were on speaking terms or not.

Tanaquis touched her wrist again. "I *am* sorry that things went poorly for you last night. I promise, I have no desire to see you hurt. And if you'd prefer not to take part in any more Praeteri rituals, that's fine. You've gotten far enough for us to talk openly about this."

Renata laid her hand over Tanaquis's. "I do appreciate that you're trying to help. I—I need some time to think. We can talk more later."

The Shambles, Lower Bank: Lepilun 12

The half-collapsed building where the Black Rose waited was empty apart from herself and Gulavka. Arkady was the one who'd found it for the Rose and held on to Gulavka while this handoff was arranged; her kids kept watch nearby. The sudden and out-of-tune melody of a skipping song, drifting through the cracked walls, alerted Ren that the Vraszenians were approaching.

"You claim to be Ažerais's servant, but you betray her and her city just like the ziemetse," Gulavka muttered from where she knelt. "There is still time to do right by her. Let me go, and all the Faces will look kindly on you."

Ren ignored the bluster. She just waited, lounging in the room's one chair, as Dalisva entered with a man at her heels.

"Lady Rose," Dalisva said, nodding in respect. "Once again, we thank you."

Gulavka spat on the floor. "This creature is a—"

"Don't make me regret not gagging you," Ren said. "Bear in mind that your alternatives to this include Derossi Vargo and the Cinquerat. I'd say you're getting off lightly."

"You fool yourself only if you think there is a difference. Betrayers, all of y— *Urk!*"

Ren tied the gag's knot tightly to prevent Gulavka from pushing it off with her tongue. It didn't silence the noise, but at least it rendered her rhetoric incomprehensible.

Dalisva looked saddened by the necessity. "Heed not her bile. Truly you do the work of Ažerais in bringing this one to us. The Stretsko are by family loyalty moved; without her connections, Branek will have a harder time convincing others to follow his lead."

At Dalisva's nod, the man hefted Gulavka over his shoulder and carried her kicking from the tenement. Dalisva remained behind. "Would that you could bring us Branek himself," she said, with more than a hint of suggestion behind the wish.

Ren huffed out a laugh. "Not that I'll admit it in public, but I have limits. The best hope for dealing with Branek is to back the man he deposed." She held up one gloved hand before Dalisva could protest. "What you heard was false. Branek and his allies turned against Andrejek without cutting knot, then lied to everyone else to cover what they'd done."

Dalisva sliced her own hand through the air, as if cutting away a tangle. "Who betrayed whom is not my concern. From the start, the plan to destroy the amphitheatre was Andrejek's."

"And who do you want in charge of the Anduske—the man who made the plan but abandoned it, or the one who tried to fol-low through?" Ren began to pace, hands locked behind her back. "I know your answer is 'neither.' But *someone* is going to lead the Anduske; they won't vanish simply because you capture their lead-ers. If Branek falls to an outside force—even to me—that will only make him a martyr to his followers. Whereas if Andrejek exposes him for a traitor, not only he but his ideals will lose credibility."

"And how do you propose to bring this about?"

Ren couldn't hold back a sigh, remembering her own cards. The Face of Light, cautioning against hasty action. "It's going to take time."

The low ceiling and mildewed walls dulled Dalisva's bark of laughter. Then she touched her brow in apology. "Forgive me, Lady Rose. I know you will do all you can to slow Branek. But simply to slow him is not enough. We must stop the Anduske themselves, for the safety of all our people."

"*All* our people?" Ren's nerves sharpened at the phrase. "Forgive me, Ča Korzetsu, but we both know that isn't true."

The formal address brought Dalisva upright. "I only meant—"

"You meant that you've gotten complacent. Maybe not you specifically, but the ziemetse, and the other cities of Vraszan. You've come to accept that Nadežra is controlled by the Liganti—you don't *like* it, but it's been that way for two hundred years, so how could it be anything else? But there was a time when nobody had to pay to experience the Great Dream. When no outsider had the power to enact a scheme like Indestor's, which almost destroyed our connection to Ažerais. And you conveniently forget that Cinquerat control isn't something that happens once every seven years during the Great Dream, or just at the Ceremony of the Accords. The people here live with it *every day.*"

Ren wanted to blame that flood of words on the rage numinat Diomen had placed her in, but they might have burst out anyway. Dalisva knew there was a human woman under the mask, one who hadn't come to the city with the Vraszenian delegation last year. Ren didn't have to pretend to be some mystical spirit. And she was tired of feeling like the only "true" Vraszenians were the ones who didn't live in Nadežra—like the people here didn't count, except as tokens to capture in a game of hexboard.

But she wasn't the only one with strong feelings. "Have the Anduske not caused worse harm, to less effect?" Dalisva's fists were clenched, her face twisted with frustration. "The last great uprising was Elsivin the Red's, and what profit came from that? Whole kretse wiped out, the Isarnah punished for their assistance. The only changes were for the worse. Fifty years have passed, but the sanctions remain."

She was right—and also wrong. With an effort, Ren lowered her voice. "It's foolish to try the same thing over and over again, hoping for a different result. The Anduske fight, and they change nothing. The ziemetse refuse to fight, and they change nothing. What if everyone tried something new...like working together?"

Dalisva's frustration softened. Wistfully, she said, "Ah, if only the Ižranyi still lived. Is that not what everyone says? Without the clan of the dreamweaver, our fabric has pulled askew." She rubbed her face wearily. "Perhaps you are right, Lady Rose. To have a dream is not enough, though, is it? The ziemetse will not reach out; the Anduske will not reach out. Each scorns the other for the blood or the mud on their hands."

It was the same obstinacy Ren had seen far too much of in the Charterhouse lately. Seeing it among Vraszenians made her feel tired. The Rook had spent two hundred years fighting an endless battle against the corruption of the nobility. Was she doomed to be the first in a long line of Black Roses, waging an equally hopeless war?

Dalisva's smile did nothing to wipe away that image. "Perhaps in truth this is why Ažerais chose you, Lady Rose. To bridge the river that has divided us so long. I will pray to An Mišennir that it is so."

Better bring a big offering. The Black Rose was just a mask to hide a half-Vraszenian face. Neither the Anduske nor the ziemetse had any reason to listen to someone like her.

She abruptly wanted to be anywhere but there, looking at Dalisva's hopeful expression. "I'll let you know if I capture anyone else useful," Ren said, and strode out of the building without saying farewell.

Isla Stresla, Kingfisher: Lepilun 14

When Grey heard Renata's voice coming through the door of Ryvček's practice room, he almost turned around and left.

The problem wasn't him being there; everyone knew Ryvček had trained him. But Renata Viraudax was a busy woman, and the Black Rose equally so—yet Arenza Lenskaya kept finding the time to visit his house, usually when he wasn't there. Grey couldn't tell how much of that was sympathy for Alinka, grieving and overworked, and how much was concern over the twisted fate she'd seen for him in her cards.

He hadn't expected her to react so strongly to that. He almost wished he could undo his trick, or take back the suggestion that she lay the cards for him at all. But she'd patterned the *Rook*. What if she'd patterned Grey, when he wasn't around? Better to give her a false answer, making sure her gift didn't winkle out the truth from the other side. So he'd suggested it, and then when he sent her gaze skittering away during that last shuffle, he'd slipped two cards from the bottom of the deck into a gap near the top.

Every time he thought of that, he remembered her white-eyed fear, the harsh rasp of her breathing as she stared at something he couldn't see. The rigid tension of her hands in his own. Who knew; maybe it would have been as bad even if he hadn't interfered. Grey had known for a long time that his fate was a poisoned one. She might have had the same reaction, *and* uncovered that he was the Rook.

But having gone to those lengths, he needed to make sure he didn't undo their benefit. Which meant his best course was to be Captain Grey Serrado at her as firmly as possible. Dull, upstanding, and duty-bound, with no time for a life beyond the Aerie.

"You come for practice?" Ryvček said when he entered. "Good. The Vigil are brawlers with swords; no finesse. You could use a polish. Or quit that nonsense and be a duelist. Skill you certainly have, and these past months—djek. More duels than even I can fight. Alta Renata, your people have become as prickly as wet cats."

In his peripheral vision, Grey saw Renata seizing a chance to catch her breath. Despite her sleeveless fencing coat, the hair plastered to her brow was dark with sweat. Still, her voice was as cool as always when she said, "I'd forgotten you two know each other."

"Since before he called himself Grey." Ryvček grinned at the pained look Grey shot her. She and Donaia were the only ones left who remembered.

"Oh?" Renata said. "I confess, I did think 'Grey' was an unusual name."

"He's Kiraly. And not very creative." Ryvček racked her practice blade and mopped her face with a cloth. A yell issued from upstairs. She looked at the ceiling with a glare that could burn through the boards. "If those two cease not their arguing—"

Cutting off the common complaint, she winked at Grey. "The pains of living with cousins. I must deal with this. Serrado, why not put the alta through her paces? A student needs *many* partners to learn from." And with that, she vanished from the room.

Vengeance for all the times you *almost stumbled on her secret*, he thought—which didn't put him in charity with her.

"Is she that suggestive with everyone?" Renata asked as the door shut them in Ryvček's trap.

"Everyone she hasn't known since they were children. Leato and I were safe. Mostly," Grey grumbled, shucking his coat and tying his sleeves down with a pair of cords. He'd come intending to ask Ryvček a question, not to spar, but leaving now would only make Renata more curious. Taking up a practice sword, he gave it a few sweeps to get the feel of its balance. "What have you worked on so far?"

He listened with half an ear as Renata named off drills. She was further along than he'd expect from a beginner, but that made sense; he knew from when he'd ambushed her in her kitchen that she had instinct and experience already. Just no formal training, and no familiarity with swords.

So far as he knew, she still had Mezzan's Vicadrius blade. She deserved its fine craftsmanship more than that kinless bastard ever had, and it would be a pleasure to help her learn to use it well.

"Three moves," Grey said when she was done. "I'll call them, and you respond as fast as you can."

Like Vargo, her biggest flaw was her inability to judge measure. She was fine when attacking, lunging at Grey from a reasonable distance, but when it was her turn to defend, she retreated farther than necessary. "I know," she said with a grimace when he pointed this out. "I'm working on it, but—"

But her impulse was to get as far from danger as possible. *At least when fencing*, he thought. In social matters, she courted danger close enough to kiss.

He reminded himself to be a boring hawk and focused on correcting her technique in as dry a manner as possible. When he finally gave her a respite, she said, "I never thanked you for your assistance during my episode of sleeplessness."

Assistance. If the Rook hadn't sent her into a panic, forced her to confess her malady, then all but shoved her into seeking help, who knew how long she might have spent dying before she told someone other than Tess? But he hoped she wasn't referring to that.

Grey tugged his glove straight, as though her words didn't trouble him. "Eret Vargo and Meda Fienola solved the problem. All I could do was share what hadn't worked for the sleepless children."

The tightening of her lips at Vargo's name was faint but visible. He'd heard rumors of a rift between them; was the strain of her masquerade starting to bleed through? Renata said, "But Tanaquis spoke very highly of your attempts—in particular, the herbal remedies. Might I ask who your herbalist is?" She hesitated, then confessed, "Donaia isn't doing well. It isn't *that* kind of sleeplessness, but...nightmares. And her appetite is poor. The Traementis physician is attending her, of course, but I wonder if different methods might not produce better results."

You know damned well who my herbalist is. "My sister," he said, letting a little of his conflict drag his expression into a frown. Would Ren pretend to misunderstand his ambiguity, or would she slip and reveal that she knew Alinka was Grey's sister by marriage? "She traveled the river growing up, and had the benefit of learning from a variety of village healers."

Renata's expression grew stricken. "I'm sorry—I wasn't aware you had a sister as well. She might not want to attend to Donaia, especially if dealing with a grieving woman would remind her of her brother's death. Though..." Was that the hesitation of a real thought? Or an artfully staged pause? "It might help Donaia—might help them both—having the company of someone who understands."

"Alinka was Kolya—my brother's—wife." No need to fake the roughness of those words. If only he could loosen the hold of the grief that strangled him whenever he had to speak of it. "But are you looking for an herbalist for Donaia, or a companion? Alinka is good at the first, but you could easily find better. For companionship..."

It was like fighting with two blades, maintaining the fiction that he didn't know about Ren, about Arenza, about all the things the Rook knew, while trying to puzzle out the motives behind her words.

Perhaps she was merely making the suggestion out of concern for Alinka—and for Grey. She'd seen herself how much strain their current situation placed on everyone, even without Koszar's presence adding danger. Alinka was even talking about returning to her family. If she had more money, more stability, then perhaps she wouldn't take Grey's niece and nephew away when her kureč came for the next Great Dream.

"They've only met once, that I know of," he said, turning over the possibility as he spoke. "Era Traementis offered us her garden to dance the kanina for Kolya's passing. Besides, Alinka has her own children to care for. Their company might not be soothing for Era Traementis."

"We aren't the best judges of that," Renata pointed out. "But it might be worth proposing to them."

"True. Ask Era Traementis first; I wouldn't want to raise Alinka's hopes. Or hurt her if the era decides she doesn't want the company of a Vraszenian widow with a toddler and a . . . spirited little girl who's fond of biting." She'd bitten Arenza during the last visit, when she was refused a pattern of her own. He saw no sign of a bruise; no doubt Ren had taken care to hide that with cosmetics.

Chuckling, Renata lifted her blade again. "Now that it's decided . . . I'd love a chance to spar properly with someone other than Ryvček. Would you help me with my sleeves?" She nodded at two pieces of fabric laid over the weapons rack.

Grey retrieved the sleeves, then slid them up her bare arms, lacing them back onto the shoulders of the surcoat. Tess had sensibly included upward-pointing caps to cover the join, so the point of a blade wouldn't skid inside. Renata might have been able to lace them herself, but not easily. And Grey had seen her use flirtation as a tool before.

It had failed when she tried it on him at the Gloria. It was annoyingly more effective now that he knew the face behind the mask.

He kept his movements brisk and efficient, without being rushed... but still, he couldn't ignore the warmth of her skin, the breath ghosting over his hands as she observed his progress. Nor the pleasant tension it created inside.

When he was done, he said, "How easy do you want me to go on you?" Sparring would at least give him a reason for his unsteady breathing.

The corners of her eyes creased in amusement. "I have no doubt you can trounce me... but don't go *too* easy. I ought to learn something, after all."

Such as whether he fought like the Rook? Grey resolved to use orthodox Liganti style, and raised his blade.

Fortunately—though part of him immediately regretted it—Liganti-style fencing was a very proper affair, especially against someone who hadn't mastered it. The straight-armed stance kept them at a distance from each other, their blades flirting back and forth, their bodies never closing or passing the way the Vraszenian style was more prone to. Grey confined himself mostly to defense, deliberately leaving openings to encourage her to practice attacking. But after a while she fell into a predictable routine, and he decided to shake it up with a small surprise.

The next time she advanced, he counterattacked like he had before, coming in toward her throat, and she parried as she had before, deflecting him out to the side. Grey responded by dropping his point, stepping in close to seize her hand, and bringing his blade around to the back of her neck.

"Just because we don't often move in," he murmured in her ear, "doesn't mean we can't."

Djek. That sounded *far* too flirtatious.

He released her hand as if it had burned him, then backed away and bowed. "My apologies, alta. I should not have presumed."

"You owe me one for that fright," she said dryly, rubbing the back of her neck as if imagining a sharp edge there. "Perhaps you might do me a favor in recompense. Have you ever heard of someone named Alsius?"

He kept his repentant expression from faltering, but the sudden thud of his heart had nothing to do with exertion. That question was no accident. Whether it was this moment or something before it—some mistake he hadn't even noticed himself making—she *did* suspect. And she'd thrown that name at him when he was off balance, to see if he reacted.

"Alsius," he repeated, as if he'd never heard of such a person before today, let alone a spirit. "Someone you know from Seteris?"

"Not Seterin, despite the name. I overheard him talking, and his accent was Nadežran. Upper Bank, though." She shrugged and adjusted her grip on the blade. "I know a name and a voice is precious little to go on. But I'd like to know who the man is, and given your Vigil resources, I thought you might be able to find out."

It was good logic whether she suspected him or not. But dutiful, upstanding Captain Grey Serrado was a busy man. "I realize I found Gammer Lindworm, and she's a legend out of a fire tale, but that doesn't make me all-knowing. If I hear anything, though, I'll be sure to tell you. In the meanwhile—" He raised his blade. "Uniat."

Lacewater, Old Island: Lepilun 21

Vargo waited patiently in a private back room in the Talon and Trick, the card parlour he owned in Lacewater. Out in the front room, slumming delta gentry gambled away their coin on nytsa and sixes, surrounded by just enough Vraszenian trappings to make them feel like they'd gone somewhere exotic. In the room next to his, a szorsa read cards and her clients alike, sifting out any useful information she might pass along to Vargo.

He couldn't hear any of it, of course. This room was meant for meetings that shouldn't be overheard.

Even the bell towers couldn't pierce its walls. Vargo kept the clock in his bones, though, and he knew his guests were late. Normally he understood how to be patient, but tonight he kept catching his fingers drumming against the table or the head of his sword cane.

His fury over the incident with Renata had faded to a sullen glow, but it had left him shaken in other ways. She wasn't a woman prone to losing self-control...yet a few minutes in that numinat had been enough to tear her mask away. Vargo had blithely assumed he could advance in the Praeteri and keep his true intentions hidden, so long as he knew what to expect. Now he wasn't so sure.

By comparison, this felt easy. A simple bit of street politics, easily solved with fists and blades.

A disc set into the door rotated—a signal that took the place of knocking. Nikory opened it, admitting a man with a missing ear: Ardaš Ljunan, Sedge's contact. Vargo felt a brief surge of irritation at Sedge for coming down with a stomach flu earlier today. This would go more smoothly if both messengers were here.

Ljunan was alone. His wary gaze flicked over them all: Vargo, Nikory, Varuni, and Merapo, who led what was left of the Cut Ears. The room had no hangings anyone could hide behind, and Ljunan shouldn't be able to see the concealed exit. But even if he did, Vargo didn't have anyone lying in wait there. This meeting would be as honest as he got.

Satisfied, Ljunan turned and nodded to someone outside the room. A moment later, two others entered.

The woman was likely Idusza Polojny. She was holding the arm of a man, not quite steadying him, but ready to catch him if he faltered. Between that and the descriptions Vargo had, he believed the man was, in fact, Koszar Andrejek—and not some decoy.

"Have a seat," Vargo said, gesturing to the only other chair. Nobody else here was likely to want to sit; they preferred to be on their feet and ready to move. Andrejek, on the other hand, looked like he needed it.

He wasted no time in doing so, nor in speaking. "Ča Vargo. I hope you take no offense if I call you not by the title of the invaders."

"Given what I know of you, Ča Andrejek, I'd suspect you of insulting me if you did."

Andrejek chuckled. "Is it true you've captured Dmatsos?"

"Is it true you're not the knot breaker rumor claims?" That

had been the hardest part of arranging this meeting: Half his knot leaders threatened to cut off a finger before striking palms with an oath breaker. Ironic that Sedge had been the one to convince them Andrejek was no such thing.

By way of answer, Andrejek unbuttoned his collar and displayed an age-worn charm, knotted from many different pieces. "If this satisfies you, then let us begin. I suspect neither of us wishes to remain here any longer than we must."

Vargo liked a man who knew how to get down to business. "You think I can help you?"

"If not the Master of the Two Banks, then who?"

That was a title he'd not heard before, but Andrejek was a fool if he thought flattery and sympathy would soften Vargo's heart. "I should have been clearer. You think I have *reason* to help you?" He knew what Andrejek wanted from him, and suspected what he had to offer, but there was power in making the other man open negotiations.

Andrejek folded his hands atop the table. "The Crimson Eyes. Tserdev is none of mine, now or before I was overthrown, but I know something of her dealings. Shelter me and mine—someplace safer than where I hide now—help me get word to those who might support me if they knew the truth, and I can share that knowledge with you."

That investment came with risks. Andrejek's information might be outdated or worthless. He might hold something vital back to protect his own. And if any of Andrejek's detractors found out Vargo was sheltering him, he'd end up with twice the enemies.

But laid against that was the chance to get rid of the gutter rats gnawing at his shoes. Vargo could go on clashing with them at the borders...or he could take a risk and strike at their heart.

Like he'd done in Staveswater. And that had turned out *quite* well.

Vargo spat in his palm and held it out. "Your pledge to give me everything you know. In return, I'll give you safe harbor for as long as you need."

Andrejek showed no surprise at Vargo's bare hand, or that he struck the bargain in street style—which was originally Vraszenian style. Leaning forward, he returned the gesture. Vargo forced a smile through the unpleasant squelching of their palms.

A smile that fled when the door crashed inward.

"Koszar Andrejek! Submit yourself to the authority of the Vigil!"

Andrejek's and Vargo's curses overlaid one another. "You did this," Andrejek hissed, yanking his hand from Vargo's.

"Why would I—*Fuck it*." Defending himself could come later. Vargo flung the table toward the hawks flooding through the door and hurled himself in the other direction, toward the back wall.

Varuni already had the door open and dove through it. Behind Vargo, the room was dissolving into chaos; he caught a glimpse of Merapo going down to an elbow in the face, and then he was in the narrow passageway that led along the back of the Talon and Trick. The canal outside came right up to the parlour's foundation, so there was no room for hawks to surround the building and no reason for them to think they should . . . but it was narrow enough to leap, for anyone coming out the hidden door.

Once again, Varuni went first. There was just enough time for Vargo to hear her swear before his jump turned into a headlong sprawl, as somebody tripped him on landing.

He rolled to his feet and found Varuni pinned to the ground. But the people holding her were not in Vigil uniforms; instead they each wore a gold-and-black armband.

Fucking Mask-damned stingers—And to think, there was a time when Vargo had believed Ghiscolo's new Ordo Apis might actually be *useful* to him, giving the damned Stretsko something to gnaw on besides him.

He recognized the blade-nosed man who advanced on him. One of the Praeteri, clearly drunk on the power of his new job. "Mede Kaineto," Vargo said.

"*Eret* Vargo." In Kaineto's mouth, the title was a different kind of insult: one that said he wasn't worthy of bearing it. "What a *surprise* that you got caught up in this."

Vargo's membership in the Praeteri had to be good for something. Stepping closer and lowering his voice, he said, "An unfortunate accident, Brother Ludoghi. I had no idea that such criminals were hiding out in the vicinity. I'm certain you can set things straight."

Kaineto's smile stretched his already thin lips into invisibility. "Of course. But I can't go against my orders." He waved at his fellow stingers. "Take them to the Dockwall Prison."

Dockwall Prison, Lower Bank: Lepilun 21

Being in jail was a different experience now that Vargo had a title. Instead of being slung into a common cell with Nikory and the rest, he got a cell of his own, on the top floor of the prison. It had a chair and everything. And a window, through which a spot of bright color scuttled. ::It's taken me over an hour to get here. What in eleven hells happened?::

Vargo's cell wasn't one of the luxurious ones meant for long-term prisoners. Though deep, it was so narrow he could lean the chair back and rest his head against one wall while propping his feet on the opposite. He'd spent the past several bells finding the perfect point of equilibrium. "Clearly, I pissed off every god associated with Quarat. And Sessat."

::So you're going to test your luck further trying to break your fool neck?:: Peabody jumped, his landing softer than a fresh pork bun to the gut.

Vargo sat up once Peabody attained the safety of his shoulder. The crack of the chair legs hitting the floor echoed through the dank stone halls and reminded him that, however it might seem, he wasn't alone.

We were set up, he said silently. *Not by Andrejek, I don't think; all three Anduske got taken. But Dimiterro must have known we'd be there, because he brought the Vigil in force. And the stingers knew to wait at the bolt door.*

::You suspect Sedge?::

No, he didn't. Not really. But...*He was the go-between. And I'm starting to doubt he was sick tonight.*

::It could also be one of the Anduske, selling Andrejek out.::

Been a lot of that going around, Vargo thought sourly.

The sound of footsteps brought him to his feet. He boosted Peabody up to the windowsill—the guards might try to crush the spider if they spotted him—then turned and straightened his coat. Two hawks stopped at the narrow window in his door, which wasn't a surprise. They were followed by Ghiscolo Acrenix, which was.

Suddenly very glad Alsius was gone, Vargo said, "Your Mercy. To what do I owe the pleasure?"

"Eret Vargo. You have my deepest apologies for this inconvenience." At Ghiscolo's nod, one of the hawks opened the cell door. The other held out the coat, journal, and satchel that had been confiscated when Vargo was arrested. "I believe there was some confusion regarding your involvement in tonight's raid. But I'm certain your presence at that card parlour was unfortunate happenstance."

"Very unfortunate," Vargo agreed dryly, shrugging into his coat and checking his journal to make certain none of his notes were missing. That they'd been read, he had no doubt, but he didn't keep anything sensitive on him. Especially not after being frisked by the Rook. "What of my guards? They should all be protected by my military charter."

"They're being released as we speak."

"And the others? Was Koszar Andrejek really hiding in Lacewater this whole time?"

Ghiscolo sighed. "I doubt it. But it bodes ill for the owner of the Talon and Trick that Andrejek was caught there."

Vargo nodded solemnly. It would bode very ill for the owner... if such a person existed as more than a false name on a few deeds and contracts. But he had no doubt that Ghiscolo knew who really owned the place. And now Ghiscolo was letting Vargo know that he knew.

His freedom wasn't the usual reach-around the Praeteri gave to their brethren, succeeding with Ghiscolo where it had failed with Kaineto. House Acrenix had claws inside their gloves.

Smiling through his fury at how elegantly he'd been set up, Vargo thanked Ghiscolo and allowed himself to be escorted downstairs to wait for his people to be released from the communal cells. He silently took note of the prison's guards and defenses as he walked through its halls.

He wasn't the only one who'd been betrayed. And there was more than one way to get someone out of jail.

Though he was going to need some help.

Isla Indestor, the Pearls: Lepilun 24

Wisps of melody drifted in through the windows as Ren crept through the Essunta townhouse. She had an innocent excuse for leaving the party—a need to use the private—and a plausible one for being not where she should be if someone caught her, in the form of a badly concealed intent to meet an unnamed suitor. But she hoped not to have to use the latter, because she was headed for the narrow servants' stair that led to the roof, and that was a decidedly out-of-the-way place for a tryst.

At least, the sort of tryst most people would imagine. Ren opened the small door and ducked out into the hot summer night.

"I came this close to pinning you against the tiles," an amused voice said behind her.

"And I came this close to thinking I'd guessed wrong—that the message I left for you about this party *didn't* sound like an invitation to do something dramatic." Ren turned to face the Rook, whose coat hung slack in the windless night.

"You think I do this for fun?"

She cocked her head, studying him. Arms crossed, shoulders tense. "I don't think it's what drives you, no. But...I do think you enjoy it, some of the time."

He didn't answer that. "So what's driven Alta Renata out of the lamplight this evening? Bored with noble games?" His words were light as a rapier, and their edge just as sharp.

She hated it when he turned that sharpness against her. Most of the time when they encountered each other, his flirtatious manner rose to the top, and she answered in kind. But then something would set him on edge or remind him that she was a noble now. It didn't matter that she hadn't grown up among the cuffs and had spent the last few months feeding him information from the inside—even setting up that chance for him to search Vargo, she still didn't know for what. When all was said and done, she'd been adopted into the Traementis. That put her among the Rook's traditional enemies.

Out of habit, she'd been speaking in Renata's accent, because she was in Renata's clothing. Now she dropped it, shifting away from the door lest a servant hear them talking. "I need your help with something. It's urgent."

The tension eased. With a tilt of his hood, he invited her farther down the narrow, fenced widow's walk that ran the length of the house. "If your 'something' is tonight, I'm afraid I'll be a bit occupied. But if it can wait until tomorrow..."

"Two nights from now. You heard about the arrests in Lacewater?" At his nod, she said, "Then here is the part you likely haven't heard. Caerulet calls for them to be executed *de Ninate*."

It stopped him mid-pace. That Andrejek, Idusza, and Ljunan would be found guilty and executed was no surprise—but it had been decades since anyone was condemned to die *de Ninate*. Passing that sentence required a four-person majority in the Cinquerat, including the support of the Iridet seat, because it meant using numinatria to kill the victim.

Slowly. Agonizingly. As a spectacle for the crowd.

The Rook's answer came as a low growl. "So as usual, the Cinquerat will deal with its problems by tossing them into a furnace numinat. Only this time it's people instead of paperwork." The iron railing creaked under the force of his grip. "What's your plan?"

He hadn't known about the *de Ninate* sentence. Ren only knew because she'd overheard Scaperto ranting at Donaia. But he agreed so readily, she wondered if he'd been considering his own rescue anyway. Another stitch in the fabric of her suspicions...because Serrado had worked with Andrejek to stop the riots and prevent the bombing.

Ren said, "I think I can arrange for a gap in the guard at the Dockwall Prison. But a one-person job this is not, especially since Andrejek hasn't fully recovered from his injuries." The old ones, or the new ones he'd taken during the arrest.

The Rook made a skeptical noise. It might have been insulting if it weren't also warranted. She'd been a Finger and a con artist, but it was a long way from pulling a street hustle to infiltrating the most heavily guarded prison in Nadežra. "I'm glad you think so highly of both me *and* yourself, but I don't think this is a two-person job, either."

It wasn't. And she should have admitted that up front, but she'd been afraid he would refuse. Or laugh in her face. He still might.

"Vargo wants the Black Rose's help in breaking them out."

He'd called the meeting as soon as he had been released from the Dockwall. And even in the guise of the Black Rose, facing him had made her gut twist into knots. He and Renata hadn't met in person since that disastrous night in the temple, conducting all their business by chilly letter. But with the Rose, his coldness was directed at the problem: how to not only break into the Dockwall Prison, but get out again with three fugitives in tow.

She could read a thousand meanings into the Rook's silence. When he spoke, his tone was far too level. "After he worked so hard to land them in there? Eret Vargo needs to make up his mind."

Ren couldn't blame him for assuming that—not when she'd wondered the same herself. "Their meeting was for alliance against the Stretsko. I had Sedge act as their go-between. He says Vargo is in an honest rage at what happened, and Sedge is my brother. I believe him."

It wasn't her faith in Vargo's anger that persuaded her, though, nor even her faith in Sedge. "Will he profit from freeing them?

Yes—but in the end, I care not. I cannot stand by and let them be killed. And I hope you cannot, either."

From the Pearls and Eastbridge came the sound of bells ringing second earth. Only a thin band of deep blue limned the horizon; the rest of the sky was as dark as the shadows within the Rook's hood.

"I have to go. The fireworks are scheduled to start soon," he said, vaulting over the rail of the widow's walk.

Her shoulders sagged with disappointment, but his next words snapped them tight. "Tell Vargo the Black Rose will have the Rook's support. And that he'll taste the Rook's steel if he so much as *thinks* of playing us foul."

Ren rocked back on her heels. He wanted her to *tell* Vargo? She'd been assuming she would have to keep his aid secret. If he even agreed in the first place, which she'd doubted. But it seemed he cared enough about the Anduske to grit his teeth and work along-side Vargo.

Or else he trusted *her* that much.

A spot of warmth blossomed beneath her ribs as the Rook crouched into a controlled slide down the tiled rooftop, catching his bootheel on the edge to stop his fall. One parting instruction floated up to her as he dropped. "When you go back down...stay clear of Mede Essunta."

What did he have planned? Her mind spun possibilities as she drew Renata's persona around her once more, as she sneaked back into the house, as she explained to a confused maid why she was in an upstairs hallway.

Outside, Mede Essunta's guests were sipping chilled wine, watching as he stepped onto a small podium and began what was sure to be a long-winded and self-important speech about the his-tory his house had of administering Nadežra's firework charter.

"Can we stand by the fountain?" Renata asked once she found Giuna and Parma. "I don't know how you endure this heat. I think I might sizzle away into a puddle if I don't get some cool water on my face."

As they moved away from the podium and down the path,

Essunta called for the fireworks to begin. Renata dearly wished to look around, to see if she could spy a moving shadow. She held her breath along with the rest of the crowd. Waiting, but not for the same surprise.

Nothing happened.

Whispers rose from the restless crowd. Essunta shot a worried glance at Eret Fintenus, his new patron, and shouted again at the barge crew on the river.

Still, nothing happened.

Essunta abandoned all pretense of calm and screamed, spittle flying, that he would see them all doing hard labor in the fields if they didn't get the fireworks started. Only then did a voice drift down from one of the riverfront house's balconies.

"Don't blame them," the Rook said from his perch on the rail, twirling something in one hand that looked more like a baton than his rapier. "I've heard it's hard to light black powder once it's been wetted down."

"*You*—you *dare!*" Essunta sputtered.

The Rook laughed. "I have it on excellent authority that I not only dare, I *enjoy* doing this. The question is, how do *you* dare, Mede Essunta? When you've demonstrated less responsibility with fire than a child."

He paused a moment to let the crowd murmur questions to each other. What could he mean? Criminal he might be, but the Rook never acted without cause.

"Fontimi should take notes," Parma muttered, sounding more amused than affronted. "He plays the Rook in the Theatre Agnasce's productions. His flair for the dramatic pales next to this."

Everyone fell silent when the Rook stood, balancing atop the rail. "You seem puzzled, Mede Essunta. And yet, didn't you have Derossi Vargo plant black powder at the Fiangiolli warehouse, on Mettore Indestor's orders? And then didn't you and Era Novrus arrange for Vargo to set it off?"

The murmurs spiked in volume. Ren's blood ran cold. *I'm supposed to tell Vargo they're working together—after this?*

The Rook's voice carried over the noise. "Deny it all you want, but we both know the truth. And I'm tired of taking the blame for the deaths *you* caused. You want fireworks? Allow me."

A spark lit the shadows, flaring red as the Rook touched it to the baton and pointed it toward Essunta.

There was a general dive for the shrubbery as everyone around Essunta realized what the Rook held. Essunta himself hit the ground—just as the Rook had given him time to do. It meant the arc of the firework didn't take him in the chest, but instead burst in a shower of glittering flame over his head.

Essunta shrieked as the sparks ate into his clothing and seared his covering hands. It wouldn't kill him...but Ren, watching dispassionately, knew it would leave scars. Poetic justice: the hallmark of the Rook.

She didn't bother to look up. By now the Rook would be gone.

Instead she comforted a distressed Giuna as best she could. And turned her thoughts to Dockwall.

10

The Mask of Chaos

Dockwall Prison, Lower Bank: Lepilun 26

The Rook lay in darkness, listening to the splash of oars and the steady pace of his own breath, marking time.

In, out. Voices from right above his head. Vargo's people—and that was the first thing he didn't like about this plan.

In, out. A more distant call, half masked by splashes echoing off stone. The second thing he didn't like: having to put his faith in Ren's assurances that the man on watch at the Dockwall Prison's river gate would let them pass. It wasn't that he doubted Ren herself…but she hadn't explained how she'd persuaded Scaperto Quientis to assist in this plan. Which version of her had persuaded him? Renata? The Black Rose? Arenza?

In, out. When he breathed too deeply, his shoulder brushed the one next to him. And that was the third thing he didn't like. Because a hammer named Ren had pinned him against the anvil of Grey Serrado's moral compass, and the result was this: him lying under the false bottom of a river smuggler's scow, packed in like a salted herring next to the man who'd murdered his brother, all to rescue a trio of Vraszenian dissidents who had very little to do with the Rook's mandate.

The cargo loaded into the scow muffled the voices, but the tenor of the conversation above was bored and routine. Then the scow began moving again, through the river gate and into the moat that divided the prison from its outer wall. Sweat ran down the Rook's face and throat from the stuffy air, but he held still until the scow stopped again, rocking gently on the current, and someone popped open the concealed hatch.

Because he was in the middle, Vargo had to scramble out before the other two could move. Ren went next, masked as the Black Rose, and the Rook came last. He found Vargo standing a wary distance away, mopping at his own face with a lace handkerchief. Tonight, that was the only sign of the nobleman about him. The rest was nondescript clothing, one visible knife, and undoubtedly several more the Rook couldn't see. And—according to Ren—the spider, riding somewhere hidden.

Vargo eyed the Rook with the expression of a man who expected this improbable partnership to end with a blade in somebody's back. "What now?"

This part would be even worse than the smuggler's hole. "We hide while your people unload the goods," the Rook said, leaping from the scow to the crumbling lip of the Dockwall's foundation. A century ago when it was new, the prison rose tall on a small islet of its own, with a numinat to keep it dry. But numinata failed over time, broken down by the flaws in their construction, and only the Point stood unchanged against the River Dežera's slow hunger. The bank had become nothing more than a tumble of river-worn foundation stones and fill, a desperate attempt to fortify the place against the rot. *Not unlike Nadežra itself,* he thought grimly as he spread his coat wide.

Vargo and the Rose blinked at his coat, then exchanged a look. "You're joking," they said in tandem.

If only. "Do I look like I'm joking?" the Rook snapped. "The shadows aren't thick enough to hide three of us on their own. Now hurry up. And keep quiet."

Ren moved first, crowding up under his arm like a barnacle, which gave her a moment to tap out a warning that Vargo and his invisible companion were plotting.

"If you bring that spider of yours, we'll find out if it can swim," the Rook said.

Vargo hesitated on the lip of the scow before reaching behind his neck to pass something to one of the disguised rowers.

Ren's chuckle was swallowed by the depths of the Rook's coat. Then Vargo was on the bank at his other side, and once again the Rook had to cozy up to his enemy.

The foundations stood exposed to the guard turrets along the outer wall, with only a few inconveniently situated hiding spots. The Rook and his two conspirators had been let off at one of those, nearest to the storage rooms on the administrative side of the building. While the scow drifted toward the loading dock, they crept in tandem along the rocks under the concealment of the Rook's coat.

"Is this an embroidered numinat?" Vargo whispered, testing the fabric like he was some altan in a tailor's shop. "I have to get myself one of these."

"You'd die making it." The Rook restrained the urge to elbow Vargo into the moat. "By all means, go ahead and try."

Pressed tight together, the three of them waited while guards thoroughly checked the manifest and the vessel, including the hole the trio had just been hiding in. Then the rowers began hauling cargo onto the dock, to be taken away by the kitchen staff and guards.

Two sacks landed easily on the planking. Then, exactly as planned, the rigged stitching on the third sack gave way, and black-and-white beans cascaded everywhere. In the chaos that followed, three shadows slipped through the service door, through the storeroom, and into the empty kitchen.

It wasn't the Rook's first visit to the Dockwall—he sometimes found it beneficial to question the inmates—so he led the way, the other two silent at his heels, except when they came to one of the numinata warding the doors. Vargo could deal with those more elegantly than the Rook could, leaving less trace of their passage.

Until they reached the door leading to the prison cells themselves. A door that had what appeared to be a brand-new numinat inlaid on its surface. One of a type the Rook had never seen before.

Well, they'd brought Vargo for a reason. The Rook gestured at the numinat. "Take care of that."

"My pleasure," Vargo said, in a tone that indicated anything but.

"Only one problem: I know that design. It has to be disabled from both sides at once."

Dockwall Prison, Lower Bank: Lepilun 26

Any other time, Vargo would have taken deep satisfaction at eliciting what he assumed was a murderous glare from the Rook. Unfortunately, they had limited time to linger here, so he merely said, "You know this place best. Any other ideas?" and was proud that it came out only a *little* smug.

After a moment of silence, the Rook sighed. "There's a dumbwaiter shaft. But the ropes aren't exposed, the walls are greased to prevent climbing, and the boards would snap under a person's weight. Scaperto Quientis has been making some regrettably effective improvements in his prisons."

"I can reduce the weight on the board. Don't know if it would hold you or me, but..." Vargo raised a brow at the Rose.

She'd been silent since the all-too-brief meeting to plan this infiltration—a meeting that began with her announcing that she'd recruited the fucking *Rook* of all people to help. Followed by the news that one of Quientis's own people would be turning coat on their behalf. As grateful as Vargo was for the assistance she provided, he didn't like the so-called Black Rose having so many layers he couldn't see.

He suspected there was a human underneath that mask, though. And like a sensible human, she hesitated before nodding. "Tell me what to do on the far side."

"The only hard part is the timing." Vargo pointed at one segment of the metal numinat, an arc sliced into Uniat's circle. "If I take that out right now, the door will warp and jam in its frame. Same on the other side. But if we take them both out at the same time, the door will open. Tap twice once you're there; I'll tap back three times, and then on the fourth beat we'll disarm it."

"I'll stand guard," the Rook said, and glided away.

Great. Vargo had to trust the Rook to watch his back while he shoved his upper half into the dumbwaiter that conveyed trays of watery porridge to the prison floors, leaving his ass hanging out like a target. The Rook didn't kill...but would he balk at letting Fulvet's guards do it for him? Vargo being caught breaking *into* a prison was the kind of justice the Rook might find amusing.

But that would leave the Anduske leaders trapped. This plan was complicated enough without adding a double cross into the mix. Not that Vargo hadn't arranged a few contingencies, just in case.

The Rose held a lightstone inside the dumbwaiter so Vargo could see what he was doing—but that meant he had to keep his thoughts carefully inside his head while he consulted with Alsius on the design. *Any problems outside?* he asked as he began to chalk lines.

::None so far. But if you expect to ride back out on the scow, you'd better move quickly. They're almost done unloading.::

As soon as I'm finished here. At least Vargo wasn't expected to go all the way to the cells. He hadn't seen any numinata in that area as he was escorted out. His next job was to create a distraction outside, if one proved necessary.

He knew better than to rush the inscription, but he wasn't so cautious backing out of the dumbwaiter. Vargo cracked his head against the lintel and bit down on a curse. A muffled noise came from the Rose. Was she laughing at him? He couldn't tell through the lace. "Your chair, alta," he muttered, gesturing at the opening.

The mock courtesy made her stiffen. She merely climbed into the dumbwaiter, though. The board creaked beneath her reduced weight but held, and Vargo closed the door. Then he began cranking the handle for all he was worth.

Dockwall Prison, Lower Bank: Lepilun 26

Ren winced as the dumbwaiter compartment juddered into motion. Its rise snuffed out the light in the shaft, leaving only the creaking of ropes and the squeaking of pulleys in the darkness. Those sounds echoed up and down the shaft loud enough to be an alarm all their own. She crouched, ready for whoever might wait on the other side of the low door above.

At the first crease of light in the dark passage, her boot shot out. Bone crunched under her heel, muffling the grunt of the unlucky guard. Lunging out, she grabbed him by the collar and twisted him into a choke hold before he could shout an alarm.

Which might have worked—except the dumbwaiter platform kept rising, leaving her a few inches and a few moments away from being bisected. Releasing the man, she pushed off and rolled to safety, the edges nipping at her toes as she pulled them clear.

She landed in a service room, facing an angry, bloody-nosed guard.

This, not Ryvček's elegant fencing, was what Ren was made for. She didn't bother rising; she just kicked hard against his ankle, then his knee. The guard yelped as his leg gave out, and she prayed nobody heard the scuffle, but one problem at a time. Ren caught him in a new choke hold as he dropped, and held it just long enough for him to go limp.

But now she had to figure out what to do with him. She had enough cord to bind him, but a gag wouldn't silence him, and he was already stirring.

Through the open doors of the dumbwaiter, she saw the platform creaking downward again, Vargo returning it to its starting position.

Ren moved fast, tying the guard's hands and stuffing a wad of cloth into his mouth. Then she heaved him into the dumbwaiter and shut the doors to muffle the sound of the platform snapping and crashing to the floor below.

Let Vargo and the Rook deal with that.

In the corridor outside, she heard a low murmur of noise from the cells where convicts destined for the penal ships were kept. For a brief instant, she entertained visions of breaking them all out—but causing that much chaos would only make the rest of the job harder. Better to strike at the ships themselves before they set sail.

Now you're thinking like the Rook. Maybe the two of them could discuss that idea once they'd finished with their current recklessness.

Ren slipped downstairs to the door and pressed her ear to it. On the far side, everything seemed quiet. That meant either the guard was dealt with and Vargo was waiting...or something had gone very wrong while she was busy.

Only one way to find out. Ren tapped twice and waited, her hand hovering above the removable piece of the numinat.

A moment later, more tapping replied, in a steady beat. *Uniat, Tuat, Tricat—*

On Quarat she pulled it free, wincing as a small shock jolted her hand.

The door swung open.

Dockwall Prison, Lower Bank: Lepilun 26

The cold-room was a safe enough place to stash the guard who'd come crashing down the dumbwaiter shaft. The Rook even left a chilled flank of goat meat wrapped in a cloth to leech away the pain of the man's busted nose—after sticking him with a dart tipped with an imbued sedative, to make sure there weren't any disturbances. By the time the Rook rejoined Vargo, the door was already open, the Rose waiting on the far side with a cocky grin.

"Thanks for the gift," the Rook said, returning her grin. "And so nicely wrapped. I didn't get you anything."

"You're giving me an entertaining evening. Isn't that enough?"

"Do you flirt with everyone?" Vargo muttered, which almost made the Rook laugh despite his doubled hatred of the man.

"Not everyone," he said. *Only her.* "I have no interest in flirting with you."

"I'm devastated," Vargo said, deadpan. "If you're just going to ignore me, then I have a distraction to arrange."

And the Rook had an escape to see through...among other things. "Go. We'll take it from here."

Vargo didn't need to be told twice. As he disappeared down the corridor, the Rook nodded for the Rose to follow. Together, they made their way up the stairs.

This was where the Cinquerat kept their important prisoners: those of high rank, and those they couldn't risk in the mass cells. Either because they might try to organize a breakout, or because they'd be murdered by their fellow inmates. The three Anduske had no rank to recommend them, but both of the latter risks were distinctly possible.

There was no way into this area that didn't pass by the first and largest cell. And from the bars in its door came a tenor voice. "If I shout for the guards and they catch you, there's a proper dinner in it for me."

"Eret Contorio," the Rook said softly. "It's been a while."

"Two years. What happened? Did you decide this information cow had dried up, and there was no more milk to be had from her?" There was a shelf below the bars, meant to hold trays of food; the man in the cell rested his elbows on it. His face was as pale as uncooked dough from years spent in a room with only one high window; his once-trimmed beard had gone to seed, grey rooting amid the dusty brown like weeds.

Ryvček was the reason Contorio had been in Dockwall for the last twelve years, the only survivor of a noble house that once held the Argentet seat in the Cinquerat—and the medallion that went with it. But although she'd put him here, she spoke of him with odd fondness. Ryvček had always enjoyed interweaving flirtation with her work as the Rook. Even flirtation with nobles.

But Grey had never met the man, and flirtations soured when left too long unattended. "For the Rook, I'd get much more than one proper dinner," Contorio said. "A whole *month* of them, at least."

"Forgive me for intruding," the Rose said, "but I'm clearly the stranger here. To whom do I have the honor of speaking?"

The Rook heard a thread of Renata's courtesy in that question. It was a ploy, and an effective one; Contorio prided himself on retaining his nobility despite his long imprisonment. "Eret Octale Contorio, last of my house," he said, sketching a small bow. "And you must be the Black Rose my guards so love to gossip about."

She feigned modesty. "My name has reached this far? I wonder what you've been told."

"Mostly that you're the spirit of the Wellspring of Ažerais. Based on that, I'll venture a guess that you're here for the new Vraszenian prisoners." Contorio's gaze cut sideways to the Rook. "I should have known better than to think he was here for *me*."

It wasn't the kind of bitterness that refused reconciliation. On the contrary, it begged for it. Contorio didn't want to call the guards; he wanted to be given a reason not to. A reason to believe the Rook hadn't simply used him and discarded him.

I'm not Ryvček. He couldn't fully mimic her panache, nor her depth of history with this man. If he failed to talk their way past this obstacle, he had another sedative dart tucked into the palm of his glove. But he would try talking first.

"Apologies for my absence," he said, stepping closer to the bars. "Quientis has made this place harder to infiltrate. But if you tell us which corridor the Anduske are being kept in, I pledge to come back and play hexboard with you again."

Contorio's eyes gleamed. "I persuaded one of the guards to bring me a book on strategy. I wager I could beat you now."

He definitely could beat *this* Rook—but that wouldn't be the one who visited him. "We'll see about that when next I'm here."

The Rose drifted closer. "I'd challenge you to a game of nytsa myself, but we left someone tied up downstairs, which means a clock is ticking. Which way should we go?"

"Nytsa, hmm?" Contorio didn't seem much moved by her urgency. "How Vraszenian of you. Tell me, Black Rose...are you really the spirit of Ažerais's wellspring?"

Her pause was so brief, the Rook suspected only he noticed it. "Not exactly," she said. "But I am born of Ažerais's Dream."

Contorio's smile was oddly hesitant. "Good enough. Will you do something for me as well?" When she nodded, he said, "Bless me. In Ažerais's name."

The Rook was glad for the shadows of his hood, which hid his surprise. Contorio was as Liganti as they came, his blood pure register ink all the way back to the northern continent. No Vraszenian had ever darkened his lineage.

As if Contorio could feel the Rook's disbelief, he said defensively, "I was born in Nadežra, wasn't I? It's foolish to ignore the local divinities. And—well. My usual gods have had twelve years to get me out of here, and see how much they've done. I dream of freedom, and Ažerais is a goddess of dreams. Why not seek her blessing?"

Freedom—something the Rook had never offered him. To the best of his knowledge, Contorio had never asked. As if he knew there was a limit on how far any friendship between the Rook and a noble could go.

An uncomfortable thought, with the heir of House Traementis standing right there.

"Ažerais is a goddess of pattern," the Rose said. "But every person has more than one future: the good, the ill, and that which is neither. May you see the Face and not the Mask."

Contorio nodded again, lifting his chin like it might keep a tear from spilling. "Thank you. They're down the left-hand corridor. Are you planning on hitting the guards over the head?"

"If we have to," the Rook said.

Contorio frowned. "Fulvet's been hiring a higher class of guard lately. They're much better fellows than the previous lot, and don't deserve cracked skulls. Hide over there—I'll distract them for you."

Dockwall Prison, Lower Bank: Lepilun 26

Ren had to give credit where it was due. Octale Contorio put on a splendid performance as a finicky, demanding nobleman who would not relinquish one sliver of his rank just because he was imprisoned. It was clearly a role he'd played before; the guards' responses as they came to his summons were weary and long-suffering, without a hint of suspicion.

It was a damn sight better than having the Rook be the distraction. By now he was well on his own way out of the prison, going to set up the route by which Ren and the Anduske would escape. He'd left her with four pieces of metal bent almost in a circle, each with a length of rope tied through one end and looped to hook over the other. Ren would have sworn the sack they came out of wasn't big enough to hold all four. *Another mystery of the Rook, I suppose.*

"Flash your lightstone when you're ready," he'd told her. "And then stand back."

She found the cells with the Anduske easily enough. But to her dismay, all three prisoners were lying motionless on the floor. One at least needed to be able to walk well enough to support someone else; otherwise she wouldn't be able to get them out.

Unlike the door downstairs, these lacked numinata protecting the locks, but Ren took the precaution of oiling the hinges before she began trying skeleton keys. The sixth one turned, and she eased the first door open just far enough to slide through.

The huddled figure didn't even twitch when Ren touched their shoulder. In the dim light, she couldn't tell who was under the tangle of filthy, half-unraveled braids. "I'm a friend," she whispered. In Vraszenian, even though it was a risk—she sounded more like Arenza in that language.

The figure moaned and turned under her hand. It was Andrejek, barely recognizable through the bruises and splits in his skin. "No . . ." he mumbled.

He was only semiconscious. Ren clenched her teeth, debating. Then she rose, pulled the cell door nearly to, and tried the next one over.

Ljunan had roused and backed into the corner of his cell. Ren held up her hands, with the lightstone in one to show her face— or rather, her black lace mask. "Thank the ancestors," he breathed when he saw her.

"Can you walk?" she asked. At his nod, she said, "Take these medicines and try to get them down Andrejek's throat. He knows you." Though right now she was more worried about him not being able to swallow than him fighting back.

Into the corridor again, and the door of the third cell. Ren glanced through the window before sliding her key into the lock—and realized the third figure was gone from the floor.

Instead of opening the door, she whispered as loudly as she dared. "I am the Black Rose of Ažerais. May the Masks curse me through nine lifetimes to come if I mean you harm."

That was enough to make Idusza edge into view. Half her face was veiled with dried blood, matting her hair and gluing one swollen eye shut, but she looked no less fierce for that. "How came you here?"

Ren briefly considered a mysterious answer, then discarded it. "With the help of Vargo and the Rook—working together."

After a beat, Idusza said, "Miracle enough for me. Get us out of here."

Dockwall Prison, Lower Bank: Lepilun 26

Stuffed once more into the scow's hidden compartment, Vargo counted the moments until the rougher water said they'd exited the river gate into the main channel.

From above him came Ladnej's voice. "We're going to be picking beans out of this thing for years to come."

Smuna's response was a snort. "Optimistic of you, love, thinking this bucket will last the winter."

She had a point. Vargo was fairly certain water was seeping in below him—or maybe that was just sweat. But at least Ladnej's uncle owned a smuggling scow, however leaky; that and his connections to the merchants who supplied the Dockwall had made this part of the plan something that could pass for feasible.

It *was* water, Vargo found when he climbed out. The wet fabric made his skin crawl. Yanking off his coat with a resigned sigh, he tossed it into the scow. "Take this thing out to Turtle Lagoon and scuttle it. Your uncle will have a replacement next week."

Once Ladnej and Smuna pushed off, he swiftly made his way along the Dockwall's north perimeter. From here he couldn't see the rooftop, but Arkady had kids loafing about a nearby inn to keep watch.

A quick glance at the washing line draped across a balcony confirmed only pale linens, no banner of red to indicate a problem. Vargo ducked behind the tilted bulk of a dilapidated sedan chair that had conveniently been abandoned against the wall earlier that evening. The shadows of the frame hid a numinat missing only a focus and a final swipe of charcoal. Cupping a lightstone in his hand, Vargo made a last-minute check to ensure nothing had disturbed the lines since he'd scribed them. The basic shape of the numinat was easy enough; pulling raw power from the Lumen always was. The complexity lay in the recursive loops that would give him a few precious seconds to run after he set the focus.

A moment later, a colorful blot landed on his head. *I expected you to be in the scow,* Vargo said silently.

::Too many tromping boots. Safer to go over the wall. I take it things went well?::

Vargo had made it out unbetrayed. By his recent standards, that was already a success. He was hoping for more, though. *Ask me when we're back in Eastbridge.*

::Do you think the Rook knows? About me?::

Keeping one eye on the washing line, Vargo sat down to wait. *Twice now he's deliberately gotten rid of you, and he locked you in my bedroom when he broke in. But he hasn't tried to crush you.* Vargo shuddered at the prospect.

::So...we assume he does, and take precautions?::

I don't know what to assume. Two days ago he would have assumed the Rook would eat glass before he worked with Vargo, and see how accurate *that* had been.

They were still enemies, though. Vargo wasn't about to forgive the Rook for accusing him of starting the Fiangiolli fire in front of every noble in the city, or for humiliating him in front of Renata. But then, he'd never had the nobility's good opinion to lose—or Renata's—so what did that matter?

A creak drew Vargo's attention. One of Arkady's kids leaned out the inn's window to tie a red rag to the laundry line. Something was happening inside the prison—something troubling enough that it called for a distraction.

Time to move.

::We could still walk away. Have the backups you put on the south wall pluck the Anduske while the Dockwall guards and the hawks tangle with the Rook and the Rose.::

Vargo's hand hesitated for a moment before he dug soft wax, a chop, and charcoal out of his inner pocket. The body-warmed wax took the chop imprint nicely.

"No, let's let this run and see how it plays out. I have my compass, my edge, my chalk, myself. I need nothing more to blow the shit out of the cosmos." Charcoal blackening his fingers, he closed the circle.

And ran like hell.

Dockwall and Kingfisher: Lepilun 26

Ren heard the rising voices as she gripped Andrejek's good leg and pushed him upward, helping Idusza lever him through the hatch that led to the prison roof. *Djek. Someone found the guard.* Or the broken dumbwaiter. Or they'd caught sight of the Rook—no, that was the least likely. And she prayed it wasn't true, because if the Rook was still inside the prison, then she and the others had no way out.

With a grunt from Idusza and a muffled sound of pain from Andrejek, he was through. Ren waved for Ljunan to follow, then swarmed up the ladder and shut the hatch behind her. It would at least delay any pursuers.

Much good may it do us. The hatch wasn't guarded, because there was no way on or off the roof. Any prisoner who escaped up here would eventually be shot by the crossbowmen on the wall or simply left to starve. No one could survive the jump to the ground, and the moat was far too shallow to provide safe landing.

All of which was written in Idusza's expression. "What now?" she hissed.

Ren reached for her lightstone—and nearly dropped it when an almighty explosion lit the night behind her.

She crawled up the low slope of the roof and found that Arkady's kids had apparently also noticed the rising alarm. Vargo's numinat hadn't quite punched a hole straight through the outer perimeter of the Dockwall, but not for lack of trying. The wall there was badly cracked, chunks of masonry fallen into the moat below, and the guards atop it were swarming.

Pretty soon that swarm would extend over the full length of the wall—just as soon as someone figured out that the very obvious attack might be a distraction. But some badly pronounced Stretsko battle cries were coming from the north, and for the moment, that had the guards' attention.

Ren slid back down to the south side and flashed her lightstone, praying the Rook was in position.

At the last instant, she remembered to duck aside.

A crossbow bolt punched through the tiles not far from her, trailing a length of rope. Ren took it and tied it around the nearest chimney before handing out the devices the Rook had given her. "Hook the metal over the line, loop the cord onto the other end, and hold on tight," Ren said. "Then jump, and you'll slide down to the outer wall."

Idusza stared at her. Ren called on years of con artist experience to exude confidence. "It will work," she promised.

But Andrejek spoke up, his voice slurred with the pain-numbing drugs Ljunan had fed him. "M'hand's broken. Can't grip."

Djek. She'd made plans for what to do if he couldn't walk—but not if he couldn't hold on to things.

Ljunan responded by pulling off his shirt and shredding it into strips. Idusza began helping him tie them together, but Ren stopped her. "Go. I'll help here. We don't have much time before the guards regroup."

Idusza's jaw tightened. She clearly didn't like leaving Andrejek behind. "He'll need you to catch him on the far side," Ren said. "*Go!*"

She didn't watch as Idusza hooked her handle over the rope and slid into the darkness. Together she and Ljunan rigged a makeshift harness for Andrejek and tied him to the handle, then pushed him away. In the distance, Ren saw two guards running toward where Idusza waited atop the wall—

—only to topple into the moat when a swirl of black fabric rose up. Ren mouthed a prayer of thanks as Ljunan leapt to safety, then followed him as soon as he was off the line.

By the time her boot struck the wall to stop her momentum, Idusza was sliding down a second rope to the street below, and Ljunan and the Rook were modifying Andrejek's harness to lower him. The Rook's arm flashed out to keep Ren from overshooting and toppling completely over.

"Good work," he said. "Can you get them down while I cut the line?"

It hadn't been shot from the wall, but from a window in a building outside the prison, high enough for the rope to clear the wall's top. *Isn't that the Dockwall warden's house?* Ren thought, before dragging her thoughts back to more immediate issues. She nodded, and the Rook began sawing at the line while she helped Ljunan lower Andrejek.

When the Rook finished, he leapt to the ground, rolling in a swift tuck across the cobbles before rising and slinging Andrejek's good arm across his shoulders. By then the prison's alarm bell was sounding, its tolling picked up by Vigil outposts across the Lower Bank.

"Follow me," the Rook said quietly. "Lady Rose, watch our flanks."

It wasn't a pell-mell run, as much as Ren wanted it to be.

Andrejek's leg wouldn't support that, and they also didn't want to draw attention. Fortunately, the Rook seemed to know every deserted alley and shadowed alcove as they crossed south into King-fisher, slipping from one to the next when no one was looking.

"I thought the Rook cared nothing for Vraszenian matters. Why would you help us?" Idusza asked as they waited for him to signal that it was safe to cross a street of ostrettas and night-market stalls.

"You have her to thank for that." The Rook's hood dipped toward Ren in what she had come to recognize was his version of a wink. "I can't court a Rose with lesser blooms, so I've plucked a few of her Lady's children instead."

Andrejek's response was harsh with pain and exhaustion. "Poetry can wait. What has Vargo to do with this? He betrayed us."

"I'm not sure that's true," Ren said. "But if it is, we'll see that he suffers for it. Along with the rest of his crimes." She glanced at the Rook, but he was watching a tangle of drunken men lurching down the lane up ahead.

Idusza laid a hand on Andrejek's shoulder. "Peace, Koszar. We have on our side the Rook *and* the Black Rose. If that's not a blessing from Ažerais, nothing is."

"I have a skiff waiting in the Little Alwydd canal," the Rook said. "We just need to get that far. Lady Rose, can you—"

Before he could finish that sentence, Ren heard the distinctive sound of people moving in lockstep. She slid to the corner and peered around it, just as a small flight of hawks drew to a halt in the street.

The light of an ostretta lantern caught the all too familiar face of Grey Serrado.

"Levinci, take four people west and sweep north," he said. "Ecchino, you and four more head east. I'll move up the center. If the alarm's coming from the Dockwall, it's probably an escape, so keep a sharp eye out for anyone acting suspiciously. Ranieri, Dverli, Tarknias, you're with me."

Ren squeezed her eyes shut. *I'm a Mask-blinded idiot. Again.*

Grey Serrado wasn't the Rook. Even Nadežra's legendary

outlaw couldn't be in two places at once. She should just stop trying to unmask him; all it brought her was the humiliation of being
wrong.

Right now, though, humiliation was a luxury she couldn't
afford. Ren darted back to where the Rook waited, and conveyed
the new danger in a tight-voiced summary.

"Serrado?" Andrejek and Idusza exchanged a look. "In the past
he has been a friend. Perhaps we could—"

"I'd rather not risk this entire endeavor on a perhaps," the Rook
said. "Especially not for a man with a *phenomenal* grudge against
me. Ill-founded or not, let's not test his patience. Lady Rose, would
you mind playing distraction while I get them to the skiff? Give the
hawks someplace to look other than the streets?"

Her gaze followed the tilt of his hood to the rooftops. Kingfisher
was a district made for the Rook: buildings huddled close and low,
with laundry lines and sheds and makeshift patios providing cover
and obstacles as needed.

Much like Lacewater—without so many narrow canals to leap.

The Rook caught her before she could reach for a handhold. He
tugged her close and murmured, "I'll leave a message in the usual
spot once they're safe. In the meantime, don't take too many risks…
but have fun."

Ren flashed him a grin and climbed.

Serrado's hawks had split up. Why was his whole damned patrol
here at once? Fortunately, the other two wings had moved away
from the Rook and the Anduske; it was only Serrado's own group
she had to divert. Ren found a loose tile on the roof and, with a
silent apology to the building's owner, nudged it until it slid down
and shattered in the street below.

His sharp gaze went not to the sound, but to where it must have
originated. Ren had ducked low enough that all he would see was
a suspicious shadow; now she waited until she heard him snap, "Up
there!"

Then she ran.

After lying cooped up in the hidden compartment of that scow, it was a pleasure to stretch her legs. From the streets below came shouts, the hawks relaying directions to each other as they fanned out. But Serrado, it seemed, wasn't content to pursue from below. A glance over Ren's shoulder revealed him on the roofs, vaulting the building's ridgeline with a confidence and agility that said he'd done this kind of thing before. Ren balance-walked across a board set between two roofs, the sign hanging from it marking a cobbler's alley, thinking that it was barely sturdy enough to support her own weight, let alone his—but he leapt the gap and remained on her heels.

Djek. If she could get out of his sight for long enough, she could pull the mask off. Underneath, she was dressed and painted as Arenza—a precaution in case she got unmasked in front of Vargo, in preference to him finding Renata underneath. Serrado might wonder what she was doing wandering around Kingfisher at this hour, but she could find some excuse. That would only work, though, if she could get away from him and down to the ground...and he wasn't making that easy.

Fine. She gritted her teeth. If she couldn't escape him, then she could at least separate him from his people. They were falling behind anyway, defeated by the odd turns of Kingfisher's streets.

Ren put on a burst of speed, veering left and leaping across to a balcony, then climbing again to a higher roof. She heard the thud as Serrado made the same jump, and she fought to slow her breathing as she waited for him to clear the eaves.

Which he did with practiced skill a street acrobat would envy. "If you keep going higher, it's only going to hurt more when you fall," he called as he sprang to his feet.

But he faltered when he spotted her leaning against a chimney, waiting. "You're not who I...You're the Black Rose."

She acknowledged it with a cheeky bow. "And you're Captain Grey Serrado. Thank you."

"For what?"

"For being obliging and following me. It's given the Anduske time to get away." Ren couldn't very well tear off her mask and reveal any of the other masks beneath it, but he'd helped Andrejek before—sheltered him, even. If he knew they were the escapees, would he close his eyes and allow them to escape?

"You—" His hand darted to his hilt and she tensed, ready to run. She'd seen enough at Ryvček's to know she'd never beat him in a straight fight, foul or fair. But then he brought that hand to his face instead, rubbing his brow like a man sorely tried by the Masks. "You helped them escape. The one night I thought I'd sleep in my own bed. Couldn't you at least have waited until morning?"

"It *would* have the element of being unexpected," she acknowledged dryly. "Along with impossible."

"All the better for the stories afterward." He edged to one side, toward the easiest jump to the next building. It was the most obvious route for her to bolt, but the easing of his manner said his heart wasn't in the chase anymore. This was for show, so she wouldn't suspect *him* of unwise sympathies. It made her want to laugh.

"So what now?" he asked. "Do you expect me to let you walk away? Or run, or leap, or . . . I don't know. Can you fly?"

"I like walking," she said lightly. "Out of your life, letting you get back to bed. Unless you insist on arresting me—which I hope you won't. I know you work hard to protect Vraszenians. I doubt you want to see three of them executed *de Ninate*."

That rumor was spreading, and the tightening of his jaw said he'd heard it. Voices were rising up again, Serrado's people looking for him; sooner or later they would spot him on this roof. Ren took the risk of drifting a step closer, so she could lower her voice. "I know you helped them after the Night of Hells. That was the right thing to do then. This is the right thing to do now."

"Captain, is that you up there?"

Ranieri's shout made Serrado flinch. Then he breathed deeply and gave Ren a tired smile. In Vraszenian he said, "For that, I joined the Vigil. Because I hoped to do the right thing."

Stepping back, he cleared the path for her escape. "Go. My people would hate me even more if I caged our Rose."

His words sent a shiver through her. Spoken in Vraszenian, his voice rich with the accents of her childhood...and accepting her among them.

I belong to them more in this mask than I do as myself.

She drove that thought away with a running leap. Behind her, Ranieri shouted again. "Captain? Did you find something? We're coming up through the house."

"No need. It was nothing," Serrado called down. "Just a cat."

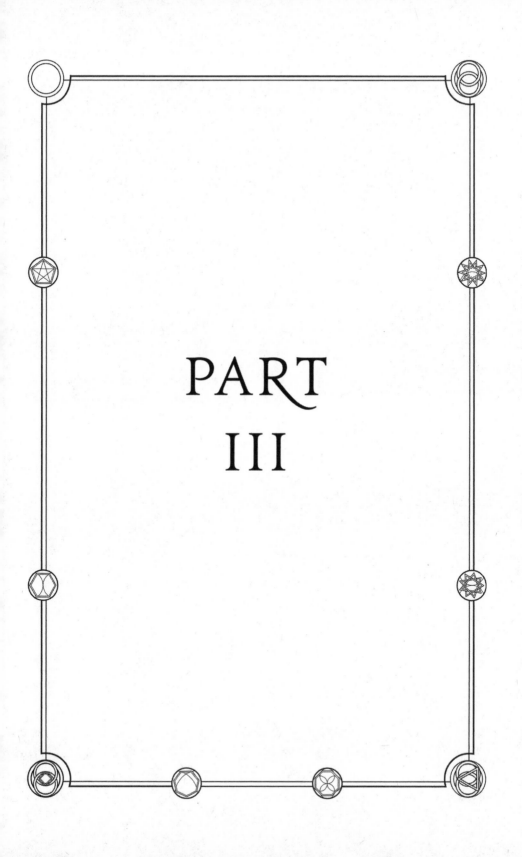

PART

III

Labyrinth's Heart

The Pearls were as different from Dockwall as a place could be, but gossip cared little for such separations. Only four hours since Tess had woken from her vigil to find Ren climbing back through her balcony doors, hardly even pausing to scrub off Arenza's face before collapsing into bed, and the parks and plazas around Traementis Manor were flooded with speculation.

Ren hadn't been conscious enough to relate the details of her nighttime prison break, only that it was a success, and something bitter about how she was an idiot who should just stop guessing. By the time she roused in the morning, the risk of other servants overhearing meant she couldn't talk at all.

But between kitchen conversations over mushroom porridge and snippets caught on the street, Tess winkled out the details. Someone had escaped the inescapable Dockwall Prison, or had tried and failed. The Stadnem Anduske prisoners had blown a hole in the wall. Or the rooftop. Or themselves. They'd had help from the inside. Or the outside. From the Stretsko. The Rook.

The Black Rose of Ažerais.

Tess wished for a third ear as Meatball tugged her along the walk that bordered the East Channel: one for the gossips, one for

Meatball's snuffles when he spotted something interesting, and one for Suilis's ramblings as the other maid walked beside her.

"—must have been the Rook," Suilis declared with a decisive nod. "Who else would have the nerve to break into the Dockwall? And I heard about what he did to Mede Essunta with that firework. Poor man—do you think his hands will heal?"

Tess made a noncommittal sound and wished she could walk the dog alone. But after a week of Suilis's whinging terror whenever she had to take out Donaia's Alwyddian wolfhound, Tess had made the mistake of saying it didn't seem like such a chore. Now that chore was unofficially shared. "After all," Suilis had blithely declared, "you're practically countrymen."

Their usual walk took them around the perimeter of Isla Traementis while Meatball examined and marked every lamppost, bush, and building stoop. If the canal walk was empty, Tess would let him off the leash to harass the gulls, but today she wasn't in a mood to listen to Suilis's yelps of fear.

Their whole friendship was like that. Tess was closer to Suilis than to anyone else on the Traementis staff, them both being new, but too many of the things the other maid did chafed her patience… and her suspicions.

Like now, when Suilis squeezed her arm and leaned in, lowering her voice to a conspiratorial whisper. "That's not the only thing I heard about the Essunta party, though. One of their maids says she saw Alta Renata coming back from meeting her secret lover."

This was a needle Tess had to thread carefully. She hated encouraging false gossip, but rumors of Renata's lover kept suitors at bay and provided the cover necessary for Ren's increasing absences.

Suilis didn't seem to need confirmation. She sighed happily, tilting her face up to the sun as if it weren't trying to broil them all alive. "Who do you think he is? Or she, though your alta seems to prefer men. I wonder where they meet up? If I had a secret lover, I'd want a nice little nest where we could be alone."

Tess might not be the con artist Ren was, able to talk people into spilling all their secrets, but that didn't mean she couldn't recognize the signs of someone else doing the same. Despite the sweltering heat, a trickle of ice went down her back.

Thankfully, Meatball could be depended on to provide a distraction. Tess loosened her hold on the lead, and he took it as permission to charge toward an unsuspecting gull. With an "oof!" of false surprise, Tess let him drag her free of Suilis's grip, then caught his collar and pulled him back with a soft command before he made a second breakfast of the gull.

"Time we head back," she told Suilis. Then, to Meatball: "Come, my lad. Let's get you back to your mistress."

When Suilis turned to lead the way, Tess pulled a chunk of dried mutton from her pocket and fed it to the hound. "Good boy," she whispered. "If I ever form my own knot, you'll be my top fist."

Colbrin was waiting for them when they reached Traementis Manor. "Keep him collared. The era wants you to bring Lex Talionis to her study." He was the only one stickler enough to use Meatball's official name.

Knowing Colbrin would want Suilis to handle the task, Tess blurted, "My alta's at an appointment, and I've nothing else to occupy myself. I can take him up." Without waiting for approval, she unhitched Meatball's lead, buried her fingers in his ruff, and led him upstairs.

She expected to find Donaia alone, or perhaps with Giuna. She didn't expect to find them both sitting across from a dark-skinned Vraszenian woman with a toddler in her lap and a wide-eyed little girl clinging to her knee.

Mother and Crone, they found us out! Tess had never met Alinka Serrado, but she'd heard enough from Ren to leave little doubt of the woman's identity.

She had to run. Get the bags. Get Ren. Find Sedge. First ship out of Nadežra, and Ren could just swallow down her seasickness.

Donaia waved for Tess to enter, then blinked in confusion. "Where is Suilis?"

The question knocked Tess's frantic thoughts off their course. "Below. She's that frightened of Meatball, so I'm the one who walks him." Only after she'd spoken did Tess realize she'd spilled on the other maid. But better Suilis for a small offense than Ren for a high crime.

Donaia frowned, but it wasn't aimed at Tess. To Alinka, she said, "This is Meatball. He's part of the family and will be joining me later at Eret Quientis's villa. I assure you, he's not as dangerous as he looks."

If this was how Donaia introduced her dog to Suilis, no wonder the maid was terrified of him. The toddler buried his whimpers in his mother's chest, and the girl silenced hers by chewing on the head of her doll.

Giving Meatball the signal to stay where he was, Tess released his ruff and ventured closer to the family. "What's your name?" she asked the girl. If Ren had shared it, Tess couldn't remember. Probably she hadn't. They had so little time for talking these days.

"Yvieny," the girl mumbled around the head of her doll. Her gaze was no longer on Meatball. Instead, she seemed transfixed by Tess's hair. "Are you Elsivin?"

Ignoring Alinka's cough, Tess asked, "Who?"

The doll was shoved in her face, all spit-sogged hair and ratty clothes. "Elsivin the Red. She's a hero."

"Is she." Donaia's cool words warned there were currents here Tess couldn't see.

To avoid them, she said, "I'm Tess, and this is Meatball. We're both from Ganllech."

"Does he bite?" Yvieny's expression walked the tightrope between fascination and fear.

Donaia's "no" tipped it toward disappointment. Tess, recalling the delight over destruction that came with Yvieny's age, winked and said, "Unless you tell him to. The princes of Ganllech use Alwyddian wolfhounds to snap a boar's legs so it can't charge during a hunt."

Paying no mind to the horrified gasps of the adults, Tess sank to her knees. "But they're well-trained to tell the difference between boars and little girls." She gestured to Meatball and he trotted up, tongue lolling in a doggy smile.

"*Gulša*," Yvieny breathed in admiration. For an instant she sounded like Ren as a child, marveling over some street magician's tricks. Keeping her hand well away from the teeth that had caught her eye, she gave his rump a tentative pat. "I bet he could chomp through a whole cone of honey stones."

"Like *that*," Tess agreed with a click of her fingers.

Now that the tension had broken, Yvieny was happy to take over explaining to her mother and brother that, see, Meatball was sweet. Meatball was harmless. Meatball could viciously maul people and chomp their legs off, but only if they were enemies. This last was accompanied by much snapping of her jaws.

Tess stood, dusting off her skirts, and stepped back to stand by Donaia. Who studied her and said, "You seem familiar with Alwyddian wolfhounds. Did you have them back home?"

"Me?" Tess's incredulous laugh earned her an arched brow. She swallowed the rest and kept her eyes downcast. "No, Era Traementis. Wolfhounds and red-points were bred for princes. But we did have a few hearth mutts with a smidge of the blood." The memory of those rawboned old hounds had kept Tess from fearing dogs the way most of Ondrakja's Fingers did. She never could convince Ren or Sedge they weren't all bad.

"There's a merchant out of Ganllech who's gotten his hands on a pair of braches," Donaia said. "He wants Meatball to act as stud for them. He's offered a pup from the first litter, in addition to a fee."

"That's a royal gift." Old Ganllechyn law had required a prince's edict for anyone else to own one.

Donaia made a pleased sound. "I'd need to leave Meatball here for the breeding. And I'd prefer to have the braches stay at the manor until the puppies are weaned. But it's clear Suilis doesn't have the temperament for it. Could I trust you?"

"It would be a genuine pleasure," Tess said. "And I'll help with the new puppies."

That thought put a bounce in her step as she left Yvieny trying to ride the endlessly patient Meatball and went to lay out clothing for Renata's appointment with Meda Capenni that afternoon.

But the bounce went dead as she went into Renata's bedroom and found Suilis inside.

"There you are!" Suilis said brightly. "And good, you've gotten rid of that beast. I wanted to ask what you have planned for your next day off. I was thinking…"

Tess kept a sunny smile up as the other maid nattered on about Nadežra's summer diversions, but underneath it was winter's ice.

Suilis ought to have been helping with the decorations for the upcoming Traementis adoption ball, not looking for Tess. *Not using me as an excuse to snoop in Alta Renata's rooms.*

She was spying. Tess had been right to suspect her.

The next time they walked the dog, she might just let Meatball terrorize Suilis. But more importantly, she would find out who that snoop was working for, and why.

Kingfisher, Lower Bank: Lepilun 27

The boards of the staircase creaked in protest under Grey's heavy tread. Masks have mercy, but he was tired. Dockwall had been a success, on all fronts; the Anduske were stowed in a safe house of Vargo's, with no one the wiser. And seeing Grey and the Rook in separate places at the same time should put any suspicions Ren might harbor to permanent rest.

But Dockwall was also the latest in a string of very late nights. He didn't remember the last time he'd gotten so much as four hours of unbroken sleep. Even when he snatched a brief rest during the day, it was too easy for some idiot or another to bang on his office door and wake him up.

So he came home. Alinka wouldn't begrudge him an afternoon nap in her bed, and with any luck, nobody from the Aerie would look for him here.

Yvie was sitting quietly for once, working on a simple button knot charm with tongue-biting intensity. Jagyi was under the table, playing some game known only to him. After an exchange of growls with Jagyi and a kiss dropped onto Yvie's hair, Grey headed up the stairs.

The door at the top was closed. Grey elbowed it open, saying, "Alinka, if you mind not—"

"Shhhh!" Alinka shot into view, simultaneously gesturing for him to keep his voice down and at the bed behind her.

Where Arenza lay asleep, half-curled on her side, one hand flat beneath her cheek.

The sight threw him almost as badly as the day he had come into the house and found her at the kitchen table. Now she was asleep in the *bed*?

Alinka hustled him back out onto the landing and eased the door shut. "What's she doing here?" Grey demanded.

"Sleeping," Alinka said tartly. "She claimed she wasn't tired— pfah! As if she could fool a healer. With her head on the kitchen table I caught her, 'just resting her eyes.' If she spent half as much time sleeping as pretending she's fine, she'd be much better off."

Grey was used to ignoring Alinka's pointed looks; he shrugged this one off with ease. "I myself hoped to rest," he said. It came out sounding more plaintive than he intended.

"That is wise," Alinka said, softening. "You can sleep in the children's truckle bed."

He swallowed a protest before it could burst free. The truckle bed? He'd have to fold himself in half to fit into that thing. Arenza was several inches shorter than he was; why couldn't *she* have taken the smaller bed?

An absurd question, and Alinka would smack him if he voiced it. "I'll sleep in the chair," Grey said sourly. He couldn't afford to forgo the rest.

"As you please." Alinka edged past him on the narrow stairs. "I'll make sure the children stay quiet."

When she was gone, Grey rested his forehead against the door, cursing silently. Then he went inside.

Arenza hadn't shifted a muscle. Either she was feigning sleep so she could observe what he did, or she really was out cold. Grey's money was on the latter. She knew how to use cosmetics to hide the weary lines, the circles under her eyes...but with her face slack in repose, the exhaustion was plain. He couldn't have turfed her out of the bed even with Alinka's blessing.

Grey knew all too well the strain of maintaining a double life, but he'd also come to know *her*. Whatever troubled her sleep was more than just her ongoing deception. It was only by comparison that she looked better rested than she had during her nine nights of sleeplessness after the Night of Hells. He wished he could prod her into seeking help, as he had then.

Prod. A kind word for frightening her into a complete breakdown. The memory of her shivering helplessness that night dragged at his conscience and made him wish all the more that he could help her now, by kinder means. Captain Serrado's relationship with Alta Renata didn't permit such familiarity, though.

Would she accept it from the Rook?

That wasn't a question he could answer today. Sighing, Grey contemplated the chair. If he put his feet up, it wouldn't be too bad. And she'd been considerate enough to curl up so the lower half of the bed was empty.

He moved the chair into position, setting it down as silently as possible. Then he pulled off his boots and stockings and shrugged out of his uniform coat, rolling up his sleeves in the room's heavy warmth. *Serve her right if I broke into her house and went to sleep in her bed.*

Thoughts like that were hardly conducive to rest. Sighing again, he settled in, propping his feet on the empty corner of the straw-stuffed mattress and laying his head on the back of the chair. It wasn't the most comfortable position, but he'd slept in worse. His eyes drifted closed.

He jolted out of a half doze with the sensation of falling, splaying his hands to catch himself. But he was safe in the chair. The sunlight had drifted less than an hour's span across the floor. As for the noise that had awoken him...

Ren was having a nightmare. Half-choked sounds slipped between her lips, and her limbs twitched, reacting to something in her dream. The tendons in her neck drew tight as her jaw clenched and released.

His first instinct was to wake her. His second was to consider how dangerous that might be. He doubted she was the type to wake gently under the best of circumstances, and if she escaped a nightmare's grip only to find him looming over her, that might frighten her worse.

"Arenza," he said. Quietly at first; then a bit louder, without result. However good she was at masquerades, he wasn't sure even she would respond to an assumed name in her sleep.

So: either shake her awake, or let her keep dreaming. She'd folded the knife-laden shawl he'd given her between herself and the wall, probably to keep Yvie from finding the blades. No other weapons within immediate reach, not that he could see. Which didn't really mean anything...but oh well. He was a Vigil captain, not to mention the city's most notorious outlaw. If he couldn't defend himself against a half-asleep woman armed with nothing worse than a knife, he should return the hood to Ryvček permanently instead of merely loaning it for a few bells.

Kneeling so he presented as minimal a threat as possible, Grey reached out and shook her knee.

She came awake swinging, as expected. But she punched like she fenced, more instinct than training. Only when her nails came near his face did he catch her wrists. "Arenza! It's all right. Only a dream."

Her eyes focused on his face. "*Grey.*"

She breathed it like a prayer. His grip eased on her wrists, cradling them like two fragile birds. She'd never used his name before. As Arenza or Renata, she always called him "Captain Serrado." But the shift wasn't a calculated decision, some part of her masquerade. For one suspended moment, she saw him, and he saw her.

Not Arenza or Renata or the Black Rose, but *Ren*. Her true face.

"I'm here," he said. The words were rougher than they should have been, snagging on the tangle of feelings welling up inside. *I just moved the moons to deceive her. I don't deserve to see this.*

He released her as she slumped, letting her sink back onto the mattress. She lay there for several heartbeats, damp with sweat, gaze skittering back and forth as if she were trying to gather up the frayed threads of her composure. He wanted to stroke the hair from her face, but he reined the impulse in. The kindest thing he could do was to wait in silence, giving no hint that he'd seen her come apart.

"I'm sorry." Ren's apology came out a rasp. Her throat worked as she swallowed, a brief hitch in the rapid pulse of her breath. "I—I hope I hit you not."

She spoke in Vraszenian. When Alta Renata Viraudax Traementatis woke in the night, did she remember to speak with the clipped accent of a Seterin noblewoman? "I train with Oksana Ryvček," he said, striving to sound unaffected. "I managed."

His weak attempt at banter called forth no response. Asking felt like presumption, but seeing her like this made his heart ache. "Would it help to talk about it?"

She managed a small shrug. "A nightmare. At least for once it was not zlyzen."

Masks knew she had enough terrors to haunt her dreams. The Night of Hells. Gammer Lindworm. The Rook himself, ambushing her when she was half-insane with lack of sleep.

She hauled herself upright with the kind of slow, weary movement he recognized all too well. If she'd been alone, she probably would have groaned. "Alinka browbeat me into lying down—I meant to take a few minutes only, to satisfy her. What time is it?"

When he told her, she shot to her feet with a good deal more energy and snatched up the shawl, flinging it around her shoulders, stuffing her feet into her boots. What engagement of Alta Renata's had she just slept through? He simply nodded at the mumbled excuse she gave, and then she was gone, down the stairs in a clatter. Alinka's startled voice rose up through the floorboards. A few moments later the door banged shut below, and Grey sank onto the edge of the bed and buried his face in his hands.

Soon after, he heard Alinka's tread on the stairs. "I roused her not," he said, the words muffled by his palms. "She woke on her own. And woke *me*."

"So she said." Alinka laid one hand on his shoulder. "You too are tired. You have no peace sleeping in your office. Truly, you could stay here."

It was a conversation they'd repeated all too often since Kolya died. But now, thanks to Ren, there might be a solution. "How went the meeting with Era Traementis?"

"Well," Alinka said. "With the dog Jagyi is a little shy, but Yvie—"

"Has a new pony," Grey guessed, and smiled at Alinka's fond but long-suffering nod. "Let's just hope she teaches him no bad habits around biting." Then a yawn overtook him. "Wake me at sunset?"

"I will." Alinka eased the door shut behind her, and the room was quiet.

He lay down with a weary groan. The bed was warm where Arenza had lain, and the pillow held traces of her scent. His palms tingled with the memory of her wrists, that moment when they lay loose and trusting in his hands.

Hoping he might see her again soon—and knowing the wish was foolish—Grey went back to sleep.

Kingfisher, Lower Bank: Lepilun 27

Ren's steps slowed as she left the Serrado house. There was no point in rushing; she couldn't possibly make it to the Charterhouse on time for her appointment in Fulvet's office, which meant his secretary wouldn't let her in.

But it had been so good to sleep peacefully for a little while. While the nightmares still found her eventually, they'd been blessedly zlyzen-free. Alinka had laid a red thread around the bed for her children, and whether it was magic or just the comfort of a familiar charm, it had helped. Even waking to find Grey there hadn't been the source of fear it would have been, not that long ago. The sight of him had brought a sense of calm—of safety. He might not be the Rook, but she'd come to enjoy his company.

Be honest with yourself, if with no one else. You more than enjoy it.

Not just the chance to be Vraszenian. Alinka and the children gave her that, or Koszar and Idusza, even if Ren could never shed the awareness that she was pretending to a legitimacy she didn't have.

But Grey...there was more to him than just the dutiful hawk. He had a wry sense of humor that rarely showed when he was in uniform, and it called the same out of her. She laughed more around him, and more sincerely, than anywhere else.

If she were smarter, she would stop visiting their house at all. But she couldn't deny herself that chance to live a more comfortable lie.

Ren was so lost in thought that she had to swallow a yelp when a man stepped up to block her way. A second yelp tried to follow when she recognized him: Nikory, the leader of Vargo's Fog Spiders. And when she reflexively glanced over her shoulder for an escape, she found two others behind her.

Nikory said, "Lenskaya. Vargo wants another word with you."

Froghole, Lower Bank: Lepilun 27

The worst five words for a fist to hear were *boss wants to see you.* Yet Sedge welcomed them when Lurets showed up at the door of his boarding house. Wouldn't drop a word about what Vargo wanted, but after the cock-up in Lacewater—a cock-up Sedge had deliberately missed, which was cause enough for Vargo to suspect him—a friendly face delivering the message said that Vargo only had questions.

His confidence took a hit, though, when Lurets brought him through the Froghole headquarters and into a back room that held Vargo, Varuni, Nikory...

And Ren.

He couldn't hide his surprise and didn't bother trying. Instead, he let it dribble into confusion. "You brought me here to get patterned?"

At least Ren didn't look hurt beyond a bit of mussing. Tense, yes, and no wonder; it was sheer fucking stupidity for her to be in front of Vargo as Arenza again. Which meant this meeting was Vargo's idea, not hers. How had he nabbed her? Sedge remembered what Tess had told him, how often Ren was sneaking off to Kingfisher to spend time with Serrado's family. Might be Vargo had caught wind of it, too.

Vargo snorted at his question. "Does this look like a patterner's shop to you? No, this is just a meeting between old friends. You said you didn't know where to find the szorsa, so I found her for you." He leaned his elbows on his desk, lips resting against steepled fingers. "Unfortunately, she's being...less than forthcoming. Almost like she has something to hide."

Ren had plenty and then some to hide. "What're you trying to ask her?" *And why am I here for it?*

"Lacewater," Vargo said. "Someone betrayed that meeting. It wasn't me, and it wasn't the Anduske. That leaves the go-betweens. You...and Szorsa Arenza here. She claims she didn't know about the meeting. Convenient, don't you think? I'd love to hear more."

Something dropped in the pit of Sedge's stomach as Vargo lounged back in his chair, tugging his cuffs straight. "You're going to loosen her tongue."

He knew immediately what Vargo was saying. But he asked anyway, because horror made him disbelieve. "You don't mean—"

"Work her over, Sedge. I know you know how."

Out in the street, someone was having a shouting match. It sounded like it was a thousand leagues away. There was only this room, and Ren in a chair, and Vargo waiting for him to beat her bloody.

Stall. He had to stall. Give Ren time to get them out of this without giving them away. "Why me? There's a half dozen others still tied in who could do it as good." *No. Wait. Don't give Vargo ideas about having some other fist hurt her.* "But you brought *me* in. What's your game?"

"My *game*," Vargo said softly, "is that I want information, and I want you to get it. You don't need to know more."

Sedge could guess without being told. Tests of loyalty were

meant to be hard. Ondrakja had taught him that, using Ren and Tess. She'd taught his sisters the same lesson using him.

He cracked his knuckles. Not threat; habit. He looked to Nikory, Varuni, even Lurets, but there was no help from them. And Ren...

Ren was braced in the chair, but not afraid. Because she knew Sedge wouldn't do it? Because she was ready to take it? Could be either, and he couldn't ask her. They were too out of practice from their days of working together against Ondrakja—only they'd never had to do *this*, because Ondrakja was careful not to push them that far.

Right up until the day she tried to murder Sedge, and Ren poisoned her for it.

Vargo wasn't Ondrakja. And Sedge had never been good at playing people, neither. He could toss the ball to Ren, though, and see what she did with it. Leaning in close, Sedge said in his most menacing voice, "You heard the man. But if you talk, you can save yourself some pain."

Ren stayed silent, her eyes telling him to do it. Was she fucking kidding? Even if he would, there was nowhere he could hit her. People—Vargo—would ask questions if Alta Renata turned up with a bruised face. But if Sedge hurt her where it wouldn't show, Ren might hate him almost as much as he'd hate himself. Because Ondrakja had always protected Ren's pretty face.

Do it. Get in with Vargo. Don't give up the con. He could almost hear her thoughts beating against him.

Sorry, Ren. En't gonna happen.

"Fuck this." Turning his back on Ren, Sedge planted a hand on Vargo's desk, displaying the fading stripe on his wrist where a charm used to be. "I en't one of your fists no more. Got cut out, din't I? And even then, I weren't the sort to work someone over on a suspicion. You show me proof she did you up, I'll plant a whole garden of purple roses under her skin. Until then, play your games on someone else. And leave her alone."

He expected cold rage. Masks knew he'd seen that often enough from Vargo, when somebody sauced off at him. Instead—incredibly—Vargo *smiled.*

"Good to know you haven't changed, Sedge," he said. Lurets looked confused; Nikory looked relieved. Only Varuni's expression remained stone. But then, reading her was like trying to decipher Enthaxn.

Sedge was slow, but he wasn't a snail. "This en't some loyalty test?" But what else could it be? And if it was, how the fuck had he passed by *refusing*?

Vargo said, "Of course it is. A man who's determined to worm his way back into my organization would do anything I said, just to ingratiate himself—and to prove his innocence."

"You thought it was me," Sedge breathed. "You thought I sold you out."

"Your bout of stomach illness was very convenient."

It hadn't been convenient at all. Sedge had to go rooting through trash heaps to find some mussels that had gone off, and then there had been all the puking that followed. But he couldn't risk Idusza recognizing him as the bullyboy she'd slugged the day she met Arenza—or Varuni paying him a visit and deciding he was malingering.

He sagged, only his braced hand keeping him from sinking to the floor. "You *asshole.*"

"Mm." Vargo's attention moved back to Ren. "Though that still leaves her under suspicion. No personal enmity, szorsa; you understand that I have to tie off every thread here. And you haven't exactly been helpful."

"Because you ask the wrong questions," she said, sounding not at all offended. "What would I gain from betraying the Anduske, or you? Seem I an ally of the hawks?"

"You visit the house of one often enough."

"A *Vraszenian* hawk. And while to the Anduske I may not be sworn, they are my friends. No, Ča Vargo, I betrayed them not. You have a patterner before you—why not ask pattern for answers?"

"Will the answer come in the form of another dropped card?" Nikory asked curtly. He had faith in patterners, and no respect for frauds. Especially when he thought they were trying to play his boss.

But Vargo merely raised a brow, intrigued. "Even a dropped card can provide information."

Ren knew better than to subject Vargo to an elaborate show. She merely took out her deck and gave it three quick shuffles, then cut and drew a single card. Whereupon her brow knitted in what looked like honest confusion. "Seven as One," she said, turning it so everyone else could see. "The card of institutions. An enemy of yours in the Cinquerat?"

"Cinquerat's five people," Lurets said.

She gave him an exasperated look. "The names are not literal."

"You can learn to be a szorsa later," Vargo told Lurets, scowling at him for the interruption before turning back to Ren. "I want to know more about this enemy of mine. How did he know about the meeting?"

He. Not *she* or *they.* So Vargo already had a suspicion of who was behind the ambush.

Ren was still frowning at the card. "You have more than one enemy, I think, in more than one place. Of your troubles with the Stretsko, many people know—and they are an institution, as much as the Cinquerat. But no, this came not from them. Perhaps..."

She trailed off in a way Sedge recognized. He wasn't surprised when Vargo said, "Give us a minute."

Sedge didn't want to leave Ren alone with Vargo, no more than Varuni or Nikory did. It was a reverse race to see who could dawdle slowest out of the room, until Vargo's glare prodded them along.

After several silent moments of everyone staring at the closed door, Varuni said, "Never should have cut you out."

"Huh?" Sedge wanted to shush her, even though Vargo's office door had been scribed with numinata to prevent eavesdropping for exactly this reason. But then Varuni's words caught up to him. His hand went to his bare wrist. "Thought you was madder at me than anyone."

Varuni made a noise in the back of her throat, something between a growl and a purr. "I was. But I also know what it's like trying to guard that asshole's back."

"It was politics," Nikory said, as much to Sedge as to her. "A bodyguard don't come back with a few scratches when the boss is filleted like a trout. Had to feed the fists some blood before they started asking why Sedge was still allowed to be walking." He redirected his gaze to Sedge. "But you din't deserve that. And you've been good despite it. I told Vargo you en't leaky, tied or not."

Sedge blinked hard. It had hurt bad when Nikory cut him out—worse than he'd admitted even to his sisters, though he was sure they'd guessed. Nikory trusting him enough to speak for him when there weren't any oaths between them was the balm he hadn't known he needed.

"Thanks." Sedge turned his head away and coughed to remove the thickness from his throat, and then they all waited some more until the door opened and Vargo gestured Ren out—with way more courtesy than he'd shown at the start.

Courtesy enough that she offered him a respectful touch to her brow. "One card alone says little. A full pattern says more. But for that...I would humbly accept your offering to Ir Entrelke Nedje."

"Just make certain I know where to send it, so I don't have to disturb you on your way home again." It was as good a promise as Vargo ever gave that he wouldn't send fists next time to pluck her off the street.

The veneer of warmth vanished a moment later. "Nikory, Varuni, back in here. Sedge, see her wherever she wants to go." He started to turn back to his office, then paused and glanced over his shoulder. "We'll talk again. Don't worry—next time it won't be a test."

The Shambles, Lower Bank: Lepilun 27

After they left Vargo's place, Ren and Sedge kept silent except for a few muttered cues. They both knew it was even odds whether Vargo had sent someone to follow them and see where "Arenza" lived; if so, she had to give him an answer. They walked to a seedy lodging house in the Shambles; then she bid Sedge goodbye, went inside, and bribed the landlady to say she lived there if anyone came asking. Then it was out the back door, to the stinking canal behind the house.

Where she found Sedge waiting on a walkway so narrow his shoulders almost pushed him off. "Nobody saw me go round," he promised. "And I en't letting you walk the whole way home alone."

"I thought to take a skiff."

"That en't what I meant, and you know it." He scrubbed at his scalp. "'Sides, nobody's poling across the Dežera today. Skiffers went on strike."

She ground the heels of her hands into her eye sockets as if that could press away the headache. *This is what Scaperto was afraid of.* A magistrate had sentenced a skiffer to death for dumping a passenger in the river when he refused to pay the fare. A slumming noble, it turned out. The punishment was egregious, and Fulvet had commuted it, but the skiffers had been whipped into a fury. It could have been Branek's work—most of the skiffers were Stretsko—but she suspected it was just more of Nadežra's tensions boiling to the surface.

By water or walking, getting home posed other problems. She didn't dare go back to where she'd stashed Renata's clothing and makeup, not right now, and maybe not ever. Not if Vargo had people watching the Serrado house. But she could hardly walk into Traementis Manor looking like Arenza.

Well, if she had to walk across the whole city, it would be dark by the time she arrived. That would make sneaking in easier.

Her attention refocused on Sedge, and the jittery tension that hadn't left his shoulders. Her memory echoed back Vargo's smooth, menacing voice. *Work her over, Sedge. I know you know how.*

There was no room on the walkway for a hug. Ren nudged Sedge off it into the slightly less cramped alley between buildings. Once they were on less precarious ground, his arms landed heavy around her. Sedge's voice scraped raw as he said, "What did Vargo say to you, in private? You're sure you're safe from him?"

She blew out a long breath. "I told him that I think it's someone in his own organization. Not you; someone else."

"That's it? He din't go after you?"

They'd been alone—the perfect chance for Vargo to intimidate or threaten her. But he'd just nodded thoughtfully, and his spider had agreed that they needed to take a closer look at their own security.

"He was never going to hurt me," she said. "When he told you to do it—"

She knew what she'd heard, and yet it still baffled her. Pulling back from the hug, she said, "That spirit of his was *outraged* at the order he gave you. And then Vargo said not to worry—that he'd stop you before you could follow through."

"But you—I thought you were telling me to do it."

Ren rubbed at her eyes again. "I read him wrong. I thought the test was to see if you would obey. Not if you would defy him." She offered Sedge a half smile. "Turns out you know your own boss better than I do."

A familiar hardness came into his jaw, and he turned as if to make sure nobody was spying on their alley. "Vargo en't my boss. Nikory said I was cut on account of politics, but..." With his back to her, maybe he thought Ren wouldn't see the sheen of a tear, or the surreptitious hand that came up to knuckle it away.

She might be a knot-traitor twice over, but Sedge wasn't. Ren touched his shoulder gently. "I'm sorry. I..."

She'd been thinking of Sedge's snapped bond as a connection she could use. Not as a broken, jagged thing that would cut him every time he touched it.

"You don't have to spy on them for me," she said. "I should not have asked you to."

He gave a one-shouldered shrug—the shoulder he wrapped now in one of Tess's imbued braces, because he'd dislocated it so often defending his knot-mates. Sedge would do anything for people he claimed as his. Even to the point of hurting himself. "Who says I'm doing it for you? I weren't ever tied to Vargo, but leastways I can look out for Nikory and the others by keeping an eye on him."

Ren bit down on the regret that surged inside. She *missed* that kind of loyalty. Not that she didn't have the loyalty of family, from Sedge and from Tess—however poorly she'd been repaying it lately—but a knot was a different thing. There had been good times in the Fingers, however badly that had ended. She missed having friends who would have her back.

She hadn't told either of them about the knot offer from the Anduske, and now wasn't the time. Ren was grateful when Sedge turned back and said, "So what now?"

"Now," Ren said, "I get back to the Pearls before Donaia deploys the full complement of the Aerie to find me. And I figure out some way to grab the clothes I left stashed in Kingfisher before Renata Viraudax's latest surcoat turns up in a Coster's Walk stall. As for Vargo..." She sighed. "I don't know."

"I'll leave Vargo to you," Sedge said, the old grin returning as he bumped hips with her. "You leave the dress to me."

Isla Traementis, the Pearls: Lepilun 27

True to his word, Sedge stuck with her all the way through the strangled traffic on the Sunset Bridge, past the skiffers in their boats chanting protests from the river; through the crowds of the Old Island, with the Vigil keeping wary watch; even across the Sunrise Bridge, as choked with people as its western cousin. It was full dark by the time they reached Eastbridge, and they only parted company when Ren pointed out that a Lower Bank fist and a Vraszenian szorsa walking the streets at this hour were just asking a hawk to arrest them for vagrancy. "I'll go the rest of the way by rooftops," she said.

He snorted. "Yeah, that's a lot safer. Naw, I know you'll be fine—go. I'll see you later."

Ren would have liked to keep his company, and not only because she'd seen Sedge even less often than Tess lately. Having him there would have meant not being left alone with her thoughts.

I don't understand Vargo. Every time she thought she had the man's measure, he did something that didn't fit. For someone in Ren's position, whose safety depended on being able to read those around her and anticipate how they would act, that was terrifying.

But she couldn't solve that riddle tonight. Right now, her priority was getting back into Traementis Manor. She would have to sneak in her own window, redo her face and clothing, then climb out again and return through the front door. And hope that in the meantime she came up with some sufficiently plausible story for where she'd been, and why she was wearing a different dress.

When she got to the manor, though, there was a shadow on her balcony.

Ren froze, wondering if she'd interrupted the Rook in the middle of delivering a message. But he sat on the balustrade, and she heard a soft murmur as he... talked to someone?

"Ah, no—*ow.* Is that any way to treat someone who's trying to help you? Sheathe your daggers, alča. You need to make a good impression."

Several contradictory possibilities warred in her mind, most of them absurd. None were likely to be answered from the ground, so she climbed the tree to her balcony.

He heard her coming and acknowledged her with a distracted nod. "Here's the lady herself." He seemed more interested in his coat than Ren's arrival. "I've been waiting a while. Do you ever sleep?"

"Do *you*?" She slipped over the railing, perching on the balustrade cornerwise to him. Was something moving in the Rook's coat?

His laugh was rueful. "Not today. I was dealing with unexpected intruders." He lifted the edge of his coat. Clinging halfway up the lining, so dark it almost became invisible, was a small fuzzball. It rolled its head back, looking at Ren from an impossible upside-down angle, and its eyes flashed like moonstones when the light caught them. A high, squeaking mew revealed a pink tongue and white, pinprick teeth.

Apparently one of the absurd possibilities was right. *Alča* was Vraszenian for "kitten."

The Rook said, "The Anduske found her in their safe house today. Unfortunately, cats make Ljunan sneeze." He tried to free the kitten, but for every claw he unfixed, two more snagged on his coat. "Fine altas keep cats, don't they? Or perhaps your kitchen could use a good mouser. Though she seems to prefer climbing to stalking... Could you—a little help, please?"

It shouldn't have taken four dexterous hands to detach a kitten from a coat, but cats had never shown much concern for logic. Once extracted, the kitten displayed no interest in being cradled and petted, but instead began exploring Ren.

Given what Ren needed to say, she was grateful for the distraction. "I had no chance to tell you—not with Dockwall being such an urgent matter—but I've learned more of the Praeteri."

He listened in grim silence as she told him about the hidden temple and the numinat Diomen had put her in. When she was done, he said, "You're sure it was your emotions it affected? Not a physical reaction? Numinata can affect the body in ways that make it feel like it's your thoughts that are the cause."

"Tanaquis confirmed it. She sees it as normal enough, but..." Ren sighed, using one hand to make sure the kitten's explorations didn't take her off the balcony. "To Tanaquis, all parts of the cosmos are normal. They divide only into 'known' and 'not yet known.'"

The Rook made a thoughtful sound as the kitten began scaling the mountain of his shoulder. "The incidents I found among Vargo's notes sound a lot like the effects of what you just described. Praeteri numinatria at work."

"He's new to their ranks," Ren said, then chewed on her lower lip, thinking. "But he knew *of* them, and I think all along his goal has been to join them. They have no one below gentry in their ranks."

Whatever the Rook might have said in response was forestalled by the kitten, who had discovered the fascinating world of his hood. Ren couldn't suppress a snicker as the tiny head disappeared into its shadowy depths; then, when he gently eased her out—with a stifled noise that suggested her whiskers had found his ear—she took an interest in the loose fall of the fabric itself.

He didn't seem inclined to ask for Ren's help this time, but after significant effort to pull the kitten free without dislodging the hood, the Rook sighed. "Two centuries of mystery, about to be undone by the cleverness of cats. Would you?" He tipped his head to Ren in invitation.

A spark of curiosity flared to life within her. All it would take was one poorly calibrated attempt to pull the cat free...and he'd never speak to her again. Ren looked at the kitten, looked at the hood, and made a face. "I will regret teaching her this trick."

Then she leaned forward and dangled her braid at prime pouncing distance.

Moonstone eyes went wide, and the skinny tail lashed. The kitten missed her leap, but wound up in Ren's lap. A stuttering purr started up, louder than she was large, as she rolled onto her back and began attacking the braid with all five pointy ends.

"Thank you." The depth of the Rook's voice suggested the thanks wasn't only for the kitten-wrangling.

Trying to keep her tone light, Ren said, "I couldn't let a mere cat succeed where I have—ouch!—failed." The last word was delivered from an odd angle, as one well-hooked paw dragged her head down.

Apparently, it wasn't light enough. "Don't feel too bad about not unmasking me. People have been trying for centuries. If I weren't good at what I do, I wouldn't still be here."

"It isn't that." Once the temptation of the braid was removed, the kitten's antics became more of a reflexes game than a knife fight. Ren kept her attention on that, not only to preserve her skin, but because if she looked at the Rook, she would lose her nerve. "I... Several times now, I've had a suspicion about your identity. Every time, I've been wrong."

"I see."

"No, you don't." She tucked her hand to her chest, out of harm's way. It was pure imagination to think she still felt the warmth of Grey's touch on her wrist. Pure folly to want more. "I—I got attached. To the idea that you might be someone I knew. The idea that...I could trust that person with my secrets. That with him, I wouldn't have to keep up the lie."

"And you don't have many people like that." The Rook distracted the kitten with a gloved finger, nearly lifting her from Ren's lap when she latched on. The scratch of back claws on leather was almost as soft as his words. "I'm sorry."

Ren managed something like a smile. "Not your fault."

His breath caught. Then he gently detached the kitten from his hand and engulfed her bat-eared head with his palm to settle her down. The tips of his fingers were a whisper away from brushing Ren's thigh.

"She'll need a name," he said. "I suggest something like Shadow Stalker or Night Vengeance."

The suggestions startled a laugh from Ren. "Who taught you the naming of cats? What about Velvet? Coal? Thorn?"

He picked up the kitten and held her facing Ren. "Thorn? Does this look like a *Thorn* to you?"

The kitten squirmed free, but not to cause more mayhem. She curled herself into an impossibly tiny circle in Ren's lap and laid the tip of her tail over her nose. Without thinking, Ren said, "Clever Natalya."

The trickster heroine of Vraszenian folklore. It was foolish for Alta Renata to have a cat with a Vraszenian name, but— "Of course, a proper cat needs three names, one for each thread of the pattern deck. Her public name will be Nox. And her secret name...to herself only will that be known."

"Like kitten, like mistress. Here's hoping the mistress will sleep as easily."

Ren didn't watch him go. She only sat with the kitten in her lap, feeling the trace of warmth where he'd touched her cheek before leaving.

A Spiraling Fire

The Pearls and Kingfisher: Lepilun 28

Ren's nap felt like it had only underscored her exhaustion. After she changed back into Renata, crept out again, and returned through the manor's front door, she fell asleep immediately—and of course woke not much later, from another zlyzen nightmare.

She lay, heart pounding, staring at the canopy overhead. Then an inquisitive *mrrp?* near her left ear nearly made her jump out of her skin. Fortunately the sound came before the whiskery sniff, or Ren might have reflexively whacked the kitten straight off the bed.

Natalya walked over Ren's face and neck with no concern for personal space before settling down in the gap between shoulder and cheek. Her skinny tail thwapped twice across Ren's lips. Then the purring began.

Ren went back out like a snuffed candle. And this time, there was nothing but peaceful sleep between that and Tess throwing the drapes open the next morning.

The sensation of being well-rested was so novel, orienting herself took a moment. Ren blinked sleepily at the bright light, luxuriating in the softness of her bed, the loose relaxation of her limbs. Yawning, she stretched like a cat—and dislodged the actual cat, who mewed with indignation.

Tess shrieked and sprang back. The mew turned into a hiss, and Tess bent to peer at the small intruder. "Mother bless me, I thought you'd bedded down with a rat!" She reached out a tentative hand, but the kitten shied back from her, taking refuge in the rumpled covers.

Renata soothed Clever Natalya while Suilis came in with a pitcher of water and filled the washbasin. "I found her in the tree when I was on my balcony last night. Poor thing seemed to be stuck." She caught Tess's gaze on the word "balcony," and got a slight widening of eyes in return. Too many of their conversations were reduced to this now, hinting at things because someone else was in earshot. She mourned the loss of the time when she could have simply said *The Rook gave me a kitten* and watched Tess melt.

It was that as much as the coalescing of the half-formed notion in her mind that made her say, "Suilis, could you fetch a saucer of milk?" Her own breakfast already waited on the table in her sitting room, but Ren had no idea if the kitten could eat it. Her experience of pets ended at the rats the Fingers had sometimes trapped to fight each other.

"Begging your pardon, alta, but I don't think Tess will thank me if she has to clean up kitten runs later. I'll bring up some trout instead." Suilis bobbed a curtsy and stepped out.

In her absence, Ren asked softly, "Can you arrange for me to be undisturbed? I need to lay a pattern."

Tess checked the hallway before returning to whisper, "Not here. Yesterday I caught Suilis snooping in your room." Her lips pressed into a flat line. "She's tried hard to be friendly with me, but I'm wise to her now."

The news jolted Ren. *If I didn't have Tess watching my back...* "Should I have her sacked?"

After a moment's thought, Tess shook her head. "I don't *know* that she means any harm. And even if she does, isn't it better that she's here to keep an eye on? No, I've a notion of how to deal with it. Don't you worry."

Before Ren could ask what that notion was, a creak from the

hallway signaled the end of their privacy. Tess straightened up. "What do you say to the jonquil surcoat with smocked bandeau, alta? I'm certain *some people* would find that quite fetching."

Ren tried to go along with the hint about her mystery suitor, but her heart wasn't in it. Watching Tess bustle about, playing alta's maid with Suilis, she thought, *It hardly counts as playing anymore.* Not when there was never any time off the stage. She'd never meant to trap Tess into a servant's life, curtsying to and fetching for her own sister... but whether she meant to or not, that was exactly what she'd done.

The weight of that reflection pursued her out the door of the manor. And although Ren had a basket of tricks good for shedding any tail, no trick could help her escape her own guilt.

But the scene in Kingfisher drove it from her thoughts. Yesterday there had been Vigil patrols sweeping the area, looking for the escaped Anduske; today it was the Ordo Apis, and they were doing more than just sweeping. The courtyard of Alinka's tenement was full of stunned people and broken belongings. Arenza barely dodged a travel chest tossed from a second-floor window. It broke on impact, scattering wedding linens, a kureč banner of the Anoškin, a bundle of embroidered black that had to be someone's koszenie, the record of their lineage.

Alinka caught her arm and pulled her away. "Say nothing," the other woman warned in Vraszenian, dragging her inside. "They know this is Grey's house and will bother us not, but I've no wish to test their patience." A last glimpse showed the family rushing to take stock of their broken belongings, before Alinka firmly shut the door.

"What are they doing?" Arenza asked, her blood cold. "Why come here?"

"They search all the districts, one by one. Seeking the Stadnem Anduske... and any who might have sheltered them."

Like Alinka. Arenza watched the woman gather up her huddled children, pressing kisses into their hair. "You did so well, alča. You and Jagyi, quiet like bunnies."

I brought this on them. Not the connection to the Anduske—Grey himself had done that, and Alinka, insisting Koszar stay until he recovered—but the sudden crackdown. And yet, how could Ren have left Idusza and the others to die?

She wanted to apologize, but couldn't. Arenza had nothing to do with the escape.

At least she could draw comfort from the plan she'd put into motion. The meeting at Traementis Manor had gone well, and Donaia was sleeping better thanks to a calming tea Alinka had blended for her. There would be a message on its way later today, inviting her and the children to come with Donaia to Quientis's bay villa once the adoptions were complete, a little over two weeks hence. That would get them all out of harm's way, until the search for the Anduske died down.

"You came not for this," Alinka said, with the determined air of someone trying to pretend to normalcy. Her grin slid toward cheeky. "But if it's Grey you came to see, he's not here."

It startled an embarrassed laugh from Arenza. "I seek him not. Only a quiet place to lay some cards—though it seems quiet is not to be found."

"The worst has passed. I will take the children upstairs." Jagyi fussed when Alinka withdrew an arm to gesture for Arenza to use the table. She wrapped him up again quickly, but the tension had broken, and a full tantrum loomed behind it.

"I can make my own tea," Arenza said, reading the hesitation in Alinka's expression as she glanced at the water warming on the hearth, the brick of tea waiting next to it. Alinka gave her a grateful smile and nudged a curious Yvie upstairs, Jagyi's wail drifting in their wake.

Brick tea wasn't nearly as good as what she drank at Traementis Manor, but the preparation was soothingly familiar: toasting a small chunk, then grinding it and whisking the powder in. That done, Ren arranged herself at the table and took out her cards.

She should have done this ages ago. But after nearly turning her brain to sausage patterning the Rook, she'd been half afraid of what would happen if she tried to pattern Vargo—because at the time, she thought he might *be* the Rook. And then, once they'd fallen out...

Admit it. You were even more afraid then. Vargo, with his spider spirit and his unnaturally fast healing, his knowledge of numinatria. What defenses might he have around him?

There was only one way to find out.

She took three deep breaths, then recited the prayers as she shuffled, cut, and dealt.

The good of his past puzzled her. The Mask of Bones, revealed; in most cases she would interpret that as some metaphorical ending. Here, it felt like a literal death. Yet the sense she got from that grinning skull wasn't a dark one—or not *only* dark. This wasn't Vargo profiting from murder...not exactly. Whoever had died, they'd made Vargo the man he was today—and that was better than what he would otherwise have been.

At the other end of the row, The Mask of Nothing formed a chilling counterpoint. It was the card of madness, in all its forms, from rash action to literal insanity, and it had appeared in Koszar's pattern as well. They didn't mean the same thing, though—at least, she thought they didn't. Vargo had brushed up against something that lay outside the bounds of rationality. The eyeless mask on the card resembled the one Renata had worn to the first Praeteri initiation, and her pulse leapt as she remembered the rage that overtook her in the temple. Was that why Vargo was so interested in the Praeteri—because of their eisar numinatria?

That left the middle. One Poppy Weeps represented pain and suffering, of which there was certainly plenty in Vargo's past. For himself as well as for others; hadn't she sensed that when they danced on the Night of Bells? He spared no one in pursuit of his goals, not even Derossi Vargo.

Ren turned over the next row. Her fingers trembled at Drowning Breath, the ill of his present. It had appeared in the pattern her mother, Ivrina, laid in the nightmare, as Ren's own ill future: the confrontation with Ondrakja and the zlyzen. The one that had killed Leato.

Ondrakja was gone. But whatever Vargo was doing, it was equally terrifying...and only partially balanced by Labyrinth's Heart in the position of good. When Ren looked at the labyrinth painted on the card, she didn't see the serenity of walking its curving path; she saw a spider's web, with Vargo at the center. He was biding his time, waiting for the right moment to move.

Unfortunately, the central card baffled her almost as much as the present row of Grey's had, laid on this same table. In that position, The Face of Song could be read as either revealed or veiled, or a mix of both—but neither made sense. On the one hand it signified love, peace, reconciliation; on the other, an insistence on painting over conflict and pretending it wasn't there. Prior to that confrontation in the temple, Ren would have thought it pointed to her own false warmth with Vargo. That was long gone, though, their conflict bared to the world.

So you're not all-seeing, she thought wryly. *At least this time the central card didn't try to scramble your brains like an egg.* The Rook was still one up on Vargo.

With the Rook at the forefront of her thoughts, she immediately felt the connection when the top row disclosed The Ember Adamant. That had been the Rook's good future, a chance for him to fulfill his mandate against the nobility once and for all. For Vargo it was ill, and a fate Ren recognized all too well. He owed a lot of debts—not of money, but other kinds—and had made a lot of promises he might not be able to keep. Ren had teetered on the brink of a fall like that as she worked her way into House Traementis. Vargo failing now would be like Ren failing Tess.

Who did he care about that much? His spirit, Alsius? There was an odd warmth between the two at times. The connection between them whispered to her from the middle card, The Face of Roses. Vargo did recover swiftly from injuries; she suspected Alsius was the reason. But in the ambivalent position, that healing came with a cost.

And the counterpart to The Face of Roses was The Mask of Worms. *That* card had occupied the central position in the Rook's future, representing the unknown poison corrupting Nadežra—a poison the Rook clearly suspected Vargo of profiting from. Was he right? She couldn't tell. Everything felt tangled up together, the threads too snarled to tease apart.

Whether he was right or not, Ren couldn't ignore the final card. The Mask of Night was Ir Nedje, the deity of bad luck—but it lay revealed. Something in Vargo's future held the possibility of averting disaster.

Disaster like The Mask of Worms. Like what the Rook fought against.

She stared at the cards, trying to feel the threads of not only Vargo's pattern, but the Rook's. She was sure they influenced each other somehow, but—

"Alinka!"

The door banged open, revealing Grey in his patrol uniform. It was almost the mirror of Ren's old nightmares, but this time her heart lifted instead of seizing with fear. And when his gaze fell on her, she saw a similar warmth, paired with relief. She wouldn't be sitting quietly at his kitchen table with a cup of forgotten tea if something had happened to his family.

"They're upstairs," she said, sweeping her cards into a pile before Grey could study them. "All is well." *Here, at least.*

He shut the door behind him and sagged against it. "Thank you." Then, as she murmured a prayer of gratitude and tucked the cards away: "Who was that for?"

Ren's answer came softly, almost drowned by the sudden noise from Yvieny upstairs as she heard her uncle. "I'm still trying to figure that out."

Kingfisher, Lower Bank: Lepilun 28

Grey didn't have to try nearly as hard as he expected to talk Arenza into staying after she finished her pattern. He could practically see her weighing her schedule and obligations, but her body showed no inclination to move. When he offered to fetch crab claws and garlic fried daybread from a stall on the Tmarin Canal, it was too much for even her self-control to resist.

Yvie pounded the claws until the table was sprayed with butter, the morning's fright forgotten. Arenza couldn't fill the gap Kolya had left at the table, but she made it a little less empty, a little easier to deal with a garrulous Yvie while Alinka tended to Jagyi. Grey's amused glance caught Arenza's several times over a gruesome detail in the long-winded tale of the terrible Claw-Cracker, denizen of the Dežera. When their fingers brushed mopping up the buttery remains of Claw-Cracker's last stand, he let her be the one to pull her hand away.

After the bucket was depleted and Alinka had taken Jagyi upstairs for a nap, Grey scrabbled for a reason to keep Arenza there awhile longer. The quiet ache in her voice last night haunted him, the wish that he *were* the Rook. He knew she enjoyed spending time with his family, being Vraszenian for once instead of Alta Renata...but he hadn't thought of his own role in these occasions. The possibility that it was his own company, not just Alinka's, that she craved.

Yvie solved the puzzle for him. When he finished washing her hands clean of butter, garlic, and bits of crab shell, she turned to Arenza. "Last time you were here, you said you would draw a card for me, and then you didn't!" She flopped across the table, a picture of woe, and twisted so she was looking at Arenza upside down. "You have to keep your promises. That's a rule."

Had Ren's manners always been so tidy, or had she picked that up from being Renata? Her hands were remarkably clean. But she still wiped them off before bringing out her cards and shuffling. "Hare and Hound," she said, flicking the card up between two fingers. "Know you the sto—"

"Clever Natalya!" Yvie said, bouncing upright. "When the evil sorcerer was chasing her, so she had to turn into a hare and so he turned into a hound and so she turned into—"

Grinning, Grey let his niece relate a mostly coherent version of the tale to Arenza while he cleared off the table. By the time Clever

Natalya had tricked the sorcerer into turning into a dream, then defeated him by waking herself up, he wasn't quite done, so Arenza moved on to card tricks. Yvie didn't have the patience for the more drawn-out kinds of street magic, designed to make the audience think their chosen card was thoroughly lost in the depths of the deck, but she was entranced by stunts like single-handed shuffling or one card seemingly leaping from the pack of its own accord.

So was Grey. The dexterity of Ren's hands as she split the cards into a two-part waterfall that flowed together again at the bottom was a beauty to watch.

"Uncle Grey does things like that, too!" Yvie shot to her feet. "Let me get the cards—"

He began to protest, but it died on his lips. He'd convinced Ren he couldn't be the Rook, and by now she knew he wasn't the strait-laced Vigil captain most of the world saw. Besides, the thought of showing off his own skill pleased him.

Though Ren—*No, Arenza; you have to keep them straight*—pouted when he used one hand to split the deck into four parts, flipping and turning them before setting them straight once more. "This is not fair," she informed Yvie. "Your uncle has larger hands."

"Let me see!" Yvie climbed up onto the table and grabbed them both, pulling their hands together to compare.

Her palm was dry and warm, and petal soft thanks to the protection of Renata's gloves. On reflex, the tops of his fingers curled over hers. They were slender, but also capable and strong. Like the finest steel, forged by Vicadrius herself.

Djek, he was far gone if he was turning poet over a woman's hands.

Then his head caught up with his heart. What was he *doing*? It wasn't just work that kept him from having a sweetheart, like Alinka thought; it was the secrets he carried. Secrets he'd worked his ass off to turn Ren away from. He couldn't hope to keep the truth from her if he let her get even closer.

And another reason, even deeper than that. *Wrong*, she'd called his pattern. Not the first time he'd heard that. He didn't want her to be another victim of the ill luck he'd carried since birth.

But her eyes were merry as she looked at him across their joined hands. "See? Very unfair," she was saying to Yvie.

He said nothing; he was too busy telling himself *Pull away* and then failing to do so. Because for a moment, Ren looked happy.

And he was, too.

Dawngate, Old Island: Lepilun 31

Renata's previous visit to the Theatre Agnasce had been on the Night of Bells, when the place was filled with a mirror maze. Now she got her first proper look at its full glory, from the gold-veined marble of the columns in its vestibule to the soft sueded leather of the seats in the hall.

Beautiful though it was, she didn't particularly want to be here tonight. Ironic, considering that pleasures like this had been one of the rewards she imagined for herself when she began her con. But these days, all she could think was that there were half a dozen better uses for her time.

Giuna had been craving a diversion, though, and Renata knew whispers were flying about her falling-out with Vargo. Doubly so after the night at Essunta's, when the Rook publicly accused him of conspiring with both Mettore *and* Sostira Novrus, and triply so after Vargo's arrest in Lacewater. The rumors hit him more than her, of course, but their association meant Renata needed to show her face in public.

Sibiliat leaned in as they passed a trio of delta gentry whispering not at all subtly behind their fans. "You know, I don't think His Grace would raise a fuss if you reassigned that charter for the river numinat."

"To whom, though?" Renata had been making an effort to show more friendliness to Sibiliat, if only for Giuna's sake, so she tried to keep her tone pleasant. "If anyone else stood ready to replace it, the West Channel would have been flowing clean years ago. I can't let personal animus ruin the chance of that now."

"How admirable." It was impossible to tell whether Sibiliat spoke sincerely or not. "Well, if you want to exact some other kind of revenge on him, let me know."

Renata nodded a greeting at Meda Isorran as they strolled through the vestibule. "I believe that particular Traementis tradition has come to an end."

"And good riddance," Giuna added.

"Something's come to an end?" The question came from Tanaquis, looking remarkably tidy and elegant in a midnight surcoat of satin-woven cotton with constellations embroidered around the hem—all accurate to their celestial placement, Tess had told Renata with a put-upon groan. "Don't tell me you're thinking of quitting the—"

In a remarkable moment of self-restraint, Tanaquis silenced herself, her grey eyes darting to Giuna.

Sibiliat came to her rescue. "Giuna, I left Grandmama waiting on the landing for Fadrin. Could you be a dear and keep her company until he arrives?"

The interactions between those two had been strained ever since Giuna made public the truth of the Scurezza murders. Now she fixed Sibiliat with a flat look. "I *know* you're getting rid of me."

"Yes, little bird, but only for a moment. And only because it's necessary."

The nickname was a misstep. Giuna drew herself up in a way Ren recognized, because she'd spent hours practicing it in front of a mirror. *Well, I'd rather she imitate a con artist than a snake.*

The snake realized her error, too. Her whisper into Giuna's ear was too loud, though; it carried to Renata's ears. "I promise, soon I will share these secrets with you."

Renata's pleasant expression grew stiff as her cousin walked away. She didn't want Giuna anywhere near the Praeteri.

She'd tried patterning the group, following the suspicion that they might have caused the Traementis curse. But she didn't know whether the ensuing lack of confirmation was due to their innocence, or the difficulty of patterning a whole group en masse.

The ill cards had been perfectly clear: The Face of Gold, One Poppy Weeps, A Spiraling Fire. Increasing their wealth and indulging their passions, without a care for those they hurt. The rest, though, were hard to interpret. Labyrinth's Heart had echoed the pattern she laid after the Traementis were uncursed—the stillness that said their troubles were not over—but what she hadn't seen from that line was The Peacock's Web. The riddle she had yet to solve, the mystery of where the curse came from.

Once Giuna was gone, Sibiliat turned to Tanaquis. "We weren't speaking of Renata's involvement with our 'illustrious circle.' But now that you mention it—it's true that we haven't seen you recently, Renata. Surely you must have received invitations?"

She had—but even if she'd been eager to return, she had no time for it. She could hardly explain her absence, though. *I was busy breaking into the Dockwall Prison* wouldn't go over well with this audience.

Sibiliat misinterpreted her hesitation. "I promise, not everything is like what you went through last time. But the Pontifex said that he sensed vengeful energy in you. He felt it needed to be released before you could progress."

Renata didn't believe in the slightest that her spiritual progression was Diomen's primary concern. She couldn't figure out what he *did* want, though. And that eyeless mask haunted her: The Mask of Nothing, the madness she'd seen in Vargo's past.

To understand its meaning, she might have to go back.

"Besides," Sibiliat added, "half the point is to make useful connections with fellow members. Meda Terdenzi could lean on Prasinet for you—get her to drop that silly insistence on double taxing electrum as both gold and silver. I hear you've been arguing with her office for weeks about that."

Tanaquis looked like she'd bitten into a sour plum. "That isn't 'half the point'—it's a *corruption* of the point."

"For you, maybe." Sibiliat cast a sidelong smirk at Renata, as though expecting her to share the joke.

A discreet bell interrupted them. Tanaquis looked around. "Something's ringing."

"Our signal to take our seats." Sibiliat's raised eyebrow questioned Tanaquis's ignorance of such cues—which neatly covered Renata's own. "If Fadrin's late . . . No, there he is." The tall, muscular Acrenix cousin had picked up Carinci and was carrying her up the stairs to their family box, while a theatre usher stowed her wheeled chair. Giuna hurried to rejoin Renata, and together they went to the Traementis box.

It had formerly been the Indestor box. House Ecchino, who administered the Novrus charter for the theatre, had painted over the Indestor emblem as soon as the house was dissolved, but the crossed triple feathers of the Traementis still gave off a whiff of fresh paint. Settling into her plush chair, Renata found she had a splendid view of not only the stage, but the other noble boxes—which, as Sibiliat might say, was half the point.

The first of the night's two performances was a reworking of a much older play, recounting the spectacular downfall of two of the first noble houses. Formed after the death of Kaius Rex, Adrexa and Taspernum had been in a constant war, their conflicts often spilling into the city in waves of blood and destruction. Until an unregistered relative of both houses destroyed them.

Renata knew the general story and had been hoping to enjoy the play. Her companions, unfortunately, were more interested in gossiping. "No surprise that Her Elegance approved this one," Sibiliat mused. "Sostira's trying to cozen Cibrial with flattery. She has her eye on one of House Destaelio's daughters, but ever since that business at Essunta's, Cibrial's been questioning whether Sostira should even hold the Argentet seat."

"Is that why Ovictus is being painted as so heroic?" Tanaquis asked, as the character in question saved a delta gentleman from assassins. "I don't recall that being very accurate to history."

Ovictus, who'd founded House Destaelio atop the ashes of Adrexa and Taspernum. "Who cares about accuracy?" Sibiliat replied, smirking against the tips of her fan. "The history of Nadežra is what Argentet says it is."

Her comment left a sour taste in Renata's mouth, ruining her enjoyment of the rousing speech Ovictus delivered as his new house register unfurled behind him like a banner.

When the audience streamed out to search for refreshments during the interval, Sibiliat said, "If you'll excuse me, I want to check on Grandmama. It's too much of a bother for her to step out, and I don't want her to feel lonely."

Giuna must have still felt miffed about being sent away earlier, because she said, "We'll go with you," and promptly hooked her arms with both Renata and Tanaquis.

They found Carinci Acrenix not quite alone. Faella Coscanum had joined her, and the two women were tearing apart the production like cats fighting over a wounded bird, while Fadrin slouched beside them, looking bored out of his skull.

"—only thing he has to recommend him as a playwright is that he's fast and cheap," Faella sniffed. "That, and his ability to kiss Her Elegance's feet on command. Every script is more tedious than the last."

Carinci nodded vigorously. "No wit, and no memorable lines. And that actor! I'll put up with bombast if the speaker is pretty enough... Do you remember the decade where Toccante played Segretto Adrexa?" She leered in memory. "Now *that* was a time to be alive. Never wore a shirt. It was glorious. Do you remember the amphitheatre staging? Winter Starvation of 173, and he's out there oiled up and bare to the waist. By Argentet's command, to distract everybody from the famine. Even had his spirit show up in the second act, shirtless and painted blue. This fellow isn't a tenth the actor Toccante was."

Faella fanned herself. "We will never see his like again." Nodding at Renata's party, she said, "But here are the children. Come, tell us what you thought of the first play."

Carinci immediately claimed Giuna's attention, grilling her in between giving Sibiliat sly, amused looks. Leaning forward, Faella said to Renata, "I haven't thanked you yet for the service you've done for my family. Marvisal was a bit put out, but she's recovered. And my brother agreed to cede all decisions about her future to me. I don't suppose *you're* looking for a wife?"

That was the other reason to avoid social gatherings: Everyone was placing bets on how long it would be before Renata married. "I'm afraid I've been much too busy to think that far ahead."

She could see Faella readying to fulfill her duty as an elder by delivering a lecture on the importance of marriage. Casting about for some way to prevent that, Renata said, "It occurs to me that you must know absolutely everybody who's ever been anybody in this city. I don't suppose you've heard of a man named Alsius?"

Complete silence seized the box. The stricken looks on Faella, Carinci, and Sibiliat's faces told Renata she'd just put her foot through a rotten board.

Carinci snapped, "Fadrin. I'm tired. Take me home." But when he came to lift her, she forestalled him with a hand. "I will assume that you are ignorant rather than cruel, Alta Renata, and will only ask that you not gossip about my son."

Her *son*? Renata knew her shock was visible as Fadrin carried Carinci out.

"Uncle Alsius passed away when I was a child," Sibiliat said quietly. "He was Grandmama's only natural-born son—she adopted my father from one of the contract wives after that. She took to her chair following his death. I don't think she's ever fully recovered from that loss."

"You couldn't know." Faella patted Renata's hand. "Nobody ever speaks of it, out of respect for Carinci. They say he killed himself—not suicide; a numinatrian experiment gone wrong—but there were also rumors he'd been murdered. I suppose Lecilla must have mentioned him. They were of an age, though they hardly ran in the same circles." She clicked her tongue.

"Yes, she did," Renata lied, and hoped nobody would ask her why.

Tanaquis chose that moment to take the conversation down an even worse path. Her eyes widening with epiphany, she said, "Could Alsius Acrenix be the father you came looking for?"

"*What?*"

That came in unison from Sibiliat and Giuna, while Faella

sparkled in delight at her unexpected banquet of gossip. "Why, Alta Renata! I thought your father was Seterin—Eret Viraudax."

"My father *is* Eret Viraudax," Renata said stiffly, grateful for once that Seterin and Liganti custom cared more about registered ties than those of blood. "I'll thank you not to insinuate otherwise, Alta Faella. As for your question, Tanaquis, no. My mother was very clear that the man who sired me was Seterin."

"And breathtakingly handsome, as I recall," Tanaquis mused. "Alta Sibiliat, was your uncle good-looking?"

Sibiliat lifted her hands helplessly. "He was my favorite uncle. I liked him, but to me he was just an old man. He dressed very nicely?"

"Old? The boy was barely past thirty. But no, he wasn't particularly handsome, unless a face buried in a book is your pleasure." Faella sniffed. "You're right about his clothing, though. Alta Renata—"

The tolling of the bell wouldn't have been enough to cut her off, except that Giuna intervened. "The interval is over. We should get back to our box. Good evening, Alta Faella."

This time Renata didn't have to be dragged; she was more than ready to go. When the second play began, she barely even saw the stage, her mind was so full of other things.

Vargo. Alsius *Acrenix.* What in the name of the Faces, the Masks, and her unknown ancestors was going on there?

She needed to tell the Rook. And then, as if her thoughts had summoned him, she saw a familiar shadow climbing one of the heavy tasseled ropes by the curtains.

For an instant her pulse thundered in her throat. But the laughter of the audience cued her even before she got a good look at his costume, which parted at the collar to reveal an enticing glimpse of his oiled chest. It wasn't the real Rook; it was Fontimi, the actor who played him in stage productions.

What he was doing in the story she didn't know, but there were hoots and catcalls as he made his way from box to box, stepping on a ledge that seemed to have been installed for the purpose, making flirtatious gestures and even kissing any audience member who would play along.

Then he was at their box and pulling a pale glove from his coat. Clearly, he'd done his research.

"I'll happily trade this forfeit for another, fair alta," he said in a pleasant baritone meant to carry throughout the theatre. Then, leaning over in an impressive display of core strength, he offered himself up for a kiss.

The hoots took over the hall, and even Sibiliat was clapping in delight. Thinking in resignation that she might as well give Faella enough gossip to choke on, Renata kissed the fake Rook.

It wasn't bad. His breath was inoffensive, and his lips were firm and warm. It was chaste enough to be cheeky. When he finished and moved on, she played to the crowd's cheers by lifting the "returned" glove and waving it.

But it called an ache from deep inside—a craving for the real thing. A kiss from the Rook himself.

Her expression felt like a porcelain mask as she sat down. *That* was even more impossible than her attraction to Grey Serrado. There was no point in chasing an enigma, a shadow she'd given up on seeing through. He might know the truth of her, but she would never know the truth of him.

It didn't stop her from wanting it anyway.

Villa Acrenix, Bay of Vraszan: Lepilun 35

The islets scattered throughout the Bay of Vraszan had long been the playground of the Liganti nobility. They allowed for more sprawling estates than the manors on the Upper Bank, with more extensive gardens... and more privacy.

The only one Vargo had ever publicly visited was the Villa Extaquium, for the Praeteri initiation. That place had made his skin crawl, because he knew too many details about Sureggio's excesses:

not just the titillating stories, but truths far more disturbing to any-one with a conscience. He might not have been able to bring himself to accept another invitation there, and never mind that he couldn't afford to be finicky after what happened with Renata in the temple.

But the invitation he received for the autumnal equinox came from Sibiliat, bidding him attend a ceremony at the Villa Acrenix instead.

Vargo watched Diomen as the Praeteri gathered at sunset on the terrace behind the villa. Even outside the theatrical stage of the Tyrant's hidden temple, the man was impressive. He was exactly the sort of person one would expect to see leading a mystery cult, with his imposing height and his deep-set eyes, his resonant voice prom-ising the secrets of the cosmos. And he hardly seemed to have aged in the last sixteen years.

Vargo, on the other hand, had made himself unrecognizable as the boy Diomen once hired to carry out an assassination.

Even with that transformation, coming anywhere near the Pon-tifex was a calculated risk. At first it hadn't been an option; although a Seterin man with a shaved head ought to have been easy to find, tracking Diomen down had taken years. Then more years to uncover the existence and activities of the Praeteri, to get himself into a posi-tion where he could enter the temple, attend the rituals, find out what game was being played where Vargo couldn't see. To become a player in that game—and, if all went well, to win.

He hadn't yet been able to make sense of their philosophy, assum-ing there even was any. The first three gates were easy to parse; like a knot, the Praeteri put candidates through challenges designed to make them earn their place. But these middle gates focused on desire, pain, rage—the one Renata had passed through—and self-ishness. How to embrace such things, and how to master them.

The numinat he'd seen during the Dreamweaver Riots had stoked people's rage, which no ordinary inscription could do. It was solid proof of what he and Alsius had suspected for years: that the Praeteri had some way of influencing people's emotions through eisar-based numinatria. He might not grasp the method yet, but he'd seen its effects all over Nadežra, in the unnatural obedience of certain people, the inflexible determination of others. He saw it in people who betrayed long-held convictions on a seeming whim, and in others whose resentments suddenly boiled over into murderous hatred.

Things like that could happen on their own. But when there was a pattern of certain people profiting, it stopped being just human shittiness at work.

"Brothers and sisters," Diomen said. "We come together once more to know our deeper selves, to reach beyond the confines of ordinary wisdom. To know the cosmos with the intellect alone is insufficient: We must know it with our hearts and with our flesh."

So much for the inscriptor's prayer. Vargo couldn't deny there was some truth to Diomen's rhetoric, though. *I have my compass, my edge, my chalk, myself...* But so far, Vargo's self had been insufficient. How did one create a numinat that called on eisar instead of the gods? With a blank focus, apparently. Which made *no* fucking sense, because a focus operated by drawing the power of the god it named. Eisar didn't have names—according to Alsius, they were just unformed emanations of the Lumen—so it followed that one couldn't call on them that way. But then how did you attune a numinat to them?

He hoped that tonight might teach him.

The purpose of this ceremony was to explore the revelation of desire. There was no numinatria involved, at least not yet; instead Diomen led them in a series of chants and prayers, then stood before each participant and asked them what they desired tonight.

Some of the answers were surprising. Ebrigotto Attravi complained of exhaustion and said he just wanted a good night's sleep. Tanaquis Fienola wanted to experience dissolution into the cosmos, though how she was going to achieve that, Vargo had no idea. But most confessed to the kinds of desires he expected: greater wealth, the destruction of a rival, knowledge of a cousin's secrets.

Vargo had his answer prepared long before Diomen came to him.

"I want to re-create the West Channel cleansing numinat. But

I don't think that's any surprise," he said with a wry grin, drawing chuckles from a few of the Praeteri.

Diomen's eyes narrowed. "A goal is not a desire, Brother Vargo. What do you want?" He pressed a hand just below Vargo's contraceptive numinat. "*Here.*"

Vargo's stomach jumped at the touch. The entirely organic rage he'd felt in the temple—at Diomen's interference and Renata's accusations—flashed through him like heat lightning. He stiffened to stop himself from forcibly removing that hand at the wrist. *I want every fucking cuff in this city to see me for what I am.*

Something better than Lower Bank trash.

But that was a truth he barely admitted to himself, and not something he'd ever say to the very people who despised him. Instead he said, "I'm not certain what I want. But I'll know it when I see it."

Diomen withdrew his hand with an avuncular nod. "It can be difficult to understand what we truly desire; often we settle for distractions and substitutes. But remember that you cannot reach your destination by looking at a map. You must walk the path."

::How does anyone listen to this arrant nonsense?:: Alsius grumbled as Diomen moved on to hear Sibiliat's desire for new experiences. ::Must I follow this charlatan all night?::

Better you than me. Alsius could eavesdrop much more easily on Diomen's conversations. They'd thought for a time that the man was a fraud, set up by a puppet master to bilk Nadežra's gentry and lesser nobility out of their wealth; in a way, Vargo wished that were true. The Praeteri wouldn't have been nearly so dangerous then. But having met the man now, it was clear he was a fanatical believer. And that meant he might speak of the things Vargo still needed to know.

Having completed his circuit, Diomen spread his arms wide. "Brothers and sisters! The Lumen has the power to bring you what you seek. For some, your desires can be satisfied here and now. For others, that lies in the future. But to achieve either, we must immerse ourselves in desire, and through experience, master it. Cast off your hesitation, your shame, your shackles! Indulge yourselves without restraint, and know the revelations of the cosmos!"

Fully half the Praeteri took that as their cue to strip. Vargo barely stopped himself from rolling his eyes. There was food and drink aplenty, and drugs of various kinds—including an abundant supply of the aža that was supposedly unavailable now—but the eager bypassed those in favor of more immediate desires. Before long, the estate rang with the groans and gasps, and the snap of the crop Parma Extaquium wielded as she rode, not her usual Fintenus or Coscanum toys, but her half brother Ucozzo. Desires easily satisfied...which in theory would lead people to something more, but Vargo couldn't see how. The only numinata he saw at work were Noctat charms some men had looped around their cocks to keep themselves hard.

Sibiliat, however, had set up the estate to cater to other activities as well. The Acrenix library was open to anyone who desired knowledge, though Vargo didn't see anyone there when he passed through. True to his word, Attravi sought out a quiet, luxuriously appointed room to sleep in, and a peek into another darkened room revealed not people coupling, but Tanaquis floating blindfolded and naked in a tub of goo.

The sight of her made Vargo pause, frowning. It wasn't any surprise that Tanaquis belonged to the Praeteri...but she'd given no hint of it when he brought her evidence of Breccone Indestris's interference during the riots, even when Vargo brought up eisar. How closely did she protect her brethren? She'd led Serrado to arrest her fellow cultist, so apparently not *too* closely. Perhaps Vargo could bait her into sharing some of their secrets.

Not while she was communing with the cosmos, though. Sighing, he worked his way back to the terrace and found Diomen gone. That left Vargo with a choice: avail himself of the library in the hopes of learning something useful from a book, or write the evening off as a routine orgy and find himself a hole he didn't mind fucking.

Instead he wound up in a chaise on a balcony overlooking the blackened waters of the bay, a Seterin brandywine in his hand, warm with the flavors of summer stone fruit. His glass was emptied to the dregs and full-faced Corillis had risen, dripping silver mist in her wake, when Sibiliat pushed aside the balcony curtain.

In a voice honey-thick with amusement, she said, "After hearing cousin Fadrin's tales, I'm surprised to find you seeking solitude."

After hearing so much gossip about her and Giuna Traementis, Vargo was surprised to find Sibiliat seeking him. Then he recalled her words to the Pontifex about new experiences. It was a story as old as the Point, that Upper Bank cuffs often went slumming in search of those.

Still, there were worse ways to spend his night than fucking his way through the Acrenix register. Finishing the last of his drink, Vargo rose from the chaise and gave her a Lower Bank once-over. "If Fadrin were here, maybe I'd be more interested."

Sibiliat leaned her hip against the railing and smirked over the rim of a goblet of pomegranate-red wine, letting him look his fill. Her kohl liner extended to sharp points, giving her eyes a sly, knowing look, and her hands, he noticed, were bare. "I've heard my cousin's boasting often enough to know he's not that good in bed."

Removing his gloves, Vargo slid his hand around hers and coaxed the goblet to his lips. The wine rolled thick over his tongue. "You've come to prove you're better?"

"I've come because I'm not the fool Renata is." Sibiliat's mention of Renata threatened to sour the pleasant taste of the wine, until her following words sweetened it. "Her loss could be my gain. My father was right about you. You are a singular man, Eret Vargo."

His touch slid down her arm, settling on her hips to pull her closer. Whatever Sibiliat wanted from him, he doubted it stopped at a quick bend over the balcony rail. But he was in a mood not to care. "Let's not bring Renata into this," he growled. Then, after a moment's thought: "Or your father."

Sibiliat set her glass aside, her laugh brushing silk-soft against his lips. "Whatever you want," she whispered, before silencing herself in his kiss.

::I hope you're having a more successful night than I am.::

At Alsius's interruption, Vargo's grip tightened, drawing a questioning noise from Sibiliat. Oblivious, the spider nattered on. ::The Pontifex's only desire seems to be listening to his own voice—and he isn't saying anything worth hearing. Shall we meet back up?::

Later, Vargo replied as Sibiliat took charge and crowded him back onto the chaise, knee pressing hard between his thighs. *You might want to stay away. I found something interesting to do.*

When he and Sibiliat lay panting and spent, she reached down to her discarded clothing. Vargo assumed she was going to dress and depart, but instead she sat up again with a lump of clay in her hands, which she divided into two pieces, giving him half. "Mold this in your hands," she said.

"Into what? Some toy for our use?" It was too small to offer much interest on that front.

Another smirk flashed across her mouth; she had a face made for it. "No—though if you want to think about that, go ahead. Shape it into a focus. And while you do, meditate on what we just did. Not the actions; the *wanting.* The craving for what's not quite within your reach. The refusal to stop until you possess it."

Her words killed all sexual desire but left him filled with a different kind of wanting. *This . . . is it? This is how it works?*

Sibiliat was shaping her own clay, eyes closed and expression as serene as if she were meditating in a temple. Which was essentially what she'd told him to do—and shit, that *made sense.* For the first time, Vargo finally understood.

Shaping the clay. The focus he'd seen during the riots was glass, but maybe Breccone Indestris had enjoyed glassworking. The point wasn't the material. For a Praeteri numinat, you didn't rely on sigils; you had to *imbue the focus.* Not the numinat, but the point at the center. Saturate yourself in the emotion you wanted to evoke, then pour that energy—the eisar drawn by it—and bind it in a physical object.

Alsius. I found it. I have it. He hoped.

Closing his eyes, he paid attention to the clay, working it with his fingers as he'd been working Sibiliat a few minutes ago. What did he want? What did he *really* want? He let it wash through him, as Diomen had said. Not the goal, but the desire: sixteen years' worth of waiting, of *wanting.*

::Excellent! What have you fou—*What are you doing with my niece?!*::

Opening his eyes, Vargo spotted Peabody's shadow-dimmed hues on the balcony rail. *Meditating. I warned you to stay away.*

::Since when does meditation involve being naked with a girl who's barely—::

She's a grown woman, old man, not the child you remember. Now leave me the fuck alone so I don't lose this!

The small lump of Peabody vanished. Hoping that hadn't broken his concentration too badly—or somehow muddied the focus with a desire for Alsius to stop interrupting—Vargo finished shaping the clay into a cabochon-domed round.

When he opened his eyes again, Sibiliat was pulling on her violet underdress and studying him with a speculative look. Vargo was very glad he'd invested in imbued cosmetics to cover up the brand on his chest, and he hoped Tanaquis's lack of inclination to gossip extended to him.

But Sibiliat's mind proved to be elsewhere. "By the way, my father was interested in speaking with you."

He paused in the act of pulling up his trousers. "What, here? Tonight? I thought he'd left the Praeteri, since he's part of the Cinquerat now."

"This is still our home. You'll find him in his office at the end of the south colonnade." Leaning over, she brushed her lips across his cheek, pausing at his ear. "Next time you want to stick it to the cuffs, don't settle for Fadrin. I'm curious whether you can take as good as you give."

Pulling back with a sly smile, she draped her surcoat over her arm and left Vargo to his thoughts.

Vargo straightened his clothes and debated reaching out to Alsius, but discarded the idea. He usually did his best to avoid bringing the spider anywhere near his brother. It was far too awkward... seeing as Ghiscolo was the one who'd had Alsius killed.

Villa Acrenix, Bay of Vraszan: Lepilun 35

"I hope I'm not interrupting, Your Mercy."

Ghiscolo's study looked out on the glow of distant Nadežra, with an entire wall of windows that surely required a numinat to keep the room from turning into an icebox in winter. He sat by those windows in an armchair of oxblood leather, a book in hand.

Marking his place with a finger, Ghiscolo glanced up. "Not at all, Eret Vargo. I was hoping you might find time for me tonight. Please, have a seat. Drink?" He nodded at the chair opposite him and the decanter on a side table, filled with the same stone fruit brandy Vargo had been drinking earlier.

"I wouldn't mind another taste of House Acrenix's best," Vargo said, watching Ghiscolo carefully as he poured. The man's pleasant expression didn't change, so either he didn't know how Vargo had spent the past hour, or he didn't care.

Vargo's money was on the latter.

Ghiscolo said, "I apologize for tarnishing your evening with a matter of business, but it's rare that I get an opportunity for true privacy. In the city, there are always servants around, or the risk that someone will interrupt with some urgent matter."

Servants who were often in someone else's pay. That was why Vargo kept no live-in help, and made sure those who visited for cleaning were well-enough compensated that they wouldn't be tempted to take bribes. He suspected Ghiscolo had already made more than one attempt to insinuate someone into his household.

"This is a familiar song," Vargo said dryly as he accepted the brandy. "Last time you had me out here for a private conversation, it was to discuss Mettore Indestor snooping into Praeteri business."

Ghiscolo toasted Vargo with his own glass. "A timely warning for which I am still grateful. And an apt comparison...because I'd like to talk to you about Sostira Novrus."

Vargo's hand tightened around his glass. Apart from his two assignations with Iascat, Vargo tried to have as little to do with House Novrus as possible. Sostira had a heart of stone, a roving eye, and nothing Vargo couldn't get elsewhere for less trouble. The last dealings he had with her led to a warehouse fire and the deaths of two men that Vargo hadn't intended to kill.

But rumor said Sostira's control of her house was faltering, especially after the Rook's accusations at the Essunta fireworks display. If Ghiscolo scented blood in the water, it made sense he'd turn to Vargo.

"Has she grown bored without Mettore to bicker with?" Vargo asked.

"She's grown unstable," Ghiscolo said bluntly, sliding his fingers through the gap between two shirt buttons as he lounged back in his chair. "To the point where the members of the Cinquerat are discussing whether Nadežra is truly best served by having the Argentet seat in her hands. Or in Novrus hands at all."

Vargo's snort set the liquid in his cup to rocking. "I don't think you can occupy two seats at once, *Your Mercy.*"

"Of course not," Ghiscolo said easily. "The law forbids it. Nor could any member of my house take the seat. We'd have to look... elsewhere."

A Cinquerat seat? The dull ennui Vargo had been feeling since Diomen asked him what he desired sharpened to a point. A heavy burst of wanting drove the air from his lungs. *Power.* Vargo didn't give a wet leech about the duties of the cultural seat—but the power behind it was enough to reshape Nadežra until the Lower Bank was every bit as good as the Upper.

He fought to keep his voice steady. "Removing Indestor took over a year, and in the end, it only worked because he put the entire Cinquerat—the entire *city*—in danger. Unless Sostira's instability contains an equivalent threat?"

He wasn't sure he had the patience to wait a year. Surely he could push it along. Like his fast-beating heart was sending the blood rushing hot through his head. Heat and blood. When in doubt, you could always turn to those solutions.

"Some threats are too delicate to make public. Sostira's marshaling her leverage to keep hold of her seat, but if someone was willing to use unorthodox means..." Ghiscolo sipped his brandy. "It wouldn't be just gratitude that person would earn. It would be respect."

The blood rush ebbed at that word, leaving the silence of clarity.

Vargo knew what he wanted, and he knew the most expedient way to get it. Better to start sooner than later. Setting his glass aside, he stood. "Thank you for your suggestion, Your Mercy. This has been an enlightening conversation. If you'll excuse me?"

"Of course," Ghiscolo murmured. He looked faintly surprised but not displeased. "Don't let me keep you."

Vargo barely heard, already striding from the study. There should be boats at the dock, waiting for guests who didn't intend to stay the night. He could have his fists gathered by midnight. He'd need information on where Sostira was, but that should be easy enough. The woman wasn't particularly subtle. Then a team of his best, enough to get in and get out fast...

::Are we leaving?:: Alsius asked, intruding on his plans. ::Good. Diomen is maundering on to Sureggio about the grand achievement the Lumen has surely destined him to make, and I'm not sure what drug Sureggio has taken. Let's go home and you can tell me what you discovered *besides* what lies beneath my niece's skirts.::

"We're not going home," Vargo said, spying Peabody waiting for him atop a topiary. He scooped the spider up as he passed. "We're going to kill Sostira Novrus."

::We *what*?::

He kept walking, ignoring Alsius yammering for an explanation, until the spider leapt free to one of the lanterns lining the path down to the dock. ::Vargo, *stop*. We're not going anywhere until you tell me what happened!::

Vargo's impatience tempted him to leave Alsius behind. Let the spider swim home if he was going to upset the plan. But then sense intervened. He might need Alsius; none of his fists were half as good at infiltrating protected locations for reconnaissance.

He stopped, rubbing his brow irritably. "Ghiscolo all but offered me Argentet if I could remove Sostira Novrus." Argentet, and through it, power. And respect. The desire for it buzzed like flies on a corpse. "Killing her is the most expedient way."

Dead silence followed.

"Is that good enough for you? Can we carry on now?"

::Vargo . . . :: Alsius's mental voice was more than hesitant. It was afraid. ::This isn't you.::

"Isn't it?" Vargo snapped. "I've killed and whored before, when it was necessary."

::But this isn't necessary.::

It is. It's just not necessary to you.

Even as he thought that—even as he turned to stalk down to the pier—Vargo hesitated. Where had that thought come from? Everything he did, every choice he'd made for sixteen years, all came back to one thing. Uncovering Alsius's murderer, the snake hiding beneath the water's surface, and freeing Nadežra from his coils.

Ghiscolo. Whose study Vargo had just stormed out of, blazing with a lust for power that had been a mere ember when he walked in.

"Fuck." He scrubbed hard at his face, as if that could scrub his brain. Unlike the rage numinat in Dmariše Square, or the one he'd pulled Renata from, this urge wasn't fading. Not anger; just the conviction that he'd be a better Argentet than Novrus was. "He did something to me. What the *fuck* did he do to me?"

::I don't know,:: Alsius whispered. ::Could there have been a numinat you didn't see?::

Under the floorboards, maybe. Or the underside of Vargo's chair, because Ghiscolo didn't seem to be affected. But its hold on him ought to have begun to fade as soon as he left.

Something on his body? Sibiliat's seduction might have been a preliminary step in the process. Vargo fought the urge to strip right there on the path and have Alsius examine him. She could hardly have tattooed or branded him without Vargo noticing. And the impulse hadn't overtaken him until he was talking to Ghiscolo. Though—

He dug the molded clay out of his pocket and hurled it as far as he could, into the night-dark water. It didn't make him feel any better.

"Let's get the fuck out of here before it hits again." Vargo reached up to the lantern, and Peabody scuttled down the bridge to his shoulder.

::Home, yes?::

Yes. Where Vargo would send notes out to his knot leaders instructing them to question any later orders to take out Sostira Novrus. Even knowing the urge was forced on him didn't banish it; it was an itch he couldn't scratch away, somewhere deep inside his head.

It was pure luck that he wasn't alone in there, or he might not have realized. "Thank you," Vargo said softly. "For being here."

::We're here for each other. Now why don't you tell me what you found before all this drama?::

Grateful for the distraction, Vargo headed for a boat and began silently explaining how to call upon eisar.

Saffron and Salt

Isla Prišta, Westbridge: Lepilun 36

Summer's heat was finally starting to loosen its grip on the Lower
Bank, and Coster's Walk was busier than ever with mid-autumn
traffic. With the breezes down the Dežera helping ease the stink of
the channel and the crowd, Tess lingered longer than she had time
for over the pieces at her favorite remnant stall. Not that she had
need of scraps these days, not with Ren's adoption and the custom of
all the cuffs who wanted to follow her fashion...but Tess wouldn't
always be clinging to Ren's purse. And no sense losing a forro over
what you could get for a mill.

No sense getting weepy over a bit of lace, either, but she found
her face clogging up as she fingered a length that would look lovely
as a ribbon in Ren's hair. *I miss my sister.* They'd had bad times
before—under Ondrakja, or in Ganllech, or when Ren couldn't
sleep—but somehow this one hurt...not worse. Differently. Like
the treasures Tess used to peer at through shop windows. Visible,
but out of reach.

She put the lace down firmly and wiped her eyes. One thing she
and Ren had in common: They were both busy. Squaring her shoulders, Tess headed for the old townhouse on the Isla Prišta, locked up
and empty since they moved out.

She regretted that they'd lived in the house mostly during winter, when the weather was dreary, the canal clogged and sluggish, the pavers dark with weeping rain. The back walk at the start of autumn was a different world. Mellow sunlight painted the stonework gold; late-blooming flowers cascaded from every window box, their scent masking any foulness in the water, and lush green moss stretched tendrils up from the waterline. A heat bloom rendered the waters a milky jade, blindly reflecting the hazy sky above.

Tess half hoped the message she'd left at the Ranieri bakery hadn't been delivered, or that it had been ignored, but no. Pavlin leaned against the canal abutment, a familiar basket at his hip. He was in one of the coats she'd tailored, and one of the imbued binders, too, by the look of it. She tried to examine him with a seamstress's eye, but her thoughts drifted to decidedly unseamstressy places... like his shoulders, and how they would feel under her hands. And how much she wanted to wrap her arms around—

Stop admiring him, you ninny. You asked him here for his function, not his form.

The smile that lit his face when he spotted her weakened her resolve. The scent rising from the basket broke it. "I wasn't certain if you'd take offense, but I brought the spice cakes you like," Pavlin said in greeting.

Tess took the basket out of habit, then poked through it for a moment to collect herself. There were spice cakes, and lemon and honey-seed besides, and tarts with custard and fruit. *Marry a man what brings you food...*

She studied the silk fall of his hair, the soft curve of his lip, trying to see past his lies and her resentment. This man. Did he have to be so *sweet?*

"If you mean to bribe your way back into my graces, I'll not accept it," Tess said sternly.

"No! I just..." He scrubbed his palms on his coat. "I know you like them."

Relenting, she said, "Sit," and perched on the canal abutment, swinging her legs over so they dangled above the jade waters. She handed him a lemon cake and took a spice for herself. They nibbled to the tune of the eave finches squabbling above and the lapping of the canal.

"You've settled well into Traementis Manor?" he asked, breaking the silence. "It must be a relief, not having to care for an entire house on your own."

Something he only knew from his spying. Tess arched a brow, and Pavlin grimaced, too late to take the words back.

Taking pity on him, Tess said, "It's nice, but I've still eleven hours' work for a ten-hour day. Just that now it's all sewing. There's my alta to dress, and Alta Giuna as well, and half the nobles of this city crying for my services."

"You could say no."

"Lending my services out helps my alta's reputation. It's the least I can do." After all, Ren was the one who took all the risks. Who'd given up her life. Who couldn't sleep or say more than six honest words to Tess for fear of discovery. If Tess's needle could ease Ren's burden even one bit, she was glad to help.

I just wish I knew when it would end.

"Do you plan to be her maid forever?" Pavlin asked, as though she'd spoken her thoughts aloud. When Tess gaped like a popped seam, he said, "I know you're grateful to her for getting you out of Ganllech, but you've said you want a shop of your own someday. It's not my business—"

"You're right. It's not," Tess snapped before he could read her other thoughts. How she feared for her sister. How lonely she was even when they were together; how each day it felt more like this trap had become their lives, and she couldn't share her worries, because Ren had enough troubles for *three* lives, and how could Tess add to them?

Sighing, Pavlin asked, "Why did you invite me here, Tess?"

She felt bad asking now, after snapping at him. But he was the one most likely to help her and not ask questions. "I think one of the Traementis servants is spying on my alta. I need your help finding out if she is, and who for."

She'd prepared for him to call her a hypocrite. *It's different*, she would say, and recite the litany of justifications she'd rehearsed on her walk from the Pearls.

But after several silent moments, Pavlin said, "You're asking for my help because if you take this to Era Traementis, she'll sack the girl whether she's guilty or not."

"Sack, or worse. Even I've heard tales of Traementis vengeance."

He hummed agreement. "And your alta can't ask for Vigil help because..." He chewed on his lip. Just as Tess was about to answer, he said, "You think the maid is working for Eret Acrenix, don't you?"

Tess's breath caught. He was so kindhearted, she sometimes forgot he was smart, too. "Alta Sibiliat already paid someone to break in and search the townhouse," she said, waving at their old home. "How did you know it's them I suspected?"

"Ghiscolo Acrenix is Caerulet now." Flicking the crumbs of his cake to the ground as an offering to the finches, he said, "Era Traementis asked for the captain instead of another hawk because she feared Renata was working for Indestor."

A laugh burst from Tess, startling the finches from their feast. "Well, the world knows *that* for a lie."

Pavlin caught her hand in his, as rough-skinned as her own, though she supposed that was from soldiering rather than sewing. "I'm sorry. Not for what I did, but for how I went about it. The captain warned me not to make it personal, but...I wanted so badly to prove myself."

It wasn't the apology she wanted, but she supposed it was the only one he could give. She'd been nobody to him at the start, and he was just a hawk doing his duty. And didn't they all have reason to be suspicious? Weren't Tess and Ren keeping secrets of their own?

Secrets that meant she couldn't reconcile with him, even if she wanted to. Not when it would mean more lying. Tess tugged her hand free and swung around, hopping down from her perch. A few crumbs scattered from her skirts.

"Her name is Suilis Felsi," Tess said, watching the birds edge their way back and start squabbling like they were a debut performance at the Theatre Agnasce. "She looks to have some Vraszenian blood, but she's Nadežran through. Leastways, she hasn't said anything about her people."

Sighing, Pavlin stood and handed the basket to her. "I'll see what I can find. Give me a couple of weeks?"

Tess nodded. His fingers brushed hers, and she couldn't say if her heart twisted for that...or for his easy agreement and the prospect of seeing him again. Mumbling her thanks, Tess turned and fled the conundrum he posed.

Why had she thought this a good idea? She really was a ninny.

Dawngate and Lacewater: Canilun 1

The Charterhouse never put Renata in a good mood. The gears of bureaucracy had ground to a slow enough crawl that even advocates with forty years' experience were threatening to quit, and all Renata's charm and tricks weren't enough to make her obstacles budge. By the time she came out, having wasted three hours waiting to see a Prasinet functionary who dismissed her petition without reading it, she was in a foul enough mood that she didn't ask where Tess was leading her to. She couldn't remember what was next on her schedule—something she was probably late to—but if she wasn't getting in a sedan chair, that meant it must be close enough to walk to.

Which was true...after a fashion.

The door Tess opened for her led not to an office, but to a room with a lightstone, a good mirror—and a set of clothing Alta Renata would never wear.

She stopped on the threshold. "What's this?"

A nudge of Tess's hip propelled her into the room. "Something long overdue, if you ask me. Which you didn't. That's why Sedge and I put the plans together ourselves. Go on with you. There's soap for your face as well." Tess waved at the clothes, her grin turning saucy. "Or have you forgotten how to dress yourself without help?"

Tossing off her own grey-and-white maid's surcoat and underdress, Tess stepped into the full skirts, twill half jacket, and woolen stockings of a girl born on the streets of Little Alwydd, while Renata—Ren—blinked. "Don't I have an appointment?"

"Alta Renata is meeting with a very exclusive and mysterious merchant from Ghus who's only in Nadežra for a few hours. *Ren* is putting on this outfit and going out to celebrate her brother's birthday."

"Sedge doesn't know when his birthday is."

"Then there's no saying it *isn't* his birthday, is there? Hurry, or he'll be beating people back from stealing our table."

Equal parts wary and bemused, Ren asked, "What table?"

"At the Whistling Reed. We're going to be customers instead of robbing them blind!" Tess grinned as though it was a treat to visit the seedy Lacewater music hall from their Finger days. And Ren realized, blushing for shame, that for Tess and Sedge . . . it probably was.

Her mind reflexively summoned objections, even as she leaned against the wall and began unlacing her tight, fashionable boots. If the Ghusai merchant wasn't real, she could and should be doing other things with this time. Donaia had made her final decisions on the adoptions, but Renata was behind on filling out the paperwork. She had letters to answer, clerks to bribe, a warehouse in Dockwall she was supposed to go inspect. Adding this to the list—

That thought stopped her dead, like she'd walked straight into a blade. *Since when did my brother and sister become just another item on my schedule?*

"Usually one takes *both* boots off," Tess said. "But if you want to wear one and go barefoot with the other, you'll fit right in at the Whistling Reed."

Ren had no idea what her expression looked like to Tess, but to her it felt like a horrible mélange of guilt and desperation. "Tess—"

Her sister took the boot from her limp hands, nodding with more understanding than she deserved. "Get on with you. I know how fast you can be when you want."

In *changing* her disguise, yes. Tess had only put out the soaps to wash away the imbued cosmetics—nothing to replace them with. When was the last time she'd worn her face bare, for more than the brief moments between masks? Her hands trembled as she worked.

With friendly impatience as soothing as warm tea in winter, Tess bundled Ren out the door. She chattered with all the familiarity of a sister and none of the respect of a maid, and the sheer bloody relief of that made Ren want to stop in the middle of the street and—

"Oof!" Tess patted her on the back with a confused hand. "What's this for?"

"I just wanted to," Ren said, pulling back from the hug. And if her eyes watered as she said that, Tess was kind enough not to mention it.

Together they pushed through Suncross's bustle into Lacewater. Ren kept her head down, even though the odds that anybody would recognize her as the fourteen-year-old Finger who'd tried to murder her knot leader were low. But she kept watch in her peripheral vision, and what she saw troubled her.

Lacewater had always been one of the poorer parts of Nadežra, with overcrowded tenements and the occasional grasping landlord who raised his rents until he drove the "undesirables" out. But it had gotten much worse since she lived there, and worse still in the last few months. She saw more beggars on street corners, ragged enough that they must be sleeping rough, their faces pinched with hunger even though the markets were flooded with the harvest. Ren kept a hand over her purse out of reflex, then wondered if she should just let some pickpocket take it. They needed those coins more than she did.

The Whistling Reed was as lively as ever, though. The noise of chatter over the sawing of fiddles and shrieking of fipple flutes shook the dust from the rafters; it hung heavy on the air, thickened in places with the haze of pipe smoke. Ren and Tess pushed along the edge of the dance floor until they reached the table Sedge was guarding. His theatrical scowl split into a boyish grin as Tess flopped into a seat and wiped imaginary sweat from her brow.

"You did it," he said, winking at Ren and sliding a mill across the stained table to Tess.

She pocketed it before grabbing one of three waiting mugs and taking a hearty swig. "I didn't even have to bind her!"

Indignation popped Ren upright on her stool. "You placed *bets* on whether I'd come?"

"No," they answered in tandem, gazes sliding away from hers.

"Just on which version of you we'd be getting." Though Sedge spoke through a lopsided smile, there was an edge of worry to it.

Tess's, too, as she pushed a mug toward Ren. "Don't be fashed with us. It's only that we've missed you."

Ren's throat ached. "I've missed you, too."

She truly had—to a depth she hadn't let herself think about, because it would only bring misery. She was playing so many roles, even this had started to seem like one of them: Ren the sister.

Before she could try to put that into words, Sedge said, "But you're here now! Tess, watch the table." With no more warning, he grabbed Ren by the wrist, his hand warm against the scar the three of them shared, and dragged her into the diamond-shaped sets of dancers.

It was nothing like the elegant dances she'd learned as Renata. There, someone would occasionally bump into her out of drunkenness or error; here, the bumping more or less *was* the dance, given how close people were packed together. She had no lead to watch carefully for the cues that would tell her which way to move—but if she stepped wrong, nobody noticed or gave a wet leech, because half the time the step was "whatever you're sober enough to manage." At first the lack of structure was disorienting. Once she warmed to it, though, it felt like putting on an old and comfortable dress.

One that stank of millet beer after somebody spilled theirs on her. But even that, she could laugh off.

Tess replaced Sedge, then Sedge claimed Ren again. By the time she was allowed to retake her seat, she drained her mug in one draw, and they were all ruddy with laughter and drink.

"I only had to smack a hand twice, going for my pocket," Tess said, shoving back sweaty curls from her face. "Is it just me, or are the filchers not as good as we used to be?"

"It's 'cause everyone knows that Ganllechyns en't got two mills to rub together," Sedge said, then laughed harder when Tess forlornly pulled out the single mill he'd given her and wiped away fake tears.

Their banter had a well-worn rhythm to it. Ren was the one out of step, sitting with her beer—sour stuff, its poor quality not disguised by the lemon squeezed into it—and trying to find something to say.

Catching the distance behind Ren's smile, Tess's laughter faded. She reached over to tuck a few stray tendrils behind Ren's ear. "Here now. Don't make us drag you back to the dance floor. My feet can't take much more."

"I'm fine," Ren assured her.

Sedge exchanged a look with Tess—another one that left Ren on the outside. And she wondered how often they'd done that lately... not because they'd grown away from her, but because *she'd* closed herself off from *them*.

Her heart surged like it was trying to leap out of her mouth in place of words. "Oh, fuck," she said, and it wobbled like the drunk shoving past their table. "I'm not fine at *all*."

She didn't start crying—but only because she'd learned years ago not to. Tears were a tool, Ondrakja had always said; they should only be used when they were useful. Her hands shook as she reached out, though, and she gripped Tess and Sedge as if they were the only thing keeping her from drowning in the river. It didn't feel far from the truth.

"You've been so busy," Sedge began.

Tess shook her head. "She has time enough to skiff over to Kingfisher for an afternoon—"

Guilt knifed through Ren again. Yes, she had—or rather, she'd found ways to make time, even though the Serrados were near strangers. Why hadn't she done the same for her siblings?

Because I can't stand to be myself.

That was the ugly truth under the mask. It was easier to be the Black Rose. Or Arenza, even though she felt like a fraud every time she passed herself off as a real Vraszenian. Or even Renata, however much that felt like a trap Ren couldn't escape.

All of those were preferable to being the half-Vraszenian liar who'd betrayed her knot twice, who'd gotten Leato killed, who didn't deserve the trust of the Traementis or the friendship the Anduske had offered or the Black Rose's mask.

The tears that came then weren't useful, at least not in any way Ondrakja would have recognized. But they had to come out, because she couldn't get the words out with them in the way, and she needed words for Tess and Sedge to understand. Which they did, even though what she said was a tangled mess. They knew her well enough to finish the half-completed sentences, to follow when she leapt from one thought to the next, to fill in what she didn't say when she told them about the knot offer she'd refused, or the hole it left when she realized Grey wasn't the Rook.

"*Djek*," Ren said when the flood finally tapered off. She'd already soaked her own handkerchief and Tess's—Sedge didn't have one— so she wiped her eyes with her sleeve. "Thank the Faces nobody likes to look at a sobbing drunk. Otherwise the whole city would know my secrets now."

"If they could hear anything over this noise," Sedge said. She'd wound up leaning into his side somewhere halfway through, and her back protested when she straightened up.

Tess blew out a slow breath. "If you can't even have a good cry with your friends without worrying about your secrets getting out, I'm thinking you need more crying, more friends, and fewer secrets."

A watery laugh bubbled up at the truth of Tess's assessment. Ren did need those things, badly. And she wasn't surprised they'd planned this—not just the visit to the Whistling Reed, but a conversation that was long overdue.

"I'm sorry," she said, holding Tess's gaze, and then repeated it to Sedge. "I've been an absolute ass to you both."

"Not an *absolute* ass," Sedge said. "I know asses that would put you to shame. You're just..."

"Trying to spin moss into emeralds," Tess suggested, refilling Ren's mug with the dregs of their pitcher and nudging it toward her. "But you can't eat neither of those, and none of this life of yours was part of our plan. So stop thinking for a moment about the con and all those things you need to do. What do you *want*?"

Ren's mouth opened, but no words came. What *did* she want? Not piss-poor beer and meat whose origins she shouldn't question. But also not a bed that was still too soft and too lonely, and cold friends who would drop her like hot iron if they knew the truth.

She'd gone into the con thinking she wanted money. In truth, it was safety she'd craved. Safety, though, was about more than living on the Upper Bank with enough wealth to pay her way out of problems. Victory wasn't being able to buy Tess a dressmaker's shop—not if it meant the two of them parting ways.

But she couldn't see a path to having everything. Wealth and status and the protections those brought, *and* her family and the ability to be herself. Nadežra just didn't work that way.

When she voiced that, Tess pulled her close into a hug, unpleasantly sweat-damp from the dancing—and yet it still felt like home. "We may not have a solution now, but we should be smart enough to get out of this mess. Weren't we smart enough to get ourselves into it? But that means no more hiding. Not from us, and not from yourself."

"And no more sniffling," Sedge said, joining the hug by slinging a long arm around them both. "At least, not tonight. It's my birthday, you know."

"Is it?" Ren asked, mustering something like her usual deadpan.

"Hey, if you and Vargo can make up birthdays, why can't I?"

Falling out of the hug, Ren tossed back the remaining beer and thunked her mug onto the table. "Then we must change the subject—and order another pitcher. I care not where I'm supposed to be right now; I want only to drink this terrible swill and talk about *anything* other than my problems."

Her stomach regretted that by the time they stepped out of the Whistling Reed, but her heart felt lighter than it had in months. Light enough that instead of hurrying back to her disguise, she lingered with Tess and Sedge, chatting and laughing—

—laughter that faded when she saw the man crouched on the stoop across from the Whistling Reed.

It was Stoček, the old aža seller who used to give honey stones to his favorites among the street children. He'd lost finger joints to the Cinquerat's punishments before; now he was missing an entire hand. Rapprecco, one of the senior magistrates, had been cracking down hard on the illicit aža trade. By the stump of his wrist and his starved look, Stoček was feeling the loss.

Ren had been one of his favorites. Of all the people in Nadežra, he would *definitely* recognize her. She ought to get out of his sight as fast as possible.

Fuck being afraid. She might be a knot-cutting traitor, but she could still do something for an old friend.

Turning toward him, Ren dug into her pocket. But before she could go pour her handful of deciras into his lap, Sedge blocked her with his body, his grip a manacle around her wrist. "What are you doing?" he hissed.

"Helping him!"

"D'you *want* him to get mugged as soon as you're gone?"

His words stopped her dead. It was one thing to toss a beggar a coin or two—but she'd been about to give Stoček what by the standards of Lacewater was a small fortune.

To Alta Renata, it was pocket change.

Frustration welled up like bile. *I just want* one Mask-damned thing *to be simple.* No politics, no unintended consequences. Just help for a man who had once been kind to her.

Sedge pressed his nose to the top of her head, then turned her about before releasing his hold. "I'll find a place for him to stay," he said. "You go with Tess. I'll see you later."

Tess slipped an arm around Ren's waist. "We'll figure something out," she said softly.

For Stoček, for herself, for all of Nadežra. Ren didn't know how to solve any of those problems. But she looped her arm through Tess's and reminded herself that at least she didn't have to solve them alone.

Splinter Alley, the Shambles: Canilun 1

This time when Vargo ventured into the Shambles to check in with his newest knot ally, he left his guards behind.

"I don't like this," Varuni said when he dumped her at an ostretta on the edge of Arkady Bones's territory.

"She's thirteen," Vargo said, laughing as he stuffed his concealed purse with mixed coins and his pockets with interesting things for the friskers to find—a puzzle box, a shark's tooth, a handful of black powder flash-crackers. "If that girl can take me down, I don't deserve to run the Lower Bank."

Privately, he didn't doubt that Arkady *could* kill him if she found reason. She had enough kids to swarm him, so long as they didn't mind taking the losses. But this was as much about how his other knot bosses saw him as it was about what she was capable of. If he took protection to talk to a gaggle of children, he'd lose what little respect he was clinging to.

"Don't worry. Arkady likes mocking me too much," he said, slipping a knife he didn't mind losing into his boot sheath. "The only thing that might take a hit is my pride." Pride was just another commodity for him to peddle, and Arkady might be the only person in a place to trade for what Vargo needed. Handing his sword cane off to Varuni—that was one thing he wouldn't sacrifice to Arkady and her grasping little flock—he sauntered alone into the Shambles.

As predicted, he was thoroughly patted down before they let him into the converted papaver den. He even lost the bottom two buttons of his waistcoat before he caught the hand nicking them off and moved it away with a soft declaration of "That's enough."

"Yeah, shove off and let him through." The crowd of children parted for Arkady. They had to; she was shorter than half of them. And just as grinning mad as always. "I already seen enough nekkid nobles. I en't no pervert like the Rook."

Vargo smiled through the urge to wince. He wasn't certain how the story of his encounter with the Rook had gotten out, but if he ever found out who'd talked, he was adding them to his list of people to ruin.

Arkady didn't lead him back to her gallery throne, where every child in her knot could witness her exerting power over Eret Derossi Vargo. Instead she took him to a cozy side room that was a threadbare version of Vargo's own office in Froghole. No hangers-on; just Arkady, Vargo, and the biggest, surliest, ugliest yellow tomcat in Nadežra—the one he'd seen at Staveswater. The tom lifted his head from an Uniat-perfect curl and cracked one sulfuric eye, a yowl simmering low in his chest.

A yowl that broke when Arkady grabbed him and draped him over her shoulder like an alta's winter stole. Vargo found himself grateful that he'd left Alsius at home. If the kids hadn't confiscated the spider, that monster cat would certainly have pounced on him. Vargo didn't want to test whether the bond between them could keep Alsius alive through *that*.

"Have a seat," Arkady said, nodding at the other chair as her raging hellbeast went as limp as an overcooked noodle. "And don't try nothing. Doomclaw the Yowler don't like cuffs anymore'n he likes biggies."

"I en't here to try nothing," Vargo said, dropping into rookery accents as he sat. "Got a job, 'n' I think you're the only one who can do it. The only one I trust, leastways."

The ever-present grin cracked into something more genuine, and a flush darkened Arkady's sparrow-brown cheeks. "Yeah, heard you been getting bent and drilled by your own people. Tired of taking it, I take it?"

Vargo chuckled at her attempt at Upper Bank speech. "I'm ready to dish it. I want to know who sold me out to the stingers."

Arkady's nails dug into Doomclaw's ruff as she thought, drawing out a stuttering purr. "You'd have less trouble with your people if you swore oaths direct to each of 'em."

Vargo eyed the rainbow of knot bracelets circling up her arms. There was even one around her neck, matching the collar buried deep in Doomclaw's rough fur. "That why you tied yourself to the cat? So he won't give you trouble?"

Her laugh cracked through the room, startling the tom. He launched off her shoulder, thumping down hard onto the floor. "Naw, it's 'cause he eats nightmares for breakfast." Her expression flickered, as if that use were more than theoretical.

"I know your turf's the Shambles," Vargo said, abandoning banter for business. "But your kids can go anywhere and nobody pays them much mind. Including the Aerie."

"If it's Aerie gossip you're wanting, I'll send Pitjin. The laundresses like her, and nobody guards their tongue around a dawn child."

They underestimate her was the unspoken meaning behind Arkady's hard look. Just like people underestimated Arkady herself. But Vargo was learning to see past the lack of years, so he asked the question he'd ask of any other knot boss. "What do you need in return?"

Sitting back, Arkady pulled her feet under her, tucking into the chair like she, too, was a surly old cat who'd found a spot of safety in a hard world. "You hear about that mad cuff who tried to adopt a whole orphanage?"

"Giarron Quientatis," Vargo said. His husband had talked him down, but the entire notion had been absurd. Enough so that Vargo had assumed Praeteri interference. He hadn't been able to find any sign of it, though.

"Got me thinking," Arkady said. "Orphanages en't great—you don't need me telling you that. Kids like you and me, we're better off on the street."

Vargo nodded. Nadežra's orphanages were too few and too crowded, and too many of their administrators only cared about how much work they could squeeze out of their underfed charges.

Arkady lowered her voice, leaning forward. "But some kids en't like us. They need to get off the street, 'fore somebody scoops them up or hurts them bad. Pitjin, for one."

He couldn't argue with that. If Arkady hadn't been protecting her, the street would have chewed Pitjin up and spat her out long since. Even so... "If you're asking *me* to—"

Arkady squawked with laughter before he could finish. "What, *you* as somebody's papa? Not bloody likely. But you're a respectable man now, en't you? I figure you know some respectable people who could use a kid. Without *using* them, if you follow."

Vargo did. He might get in trouble if somebody accused him of circumventing the orphanage charters, but... "Bring me the name of the person who sold me out, and I'll see what I can do." He'd do the latter anyway, but he didn't much fancy starting a new round of bargaining with a girl bidding fair to someday replace the Stretsko as his biggest competitor.

He spat in his hand and held it out. Hocking an impressive and entirely unnecessary loogie into her own palm, Arkady grinned and squished her hand into his. "You got it!"

Isla Traementis, the Pearls: Canilun 1

After Ren's afternoon with Tess and Sedge, pulling Renata's persona back on was as painful as shoving her feet back into fashionable boots. She barely listened to the footman as he told her there was a visitor waiting in the library. He must have said who that visitor was... but it hit like a shock of cold water when she walked in and found Diomen standing like a statue in the center of the floor.

A second shock came when he addressed her with her title. "Alta Renata. I'm glad I found you at home." He swept one hand to the opposite shoulder and bowed in the Seterin style.

In hindsight, that much beer was a mistake. Closing the door bought her a moment to gather herself before saying, "Altan Diomen? Eret? I'm not sure how to address you outside... the usual context." It felt wrong to have him standing here, in Traementis Manor. Like an ordinary visitor. But unless he was able to dim the burning intensity of his gaze, nothing about him seemed ordinary; the servants would gossip about this for days to come.

"Master will suffice. Worldly titles mean nothing to me. The Lumen has blessed me in other ways." He regarded her with that unsettling gaze, hooded and unblinking. "It has blessed you as well. My only wish is to help you see it."

Conflicting impulses warred within her. "When you brought me through the second gate, you said it was your duty to remedy the gaps in my education. But when you put me inside that numinat in the temple, you treated me as if I were still an ignorant initiate, explaining nothing at all. Now you claim you want to help me see my blessings—but how?"

"I erred that night, yes. I fell to my zeal, instead of mastering it. May we sit?"

His response was neither answer nor apology, but there was no profit in being hostile. Renata gestured him to one of the high-backed chairs and took another, making sure the light from the windows fell on his face, so he couldn't retreat into shadow. "Then educate me, Master Diomen. Speak plainly of these blessings, these gifts."

His hand made a slow sweep of their surroundings. "Places such as this are profane, and not meant for such secrets. It would be far better for you to rejoin our circle. I came here today hoping to persuade you to do so."

"Master Diomen, I've been given a variety of reasons for why I should wish to be a part of your circle. The political benefit of having such allies—but I can manage House Traementis's business without that. The answer to a question Meda Fienola and I have been investigating—but that, we have already achieved." *After a fashion, at least.* Even if Tanaquis was right about eisar, that didn't tell her who had cursed the Traementis. "And finally, the deeper mysteries of the Lumen. But I am not an inscriptor. So if you wish to persuade me to return, you will need to convince me those mysteries are worth what I went through that night."

There was a fourth reason, of course: Vargo, and whatever goal he was pursuing. But she wasn't about to admit that.

Diomen frowned. "The mysteries of the Lumen are not merely about inscription. Can you honestly say that you do not wish to understand yourself better? Your education in Seteris was lacking, but surely it was not so barren as to strip you of all interest in self-discovery."

Weaving his long fingers together in a net, he said, "The threads of the Lumen connect us all, sometimes in obscure ways. They brought you to our sect, and they brought you to that circle. Will you step off that path before you've followed it past the point illuminated by your present understanding?"

His words and gestures held an echo of pattern imagery, and once again, she wondered what he might have heard, and from whom. "Tell me, Master Diomen. What have *you* discovered about yourself, past the edge of illumination?"

"My path is not your path. But if it will help you to see another's..."

The weight of his gaze lifted off her, drifting to the sunbeams that cut through the windows. From the flicker of his pupils, she couldn't tell if he was searching his past, or only following the dance of dust.

In the silence, the air became so still that when he spoke at last, the dust motes shifted with his breath. "When I left Seteris, I thought I was the enlightened one, bringing my knowledge to beat back the darkness." Diomen waved at the window as though implicating all of Nadežra in his past self's disdain. "You surely must know what I mean. Every person from Seteris comes to Nadežra with certain... opinions."

"Disdain, contempt, pity. Yes. Go on."

"These opinions are foolish."

She didn't bother stopping her eyebrows from rising. Diomen said, "I do not speak of politics or culture, but of wisdom. We Seterins are the inheritors of the great wisdom of Enthaxis—but we have allowed that inheritance to ossify. We behave as if we know all there is to know about the Lumen, the numina, the divine sigils we use to call on the Lumen's grace. But as you yourself have experienced, there is more to numinatria than the mere channeling of heat and force and sound. There are emanations we have no names for."

A chill ran down her spine at the memory of rage. "You mean eisar."

"Eisar are the smallest part of what I mean. I cannot unfold to you all the secrets of the Praeteri; it is for good reason that one must pass the Gates of Revelation before entering into the Great Mysteries. But I can tell you that when I came to Nadežra, I discovered there is wisdom outside the rigid boundaries of Seterin orthodoxy. There is *power*."

The sunlight made Diomen's eyes gleam with the fervency of his words. Studying that gleam, Renata thought, *He's sincere.* This wasn't the pitch of a charlatan; it was the sermon of a true believer. And she understood why Tanaquis might find the Praeteri worthwhile.

She understood why Vargo might, too.

Renata kept her voice steady as she said, "What if I have no interest in power?"

"Power is a means to an end, not an end in its own right. Is there truly nothing you desire? Nothing lacking in your life? Nothing you wish to achieve?"

Nothing the Praeteri would want to give me. Numinatria could not provide the feeling of safety she craved, the safety she'd lost the night her childhood home burned down. Nor could it resolve the conflict inside her. The gap between Renata Viraudax and Arenza Lenskaya, with Ren drowning in between.

Diomen was waiting, watching her with those too-intense eyes. Her stomach churned uneasily, though she couldn't say how much of that was him, and how much was the Whistling Reed's beer. What was he driving at? What secret did he think she was holding back?

Renata said, "I'll grant you this, Master Diomen; you've given me a great deal to think about. When is your next ceremony?"

"Two days hence," he said without hesitation. "The night of

Canilis Tricat. Meda Fienola leads a small group in celebration of the minor holy days."

Renata frowned. The adoption ceremony was also scheduled for the third day of the third month. With Tricat being the numen of family, everyone agreed that was the ideal timing. Although the ceremony would be in the afternoon, the celebratory ball was that night. Was Tanaquis intending to leave early? Very likely, she supposed; a numinatrian ritual was more Tanaquis's preferred sort of celebration than a ball would be.

"I'm afraid my duties prevent me from attending that night," she said. "But I will speak with Tanaquis and see whether there's another I might join you for. Next month for Suilis Quarat, if nothing else."

"I hope to see you sooner." Diomen stood, looming over her. Renata stood as well, refusing to give him such an advantage.

And she made a point of giving him only the minimal curtsy expected from an alta to a commoner. "We shall see, Master Diomen."

The Aerie, Duskgate: Canilun 1

When Grey stalked into the Aerie, he was tired, bruised, and pissed off. The entirety of Nadežra seemed in a mood to pick a fight with the first person who breathed at them wrong; this time the spark had been a puppet show in Remylk Square. Whether it had actually mocked House Destaelio or not, Grey didn't know and didn't much care. Somehow that had escalated into a full brawl, and by the time Grey's patrol put that down, the puppeteers had gone missing.

Grey found them in a neighboring alley, in the custody of Lud Kaineto. Who claimed to be questioning them over possible Anduske sympathies, as if criticizing the Cinquerat made one a radical.

These stingers of Caerulet's were becoming more and more of a problem.

I should have known better than to trust those soft words. Grey had wanted to believe Caerulet's promise that he wasn't looking for scapegoats. He'd wanted to believe Nadežra *could* change—that he could help change it, from within.

But lately he felt like the only good he did was when he was wearing a hood.

He planted one hand against the Aerie's stone wall and made himself breathe deeply. The Rook's anger surged up within him more and more these days. Ryvček had warned him: Many who wore the hood wound up losing themselves to it. She'd taught him to cultivate a separation between his two lives, to be Grey when he was Grey and the Rook when he was the Rook. But he wasn't as good at the divide as she was. Ryvček had survived for over twenty years, then achieved the rare feat of letting go. Grey doubted he would last half so long.

With those thoughts roiling in his mind, he was less than pleased to enter the main room and be accosted by Rimbon Beldipassi.

"Captain Serrado!" The man hurried forward with his usual broad smile and ready hand, clapping Grey familiarly on the shoulder. "Just the man I was hoping to see! In fact, even more perfect than I'd realized—how intriguing. Can I bend your ear for a moment?"

"If you're offering me a business opportunity, Mede Beldipassi, I'm afraid I'm busy." It was a coin toss whether it would be some new business scheme, or complaints about troubles with an existing one. The turmoil among the Lower Bank knots had already collapsed one of Beldipassi's concerns in Kingfisher—not that he seemed to care. He always had three more to replace it.

Beldipassi leaned closer. "No, no, not that. Something a bit more...private. Is there somewhere we can talk?"

"My office is this way." If nothing else, the cramped space might encourage him to be brief. But in case it failed: "Coffee?"

At Beldipassi's nod, Grey diverted them past the officers' nook to secure two cups, then headed upstairs. Someone had dumped a box of confiscated possessions from the Kingfisher raids on his desk: items too worthless for any hawk to pocket, which would be sold off through a shop in Suncross. It made his office seem even smaller. Grey hesitated in the doorway before shifting the box to the hall outside and ushering his unwanted guest in.

"This is where you work? How—ah—cozy." Beldipassi resorted to putting one foot up on a stack of reports so he could lean aside for Grey to shut the door. It placed them awkwardly close together, but unfortunately, he didn't seem to mind.

"Now, this will sound a little strange, but hear me out. I understand that there's nobody in Nadežra more dedicated to finding the Rook than you. I need you to—well—help *me* find him. For a conversation. Set me up as a sort of bait, maybe. And then once I've had a chance to talk to him, you can swoop in and capture him! Profit for everybody."

Grey stared, half expecting one of his fellow captains to pop their head through the doorway and shout *Surprise!* But nobody did, and Beldipassi watched him with an air of eager conspiracy, as though his proposal made *any* sort of sense.

"I don't have time for pranks, Mede Beldipassi," Grey said, reaching for the door.

"This isn't a prank!" Beldipassi leaned against the door, though that might have been for lack of anywhere else to go. "I'm quite serious. I have—oh, it's difficult to explain. You heard about my cabinet of curiosities, yes?"

Everyone had, for the brief window of time when it was popular. "I have. Please get to the point."

"That's what I'm trying to do. I collect old things; history is a passion of mine. And a while back I came into the possession of a fascinating artifact—something I never put on display. I believe that the Rook, being immortal, is the one person who might be able to tell me more about what it is and where it came from. I don't mind if you capture him afterward, but I need the chance to speak with him first. Please! I'm prepared to pay handsomely, if that's your concern."

It stank of a trap. It wasn't possible that what he was looking for would just land in his lap.

Still, he had to ask. "What sort of artifact?"

"A numinatrian piece that fell into my hands while I was putting together my exhibition," Beldipassi said. "A medallion. At one point somebody welded a loop onto it so it can be worn as a pendant, but there are remnants along the sides that make me think it was once part of a Seterin-style chain of office."

Forcing himself to act normally was the hardest thing Grey had ever done. He backed into his chair, gestured Beldipassi to the guest chair he tried to keep clear for Cercel's use, and took a long draw from his mug to steady his heart—never mind that coffee usually had the opposite effect.

"You heard about the Rook's accusations the night of the Essunta attack?" Grey said, setting his cup gently back on the table. At Beldipassi's nod, he lowered his voice. "This doesn't leave my office, you understand. But... a few nights later, the Rook paid me a visit."

It was like watching a small child react to a good storyteller. Beldipassi's eyes went as wide as Jagyi's. "Of *course*," he breathed.

The fish was on the hook. "He offered to help me avenge my brother. So if you're serious about this, Mede Beldipassi... I have a way of getting a message to him."

"Yes! Please do! Er—I suppose that means you won't be trying to arrest him afterward. Probably for the best; he would blame me. Quite rightly, as it happens. Yes, better to keep this all friendly. As friendly as a meeting between him and someone like me can get, that is." His nervous laugh was almost a giggle.

If this was a trap, then Beldipassi was an ignorant tool in someone else's hands. Grey would have to take extra care—but that was a concern for later.

Because there was a chance, however faint, that Beldipassi held not just a relevant thread... but the first loop in the process of undoing a knot.

He'd thought all along that Vargo might have it—Vargo, who according to Ren was somehow tied to the ghost of Ghiscolo's *dead brother*—but so far his searching had turned up nothing. And he'd be an idiot if he let that assumption blind him to this opportunity.

"I'll see what I can do," Grey said. "If I'm able to arrange something, I'll leave a message with the place and time at your house." Already he was considering options. And risks. And precautions.

Beldipassi stood and wrung his hand. "Thank you, Captain Serrado."

No, Grey thought, barely able to contain his smile. *Thank* you.

Charterhouse, Dawngate: Canilun 2

The meeting was supposed to be an ordinary business matter. House Indestor's charter for the translation of foreign books had been granted to the Traementis after Indestor's dissolution, but it had gotten caught in the bureaucratic snarl of the Charterhouse for months. Renata thought she was visiting Argentet's office to sign the necessary documents that would finalize the transfer.

She knew as soon as she walked in that Sostira Novrus had something else in mind.

Like the other Cinquerat offices Renata had been in, Argentet's overlooked a central atrium, a small stamp of greenery caged in marble and stone. Instead of taking the position of authority at her desk, Sostira led Renata out to the small balcony behind, where a carafe and cups had already been laid on a table. In the courtyard below, several clerks argued, their voices echoing off the walls.

Renata accepted the coffee Sostira poured with a graciousness as false as her hostess's. After doctoring her own cup with honey and a liberal dollop of cream, Sostira said, "We'll get to your charter concerns in a moment. But first... though we haven't had a chance to speak privately since the Indestor trial, I've heard rumors that you and Eret Vargo are no longer on good terms." Her smile as she sipped the bisque-pale coffee was the satisfied one of a woman whose schemes had paid off after too long a wait.

Benvanna Novri had been at the initiation ritual in the temple. Of course she would have mentioned it to her wife. Renata made herself smile and said, "I don't believe I thanked you for your warning on the day of the Indestor judgments, Your Elegance."

"No, I don't believe you have." Sostira let that hang just long enough to resemble a threat. Then she said, "But since House Traementis is eager to show their gratitude, I hope I can count on their support during these trying times."

She might have simply meant the tensions and unrest in the city. But the Rook's accusations against her had rekindled the resentment Mettore Indestor once stoked against her house. And not just in the streets, but within the Charterhouse... and House Novrus itself.

The last thing Renata wanted was to dive headfirst into the center of such a tangle. She tried for flattery instead. "Small dogs may yap, Your Elegance, but there's nothing to fear from their teeth."

Setting her cup down with a decisive clink, Sostira said, "Wolves, my dear. Don't mistake us for anything else. We're all wolves. And unless you wish to feel *my* teeth, you'll use your confounding popularity to shore up my support."

The harshness of her response took Renata aback. "Your Elegance—"

"Do not take that for an idle threat, Alta Renata, nor the desperate flailing of a woman in peril. House Traementis's fresh reputation rests largely on your shoulders. Cross me, and I will bring you down. And your new family will fall with you."

Renata's pulse leapt as if she were in battle. Which, in a sense, she was. What leverage did Sostira have, or imagine she had? This was the moment where ordinarily Renata would expect a blackmailer to hint at the nature of her leverage, but Sostira gave no specifics. Yet she also spoke with utter confidence: not the bravado of someone making a bluff, but the certainty of someone with a weapon in hand.

Nodding in satisfaction at Renata's speechlessness, Sostira stood and made her way back inside, pulling a folder off her desk. "But enough of personal matters. You came to settle business. It took considerable effort on my part to push this through, but here's the foreign translation charter. You only need to sign and put your seal here."

Out of sheer defensive reflex, Renata read the entire document Sostira laid in front of her, because she wouldn't put it past the woman to have drafted an additional clause binding House Traementis to support Novrus. But the text was as it ought to be, and she silently did as told.

"A pleasure as always to see you, Alta Renata," Sostira said, even walking her out as though they were more friends than acquaintances—let alone possible enemies. "Please pass along my regards to your aunt."

And with that strange farewell, she left Renata alone in the autumn-chilled atrium of the Charterhouse.

14

The Mask of Mirrors

Isla Traementis, the Pearls: Canilun 3

On the holy day of Canilis Tricat, House Traementis more than doubled in size, with four new adoptions.

"Quarat," Tanaquis had said, nodding in approval, when Renata told her about Donaia's final choices. "A good number for growth." She would be the first; the second was Nencoral, a distant cousin of House Fintenus with significant trade connections; the third was Idaglio Minzialli, a rich delta gentleman whose current family had forbidden him to marry the man he loved.

The fourth was the man in question: Meppe, formerly of House Indestor.

Renata had pushed for both Meppe and Idaglio. Apart from Mezzan, who'd somehow managed to secure a job with the Ordo Apis, the former members of House Indestor had not fared well since their dissolution. Many ran afoul of the Vigil for crimes real or imagined, or received missives from Prasinet's office, claiming they owed vast sums in unpaid taxes. Several had died, and no one was in a hurry to inquire whether it was of natural causes or not. As Renata pointed out, nothing would more clearly show that Traementis had shed its old ways than embracing one of their former enemies—and Meppe genuinely had bureaucratic skill to recommend him.

Earlier that day, all of them had gone to the Pearls' Tricatium so that Utrinzi Simendis could inscribe each adoptee into the register with their new Traementatis name. Now the doors of the manor were flung wide for the first party it had hosted in many years. While the staff hurried to prepare, the new adoptees took over the second-floor rooms to change and prepare for the evening's celebrations.

Ren still might not be able to talk freely with Tess, but that didn't mean all conversation was impossible. "I heard someone from a certain bakery came by yesterday with a basket of samples for the cook to try," she said as Tess draped a sheer cape of amber silk over her shoulders. "Is there any chance we might see more of those buns in the future?"

She didn't even attempt to veil the innuendo, and the blush in Tess's cheeks undercut the answering glare. During that afternoon at the Whistling Reed, Tess had mentioned putting Pavlin on Suilis's trail. She'd done her best to be businesslike about it, but Ren could tell the ice of Tess's anger was thawing. And underneath...

Tess sniffed. "Foolish man—as if it made sense to carry bread all the way here from the Lower Bank."

"People have gone farther for a taste of something sweet."

Under the guise of adjusting the topazes sparkling in Renata's hair, Tess flicked her sister's ear. "I'll go see if everyone else is ready, alta. You stay here—don't want you trampling in *too soon*."

Ren touched her heart in apology, and got a quick smile as Tess went out the door. *I hope they work it out*, she thought, settling her flimsy net mask over her face. Based on Grey's comments, Pavlin seemed like a genuinely good man. Tess deserved someone like that.

Then she drew a deep breath, and settled Renata's mask over her mind.

There should have been a celebration like this for her adoption, but it had been too soon; even this was too soon. But Renata's job was to help move the house past that, allowing Donaia to retire gracefully from the public eye for a while. So when the time came, she descended the stairs and waited in the hall while Colbrin announced each of the new members of House Traementis:

Tanaquis and Nencoral and Idaglio and Meppe, and then, like the
resolution of a musical crescendo, herself.

Renata moved into the open doorway and, with a languid tug
at its tie, let her flimsy capelet slip from her shoulders and into the
waiting footman's hands.

A tide of gasps and murmurs lifted her lips in a satisfied smile.
The warm ballroom lighting gave depth and richness to the bronze
silk of her surcoat and caught the sparkles of the green spinels worked
into the sheer embroidered overlay. But what people were staring at
wasn't her dress; it was her shoulders and arms, completely bare save
for a powdering of pearl dust.

*I used my sleeves at the Gloria to catch their interest. Now my lack of
them will hold it,* she thought in amusement as Donaia, resplendent
in a new surcoat of quilted amber taffeta, handed her a glass of iced
wine. Donaia murmured, "I leave it to you to welcome them, my
dear niece."

It was like stepping into everything she'd dreamed of. The ballroom had been oiled and buffed until every bit of the woodwork
gleamed like warmed honey. With a murmur of *The budget!* and a
pert wink at Renata, Tess had hired her old tatting circle from Little
Alwydd to assemble a mass of fabric flowers from the scraps left over
from the Traementis ladies' gowns. Silk lobelias and begonias, velveteen peonies and dahlias cascaded down the walls—some doused
in compounds imbued to keep away the insects that swarmed along
the canals in autumn's last gasps of heat, others with perfume to
mask that. Miniature colored lightstones flickered among the flowers, transforming the stuffy and outdated ballroom into an airy out-
door plaza, and below them lay bountiful trays of cold meats and soft
cheeses, berries sparkling with crystallized sugar, dipping creams
flavored with mint and basil.

Everything I ever wanted, and more. It should have been a happier
thought.

Perhaps some hint of that shadow bled through as she freed herself from the initial round of conversations. "Dark thoughts?" Tanaquis asked, wandering up to her side. Renata's new cousin wore a

thin arc of lace fixed to the skin around her brow and cheekbones; it suggested a mask without actually masking anything. "It occurs to me that it might be good to conduct some kind of cleansing ritual for all the adoptees. I know for certain that you, Donaia, and Giuna are free of the curse, but who's to say whether something doesn't linger in the Traementis name?"

Even in the day's remaining heat, that type of chill wasn't welcome. "Do you think that's a risk?"

"Let's be safe, not sorry." Tanaquis patted her shoulder. "I'll be leaving soon to attend a ritual with our illustrious friends—unavoidable timing, I fear; the stars don't dance to our schedules—so don't worry about it for tonight. We can arrange something later."

She swept off as if such concerns could be laid aside as easily as an empty wineglass. Her departure gave Renata a clear view of Scaperto Quientis, standing temporarily idle. *I should go talk to him,* she thought. Except she couldn't say any of the things she wanted to: gratitude for his help with the Dockwall infiltration, and apology for the Black Rose scaring him out of his skin the night she broke in to ask for that help.

A beckoning hand instead drew her over to where Donaia stood in quiet conversation with Grey Serrado, resplendent in his dress vigils. "I was just thanking Grey for the services of his sister-in-law," Donaia said, catching Renata's arm. "Have you met her charming children? No, you wouldn't have. Darling little girl, and the boy is so sweet." Her eyes misted with tears. Between that, her flushed cheeks, and the thick honey of mead on her breath, it seemed clear that Donaia was rowing in her cup from happiness to heartache. The pat she gave Renata's cheek confirmed it. "You must have been as sweet. Truly, your mother didn't treasure you as she should."

"Perhaps we should find Giuna," Grey said, gently prying Donaia off her.

"No! No more hiding back here. You should dance. The two of you, together. Look, there's Scaperto. I need to talk to him about dog breeding. Go on with you." With a final push, she tottered off.

Renata breathed out a soft laugh. "Well, we can't disappoint her.

And I've danced very little tonight—too busy fending off people asking something from me."

"I ask nothing but that you avoid my toes," Grey said with a smile, and bowed for her to precede him to the floor. A progression dance was already underway, leaving them to wait in awkward silence at the edge until the sets shifted and the dance swept them up.

The first figure was a promenade in the sagnasse hold. Which they'd danced before, in this very room...but things had been so different then, back when he was a stranger and a threat.

When she hadn't yet seen him through Arenza's eyes.

His arm lay across her shoulders with exquisite delicacy, barely making contact. She said, "You needn't worry about your coat, Captain. The pearl dust is imbued; it won't rub off."

"Yes." He coughed lightly. "Yes, the pearl dust is my concern."

She unwound from the hold and came face-to-face with him. His gaze was studiously on their hands, rising to clasp—as if Captain Grey Serrado, a swordsman trained by Ryvček herself, were afraid he might miss. Or as if he were afraid to let his attention rest on the expanse of bare skin across her collarbone and shoulders.

As their gloved palms came together, Ren briefly lost where she was. She was back in Kingfisher, her bare hand against Grey's, the tips of his fingers curling warmly over her own.

The silent prayer of *Ir Entrelke, let him not remember that* drowned under the wave of heat that swept her from head to toe. She wanted to lace her fingers between his, use that to draw him closer...

"I didn't think you could cause more ripples than you did at last autumn's Gloria," Grey said as they circled each other around clasped palms. The scent of coffee hovered over him like perfume, far more pleasant to the nose than to the palate. "But I underestimated you."

His gaze flicked briefly to her bare shoulders. Scrambling to be Renata, she said the first thing that came into her head. "Are you flirting with me?"

"Make no mistake, Renata," he said, his voice deepening. "When I flirt with you, you'll know."

Though his accent remained Nadežran, it was the register he

used when speaking Vraszenian, and that familiar rumble held more than just words. He wasn't masked—Vigil officers never were, in uniform—but although his expression remained controlled, his body said what his face did not.

He *was* flirting. And he meant it.

She was grateful beyond words that the dance separated them briefly; it gave her time to regain her wits and her tongue. Which was fortunate, because the next segment involved an intricate change of holds. "Sunwise, Captain Serrado," she said with a suppressed laugh when he began to turn the wrong way.

He chuckled and corrected by way of a dizzying flourish that brought her closer to him than the dance required. The music drifted to a close as they grinned at each other over joined hands.

"That's a Liganti dance, a Vraszenian one, and now Liganti again that we've shared," he said, releasing her for the bow and curtsy. "I look forward to continuing the pattern."

He left her breathing too fast and trying not to think about the twelve kinds of impossibility that faced her.

Orrucio Amananto chose that moment to scrape together his courage, asking her to partner him for the next call. And if the gossips noticed her distraction—which she had to assume they did—she couldn't quite bring herself to care.

Isla Traementis, the Pearls: Canilun 3

One benefit of not giving a shit about cuffs or their courtesies was that Vargo felt free to ignore the carefully worded snub that had arrived from Era Traementis yesterday. A polite note mentioning a musical evening at the Rotunda that he might enjoy: cuff code for *We can't take back your invitation, but don't show your face here.*

Vargo donned his finest coat and a mask of thin crimson netting, then took a sedan chair to the Pearls.

He timed his arrival at the Traementis threshold for a moment when the majordomo was called away and some hapless footman had responsibility for collecting the invitations of any latecomers. The man recognized Vargo, if his wide eyes and trembling hand were any indication, but didn't dare turn him away.

In this world, a hard smile worked as well as a knife to someone's throat.

Vargo kept that smile in place as he entered the ballroom and surveyed the crowd. As he'd intended, the blood-bright velveteen of his coat drank the light and drew their gaze. Vargo gave himself two bells at most before Renata found a way to elegantly give him the boot; he wanted to make certain he was seen—an invited guest of the Traementis—before she did it.

Hate me all you want. I may be a bloated tick, but you en't burning me out now. He'd come so close after so long, with an ennoblement charter, entry into the Praeteri, learning about the eisar and whatever Ghiscolo had done to his mind. He wasn't going to let a bit of disdain and an unproven accusation of murder bring him down.

::It won't,:: Alsius said. He wasn't hiding in collar shadows but rode proudly at the center of Vargo's neckcloth, like a pin holding it in place. A bright, eight-legged splash of moral support. ::Gossip passes faster than river trash, and there's always new dirt to replace it. We just have to wait this out. You'll see.::

Patience. Always more Alsius's strength than Vargo's.

When nobody came forward to greet him, he lifted his chin and ventured farther into the room. Aghast at his presence—or maybe just his presumption—the gossiping cuffs parted for him like the Dežera for the Point. He'd been too busy with prison breaks and Lower Bank problems to give fuel to the resentment lit by the Rook's accusations and Renata's invective, but now it flared, fanned by the whispers that followed him as he made a circuit of the ballroom.

::We'll stay long enough to show that the rumors don't concern us,:: Alsius said.

They don't. En't none of them any better than me. Ligs wear gloves 'cause their hands are stained with blood.

Still, Vargo wasn't foolish enough to invite a public rebuff by approaching anyone. Not Tanaquis or Benvanna, his sponsors for the second and third Praeteri gates; definitely not Ghiscolo, after whatever had happened at his villa. The circle of cuffs he could actually talk to was rapidly shrinking to a dot.

Which left him all the more astonished when someone approached *him*.

"So, even the jaded Eret Vargo can be surprised?" Iascat Novrus murmured. The silver lining his eyes made them unnervingly bright as he took Vargo's hand and led him into the swirl of dancers. "Close your mouth unless you mean to use it."

His tone was far more confident than Vargo was used to hearing, and carried a hint of Sostira's steel. It startled Vargo into complying as Iascat pulled him into the hold for a couple's dance—one slow and sweeping enough to grant them as much privacy as could be had in the midst of a crowd.

But not for long. "I don't need a pity dance," Vargo said, stamping out the brief flash of gratitude that people were staring at both of them now, instead of him alone.

"And I didn't need a pity fuck, but here we are."

The hardness of Iascat's delicate features lasted a few beats more before it cracked. "I won't lie. Watching you silently tell us all to go fuck ourselves is painful... but that's not why I dragged you out here."

"Oh?" Of course Iascat didn't want Vargo; he wanted something *from* him. That was a dance Vargo could perform without stumbling. "How can I serve?"

"Your falling-out with Alta Renata. Nobody seems to know the details, but I can guess." Iascat's hand shifted on Vargo's back, subtle cues to guide him around possible collisions. "She found out the invitation you gave her for the Ceremony of the Accords came from Mettore Indestor."

Vargo's grip tightened. "How did *you* know that?"

"Because my aunt's the one who told her. After the trial. She was quite upset when nothing seemed to come of it, but I suppose Renata was just biding her time."

Yes. Smiling through her hatred, until a Praeteri numinat set it free.

Much like Vargo was smiling now. But it wasn't hatred he masked; it was the insistent voice that kept whispering for blood at Sostira Novrus's name. "Why are you telling me this?" Iascat could have sought Vargo out anytime since Veiled Waters if he'd wanted. Doing it now meant he'd found a reason.

Shifting closer than the dance called for, Iascat said softly, "My aunt has been looking into Renata's background. There's a diplomatic packet arriving from Seteris tonight with some kind of important information—something Sostira thinks she can use against Renata. Something *you* could use to keep the Traementis from cutting you out."

Or to hurt Renata the way she'd hurt him. Not publicly; no, that would be a foolish waste of valuable leverage. But Sostira wasn't the only one who knew how to profit from blackmail.

Vargo hoped Iascat took the rigidity of his hands as anger at Renata. He couldn't very well explain that he was afraid of every thought he had related to Sostira. *Do I want to make use of this because it's useful? Or because fucking eisar are influencing my mind?*

He'd taken a good look at himself in the mirror before coming here tonight, and knew that the kohl around his eyes, overlaid with a strip of crimson gauze, loaned his gaze a menacing intensity. He turned that intensity on Iascat now. "That doesn't address what *you* want."

The dance was circling to an end. Iascat pressed his cheek to Vargo's, his net mask a rough contrast to the soft skin beneath. He whispered, "My aunt has grown more erratic this past year. Novrus is starting to have more enemies than friends. Many in the family think it's time for her to gracefully retire. When that happens, House Novrus hopes to find a strong ally in House Vargo."

Fucking hell. Vargo was beginning to think getting rid of Sostira *was* a good idea, just so he could have some peace in his own head. Swallowing down the need to unseat her felt like swallowing a rock.

If Iascat noticed anything strange in his demeanor, he didn't comment. He only pulled away and bowed over his hands. "The *Stella*

Boreae, in Whitesail, on the late tide." A wry smile touched his lips. "Try not to kill anyone."

Isla Traementis, the Pearls: Canilun 3

Dancing with Renata had been a foolish move, and Grey was lying to himself if he pretended it was one he couldn't have avoided. There were a dozen ways out of obeying Donaia's tipsy order. He'd just chosen not to take any of them.

All around the room, fans were hard at work, both cooling their holders and covering the tide of gossip. Renata wasn't the only person to dance with Grey; Parma Extaquium saw no reason his Vraszenian ancestry and lack of rank should stop her from enjoying an aesthetically pleasing view. But Parma wasn't the heir to her house.

Nor had she bared her shoulders to the world, in an invitation that made Grey wish he wasn't wearing gloves.

That pleasant regret burned away when his gaze caught on a crimson coat across the room, a gauze mask covering kohl-edged eyes that glittered with disdain, and a smirk that invited anyone to take exception.

Renata was out in the gardens, but it took Grey less than a minute to find Donaia, still bending Eret Quientis's ear about her dog. "What is Vargo doing here?" he hissed.

Apparently Donaia had managed to overlook what everyone else had long since noticed. She followed Grey's jabbing finger, and her surprise darkened into fury. "After I specifically told him to find another engagement for this evening? The *gall* of that man." She gathered up her surcoat like she meant to march across the dance floor to challenge Vargo herself.

Quientis stalled her with a hand on her shoulder. "Donaia, I sympathize with your disgust. But perhaps the captain's grudge against him is more..." He left the suggestion hanging, but Grey could finish it well enough. *Warranted. Legitimate.* And less likely to bring scandal down on House Traementis. If Vargo were the type to go quietly when invited to leave by the majordomo, he wouldn't be here in the first place.

"An excellent point," Donaia said, dropping her skirts and laying her hand over Quientis's. "Captain, I know you're off duty, but can I ask you to inform Eret Vargo that his presence is required...anywhere that isn't here? Quietly, if you can. And preferably before it ruins Renata's night."

He hadn't been looking for an opportunity like this, but he wasn't going to refuse it when it came wrapped in Donaia's approval. "Era Traementis, it will be my genuine pleasure."

Vargo saw him coming. The deep blue of a Vigil coat stood out among the paler shades of Liganti fashion, and Grey made no attempt to drift with the flow of the room. He cut straight through, fetching up just close enough to Vargo to be slightly inside the man's personal space. "Eret Vargo," he said, the heels of his boots coming together with a snap—but he omitted the bow a Vigil captain owed to the head of a noble house. "Let's step outside."

For an instant he thought Vargo might refuse, and this would happen right here in the ballroom. But Vargo swung one arm wide in mocking invitation, and the wind of whispers pursued them out the door.

Once in the hall, Vargo's step slowed as if to stop, but Grey clamped one hand on his arm and kept them moving toward the front door. Not for long—Vargo twisted free a moment later—but it was enough to get the message across. They both knew that what was coming shouldn't have an audience of cuffs.

In the plaza outside, he shoved Vargo into the shadows between two carriages. The man spun to face him and asked in a deceptively pleasant tone, "Is there a problem, Captain Serrado?"

Until that moment, Grey hadn't been certain how he wanted to deal with this. That mockery of innocence decided him. An instant later Vargo was doubled over, dry-retching from the force of Grey's blow.

A hand on his shoulder kept him there. Fingers digging into the hollow of Vargo's collarbone, Grey said, "I know, I know. Assaulting a noble is a crime. Feel free to bring charges before the high commander. I hear he's not terribly fond of you."

Sucking in a breath, Vargo drew back for a retaliatory strike, but Grey knew the dirty tricks of street fighting. With a step to the side and a swift joint lock, he had Vargo against the side of a carriage, one forearm barred across his throat. The spider had scuttled to the safety of his shoulder. Grey ignored it. A king peacock's venom might be agonizing, but the creature showed no sign of wanting to bite him, and talking mind to mind wouldn't save Vargo right now.

"There is indeed a problem," Grey said. The fury he'd kept caged for so long shredded his voice. "The *problem* is that you murdered my brother."

"So like everyone else, you believe the Rook's accusations without pr—"

"Don't," Grey snarled, pressing harder. "I know what I know. You planted the powder. You set it off. Don't add insult by denying it."

Vargo's throat moved under Grey's arm, his chest rising and falling rapidly as he struggled for breath. "Nobody was supposed to be inside," he said, so faintly Grey would have missed it if they weren't breathing the same air. His eyes fluttered shut. "I didn't know."

"And that *excuses it*?"

"I never said that." The red veil of Vargo's mask added fire to his glare, like he was daring Grey to add more pressure, to take this to its obvious conclusion.

Even in his rage, Grey remained aware. A shift of movement off to the side was Varuni, but so far she was only watching. She had to have known this was coming—must have known ever since the accusation became public—and Grey had no doubt that if he tried to kill Vargo, she would intervene. Until then, however, she appeared willing to let them have this out.

Part of him wanted to try. The Rook didn't kill, but Grey Serrado might.

What stayed his hand wasn't that oath, nor his conscience, nor the practical challenges of trying to commit murder in front of Vargo's bodyguard. It was the self-destructive defiance of Vargo's expression. Like he would actually welcome it if Grey lashed out again.

Which meant that the best way to hurt Vargo right now was to refuse.

He shoved himself back. "Your presence here is unwelcome. Take yourself somewhere you're wanted." Dusting off his gloved hands like he'd taken out the trash, he added, "Assuming such a place exists."

The muscles stood out in Vargo's throat as he clenched his jaw—but he was resilient enough to survive for years on the Lower Bank. With the precision of someone reassembling his defenses, he straightened his coat, shot his cuffs, and retrieved the spider from where it had fled to the edge of the carriage window, setting it back onto his shoulder.

"We both know it doesn't, Captain," he said. "But I won't trouble you any longer. I have business to attend to."

With a nod as though they'd just had a pleasant conversation, Vargo waved for his guard and a sedan chair, and left.

Isla Traementis, the Pearls: Canilun 3

Growing up, Giuna had always associated the Indestor name with hostility. So when Renata argued for the adoption of Meppe, the former Indestor cousin, Giuna's reflexive thought had been that the Dežera would flow backward before that happened. Not only because of her own resistance, but because of her mother's: Donaia had always been less flexible, less forgiving, than either of her children.

But Renata talked them both around, and looking at Meppe Traementatis now, Giuna was glad she had. Happiness effervesced through him like bubbles in sparkling wine, carving ten years off his clerkish, lined face. His new cousin Idaglio was more sedate but no less delighted. And Giuna wasn't so sheltered that she didn't recognize the eagerness thrumming between them. Meppe would be moving into Traementis Manor tomorrow, out of the rented room he could barely afford, but when she approached the two men and asked, "Would you like me to arrange a guest chamber for you both tonight?" they couldn't accept fast enough.

Speaking to the servants gave her a welcome excuse to leave the ballroom for a little while. The gossip had taken a more vicious turn after Vargo showed up; someone claimed he and Grey Serrado had gotten into a fight out in the plaza. Giuna didn't want to think about that—didn't want to think about Kolya, whose polite manner never stopped him from teasing her in a friendly way. Kolya, who had died so horribly . . . and the rumors said it was Vargo's fault . . .

"I have a price, though."

The voice was soft, and it came from a room that should have been off-limits. Giuna's delicate slippers made no sound on the carpet as she slowed.

The reply was immediately familiar: Sibiliat's most honeyed tone. "Looking ahead to the moment Sostira casts you aside? You're wise to prepare your landing."

"I'm not going back to House Ecchino." Now Giuna recognized the first speaker as Benvanna Novri, sounding much more intense than usual. "I want to be adopted into the Acrenix."

A stifled laugh from Sibiliat made Benvanna's voice rise in pitch. "I can be useful! I got Magistrate Rapprecco into a numinat of zeal, and now those kinless Essunta bastards have no aža trade to profit from on the side. But Sostira brushed it off when I told her."

"That may be true, but I can do that sort of thing as well as you can." *Better*, Sibiliat's tone implied.

"Which is why I'm offering something you *can't* do. Promise me adoption—in writing, if you please—and I'll tell you what I know."

Giuna shouldn't be eavesdropping. But they were in *her* house . . . and the edge to the conversation worried her. She eased closer to the door as Sibiliat said, "I'd have to consult with my father first."

"There's no time for that. He's already left. You're his heir; your written promise will stand. But you need to act on this tonight, or you'll miss your chance entirely."

Silence. Giuna could imagine the expression on Sibiliat's face, the narrow-eyed focus she took on when considering politics. "What's so valuable, and so urgent?"

"Information on Renata Viraudax's past."

Giuna's heart thumped so loud, she feared Sibiliat would hear it.

A faint rustling and scratching, as of someone scribbling a quick note. "There. Now tell me."

"I don't know the information myself," Benvanna said. "Sostira got word that her agent in Seteris would be sending along a letter from Eret Viraudax. That's expected to arrive in Whitesail on the *Stella Boreae*, late tonight. Sostira beds down early; if you send someone to collect it before the morning, you can claim it for yourself."

"And then what?"

Benvanna's tone became venomous. "Do whatever you like with it. Sostira may be fickle, but she wouldn't have cooled on me so fast if that Seterin snot hadn't come along. I know you'll cut her down to size."

The rustle of fabric warned Giuna. She barely managed to slip into the nearby bathing chamber before Benvanna barreled out of the room, followed more slowly by Sibiliat.

But she had plenty of time, peering through the slatted opening that released the steam, to observe Sibiliat as she stood and thought.

These past months, as they grew closer and Giuna grew more confused, she had made a serious study of Sibiliat's expressions. Not just the ones that showed on her face; those were almost always lies, or the occasional calculated truth. But Sibiliat had a habit of dancing with her hands when deep in thought, like she was playing an instrument or fighting a duel.

Giuna watched, heart sinking and tears rising, as Sibiliat's fingers worked through her options, weighed the costs and gains, and came to a decision. Watched until Sibiliat strode down the hall and rounded the corner.

Slipping out of the bathing room, Giuna crept downstairs after her, where she watched Sibiliat catch the attention of her cousin Fadrin and send him off with a hurried whisper.

Before she could decide on a course of action, Sibiliat turned and saw her. "Ah, there you are!" Her smile was a lie of delight. "Come dance with me."

Giuna slipped out of her grip, puffing up with indignation like the little bird Sibiliat so often called her. But she willed herself to smooth down her anger. "I've just come from a round of Parma's haranguing," she said. "I wanted to check on Mother. Have you seen her?"

Tell me. Tell me. You said you'd set aside your suspicions for my sake. Don't break your promise.

Sibiliat flicked Giuna's concern aside with casual cruelty. "Last I saw, Donaia was rosy in her cups and 'furthering relations' between Traementis and Quientis. She doesn't need you mothering her. Come dance!"

"Later," Giuna said, putting her off with a wan smile and turning her head so Sibiliat's kiss landed on her cheek. "I promise."

This is what she is. She told you herself, months ago. She manipulates people.

So did Renata. The difference was, Renata was on Giuna's side. Sibiliat was the Acrenix heir.

And House Acrenix was nobody's friend but their own.

Gut churning, Giuna fled Sibiliat's company and went in search of her cousin.

Eastbridge, Upper Bank: Canilun 3

Even by the Rook's standards, he was early in heading for the place where Grey had arranged the meeting with Beldipassi. After the confrontation with Vargo, he couldn't bring himself to loiter around the Traementis party any longer; grim satisfaction had chilled the glow of his earlier mood.

He donned his hood, then checked Renata's balcony for messages before leaving. All he found was the kitten standing with her paws braced against the glass of the door, mewing to be let out.

"I'm afraid I must leave you to guard your mistress, Clever Natalya," he said.

It was the meeting itself that drew him out so early, though. If Beldipassi held a piece of the Tyrant's poison, then all the signs pointed to that piece as the start of the cycle—and that might be just what the Rook needed to finally move forward on the goal that had motivated him for two centuries.

That very possibility drove him to be even more wary. If this whole thing was an ambush, he wanted to know where every obstacle and exit was... and lay a few traps of his own.

Parts of Eastbridge retained their Vraszenian stamp, with two-story courtyard houses that had once belonged to various kretse. Others had been rebuilt in the Liganti style, townhouses lined up in a row like books on a shelf, separated by the occasional manor. It wasn't the best area for the Rook to operate in. But Beldipassi had moved here just after the solstice, into a small manor whose back garden was the most suitable place to meet. Familiar enough not to make the target feel vulnerable, but open enough for the Rook to escape if necessary. He studied it from a nearby roof, noting the trees, the gate, the architecture of the house. There was a small fishpond, and the Rook had a sachet of an imported Arthaburi compound that reacted quite brightly with water; that would be useful if he needed a distraction.

It seemed... not *safe*. He wasn't foolish enough to think that. But acceptable, so long as he made a few preparations.

Grey had spent the afternoon studying maps, familiarizing himself with the terrain. Now he checked that against the situation on the ground, identifying several escape routes and clearing them of obstacles, jamming locks open for quick access. He loosened an area of roof tiles until a foot would shove them free; laundry lines cleared of linens and lowered made for barely visible garottes. A heavy shade break over one of the garden courtyards would collapse with a single kick to one of the support poles.

He was on his way to lay another trap inside a perfumery—one that sold a few compounds that escaped Prasinet's tariffs, and therefore had a hidden exit through the side wall into the neighboring wig-maker's—when he made himself stop. *You didn't do half this much preparation for Dockwall.* At this point he was just working off nerves. In ways that would cause headaches for ordinary citizens later on, no less.

Time to settle in for the boring part. The rooftop he'd been on before would do; he'd see when Beldipassi returned home from the Traementis ball. Which also meant he could see if the man was bringing anyone extra.

The Eastbridge bells, their clappers padded for the earth hours, softly rang midnight. The respectable entertainments had closed, and anybody who wanted something less respectable had gone to the Old Island. Nobody should be up and about, and Grey had made certain the usual Vigil patrols would be dealing with misfiled complaints on the other side of the district.

Yet from the street ahead came the muffled sound of footfalls.

The Rook slipped down an alley, only a slight detour on the way to his destination. Or it would have been—if shadows up ahead hadn't spoken of someone there, as well.

It could be coincidence. On the night when he was supposed to meet Rimbon Beldipassi, though, he didn't believe in coincidences.

A setup? Maybe not on Beldipassi's part; nobody had been waiting for him at the house. The shadows didn't have the silhouette of Vigil uniforms; they might be some noble's house guards, or mercenaries.

Who they were didn't matter right now. He needed to draw them away, shed them, then circle back to see if the meeting could be salvaged. There was plenty of time.

To that end, he let the people at the end of the alley spot him before he darted off. They obliged by following, and with the numinatria of his mask thinning the darkness, he got enough of a look to know his pursuers were professionals. Well-armed, moving well, and masked so no one could identify them.

Moving all too well. It took him longer than it should have to realize that he wasn't leading them away: *They* were herding *him*.

Even as that thought formed, something fell on him from above.

It burned like hoarfrost, even through the layers of his clothing. Something heavy and enveloping—and it *clung*, wrapping unnaturally around his arms and legs. The Rook struggled to free himself, but it was hopeless; he only became more entangled.

A net—but not an ordinary one. The strands sank tendrils of cold into his flesh, like roots seeking water. When he tried to take a step, his legs gave out and he dropped to one knee.

His pursuers circled him, watching their trap do its work. "Mark this one in the books," one of them said, laughing. "Two hundred years, and the Rook's finally been caught. Go set the snare for Beldipassi. We'll deliver the Rook...if he lives that long."

The net was growing tighter. It had to be some kind of numinatria—the shape of the strands inscribing the figure—which meant that if he broke it—

He got his fingers into a gap, but the net resisted his attempts to tear it. Imbued, maybe. Had someone died to craft this trap?

The trap that would finally kill him. He couldn't throw off the net, he couldn't break it, and with every passing moment its weight grew heavier on both body and mind, plunging him under the dark surface of despair. He tugged again at the net, but feebly, knowing there was no point.

Grey knew there was no point. But the Rook did not give up so easily.

He had outlasted every person who wore the hood. He was born from determination in the face of despair. He was something like a spirit—but one created again and again by those who became him, who imbued the outward facade of the costume with the energy and conviction of their performance.

It didn't matter what it cost the man inside. The Rook would not die here tonight.

Human weakness folded in on itself, hammered into the steel of that immortal drive. Hands tightening, arms flexing as if to bend iron bars, the Rook pulled at the constricting strands. Sparking energy in all directions, the net tore—then dissipated in a cloud of black smoke, as if it had never been.

Its effect wasn't gone. He could feel it in his flesh, slowed but still burrowing, still draining. His attackers didn't know that, though, and they flinched back as he rose to his feet.

"Don't lay your wager before you see your cards," the Rook said, retreating slowly through the threshold of a courtyard house and across the garden inside. It funneled his enemies into a clump, but that wasn't why he chose this route. "You haven't caught me yet. And I've got a net of my own."

Kicking the pole at his back, he flattened himself against the wall as the heavy canvas awning fell on the cluster. While they struggled underneath the weight, he dashed across the lumpy terrain, using their covered bodies as a stepping stone to launch himself back into the street.

Not everyone had followed and been caught. The Rook's sword flashed out, not sparing flesh and blood. One man screamed as his blade fell to the ground, the hilt still gripped in his severed hand. By the time the Rook broke through their line, the ones under the canvas were free, and they pounded after him as he slammed through the door of the perfumery.

But they couldn't see in the dark like he could, and they didn't know where the hidden exit was. As they staggered to a halt inside the building, the Rook eased shut the panel in the side of the false cabinet and slipped like a ghost through the wig-maker's shop, toward the door that let out onto an adjoining street.

Free—for all the good it did him. His muscles twitched with warning shocks of greater agony to come. Whatever that net had done to him, it hadn't stopped working; it had only been slowed. But he still had to make his rendezvous with Beldipassi, had to stop the next stage of the plan.

Not like this. Not on my own.

Grey fought his way up, out of the drowning shadows that had overtaken him. The Rook had gotten him out of the net, but he couldn't afford to lose himself permanently to that power. *I need help.*

Ryvček. But she lived in Kingfisher, clear across the river; under the best of circumstances it would have been difficult for him to get there and back in time. With pain ripping along his body like swarms of flame ants underneath his skin, burning away his strength, there was no chance.

Without help, though, Beldipassi would fall to the trap that waited for him. And as for what he held...

The hopelessness eating into his bones wasn't just logic at work; it twined like a snake with the exhaustion and pain that drained his strength like someone had opened a vein.

No. This couldn't be the night it ended. Not when they were so close to the goal they'd pursued ever since the Rook became something more than a scrap of wool and a young woman's grief-stricken anger.

It wasn't only the effect of the net that made him lurch into a wall as he began walking. The Rook didn't just have a mandate; he had the ghostly traces of the men and women who'd bound themselves to that role. Those traces gave Grey strength... but they also fought him now, as he forced himself north.

Toward Traementis Manor.

15

The Liar's Knot

Gut still aching from Serrado's sucker punch, Vargo led Varuni through the maze of warehouses and wharves that made up riverside Whitesail. He was wearing a coat bought off one of the sedan chair bearers; his own coat and Varuni's chain whip were on their way back to his Eastbridge townhouse. Nothing to mark the two of them as Eret Vargo and his bodyguard.

Although most of Vargo's shipping ran out of Dockwall, he'd been a smuggler long enough to know his way around the port offices of Whitesail. A decira in the pocket of a night watcher bought word that the *Stella Boreae* was still at anchor in the bay awaiting port authorization... but a dinghy had come upriver and docked near the Novrus warehouse office.

"Better if we had a few more people," Varuni said as they surveyed the darkened building. Her hand brushed over the place her whip normally coiled.

::She's right,:: Alsius said, his legs twitching against the back of Vargo's neck. ::We should wait until—::

"I'm done with waiting," Vargo snapped. He'd sent a message along with his coat, but the time it would take to get to the Froghole den or his Dockwall warehouse was time for Iascat's promised information to slip out of Vargo's grasp.

He and Varuni pressed themselves against a wall as footsteps approached. Not the irregular beat of people walking normally, but the heavy and rhythmic tread of chair bearers. Peering around the corner, Vargo saw a sedan chair approaching with two guards flanking it. Black cloth covered the crest on the side, but the red-lacquered panels were familiar enough on their own.

The reason for the identifiable chair became obvious as soon as the bearers set it down. House Acrenix had people who understood subtlety and delicate operations...but Fadrin wasn't one of them.

Vargo's lips shaped a curse. He didn't know how Fadrin had learned about the message, but nothing else would have brought him to this part of Whitesail at this time of night. *Seems like everybody wants leverage over Renata Viraudax.*

He edged back so Varuni could size up the situation for herself. "Doable?" he asked quietly.

She wasn't reckless like some of his fists, so invested in proving her toughness that she charged stupidly into situations that would overmatch her. She held still, massaging her knuckles, calculating odds.

Then she nodded.

"Let's do it," Vargo said. He was looking forward to finally *throwing* a punch tonight.

Neckcloths served as makeshift masks, though they weren't enough to provide total anonymity, especially with an Isarnah woman at his side. And Vargo couldn't risk being identified. Ghiscolo Acrenix was the pot for every gamble he and Alsius had made since the night they met, and Fadrin was a card Vargo couldn't afford to sacrifice.

So while Varuni kicked over a crate to make a distraction in front, he slipped up behind Fadrin, taking extreme satisfaction in blinding him with a handful of mud slapped across his eyes. Four-on-two still wasn't a fair fight, but with Fadrin swearing and scrubbing at the grit on his face, Vargo had less to be concerned about when one of the chair bearers hooked a finger under his mask and clawed it down from his nose. He unhooked it with a twist of the bearer's arm, followed by an elbow to his throat. A drumbeat of meaty thuds and low grunts said Varuni was doing what she did best: taking care of the guards quietly and efficiently.

With one chair bearer retching for breath, the other looked around, weighed his odds, and ran. Vargo might have gone after him, but Fadrin had regained his feet, if not his vision, and charged blindly. Vargo locked him close in a shoulder-to-shoulder hug and brought his fist up again and again, tenderizing Fadrin's gut and bits farther south. When Vargo's arm became the only thing keeping Fadrin up, he was about to switch to the ribs and the face—but Varuni pulled him off, and Alsius's shouting finally pierced the need to break his knuckles on someone else's bones.

::—that's enough! I agreed to come here, but it wasn't for *this*.::

No. This wasn't what Vargo had come for. But it was what he'd needed.

Shaking the pain out of his bruised hands, he nodded his thanks to Varuni. She understood. Just like she'd understood enough to step aside and let Serrado deliver his hits.

"What do we do with them?" Varuni asked, crafting makeshift bindings out of the neckcloths and the bunting from the Acrenix sedan chair.

Vargo wasn't sure how long it would take him to find the papers, and he didn't want this lot having a chance to draw attention. He jerked his chin at a nearby dinghy, and Varuni hoisted one of the men over her shoulder.

They'd loaded three and were going back for Fadrin when Vargo's gaze fell on the sedan chair. It was lightweight. Well-made. And wooden.

Keeping his voice rough and unrecognizable, he said, "I bet that thing would float."

They sent Fadrin off in style, floating downriver in his remarkably seaworthy sedan chair, with the dinghy following behind—leaving its paddles on the dock. Watching it go, Vargo said, "Remind me to give you a raise."

"You're not the one who pays me," Varuni reminded him. The twitch of her lips was as good as a laugh from anyone else. "We should move. Before we have to deal with whatever problems that noise brings."

Whitesail, Upper Bank: Canilun 3

Ren knew what the gossips would say. Derossi Vargo had shown up at the Traementis adoption ball and been escorted out scarcely one bell later by Captain Serrado—the man whose brother he'd murdered. Shortly after that, Alta Renata had retired to her room, apparently fleeing what should have been a night of triumph.

She didn't care what explanations they invented for her absence. The worst would pale next to the truth, if it got out: that Renata Viraudax Traementatis had been a fiction from the start.

Her mind had begun shuffling possibilities the moment Giuna told her what she'd overheard. By the time Ren changed into inconspicuous clothes and climbed down from her balcony, she knew exactly what the threads of her future looked like.

Learning she wasn't a Viraudax didn't mean people would know she was half-Vraszenian. She could still pass herself off as Letilia's daughter, even; that part didn't require noble Seterin connections. There would be no legal difficulty, because what mattered under Nadežran law was who had signed the contracts, not what past that person claimed. Nor could she, as a registered noblewoman, be tried for the crime of having previously pretended to be one.

But none of that would matter. This was what Sostira had threatened, and why the woman had been both vague and certain: She knew something damaging was on its way, but not what form that damage would take.

And Sostira was right to be confident. The scandal of having adopted a liar like her would destroy House Traementis's newfound credibility. And if Donaia threw Ren out—which was all too likely—a trial would become a very real danger.

So that was the ill of her future. It was up to her, now, to ensure she saw the Face and not the Mask...by getting those papers before anyone else could.

She arrived in Whitesail to find the competition for that prize was dismayingly fierce. Bad enough, though not unexpected, to see Fadrin Acrenix getting out of a sedan chair with several people at his side; Giuna had told her Sibiliat wanted the papers, and given the need for haste, it wasn't surprising that she sent her cousin. But then two figures sprang from the shadows and went to work on the Acrenix crew—and even though they were masked, she'd spent enough time watching Vargo to recognize his movements.

Djek. How had *he* found out about the papers?

It didn't matter. Vargo wouldn't hesitate to use any leverage he had; she could no more let him get hold of them than anyone else. But he was unwittingly doing her the favor of taking care of Fadrin and the others, and while everybody else was distracted, she had the perfect chance to act.

Ren knew which office to go for. Her lightstone was shielded like a thieves' lantern, casting its illumination only where she wanted it. She swept it around the interior, noting desks, cubbyholes, cabinets, an incendiary numinat for disposing of waste paper. Once she found the packet from Seteris, one toss would preserve her secret.

For now. A message sent once could be sent again. She'd hoped to forge a replacement letter once she saw the real one, but there was no time for that now. And if Sostira kept pressing—or anybody else, for that matter—then sooner or later the truth would come out. All Ren was doing was buying time.

Better to have time, though, than to face that crisis tomorrow.

She was swift in her search. The Novrus office wasn't as well-organized as anything under Indestor control, but it wasn't a shambles; it didn't take long to find the cabinet where important packets were kept. Ren tore open the one on top, spilling papers onto the floor, and found a letter marked with the seal of House Viraudax in Seteris.

Her triumph was short-lived. A board creaked in the hallway

an instant before she heard Vargo's mocking baritone. "Lady Rose. What possible interest could Ažerais have in the business of a Seterin alta?"

He leaned against the doorway—blocking it—and in the shadows behind him, Varuni cracked her knuckles. Over his shoulder, Vargo said, "Make sure the Rook isn't about to drop in on us. I can handle her."

His tone wasn't exactly a threat. After all, hadn't he and the Rose worked together before? But Vargo's expression in the dim light was as unforgiving as she'd ever seen it, and he absently massaged one hand, the action of a man who'd been employing it as a weapon. There was no hint of the cuff about him now, in his clothes or his bearing. This was the crime lord who'd taken over the Lower Bank.

One Poppy Weeps. He'd caused plenty of pain in the past, and that wasn't behind him now.

She tried for the Black Rose's usual careless tone. "Thanks for taking care of the others. Whitesail's oddly busy for this time of night."

"Sostira's ship has more leaks than she realizes." Edging into the room, he closed the door behind him. Not locked, but it was another barrier to slow her down if she fled.

Ren couldn't see the spider, but she heard his voice. ::Vargo, if she gets away with that letter—::

::She won't.::

::Even if that means making her an enemy?::

::I already have plenty of those. What's one more?::

Ren's pulse spiked. That bleak tone didn't offer much hope for her getting out of here with the letter in hand, and she was too far from the incendiary numinat to throw it with any accuracy. Nor did she want to imagine what Vargo might do if she tried.

But she'd talked her way out of worse situations. "I imagine we both have a use for the information in here. As I recall, I gave you Dmatsos Očelen back in Staveswater. You still owe me for that—so how about I take this, and we call it even?"

The curt shake of his head didn't pause for even a moment of consideration. Vargo, advancing, backed her into a corner between desk and cabinet. "I'm not here for deals or trades or favors. Whatever interest you have in Renata Viraudax, mine takes precedence. Hand it over. Now."

::Before someone else shows up,:: the spider added.

When she still hesitated, a knife flashed into Vargo's hand. "After the way my life has gone lately, I'm done fucking around. You've been useful to work with, but if I have to, I *will* fight you for that letter."

And he would win. Ren had a knife, too, but she couldn't have taken down Fadrin and the others the way he had. Even without Varuni to back him up, Vargo could beat her. Then she wouldn't have the letter *or* any trust between him and the Black Rose.

But if she gave it to him, that knife would be at Renata's throat.

Deal with that when it happens. It's that, or lose right here and now.

Good, rational thinking. None of which made it any easier for her to seal her fate by handing Vargo the letter.

For the briefest instant Ren thought about rushing him while he was distracted, looking down at the envelope. But before she could, a casual flick of his wrist sent the letter flying—into the incendiary numinat.

Fire surged abruptly, then died away.

It was too sudden for her to do anything more than yelp. Or for her to read the complicated expression on Vargo's face, before it sank back into shadow. "I don't know why you want leverage against Renata," he said. "I'm guessing the Rook asked for it. But I'm warning you now: Leave her alone, or we *will* be enemies."

His words were a pattern she couldn't read. "But—" All her eloquence had deserted her; she stared at the ashes drifting out of the numinat. "Why come all the way here, just to destroy it?"

Vargo sheathed his knife, as though she wasn't any sort of threat anymore. "Because I'm the only one I trusted not to fuck it up."

"You didn't even read it." Renata had torn into him with every vicious word she could find, unleashing all of her pent-up rage—at him, at Nadežra, at everything she'd suffered—and he'd just protected her. "You could have used—"

"No. I really couldn't have. I've made that mistake one time too many." He ran a palm down his face as though trying to pull a mask over the bitter lines there. "Her secrets are her own."

A performance. He's doing this for your sake, because he knows who you are.

But even the most suspicious part of her, the part that saw the world as a constant dance of manipulation, didn't believe it. Vargo had no idea who the Black Rose was. And he had no reason to think Renata would ever know what he'd done here. He was protecting her because—

Because she *hadn't* been wrong, when she believed that she mattered to him. That he cared what happened to her, and didn't just see her as a tool.

Yes, Vargo had used her. He'd sent her into the Charterhouse, knowing Mettore wanted her there, and he hadn't told her either before or afterward. He kept things hidden from her.

But he also regretted hurting her.

Vargo's gaze flicked up. "Go home. Or back to Ažerais's Dream, or wherever it is you bed down." His hand touched his stomach, and he winced. "Masks know that's where I'm headed."

Then he turned and walked out. And Ren stood where she was, not breathing, until a shout outside reminded her she was somewhere she shouldn't be, and she ran.

Isla Traementis, the Pearls: Canilun 3

Light and music still drifted from the windows of Traementis Manor, though the crowd of carriages out front had thinned. The upheavals of the evening hadn't prevented Nadežra's elite from enjoying themselves late into the night.

Ren was cautious as she entered the side garden overlooked by her balcony, but there was no sign of any guests having migrated there in search of privacy. Her windows were dark, signaling to all the world that Alta Renata was asleep. The moons shed enough light for her to make her way silently through the flowerbeds and trees.

Not enough to keep her from almost tripping over the dark figure on the ground beneath her balcony.

The Rook roused at her choked-off cry of surprise. He shoved himself up with his elbows, then with his fists, but made it no further than sitting. "Good. You came down. I was about to climb up. How late is it?" Exhaustion threaded through his voice, and the hood dipped and swayed like a drunkard's as he took in the dark garden around them, the moons headed for the horizon. "Too late. Fuck. It might be too late."

Ren crouched at his side. If he'd been too dazed to notice her approaching along the ground, instead of from above—"Too late for what? And what *happened* to you?"

"Beldipassi. There's no time. Help me stand." But even as his gloved hand landed on her shoulder, shaking and too heavy, he slumped against the manor wall like a man who'd given up. "There's...no time."

"Rimbon Beldipassi? He's in trouble?" Ren wasn't sure how to measure the health of a man cloaked in shadow, but she didn't need to be a physician to know the Rook was unwell. "Or he hurt you?"

His laugh creaked like a gallows rope. "Ambushed, on my way to meet him. They're going after him next. Garden of his house. Pomcaro Canal, in Eastbridge. I need...*You* need to help him."

That was clear enough. Whatever was wrong with him, the Rook was in no state to be doing anything. Ren had the Black Rose's mask in her pocket—but when she drew it out, the Rook caught her wrist.

"No," he said. "Beldipassi expects the Rook. Won't talk to anyone else."

Ren went still. Given time, she could assemble a Rook costume; people wore such things to parties, thinking it made them daring. But he'd said it himself: There *was* no time.

His hand rose—then hesitated, trembling. "No questions. I'll explain later. Don't waste time. The hood will help."

She wanted to tell him to stop, that she'd given up on guessing, that she didn't want to know. But before she could find the words, he dug his fingers into the wool.

It was like watching her own transformation from the outside. The black leather and silk and wool poured off his body, draining upward into the hood. In the shadows of the garden, the blue fabric of his coat was almost as dark.

She knew, even before it finished. Even before he lifted his head and extended one shaking hand, offering the hood to her.

Grey.

"Go," he whispered.

His strength was fading. When she took the hood, his head fell back against the wall, eyes sliding shut in a grimace of pain.

Grey Serrado. And he looked like he was dying.

But he'd begged her to go.

She pulled the hood on, and went.

Eastbridge, Upper Bank: Canilun 3

Ren wasn't alone.

The hood might work like her mask, but there was far more to it. Her steps were unnaturally silent as she ran; when she dropped from the top of the Traementis Manor wall, the impact was cat-soft. The shadowed streets and canals unfolded their secrets to her eyes.

And there was... *something* there. Not a thing she could converse with, the way Vargo did with Alsius, but a presence nonetheless. The Rook was more than just the men and women who'd played that role; it was the hood and the coat and all the components that made up the disguise, all coming together to form something greater than the assemblage of parts.

It was aware of Ren.

And it did not accept her.

I'm on your side, she thought fiercely as she slipped southward toward Beldipassi's house. *I'm trying to help.*

No answer. She didn't expect one. But nothing fought her, either, and so she went on. Trying not to think about Grey, about the fact that she'd been *right* and he'd somehow tricked her. Trying not to think about the fact that he was dying.

She could feel it, distantly, like the resonance of a harp string next to the one plucked. She might wear the hood, but *he* was the Rook's bearer. And something connected them still—something weakening badly, now that the two had been separated.

Ren had to finish this, fast. Before it was too late for him.

But she also had to be careful. Ren's steps slowed as she neared the Pomcaro Canal, with Beldipassi's manor up ahead. The streets were deserted—

Not quite. Someone crouched on a balcony, with a good view of Beldipassi's garden and the northern approaches.

At the sight, a tension built in the Rook. Ren could translate it well enough. *I won't kill*, she promised.

And she didn't have to. When the Rook had used his coat to conceal her and Vargo in Dockwall, she'd seen three darts tucked into a reinforced inner pocket. It wasn't hard for Ren to climb the building and get above the watcher. He had a crossbow in his hands, but he wasn't looking up; one quick flick sent the dart into his shoulder. A moment later he slumped.

Where there was one, there might be more. Despite the urgency, she circled south and found another watcher there. Only those two; any other traps must be inside Beldipassi's garden.

Grey's worries of *too late, too late* haunted her as she approached and heard voices. She recognized Beldipassi's. The other sounded familiar—bombast toned down to a whisper—and too large for his garden stage. "I don't mean to rush you, Mede Beldipassi, but you should know I'm not often one to give command performances."

As Ren levered onto the garden wall and caught a glimpse of the speaker, the urgency driving her flickered with an impulse to laugh.

"Yes, yes, sorry." Beldipassi's ornate lounging robe of silver-shot brocade caught the light of both near-full moons, making him an easy beacon to see in the dark. He twisted the sash in his hands. "It's just... I expected you to be... different."

"If you're hoping I'd flirt with you, I'm afraid I save that for lovely women." The false Rook sauntered closer, tugging Beldipassi's sash from his hands and using it to draw him closer. "Now, you've teased me enough. Shall we get to it?"

She knew her own entrance cue when she heard it. With a very satisfying flutter of the coat, Ren vaulted down into the garden.

"By all means," she said. "Let's get to it."

She heard her words in a double layer: her own familiar voice, and the deeper tones of the Rook. Beldipassi yelped, tried to retreat, and stepped on the hem of his robe, tumbling unceremoniously onto his ass. The false Rook also backed away, but he managed to keep his feet.

"You—" he said, and for a moment his voice wasn't nearly so deep and resonant. Then he regrouped. "An imposter!"

Ren laughed. "Really? That's your line? Though I suppose you don't have any better option, at this point."

"Ah, but isn't a point always an option?" the false Rook cried, drawing his sword and setting himself between Ren and Beldipassi. Sotto voce to the man behind him, he hissed, "You should hand it over to me before this thief tries to make off with it. Or with you. Or with your life."

"But th-the Rook doesn't kill," Beldipassi said, scuttling backward and casting confused looks between the two hooded figures.

"Yes," the false Rook explained patiently. "Which is why you're safe with *me* and not with this charlatan."

Ren rolled her eyes before remembering no one would be able to see it. The Rook's sword had come along with the gloves and boots and coat; she drew it and took a stance, point dipped low. "I don't have time to waste on this."

"Then let us end it!" the false Rook said triumphantly, and leapt forward.

She didn't bother parrying. Based on the voice and the behavior, she suspected she knew whom she faced; sure enough, his flashy swings were too far away to really threaten her. She retreated one step, two—then caught his blade with her own, binding it against her quillon. A simple twist of her wrist sent his sword clattering to the gravel of the path, and she followed up with a hilt-punch to his face.

This time the false Rook did go down. And his hood, unlike the real one, slipped off his head.

She might not be able to win against Grey or Vargo...but against an actor from the Theatre Agnasce, her skill was more than sufficient.

"Give me that," she said, yanking Beldipassi's sash free of its loops, then roughly binding the actor's hands and feet like a market hog. His nose dripped blood into the garden dirt. The sense of a thread ever unraveling robbed Ren of any delight in her victory: Every moment wasted here was another moment Grey wasted away.

It made her words to Beldipassi curt. "Someone found out about this meeting. Enough to ambush me and try to get to you. Just what do you have, Mede Beldipassi, that so many dangerous people are interested in it?"

"I don't know," he whispered, hand dipping into the deep pocket of his robe. "I hoped you could tell me. Because you're so old. I mean, the Rook is. And you're the Rook, right?"

With another confused glance at the bound man bleeding on a cluster of marigolds, Beldipassi pulled out a wad of white silk and began unwrapping it. "I collect things, you know. Like my exhibition. I found this old numinatrian piece. It's special. I mean, all the things I collect are special, but this..."

The last corner of silk fell away, revealing an antiquated-looking gold medallion, many-sided and etched with a sigil in archaic Enthaxn script at the center.

A medallion very much like one Ren had seen before.

As had the Rook.

She couldn't have reached for it if she wanted to. Her muscles were locked tight by that wordless presence—by the simultaneous awareness that *this* was the poison the Rook existed to fight...and that Ren herself had held such poison, not long ago.

"Illi. For beginnings. I thought it would bring my endeavors luck, but..." Beldipassi's whisper grew hoarse with fear. "I think it does more than that."

The medallion she'd stolen along with the rest of Letilia's jewelry when she fled Ganllech had been cast in bronze and etched with Tricat instead of Illi, but otherwise it was identical: the many-edged sides, the flat silhouette, the minute signs of wear that spoke of great antiquity.

Gammer Lindworm had torn it from Ren's neck in the nightmare. Ren had returned the favor at the amphitheatre when she pulled the knot charm loose. So far as she knew, it was still there.

The pressure in her head eased slightly. *Because I don't have it anymore*, Ren realized. *But—the Rook was right to suspect me.*

Now wasn't the time to ask the thousand questions swarming in her throat. She wasn't the real Rook; that man was dying in the gardens of Traementis Manor. Ren folded the white silk back over the medallion, careful not to touch it, and closed Beldipassi's hand around it. "You're right to be afraid. People have tried to kill me tonight because of this. They may well try to kill you, too."

She thought fast while Beldipassi whimpered. The actor must have been sent to lure him into handing over the medallion. If he failed, there would be a backup plan. But how could she protect Beldipassi and Grey alike?

Ren pivoted and crouched over the actor. Fontimi, that was his name—the one she'd kissed at the theatre. She let her shadow fall across him, and knew the intimidation was working when he cringed against the gravel. "Fontimi. Whoever hired you for tonight won't be pleased with your failure. You have two choices: find out whether their displeasure is lethal, or go with Beldipassi to safety."

"What safety?" Beldipassi yelped as Fontimi nodded vigorously.

Not Traementis Manor. If the Rook had hiding places, she didn't know where. She could only trust her instincts, and the picture that logic was swiftly assembling in the back of her mind.

"Isla Stresla, in Kingfisher," she said. "Oksana Ryvček's house. Tell her the Rook sent you."

The Pearls and Eastbridge: Canilun 3

She ran back north.

Stealth be hanged; it would hardly be the first time the Rook had been spotted on the Upper Bank. Only when Ren neared Traementis Manor did caution reassert itself. She eased over the garden wall, praying to Čel Kariš Tmekra that she wasn't too late.

Grey was where she'd left him, slumped against the wall. His chest barely moved, but he still lived.

With the Rook enhancing her sight, she saw now what she'd missed before: lines arcing up from his collar and across his face. Ren dragged his coat and shirt open and saw they continued downward onto his chest; when she pushed his sleeve up, she found them on his arm.

Lines like numinatria—except these shifted as she watched, sliding beneath his skin like worms.

Ren dragged the hood off, a gasp shuddering out of her as the Rook went away. There was magic of every kind worked into the components of his disguise. Not just imbuing and numinatria—a combination she'd have to think about later—but something like pattern, too, like the threads she'd seen that night in the amphitheatre. Outside the dream, she couldn't see or manipulate them, but she hoped that restoring the hood to Grey would do some good.

He didn't stir, though. Not even after the Rook lay before her again, shadowed and unreadable.

"Come on," Ren whispered, gripping his shoulders. "You have to tell me what happened to you. How do I fix this?"

An ambush, he'd said. Some kind of numinatria.

Tanaquis. But she'd left for that Praeteri ritual—would she be back in Whitesail by now? Or Ren could try the temple—

No. It would take too long, with no certainty of finding Tan-aquis in either place, and too much risk of the Praeteri. Grey couldn't survive that kind of mistake.

That left only one inscriptor.

Despite the horror of Grey dying beneath her hands, Ren bit down on a hysterical laugh. It was all well and good to believe that Vargo regretted hurting her... but that didn't answer all her other questions about him. Let alone what would happen if she showed up on his doorstep with Grey Serrado.

None of that matters. She would kiss the ground Vargo walked on if that was what it took to make him help.

But Ren couldn't run all the way to his townhouse carrying an unconscious man. She pulled the hood off Grey; then, on further consideration, she wrestled with his Vigil coat until it came free. No sense making him any more identifiable than he had to be.

She stuffed the coat under a bush and went out into the plaza. By now the ball had ended, but the lights at the front of the manor hadn't been extinguished yet; to her relief, two chair bearers still waited in the hope of one last passenger. Ren dug in her pocket, finding the money she'd taken to Whitesail in case she needed to bribe anyone, and shoved it at the larger of the pair.

"I have a sick man who needs transportation to Eastbridge," she said, remembering at the last instant to use her Seterin accent. "This is for the journey—and your discretion."

For almost a forro in assorted coins, they were delighted to com-ply. They loaded Grey's unconscious body into the chair, and Ren jogged alongside as they threaded a path across the bridges and canals of the Upper Bank to the Isla Čaprila.

At her direction, they left the chair at the base of the steps and retreated to a respectful distance while Ren pounded on the door. She dragged herself back into persona just in time for Varuni to open the door.

The set of the bodyguard's shoulders wasn't promising. "It's late, Alta Renata. Eret Vargo is in bed." *And not interested in seeing you*, her tone implied.

"Wake him," Renata said. "Please. I wouldn't trouble him if it weren't urgent. I know he has no reason to help me—I know I've given him every reason not to—and I'll owe him whatever he likes afterward, but—"

Varuni stepped aside, and Vargo appeared in her place. It was clear he'd been listening from just out of sight; his gaze was level and unreadable. "It must be something urgent indeed, to bring *you* to my door."

Even apologies might be a luxury she couldn't afford right now. Renata simply descended the steps and flung open the door of the sedan chair. The light from Vargo's front hall spilled in, showing Grey's slumped form.

"He's dying," she said. "And it's some kind of numinatria. *Please.*"

She expected questions, and had a lie waiting on the tip of her tongue.

Vargo only said, "Let's get him inside."

Eastbridge, Upper Bank: Canilun 3

"There's a lounging couch in my bedroom. Drag it into my study," Vargo called to Renata as he backed up the stairs, hugging Serrado's torso while Varuni carried his feet.

Peabody hopped onto the man's chest, trying to nudge his shirt open wider. ::We'll need to strip him to see the full shape of the curse. Strange that it hasn't settled.::

Strange, and lucky, Vargo thought. A curse that had fully dug in wouldn't have left such obvious traceries.

Together he and Varuni hauled Serrado's limp weight onto the couch. Vargo said, "Get the restoratives—anything we can pour down his throat. Renata, how long ago did this happen? *What* happened? Anything you can tell me might help."

::Anything she keeps back could hurt,:: Alsius added as Vargo checked Serrado's pulse. It was too faint to feel, but a weak, rattling breath confirmed that the man wasn't dead yet.

I don't know why she came to me for help, he told Alsius, *but I'm not going to scare her off with something that sounds like a threat.*

"I...I'm not certain," Renata said. The lack of conviction sounded odd, from a woman whose usual tone was cool silk over steel. "I brought him immediately after finding him in the garden, but he might have been there for a while. Perhaps an hour?"

Vargo started cutting Serrado out of his clothes. Any other time, he would have taken a perverse joy in destroying a set of dress vigils—but when the shirt fell away, shock overrode everything else. *Alsius, is that—*

::The same curse that killed me. Yes.::

The traceries shimmered through Serrado's brown skin like stretch marks of iron-dark hematite. Ninat, attacking his life energy; Quinat, sapping his health. Even just touching the lines, though, Vargo felt the difference: not just physical pain, but the inescapable agony of the spirit within.

The sort of agony that could only be created by eisar. "Renata," Vargo said softly. "Is there a reason why Captain Serrado would have enemies among the Illius Praeteri?"

The answering silence stretched long enough that he glanced up. Renata looked utterly stricken. At his pointed glare, she stumbled into speech. "I—no. Not that I'm aware of. This...Is this like what Diomen put me in?"

::If Ghiscolo wanted him gone, there are easier ways to do it.::

"Not important right now," Vargo snapped, at himself as much as anyone. A distorted gap centered on Serrado's left shoulder and dragging down his arm explained how the curse hadn't killed him before Renata discovered him. He'd somehow managed to tear through a section of it as it dug in, slowing its effect.

But a slow death was still death.

Varuni returned with the restoratives. While she propped Serrado up and enlisted Renata's help in massaging tonics down his throat, Vargo escaped to his workbench, putting his back to the room while he thought.

::You know those medicines won't slow it for more than a bell.

We've never tested our theories for how to counteract this, and even you on your most reckless day can't freehand a numinat fast enough to save him.::

So we let him die? Vargo started assembling his tools. Ink and brush instead of chalk. A soft cloth for blotting. A thin metal drafting template so he didn't have to resort to compass and edge for his basic geometric forms. What focus would be best? Svalthu was an aspect of Tuat, the one Alsius had used on him sixteen years ago. Vargo sorted through his chops and found the right one, fingers brushing over the raised, wax-stained marble.

::There's no 'letting' involved.:: Alsius's voice was gentle, and full of regret. ::The curse has drained too much. Unless you propose to sacrifice Renata or Varuni to buy time, he *will* die.::

"Not them," Vargo whispered. Aloud. To make it real. Because he couldn't believe he was even fucking proposing this. Setting the Svalthu chop back in its box, he pulled out the chop for Teruv instead.

Teruv, an aspect of Tricat. Because what would kill one or two, three might survive.

Alsius's voice became shrill. ::Have you gone completely mad? Stop. Put that down. I will not countenance this. You could kill us both!::

We've survived worse. And it would give us the time we need. Vargo swept his tools onto a tray and carried it over to the lounging couch. Varuni had finished cutting Serrado out of his breeches, leaving only his smalls, and now was cleaning up the various bottles. Renata sat tense, watching Vargo with an odd look. Half-worried, and that made sense—but half-wary, as if she were afraid of what he might do. She must have heard about Serrado punching him.

Alsius saw the connection, too, but from the other side. ::Just because you feel guilty about his brother—::

"I do."

"Vargo?"

He ignored Varuni's prod. *I won't do this if you don't agree to it,* he told Alsius. It took all his will not to add that it was more choice than Alsius had given him.

But then, guilt had motivated Vargo the first time, too.

He stalled, setting out the ink and the other tools onto the table Varuni had dragged up for the medicines. *Alsius?*

::It...would be a chance to examine the death numinat at our leisure. Well, not leisure, since we'll be in considerable pain and metaphysically bleeding like slaughtered pigs, but you understand what I mean.::

Vargo choked down a laugh. *So, we're doing this?*

::Why do I let you talk me into these things?::

Because you're a softhearted old man.

::Soft*headed*, more like.::

Vargo uncapped his inkwell, raising his voice to spin a lie for Renata. "I'm going to inscribe a temporary Quinat numinat on him. It should keep his health stable while I remove the curse." He took one of the half-full bottles from Varuni and downed it, ignoring the vile taste. A moment later his senses shocked awake like he'd drunk a whole pot of coffee in one gulp. Serrado's pallor, Varuni's scowl, Alsius's skittering, Renata's masklike tension: all were cut as sharp as panes of glass in the Sebatium.

"I have my compass, my edge, my chalk, myself. I need nothing more to know the cosmos." Vargo set his template and brush to Serrado's bare shoulder.

The cold sweat made things harder, threatening to blur his ink. Without being asked, Renata used a cloth to blot it away. Vargo worked fast, both from a sense of urgency, and to keep himself from reconsidering. Quinat for health—a mere handkerchief to stanch the sucking chest wound draining the life from Serrado—balanced by Tuat and both linked to Illi, joining Serrado to the inscriptor's self. Or in this case, selves. He didn't use a wax seal for the focus; instead he painted the Teruv chop with ink and printed it directly onto Serrado's skin.

Despite everything, an odd pride glowed through him. What he was about to do, no other inscriptor in Nadežra could do. Not if they hoped to survive.

He closed the circle of Uniat, and the mark on his chest seared like someone pressing a branding iron into his flesh. For an instant he went blind with pain—just like he'd done in an Eastbridge study, sixteen years ago.

But Serrado's breathing grew steadier. Now Vargo had time. "Let's get him onto the floor."

This time he let Varuni and Renata do the carrying. With his and Alsius's joined life energy pouring into Serrado, Vargo didn't trust himself not to drop the man, and he didn't want Varuni realizing what he'd done.

After that, the process shattered into moments of hard-edged focus, each one careful and precise, but disconnected from the others. A step, and a step, and a step. He etched two wax blanks with simple Quinat figures, leaving the Uniat line just short of closure; he would have liked to make three, but he couldn't craft one small enough for Peabody, not with sufficient precision. The connection between him and Alsius would have to be enough. The growing pain was an odd sort of blessing: There was no chance of Vargo losing himself to imbuing anything, not when each breath carved its way into his lungs before rasping back out. When the blanks were prepared, Vargo began scribing a counter to the curse, a complex net of lines through the prismatium framework laid into the floor.

Then he had to pin the curse down on Serrado so it could *be* countered.

That was a bad moment for everybody involved: Vargo bit down on a scream, and Serrado went into a seizure. So did Peabody, twisting onto his back with legs twitching, but fortunately neither Renata nor Varuni noticed; they were too busy holding Serrado down, keeping him from spasming right out of the numinat.

Pinning the curse made the pain more visceral, a Primordial agony Vargo couldn't ignore. Blood welled in his nail beds, and he had to hold one hand steady with the other to join Ninat to Illi, passing the energy of the curse back into the cosmos while a recursive loop fed Serrado's life back through Illi to Uniat.

Simple, really. The only way to remove a death curse was to let it finish what it started. The only way to survive it was to be reborn.

Varuni saw the bloody fingers and the shaking of his hands when he passed her one of the prepared wax rounds. Vargo spoke before she could say anything. "In a moment, you'll need to put one of those on Serrado's chest and one on mine, over the heart, and close the circle. Just press your fingernail into the gap."

Renata pulled off her gloves and took the other round from him. "Why? What will this do?"

"Restart our hearts," Vargo said, and activated the numinat.

Eastbridge, Upper Bank: Canilun 3

Varuni was lunging for Vargo even as he collapsed, filling the air with what Ren presumed were Isarnah curses. That left her to dive for Grey—and for one horrible instant, haste made her hand slip, the wax sliding from his chest to the floor. But she slammed it back in place and dug her fingernail into the gap in the circle, and the jolt that ran through her hand was nothing, because Grey gasped in a sudden breath of air, and he was alive.

She wrenched around and saw Vargo was breathing, too, and something like awake, because one blood-smeared hand batted feebly at Varuni as if that mothlike touch could move the very angry brick looming over him.

"Peabody," Vargo managed, more groan than word, and flinched when Varuni scooped the limp spider off the floor and dumped it into his lap.

"Can you believe this asshole?" she ranted at Ren. "Cares more about a bug than his own life!"

::Alsius?:: Vargo's mental call was as weak as his physical voice.

Two fuzzy legs lifted and waved like surrender flags. ::Mm'fin. S'rado?::

Vargo struggled to sit up. "How is he? Serrado? Did it work?"

"He's alive," Ren said, and felt her own hands tremble. "Unconscious still, but the lines from the curse are gone."

Relief and exhaustion made her stupid; she pronounced the *r*'s too distinctly for a Seterin accent. But Varuni was occupied with chewing Vargo out, and Ren didn't think either he or Alsius were in any state to notice.

"Good. That's good." Vargo nodded longer than he needed to, cupping his spider carefully to his chest. Without bothering to rise, he wiped away a portion of the circle on the floor, then rolled a bottle of liniment toward Renata. "Use that to remove the numinat on him."

::Does it matter? It's 'nnert.::

::Do you want a hawk listening in on our conversations?::

::Hmm. Point.::

She dragged her gaze away from Vargo—from the layers of clothing that covered the brand on his chest. A brand Tanaquis thought connected him to Alsius. And they had used that connection to save Grey, risking their own lives to keep him from dying before they could undo the curse.

The same curse that had also killed Alsius.

She had a thousand new questions, and no chance to ask them. Instead she found a rag and wiped the ink from Grey's skin, as gently as she could, even though there seemed no risk of him waking.

By the time she was done, Vargo had regained his feet. Even without Alsius offering commentary, Renata could tell it must be sheer force of will that pushed him upright; she knew all too well what it felt like to hide the full extent of one's weakness.

Before she could speak, Vargo said, "You promised whatever I like in return."

She stood, hiding the knot of worry that tightened inside. "I meant it."

"Then you don't tell Serrado I had anything to do with this."

She was too tired not to gape at him, and gaping was the appropriate response anyway. "What?"

"Not a word. I don't care what you say. It's possible he won't even know what hit him. But you weren't here, and I didn't do anything." He scowled down at Grey, absently rubbing his own stomach. "It would be awkward, and I don't need that shit."

Awkward? It might be the one thing that could ease the fury over Vargo's involvement in Kolya's death. But Vargo hadn't hesitated before issuing his demand, even though he had leverage to get anything he wanted out of Renata.

Just like he hadn't hesitated before throwing that letter in the fire. Or before risking himself to save Grey.

They needed to talk. She had no idea what to say, though, nor the energy with which to say it—and Vargo, she suspected, needed to collapse as soon as possible. "Understood," she said faintly.

"Good. Varuni, can you handle delivering Serrado to his house? I trust your discretion." Lurching to a sideboard, Vargo splashed something the mellow gold of warm honey from a decanter into a glass.

"Sure." Varuni's expression didn't change, but she waited just long enough for Vargo to lift the glass to his lips—deliberately, Renata was sure. "As is, or should I put some clothes on him first?"

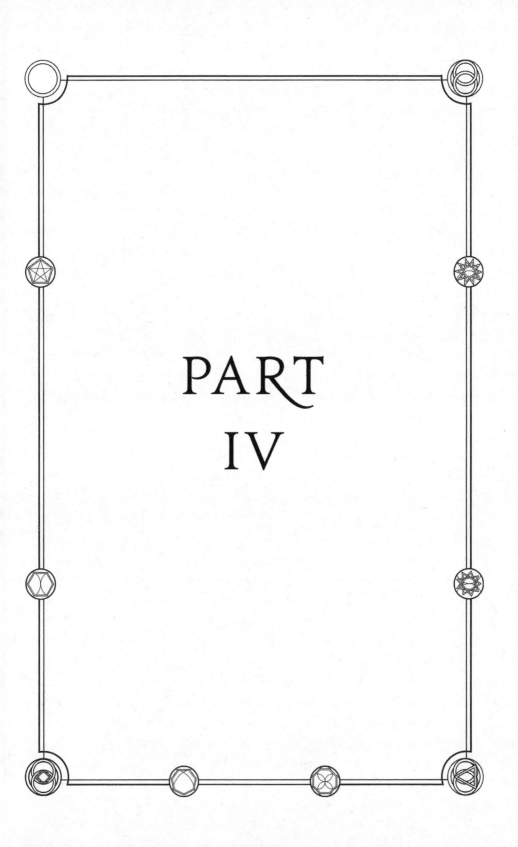

PART

IV

The Constant Spirit

Isla Traementis, the Pearls: Canilun 4

Ren meant to stay awake after she climbed back through her window, even though the hour was appallingly late. It seemed impossible that the ball had been earlier that same night; so much had happened since then, a month might have passed. She needed to think.

She changed into her sleeping robe, sat on the floor at the foot of her bed to dangle and drag the sash for Clever Natalya's amusement—and woke to find a snoozing ball of fur in her lap and Tess and Suilis exclaiming in concern.

"The letter from Seteris?" Tess whispered urgently once she'd sent Suilis off to refresh the washbasin water and get breakfast for the kitten.

"Destroyed," Ren said, wincing at a series of thumps just past her door.

"Folks moving in, folks moving out. 'Twould save our bones a lot of aching if the new cousins were the ones going to Quientis's villa," Tess said briskly, just as one of the other maids came in to ask whether the alta would be coming to see Era Traementis off.

Downstairs, Renata found a scene too well-organized to be called chaos, despite its flurry. Colbrin was directing it all, instructing an ant brigade of footmen, some in Quientis livery, carrying trunks to a cart waiting outside. Bemused, Renata said, "Is Donaia going to the bay for a rest, or moving to Seste Ligante?"

"I didn't know what she'd want." She turned to find Giuna hovering nearby, hands twisting. "It just seemed easier to—well—pack *everything.*"

The hand-wringing wasn't all for Donaia's departure, though. More quietly, Giuna said, "The problem I told you about last night. What are we going to do about it?"

We, not *you.* Ren still struggled with hearing that kind of speech from anyone other than Tess or Sedge. Too many years of *only* having those two. And Giuna hadn't once asked what in a letter from Seteris could be used against her.

"It's been taken care of," Renata said, and then Alinka's arrival gave her a blessed excuse not to try and explain what had happened in Whitesail.

"Please forgive me for being late," Alinka said, shepherding her children ahead of her. Yvieny immediately went bounding off, shouting for Meatball, while Jagyi sucked his thumb in quiet wariness. Directing her words equally to Colbrin, Giuna, and Renata, Alinka explained, "My brother by marriage was...not well this morning."

As Giuna went to corral Yvieny and the dog, Renata drew Alinka to the side. "I hope it's nothing too serious." *He must be all right, or surely she wouldn't be here.*

Alinka laughed awkwardly. "No, just—worse for the wear from drink. Which normally is not his way," she added hastily. "He said he had an...unpleasant encounter last night."

Relief unfurled inside Ren. *He's awake enough to talk. And perhaps to lie.* While she didn't know what had transpired between him and Vargo outside the manor, in his shoes, she would have blamed everything on that.

But a bitter thread wove through the relief. Yes, Grey Serrado was a very good liar.

"He asked me to give this to you," Alinka added, handing over a sealed envelope.

Renata shoved the envelope in her surcoat pocket before anyone else could note it, just as Donaia wandered in blearily. She held her head as though she wasn't quite sure it would stay on without help. "And people accused *me* of having too good a time last night," Renata said with mild amusement, helping Donaia sit away from the commotion and fetching her a pot of strong tea.

"You are a malicious spirit, sent to torment me," Donaia grumbled, crouching over her cup as though it contained the elixir of life. "How can you be fresh as a flower when I feel like a trampled weed?"

"Youth," Renata said succinctly, and Donaia laughed so hard she snorted her tea.

"Forget a spirit," she said as she wiped her chin. "You're one of the Primordials, set loose from the gods' binding. Go do something useful, since you're so young and spry. There'll be time for goodbyes later."

Renata circled her fingers the way a Seterin would to banish the ill luck of naming the Primordials—and interlaced them like a Vraszenian once Donaia couldn't see. Then she went to help organize the chaos.

Donaia had perked up by the time Scaperto Quientis arrived a short while later. Renata gathered that he'd escorted Donaia upstairs the previous night...then left soon after, having seen her safely into the hands of Suilis. His manner as he led her out the door to a waiting carriage showed a similar mix of concern, courtesy, and gentle teasing. Giuna followed, to see them off at the dock.

With the villa party gone and the new cousins yet to move in, the manor seemed very empty. As Renata sat at her desk to glance through the morning's messages, a crinkle from her pocket reminded her of the envelope Alinka had given her.

She pulled it out with reluctance. So many things it might hold, and so few of them anything she wanted to see right now, with her feelings so tangled. Grey Serrado was the Rook; Grey Serrado had tricked her. The old hurt rose up, choking her, and she swallowed it down. *This is probably instructions for returning the hood.*

But there would be no rest while she wondered at its contents. Steeling herself, Ren broke the seal and unfolded the envelope.

Something fluttered loose, and she caught it by reflex. A rectangle of stiff paper, painted on its back with the spindle, shuttle, and shears of the three threads. A pattern card. And when she turned it over—

The Constant Spirit.

Ren almost dropped it again. That wasn't a usual part of a pattern deck, not anymore. It was one of the seven clan cards, which had fallen out of use after the destruction of the Ižranyi—when, according to the legends, every Ižranyi card had gone blank. After that, most szorsas had stopped using the clan cards entirely.

This wasn't the Ižranyi card. It was the card of the Meszaros, representing the virtues and failings of that clan. They were the Children of the Horse: stubborn and slow-witted, their detractors said, but also hard-working...

...and honest.

The message inside the envelope was only three words.

When you're ready.

Kingfisher, Lower Bank: Canilun 4

Alinka was a skilled herbalist. Thanks to the tonics she'd given him before she left, Grey was only nursing the memory of a headache by the time a soft knock sent him to the door.

His muscles ached—his *bones* ached—and a reddened splotch on his chest stung like a burn he didn't recall getting. But he was alive, and had somehow landed on Alinka's stoop for her to find in the early dawn hours, wearing unfamiliar clothes and stinking of zrel as though a bottle had been summarily dumped over his head.

He had so many questions. All of which fled when he opened the door and saw Ren—as Arenza—standing on the other side.

She held herself stiffly as he silently gestured her in, barely nodded as he offered tea. He felt her gaze on his back while he ground up pieces off a brick and whisked it into something almost too strong to be drinkable. She looked like she needed it, and Masks knew he did.

She still hadn't spoken by the time he placed cups on the table. *Why should she? You're the one who promised her honesty.*

"You got my message," he said, then shook his head at the stupidity of that opening. "I—"

"I assume you want this back," she said, and laid the Rook's hood on the table like the accusation it was.

Grey pushed the hood aside. "I wanted to make certain you were safe. Last night..." She sat too far away for him to reach out, and might not welcome it if he did. They'd grown close in their various personas—Captain Serrado and Renata, Grey and Arenza, the Rook and the Black Rose—and he knew her well enough to guess at her thoughts.

Vargo had played her. He'd made her believe in the possibility of friendship, while the whole time he'd been using her. Right now, she would be wondering if Grey had done the same.

Had she understood the meaning of the card? She was a szorsa, but the clan cards weren't common anymore. Grey took a steadying breath and said, "I can't apologize for not telling you before. I have an obligation. But...I never set out to hurt you. And honestly, I'm glad you finally know. I don't *like* lying to you."

"I believe you."

Her reply was so quiet, for a moment he wondered if he'd imagined the words he wanted to hear. But then her masklike expression cracked into something that wasn't quite a smile, but wasn't bitterness, either. "You gave me a kitten," she said. "Because of my nightmares. Yes?"

Grey nodded. It was an old Vraszenian superstition, alongside a red thread to keep away the zlyzen. Cats defended against nightmares, chasing them down like little mice.

She ran her thumb across the edge of her teacup. "The Rook knew not that I was having nightmares. Grey Serrado did—but he couldn't give Arenza a cat, not when he might later see it at

Traementis Manor. You helped me, in a way that meant I would never know you had." A huff escaped her. "A lot of that going around these days."

Before he could ask what she meant by that, she met his gaze and said, "Even at my most suspicious, I cannot see anything in that other than kindness."

The heartfelt ring of her words brought an unexpected catch into his throat. Had her life seen so little spontaneous kindness that a kitten for her nightmares took on such importance?

"Has it helped at all? The kitten?" He didn't think so. She looked almost as exhausted as she had after the Night of Hells. However long of a night it had been for him, hers must have been even longer.

Now her expression lightened into a soft smile. "Yes. Though only when I actually *sleep*, which I did very little last night. Aren't you going to ask what happened?"

Grey wanted another quiet moment to savor the comfort of her forgiveness, but his life didn't allow for many of those. He forced himself to break away from that smile, gaze settling on the hood. He took a sip of tea—too hot, too bitter—and said, "Is Beldipassi safe? Did he have...anything?"

"He is safe, and he has a numinatrian medallion. Something the Rook recognized." Ren's voice tightened. "As did I."

"You've seen one? Was it the Tricat medallion?" He'd initially abandoned that suspicion when he learned she wasn't truly Letilia's daughter. But if she'd had it, all this time...

Grey knocked his cup over, reaching for her wrist. "Tell me you have it still."

The force of his reaction made Ren recoil, slipping out of his grasp. "Not anymore. I lost it. And—am I right to think it's the source of the curse on House Traementis?"

"Yes." His fear turned queasy, spreading cold through him like the spilled tea across the table. Once a family lost their medallion, there was no hope; the repercussions would eddy outward until they struck everyone in the register. It had taken down multiple noble houses in Nadežra's history—was doing the same right now to the former Indestor.

When he'd inherited the hood, he'd learned the truth about House Traementis's ill fortunes, but he'd been helpless to do anything to stop their fall. Renata's adoption seemed to have turned things around for the Traementis. But if she'd had the Tricat medallion and then lost it . . .

He mopped up the tea, hands shaking. The nightmare had started again. *Not Ren. Please, Masks have mercy on us all—not her, too.*

Before he could make himself speak, Ren's hand twitched toward his own. "We are not under it anymore! Tanaquis was able to remove it. Ask me not how; all I know is that she used as her focus the cards that had shown me the curse."

"Thank the Faces." He shut his eyes and took the not-quite-offered hand, his skin cold against her warm fingers. Until Leato's death, he'd hoped the Traementis's store of ill luck had run dry. The idea that the curse might have been renewed by a second loss of Tricat was gut-wrenching. But after a lifetime of resenting charlatans and women with good intentions but no gift, he'd finally met a szorsa truly blessed by Ažerais. And it seemed pattern could do what numinatria on its own could not.

If only pattern could solve all of Nadežra's problems. "Where did you lose the Tricat medallion? When? We have to find it. It's . . ."

He hesitated. She'd worn the hood. She'd gleaned something of the medallions' importance. But sorting through the Rook's memories was hard even for their chosen bearer, never mind a substitute—especially when reaching for those memories meant giving more of oneself to the role. "The medallions are connected to Kaius Sifigno. You know the stories of how he couldn't be stopped, couldn't be killed . . . It wasn't just exaggeration. His chain of office was a set of medallions, one for each numen, all linked. It held power enough to let him take all of Vraszan. The chain—the Uniat piece—broke when he died. The various nobles around him stole the pieces."

Had it felt like this for Ryvček, when she finally had a chance to share the weight of that secret with someone else? Ren's eyes were wide as his flood of words continued. "People have been fighting and killing each other over the medallions ever since. The woman who created the Rook knew that power would go on poisoning Nadežra. She drove herself to annihilation, trying to recover and destroy those pieces, but the Rook...continued." Not quite a spirit, not quite a ghost—all three parts of her soul caught in the weave of the hood. In becoming the Rook, she'd done more than create the pieces of a disguise; she'd created an identity, a persona. And she'd imbued it so deeply with her passion that afterward, there was nothing left of her—not even a body.

At least those of them who wore the hood afterward didn't pay as high of a price.

"That's why you suspected me," Ren breathed. "Rightly, as it turns out. But I—I swear, I knew not what I had. It was among the jewels I stole from Letilia when I left Ganllech. She must have stolen it from the Traementis when *she* left."

As Ryvček had always suspected. The decline of their house started with the flight of one spoiled brat.

"Where is it now?" Grey asked. To have *two* medallions within reach... "And where's Beldipassi? What *happened* last night?"

Ren quirked one eyebrow at him, amusement softening her mouth. "You ask three questions at once. Which should I answer first?"

"You could have answered two of those instead of giving me sass." He fought a smile. "Where's Beldipassi?"

"With Ryvček." As Grey's shoulders relaxed, Ren nodded. "Then I guessed correctly. I knew she was your teacher, and—tell me. Was she the one in the hood when I escaped the prison?"

"Have you any notion how hard we worked to set that up? All my efforts to hide, and still you suspected. We tied ourselves in knots to lead you off the scent—but here it all falls apart in a fortnight." Grey released her to run a hand through his hair, sighing. "So, Ryvček has Beldipassi. What of his medallion? And Tricat?"

"His looked to me like Illi in its zero aspect. I left it with him; I liked not the idea of taking it myself. But whoever set things up last night sent a fake Rook to speak with him—Fontimi, the actor from the Theatre Agnasce." Faint laughter shook her shoulders. "He was *terrible*. I can only hope I looked not so foolish. He went with Beldipassi; I convinced him the alternative was being killed by his employer. As for Tricat... Gammer Lindworm tore it from me during the Night of Hells. It fell when I pulled her knot charm off at the amphitheatre. I—" Ren grimaced. "It never occurred to me that I should pick it up."

He could hardly blame her. And it was better for her that she didn't have it.

Worse for everyone else, though, if it was lost in Ažerais's Dream.

A brief silence fell. Yesterday Grey had been dreading the quiet of these rooms, without Alinka and the children to distract him. But it was warm, and the quiet was a gentle one, and he was less lonely than he'd been in years.

Because of Ren.

He couldn't say that to her, not yet. Instead he asked, "How is it I still live? That curse should have killed me."

Ren's teacup reversed course, thunking onto the table rather than rising to her lips. She opened her mouth, then caught herself; he could see the internal argument as she hesitated. Finally she shook her head. "I... cannot bring myself to lie. This is the first honest conversation we've had; to stain that would be wrong. But... I also cannot tell you."

Her refusal sharpened his curiosity. What could have saved him, that she was unwilling to confess to? Not a medallion; Tricat was gone, and Beldipassi still had his. Tanaquis Fienola had dealt with the Traementis curse; perhaps Ren had gone to her again? Or the curse hadn't been as bad as he'd thought—after all, he *had* damaged it. But there would be no reason to hide that, if so. Something to do with pattern? For all he knew, Tess had employed some arcane Ganllechyn stitch-witchery.

Grey forced himself to stop. Even if he guessed right, she wouldn't tell him, and by trying to guess, he was pushing at the boundaries of her secrets. He'd done that more than enough already.

Especially since there was an unspoken question beneath her words. *Do you trust me?*

With his mission, and with his life. He'd decided that last night.

"Then I will press not," Grey said.

Ren fiddled with her teacup. "Your Vigil coat—I forgot to bring it. I will send that along. And—" She hesitated, then reached into her pocket and drew out The Constant Spirit.

He laid his hand over hers. "That was meant as a gift. Keep it."

"How came you by it?"

It was fascinating, listening to the subtle shifts in her wording. She was disguised as Arenza, but speaking as Ren: her accent fainter, sliding in and out of the markers of Vraszenian speech. When she spoke of pattern, those elements strengthened—and his own voice was responding, easing out of the Nadežran accent he assumed all too easily these days. "It belonged to my mother."

"Your mother was—" Ren caught herself.

"Meszaros? Yes, this Kiraly has the blood of a plodding horse." He smiled at her discomfiture. "I know what you meant. Yes, she was a szorsa, though she lacked your gift."

"A szorsa? But you..." Ren's lips pressed together.

Her diplomacy was more than he deserved, when he hadn't exactly made his disdain a secret. Scrubbing exhaustion from his face, Grey said, "My issues are not with szorsas, but with frauds. Ažerais's gift should be honored."

Bitterness edged those words—his grandmother's words. But now wasn't the time to burden Ren with the weight of his past. Forcing his voice to lighten, he said, "This tea is barely drinkable. What say you to something better?"

Thankfully, she let him change the subject. And the amused tilt of her lips was as bright as the sunlight coming through the window. "Better? Is it wise to be drinking alcohol so early in the day?"

"Who said anything about alcohol?" he asked, retrieving the packet Alinka had left behind for him. He knew whom she'd meant him to share it with. Collecting the cups, Grey said, "What say you to spiced chocolate?"

Isla Traementis, the Pearls: Canilun 4

The sweet warmth of the chocolate stayed on Ren's tongue as she left Kingfisher, changed personas, and took a skiff to the Upper Bank. It was more than taste; it was the odd, not-quite-comfortable comfort of having sat at Grey Serrado's kitchen table, with no masks between them.

It felt like being naked for the first time with a lover. Except that he'd apparently known the truth of her for months now, ever since the night the Rook had invaded her kitchen. And he accepted it. All that time spent fearing he would turn on Arenza if he knew who she really was...but he'd known all along.

Had he feared the same from her? That she would hate him for lying? Ren understood why he had, though. And while the bruised part of her soul kept bracing for something else to hurt, inch by inch, breath by breath, she'd relaxed into the novelty of being herself around someone other than Tess and Sedge.

If only the discovery of his secrets didn't come with the news of an ancient poison eating away at Nadežra.

The Mask of Worms, in her pattern for the Rook. Kaius Rex's chain of office, shattered into pieces, but each still holding a fragment of the original power. Sibiliat had claimed the medallion Ren stole from Letilia was an Acrenix family heirloom, but Ren doubted it, and Grey had confirmed. The Acrenix showed no sign of the type of decline that would have accompanied such a loss. In fact, he now suspected them of holding the Quinat medallion—and possibly Sessat as well, lost in the fall of House Indestor.

She stopped halfway up the river stair, one hand against the damp stones to keep herself steady. *The fall of House Indestor.*

Meppe.

People stared at the fine alta running, but she didn't care. Renata slammed through the front door of the manor, shouting, "Meppe!"

Suilis popped into view. "He's in Era Traementis's study, alta."

Where Renata had sent him to start work on their ledgers. Meppe had all but glowed at the prospect; he genuinely seemed to enjoy the straightforward tedium of clerical work. When she burst into the study, he overturned his ink. "Renata—"

"You're coming with me to Whitesail."

Isla Stresla, Kingfisher: Canilun 4

Grey would have liked to burrow back into bed after Ren left, but that was a luxury he couldn't afford. He only took the time necessary for a basin wash and a shave before carefully folding up the hood and heading for the opposite corner of Kingfisher, where Oksana Ryvček lived.

The midday streets were oddly quiet, even in the market plazas. He passed shopkeepers fretting on their stoops in search of custom that wasn't there, returned the wary nods of a few carters who recognized him even out of uniform, but the homey buzz and bustle of Kingfisher was absent. Ever since the Dockwall escape, the Vigil had been patrolling the Lower Bank with more vigor than usual, and the Ordo Apis kept breaking into places to search for the missing prisoners. Supposedly following up on leads, but Grey suspected at least half of it was random strikes to keep people afraid, so that no one would shelter Andrejek.

Which meant it was accomplishing nothing at all. Grey didn't much like leaving the Anduske trio in Vargo's hands, but he'd seen firsthand the precautions the man was taking. *Nobody* was going to find them anytime soon. Which was a good thing, since Koszar's new injuries had set his plans for confronting Branek back almost to where they'd been after Veiled Waters. The only thing weighing in his favor was that Branek blamed Prazode for not protecting Gulavka, Prazode blamed Branek for blaspheming against Ažerais, and the resultant infighting would keep the Stretsko busy for a while. Ren's doing, she'd admitted over chocolate.

A wry smile of admiration tugged at his mouth as he climbed the steps of Ryvček's townhouse. His teacher must have set one of her cousins to keep watch, because he'd barely released the fox-headed knocker before the door opened.

"She's in the training room," the girl told him, as though that wasn't always where Ryvček was. With a nod of thanks, Grey went to the back of the house.

"You had an exciting night," Ryvček said in greeting, not pausing her usual drill.

"Beldipassi?"

"Comfortably ensconced in my attic. And Fontimi in the cellar, not so comfortably bound. He started second-guessing his cooperation around breakfast." She swept a bow to her imaginary opponent before racking her practice blade and drying her sweat-damp face with a towel. "After two decades failing to achieve anything of note, I'm glad to be included, but also surprised. Why send them to me?"

Grey closed the door against possible eavesdropping. "I didn't send them. Nor did our hooded friend. Whoever hired Fontimi was waiting with a numinatrian curse that nearly killed me. Ren was the one in the hood last night."

He knew Ryvček well enough to expect her laughter, but that didn't make it any easier to sit through. "After all the work we—"

"I know, I *know.*" He folded his arms and glared at her. "You could take this seriously. I nearly died."

"Nobody dances the kanina for you today."

He understood her blithe attitude. Every Rook courted death; she was one of the few who'd survived long enough to retire. If he *had* died, she would mourn him—but since he lived, why worry?

Ryvček hadn't felt that curse. The foul *wrongness* of it, leeching away his vitality, burrowing into his bones. It wasn't only pain; it was the loss of the desire to live.

Her laughter died as he explained how he'd escaped the net. "You gave yourself to the Rook? Grey—"

"It was the only way. He wanted to continue. I...did not. But once he got me past that, I regained control." He met her gaze, letting her search as if she might find some hint of the Rook's shadow there. He wasn't sure she wouldn't.

Most people thought of imbuing as relating only to crafting, the making of physical things. Some could imbue performances instead, achieving feats of supernatural strength or dexterity; Ryvček had taught him to do it with fencing.

The connection between the Rook and his bearers went beyond even that. They didn't imbue him as strongly as his maker had—they didn't have to, with the framework already there—but they added to it, a new layer with each person who wore the hood. And unlike numinatria, imbuing didn't pull its power from the outside. It came from within: a thread of the spirit, woven into what they made. That was why imbuing the inscription of a numinat was lethal. Pouring too much of oneself into the Rook...

Other bearers had lost themselves to the hood, never removing it, never resting. Or thinking as the Rook even as they carried on their normal lives, until there was nothing left of the original person. Ryvček had told him, again and again, that he needed to hold some part of himself back.

Last night he'd held nothing back.

If he hadn't, he would likely be dead. But there would be consequences for his choice.

What Ryvček saw must have reassured her, at least for now. "So you just gave Renata the hood? And the Rook..."

"Tolerated her," Grey said. "But didn't accept her." The Rook chose his own successor and bound them with ties that lasted after death. Ryvček told him once that she thought the Rook claimed their szekani—the part of the soul that was supposed to go into Ažerais's Dream.

That was fine. It wasn't like his kin would summon him with the kanina anyway.

Ryvček's eyebrows rose. "For a real chance at this, it seems even our hooded friend will compromise. Who will you terrify first, the actor or the fool?"

"Actor. The longer we keep him, the less likely it is he'll survive if we release him." Fontimi was an oblivious tool in the schemes of the nobility and, Grey suspected, an expendable one. That wasn't a crime worthy of death.

Ryvček smirked. "In that case, I think a bit of stagecraft is in order."

Grey met that smile. Ren was right; some parts of being the Rook were definitely fun. "Rooftop?"

"Rooftop."

He went through the motions of farewells and leaving before circling around to the narrow gap between Ryvček's house and her neighbor's. Pulling the hood out, he smoothed the wool with a reluctant hand...then made himself slip it on.

Shadow impressions of the night before swept over him. No clear memories, but a grudging sense of forbearance when Ren donned the hood. Amusement when they faced off against a second imposter. Triumph when Beldipassi showed them the medallion.

And simmering mistrust when Ren recognized the similarity to a medallion she'd once owned. Even if she hadn't known what she held, even if she hadn't consciously used it, that power had tainted her.

Yes—and then she let it go. Not voluntarily, not the first time, but she'd left it behind without a second thought during the confrontation at the amphitheatre. As much as a part of him wished she hadn't—how were they going to get it back?—what the Rook hated above all was the lengths people would go to for that power. Walking away, even in ignorance, was a mark in her favor.

Setting thoughts of Ren aside, he braced himself against the walls and chimney climbed to the roof.

The flat rooftop deck was built as a nighttime refuge from stuffy summer air. Today fitful gusts off the Dežera, bearing the first bite of autumn's chill, set the Rook's coattails snapping. A moment later, Ryvček shoved a blindfolded man through the roof hatch—still dressed in the remnants of what was clearly meant to be the Rook's disguise.

"You should have kept to your usual stage, Fontimi," he said as Ryvček pushed the man onto his knees. "I don't take kindly to imposters."

He knelt before removing the blindfold, so the actor's first sight was the depthless shadows of the hood. Fontimi's swallowed shriek came out as a frog croak.

"Thank you for your assistance, duellante," the Rook told Ryvček, standing but keeping his attention on Fontimi. "You can leave him to me."

"Just leave no mess for me to clean off my stoop," Ryvček said, with a meaningful glance at the drop to the street below.

The Rook let his tone sink into playful menace. "That depends entirely on my imitator's cooperation."

"I'll cooperate! I'll cooperate!" Fontimi babbled as Ryvček left the roof. "What am I cooperating with?"

Intimidation worked much better than pain for persuading people to talk. Intimidation, and the promise of help if they played nice. "You're going to tell me who hired you, and what you were hired to do. Answer honestly, and I'll protect you."

"Nillas Marpremi! He hired me. Gave me this costume, too. It's much better than the one I wear on stage. You wouldn't believe how flimsy that thing is, no lining or anything. And nobody would believe me as the real Rook if I were flashing my chest—" Fontimi caught himself, sweating. "You don't care about that part. Marpremi hired me to get some kind of medallion. Said I should talk Beldipassi into giving it to me, or taking me to wherever he'd hidden it if the thing wasn't on him. Kind of implied I should beat him up if he didn't hand it over, but I wasn't sure I would do that part. Marpremi wasn't paying me that much, and besides, I only know stage combat."

"Then what?"

"Once I had it, I was supposed to go to the fountain in the Plaza Giotraia and deliver it to Marpremi. By now he'll know something went wrong."

If it hadn't been for the death curse, the Rook might have chalked this up to ordinary business. The zero-aligned Illi medallion was nearly impossible to track down; it changed hands too frequently, cursing those it left behind. His predecessors had only been able to trace its path by the devastation it left in its wake.

But the ambush was far too sophisticated for a man angling to be the medallion's next holder. He suspected Marpremi was a middleman working for someone else. But who?

Vargo didn't have Illi-zero after all—but maybe he wanted it. The man was certainly a skilled inscriptor. Skilled enough to scribe the curse that caught the Rook?

A few more questions proved that Fontimi knew nothing else of use, and the Rook's impatience to question Beldipassi next made him brusque. "Mistress Ryvček will give you some coin and a change of clothes," he said. "I suggest you hire on with the next traveling show leaving Nadežra and not return for . . . a while. If ever."

"But—" Fontimi's expression crumpled into disoriented shock. "My career is here in Nadežra. My *life* is here."

In the grand scheme of things, this man's losses were nothing. But this was what the struggle over the medallions did: It ruined people's lives, in ways great and small.

"That life will be very short if you remain," the Rook said, tying the blindfold back in place. "The choice is yours." He knocked on the rooftop hatch and waited until Ryvček had bundled Fontimi away.

For Beldipassi, different tactics were required. Ryvček's attic was one of her stashing places for her seemingly endless series of cousins who rotated in and out of the house. It had a single window, just barely large enough to admit passage, but the Rook had squeezed through smaller. If the effort made his arms tremble with residual weakness, Beldipassi didn't have to know.

He found the man dozing in a reading chair, dressed in an ornate lounging robe, open book fallen into his lap. Beldipassi startled awake when the Rook removed the book and perched on the footstool.

"*Ten Summers in Seteris*," the Rook said, examining the title page before setting the book aside. "Are you fond of poetry, Mede Beldipassi?"

"I prefer history, but it was the only book in here." Rubbing sleep and astonishment from his eyes and a bit of drool from his chin, Beldipassi said, "You came back."

"You have something of great interest to me."

"This?" Digging into the pocket of his robe, Beldipassi pulled out a timeworn medallion. "If you want it, you can have it. After last night, I want nothing to do with it."

The disc of gold was both familiar and not, something the Rook had seen but Grey had not. Nausea rolled through him at the sight, and he fought the urge to back away. Only two centuries of poise kept his voice steady. "I'm afraid it's not so easy as handing it over."

Beldipassi shivered, fingers curling protectively around the disc. Would he really have surrendered it, if the Rook had reached out? Whatever gave the medallions their power, it was seductive. The more a person used one, the harder it was to give up, like an addict with their drug. "What *is* it? I saw you at Essunta's party, and I knew—I'm not even sure how—I knew you could answer that question for me."

No question that Beldipassi had made use of the medallion, then, knowingly or not. "It gives you insights into the people around you. It guides you to the things you need to accomplish your goals."

Beldipassi examined the medallion as though for the first time. "Ah. I thought it was just lucky, but that didn't make sense for an Illi medallion. Luck is Quarat's domain."

"It has nothing to do with luck. With a deep enough understanding of numinatria, you can even make those around you want whatever *you* want them to." The Rook nodded when Beldipassi blanched. "You said you prefer history to poetry. Can you tell me what Houses Persater, Contorio, Taspernum, and Adrexa have in common?"

Fingers tightening around the medallion, Beldipassi whispered, "They all died."

"They all used—then lost—a medallion from the Tyrant's chain of office. Like the one you're holding."

Beldipassi dropped the medallion.

Then he shrieked and snatched it up again. "No! I didn't mean it! I only dropped it—tell me that's not the same as losing it!"

A laugh ghosted out of the Rook. "If only. I could have set my hood aside ages ago if people had to keep the medallions in their possession at all times. No, ownership is more than mere contact. Do me a favor and place it back on the floor."

Beldipassi obeyed with alacrity, then retreated even faster when the Rook drew his blade. The odds of this working were vanishingly small . . . but he couldn't not try.

This wasn't the first medallion the Rook had managed to find in his centuries of effort. All previous attempts to destroy them, however, had failed. He had two theories as to why: Either they could only be destroyed when all brought together, or the destruction had to start at the beginning. With Illi-zero.

Taking his sword in both hands, he slammed the point into the medallion.

Ordinary gold would have given way. An ordinary blade would have snapped. Neither happened: The Rook's imbued sword bent and then sprang back, and the medallion showed not so much as a scratch.

Biting down on a curse, he sheathed his sword once more. Numinatria had made the medallions; it would almost certainly take numinatria to unmake them. He would need to either find an inscriptor he trusted enough for this . . . or sink himself deep enough into the memories of past Rooks that he could see what they had tried before.

Both held more than a hint of danger. And neither was something he should attempt today.

Sighing, the Rook said, "Mede Beldipassi, I'm going to ask you to do something very difficult."

Beldipassi's throat flexed as he swallowed. "You're going to make me keep it, aren't you?"

"Until I can figure out how to destroy it. Keep it, and not use it—which will be the harder part."

"Don't think about what I want? Oh yes, *that* should be easy."

Beldipassi's snide response dulled into fear with his next question. "What happens to me if you destroy it? Will I..."

"You're in luck. I know a way to remove the curse." The Rook wondered at that luck—if it was somehow due to the medallions' influence, if he might not have learned about Fienola's discovery if he hadn't worked with Ren the night before. Ren, who used to hold Tricat.

A man could go mad, wondering where that influence ended.

It might even be responsible for the ambush. "How did someone know to send an imposter?" the Rook asked. "Who did you tell about our meeting?"

"Nobody!"

The answer came readily, but he didn't believe it. The Rook merely looked at Beldipassi in silence until the man squirmed and said, "Just my valet. I wanted him to know not to disturb us!"

The Rook's teeth clenched so hard they ached. *His valet. But for that stupidity...*

He wouldn't have almost died. He wouldn't have revealed himself to Ren.

Maybe things had worked out for the best after all.

"Your valet is almost certainly in someone else's pay. I'll look into it. Meanwhile, I don't recommend going home."

Beldipassi blanched. "No, but—will I live in this attic? For how long?"

Not the attic. Sooner or later people would gossip about Ryvček's reclusive boarder. Given the reputation she'd built over the years, it was likely that some people already suspected her of being the Rook; keeping Beldipassi here would only increase that risk.

But where? He couldn't send the man away, like he'd done with Fontimi; he had to make sure this medallion didn't slip through his fingers. Beldipassi couldn't hide with Grey, though, because he needed someone around to watch him. Nor with Ren, either, because then there were too *many* people around.

Someplace a person might take a room, without it being an item of gossip. Someplace he could trust.

There were no good options. All he could do was choose the least flawed one.

"I'll send Grey Serrado to you," the Rook said. "He'll take you elsewhere. I need your oath on whatever you hold most dear that you will *stay there*, and not tell anyone where you are or what you have."

Falling to one knee with a hand over his heart, Beldipassi said, "I swear on my collection of golden walnuts from the Tomb of the Shadow Lily!"

That would have to do. Meanwhile, the Rook needed to change back into Grey and have a chat with Dvaran about a temporary lodger at the Gawping Carp.

Whitesail, Upper Bank: Canilun 4

Renata didn't stop to consider whether her new cousin would be ready to receive guests. Fortunately, Tanaquis didn't recognize ceremony well enough to stand on it. Instead of letting Zlatsa show them to the salon to wait, Renata hauled Meppe up to the garret observatory. Then she stopped at the doorway in bewilderment.

Sprawled facedown on the polished floor in nothing but chalk-dusted trousers and a fitted shirt, Tanaquis clutched a stick of chalk in each hand—and also between the toes of each foot. Her limbs swept up and down, tracing sweeping arcs onto the slate. At Meppe's croaked giggle, she lifted her head and blinked in confusion.

"Was there something I was supposed to do that I've forgotten?" She rose to her knees and removed the chalk from her toes.

Despite her urgency, Renata couldn't help but ask, "What are you *doing*?"

"Hm?" Tanaquis followed Renata's glance to the chalked arcs. "Oh! Chalking the dimensions of a personalized numinat. Of course, you can use standard measurements—most inscriptors do—but I've found an organic approach can be more effective when determining the terminus of the spira aurea in relation to—"

"Right. I understand now," Renata said, before Tanaquis spiraled off herself. "I brought Meppe because of that matter you brought up last night. The cleansing?" Turning to Meppe, who was looking utterly adrift, she improvised, "Tanaquis was concerned that, because the Indestor register was burned rather than being properly undone, there might be some negative effects for you. I wanted to make certain we dealt with that as soon as possible."

Tanaquis had stood, and was hopping on one foot as she tried to wipe a rag between her toes. "That's not—Oh. Yes." She turned a brilliant smile on Meppe; Renata only hoped it didn't look as false to him as it did to her. "Burned register. Let's fix that. Renata, would you, ah, oblige me by getting that . . . thing you used before?"

She had a deck with her, the replacement she was using for her mother's. Stepping over to the table, she pulled out the cards and shuffled them, her back to the others so they wouldn't see her lips moving in silent prayer to the Vraszenian ancestors. Then she drew a single card: Sword in Hand.

"Do you always shuffle seven times?" Tanaquis asked as she handed it over. "Fascinating. I wonder if there's some relation to Sebat. What does this one mean?"

It means I've taken up the Rook's crusade. "It's the card of commitment," Renata said. "I think in this instance, it signifies Meppe's commitment to his new house."

Tanaquis frowned at the card. "Before, you drew three."

Because she'd been laying a three-card line for House Traementis. But also for the curse laid for Tricat, whether she knew it or not. "I think," Renata said, then hesitated. If the Rook was right about Mettore holding Sessat . . . "For Cousin Meppe's new loyalty, it ought to be six this time."

"Fascinating. I'll wipe down the floor."

Reeds Unbroken, Pearl's Promise, The Liar's Knot, Aža's Call, A Spiraling Fire, Drowning Breath. She explained the cards while Tanaquis cleaned the boards: endurance, reward, trust, illusions, passion, fear. Or if they were veiled, the dark sides of those concepts. "I'm not sure how to interpret their significance, though. There aren't any six-card layouts that I'm aware of."

"We'll work with it anyway and see what happens," Tanaquis said cheerfully, presenting Meppe with four sticks of chalk. "Right, cousin. Off with your boots."

When Tanaquis removed the curse from Donaia, Giuna, and Renata, the numinat had been prepared before they arrived at the townhouse. Now, twice in less than a day, Renata was treated to the spectacle of a master inscriptor laying down lines that could save a life.

Tanaquis didn't work like Vargo. Her mutterings were all to herself instead of to an Acrenix ghost, and devoid of any profanity or frustration. Where Vargo's movements were calculated and precise, Tanaquis danced barefoot around the figures she was chalking, each step and figure leading fluidly into the next.

"I dabble in numinatria, you know," Meppe said to Renata, fiddling with his boots as though uncertain whether he was allowed to put them back on now that he'd made his bird wings on the floor. "I've never understood how an inscriptor could get so lost in their work that they imbued a numinat by accident. But this..."

"Don't worry," Tanaquis said brightly as she skipped out of the circle to examine her work. "I'm not quite ready to know the cosmos *that* intimately."

The process of uncursing Meppe seemed much less dramatic than Renata remembered. Because there was only one of him? Because he was less intensely cursed? Or because she was an outside spectator? Regardless, it was a relief when Tanaquis declared the process complete. Meppe, still bemused, stepped out of the framework and finally put his boots back on. "Thank you for humoring us," Renata said, favoring him with her most dazzling smile, before remembering that Meppe only had eyes for Idaglio. "My apologies for interrupting your day. Tanaquis, would you mind if I stayed to consult with you on a separate matter?"

"Of course." Tanaquis glanced down at her chalk-streaked trousers and bare toes. Then her stomach grumbled audibly. "Perhaps you could find us food while I put on clean clothes?"

Renata accompanied Meppe outside, then came back a short time later with the corner ostretta's errand boy at her heels, bearing a hamper emanating all sorts of tempting smells. The actual taste proved less impressive than the scents advertised, but she'd eaten far worse in her time. Tanaquis joined her, now wearing a surcoat with an ink stain at the knee, and tucked in like she was a fireplace someone had forgotten to supply with coal.

"That was fascinating," Tanaquis said after she'd removed and eaten the filling from her dumplings, then moved on to the limp, steamed wrappers. "Last night I called the cleansing precautionary, but there's no question it was necessary." She finished rolling a wrapper and studied Renata with an intensity that would have made most people squirm. "Also interesting that you correctly identified the source as the Indestor register. Did you learn that from your pattern cards?"

Eating while having such conversations was useful; the time spent chewing and swallowing covered any hesitation. "To be honest," Renata said, "I made that up. I didn't want to tell Meppe the Traementis used to be cursed. But I had a dreadful nightmare about him last night, and it put me on edge."

"Quite a lot of nightmares going around," Tanaquis murmured, rolling another dumpling wrapper into a ball, heedless of the grease on her fingers. "Just Meppe?"

Renata nodded. Grey had told her a good deal more over their cups of chocolate; he didn't think House Fintenus had a medallion. Half of them tended to be in the hands of the Cinquerat: Tuat with Argentet, Tricat with Fulvet, Quarat with Prasinet, Sessat with Caerulet, and Sebat with Iridet, following the numinatrian associations of those seats. Many of the others could be tracked by the way the numen's influence spilled outward through the holders' registers. Quinat and Ninat had been difficult to locate, but the hedonism of House Extaquium's members pointed toward them having Noctat, while the social dominance of Coscanum suggested they had the Illi medallion that represented ten. And until Beldipassi approached him, Grey had suspected that Vargo's extraordinary rise was driven by the other half of Illi, representing zero.

But knowing where the medallions might be wasn't enough. He needed to destroy them. And while that process might start with

Beldipassi's Illi-zero, if she could get Tricat back for him—make up for her mistake in losing it . . .

In a rare show of empathy, Tanaquis said, "I could check the household again to confirm, but I would hate to add to Donaia's worries if she were to find out." She frowned at her lumpy dumpling ball. "I suppose we'll have to rely on pattern."

By now Renata was used to the aura of mingled curiosity and dissatisfaction that surrounded Tanaquis whenever pattern came up. It drove the woman mad that she couldn't neatly slot its intuitive workings into her ordered cosmos—and not for lack of trying.

Wiping her own fingers clean, Renata said, "If it's any comfort, the other puzzle I have for you may well need a numinatrian solution. Do you know of a way to bring a physical object out of the realm of mind?"

"You mean like your prismatium mask?" Tanaquis leaned forward, nearly upsetting the table and its platters. "Not yet. Vargo provided very scant details of his experience. Protecting your privacy, when there are things to be *learned*! I'd hoped his involvement in the Praeteri might pry it out of him, or that *you* might, but—"

Tanaquis drew back. "I forgot. You had a fight."

Renata wasn't about to share details of the Rook's purpose with Vargo, even if the pattern she'd laid had indicated that he might somehow be involved. Not that she would tell Tanaquis, either— but she had much more confidence in her ability to sell Tanaquis on a false story. "During the Night of Hells, I lost a numinatrian medallion I'd been wearing. I'd like to get it back."

"By some means other than dosing yourself with ash and falling in? Hmmm. Apart from that mask, I've never heard of someone bringing an object back from a spirit trip. Do you still have it?"

"The mask? Yes."

"Have it sent here. I'd like to study it." Tanaquis tapped her knee, overlaying the ink stain with grease.

Renata gathered herself to leave. "I'll do that right away."

"What's the nature of the medallion?" Tanaquis asked suddenly.

"I'm not sure what god it invokes—I've never really learned the sigils." Perhaps Grey would be able to answer that once he got a good look at Beldipassi's. "But it was a fairly simple configuration of three overlapping Tricats."

Tanaquis hummed. "So Tricat in a tripled arrangement, left in the realm of mind. Fascinating. Why didn't you mention this in the account you wrote for me after the Night of Hells?"

Djek.

At least it made sense to be taken aback. "I didn't think it was relevant. You wanted to know what sorts of scenarios we'd encountered and so forth; it didn't occur to me that you would want to know I'd lost a piece of jewelry."

"Not relevant!" Tanaquis's voice rose in pitch as she shot to her feet. "What sort of nonsense are they teaching in Seteris these days? A physically embodied numinat in the realm of mind? Who knows what ripples that might cast into the real world! And by ripples, I mean floodwaters. Tricat tripled, and brought there by ash... It would mean the breakdown or unhealthy growth of familial and communal bonds. Failures of justice. Inability to compromise. Veng—"

"*Oh.*" Tanaquis fell back into her chair as quickly as she'd risen. "Not might. *Has.*"

Some realizations hit suddenly, like a knife to the ribs. Others took longer to sink in... but left you bleeding just as badly. "You mean—" Renata couldn't have stood to leave if she wanted to; her knees wouldn't hold her. The grinding breakdown of business in the Charterhouse; Branek trying to bind all the Stretsko to the Anduske; even well-intentioned things like Giarron Quientatis's rash attempt to adopt an entire orphanage.

And inexplicable horrors like Meda Scurezza slaughtering her entire family.

"No," she whispered. "Surely one piece of numinatria couldn't be responsible for all of that."

Not even something that belonged to Kaius Rex?

Tanaquis's eyes had taken on an all too familiar glow as the tide of her own thoughts caught her up. "Responsible? No more than the rain is responsible for weeds growing. Numinatria in the realm of mind—but don't Vraszenians call it Ažerais's Dream? A place of pattern. What we're seeing right now might be the result of those two things working in tandem. Which means it *is* possible!"

"*Tanaquis.*" Renata leaned forward to grip her wrist, fingers digging in. "If this is causing problems in the city, we have to get it out of there. How do we do that?"

She had to get it back. Not just to help the Rook. Because she had lost the medallion—let it fall to the ground, unheeded and unimportant, when she turned the zlyzen against Gammer Lindworm—and who knew how much of what was happening in Nadežra right now was her fault.

"I don't know," Tanaquis said with an excited grin. She tamped it down when Renata's grip tightened. "I don't know *yet*—but you have pattern, and I have my compass, my edge, my chalk, and myself. Together, we can figure it out!"

17

One Poppy Weeps

Isla Čaprila, Eastbridge: Canilun 5

Renata made it to the foot of Vargo's steps the next morning before she wondered if this was a mistake.

But she was here, and if she backed out now, she wasn't sure she would find the courage to try again. Climbing the steps, she rang the bell with more confidence than she felt.

No answer came. After pulling the chain twice more, she was about ready to try his Dockwall office when the door was yanked open.

Vargo looked like he'd played sixes with death and lost every hand. His hair was lank with oil, his bloodshot eyes smudged with kohl two days old. Wrapped in a sumptuous lounging robe of blue and green brocades in a patchwork quilt, the collar open enough to show the scar slashing down his neck, he looked like what the world called him: street trash in the guise of nobility.

He stared at her as though he couldn't dredge up the energy for a proper scowl. "The fuck do you want?"

"I—" She was off to a splendid start, not even able to offer a worthwhile greeting. "I wanted to make sure you were all right."

"I'm alive. I assume Serrado is, too, or you'd have come by sooner." Scraping fingernails through his stubble, he stood aside. "Well, come on. En't gonna do this on the stoop."

He led her to the back of the house and the morning room where the two of them had breakfasted together, what seemed like a lifetime ago. A bowl of congealing tolatsy sat on the table; the small warming numinat on the sideboard held a basin of gently steaming water instead of a teapot. The razor and soap waiting alongside said Vargo had been preparing to shave, but he ignored them in favor of slumping onto one of the plum velvet couches. "Don't have coffee for you. There's tea if you feel like brewing it." He waved at the sideboard.

It would provide a distraction and something to do with her hands, but Renata sat instead. "I thanked you the other night, but given the state you were in, I'm not sure if the words registered."

"They registered. You're welcome. Don't mention it, but I think I already covered that." The lift of his scarred brow added, *Anything else?*

"I've told Captain Serrado nothing," she assured him. "But— well, I expected *you* to have questions."

Vargo merely shrugged. "Our business is the river numinat. Unless this has something to do with that, what does it matter?"

It matters because you nearly died saving him. And because the story she'd crafted to explain Grey's state was designed to draw Vargo out, offering footholds for getting him to talk about other matters.

But if he wasn't going to ask, she would have to prod. "You mentioned the Praeteri that night, when you saw the marks on Captain Serrado. Why?"

"Praeteri numinata can do some unpleasant things. As you found out the hard way. I was going to warn you about that, but I was too late." He toyed with the spoon in the congealed tolatsy, standing it up in the rice porridge and watching it slowly list to one side. "As for death curses, who knows what sort of secrets are shared past the gates we've seen? It seemed a logical deduction."

That was far from the whole truth—but she could hardly admit she'd overheard his conversation with Alsius. Nor, for that matter, could she bring up the absurd possibility that Alsius was somehow the spirit of Ghiscolo's dead brother inhabiting the body of a king peacock spider. She wished one of them would make a mental comment, but either the spider wasn't around, or she'd somehow lost the ability to hear them.

Too many secrets between them. Hers as well as his. "What happened in the temple that night...it took me by surprise. I'm not sure what Diomen wanted to achieve; I can only hope he didn't get it. And that you'll forgive me for saying such things to you."

A laugh ghosted from him. "Apologizing for speaking the truth? Fine. You're forgiven. I figure I owe you after..."

It was almost exactly what he'd said when she came to him after her sleeplessness was cured. Vargo must have heard the echo, too, because he grimaced and muttered, "I didn't know what Mettore was going to do. I didn't think you'd be hurt." Mouth twisting, he added, "Saying that a lot these days."

His forgiveness came too easily to be real. In the temple she'd spoken with the intent of wounding him—and it seemed she'd succeeded. A sudden impulse of regret made her say, "I won't pretend that night wasn't horrific. But what cut most deeply was believing you didn't care. After I found out...I overheard you talking to Ghiscolo Acrenix. He asked if I was going to be a problem, and you—you said, 'I don't get attached to my tools.'"

Vargo's jaw tightened. In a low voice, Renata said, "After that, I thought I'd misread you completely. That everything between us had been a lie from the start."

"No reason it should occur to you that I might be lying to Ghiscolo, instead."

"In that moment? When I'd just learned about your deal with Mettore? No. You sounded very convincing, and you have a certain reputation." She slid one hand into her pocket. "A reputation that is not unfounded...but also not the whole story."

Hoping the trembling of her hand didn't show, she laid the mask of the Black Rose on the table.

The possibility of admitting that truth to him had crossed her mind yesterday, on her way back from Kingfisher. She hadn't been at all sure she would do it, though—not until he'd delivered that bitter, resigned reply.

She suppressed the urge to snatch the mask back as Vargo picked it up. He let the fabric slide like petals through his fingers, then held it up and studied her through the lace, as though looking for hints of the Black Rose in Renata's tense expression.

With a sudden gesture, he let the mask drop. "Now I understand why you brought Serrado to me—but I'm still confused. You hate me...so you've been helping me?"

She sighed and rubbed one hand over her face. "It began as spying on you. After Sostira told me what you'd done, I wanted to keep a closer eye on what you were doing. Especially when you thought I wasn't around."

"Sostira." A flush darkened Vargo's skin, and a hint of murder glinted in his eyes. Lurching to his feet, he went to the sideboard and fell silent for the time it took him to swap the basin for the teapot and measure out the tea.

When he spoke again, something unsteady threaded through his voice. "There's your real enemy. She's a danger to you as long as she holds Argentet. I can only destroy so many packets from Seteris before one gets through."

A small noise escaped her, and Vargo turned to look. "What?"

Three different responses rose to her tongue, all of them delicate, political—manipulative. But she was tired of dancing around things. "I'm trying to figure you out, Eret Vargo."

"I en't that complicated a man, *Renata*." The emphasis on her name, bare of title, deliberately mocked the respect she'd just paid him. As did his slipping accent. "You said it yourself. I'm a jumped-up Lower Bank rat. Anyone from Froghole to Dockwall could tell you what I'm about. The problem is, you cuffs en't got a shit-crusted clue what people are like when they weren't born with a pair of gloves shoved up their ass." He punctuated his self-assassination with a shark's smile.

Then his speech shifted back to studied elegance. "Thank you for your apology, but we both know what you said in that Praeteri numinat was the Lumen's own truth. What's the saying? 'There's no washing off Lower Bank filth.'"

She rose to her feet, facing him across a breakfast room that suddenly felt both too small and very large. Vargo merely arched his brow again, as if daring her to refute him.

Instead she nodded at the abandoned basin of water resting next to his forgotten shaving tools. "May I?"

He shrugged and went back to his seat, dropping down hard enough to make it creak, while she dipped the block of soap into the basin. Working it into a lather, she said, "Perhaps you're right, and there's no washing it off." Her hands muffled her voice as she rubbed them over her skin. "Nothing about Nadežra is clean, from Lower Bank to Upper. But this is and always has been a city of masks."

That last line was delivered in her own accent, and she turned toward him with her face scrubbed clean.

Vargo jerked upright, gaze flicking to the sideboard as though searching for the cosmetics behind her transformation, before fixing again on her. When she laid out the Black Rose's mask, his expression had been guarded. Now it was raw, open confusion.

He stood, slowly. "The fuck is this?"

"My name is Ren," she said, her throat tight. *What have I done?* "I was born in Lacewater and trained as one of Ondrakja's Fingers. Never in my life have I been to Seteris. I am a con artist."

"You're..." His breath hissed through his teeth. Vargo wasn't a stupid man, nor an unobservant one. She watched as he unraveled the knot. "You're Lenskaya. And if you were a Finger, then Sedge..."

"Is my brother." She tipped her wrist upward, showing the faint line of the scar.

She forced herself to hold still when he grabbed her hand and studied the scar like it would reveal another layer of secrets. Her fingers were soft after almost a year in gloves, his calluses rough against them.

He released her as though he'd picked up a dead fish. "How nice for you." There was something ugly about the way he glared at her wrist, and something uglier still in his voice. "So we're both liars and hypocrites. Are *you* a murderer, too?"

She'd taken her mask off. There was nothing to hide behind when that knife slid between her ribs. *Leato.*

The flinch shook her whole body, and Vargo's expression transformed on the spot from anger to horror. "*Fuck.* Renata—Ren—I—"

He froze halfway through reaching out, like he didn't know how to comfort instead of harm. Like he didn't know if he *could.* For an instant she stared at his hand. Then Vargo started to withdraw—

She caught him, clutching his fingers in an awkward grip. It was the only thing she could think to do, because for once in her life, no words would come. She'd meant for the revelation to ease the tension between them, to prove that she *did* understand. Instead she'd hurt him—again—and he'd done the same.

But that hand spoke a different truth. The friendship she'd once believed in, even if they both kept doing their best to break it.

Vargo stood, hardly breathing, looking at their hands. It lasted long enough for Ren to start feeling embarrassed, and to search for something to say; then Vargo broke the silence. "I...need a drink."

She let go, and he went to the sideboard. From its depths came a dusty, full-bottomed bottle of fortified wine. He filled one of the teacups, then held it out like a peace offering.

Fuck it. Ren knocked the contents back like the Lacewater rat she was.

Vargo refilled her cup, then took a swig directly from the bottle and clutched it to his chest as he sat. When he finally broke the silence, his voice was hoarse. "Let's start again? I'm Vargo. Lower Bank knot boss, recently ennobled. And an ass who sometimes says things he regrets. You?"

She laughed unsteadily. "Ren. Arenza Lenskaya really is my name, but I use it now only when...well. You know. Also Renata Viraudax Traementatis, fake noblewoman, and the Black Rose. Though I planned that last one not."

His smile was grudging, but real. "Not a fake noblewoman; I watched them add you to the register. Shit, that was an even bigger coup than I realized. Sit down. Stop making me look up at you. I died the other day and only woke up a few bells ago."

Sitting felt like an excellent idea. Vargo took another swig, study-ing her. Abruptly, he said, "How old *are* you?"

She fought the urge to touch her bare face. "I'll be twenty in Equilun."

"Fuck me. I knew you were younger than me, but under that makeup, you're still nipper-cheeked. I feel like an old man now." He eyed the bottle as if trying to gauge whether it would be enough to get them through this conversation. "How the hell did you infiltrate the Traementis like that?"

"I was Letilia's maid for five years. After Tess and I fled the Fin-gers." No way in hell was she going to admit to Vargo that she was a knot-traitor who'd poisoned Ondrakja. Not right now, anyway. "Think you that I will answer all your questions, and ask none of my own? What is your interest in the Praeteri?"

His breath huffed out. "Destroying them, if I can."

The fortified wine was hitting fast enough that her eyebrows rose. Vargo said, "I mean, I also want to know how they're doing what they do. There's a type of spirit called an eisar—"

"Yes, Tanaquis said."

"Did she also tell you the Praeteri are using that shit all over Nadežra to bolster their own power?" He grimaced and drank again. "Probably not. She might be the only person in that cult who's actu-ally there to study the mysteries of numinatria. They've been doing it for years, though—I'd show you my notes, but the Rook burned 'em. The first time I was able to lay eyes on an active eisar numinat was during the Dreamweaver Riots. But the whole reason I became a cuff was so I could get an invite to the Praeteri and see how they make the damn things."

Then he glanced around the plush comfort of his breakfast room and snorted. "Well. *Part* of the reason."

Ren could hardly cast stones at anyone for wanting luxury. She sipped the wine: rich and dark, smelling of summer cherries, and nothing either of them could have afforded in the past. Vargo said, "My turn. Why the Black Rose? What was a con artist doing at the amphitheatre that night?"

"Initially? Being a prisoner. Mettore's plan required using ash to poison someone conceived during the Great Dream. He had two: me and—"

Ren stopped, suddenly cold. *That's how Mettore knew.* For ages she'd wondered how he could possibly have guessed—especially with Arkady. But Grey had said those who held medallions could tell when someone or something would be useful to their goals.

She took a gulp of her wine, washing down her fear. "The curse on Grey. You recognized it, and as more than just Praeteri work. You—" There was no good way to lie around it. As Vargo reached across to fill her cup again, she said, "I can hear your conversations with Alsius."

The wine nearly splashed over her hand. Vargo cursed and stopped pouring, then belatedly dug out a wrinkled handkerchief and tossed it to her. While Ren blotted up the spill, he said, "How the *fuck*—"

"Veiled Waters. You had collapsed. I could see a thread connecting us. I—strengthened it. Somehow. And since then, if I am close enough, if I pay attention...I can hear." She glanced around. "Except I cannot hear him now."

"That's because he's still passed out. Shit! I *told* Alsius I heard a voice that night." Vargo sank back on the couch, staring. "I'm going to lose my mind obsessing over every conversation we've had in your presence since then."

Then, midway through another swallow, he coughed on the wine. "Is it only him you can hear, or—" His eyes narrowed as though he was thinking at her very hard.

"Only the two of you together." Ren waited until he set the bottle down, then asked, "Is he really Ghiscolo's brother?" When Vargo nodded, she said, "And he was killed by the same thing that almost got Grey."

"Seems you've heard plenty."

"But with Ghiscolo you still work." Her speech was getting more Vraszenian the emptier that bottle became.

Vargo snorted. "Gotta get close enough to your enemy to slip the knife in. Sixteen years ago, he tried to murder Alsius with a death curse. Same one that was laid on Serrado. How did he stumble into it? That's no simple thing to drop on just anyone. There's a thousand easier ways to kill a person."

Ren hesitated. It was the other side of the coin Grey had flipped to her: secrets she couldn't share, because they weren't her own.

Before Vargo's expression could shutter the way it so often did, she spoke her thoughts. "I would tell you if I could. But that secret…"

"Isn't yours. Got it. Out of idle curiosity, what lie were you planning to feed me if I asked before we started being all honest-like with each other?"

"That he was assisting me by investigating the Ordo Apis."

Vargo traced a numinat into the dust on the side of his bottle, then wiped it away half-complete. "Alsius didn't fare as well as Serrado. His spirit got trapped in the body of my pet spider, and we wound up connected." He tapped his chest, where the numinatrian brand lay hidden. "Once we realized there was no freeing him without killing us both, we started investigating who was behind the curse. The trail led to Diomen. Guebris, the old Acrenix head, had brought him to Nadežra, and was acting as his patron. Alsius thought Diomen was a charlatan, using trickery to control his father. Turns out his tricks are real. But we found out that while Diomen may have crafted the curse, the assassination wasn't his idea."

"Ghiscolo."

Vargo nodded. "He started up the cult after he took over House Acrenix. So the plan's been, learn their secrets, then once I've got those, kill Ghiscolo and Diomen. Then see about making this city less of a shithole."

Assuming he could pull all of that off without being arrested and executed himself. But Ren knew better than to point that out, and Vargo went on in a deliberately lighter tone. "That's tomorrow's business, though. Today is for removing masks and washing off mud and whatever other metaphors you care to add to the pile."

He topped up her cup, then clinked his bottle against it, hard enough to spill again. Ren looked for his handkerchief before giving up and licking the droplets away. Vargo watched for a moment like a man who hadn't eaten his morning porridge, then grumbled, "I am not sober enough *or* drunk enough for this," and took another swig.

She'd had enough of the wine to snicker at his comment. "The rest of my business can wait also. What say you to the idea of getting drunk and telling each other more things? I have of late been strangely honest, and it feels . . . good." More than good. Like—

Like it was all right to be herself.

"I've got nowhere else to be. And no particular desire to get off this couch." Kicking his slippered feet up onto the cushions, Vargo turned his sprawl into a shameless, full-blown lounge. "So. *You* were one of the famed Lacewater Fingers? Start there."

Isla Čaprila, Eastbridge: Canilun 5

The message Tess received was brief, cryptic, and worrying.

Bring my makeup to Vargo's.

Ren had left for Eastbridge at midmorning. Now it was well after noon, and she'd missed two appointments. What had gone wrong? Why did she need her makeup? If it was bruises that needed covering up—if that man had hurt her—

The heavy thump that came a moment after Tess knocked on the door put her heart in her mouth. But after it . . . was that a *giggle*?

Before she could fret more, the door swung wide to reveal a *very* drunk and disheveled Vargo, clinging to the frame. "Tess!" he exclaimed. "I hear you're a wanted criminal in Ganllech!"

"Wha—" Tess stared past him to see Ren sitting on the floor of the hallway . . . without a spot of makeup on.

Her sister waved one hand loopily in Tess's direction. "He knows everything. Long story. Come inside. Vargo believes not that I can put my face on while drunk; 'm gonna prove him wrong."

Charterhouse, Dawngate: Canilun 6

Vargo woke the next morning wishing that the truth in wine didn't come with predictable consequences. Yesterday he woke up feeling like death because he'd died. Today, he only wished he had.

::It's your own fault for letting me sleep through important conversations,:: Alsius grumbled. After two days of his own dead sleep, he'd woken up chipper—until Vargo relayed the reason for his hungover state. ::A conversation I actually could have *participated* in!::

"Please, not so loud," Vargo said, mixing up a concoction of pear juice, ginger, and willow bark that had never let him down. Perhaps he should send the recipe to Traementis Manor.

He could understand Alsius's enthusiasm. For sixteen years the old man had precisely one person he could talk to; the prospect of being able to double the size of his social world made him giddy. And, true to form, Alsius was salivating to learn how it had been done, pronouncing Vargo's secondhand and hungover explanation "quite insufficient."

But the eagerness still rankled, for reasons Vargo preferred not to examine too closely.

He let the flood of questions go mostly unanswered while he bathed, shaved, and debated spending another day in his robe. He'd already let business slide for two days, though—three more than he could afford—so eventually he dressed. Then he sent a messenger boy to the Isarnah compound in Floodwatch, letting Varuni know he was feeling well enough to make himself into a target again, and would meet her at the Froghole headquarters.

::Could we make a brief detour to Traementis Manor before that? I should like to pay my respects to Renata personally.::

"Give the woman a chance to rest before giving her reason to regret having said anything." It came out more sourly than Vargo intended. "We'll see her soon enough, but business won't wait."

Just as Vargo was pulling on his gloves, however, a messenger in Charterhouse livery arrived with a summons he didn't dare ignore.

Visiting the Charterhouse made Vargo want to take his hangover and crawl back into his deathbed. Bureaucracy that usually moved turtle slow had become mired to the point of stagnation. Vargo would have suspected Praeteri influence, except that it wasn't like the usual push and pull of warring delta houses. *Nobody* could get anything through, not even with help from their friends in the cult.

The liveried messenger whisked Vargo past the morning crowd of petitioners and advocates clogging the main atrium. Past the doors of the Cinquerat's public audience chamber and the archways leading to their offices, to upper-level halls that echoed with the somber hush of infrequent use.

::Maybe he's leading us into an ambush.::

The way things have been going lately, don't joke, Vargo thought as they passed through a set of polished doors of cherrywood and into a more intimate version of the audience chamber below. There was no spectator's gallery, the Cinquerat thrones were understated rather than ostentatious, and instead of house benches for the nobility, comfortable chairs had been set up in rows.

They weren't the first arrivals. Among the quietly chatting cuffs, Vargo spotted Faella Coscanum and her brother, Paumilla Cleoter and her heir and spare, Sibiliat and Fadrin Acrenix—Vargo quickly looked away before he caught their attention—and...

::Look, there she is! Renata! I mean, Alta Renata. Do forgive my manners. It's just been so long since I've had a proper conversation—::

I talk to you every day, *old man,* Vargo grumbled, even as he felt his face warm. This was the sort of thing Ren had been privy to for months. He preferred to not think about what she might have overheard.

From the stiffening of her spine, she definitely heard Alsius shouting for her, but if she tried to reply, nothing came across. Peabody tickled Vargo's neck as he crawled out of hiding and raised his colorful abdomen in an attempt to catch her attention.

::Why isn't she saying anything?:: he asked mournfully.

I don't think she can. Vargo ignored the welling of petty satisfaction that at least some things remained private. *We can ask later. Right now, I'd like to know why everyone was summoned here.*

::Representatives from all the noble houses? Someone must have invoked their right to a private tribunal.::

Dread settled over Vargo as his gaze swept the gathering again, searching for some hint of who might have done so, and why.

He wished he and Renata—Ren—had spent a little less time drinking the previous day, and a little more time planning. She hadn't approached him here; were they going to keep up a facade of estrangement? It might be useful, if only because people would wonder at a reconciliation so soon after the events at the Traementis adoption ball.

It meant he had to fight to keep his gaze from drifting toward her, though. Even knowing the truth, he could barely make himself believe the woman talking to Parma was the Lacewater rat he'd met yesterday, much less the Vraszenian szorsa he'd hauled in for interrogation. Unlike him, she didn't wear the marks of hardship openly; she'd had a mother for her early years, and then after that, Ondrakja had made sure to protect the asset of her "pretty face."

Vargo's skin crawled, remembering the loathing with which Ren had uttered that phrase. No wonder she preferred to be admired for her clever mind.

But the real marvel was in her bearing. She inhabited her role as naturally as breathing—as if she believed without question that she was every bit as good as those around her. As if it never crossed her mind that *they* might question it, either.

He was staring, despite meaning not to. Vargo nudged Alsius back under his collar before anyone could see him, then turned away and dropped heavily into the single chair set aside for his one-man house.

A few other nobles had trickled in; now two of the Destaelio daughters—the only two not currently traveling on their mother's business—nodded to the doorman to close the doors behind them.

Once everyone was seated, Sostira Novrus stood up.

Vargo's hands tightened on the arms of his chair. He still couldn't look at her without thinking, *I would do the job better.* Not because he had any passion for Argentet's duties; if someone offered him the

Cinquerat seat of his choice, he would take Prasinet or Iridet or even Fulvet first. No, it was because *he* wouldn't get caught up in petty feuds. *He* wouldn't estrange the city's Vraszenian residents for no better reason than prejudice and greed. If he had her power—

::Steady, my boy.::

Grateful for Alsius's stabilizing presence, Vargo sat up as Sostira began to speak.

"I thank you all for attending this tribunal, and I won't waste your time. Three nights ago, someone broke into the Novrus shipping office in Whitesail and destroyed a certain letter. My fellow Cinquerat members have already reviewed and accepted the testimonies of several witnesses as to the existence of this letter and the tampering with the cabinet where it was stored, and the ash around the incendiary numinat used to destroy it."

Cibrial Destaelio and Scaperto Quientis looked distinctly pained at Sostira's words, but none of the Cinquerat denied her claim. With a smug lift of her chin, Sostira continued, "The missing letter was from Eret Ebarius Viraudax, the father of Alta Renata Viraudax Traementatis."

::This is bad.::

Vargo agreed...but he was also very aware of Renata sitting across the room, listening to everything they said. While Vargo was used to Alsius's gloom, she wouldn't be. *Nonsense. Any evidence Argentet might have is circumstantial at best—*

::Sostira Novrus isn't a fool. She wouldn't bring this to tribunal unless she was confident of her proof.::

Wouldn't she? Iascat had said his aunt had grown more erratic. He was there, too, watching Sostira with his lips pressed tight.

But most people's attention was on Renata, who listened to Sostira's accusation with exactly the kind of raised brows one would expect from a woman suffering a baseless political attack. Now she said, "Your Elegance, I find it troubling that you've apparently gone digging into my family situation behind my back—all the more so because I can't imagine *why* you would. I'm a registered noblewoman of Nadežra, and moreover one who hasn't committed any crime. But regardless of your motivations, I swear beneath the Lumen's light that I have destroyed no letter intended for you."

"Then perhaps you would be so good as to account for your whereabouts the evening of the Traementis ball."

A faint line of puzzlement creased Renata's flawless brow. "At the ball, Your Elegance. Yes, I retired early—but not because I needed to run off to Whitesail. I've simply been very busy of late, and I knew that beginning the following morning, the duties of the head of house would fall upon me. I thought it wiser to get some sleep."

"Did you?" Sostira pivoted to look at the man on her left. "Does Fulvet have a response to that?"

Dragging in a breath as though it contained broken glass, Quientis said, "I spent much of the evening in Era Traementis's company. At around midnight, she wished to retire for the night—and to say good night to her family. Alta Renata was nowhere to be found. We searched everywhere, including her room. It was nearly seventh earth before Era Traementis gave up and allowed me to put her to bed."

Now Vargo had to hold in his own gloom-filled thoughts. Lies had their uses, but honesty was the sharpest blade. Quientis's testimony was effective because he was so clearly speaking in spite of his preferences. No doubt Sostira calculated that when she maneuvered Renata into the lie.

She waited for the whispers to die down before returning her attention to Renata. "A crime against a head of house and a member of the Cinquerat is no small thing. One might even consider it treason. Would you like to amend your statement, Alta Renata? After all, everyone here knows how convincing you can be."

::Well played,:: Alsius said quietly. ::If she tries to talk her way out of this, she'll only look more guilty.::

Vargo's fist clenched. He couldn't say whether the desire to strangle Sostira was natural, or a product of the urge that had buzzed in the depths of his mind since that night at the Villa Acrenix.

Renata made no attempt to revise her lie. Instead her expression hardened. "Treason, Your Elegance? That's a strong word to employ so casually. Just what am I supposed to have destroyed, that poses a threat to Nadežra itself?"

"I think you and I know exactly what was destroyed, and why you might risk sneaking away from a ball you were hosting to do so."

Talking around the content of the letter would only make everyone more curious as to what might be in it. If that curiosity was whetted, Vargo suspected twenty more letters would go out on the next tide, asking Eret Viraudax about the daughter he didn't have.

There was a way to stop Sostira...and possibly nudge circumstances enough for Cibrial Destaelio to wrest Argentet out of her hands. Vargo's motives might be tainted by the urge Ghiscolo had planted, but in the end it didn't matter. Even if it helped Ghiscolo, it also helped Ren.

"I'm afraid you've accused the wrong person, Your Elegance." Vargo stood and thumped his sword cane to draw the room's attention. "Alta Renata didn't destroy your letter. I did."

Before he could lose his audience's attention to a furor of speculation, Vargo added, "And I wasn't the only one there that night. Fadrin Acrenix was attempting to break into your office as well. I greeted him with a fist to his biscuits."

"That was you?" Fadrin snarled, leaping to his feet. The scrapes and bruises from the beating Vargo gave him had blossomed in the intervening days. Not even makeup could entirely hide them from those who were looking—as everyone in the room now was.

"Sent him floating down the Dežera in the Acrenix sedan chair. The red-lacquered one. I'm certain if you examined it you would find water damage. Assuming it isn't at the bottom of the river." Vargo's taunting smile invited Fadrin to reinforce his claims with physical retribution.

Tragically, Sibiliat succeeded in dragging her cousin back down. Vargo turned his attention to the Cinquerat, avoiding Ghiscolo's cold stare. "If treason charges are to be made, then it's House Vargo and House Acrenix that should shoulder them. But I took the liberty of examining the contents of the letter from Eret Viraudax before I destroyed it. I didn't find anything anybody could use against his daughter—which I assume was your aim."

Fighting laughter, Vargo bowed in Renata's direction. "Your father sends his regards and hopes you remain in good health. Your mother...is also well."

Renata's mouth soured at the reference to Letilia, while Sostira snarled, "All this proves is that the two of you colluded—"

"The two of *us*?" Vargo laughed incredulously. "Here I thought Argentet knew everything that happened in Nadežra. No, Your Elegance—I just can't let other people take credit for my achievements."

Half the chamber was talking now, but from what Vargo could hear, more of them were talking about him and the Acrenix than Renata, and Ghiscolo was glaring murder at Sibiliat and Fadrin. That was victory enough for the moment. *Fuck you for whatever you did to me that night.*

Sostira tried to regain the floor, but the tumult continued until Cibrial Destaelio stood up. "Under the circumstances," Prasinet said, projecting her voice firmly over the noise, "I believe this is a much smaller matter than Her Elegance claims. For interfering with the correspondence of a Cinquerat seat, I propose that House Vargo be fined two hundred forri. For attempted interference, a fine of twenty forri to House Acrenix. Alta Renata, do you wish to bring a complaint against Era Novrus for false accusations?"

In her shoes, Vargo would have said yes. But he couldn't trust his own judgment.

"Thank you, Your Charity, but no," Renata said, keeping her eyes on Sostira. "I believe any dispute between us can be settled by other means. Oksana Ryvček has offered to stand for me if ever I have need of it."

Sostira flinched at the implied threat. Fighting a smile, Prasinet moved on. "Altan Fadrin, do you wish to bring assault charges against Eret Vargo?"

"He doesn't," Sibiliat said, before Fadrin could respond. Her cousin nodded with his jaw clenched tight. Vargo wondered if he would also be receiving a duel challenge soon—and if Ren could talk Ryvček into representing him, too.

Destaelio nodded crisply. "Then what is the verdict of my peers?"

Quientis concurred almost before the words were out of her mouth, followed by Simendis. With two Cinquerat members recused, that made for a unanimous verdict, and they wasted no time in declaring the affair ended.

Which was by no means the end. Renata was swarmed by those eager to express their sympathy—or just to get as close to the gossip as they could. Vargo, as usual, had a clear path to leave. For once, he didn't mind being shunned by his peers.

But when he slipped from the tribunal chamber, he found that not everyone was avoiding him.

"I wish I could have seen you nut-punch Fadrin," Iascat said as Vargo approached.

"I can do it again if you'd like. Once will never be enough." Vargo shifted so he could keep an eye on the door. The last thing he wanted was for Iascat to lose his chance at ousting his aunt because he was caught consorting with the enemy.

Yet another desire he couldn't trust.

"I'm just glad nobody thought to ask how you found out about the letter." Iascat's full lips flattened into a bitter line. "Though I'm certain my aunt knows."

"I wouldn't have given you up."

"Then why does it feel like you have?"

Before Vargo could respond, the doors behind them creaked. Iascat gave him a last, unreadable look, then strode off.

Renata was leaving, surrounded by a cloud of others. Vargo crossed his arms and lounged against the wall, giving her his most insolent look—but to Alsius he said, *I did that to help Renata, but I'm not certain it wasn't driven partly by the compulsion Ghiscolo somehow put on me at the last Praeteri meeting, to undercut Sostira Novrus and take her place. It's a good thing you helped counteract that, or I might have killed her by now.*

::I assumed as much. Why are you telling—Oh! Very clever. Farewell, Alta Renata. I do hope we have a chance to speak soon!::

She couldn't respond, of course. But Vargo saw a cloud flicker behind that serene mask, and he wondered what she knew that she hadn't told him yet.

Kingfisher, Lower Bank: Canilun 8

"Captain," Ranieri said, "wasn't this stuff supposed to be sold off?"

He hefted the box, settling it onto his left shoulder this time, having already exhausted the right. Grey felt a little bad making his constable carry the whole weight—but at least it was getting lighter as they went.

He glanced at his notes, identifying the items and who they'd been taken from. "Goods confiscated by the *Vigil* are supposed to be sold."

"And these—"

"Weren't taken by the Vigil. The Ordo Apis is a separate organization, and according to Alta Renata, their charter doesn't include anything about the disposition of items. They didn't have the right to take them in the first place, so they don't have the right to sell them now. And neither do we." That also applied to the ones his fellow officers had pocketed, but Grey was already pushing a boundary by returning these things to their owners.

Cercel had questioned him for formality's sake when Gil Vasterbol complained. Grey had cheerfully pointed out the limitations in the charter that allowed Vasterbol to sell hawk-confiscated goods through his pawnshop, and topped that with a comment about repairing Vigil relations in Kingfisher. The former shut Vasterbol up; the latter left Cercel nodding thoughtfully.

There was no doubt that teaming up with the Black Rose had helped the Rook in his mission, but Grey had never let himself consider how satisfying it would be to join forces with Alta Renata.

Or how distracting, he thought as he backtracked to the tenement he'd walked past while thinking of her.

Many of the people whose doors they stopped at were reluctant to open them. Some of those doors still bore scuff marks and boot-prints from stingers kicking them down. And while nobody dared to spit on him and Ranieri, thanks were as rare as dreamweavers in winter.

"A little gratitude wouldn't go amiss," Levinci grumbled when they returned to the wagon for another load. With Lud Kaineto gone, Grey had needed a new lieutenant. He would have preferred to promote Ranieri, but a baker's boy with mixed ancestry over a delta son...at least with Levinci in Kaineto's place, Grey's other troublemakers had become less obnoxious. But they would never understand the silt of resentment settled along the Lower Bank.

"I'll hang a medal on you when we get back to the Aerie," Grey said, pointing out another bag for Ranieri to carry.

As they headed to the next street on his list, Ranieri said, "Captain, would you consider the Oyster Crackers dangerous?"

"It depends on what kind of danger you mean. They're thieves, not killers; they prefer to slip in and out without being seen. Why do you ask?"

"Something Tess asked me to look into." Ranieri became very occupied with the bag on his shoulder. It was an obvious enough excuse for distraction that Grey didn't press. He was just glad to hear the two of them were talking, after the rift that came on the heels of Tess discovering Pavlin was a hawk—as long as it didn't mean Tess was looking to return to a life of crime.

His good mood soured when he looked up and found Kaineto approaching with three other men, all wearing the gold-trimmed black armband of the stingers.

Kaineto's liver-pale lip curled in a sneer. "Serrado. Your presence is required for questioning."

Grey motioned for Ranieri to stand back. "Regarding what? I'm on duty right now."

"Ordo Apis business supersedes your duty. Come with us—unless you want to cause more trouble for Kingfisher."

Grey glanced around. The street was quiet but not empty; everybody in sight was watching warily, ready to bolt.

Kingfisher had seen enough trouble at the hands of the stingers. "We're almost done here anyway. Ranieri, tell Levinci he has
command."

"Captain—"

A twitch of Grey's hand stopped the protest. "Do your work,
Constable. I'll see you back at the Aerie."

He hoped that was true.

Suncross, Old Island: Canilun 8

Grey had a good guess as to what was coming. The stingers had
been formed to deal with the Stadnem Anduske; he was Vraszenian, and he'd worked with the ziemetse last year. Never mind that
the ziemetse considered the Anduske almost as much of a threat as
the Cinquerat did. In the eyes of Liganti cuffs like Kaineto, every
Vraszenian was the same.

He had stories prepared, both if they knew he'd helped Andrejek
after the schism, and if they didn't.

He didn't get to use either of them, because his guess turned out
to be wrong.

Kaineto and the others took him to the plain-faced building in Suncross that the stingers had claimed as their headquarters.
They'd already confiscated his sword, his knife, and his sap; they
didn't search him beyond that. *Stupid. But lucky.* The pocket that held
the Rook's hood was well-hidden, but that didn't mean a determined
search wouldn't find it. After today, he wouldn't risk that again.

They marched him into a small stone room, forced him into a
chair, and tied him to it. Although a numinat was painted on the
flagstones beneath him, Grey didn't think it was active. The focus
would be underneath his chair, so he couldn't see if it was in place,
but he didn't feel any different.

"Is this really necessary?" he asked, allowing his irritation to
show. If tying him up was their starting move, then playing nice

wasn't on the agenda. He fixed his glare on Kaineto. "Or are you just having fun being petty?"

"Yes. To both of those questions. And now perhaps you'll answer mine. What do you know about the disappearance of Mede Rimbon Beldipassi?"

It felt like the chair had been dropped into a Depths sinkhole, with Grey still bound to it: the airless cold shock of fear. *Djek!* Ryvček was always warning him about keeping separate lives, and at least a dozen hawks must have witnessed Beldipassi seeking him out at the Aerie. But it was a leap from that to this.

Marpremi, the man who hired Fontimi, had been found floating in the Pomcaro Canal, but Beldipassi's servants had all vanished. Had one of them—

"His valet claims you arranged a meeting for him, and he hasn't been seen since. I'll ask once more. What do you know about his disappearance?"

"Nothing beyond what you've already said," Grey answered. Had they learned whom the meeting was supposed to be with? If so, let them be the ones to admit it. "I didn't even know he was missing until you told me. He doesn't live in Kingfisher, so he isn't my business."

Although there was an empty chair facing Grey, Kaineto remained standing, the better to lean in. He wasn't good at being intimidating, but the circumstances lent him a menacing air. "You might want to rethink that answer."

"There's no rethinking the facts."

"With the right pressure, a man can be made to rethink anything." Kaineto straightened and gestured to one of his fellow stingers, a woman Grey didn't recognize. She handed him a small, round object. It wasn't marked with a god's sigil, and Grey's body tensed. *Praeteri numinatria.*

Kaineto crouched to slot it into place under Grey's chair, then backed away and let the woman paint shut the activating circle. He grinned at Grey, a pure display of teeth and malice. "We'll leave you to consider."

Grey let his head sag as they shut the door on him, tensing for whatever the numinat was meant to do.

He couldn't feel anything. And that was all the more insidious, because Kaineto wouldn't smile like that if it weren't something awful. Grey knew those smiles; he'd grown up with them, little knives slicing shallow cuts over and over so the wounds never healed and scars never formed. An old woman's smile tearing through you with the sharp edges of every card she drew, leaving you open and bleeding, empty and hollow. In the face of that, death didn't seem like such a terrible alternative, and you understood why your mama might hold you under the cold water, might wade in herself and never come back up. *Your fault, your fault, your fault* eating away at him like ripples against the shore.

Grey shuddered, rattling the chair's legs against the floor. He dragged in a breath, but his lungs felt too tight to hold anything.

No. Kolya had gotten him out. They'd fled to Nadežra and pretended they were hiding from people who didn't care enough to look for them. But Kolya cared. Leato cared. Donaia cared.

Dead. Dead. And the third dying by inches after so many losses. He'd misled one brother, failed the other, and could do nothing to help a woman too good to mother one such as him. Grey hadn't fled the suffering; he'd brought it with him and inflicted it on the people around him. Just like them. Just like *her*. And Ren would be next.

A sob tore from his throat. He was shaking so hard his chair toppled sideways, his shoulder wrenching and bound wrists bending as he slammed into the floor.

Someone pulled him upright. Set him back inside the numinat. Walked around and sat down to face him.

Ghiscolo Acrenix.

"Captain Serrado." Ghiscolo sighed as if disappointed. "I wish it hadn't come to this."

For the briefest instant, when he was on his side and out of position, Grey's head had cleared a tiny bit. Enough to know that these thoughts were the work of the numinat—attacking not his body, but his mind, dragging him down into a pit of heart's pain.

Ghiscolo leaned forward and spoke quietly. "I know you arranged that meeting for Beldipassi. I know you're in contact with the Rook. Tell me how to find him."

Grey wasn't the first person to be tortured over that question. "No."

"I don't like doing this, Captain Serrado. But I have a duty to this city. A duty to bring order to Nadežra, and to lead its people to the best of my ability. I believe the Rook has Mede Beldipassi—that he kidnapped the man from their meeting. A meeting you set up. I'm surprised you of all people would work with the Rook in secret."

Kolya, burned beyond recognition. Grey leaned into that memory, into the agony it brought, because that was a shield against Acrenix's probing. "I want my brother avenged," he snarled. "The Rook can help with that."

Sighing, Ghiscolo placed his hands over his heart. "You don't have to suffer like this. It can end at any time, if you tell me what you know. Where Beldipassi might be. Where the Rook might have taken him. In return, I'll help you get revenge on Derossi Vargo. You'll finally be able to heal."

Vargo pinned against the side of a carriage, Grey's arm across his throat. The way his own father had pinned him, so many times. *I'm as bad as he is.*

Ghiscolo's words tugged at him, sweet and tempting. *The pain can end. You can heal.*

Two of Ghiscolo's fingers had slipped between the buttons of his shirt. He wasn't touching his heart.

He was touching his medallion.

Panic pierced the fog of Grey's agony. After that business in the Charterhouse, Ren had passed along word of what Ghiscolo did to Vargo. He didn't merely have a medallion; he knew how to use its full power, controlling the desires of others. This was Quinat, the numen of power . . . and also of healing.

The Rook was immune to that influence—but Grey wasn't the Rook. Not right now.

He didn't have time to think about Ryvček's warnings. The medallion's power was feeding his desire for an escape from the agony of the numinat, until it overwhelmed everything else. Already his mouth was opening.

The hood was inside his uniform, just above his heart.

Help me.

And like before—like the night he was ambushed; the night Ghiscolo must have sent the stingers to ambush him, because Ghiscolo knew about the meeting, Ghiscolo *knew*—Grey gave himself over to the shadows.

"I can't tell you what I don't know."

Ghiscolo leaned even closer. "Don't you want this to end?"

"*Yes.*" It wasn't artifice; it was truth. The Rook wanted the suffering to end. For everyone, himself included. The despair of the ambush numinat had sunk its claws in only shallowly, because the Rook was a rejection of the idea that nothing could be done—but that rejection was born of pain. Grief and loss and horror were the foundations of this house, and all the shades who inhabited it had built its walls higher with their own suffering. But someday, the Rook prayed, that house would fall.

"Then tell me—"

"There's nothing to tell. The Rook found me, not the other way around. I can't give you what you want."

Ghiscolo's jaw tightened. "Captain Serrado—"

With a slam like thunder against stone, the door to the Rook's left swung open, revealing a woman as tall and immovable as the Point. "What is going on here?" Cercel demanded.

Her righteous fury doubled when she saw Ghiscolo. "Your Mercy," she said. "Why has one of my captains been brought in for questioning? I was told it was Anduske related, but your men seem to think it has to do with the disappearance of a delta gentleman." Through the blurring of his tears, the Rook saw Ranieri and Kaineto trading scowls.

Standing, Ghiscolo withdrew his hand and smoothed the pucker from his shirt and waistcoat. "You're questioning Caerulet?" If not for the leashed anger behind it, his smile would almost have looked genial.

"I would not presume." Cercel's bow was a sop to that anger. "But I do question the overreach of the Ordo Apis. I've read their charter, and it clearly restricts the scope of their powers to issues pertaining to the Stadnem Anduske's activities in Nadežra. If this is regarding a gentleman's disappearance..." Her smile was pure steel. "That's a matter for the Vigil."

Ghiscolo nodded. "Which also falls under my purview—"

"Your purview, but not your direct authority. If you want to detain a Vigil officer, then speak with High Commander Dimiterro. Which you have not done."

The Rook let out a stifled moan. Cercel's attention shot to the floorboards, and her face went white. "Are you *torturing him*?"

Before Ghiscolo could answer, she snatched out her dagger and raked it through the numinat, breaking the encircling line. Light flashed, and the miasma of suffering vanished.

"Constable, help the captain," Cercel said, handing her knife to Ranieri, who quickly cut the Rook loose and helped him stand.

That hand on his arm was salvation. The Rook was on the verge of pulling out the hood, armoring himself in those layered defenses. It would destroy Grey Serrado's life, but that didn't matter. Ghiscolo was *right there*. And the shock of the Rook appearing in their midst would buy him the opening he needed.

But Ranieri's hand was on his arm, slowing his reach for the hidden pocket. Just long enough for Grey to drag himself back under control.

I am Grey Serrado. Not the Rook. Not here, not now.

His conviction held. For the moment.

Cercel faced Ghiscolo with the rigid correctness of an officer. "I will, of course, be reporting my actions to High Commander Dimiterro and submitting myself to any censure he feels necessary." As she stepped back to allow Grey and Ranieri to pass, she gave the whole room, Caerulet and stingers alike, a scathing look. "In accordance with the law, of course. Good day, Your Mercy."

Aža's Call

Eastbridge and the Pearls: Canilun 9

In the years that had passed since she was part of the Fingers, Ren had forgotten: Some kinds of cons were easier to pull off when you had more people helping.

She legitimately *had* gone to talk to Vargo about demonstrating a model of the river numinat for Donaia and Scaperto. And anyone asking would learn that their meeting had gone on for quite some time, due to arguments over his approach. But the actual conversation lasted barely a bell, and after that, a Ganllechyn woman slipped out Vargo's back door to meet up with Tess and Sedge.

Tess groaned when she saw Ren in the striped woolens of her country. "Just don't try to do the accent," she begged. "I've heard you be Vraszenian and Seterin and Liganti and even Isarnah, but your Ganllechyn is a pity." She *tch*ed. "And you living there five years..."

"Does she *still* sound like one of them puppet show characters?" Sedge asked.

"Worse! She sounds like me!"

"Ooch, that's enough from the both of you." Grinning at their paired groans, Ren linked her arms through theirs. Her makeup gave her fuller, rosier cheeks than nature ever had, but Tess was right about the accent; she couldn't hear it in her head or feel it on her tongue except as her sister's voice. "Fine. I won't try the accent. The point is, this way I don't have to worry about being seen by anybody who knows me. Let's go!"

For all her lighthearted tone, Ren felt faintly guilty as they headed off. Spending this time with Tess and Sedge meant missing "family dinner" at Traementis Manor—a ritual Giuna had insisted on after the adoptions, and one Renata couldn't admit to loathing.

It would have been easier if Donaia had stayed. In her absence, Renata had to take her place at the head of the table, with Giuna and Nencoral and Meppe and Idaglio, and Tanaquis on the one occasion so far that she'd joined them. Keeping her posture perfect while course upon course was served dragged up memories of Ondrakja's training exercises, where she taught her favored Fingers to pass themselves off as cuffs or infiltrate houses as staff. The lack of mildew in the carpet and the fine cooking of the various dishes didn't stop it from feeling like one of Ondrakja's tests—with all the implied consequences for failure.

Meals had been more comfortable before the adoptions, when it was only her and Donaia and Giuna, dining less formally. But even that just made her yearn for the happy memories of her childhood, sitting at the table where Ivrina laid patterns for clients during the day, with Ren herself small enough that her feet didn't touch the floor. Or those few precious evenings in the Serrado house, with Grey singing nonsense at Jagyi while Alinka panfried lotus root and crispy bluegill and Ren kept Yvie distracted.

Thinking about Grey was a mistake. He'd left a terse note on her balcony, giving her some of the story; gossip had provided other fragments. Between the two, she could imagine far too well what Ghiscolo had done to him. Part of her wanted nothing more than to rush across the river and confirm with her own eyes and hands that Grey wasn't permanently hurt.

But he'd told her to stay away for now. The odds were too high that Ghiscolo had people watching him, looking for anything that might lead to Beldipassi or the Rook.

Those thoughts weighed her down as she and her siblings purchased street noodles from a stall near the Rotunda, then found an empty river stair to perch on while they wolfed them down. "I know we can afford a proper table now," Tess said between slurps, "but they taste better this way."

"That they do," Sedge said, eating a pepper as red as sunset that he'd requested special from the cart.

"Like you can taste anything but fire." Laughing, Tess knocked gently into him.

Ren bent her head to her own bowl. She hadn't considered, when she started being honest with the people around her, that it wouldn't actually solve all her problems—not when some of those people had secrets of their own. Would Grey let her tell Tess and Sedge the truth about him? Or more to the point, would the Rook?

Lacking an answer to that, she chose instead to fill Sedge in on what had happened with Vargo in Whitesail, and the conversation where she unpeeled all her layers for him. Sedge was so busy chewing on those revelations that when the clock towers chimed the tenth and final sun hour, he had to hurry up and shovel his cold noodles down at speed.

Handing his bowl off to Tess to return to the vendor, he said, "Guess that explains why I've been summoned to Froghole tonight. Don't know how I'm supposed to look the man in the eye, knowing he knows I know. You sure he en't holding a grudge?"

"He'd better not, or he'll answer to me," Tess said, making them both grin. "Go on with you, then. I've got to get this one changed and back home."

Home. That word stuck in Ren's mind as they returned to Vargo's townhouse, made the switch back to Renata, and headed north to the Isla Traementis. Was the manor home? Had the Westbridge townhouse been home, or the lodging house in Lacewater before that? Or had "home" vanished in flames when she was six—and if so, what would it take to build it anew?

Those thoughts dogged her as she came inside and hurried to the staircase. Partway up, Giuna's voice caught her. "Renata!"

She turned and found Giuna hovering at the newel post. Seeing that Renata had stopped, Giuna came to join her. "I swear, you've been dodging me since—Are you going to tell me what happened?"

"With what?"

"Whitesail! That letter from your father! I heard about what happened in the Charterhouse, with Her Elegance accusing you, and Vargo saying there was nothing in the letter. I know there must be more to the story. And you just spent all of dinnertime at his house. What's going on?"

The hall was empty, with no one else to hear. "It's taken care of, at least for now. You don't need to worry."

Giuna caught her arm as she turned away. Not her usual bird-like plucking; this was a solid grip. "No," Giuna said, her voice low but intense. "We're working together, remember? Soon I'll be eighteen, and I'll be Mother's heir. I need to understand our family's affairs, not to be protected from them. And whatever's going to happen, we'll stand by you."

Would you stand by a half-Vraszenian criminal from Lacewater?

Of course not. They never would have let Ren in their front door.

It wasn't bad enough that she'd gotten Leato killed. Her masquerade was putting House Traementis in danger. The only way out of that was to survive until Giuna came of age, and then—

Then what? Leave the Traementis? Leato's face rose up in her memory, his reaction when he learned she'd been an imposter all along. *Do you even know how much it meant to us, gaining family for once instead of losing it?*

They had other family now. Meppe, Idaglio, Nencoral, Tanaquis. With the exception of Tanaquis, though, how much personal warmth was in those bonds? Building a true relationship there might happen, but it would take time. Renata had been through fire with Donaia and Giuna. She wasn't a good enough liar to convince herself that walking away wouldn't hurt them.

Some part of that must have shown through, because Giuna touched her arm again, this time a gentle lead. Together they went into Donaia's study, and Giuna closed the door before sinking into one of the new chairs, upholstered in sueded brown leather. "Tell me," she said. "Don't treat me like a child."

That was it, Renata realized—or at least part of it. Her own childhood had ended the day she became a Finger, if not when the fire sent her and Ivrina onto the street. Some part of her envied Giuna's sheltered life and wanted her to keep it for as long as she could.

But that was foolish and unfair. Giuna had been through hardships of her own, even if they didn't involve starvation and abuse. She wasn't a little bird in a cage.

Renata scrubbed one hand across her eyes, trying to think what she could safely say. Not everything; never that. But enough to arm Giuna and House Traementis against the risks.

"Vargo did destroy the letter," she said. "For my sake. We've reconciled, though we're keeping that concealed so Novrus can't prove we're colluding. As for its contents..."

There was a simple way through that one, like the trick knots that came apart when you pulled in the right place. "I imagine it said that Eret Viraudax has no daughter named Renata. Your mother already knows—he isn't my father. That's what Tanaquis was talking about at the Theatre Agnasce. Letilia was pregnant before she left Nadežra, courtesy of a total stranger during Veiled Waters. But I told your mother Eret Viraudax adopted me, and that part is a lie. He took my mother as his mistress, nothing more. Not even a contract wife."

"But you're ours now. None of that should—" Giuna struck the arm of her chair in frustration. "Stupid. They'll make it matter, won't they? And you and Meppe are already struggling enough, trying to get all the new charters in order. Mother won't care—I know she won't, beyond admiring Eret Viraudax's good sense—but others will."

The weight of it dragged Renata down. "I don't see a way out of this, Giuna. Short of falsifying a letter from him that somehow persuades everyone there's nothing interesting about my past... the fact is that I've lied, and eventually those lies will out. When they do, they'll hurt the rest of you—which is the last thing I want. It's death by a thousand pricking needles." Once upon a time, she wouldn't have cared.

But once upon a time, her intent had been to siphon money off what she thought was a house so wealthy they wouldn't miss it, then vanish without a trace.

Giuna was already shaking her head. "Not if we change their needles into...noodles?" She giggled, then schooled her expression into seriousness. "We could. You've already stumbled on how. There are still whispers about what Tanaquis let slip at the theatre, and not all of them are about Alsius Acrenix. If you take control of the whispers, everyone will be so busy wondering if your blood father is in Nadežra that they won't care when it comes out that Eret Viraudax isn't. When people are starved for gossip, feed them what you want them to eat."

It was the last response Renata had expected. And it was something she should have thought of herself.

No matter how often Giuna told her they were family, her thoughts still didn't go to the Traementis in her moments of need. Not after so many years with Tess and Sedge as the only ones she could trust.

But now there was Grey, and Vargo. And Giuna, at least in part, even if she didn't know who Ren really was. Donaia, and Tanaquis as well. Even Dalisva, after a fashion. When Ren stopped and made herself count...she actually had a startling number of allies.

It eased some of the tightness inside. "That's an excellent thought, Giuna. But before you ask, no: I haven't the faintest clue who my father is. Nor do I particularly care. Neither history nor register binds me to him, after all."

Catching her in a crushing hug, Giuna said, "You're bound to *us* now. And we won't give you up that easily."

A moment later, Renata was free, and Giuna was flushed and sparkling with ideas. "I'm meant to play bocce with Bondiro and Marvisal tomorrow. I can let something slip for Alta Faella to chew on. Once you've hooked her, all the other fish will follow. Oh, and Tess is making a dress for Avaquis Fintenus, isn't she? I'm certain she'd be happy to gossip."

For the briefest heartbeat, Renata felt a chill. They were in Donaia's study, where in the nightmare she'd ruled over the Traementis like Ondrakja over the Fingers.

But it didn't have to be like that. Giuna was an ally, not a minion. No one would be punished for disappointing Ren. She wouldn't use people and then throw them away.

Giuna leaned close, peering at her. "Are you still worried?"

"No—well, yes, but I'm sure what you said would help. It's only…" Saying it was like slowly committing her weight to a rope, unsure if it would hold. "Twice now I've told you, by the way, I lied. About my finances, and now about my father. Despite that…"

"I haven't turned on you?" Giuna rolled her eyes. "I know; I'm a disgrace to the Traementis name. Hardly a vengeful bone in my body. But, Renata—it doesn't bother me that you weren't rich, or that you don't know who your father is. The only thing that bothers me is that you haven't felt like you can trust me with the truth."

Because the truth is so much bigger than you know. Stepping over a small pebble was far easier than climbing a wall. And yet…

For the first time, Ren found herself wondering if Giuna might climb that wall after all.

It wasn't a decision she could make tonight, nor even tomorrow. Maybe not until after the medallions were dealt with. But the thought was there, and she hadn't laughed it out of her own skull.

And it made one little truth burst out. "Does family dinner have to be so dreadfully *stiff*?"

Giuna blinked in surprise, then ducked her chin in embarrassment. "I was trying to make it like it used to be, back before…but we're not who we used to be before, are we? We're a new House Traementis. And you're right, it *is* pretty dreadful. Meppe and Idaglio excusing themselves as fast as they can so they can enjoy each other's company, Nencoral hardly saying two words—no wonder Tanaquis doesn't join us. Yes, we can change it."

Renata threw her arms round her cousin for her own hug. "Thank you. For that, and so many other things."

Froghole, Lower Bank: Canilun 9

Sedge was pretty sure the moons were setting in the Erassean Sea these days. Ren—his closemouthed sister, who held her secrets tighter than a mussel with its pearl—had apparently spilled everything to Vargo, the man she'd been out to destroy only a few months before. If *that* was possible, anything could happen.

But the atmosphere in Vargo's Froghole headquarters reminded him life wasn't that easy. When Sedge arrived as summoned, all the Fog Spiders were gathered there, but nobody would look him in the eye. Not even Nikory.

So much for forgiveness. He'd been dumb to ever wish for it. *Hope Tess will avenge me proper.*

His sisters or his knot: Sedge had made his choice. He wasn't about to let anybody see how much it made him bleed inside.

Vargo was alone in his office; even Varuni left, shutting the door behind her. Sedge's spine knotted with tension. The spice and grease of the noodles he'd devoured too quickly roiled uneasily in his gut. *Guess we're talking about Ren.* At least Vargo was keeping that truth to himself.

"Yeah?" Sedge said after the door shut, crossing his arms like his time had a price Vargo hadn't paid. It was even sort of true.

"So." Vargo's enigmatic stare broke into a smirk. "Sister?"

"Oh, fuck you." If that was how it was going to be, Sedge wasn't going to stand around like a brown-beaked hawk. He dropped into one of Vargo's chairs with a belligerent thrust of his chin. "Don't go sending summons to my flophouse if all you want is to gossip like a Seven Knots gammer. I en't one of your fists no more."

"I'm just recalling all those times you made moon eyes at Tess. *Also* your sister, I understand."

"To hide the truth—and if you go making moon eyes at either of them, I'll black at least one before Varuni adds mine to her marble collection." In spite of everything, a smile tugged at Sedge's lips. Vargo had always kept a bit of distance between himself and his fists, but you didn't spend years bleeding with and for another person without some level of camaraderie building up. Sedge found himself slipping into it like his favorite boots.

The quirk of Vargo's scarred brow questioned whether he was even capable of anything resembling moon eyes. Sedge had to admit, he couldn't imagine it. Lust, sure; romantic goop, not so much. Vargo said, "It explains a lot. Though I'll admit, I didn't think you had that kind of deception in you."

"Learned from the best," Sedge said curtly, and let Vargo wonder if he meant Ren or Ondrakja.

Vargo nodded. "You have to admit, though, it creates a problem. You've got secrets you can't share with a knot."

And there it was, as bare as the face Ren had shown Vargo. Sedge wondered if she'd considered that it weren't just *her* secrets she was exposing when she confessed.

But too late now, and the accusation cut deep. Maybe Sedge didn't betray his knot oath when he protected Ren over Vargo on the night of Veiled Waters...but he'd broken it before that, hiding her identity when she got involved in Fog Spider business.

He shrugged stiffly. "Don't see how it's a problem. I en't sworn to a knot no more."

"You could be."

Sedge's breath hitched as Vargo went on. "Nikory wants to tie you back in. Now that I know about Ren, you can consider your secrets duly shared."

It wasn't uncommon. Knot oaths might say "no secrets between us," but that didn't mean everybody knew everything. The leader of a knot stood a bit higher than everybody else, and sometimes that person knew things others didn't.

Problem with that was, Vargo wasn't Nikory's knot leader. He wasn't anybody's—because he hadn't tied himself to nobody.

Forcing the word out felt like the time a bonesetter had to pull one of Sedge's teeth, but he made himself do it. "No."

Vargo's expression shuttered. No more genial comrade; Sedge was now facing the man who'd taken the Lower Bank because he didn't take "no" from anyone. "Why not?"

" 'Cause you en't tied into the Fog Spiders. You can't say it's okay to keep my secrets from a knot you en't in. Being cut out reminded me that knot oaths mean something. Least to me, if not you."

Sedge almost regretted that last sentence—almost, but not quite. Because instead of getting hard or angry, that shuttered expression cracked a little. And instead of responding, Vargo sat for a moment, drumming his fingers on his desk. Sedge wondered if he was talking to the spider.

"They mean something," Vargo said...but nothing more.

Long enough to make Sedge fidget and finally break the silence. "Guess that's that." The chair creaked as he started to rise.

"What if I promised to keep Ren out of Fog Spider business?"

Sedge sank back into his seat, not quite certain he'd heard right. "En't you working with her?"

"Not out of *my* business," Vargo clarified. "But as you pointed out, I'm not a Fog Spider. Your problems come up when you have to stand in front of Nikory and your knot-mates pretending 'Arenza Lenskaya' is just some patterner you yanked off the street. If that stops happening—if Ren, in whatever guise, stays clear of *that knot*— then your sister isn't Fog Spider business, and you're not obliged to talk."

It was still a bit of a dodge. On the other hand, Vargo was sitting there offering to inconvenience himself just so Sedge could feel like he was doing right by his word.

Vargo had secrets, too. Like that spider of his, and whatever made him want to become a cuff, and a lot of other things Sedge told Ren he didn't want to know.

Maybe the reason Vargo didn't tie himself to nobody wasn't that he didn't respect knot oaths. Maybe it was because he *did*.

In the end, it came down to what Sedge owed Nikory. He said,

"I'm gonna tell Nikory there's something I'm holding back. But that it's your business, too. If he's okay with that, then—yeah. I'm game."

"Don't sound quite so enthusiastic," Vargo drawled, opening a drawer and pulling out a small, shimmering vial.

That was the moment it really hit. Because just like oaths, aža wasn't something Sedge took lightly. His hand trembled when he reached for the vial, and he wasn't even ashamed.

"Go on out," Vargo said softly. "Your knot's waiting."

Froghole, Lower Bank: Canilun 9

Vargo would have preferred to wait out Sedge's reinitiation from the shelter of his office, but most of the fists thought Nikory was tied to Vargo. It would look strange if he wasn't present—like Vargo was ambivalent about bringing Sedge back.

The ambivalence had nothing to do with Sedge. Watching an initiation felt like being a boy on the street again, looking through the windows of a shop or an ostretta, seeing all the things he couldn't have.

At least nobody would find it odd that he stationed himself at the edge of the room, lurking in the shadows. The enigmatic boss spider keeping an eye on them all.

::Well, now we're certain we can trust Sedge,:: Alsius said from his own shadowy hideout in Vargo's collar. ::How long before Nikory can make him his second, do you think?::

That had been part of the debate over tying Sedge back in. Nikory wanted to install him right away, but Vargo pointed out that Sedge's life would be simpler if he eased in before getting dragged to the center again. Knot memories weren't long, but they could get tangled around issues of seniority.

And there were a few who would always have such issues— mostly the older guard from Ertzan Scrub's days who raised a fuss when Nikory took over and allied them with Vargo. Those people hung back now, while the younger men and women clasped hands with a grinning, aža-spun Sedge and reaffirmed their ties and oaths with a lot of teasing and good-natured insults.

A year, maybe, Vargo replied after consideration. *Depends on how things play out with the Stretsko. Assuming Andrejek recovers and can talk them down—get them out of our turf—people will remember Sedge brought us that thread.* The beating Andrejek had taken in Dockwall had set those plans back, but frankly, Vargo was just as glad to have some breathing room to clean his own house first. Until he found out who in his knots was playing both sides of the river, he was just asking to be sold out again.

::We should ask Renata. I mean, Arenza. I mean . . . bother. What should I call her?::

Vargo's shoulders shook with repressed laughter. A few of the fists caught his smile and returned it tentatively. Let them think he was pleased at Sedge's reinstatement, rather replying to someone they couldn't hear. *Ren for her face. Otherwise, whatever name matches the mask she's wearing. What do you want to ask her?*

::I'm fascinated by her claims about pattern. Perhaps she can advise us on the timing.::

I don't think it works like astrology, Vargo thought, straightening as Varuni approached. Getting a read on her was always tough, but the set of her shoulders said her intent was business, not a chewing out for whatever asshole thing Vargo had annoyed her with this time.

She kept her voice low. "Arkady Bones is outside. Says she has news for your ears alone."

Arkady didn't enter with her usual swagger. She stuck like a burr to Varuni, keeping the Isarnah woman between herself and the celebrating Fog Spiders, and followed Vargo into his office with none of the expected boasting or commentary on his headquarters. She barely even shrugged when he told her he'd found a possible home for Pitjin and he had some leads for a few of her other kids that needed shelter.

"Any of your people know I was looking into your business?" she asked once they were alone and the door closed. Even then, she spoke softly.

"It defeats the purpose of having someone outside my organization look into it if I admit that's what they're doing."

"Right. Smart," she breathed, fiddling with the patchwork coat sleeve that hid her knot charms. "Yeah, so it's like this. You're gonna wanna leave here real quiet and quick. Tell 'em I came crying to you like a little baby, whatever. We just gotta get out without anyone coming with. Maybe that Isarnah. Not sure what her deal is."

"I trust her."

"Trusted your knot leaders, too, and look where that got you, porridge-brain."

"What do you mean?"

"Nikory's the one who marked you for the hawks."

Any amusement at Arkady's skittishness chilled at those words. She was serious, and she was scared. But she'd still come into enemy territory to warn him.

Even then, he couldn't quite make himself believe it. "Impossible. He hates the Vigil."

"Fine. You stay and see if those fists out there are loyal to you or to *him*. But I wouldn't take a soft bun for you, much less a knife. I'm scarpering."

"Not before you tell me how you found out."

Arkady glanced over her shoulder as if she expected Nikory to come through the door. "Visits szorsas, don't he? People spill all kinds of things to them. He went to one all in a lather after you got nabbed, saying he din't know what to do now."

Not Ren; she would have warned him. Vargo could ask for the szorsa's name, track her down, question her... but that would mean leaving Nikory where he was. And Vargo couldn't let that knife stay at his back any longer than he already had.

"Scarper," he said. "I'll deal with this."

By the time Varuni brought Nikory in, Vargo was ready. He had knives to hand and ice in his heart. He didn't enjoy killing—and he'd enjoy even less explaining the necessity to Sedge and the Fog Spiders—but you didn't keep Lower Bank knots in line by being soft.

Nikory came in readily, no suspicion at all. His pupils were aža-spun, a doped grin lingering in the wake of the laughter still ringing through the main room.

Until the door closed and Varuni put her back to it, and Vargo said with no humor at all, "Have a seat."

Vraszenians said aža gave true visions. Vargo didn't know if he believed that, but he didn't doubt that it helped people make intuitive leaps over gaps too big to cross sober.

"Fuck. You know," Nikory whispered.

A heartbeat later, he sank to the floor and began sobbing.

Vargo stared at Varuni, who stared back at him, as though one of them had an explanation. Meanwhile Nikory was babbling, or trying to, between heaving sobs so harsh they shook his whole body.

::Vargo, this...is not normal.::

No fucking shit. Rounding his desk, Vargo crouched next to Nikory. If this was a ruse to bring him close enough for knifing, Nikory was wasted in Froghole. He should be headlining at the Theatre Agnasce.

"I—I—" Nikory could barely form words through the retching gasps. "I don't even know why—it bothered me, yeah, but—I just— I couldn't—"

"Try breathing, then talking," Vargo said, passing Nikory the clove-scented cloth he used on warm days when their headquarters' old life as a fishery rose up like a ghost from the floorboards.

After cleaning his face and catching his sobs, Nikory stared down at the soiled kerchief like a man looking at his own shroud. But when he raised his chin, his expression was unexpectedly fierce.

"You en't tied to us," he said. "You pretend you are, but it's all lies. You let folks like Sedge think you've got loyalty and bonds, that you'll have our backs the way we've got yours—but you en't never taken an oath. I knew that when I took over the Fog Spiders, and I was willing to live with it then, but lately—" His hand clenched hard on the handkerchief. "They deserve better than you."

Vargo's voice sounded cold even to his own ears. "So you'd take my place."

"No! Or—I don't know. It en't about taking over. It's about what we owe each other. I want them to have a real knot. If that's the Fog Spiders on their own and your organization gone..." Nikory trailed off. In a dull, hopeless voice, he said, "I kept your secrets. Even when they wanted to know what went down with the Stretsko in Seven Knots. You know why they let me go? As a favor to *you*. And I walked out of there thinking, why the fuck am I being so loyal to a cuff?"

They—not the Fog Spiders. The Ordo Apis.

Caerulet's stingers.

"Nikory." Vargo waited until the man's eyes were on him. "This is important. Did you talk to Ghiscolo Acrenix?"

Nikory nodded miserably. "Back in Colbrilun, when I went to spring Lurets from the Aerie. Acrenix told the stingers we wasn't to be touched 'cause we're *yours.*" His mouth twisted around the last word like he'd tasted something foul.

::You don't think—::

I very much do.

::But whatever he used on you seemed more Quinat's domain. This feels like Sessat.::

Sessat, the strength of the many, the numen of friendship and organizations. What Vargo had felt was Quinat: the hand that holds the world, the numen of individual power and personal achievement. *Something tells me Ghiscolo's gone farther into his research than we suspected.*

But Praeteri numinata didn't make something out of nothing. *Willing to live with it*, Nikory had said. That wasn't the same as being happy about it. And hadn't that been the crux of Vargo's conversation with Sedge?

He'd called Nikory in here expecting to ask someone to carry the body out. But Nikory's accusation was a fair one—and as for the decision to act on it...

"It's not your fault."

Vargo's words fell like lead into the silence, calling Ninat to the last of Nikory's hitched sobs.

Nikory stared like Vargo had just turned into a fish. "You take aža with the rest of us when I wasn't looking? I tipped the Vigil to the Lacewater meet. I can't explain why—"

"I can. Acrenix did something to you. It's probably still there. I *know*." Sinking back against his desk, Vargo scrubbed at his face. "He did something similar to me. That's why I told you and the others to question any orders I gave about taking Sostira Novrus down." He tensed to resist the impulse—

—but it didn't hit like he expected.

Still there, sure; the thought of himself in Argentet's seat still looked like a good one. But it wasn't clutching at his throat the way it had before.

A whispered curse broke that distraction. It came from Varuni, and when Vargo glanced up, even her stony mask couldn't hide her alarm. *Possibly I should have told her about that.*

"I'm dealing with it," he said. Vargo wasn't going to lose the Lower Bank or his ennoblement charter. Not to Ghiscolo fucking Acrenix. Not to *nobody*.

"Ask a szorsa for help," Nikory said eagerly. "Lenskaya, maybe. I got a charm from one, and—it's helping. I think. The feeling en't as strong now." He interlaced his fingers in the sign for luck.

Just as it wasn't as strong for Vargo. "Did it fade gradually, or all of a sudden?"

"Sudden-like, yeah. 'Bout two days after you got nicked."

More than a month after Nikory himself was affected. For Vargo, it was less than two weeks. What triggered the shift?

He didn't know, but it didn't change his next moves. "Not Lenskaya; I won't be involving her in our business anymore. But I'll look into getting a charm. Meanwhile, Nikory, you tell Sedge and nobody else about what happened to you—but *everyone* stays away from Acrenix. Not just Ghiscolo, but anybody in that register."

::And the other Praeteri?::

So far, Ghiscolo seems to have kept this power for himself. Let's hope that stays the case. Vargo stood, brushing dust from his knees and ass. Nikory scrambled to his feet, tentatively holding out the damp and snotty kerchief. At Vargo's lifted brow, he crumpled it in his hand.

"I—" Nikory hesitated. Then: "I was sure I was a dead man."

If Vargo hadn't gotten bored at an orgy, Nikory might have been. "You're not," he said. "But Ghiscolo Acrenix sure as fuck is."

Villa Quientis, Bay of Vraszan: Canilun 10

As the small boat bucked its way across the choppy waves, Vargo leaned in and murmured to Ren, "Are you feeling all right?"

She didn't answer immediately, because she wasn't sure what would come out if she opened her mouth: an answer or her lunch. Only when the nausea ebbed did she say through her teeth, "The sea and I don't get along."

"Oh." Vargo looked surprised, then sympathetic. "I could have asked Donaia and Quientis to come into the city, instead of us going to them."

"No," Ren said, then bit down briefly before continuing. "This is supposed to be her retreat. And a bit of seasickness won't kill me." If it could, it would have done so on the journeys to and from Ganllech.

She pulled herself back into persona as they arrived at the villa's dock. Two Quientis footmen waited there; once they'd helped Renata and Vargo onto dry land, they shouldered the crate that was the reason for this visit, and led the two of them up to the house.

Vargo was a careful man. He'd tested his theory of layered numinata for cleansing the river before he ever approached her, at least on a simplified scale, and he'd built another model of more refined design after his consultations with Tanaquis. But since he was still technically administering a Traementis charter, granted by Fulvet, he wanted to demonstrate it for them before he began assembling the enormous version that would span the West Channel.

Scaperto was too gracious a host to rush directly to business, even if he still didn't entirely trust Vargo. "You must join us for afternoon tea," he said after he greeted them. "Please—Donaia insists."

Although Donaia had left for the bay less than a week before, she was already looking better. Her hair was properly cared for again, silver shining through auburn, and she no longer moved like she was dragging a great weight behind her with every step. She still fell silent at moments in the conversation, especially when Scaperto spoke about members of his family, but she looked...

Alive again, Renata thought. And then, seeing the way Donaia smiled at her host: *In ways she perhaps hasn't been for a very long time.*

But Vargo was impatient, and so before long he excused himself to oversee the setup of the model in a long trench dug for the purpose. Renata updated Donaia on House Traementis business while he took measurements, made adjustments, and had the servants set up a windbreak when the bay breezes shook the half of the spiral arching delicately over the surface of the trench.

"The winds over the Dežera can be strong, and you won't have any breaks to shield against it. Won't that be a problem?" Scaperto asked, eyeing the prismatium arch with concern.

"I'll put Tricats on the supports. But I've also added an extra Sebat figure here." Vargo ran a finger along a curve of prismatium that scattered rainbow light from the sun beating down. "People think of it as purification, but it's also the harmony of the spheres. The winds will excite that harmony and make use of it." With a wry chuckle, he added, "It may get a little noisy at times, but the music should be pleasant."

Scaperto still looked dubious, as well he might. Numinata that worked fine in miniature didn't always scale up—the reason the river numinat was so difficult to replace. But the sludge the servants had prepared at Vargo's instruction was far more contaminated than even the West Channel; if the figure worked on *that*, then its larger cousin should be able to handle the Dežera.

So they all hoped, anyway. Nobody would know for sure until Vargo had built the full thing.

The scent of the sludge ripened in the early autumn sun as Vargo fiddled with the mechanism that would drop all seven foci into their respective layers at the same moment. Donaia used the back of her glove to blot at the sweat beading her brow and lip, until Scaperto handed her a linen kerchief.

::Moment of truth.::

Renata heard Vargo's voice, and it took her a breath to realize it was a thought directed at Alsius rather than anything spoken aloud.

He shifted the block on the mechanism, and seven foci of rainbow-shimmering prismatium slid down their chutes and slotted into place. The hairs stood up on Renata's arms, energy vibrating under her skin like heat lightning. Then, with a hum and a snap, it dissipated, leaving only the warmth of the day and the shirring of cicadas.

And the water, set loose to flow through the numinat, came out...

Somewhat cleaner, she thought. More translucent than opaque. But still nothing she would want to put her hand in, much less drink.

"Perhaps if you ran it through again?" Donaia no doubt meant the suggestion kindly, but it still acknowledged the unspoken truth: The numinat had not performed as Vargo had promised.

The scar through Vargo's brow puckered as he raised it. He looked so composed, Renata almost wondered if she'd imagined the disappointing result. When she looked at his shoulders instead of his face, though, she saw the anger he was masking. "Thank you, Era Traementis, but unless the Dežera is willing to flow backward for our convenience, I'm afraid that won't make a difference."

::I don't understand, Vargo. The previous model worked perfectly!::

Scaperto cleared his throat. "I'm afraid this is... not what I'd hoped for, Eret Vargo."

His tone wasn't as suspicious as it might have been, but Renata still heard the current beneath. Nadežra was full of people promising more than they could deliver; she'd done it herself, as part of a hundred cons. He would be wondering if this was more of the same.

"Something must have gone wrong," she said. "It worked perfectly when I saw it. But that was a different model. Perhaps this one was damaged in transport?"

Vargo's gaze flicked to her. She'd seen no such thing; this was her first demonstration, too. But if Alsius said it had worked, then she trusted them.

His startlement only showed for an instant before he picked up the thread of the conversation. "It wouldn't have worked at all were that the case. I'll need to analyze what went wrong. Your Grace, Era Traementis, I do apologize for wasting your time this afternoon."

"Not a waste. We had a lovely lunch." Donaia slid her hand into the bend of Renata's elbow. "And you forced my niece to come for a visit."

Scaperto frowned. "You'll need to delay moving forward on construction until we know why the model didn't work."

"Of course." Vargo spoke as though welcoming the setback, hands open and shoulders relaxed. Nothing to indicate the proportions of this disaster. "I wouldn't dream of wasting public funds on something I wasn't certain would work."

The noise Scaperto made sounded less than confident. As Vargo began dismantling the model, Renata saw a flash of color scuttle up the prismatium: Peabody, examining it more closely. *How well can spiders see?*

Well enough, it seemed. ::Vargo, the metal. Do these colors look right to you?::

Vargo's hands paused in their work. ::They do. Why?::

::They seem off to me. As if something went wrong in the transmutation.::

::Then . . . I didn't fuck it up.::

Vargo's back was to Renata; all she could see was the fabric of his coat, easing from its taut line as some of the tension bled out. And his mental reply held everything his face hadn't shown: the fear that he *couldn't* deliver on his promise. That he'd staked not only his public reputation but his opinion of his own skill on this endeavor, and come up short.

::Your inscription was perfect,:: Alsius said gently. ::The problem is in the metal.::

Vargo's reply sounded like a curse. ::*Sabotage*.::

Donaia was still talking, trying to lead everyone back into the house for tea. Renata patted her aunt's hand and said, "I'm afraid we can't stay. Eret Vargo will need to talk to Iridet."

Eastbridge, Upper Bank: Canilun 12

The man Iridet sent to inspect the prismatium workshop two days later found nothing, and neither did Vargo himself. But as Vargo growled to Renata afterward, that meant absolutely nothing. "They knew we were coming," he said. "If there was anything to hide, they would have hidden it by then."

And there was almost certainly something to hide. Vargo's prismatium was coming from multiple workshops, because of the quantity he needed. His first model—which he insisted on demonstrating for Renata after the sabotage, and which worked as advertised—came from House Terdenzi. The prismatium he'd gotten from Amananto, though, was flawed somehow. Ren couldn't follow Alsius's technical explanation, but the takeaway was that the metal was about more than its rainbow sheen of colors. The shipment Vargo had received was flawed...in ways that remained imperceptible until the power of the Lumen flowed through and exposed them.

It might have been an accident. Vargo didn't believe it, though, and neither did Ren. Which was why the Black Rose now lurked on an Eastbridge rooftop, waiting for a second shadow to join her.

Of course she didn't hear him coming. "You told *Derossi Vargo* who you are?"

Looking at the Rook was unspeakably strange. Even knowing who was inside the hood, she couldn't spot anything identifiable in either his face or his voice. Then again, having this conversation with Grey might not have been any easier.

She sighed. "We've finally been honest with each other—on both sides. There's no denying the things he's done..." Not just to her. To Kolya. Ren pressed her lips together, then said, "But about his motives, I was wrong. He wants to bring the Praeteri down, and to make this city a better place. And I believe he has no medallion."

"He doesn't." That came quietly enough that she almost didn't hear it. After a hesitation, the Rook crouched on the rooftop at her side, close enough to be pleasantly distracting. "Ghiscolo used Quinat on him, too. It can't make something from nothing; Vargo must want power already, for him to have responded so strongly. But anyone who has a medallion would be immune to that influence."

She could believe Vargo wanted power. *Can you imagine what this city might be if everybody just did their fucking job for once?* It had been part of a rant, halfway through their drunken afternoon together. But there was a difference between wanting power for one's own benefit, and wanting it for the sake of others.

Sometimes there was a difference, anyway. Kaius Rex's poison tended to blur that line.

"I ask not that you trust him with your secrets," she said. "Only that you trust *me* to be right about him. I laid his pattern, and now much more of it is clear. He can help us—you—do what the Rook was made for."

After a moment, his gloved hand came to rest over hers. "I do trust you. Now, what are we here for?"

She explained as they made their way toward the Eastbridge Sebatium. The roof of a bookbindery next door made a good vantage point for checking the area—and the shadowed recess of a dormer window made a good hiding spot when someone unexpectedly turned the corner and headed for the temple.

"Hello, Meda Amananto," Ren whispered as a swaybacked old woman trailing several scarves hobbled up to the door and unlocked it. "Whatever are you doing here at this time of night?"

"Good thing you invited me to back you up," the Rook murmured into her ear. "She looks *very* dangerous."

The tickle of his breath, the pressure of his chest against her back... They'd laid aside their masks, but Ren didn't know where that left *them*. Or what was even possible, given all the complications that surrounded them.

She only knew what she wanted, with an ache that went through her from head to foot.

The Rook asked, "Shall I sit on her while you ask questions, or would you prefer to be the bully?"

Steadying her voice, she said, "Cuffs expect it from you. I'll be the nice one."

"As my Lady Rose wishes." His scent lingered as he slipped away to climb through one of the windows of the Sebatium. And the sensation of his glove, brushing her cheek.

Ren dragged her wits together and followed him inside.

The old woman was Orrucio Amananto's grandmother, Orruciat, and her workshop was in an upper chamber of the Sebatium. An open door and a muffled squeak told Ren the Rook hadn't waited, trusting she'd be hard on his heels.

She entered to find him gripping Orruciat in a lock, with one hand over her mouth. "Now, now," Ren said, dropping into the Black Rose's voice. "Surely there's no need for that."

The Rook huffed a laugh. "She may look like a kindly old granny, but her elbows are sharp and she knows how to apply them."

As if to underscore his point, Orruciat tried to stomp on his foot. When he evaded that, she twisted her head free of his muffling hand. "Let me go, you ruffian, or I'll garotte you with my scarf!"

She almost stumbled into the purification basin when the Rook complied. Catching her balance, she straightened the scarves like a huffy pigeon. "Impudent boy."

Ren stifled a laugh and held up one gloved hand. "We aren't here to hurt you, Meda Amananto. We're only curious what you're doing here so late at night."

"What business do you have with my business?" Taking out a pair of spectacles, she slipped them on and peered at Ren. "And who are you? Never heard stories of the Rook having a sweetheart. Watch yourself, my girl. Can't trust a man who doesn't show you his face."

"Who says I don't?" the Rook asked, and Ren heard the echo of Grey in his laugh.

"You shush. I've nothing to say to you. You!" She leveled a crooked finger at Ren. "Do you know who's been tampering with my prismatium?"

Her indignation could have been a facade, but Ren doubted it. "That's what we're here to discover. If we may?" She gestured at the numinat laid into the floor.

Orruciat wavered visibly, then stepped aside, turning so she could keep the Rook in view. "Just so long as *that* one doesn't break my hands if he doesn't like what he finds. I made it correctly—my word to the Lumen. I would *never* disrespect the Great Work. If something went wrong, it wasn't me."

Ren made a grand display of pointing at the door, and caught the playful shrug the Rook gave her as he made a grand display of grudgingly complying. When he was leaning against the frame like an ornamental column, arms crossed over his chest, she came forward and began to examine the numinat.

What she expected to find, she didn't know. If there was anything wrong with the prismatium or the way it had been set into the floor, Vargo and Iridet's inscriptor would have found it—or Orruciat would have. The figure wasn't active, but the metal shone like a rainbow in the glow of the lightstone fixtures. "All the work has been done here?"

"Right here," Orruciat confirmed. "And the floor is new-laid, too—no warping to worry about."

The floorboards weren't emitting so much as a sigh when Ren stepped on them. But she heard something else, so faint it was almost inaudible. "Does anyone else hear that?"

Silence from the other two. Then the Rook said, "Hear what?"

"Music." Ren turned her head, trying to locate the source. "In the distance, maybe. It's..."

She trailed off to listen better, but the sound remained maddeningly faint. If it wasn't in the room, though, it wasn't relevant. She shook off the tingle dancing across her skin and looked up, as if Vargo might have missed a second numinat painted on the ceiling.

When her head came down, the metal in the floor looked different.

Ren knelt to examine it more closely. Still a rainbow of colors, red and gold and green and blue and violet—but parts of it had dulled. No, not dulled; simply changed. Where there had been orange and turquoise, the prismatium now gleamed more like the steel it had previously been, shading from polished grey to shining white. The colors of the Vraszenian clans: Anoškin white and Kiraly grey replacing the outsiders.

"There *is* something wrong," she murmured, and tugged off her glove to touch it.

Or tried to. Her glove wouldn't come off.

She looked at it, frowning. The black leather seemed to have fused with her hand, giving her no slack to pull. And the cuff now blended seamlessly with her sleeve. As if—

As if it wasn't something she was wearing. As if it was just…her.

"What's wrong?" the Rook asked, straightening from the doorway. Orruciat made a warning sound at him, but he paid her no heed.

"Nothing's wrong." Nothing except her own foolish refusal to see until now.

She remembered that moment in the dream, when she reached for a way to hide her identity from Grey. Except…that wasn't what Ažerais had given her, was it? Hadn't she thought, more than once over these past few months, that she felt the happiest, the most free, when she wore the Black Rose's mask? Renata was a lie, and so was Arenza, but the Black Rose was real.

This was a gift from Ažerais. Not a mask to hide her true self; a transmutation, a way to make something better out of the impure metal that was Ren. *I am born of Ažerais. Conceived on the Great Dream. Perhaps this is what I was always meant to be.*

"Are you speaking Vraszenian?" Orruciat snapped. "I don't understand that gibberish."

The Black Rose must have spoken her thoughts out loud, in the only language she was meant to speak. But to communicate with the old woman, she would have to sully her tongue. "You understand me not because you belong here not."

"Who doesn't belong here?" The bent old woman shook like a cypress tree in a strong wind. "Don't get pert with me, missy! It's *my* workshop."

"And it is my land!" The Black Rose surged at her, arm raised. She didn't have her thorns, but to cleanse this place of an old woman, she didn't need them.

Her strike glanced off the Rook's back instead. He shoved the protesting Orruciat out of the room, slamming the door behind her, then returned to catch the Black Rose's wrist.

"Ren," he hissed. "What's doing this to you?"

"I am not Ren," she spat back in Vraszenian. "She was broken, flawed. Our goddess has remade her into something better. She made me to defend this place, just as someone made you to take down her enemies. Why deny you the truth? You are the Rook, down to your bones! Accept it, as I have done, and be who the Faces and Masks mean you to be!"

His grip jerked and went slack. She twisted free and retreated, closing her eyes. Chasing that music. It was stronger now; it grew as she stopped fighting against her nature. She had always been the Black Rose, even if she hadn't known it. Ren was just as much a performance as the others. And that music—it was the song of the dreamweavers, the voice of Ažerais, which she had been deaf to for far too long.

But she was listening now. And she would never close her ears again.

The music splintered like wood. Ren's eyes flew open.

The Rook had slammed the hilt of his sword into the floor, cracking the boards. Wedging the blade into the crack, he set his boot as a fulcrum and pried up a central section of the numinat in a ragged maw of wood and bent prismatium.

A plug of rainbow-swirled glass pinged and bounced across the floor, stopping at Ren's toes.

She wanted to weep for the dream that had just slipped through her fingers. The pure, unwavering certainty of the Black Rose, leaving behind all the messy imperfections of Ren. And at the same time...now that it was gone, that certainty terrified her.

The door burst open again, and Orruciat made a croaking sound like a stomped frog. "What—you—my numinat!" Dodging the

Rook, she sagged to her knees next to the hole he'd pried into her pristine new floorboards.

New, she'd said. Ren bent to pick up the bit of glass at her feet with one shaking hand.

"Praeteri," she whispered, nausea twisting in her gut. Her glove was a glove again—as it had always been. She should have recognized the signs. But this one had felt so good, so *right.* Not like the rage she'd fought to keep in, that night in the temple; just her rationality slipping away like the ebbing tide. Turning her around until she didn't know what was real and what wasn't.

It didn't seem to have hit Orruciat nearly so hard. But the old woman didn't spend her life tangled in a knot of lies, playing dream-weaver's nest with the truth.

Ren recoiled as if the focus were a viper. The Rook caught it before it could hit the floor. He toed over one of the boards Orruciat was mourning; on the bottom side were painted markings. Lines of another, hidden numinat. "But to what purpose?"

Ren couldn't answer past the tightness in her throat. *How many times will they invade my mind?*

Orruciat answered for her, sobs quieting into a huff. "That... that's not right." On hands and knees, she crawled to an undamaged part of the transmutation numinat. "This...this should be earthwise, not sunwise. How did I not see that?"

Ren forced herself to look at the blank focus the Rook held. A Praeteri focus—and those, unlike ordinary numinatria, could affect the mind.

"Delusion," she said, meeting the Rook's gaze in the shadows of his hood. Searching for Grey underneath: the man, not the mask he wore. "Warping your perception of reality. You aren't to blame, Meda Amananto."

The Rook's reply was as soft as the shadows, but as sharp as steel. "We know who is."

Westbridge, Lower Bank: Canilun 13

Grey didn't go home that night.

He clawed the hood off as soon as he parted company with Ren, and stood, shaking, with it in his hands. He kept hearing Ren's voice, declaring herself to be the Black Rose in truth. Those Praeteri bastards had gone inside her head again, and if whoever was responsible for that hidden numinat were in front of Grey now, the Rook's oath not to kill might not stay his hand.

The Rook.

Accept it, as I have done, and be who the Faces and Masks mean you to be!

A shudder ran through him from head to toe. For just an instant, when she said that...

It wasn't only the Praeteri numinat at work. Every time he put the hood on, the ledge beneath his feet got narrower and narrower. He ought to look for a successor, as Ryvček had done—but who? Ranieri? Sedge? Andrejek? There was no one he trusted with this. And the end was within reach; so Ren promised him, and so he had to believe.

He walked the streets until the towers rang first sun. Then he forced himself to draw the hood back on, and went to find the best protected and least interesting person in Nadežra.

Even by the standards of his Iridet predecessors, Utrinzi Simendis was a recluse. Except when Cinquerat business dragged him to the Old Island, he spent his days in his small manor on the edge of Owl's Fields, surrounded by layers of defensive numinata. The Rook had tried to infiltrate several times, but never made it past the retaining wall surrounding the property. Iridet's Charterhouse office was less secure, but so little used the servants hardly bothered to dust it.

But the man did have one vice. And Viljin Dmariskaya Gredzyka, proprietor of the Gredzyka Exotic Goods Emporium, owed the Rook a favor.

"I'm sorry, Your Worship," she said as she led Utrinzi Simendis into her parlour. "He said he only wanted to talk, and I..."

Simendis had gone very still at the sight of the Rook. After several heartbeats passed without violence, he moved enough to nod at Gredzyka. "Thank you for your honesty. You could have claimed he threatened you. I suppose this means you have not, in fact, found a seven-stringed zither for me?"

"I did!" She gestured to a battered leather case leaning against the settee, then clutched that hand to her chest. "I hope—I hope you'll have a chance to play it."

"That depends on His Worship," the Rook said softly. He'd doused the lamp, creating a pocket of shadow between the window hangings and the display shelves. "I'm here about someone else's sins. The question is whether he'll do anything about them...or cover his eyes, as he so often does."

Gredzyka left reluctantly. Simendis was one of her best clients; the Rook could only assume that house in Owl's Fields was stuffed to the rafters with imported musical instruments. The man apparently loved them so much that he had the single-minded audacity to open the case Gredzyka had used as bait and lift into his lap an elegant instrument of lacquered wood, stringed with twisted silk.

The Rook watched him warily. Some Iridets—or rather, some holders of the Sebat medallion—had orchestrated religious purges across Nadežra; they were the reason no labyrinths survived on the Upper Bank. This one seemed content to be useless. But that wasn't the same as ignorant, and although Simendis's hands were on the strings, his eyes were on the Rook.

Or rather, on the subtle numinatrian embroidery along the edge of the hood.

Rather than wait to see if the man could unravel his own secrets, the Rook spoke. "The Illius Praeteri. What do you know of them?"

Simendis plucked one string, contemplatively, and adjusted a tuning peg. "A numinatrian mystery cult. My protégé, Tanaquis Fienola, is a member. As are a number of our leading citizens."

Silence fell, except for the plangent note of another string. The Rook said, "That's it?"

"I take it from your tone that there is something more you think I *ought* to know."

Only respect for good craftsmanship and his cordial relationship with Ča Gredzyka kept the Rook from breaking the instrument across his knee. "As Iridet, I would think you'd be concerned with the fact that the Praeteri are using unlicensed numinatria all across Nadežra. And yes, it *is* unlicensed; I broke into your office to examine the charters there."

Simendis shrugged as if the break-in was only to be expected. "It's impossible to track or control every use of numinatria. But I take it these particular uses are of concern."

The Rook began counting them off, switching between hands as he ran out of fingers. Ren had left a list on her balcony a few days before; some of the items on it matched the ones that survived the booby trap in Vargo's office.

It had the desired effect on Simendis. There was no more tuning; the man's hands went flat on the strings, and his eyes shut as though he were meditating. His expression, however, was anything but serene.

When the list was done, Simendis wet his lips, then spoke in a whisper. "Eisar. She . . . did not tell me that."

Fienola, the Rook presumed. He reined in the urge to drag Simendis out and hang him by his ankles from the Dawngate. "This is what happens when you abdicate your job to other people, *Your Worship*."

Simendis opened his eyes and studied the Rook. "I wonder. How much do you know of such things?"

"More than you, apparently."

"I doubt that," Simendis said, in a nearly inaudible voice.

Or the Rook could punch him a few times, right here. Leather creaked as his hands tightened into fists—but beating up an old man wouldn't accomplish anything. Instead he growled, "Worms breed in dark places. This needs to be dragged into the light. I'm counting on you to do it." The Rook leaned close enough for his hood to eclipse the light. "Clean your house, Your Worship. Or I will."

He would have left it at that. But before he could slip out the back door, Simendis spoke again. "You aren't in the habit of polite conversation with members of the Cinquerat. I presume you've come to me because you recognize your own limits—but have you considered my own? Iridet commands no military force. I rely on Caerulet to supply what is needed. That will hardly work in this case."

The Rook stopped. That was the objection of a man who actually *wanted* to root out the cult.

He fought with himself internally, and couldn't even say for sure which side of the argument was the Rook, and which was Grey Serrado.

"Derossi Vargo," he said at last. "He's infiltrated the Praeteri. And he holds a mercenary charter—granted by the previous Caerulet."

Touching his hood in a rare gesture of respect, the Rook left Utrinzi Simendis to his business.

19

The Ember Adamant

Isla Traementis, the Pearls: Canilun 13

When Renata reentered her bedroom after breakfast the next morning, it took her a moment to notice that Clever Natalya was making futile kitten leaps up the wall, claws scratching at the smooth birch panels. Renata, following her unwavering gaze, saw a familiar splash of color clinging to the molding, safely out of Natalya's reach.

How Master Peabody had gotten into her room she didn't know, but he made far too tempting of a target for the cat. Renata interposed herself, and Peabody flung himself onto the front of her surcoat. Covering him with one hand, she hurried out to the sitting room, where Tess was sorting through her morning correspondence, and shut the door behind her.

She expected a flood of enthusiastic and overly proper greetings and thanks to follow, but after a moment of bobbing in place on her shoulder, he scuttled down her arm and waved his front legs toward the desk. Tess's eyes widened at the sight. "Is that—"

The door to the sitting room was closed, but Tess caught herself all the same. Renata came closer, letting Peabody scuttle down to the desk and herself whisper to Tess. "Yes. I've no idea what he's doing."

The spider had climbed onto the stack of letters and was

laboriously trying to nudge the top one off. When Tess moved it away, he retreated to the one below, and repeated this process until he got to a flat package a little too thick to be the usual invitation or letter. Then he hooked one leg through the ribbon tying it closed and threw his minuscule weight into a futile effort to undo the knot.

The package was from Vargo. Brushing Peabody gently aside, Renata untied the ribbon and found herself in possession of a folded piece of fabric that, once shaken out, proved to be a painted numinat with a note.

Put the focus in the middle and pin the cut bit together.

Tess cleared her throat. "Seeing as how winter's coming on, would now be a convenient time to discuss additions to the alta's wardrobe? It'll be a difficulty to get the best fabrics with Eret Vargo's warehouse closed to us, but I've an idea for..."

She launched into a thoroughly detailed account of the state of the textile trade in Nadežra while Renata, grateful, sat on the floor behind her desk. The focus was pinned to the corner of the fabric; she arrayed everything according to Vargo's instructions, then used the pin to close the encircling line.

No sooner had Peabody jumped into the middle than a flood of words swept through her mind.

::—working? Please say it's working. We weren't certain if you would be able to hear me away from Vargo, since your connection seems to be through him. You must tell me how you did it; the details he provided were scanty at best. You're so quiet. Oh dear, perhaps you still can't respond. Blink! One if you can hear me, two if you can't. No, wait. That makes no sense. Two if you can hear me, three if—::

"I can hear you," Renata said, fighting a smile. So long as she kept her voice to a whisper, nobody would hear her over Tess waxing rhapsodic about the weave of a particular heather-fine twill shipped in from Ganllech.

::Oh! Yes, I suppose you could answer like that.:: His front limbs curled bashfully up against his mouth, but a moment later he was off again. Raising his brightly patterned body in a reverse bow, he said,

::Where are my manners? Altan Alsius Acrenix, at your service. A sheer delight to make your acquaintance properly. We have so many interesting topics to discuss—I do hope this isn't an inconvenient time. It may not be far from Eastbridge to the Pearls, but it isn't precisely an easy jaunt for me. Quite a few birds out at this time of day, and I feel so cruel when I have to bite them. My venom is very painful, you know. I could refrain from using it, but that would defeat the purpose, wouldn't it?::

"I thought the two of you were indestructible."

::I'd rather not test that in the digestive tract of a seagull.::

She stifled a laugh at his prim reply. "That's fair. I'm sorry about the cat."

::I suppose you're attached to her?:: At Renata's lifted brow, he shook himself. ::Can't be helped, then. Now that I know that beast is a danger, I'll take precautions. Vargo thought it would be convenient were I the one to relay messages between you. I am *so* relieved you set your estrangement aside. And quite scandalized! I knew Letilia, you know. Not well. But I must say, I always felt you were too interesting to possibly be related to her. Meaning no insult. Though I suppose you wouldn't take insult, since she's not really your mother.::

There would hardly be any risk of someone overhearing her when every ten words from Renata invited a thousand from Alsius. But if the only person he could talk to was Vargo, she hardly blamed him for being excited about this new opportunity. "May I ask... how did you end up like this?" She gestured at the peacock spider.

::Ah, that.:: He shuffled around, his movement curtailed by the borders of the numinat. ::I understand you heard the conversation the night you brought Captain Serrado to us? Mine was a similar situation. A curse my brother sent to kill me.::

How many people in Nadežra would believe that, when Ghiscolo seemed so affable? "That part, I know. But I've never heard of a situation like yours." She hesitated, then said, "If I'm prying too far, I apologize, but... I misjudged Vargo rather badly. I'm trying to mend that. And you're clearly a vital part of his life."

::Vital, hmm.:: Tucking his legs close, Alsius settled into a little lump opposite the focus of the numinat. His four main eyes shone like polished onyx. ::It didn't start that way. You see, Vargo was the messenger boy who delivered the cloak that held the curse. And I... I was more concerned with my own survival than his. If it weren't for Master Peabody—the original, I mean—tucked in Vargo's pocket, matters might have fallen out very differently.::

He went silent in contemplation, save for the faint whisper of his front legs against his mandibles. ::If you wish to understand Vargo, then you only need know that the unintended consequences of his actions trouble him more than he will ever admit.::

The Night of Hells. Kolya Serrado. Undoubtedly others she would never know about. But from the weight in Alsius's voice, he wasn't the only one who felt that way. While she knew very little about numinatria, she could speculate: Alsius Acrenix, trying to save his own life without concern for the messenger boy... If it was possible for a spirit to be transferred to a new body, she doubted it was the spider he'd been aiming for.

Yet somehow they'd gone from that to the oddly familial relationship they had now. "Am I right in thinking you had a hand in his rise?"

::Eight of them,:: Alsius said with a mental chuckle. ::It took quite some effort to mold Vargo into someone the Praeteri would accept into their ranks, but I was right to be concerned about what they do—as you yourself have experienced. And now with...Did Sedge relay to you that Ghiscolo somehow influenced Nikory as well? Though it's faded, for both of them. Vargo says the immediate pressure eased off quite abruptly a few days ago, though the impulse lingers. We're not sure why.::

She breathed out, understanding. "He tried to use it on Grey Serrado last week. Fortunately, Captain Serrado didn't know what Ghiscolo wanted to hear."

Alsius's feet tapped. ::So perhaps he can only affect one at a time? That's reassuring, I suppose. Inasmuch as anything about this can be reassuring. I wonder who he used Sessat on, after Nikory? You'd be wise to stay away from my family. Well, Sibiliat and Mother are mostly harmless.::

Harmless as vipers. The influence of the medallion Ghiscolo held would bleed out into his whole register, a desire for authority and power. How was it that the Acrenix had never taken a Cinquerat seat before now? Either they'd come into the Quinat medallion only recently, or the link between that numen and excellence meant they'd played their game *very* well. Didn't House Acrenix have influence all throughout Nadežra, without ever showing their hand openly?

And if Ghiscolo had Sessat now as well, that explained a great deal about his actions as Caerulet. He'd fallen very rapidly into the impulses of that numen. As bad as one medallion was, maybe it was worse to have two.

Renata hesitated, trying to think of a way to share her concerns with Alsius without saying anything about Kaius Rex's chain of office. Before she could, Alsius shook himself. ::You don't need me to tell you about dangers to avoid. You're adept enough on your own. Quite astonishing, what you've made yourself into with no help at all. I'm very pleased you're our ally. Speaking of which, is there any chance you might have a word with the Rook? I've never much cared about that vigilante, but it upsets Vargo, you know. And our plans, of course.::

If Alsius thought she'd done this with no help at all, Vargo must not have told him about Ondrakja. Or else—and this was possible—Alsius wrote Ondrakja off as insignificant, since after all, she hadn't been a noblewoman. However genial his manner, he'd grown up a cuff, with all the assumptions and arrogance that meant. *And perhaps some lingering traces of Quinat.*

But they would have marked him as dead in the register, so he wouldn't be affected now. As for his request...she hunched over the numinat, so she could speak just above a breath. "The Rook wants Ghiscolo taken down. And the Praeteri. So long as that remains, Vargo need not fear."

::Thank you. I'm glad Vargo has you for a friend. That boy is entirely too serious, though I'll never admit to saying it.::

A sound in the corridor interrupted Tess's monologue: one of the junior maids, calling out to someone else. Peabody uncurled from his huddle but stayed in the numinat. ::Before I go—and if it isn't too much an imposition—I do have a favor to ask.::

Renata answered with a brief, inquisitive noise, peeking around the desk in case she needed to sweep her floor clear—numinat, spider, and all.

::I'm very impressed with Tess's work. Since she's here, would you ask if she might be willing to make me a pair of gloves? Or rather, four pairs?:: He raised two of his legs in cheerful semaphore, though the voice in Renata's head was a mournful wail. ::Sixteen years now, I feel as though I've been walking around naked!::

Eastbridge, Upper Bank: Canilun 13

Ever since the adoption ball, notes from Sibiliat had arrived at Traementis Manor, inviting Giuna to one thing or another. Every single one, Giuna consigned to the hearth in her mother's office.

Until she accepted that she couldn't dodge them forever, and sent back a note of her own.

Securing a table in the atrium of Ossiter's was easier than she expected. Her mind still lived in the days when the Traementis name couldn't buy her an unmatched glove, much less attention at an exclusive business. Armored in one of Tess's newest designs, a split surcoat of copper net weighted down with a spray of pink tourmalines that matched the gown underneath, Giuna made sure to arrive early.

For so long she'd been the little bird. The minnow. The one who stood meekly and quietly in the shadow of her elders. Today, she took her cue from her cousin. Renata would position herself to catch the light—the better to make certain every eye was on her.

"Giuna! You made it," Sibiliat said in greeting when she arrived, as though Giuna were a pet who'd come when called.

But Giuna refused to be thrown off her footing. She dodged

Sibiliat's attempt to take her hands, pulling out the chair that would leave her guest squinting into a sunbeam. "I would hardly invite you out and then not show up."

That cool reception dampened Sibiliat's condescending effusiveness. She sat, then discreetly tried to adjust her chair so she could look at Giuna without scowling from the brightness.

Waving for a server to bring the wine she'd ordered, Giuna prepared a plate for Sibiliat of autumn fruits, nuts, and cheeses. And she let Sibiliat look her fill. She didn't have the skill to hide from those sharp eyes, so why bother? Let Sibiliat see. Let her think she could fix what she'd broken. Let her try.

"You're angry with me," Sibiliat murmured after the server had poured them both a chilled white wine as bright as an autumn afternoon. Sucking on a candied hawberry, she slid her gaze away from Giuna to study the atrium, cataloging the witnesses to their little drama. So far it was a pantomime rather than a play, Sibiliat keeping her voice low enough to deny them dialogue.

Giuna took her time selecting a creamy soft cheese to spread across a thin round of toast. "Whyever would you think that?" she asked. Usually when she spoke, she couldn't hide the sweetness, but now it felt as false as ivory teeth. "Unless you think I've some reason to be angry. Perhaps something your family recently did against mine?"

"Damn Fadrin for a fool." Sibiliat's glass clinked hard against the table when she set it down after a too-large swallow of wine. "You know what an idiot my cousin is. My father can barely control him. Trust me, he was soundly reprimanded for—"

"I *heard* you, Sibiliat." Giuna folded her hands to keep them— and her voice—from trembling. "The night of the adoption ball. I heard Benvanna offer you something on my cousin, and I saw you send Fadrin off to retrieve it."

Sibiliat offered Giuna a tentative smile and her hand, as though there were still anything to salvage. "Little bird—"

"*Don't.*" Giuna's voice rang through the atrium as she smacked Sibiliat's hand aside.

Now there wasn't an eye in Ossiter's that wasn't watching avidly. Keeping her spine straight, Giuna brought her voice back down to a murmur. Let their audience fill in the quiet with their own assumptions. "I am not a bird. Or a minnow. Or a puppy you can train to be your loyal hound. I am not a child, and I neither asked for nor want your protection. You've lied to me, and you've claimed to lie *for* me—but the truth is that you only lie for yourself. I am done with the lying, Sibiliat. And I am done with you."

Her cheeks were hot even though she hadn't taken a sip of wine. It felt good, saying the words she'd practiced and having them come out exactly as intended. She almost wished she'd spoken loud enough for everyone to hear.

But no. These words were meant to sever ties, not to flay the pride from someone who didn't know what it felt like to be hurt.

Giuna took a single sip of wine, then dabbed her lips with her napkin. "I'm leaving this afternoon to spend a few days with my mother at His Grace's villa. When I return, I'll be occupied with learning to take over my duties as the Traementis heir. Too busy for frivolity; you needn't bother sending any more invitations. It would only be a waste of paper."

With that, she'd said what she needed. There was no reason to stay.

But Sibiliat caught Giuna's wrist as she rose, and her own voice sank to the low, hard note she usually tried to keep Giuna from hearing. "Are you certain of this? You don't want me as your enemy."

"Enemy?" Twisting her arm in a move Leato had once taught her to escape bullies, Giuna broke Sibiliat's grip on her. She smiled. Even managed a genuine laugh. "So dramatic. Who said anything about enemies? Aren't you the one who loves to point out that House Acrenix is *everyone's* friend?"

"But—"

"There's no reason we can't be cordial in public." Leaning over the table, Giuna set her lips to Sibiliat's ear. "As long as you remember this. You might be Acrenix...but I'm Traementis. We protect our own. When you threaten my family, *that* is when you become my enemy."

Pulling back, she caught a flash of fear in Sibiliat's eyes, quickly veiled. No, the Traementis reputation was not forgotten.

With a satisfied smile, Giuna paid the bill and left Sibiliat alone on the stage.

Isla Traementis, the Pearls: Canilun 14

Tess was in her tiny workroom, blocking out the pattern for Faella Coscanum's winter surcoat, when Suilis brought news that Pavlin was waiting in the kitchen yard.

"What happened to the brute? This one's pretty enough, but the other had shoulders I could die over," Suilis said, poking through Tess's notions basket. Even though it held nothing more incriminating than a length of embroidered facing smuggled out of Ganllech, Tess snapped the lid shut like it was a turtle looking to take a finger.

Suilis mistook her urgency for ire, holding up a placating hand. "Not that I'd try for Sedge without your nod."

"You're welcome to him," Tess said, smoothing her curls and biting color into her lips. "But fair warning: Between his kisses and Meatball's, I couldn't tell a lick of difference."

You'll thank me, Sedge, she thought as she dragged a shawl of cranberry-shot tiretaine over her maid's uniform and went downstairs. Even if Suilis turned out to be no more than she seemed, she wasn't Sedge's type. Anyone with eyes could see that Tess's brother preferred them quiet and vaguely menacing.

Pavlin stood with his face turned up to the sun, the golden light bringing out the warmth of the wool coat Tess had tailored for him and the honey of his hair. Tess couldn't understand Suilis's criticism at all. Those shoulders looked plenty broad.

Maiden and Mother, get ahold of yourself. You're the ninny who pushed him off.

And he'd not pushed back. Tess was wise enough to appreciate that respect...and fool enough to wish he'd done it anyway.

"You've news for me?" she asked, striving for and failing at severity.

Pavlin nodded, holding out a basket of cakes for her. "Though I wish I didn't. It'll chase away that smile."

And there he went saying things like that, and how was Tess supposed to avoid becoming entirely a fool?

But never so much a fool that she didn't worry about who might be listening from one of the windows. "Not here," she whispered. Fishing two cakes from the basket, she stashed the rest in the kitchen and led him along the route she usually took when walking Meatball.

The autumn winds blustered, making Tess glad for her shawl, and the warmth of the spice cake on her tongue, and Pavlin acting as a break as they meandered down the river walk, answering her questions about his family and the bakery as though nothing had changed between them. She let a sigh join the wind as they came to the Becchia Bridge and turned to head back. She could only pretend for so long that she was an alta's maid out with her courting constable.

"I was right, then?" she asked after silence had settled too long between them. "About Suilis?"

Pavlin stopped and leaned his elbows on the river wall, forcing Tess to stay as well. The winds whipped lace froth on the rippled gold of the Dežera. From this distance, even Staveswater looked like a picturesque ruin of smoke and seagull nests.

He said, "She's been a housemaid before—mostly daywork—but that's not her real job."

The confirmation chilled Tess more than a few river gusts. She clutched her shawl tighter. "And what is?"

"She's tied into the Oyster Crackers." His searching glance was punctuated with a nod when she frowned at the name. Who wouldn't recognize it? One of the most legendary Upper Bank burglar crews. Fingers dreamed of earning an invitation into their ranks, the way they dreamed of meeting the Rook.

You've managed the latter. Doubt Suilis is sussing you out for the former.

Pavlin's next words were the last stone atop the burial cairn of Tess's optimism. "She's part of the team Sibiliat Acrenix hired to toss your house in Westbridge."

Tess's fingers dug into her arms. "When my alta was recovering from her sleeplessness."

"*And* during the Dreamweaver Riots, when you..."

She didn't need the words he swallowed. Tess recalled too well the fear that had taken her when she heard the breaking window, the thump of furniture overturned. That fear drove her into the streets—and the cordon Pavlin held with his fellow hawks.

He was fidgeting, shoulders hunched and soft hair hanging over sun-warmed eyes. "Tess, I—"

"Would you have told me?" Suilis's betrayal didn't hurt, which forced Tess to admit to herself why Pavlin's had. Only he had the power to make her feel vulnerable. "If I hadn't met you that day, would I even know now?"

"Yes."

"Why?"

"Because I was sorry for lying from the day we met."

Her heart twinged. *I could just as well be saying that to you.*

Pavlin babbled on to fill her silence. "You have every right to be angry—"

"No. I'm a hypocrite, being angry," Tess murmured, then realized what she'd just said. No taking it back; she swiftly considered what she could tell him. Not Ren's secrets, no. But...maybe some of her own?

In a soft voice, she said, "You weren't wrong to suspect something amiss. You or the captain. My alta and I fled Letilia's house with a casket of jewelry and little else." Even true, it still tasted like a lie. "There's more to the story—but that's not mine to tell."

His hand caught hers. "You don't need to tell me anything."

"I do. If I want..." She met his liquid gaze, then couldn't look away. "I do."

She wanted. Honesty and spice cakes and a shop of her own that wasn't a cramped workroom in someone else's house, a kitchen to hang her sampler while she fixed his poorly tailored coats and sewed binders for his comfort. His eyes on hers, his lips on hers, and so much more, even if it did make her a fool.

Maiden help me become a mother. It was an old Ganllechyn sweetheart's prayer, and maybe she didn't want quite all that *yet.* But she could imagine it happily enough.

Tess said, "I was born in Ganllech, but I grew up in Nadežra. There." She waved across the channel to Lacewater. "I was one of Ondrakja's Fingers."

At his look of disbelief, Tess dredged up the tears that always came so easily. Not the real ones that left her face patchy red and snot-slick; the false ones that made her eyes shine and her lip tremble enough to shake coins from the pocket of any slumming cuff. "Her best pity-rustler."

After a moment's shocked silence, Pavlin dug through his coat. He came up with a few centiras and pressed them into her hands.

"What—?"

"Don't look at me like that; I don't think my heart can take it. Lacewater's best pity-rustler."

Tess giggled, blotting away her false tears with one hand. The other was still entangled with Pavlin's, and she wasn't inclined to ever let go.

"What do you intend to do?" he asked after they'd spent too long grinning foolishly at each other. "About Suilis, I mean. Can I help?"

Tess would need to talk to Ren, but already a plan was forming. Suilis wanted information about Renata's secrets? Then Tess would become a font of them . . . and see what bait attracted her the most.

She said, "The Oyster Crackers. Suilis is probably passing what she learns through them. Do you think you can find out where they lodge?"

"I can try." Pavlin lifted her fingers to his mouth. "If only to keep you from seeking them out yourself."

His breath warmed her skin against the autumn's chill. Sweet Maiden, but this was unfair. Tess tapped his lips in reprimand before he could tease away her determined mood. "As though I'd do anything so senseless." Leave the hero's doings to Ren. Tess preferred her life quiet, uneventful, and deception-free.

And she preferred having Pavlin in it. "Come along," she said, tugging him in the direction of home.

"Where are we going now?" he asked, though he followed her readily enough.

"My workroom. I'll need accurate measurements if I'm to make you a proper constable's coat."

Whitesail, Upper Bank: Canilun 14

Ren was almost late to her appointment at Tanaquis's house. She'd gotten caught up in writing letters to Donaia and Scaperto, explaining the interference found at the prismatium workshop— interference Orruciat had obligingly reported, saving Ren from having to come up with a reason for how she'd learned of it—and if her window hadn't been open, the ringing of the nearest clock tower might not have caught her attention.

She hurried north and found she wasn't the only person running late. Vargo was disembarking from a sedan chair as her own bearers trotted up, and he waited while they set her down and received their payment. In keeping with the facade that they were doing business together only reluctantly, he limited his verbal greeting to a chilly "Alta Renata."

But over his link to Alsius, she heard him say, ::Is this about more Praeteri shit?::

Ren almost hadn't told him what happened to her in the prismatium workshop, because she knew he wouldn't take it well. But it seemed a pity to go back to the days when they hid things from each other. In his mental voice now, she could hear the leashed fury of a man who'd had enough of sitting at the center of his web and was about ready to kick someone's teeth in for a change of pace.

Heading for the townhouse, she said, "Not that. Business of my own, and tricky enough that I need both Tanaquis and the two of you to help untangle it."

"At this rate, we're going to have trouble keeping up the pretense that we're at each other's throats."

They could stage some kind of hostility, but the prospect made Ren tired. She was already playing with three decks of secrets; she didn't need to add a fourth. "Giuna's working on pulling the fangs from anything Sostira might dig up on me. I say we behave as normal, and let people assume I forgave you after you sank her attack in the Charterhouse." It was only off by a day or two.

Inside the townhouse, Zlatsa waved them upstairs with a surly mutter of "Unless you want to wait in the parlour until dusk." Her scowl softened when Vargo handed her two deciras and instructed her to bring refreshments from the nearest ostretta.

Compared to her odd behavior at Renata's last visit, today Tanaquis was practically sedate. Perched like an owl on a rung of her bookshelf ladder, she looked as though she'd gotten caught up in reading and hadn't bothered to finish her descent. She lost her balance when Vargo cleared his throat, and would have toppled if he hadn't lunged forward to steady her. The book hit the floor with a thud. Tanaquis shook off Vargo's hold and scrambled to retrieve it.

"Don't worry about me!" She carefully smoothed out the pages, checking them for damage. They were old enough to crumble at the edges, and she clicked her tongue. "I really should make a copy of this to preserve the original."

::Is that Mirscellis's *Mundum Praeterire*? How did she come by that? I spent a small fortune acquiring mine.::

The other reason for not continuing the pretense of estrangement was that Renata wasn't sure she could maintain her icy facade while listening to Alsius's ramblings. It was only a pity that Tanaquis couldn't hear him, too; the pair of them would have gotten on like the Dežera in flood.

With the book's well-being secured, Tanaquis blinked at her visitors. "Did we have an appointment? I'm afraid now isn't a good time."

She sounded more irritated than upset, but it still gave Renata pause. "Is something wrong?"

"Utrinzi said..." Tanaquis made an impatient noise. "It seems the Rook paid Eret Simendis a visit yesterday. How that man—if indeed he is a man—found out so much about the Praeteri I don't know, but I got dragged into the Charterhouse for a tongue-lashing such as I've not had since childhood. His Worship is *very* upset that I didn't inform him more thoroughly about the nature of the numinatrian work our circle conducts."

Vargo managed something like a sympathetic expression, but silently he asked, ::Did you send him, Ren? Never mind—you can't answer that.::

"Oh dear," Renata said. "Is he simply angry that he didn't know, or—"

"He's determined to break the cult up." Tanaquis laid the book gently down. "I'll miss it, I suppose...but I've learned all I can, and it seems most of the members were using our arts quite irresponsibly. He instructed me to talk to you, Vargo."

That sudden swerve made his eyebrows rise. "Am I under arrest for being part of the cult?"

"No, you're to do the breaking. He wants as many other members as possible arrested, preferably in the midst of a ritual. I have a charter for you here somewhere—Ah! There it is." She fished a packet out from under an astrological chart, held shut by the seven-star seal of Iridet. As Vargo accepted it, she added, "Apparently you come recommended by the Rook."

The sound that slipped from him suggested he might be choking on his own tongue. Tanaquis thumped him absently on the back and turned to Renata. "I remember now. Yes, you did ask to meet at this hour. Why is Vargo here?"

"Because this may require both your minds—and because he and I have mended our rift."

Tanaquis looked like she was scribbling notes inside her own head. "Interesting. Perhaps not all the effects are negative ones."

"Effects?" Vargo paused in the act of stowing Iridet's charter in his satchel.

"That's what I need to discuss with you." Renata gave him the same explanation she'd given Tanaquis, about the numinatrian jewelry she'd lost in the dream.

Halfway through the recital, Alsius said, ::I read her testimony when we were investigating her sleeplessness. Wasn't she supposedly in Seteris, having nightmares about being her mother's maidservant?::

Vargo leaned forward to pour the tea Zlatsa had brought, concealing from Tanaquis's view the smile tugging at his lips. ::Perhaps we might hear the true tale later.::

While Renata went on, Tanaquis set a number of small cakes on her plate in an order comprehensible only to her. By the time Renata finished, she still hadn't eaten any of them; she was too eager to add her own thoughts. "Under normal circumstances, I'd merely be curious about a numinatrian piece falling into the realm of mind. But the evidence suggests this is a piece of some power, or something in the realm of mind acts as a great amplifier. Or both."

::That explains the Mirscellis.::

"That explains the Mirscellis," Vargo echoed.

Eyes bright, Tanaquis asked, "Oh, you've read it?"

"I've heard summaries." His drawl left Renata in no doubt as to whom those summaries came from.

Before Tanaquis could embark on what looked to be a lengthy exploration of numinatrian history, Renata said, "She believes that my jewelry being in the realm of mind is affecting all of Nadežra—to the city's detriment. Which is why I'm hoping the two of you can tell me how to get it out of there again."

Tanaquis swiped the icing off the top of a cake and licked it thoughtfully from her finger. "Nadežra. Hmmm. Have either of you heard of similar problems elsewhere? Through your trade connections and such?" When Vargo and Renata exchanged glances and shook their heads, she said, "That suggests the medallion might actually be here, instead of in Seteris. We know the realm of mind has denizens—spirits and the like; perhaps they've moved it. How fascinating!"

::Fascinating, indeed!::

"As *fascinating* as this all is," Vargo said in a tone as dry as next-day bread, "I'm more interested in how we retrieve it. Mirscellis only ever traveled in spirit."

"You brought back Renata's prismatium mask," Tanaquis pointed out.

"And I still don't know how."

The pinch of Tanaquis's mouth said she still didn't find that a satisfying answer. Diverting her, Renata said, "I lost the pendant under more or less the same conditions as the mask. Perhaps a spirit journey like Vargo's could bring it back the same way? Even if we don't understand how."

She couldn't follow half of the flurry of conversation that followed, even the parts where Vargo repeated Alsius's interjections. The general consensus, however, seemed to be that nobody thought it likely. Not with that fragment of her spirit no longer present in the dream.

"There are other possibilities, though," Tanaquis said, brightening as she turned to Renata. "Vraszenians call the realm of mind 'Ažerais's Dream,' and there does seem to be some connection with pattern. Perhaps we could experiment more with using cards as secondary foci. Is there one you'd recommend for this purpose?"

Of course she saw this as an opportunity to further her research into the intersection of pattern and numinatria. Renata sighed. "Yes... but unfortunately, it's out of the question."

"What? Why?"

"It's one of the clan cards I told you about—the ones that fell out of use. And it wouldn't simply be a matter of finding a copy. It was the Ižranyi card, and according to the stories, all copies of it went blank when the clan died." Nobody knew why, but they assumed it was a consequence of the Primordial horror that obliterated the people. "That's why the clan cards are rarely used these days, even though the other six survive."

Tanaquis drew breath, no doubt to dive into the sinkhole of mystery Renata's words had just opened. Vargo's words snagged her by the collar. "What about ash?"

It was the obvious answer. Aža let a person see into the dream, but ash let them interact with it physically. Tanaquis had mentioned it before; Renata had known it would come up again.

Even braced for it, she couldn't hide the shudder that went through her at the thought.

"I do have access to Iridet's confiscated samples," Tanaquis said slowly. "And Renata traveled there bodily on a double dose—"

"I meant myself," Vargo said. "Using something like the numinat in the Great Amphitheatre. I crawled across the whole thing and made extensive notes afterward; I think they're enough to let us re-create a similar effect. So long as we're not stupid enough to leave out a proper containing circle and don't use the fucking *wellspring* as a focus, it should be safe." Taking in Tanaquis's offended look, Vargo cleared his throat. "Apologies for the language."

"I don't care about your fucking language," Tanaquis said, with a crisp precision at odds with her profanity. "But copying that numinat…"

The way she trailed off was all too familiar. Finally, with grudging respect, she said, "It makes sense."

Vargo looked smug. Renata threw cold water on that by saying, "If no other plan will work, then so be it. But I'm the one who lost the pendant. *I* will retrieve it."

She didn't want to. She would have preferred to pull out her own fingernails and salt the wounds afterward.

But Vargo didn't know what the medallion was. If he took it…

"I concur," Tanaquis said briskly, cutting off Vargo's protest. "Given your respective birth dates, Tricat's associations, and Renata's previous connection with this piece, she has a greater chance of success."

::You could always lie about your birthday again.:: Alsius's snide comment to Vargo made Renata choke on her tea.

Tanaquis swept the food aside to lay a sheet of paper on the table, and she and Vargo bent over it to begin drawing lines and arguing. Renata stood up and drifted over to a window, using that as her excuse to put her back to the room, so no one could see the dread she was fighting.

Almost no one.

The bright splash of Peabody crept up onto the windowsill. ::If you whisper very quietly, Tanaquis won't hear you; she's busy impugning Vargo's memory. Are you all right, my dear?::

Ash. That desecrating poison coursing through her body again, warping everything to nightmares. "I will be."

::Are you certain?::

Not in the slightest. But—"I have to fix this. Gammer Lindworm had the medallion; I pulled it from her during the fight, and I didn't think to pick it up."

::I see.:: Alsius paused, legs dancing restlessly. ::Then let us speak of more pleasant things.::

She was happy to let him natter on, filling the time with any thought that came into his head, speculating whether that copy of Mirscellis's book might be his own, sold off after his death. Vargo didn't even complain about the distraction—not until Alsius asked, ::And how are the gloves coming along?::

::Gloves?:: That interruption came not from Alsius, but from Vargo. Renata glanced over her shoulder. Tanaquis was huddled over their scatter of notes, but he sat straight, arms above his head and mulberry coat stretched tight across his shoulders.

::I requested that Mistress Tess make me some.::

Vargo was removing his own gloves, hopelessly streaked with graphite, charcoal, and chalk from the afternoon's activities. His coat followed, and then he hunkered back down to work. ::How would they be gloves? You don't have thumbs. Mittens, at best.::

::I beg your pardon!:: Alsius said, indignant. ::If they go on my hands, they're gloves. My thumbs or lack thereof do not enter into it.::

::Feet. Not hands. They'd basically be socks.::

Their banter was an effective enough balm that when Tanaquis straightened and cracked her back, Renata was able to speak with convincing equanimity. "I'd like to make some arrangements regarding Traementis business before we do this, since Giuna is visiting her mother in the bay, and I don't know how long it will take me to recover."

Tanaquis rolled up the final draft. "The inscription will take a while, anyway. I'd prefer to do it in the amphitheatre, but I doubt Her Elegance would allow—Oh! I can use the temple. It sits more or less under the amphitheatre, and I won't have to worry about others trampling through. I'll do that this afternoon, once I've sent a message to His Worship about the ash samples."

"Then I'll retrieve my kit and meet you there to help." Shrugging back into his coat, Vargo diverted past Renata to scoop up Peabody. "Shall I escort you out, Renata? And while I'm at it…I don't suppose I could interest House Traementis in adopting some darling Lower Bank orphans?"

Temple of the Illius Praeteri, Old Island: Canilun 14

Learning numinatria under the tutelage of a spider meant Vargo had never practiced cooperative inscription—at least, not with anyone who had a body he could bump into. Working with Tanaquis was surprisingly easy, though. She had an intuitive understanding of how each curve and line should flow into the others, and a concentration that was frankly daunting. She didn't criticize his own technique, either, and she brushed her hands off with dusty satisfaction once they'd finished and stood aside to admire their handiwork.

From the point of Illi-zero, the spiral cycled through the sequence of numina Vargo had crawled along that night at the Great Amphitheatre, each secondary figure dormant and waiting for its focus. The whole was encased in Quinat, encased in Illi-ten—body and spirit. Plus a containing Uniat for mind, because he wasn't the madman Breccone Indestris had been.

He was a different sort of madman.

::I don't suppose there's any talking you out of this,:: Alsius said as Vargo followed Tanaquis out of the Praeteri temple.

Vargo didn't bother pretending he didn't know what Alsius meant. *If you thought there was, you would have tried already.*

Alsius hadn't. Other than offering a few suggestions while Tanaquis and Vargo inscribed the numinat, he'd said very little since they left the townhouse in Whitesail.

"I'll head to the Sebatium now to see about collecting the ash," Tanaquis said once they were free of the tunnel and back in the empty Suncross storefront that hid the entrance. "And send a note to Renata that we're ready when she is. Shall we meet again tomorrow morning at third sun?"

"Not earlier?" Vargo teased, surprised she was showing such restraint.

Tanaquis laughed. "Even I know not to bother Renata before she's had her morning coffee."

But Renata—Ren—had admitted to Vargo that she despised the stuff and only drank it to maintain her ruse as a cultured Seterin noblewoman. She did that often, he was coming to realize. Forcing herself through things she disliked, even feared, because she had to.

He wasn't going to let fetching the pendant she'd lost be one of them. That woman had suffered enough nightmares because of him.

Vargo asked Tanaquis, "Are you certain it's safe to leave the numinat alone for the night?"

Surprise chased off her amusement. "Why wouldn't it be? The temple is secure from outsiders, and none of the Praeteri would disturb a numinat they found there."

"Of course." The concern was secondary to Vargo's main worry, that Tanaquis would decide to return early to check on it. Her naive confidence gave *him* confidence that he'd be able to proceed uninterrupted.

After putting her in a sedan chair and bidding her farewell, Vargo bought a quick dinner of fried scallion cakes and crispy bluegill at a corner stall, waiting a bell to make certain Tanaquis didn't return. For all her focus, she also seemed entirely capable of forgetting something and doubling back to retrieve it.

Then he made his way back into the temple, and the central chamber where they'd inscribed the numinat.

::At least bring me with you,:: Alsius said as Vargo finished setting the foci and closed the circle that would activate the numinat. It hummed to life, the charge lifting the hair on his arms as he pulled out a vial of ash. Iridet wasn't the only one who'd kept a sample handy after most of the street drug was destroyed.

"Do you want to risk guessing at the safe dose for a spider?" Vargo asked, grimacing, after he'd choked down his own dose. The ash sat unpleasantly in his gut, though perhaps that came from the knowledge of how the stuff had been made rather than its actual effects. Those, he knew from bitter experience, took roughly a bell to kick in. "Besides," he added as he repacked his inscriptor's kit and slung the bag over his shoulder, "if you come along, who's going to say kind words over my body at the Ninatium when this fails?"

::Not I,:: Alsius said primly.

Vargo smiled at all the things left unsaid. "You mean, your words won't be kind?"

::I mean there won't be a body to say them over.::

They both fell silent, neither one voicing what Alsius really meant. *Don't fail.*

The charge in the air slowly strengthened to a faint hum, and the lines of the numinat took on a scintillating glow, like they'd been chalked with prismatium. Setting Peabody safely onto a column base, Vargo stepped past the containing circle and onto the path of the spira aurea where it intersected Illi-ten.

The spiral stretched before him like a road. The longest argument they'd had over how to do this had concerned the sequence of the numina, with Alsius shouting in Vargo's head that walking the path backward was sacrilege, and Tanaquis stubbornly maintaining that the paradox of starting the path at its terminus was a necessary element. An argument Vargo finally ended when he pointed out that the outermost numen on the amphitheatre numinat had also been Ninat.

He saw the truth of Tanaquis's insight now as he passed along Ninat and the air around him shifted like a veil parting between one world and the next. If Illi-ten was the gateway, then Ninat was the guard.

But he also understood Alsius's concerns. This inverted path was meant to be traversed by the spirits of the dead. Supplicants at a temple walked the numina up the central aisle when they entered, but exited along the bare side aisles. The Lumen's judgment weighed on Vargo as he broke the taboo; it pushed down on his shoulders, slowing his steps to a slog, stealing the breath from his body. It was like swimming against the Dežera in flood. The world around him grew dim, dark, until he was the only thing left. Then even that was stripped away, flesh dissolving, thoughts fading, spirit scattering like leaves in the water.

Until it all slammed back with a painful jolt as he stumbled into the wine-dark twilight of Noctat.

Vargo took a moment to fill his lungs, wiping the cold sweat from his brow. A few weeks ago he wouldn't have recognized these sensations, but now he knew them too well. He'd felt this the night he'd killed himself and Serrado, that moment before the jolt when his life faded—the moment when he grabbed on, leaned into the burn, the physical pain a reminder that he still lived.

Other sensations bombarded him as he pushed on through Noctat: Sibiliat wrapped warm and wet around him, Fadrin's hand, Iascat's mouth, nails down his back and broken glass slashing his throat. The ache when Ren licked sticky wine off her fingers like the river rat she was under her mask; the impact of Serrado's fist driving into Vargo's gut and the bar of his arm cutting off breath. There was no pleasure or pain in this vision of Noctat: just sensation, reminding him that the separation of mind and body was an illusion.

An illusion that shattered like a prism into rainbow light as Vargo escaped Noctat's allure and spun into Sebat.

It was the bliss after orgasm, the floating haze of papaver smoke, the shimmer of aža. Vargo was aware of his entire self, but from a distance he could see the cracks running gold through him.

Cracks—and threads finer than silk.

Alsius?

The threads vibrated with Vargo's thought, like chords struck, rippling out beyond sight. No answer came, but the returning ripples were enough to reassure him that he wasn't alone.

Never alone. The cord that connected him to Alsius was spun of guilt, affection, purpose, familiarity, instruction, need. Vargo never would have chosen it, but he couldn't regret it. Sebat: perfection in imperfection.

He spider-climbed that line into Sessat. All around him were strung complex nets of endless connected nodes: tangles, knots, looms, an entire cosmos built between warp and weft, and Vargo with only two threads to cling to. One thick and sturdy under his feet, the road of the spira aurea; the other a gossamer-thin wire of steel in his hands.

Ren. He could sever it here, undo whatever he'd done when he brought her soul out of the realm of mind. Whatever she'd reciprocated and strengthened during Veiled Waters. He could free her from the web that had tangled him and Alsius for sixteen years. But even thinking it, Vargo could imagine the fury of her response. That wasn't a choice he should make alone.

She was going to be pissed enough at him as it was. Smiling, he laid his hand on her thread and used it as his guide as he passed from Sessat to Quinat.

His hold tightened as the blue-tinged mindscape dimmed to a malevolent red, sliding blood-thick and warm against his skin, pulsing in time with his heart. The ash was sinking its claws in deeper, and need and revulsion lodged in his throat, choking him like that alien urge to unseat Sostira Novrus. Only the prismatium path beneath his feet and the steel wire in his hand kept him steady and on course, passing through the blood tide of Quinat into the green fields of Quarat.

It should have been beautiful, a relief after the ominous pressure of Quinat. But with ash coursing through him, the farther Vargo walked, the more he smelled the rot under the honey-thick air, felt the mulch of dead vegetation under the verdant growth. Excessive wealth was built on the poverty of others. Bounty came from seeds planted in corpse-rich soil. Vargo knew. He'd been the soil, the seed, the fruit, the farmer. He might eat at the table now, but it was laid with his own death feast.

Nausea roiled his gut. His own feast, and that of countless, nameless others.

Not all nameless, he realized as he passed from lush Quarat into the sunbaked desert of Tricat. There he saw shades he recognized, their faces twisted with fury. Leato Traementis with Donaia, Giuna, and even Renata arrayed behind him. Kolya Serrado standing next to his brother. So many fists and knot bosses who'd been trampled in the course of Vargo's rise.

And Alsius Acrenix, looming on the path ahead, wearing a face Vargo hadn't seen since he was a boy. Alsius had seemed old then, to Vargo's childish eyes. But he'd only been a few years older than Vargo was now, barely thirty when he died.

When I died? You mean when you killed me. Now you owe me. It echoed through his mindscape, a thread crossing at a tangent that led from past to present to future.

"I owe a lot of people." Vargo's voice rippled out along that thread. *I've killed a lot of people.* It planted a chill under his skin that he couldn't shake no matter how hard he shivered. Justice fell under Tricat's purview. So did vengeance.

Beyond the faces, at the edge of those ripples, other eyes watched. Eyes set in shadows made of teeth and claws and backward-bent limbs. The scars down Vargo's back burned as he hunched his shoulders to avoid being seen, until Tuat's moonlight washed over him and hid him from sight.

The vengeful shades were gone, leaving Vargo on the spira aurea—alone. Given the patterns of the other numina, he'd expected to see...someone. Tuat's self-in-other. But while Vargo stood in Corillis's silver-blue light, the copper mirror of Paumillis reflected nothing.

He supposed it made sense. He stood on the borders between everything: neither Liganti nor Vraszenian, neither hero nor monster, a cuff who was Lower Bank scum. He fit nowhere. He had connections, but did any of them really mean anything? To those around him he was an obstacle or a tool, nothing more. Even Alsius had only taken him on because he was useful, a means of first investigating and then avenging his own death. Vargo was what he needed to be—what other people needed him to be—to do what needed doing.

And what he needed to do now was not get caught up with his head planted in his ass. Vargo stepped through a mirror's pane, becoming his own reflection and passing to the Illi of the self—

—and nearly toppling into the wellspring, glowing like one of Ažerais's roses in the middle of the amphitheatre.

The mist that surrounded it was a radiant veil, coyly hiding the waters themselves. But the sickly, poisoned cast it carried during Mettore's attempt to destroy it had washed away, leaving the light pure and shimmering. That light shone through all the visions of different amphitheatres laid atop each other, plays and festivals and the bloody entertainments of Kaius Rex, each as thin as a pastry layer—but not moving. They were fixed in place like paintings.

In all of them, a small circle of bronze glittered only a few paces away from the glowing wellspring.

Relief flooded through Vargo: that he'd found it so easily, that it hadn't fallen *into* the wellspring. Skirting the lip, he bent to pick it up.

In the days before he met Alsius, when he'd been a runner for any sort of job that paid, some of the rats he'd run with had a game of gluing coins to the stoop of a rich merchant's shop. Sometimes as a distraction for a quick dip and pass, sometimes just for the amusement of seeing a cheese-eater dirty their gloves trying to pry a mill free, and then huffing and pretending they didn't care when they failed.

Vargo felt the frustration and embarrassment of those cuffs now. Face burning, he stripped off his gloves, dried his sweaty hands on his coat skirts, and tried to dig his nails underneath the pendant. Then he drew out his boot knife. Then the metal form he used to trace basic numinata.

By the time he'd failed to pry it up with every compass, edge, caliper, and instrument in his inscription kit and every curse word he knew, Vargo was hot, sweaty, and shaking with irritation. The thing was still stuck fast like it had been welded there.

"Fucking Tricat," he growled. Immobility: the same Mask-damned facet of that numen that had been poisoning the Charter-house for months.

Unlike when he'd come here to retrieve the missing part of Ren's spirit, though, he knew how to deal with this. Out came the tools again, Vargo tracing a new spira aurea on the ground, with the medallion at its heart. But he drew it sunwise, so that the triangle he inscribed within the numinat inverted Tricat's basic meaning. Not immobility, but movement.

He kept his head down as he worked, grateful that the medallion also seemed to be keeping everything around him fixed in place, so he didn't have to worry about his nightmares attacking him. It was a simple figure. He set a new record for speed of inscription, and this time when he touched the bronze disc, it came up easily.

Vargo stuffed it into his pocket and stood, joints aching, wondering if he would need to reinscribe the damned temple numinat—this time the right way round—to get out of here.

With the medallion moved, the fixed layers around him came unmoored. The ground rolled beneath him, and by the time he caught his balance, he was in the amphitheatre as it had been that night during Veiled Waters. But now, two numinata were inscribed on its floor: the one he'd dismantled, and the one he'd walked to get here.

Here, where shadows flowed down the tiers of the amphitheatre like a tide of monstrous insects. Backward-bent limbs, tatters that were neither flesh nor fur, claws that scraped and ticked across the stone as they crept closer.

The scars on his back burned like they'd been reopened, the pain only made worse by a wave of nausea when the mold-damp stink hit him.

I'm a fucking idiot.

He'd taken ash—and the zlyzen had come for him.

20

Coffer and Key

Isla Traementis, the Pearls: Canilun 14

Ren was having another nightmare.

It still happened, though not as often as before. A kitten couldn't truly keep everything away, any more than a thread labyrinth could, or a red thread around her bed. But her sleep had been better, if not every night.

Tonight was one of the bad nights.

The zlyzen—always the zlyzen. Only this time they weren't after her: It was Vargo they tormented, circling around him like a living Uniat, their claws clicking, their joints bending the wrong way. Ren tried to reach out—

—and came bolt awake as Clever Natalya landed on her head.

She convulsed and sent the cat flying with a yowl of indignation. Ren sat up, swearing, wondering what in Ninat's hell had possessed Natalya to attack her like that. In the moonlight coming through her window, she could just make out the darker shadow of the kitten leaping back atop the bed and rising onto her hind paws to bat at something on the curtains.

Something *climbing* the bedcurtains, scuttling upward for dear life.

Ren had no Mask-damned clue what Peabody was doing in

her bedroom at this hour. With her heart still pounding and her thoughts muddled by the nightmare, she lurched to her feet just in time to stop Natalya from scaling the curtains after him. Peabody took refuge on her shoulder and Ren stumbled to the floor, trying to remember where she'd hidden that cloth numinat.

By the time she had it out and assembled, the heat of surprise had chilled to fear. No, Vargo wasn't here. Which, she presumed, was why Peabody had jumped onto her head: perhaps in a futile attempt to wake her, or in a reckless bid to lure Clever Natalya into doing it for him.

She slung the kitten into the sitting room and closed the door. As it clicked shut—

::—realm of mind, but something's gone wrong. He can't talk to me across the boundary. I can only tell that he's terrified, and it isn't just the ash—though that's bad enough—things seemed like they were going as well as they could, but then suddenly—::

"Alsius!" With an effort, Ren dragged her voice down to a murmur, and thanked the Faces that she still lived on the guest side of the manor, without anyone in the neighboring rooms. "Start at the beginning."

The tiny lump of the peacock spider quivered in the numinat. ::Vargo didn't want you to have to take ash again, so he's retrieving the pendant for you. Only he's not back—something bad has happened.::

Ren sat down hard on the floor. *Retrieving the pendant.* Masks have mercy—was that Vargo being altruistic? Or was it the medallion's corrupting power, luring him in? She didn't know, and it almost didn't matter; bad enough that Vargo might have it now.

But even *that* wouldn't matter if he was caught in the dream. A nightmare he'd gone into for her sake.

::Please, you must help him—::

"Of course I will." Ren shoved herself back to her feet, looking around her room. What did she need? Clothing. The Black Rose's mask. Her pattern deck. The portable cosmetics kit she'd started carrying after that drunken afternoon. She scribbled a quick note to Tanaquis; she could wake Tess on her way out, get her to take it to

Whitesail. Hopefully Tanaquis had Iridet's ash samples by now, or could get them.

At the last moment, she thought to shake Alsius off the cloth numinat, unpin it, and fold it into her pocket. He leapt onto her arm and scurried up to her shoulder, silenced now—but this way he'd be able to instruct her when she got to the Praeteri temple.

Outside, the cool night air shocked her the rest of the way awake. Praying she wasn't too late, Ren set off for the Old Island at a run.

Temple of the Illius Praeteri, Old Island: Canilun 14

The temple was eerily silent. Ren hadn't liked the place when she came here for her initiation—not when she was blindfolded, not when they told her it had been used by Kaius Rex, and especially not when Diomen put her in the rage numinat.

But she liked it even less now, with a figure chalked onto its floor that she remembered all too well from the confrontation in the Great Amphitheatre.

The only sign of Vargo was a tiny vial and cork discarded on the floor, bearing the faint, sickly traces of ash. She would recognize that poisoned iridescence anywhere. Ren forced herself to pick it up, but back when Breccone Indestris had been selling the excess on the streets, it had only been distributed in single doses. Vargo hadn't left any for her to use.

Which meant waiting for Tanaquis. How long would it take Tess to reach Whitesail? How long to rouse Tanaquis, and for her to get herself to the Old Island? Ren paced restlessly around the numinat, thankful that at least this time it hadn't been painted in dreamweaver blood, that it wasn't glowing and trying to shred the world.

Peabody leapt from her shoulder and did an agitated dance on the floor. Ren guiltily dug the cloth out and reassembled it.

::It's getting worse. Don't you understand—he's on *ash*. It subjects you to all your worst imaginings. For a man like him—::

Ren shared far too many of Vargo's unpleasant experiences not to understand. "Is he being hurt, physically?"

Alsius twitched. ::I—I don't think so. But—::

"That's enough for now." As long as the zlyzen hadn't found him yet, weren't tearing into him the way they'd torn into Leato. As long as Ren could get to Vargo before they did. She didn't know where the zlyzen had gone after they turned on Gammer Lindworm; perhaps they always lurked in Ažerais's Dream, monsters of Vraszenian legend that children feared and adults pretended not to. Ondrakja had leashed that threat, but Ren had cut those ties and the zlyzen had vanished. If Alsius didn't sense Vargo being injured, she could cling to the hope that they hadn't returned.

Alsius leapt toward her, then scuttled back into the numinat, where he hunched miserably. ::I think he's sick. Alta Renata— Ren—*please*. Your people call the realm of mind Ažerais's Dream. You yourself have some kind of connection to it. Isn't there anything you can do?::

"I don't have—" she began helplessly, but the protest died on her lips. *Ash.* She didn't have ash . . . but she could try something else.

::Where are you going?::

If Alsius said anything after that, then she must have passed out of the range where she could hear him. Ren darted into one of the side chambers and fumbled until she found the cover for the lightstone sconce and pulled it open. Yes, she'd chosen the correct room. This was where the celebratory feast had been laid, with its cabinets and supplies—

Including a small bottle of aža. For the first time in her life, Ren had reason to be grateful to Sureggio Extaquium and his appetites.

::Yes!:: Alsius said as she returned. ::Wait—will that do it?::

"Maybe," Ren said, measuring a small dose of aža into her palm. Ordinarily one put it into wine or some other drink, but she didn't want to waste time. She tipped the shimmering powder straight into her mouth and choked it down.

Aža only let one see into the dream, not touch it bodily. But there was the numinat, and she was conceived on the Great Dream.

Perhaps those two together would be enough. "Where should I stand?"

::Do you see where the spiral meets the edge of the circle? Start there—wait! Take me with you!::

Ren looked dubiously at the spider. She understood his desire to help, but even so . . . "Have you taken aža in that form? I wouldn't know how much to give you."

All eight legs curled in frustration. ::That's exactly what Vargo said!::

"Then maybe he was right."

But her mind whispered, *How would you feel if it were Tess in danger, or Sedge?*

That didn't make dosing Peabody a good idea. Instead she said, "You're his anchor, Alsius. In mind as well as body. He needs you here, unaffected. What would happen to him if you went off into your own dreams?"

:: . . . You're right, though may the Lumen burn you for it.::

No further arguments. Ren went to the place he'd indicated, took a deep breath, and began walking the spiral.

Nothing happened.

"Is it still active?"

::Yes. Aža must not be enough. Curse it! Where's that damned Fienola woman?::

Before Ren could reply, the world around her began to change.

Beneath her feet, the floor rippled like the surface of a pond. In that surface she saw a reflection—but of course when she looked up, she saw nothing but the arched stone of the temple. It was as if the floor were reflecting something much farther away, in both distance and time.

The labyrinth that had once been carved into the surface of the Point.

The path of it wound around her, a looping, serpentine curve, glowing faintly to Ren's aža-spun sight. When she crouched, though, she felt nothing but stone beneath her fingers.

::What is it?:: Alsius demanded. ::What do you see? Oh, why couldn't you lay this cloth closer to the numinat!::

Ren stepped outside the chalked lines and dragged the fabric over, even though it wouldn't do any practical good. "The aža's showing me something. A labyrinth. I'm going to walk it."

::A labyr—What, *in* the numinat?:: Despite his worry, a familiar speculative note entered Alsius's voice. ::I've always wondered about those. Whether they might not be some folk version of numinatria, like the old Ganllechyn stitch-witches. Might it lead you to Vargo?::

Until Tanaquis arrived, trying was Ren's only option. "If this works, I don't know how long I'll be gone. Should I leave the cloth out? I don't know if you'll be able to use it to talk to Tanaquis, or if you'll want to."

He fretted for a moment with his two front limbs. ::No, I suspect it won't work. We have theories about that line between—Oh, that doesn't matter right now. It will only make her wonder. Put it away. We'll be able to talk without it once you return with Vargo.::

Ren was grateful for his determined certainty. Even without ash, she was going into something unknown, and probably dangerous.

Assuming this even worked.

He skittered off the cloth, and she unpinned it and tucked it away. Then, with a silent prayer to the Faces and the Masks—and to Ažerais herself—Ren began to walk the labyrinth's path.

Inward and outward, sweeping close to the center, then spiraling away again. She fixed her gaze on the radiant line ahead of her, thinking about Vargo. About the connection between them. A silvery thread that Vargo himself had spun when he rescued her spirit, and Ren had strengthened when he collapsed in the battle.

One final turn, and the path brought her to the center, where in an ordinary labyrinth there would have been a bowl of purifying water.

She lifted her gaze, and found someone kneeling in front of her.

The Aerie, Duskgate, Old Island: Canilun 15

The call for a general muster came while Grey was in the middle of requisitioning new dress vigils, replacing the ones "unavoidably destroyed" the night of the Traementis ball.

Trying, at least. Cauvis had been an immovable rock long before the Tricat medallion started infecting Nadežra. "We'll continue this later," Grey told the quartermaster on his way out of his office. "Or perhaps Commander Cercel will speak to you instead."

The threat didn't make a dent in Cauvis's resolve. "I'll tell her what I told you. New formal uniforms are issued in Apilun. You'll have to wait until then."

Grey left before he strangled someone. Cauvis. Himself. The former would be a pleasure, but the latter might be a greater relief from the building tension.

In the days since Cercel rescued Grey, nothing had come down from High Commander Dimiterro's office—not a reprimand, not even an inquiry. Cercel tried to wave it off by saying Ghiscolo must have realized he overstepped the bounds of his office, but Grey doubted she believed that any more than he did.

The main hall of the Aerie was still filling as Grey found Cercel's section in the crowd. The other captains under her were already there with their lieutenants and constables, including Grey's own people.

"What's going on?" Grey murmured to Ranieri. Many of the faces throughout the room reflected his confusion.

Not the commanders, though. Every one of them wore the stoic mask of those following orders whether they liked them or not.

Cercel overheard him. Her jaw was set so hard, he feared she would crack a tooth. "The high commander will tell you soon enough, Serrado."

When everyone had assembled, Dimiterro descended to the staircase landing, from which he could survey the whole room. He waited until absolute silence had fallen; then his voice boomed out.

"Men and women of the Vigil. In the last year, Nadežra has seen all too much upheaval. Not just the usual crimes and disturbances, but actions from an organized group of malcontents, who will be satisfied with nothing less than the overthrow of the Cinquerat itself. They have raided our prisons, attacked our nobles, and even attempted to bomb the Great Amphitheatre."

The Anduske, then. New instructions for how the Vigil was

to deal with them? The influence of the Sessat medallion seemed to have overtaken Ghiscolo quite rapidly, hardening his easygoing manner into a relentless impulse toward order.

I should have gone after him when I had the chance.

Grey's hands, linked behind his back, balled into fists. But whether it was Ghiscolo he wanted to strike or the phantom in his own mind, he couldn't say.

Dimiterro was elaborating on the villainy of the Anduske and the importance of stopping them. Right on schedule, he pivoted to his new point—but the instructions weren't what Grey expected.

"In order to deal with this threat," Dimiterro said, "His Mercy Ghiscolo Acrenix formed a new organization, the Ordo Apis. But they are a small group, and cannot address the problem all on their own. Because of this, their charter has been amended. Effective immediately, they have the right to commandeer and direct Vigil resources, whether those be weapons, information, or personnel. If you receive orders from a member of that group, you are to obey them quickly, eagerly, and to the best of your ability."

Grey's stomach dropped. Dimiterro didn't look in his direction, but he felt the weight of that attention all the same, and he saw the invisible hand that moved the high commander. Cercel had pointed out the boundary Ghiscolo was crossing...so Ghiscolo had redrawn the map.

This is what they do. Nadežra will never be free as long as they wield the Tyrant's power. Anger burned through Grey with all the pain of the curse that had trapped him, of the numinat the stingers had used against him, of the memories and fears and depths of despair he'd been forced to relive. There was no line between the Rook's fury and his own.

He wasn't the only one reacting. The hall filled with murmurs of discontent, and a few of Grey's fellow captains even raised their voices in protest above the silence of their commanders. Too few, though. In the faces around him, Grey saw shock—but the sort of shock that would ebb into reluctant compliance. Although the stingers weren't a part of them, the order had come from above; it would be obeyed.

Before he realized he was moving, Grey slammed his fist down on a nearby desk, the sharp sound echoing through the open hall, and stepped into the empty space under Dimiterro's landing.

"Becoming a hawk was never easy for me." Grey spoke loudly over the grumbling of his fellows. "Not as a constable, and not as I worked my way up to captain. But I took that as a challenge to work harder—because I believe that the Vigil has a purpose. To serve the people of Nadežra."

His gaze swept the room, catching the eyes of constables, lieutenants, captains. Commander Cercel. "Last Epytny, the stingers took me during my patrol and tortured me for information I didn't have. They *spit* on our purpose. And handing the Vigil over to them spits on every person who wears our emblem. So as long as this order stands, I *won't* wear it."

In one swift move, Grey shed his hawk-marked coat, then laid it gently over the nearest desk, making certain the collar with his captain's hexagram pin was on the topmost fold.

Dimiterro's voice cracked like a whip. "*Captain* Serrado. If you think you can walk away from your duties and come back to them whenever you like, you are very much mistaken."

"And if you think I'm going to bend my head while you gut what the Vigil should stand for, *you're* the one who's mistaken." The fury surged, but Grey forced his voice to remain clear and hard. "Caerulet may have the authority to create his secret police, and he may have the authority to tie the hawks to their wrists. But I'm not going to help him."

"Neither am I!"

Ranieri's voice cut through the room, high with tension. Grey pivoted and saw him removing his coat. "I was there when the stingers took Captain Serrado. They had him tied to a chair inside a torture numinat. That *isn't right.*"

Pavlin's coat joined Grey's. Dverli's and Tarknias's followed, and even Levinci laid his down, his shoulders hunched against the glares of his fellows.

"Guess we know our friends from our enemies now," Ecchino

said, mild enough to mask the threat under his tone, but loud enough to be heard.

"This isn't about friendship," Levinci said. "It's about keeping cuckoos out of our nest."

"No." Cercel stepped forward, shrugging her coat off. Her hand trembled as she set it atop the growing pile, but her expression remained resolute. "It's about holding the Vigil to a higher standard, instead of letting it be dragged down into Cinquerat politics."

Her words were a sluice gate, opening the way for the flood. Those removing their coats were still a minority, and in some cases their friends grabbed at the fabric, trying to argue them out of it...but Grey's unit was no longer the only one with defections. Although Mettore's corruption and Ghiscolo's brutality had wormed deeply into the Vigil, not everyone was tainted. He even saw two other captains quitting, Atsarin and Calivaris. Both of them Cercel's people.

Dimiterro didn't hurl threats or try to stop the rush. He just waited until the last coat hit the floor, then spoke in a voice ugly with rage. "Get out. Get the *fuck* out of my sight. You're spineless traitors, the lot of you."

Far from spineless. It took courage for them all to walk out of the Aerie, past their former fellows who snarled curses or even spat on them as they went. Then they were outside in the plaza, breathing the chill air of fall, and Grey tried not to shake as he looked around and saw what he had done.

Unsurprisingly, it wasn't him the defectors flocked to. He might have started it, but he was still Vraszenian, and only a captain. Cercel was the one swarmed with questions, ex-hawks demanding to know what now. They seemed to think this was a simple protest, leverage to make something change—that after the problem was fixed, they would go back.

Maybe they would. But he wasn't going to.

The huddle around Grey was smaller. Levinci departed immediately, arms wrapped around himself as though he already regretted shedding his coat. Grey sent the rest home with a promise to call on them tomorrow. He might have set aside his command, but they were still his people.

When Pavlin would have followed, Grey stopped him. "Are you and Tess back together?" He should get a message to Ren, but Grey Serrado, formerly captain, didn't have any reason to notify Alta Renata of his change in circumstances. Showing up at Traementis Manor in his shirtsleeves would only invite gossip.

And doing it in the hood might invite problems.

"I—I don't know if we're *together*, but—" Pavlin glanced up at the looming bulk of the Aerie and grimaced. "She was making me a new patrol coat, better tailored. I guess there's no point now."

Perfect. Grey wouldn't have to come up with a reason to send Pavlin. "Go to her. Nothing else you can do here, and if she passes the news to her mistress, Alta Renata might be inclined to offer her support."

Pavlin saluted by reflex, then stopped, wincing. Grey clapped him on the shoulder and offered him a weary grin. "No formalities, Pavlin. We're past that now."

His former constable nodded and ran off, and Grey turned to find Cercel approaching. The word popped out of his mouth before he could stop it: "Commander."

Her own grin was wry. "Not anymore, thanks to you. No, don't apologize—you did the right thing. I've tried to push back against the problems in the Vigil, but..."

There was no need to finish that sentence. They both knew how little one person could do.

Cercel shook herself, as if casting off an unwanted cloak. "Join me for a drink?"

"I'd be honored, Meda Cercel."

The use of her gentry title made her snort. "Call me Agniet. Come on; I know a good place in Suncross."

Temple of the Illius Praeteri, Ažerais's Dream

For half an instant, Ren's heart leapt—but the figure in front of her wasn't Vargo.

It was a Vraszenian woman, a szorsa, her hair woven into a crown with thinner braids cascading from it like water. She knelt in front of Ren, shuffling her cards, while all around her stretched the lines of a numinat.

Not the one Tanaquis and Vargo had inscribed. Something different, with boxes marked for secondary foci, connected by radiating lines to the center and the containing circle. Where the szorsa knelt was the central focus.

Ren glanced down and saw she was still dressed in Renata's clothing, presumably with Renata's makeup on her face. Ignoring that, she spoke in Vraszenian. "For interrupting I beg your pardon, szorsa. I seek someone. Can you help me?"

The szorsa startled, blinking up at Ren as though *she* were the apparition. Her clothing was strange: her blouse buttoned at both shoulders, a style Ren had only seen in plays meant to depict Vraszenian history, and its high collar was embroidered in the colors of all the clans. "I knew not that any Seterins spoke our tongue, or followed our Lady's path. Should you not be flying off into your Lumen?"

Ren grimaced. "What you see is a mask. I am—" Her tongue stuck for a moment, thinking of all the time she'd spent masquerading to Alinka, to Idusza, passing herself off as something she wasn't. But this szorsa didn't need to know her tangled history. "Vraszenian. And not dead...I hope."

"You walk the dream waking. Is it that time again already?" The woman glanced up at a sky of stone lit by flickers of phosphor and ripples of sourceless light. "No, our Lady still sleeps. What brings you here? If kin you seek in the dream, it is the kanina you should be dancing."

Her frown was kind, like a mother scolding her child. Softly, she added, "You would not wish for your čekani and dlakani to be trapped here."

The other two parts of Ren's soul. She swallowed and said, "Not kin, but a friend. I cannot leave him. For my sake he came here—in the flesh, as I have done. I thought to find him here. This figure you sit in—know you what it is?"

The szorsa glanced at it and shuddered. "An echo of the past that is yet to be. Something to the dream has come that, like pattern, sees past, present, and future."

Tricat. One of Tanaquis's first observations about the connection between numinatria and pattern had been that the three rows of a full pattern echoed Tricat's association with time.

"You seek guidance." The szorsa's voice prodded her from her thoughts. The phrase was as old as Vraszan—one Ren knew well.

She dug in her pocket and found a decira. The szorsa's offering bowl sat in front of her knees, catching the reflected light from above; Ren knelt and placed the coin in the half for the Face, Ir Entrelke. "May I see the Face and not the Mask."

The shuffling of cards and murmuring of prayers followed, a gentle and familiar lullaby. But instead of the three-card line Ren expected, or even a nine-card spread, the szorsa began dealing her cards in an unfamiliar pattern: six in a circle, with a seventh at the center.

"What is this layout?" Ren asked.

The szorsa's fingers paused on the first card, at the base of the circle. "You have never before seen a wheel?" She clicked her tongue. "Rarely is it used, since the clan cards fell out of favor...but it is the best guide for understanding your place in the world. Other patterns are paths or tapestries. The wheel represents the wagon that carries you. See."

She turned it over. Sisters Victorious: the card of courage. "The position of the Horse reveals what you have, and who stands beside you," she said. "For your sake your friend came here; for his sake you follow him. Both of you are brave, and this courage you will need to face what lies ahead."

Ren tucked her legs tailor-style under herself and leaned forward. The last time a szorsa had patterned her, it was a woman working for Vargo at the Talon and Trick, with no discernible gift. Who was this stranger, reading for her now—other than the spirit of a szorsa long dead and gone?

The szorsa's hand moved sunwise to the next card. "The Rat position shows what stands in your way, and who stands against you."

Ah—one card for each clan. First the Meszaros; now the Stretsko, with The Mask of Ashes. The szorsa said, "You seek more than your friend—but what you seek is a danger to you. A thing your enemies have also. A source of destruction, tearing things apart."

Like the zlyzen had torn Leato apart, and Vargo during the battle at the amphitheatre. Charred and blackened wood showed through the mask's grey surface, calling to mind her nightmares. Ren shivered.

The card for the Anoškin was Jump at the Sun. A leap of faith. "The Owl for the wisdom you must remember. Without risk, there is no gain. When the time comes, you must do the thing you fear, the thing you believe you cannot."

Story of my life, Ren thought with mordant humor.

Most of the myths about Ažerais's children said they were born in pairs of twins, meaning Varadi came next. "The Spider for the question you must ask."

Ren had wondered before if Vargo had Varadi blood. From what she knew of his past, even he couldn't say for sure; she had the impression he'd acquired Peabody—the original Peabody—as a kind of talisman. Would the unanswered question be about Vargo himself?

Warp and Weft said otherwise. For the first time, the szorsa lifted her eyes from the cards and met Ren's gaze steadily. "The card of union. You know what it will mean, if you take back what you seek. Some threads bind us to those we love; others bind us to danger and harm. Are you prepared for what this joining brings?"

The medallion. Ren had kept her thoughts so firmly on the need to retrieve Tricat, she hadn't let herself think about how that would link her to it again. Would she be forced to bear Tricat until the Rook was ready to destroy it? How long would that be? What would it do to her in the meanwhile—and to the Traementis?

Ren's whisper came out dry and uncertain. "I am. I—I must be."

Any good pattern-reader knew to move along before a client could spiral too deeply into their own thoughts. "The Fox for the reward you earn," the szorsa said with an enigmatic chuckle. The card revealed for the Dvornik was The Face of Roses, beautiful overlapping petals and vivid green eyes. "If the poison is drawn out, the wound can heal."

Her pleasant expression dropped, and her hands trembled. "You know what the poison is."

The Mask of Worms. She'd seen that card in the Rook's pattern, and its Face counterpart in Vargo's. The corrupting power of Kaius Rex's broken chain of office had woven itself throughout Nadežra— but there was a chance to cut it from her city's flesh.

So far, the wheel layout had gone in alternating moods, the good cards preceding the bad. Next would be the Kiraly, and Ren wasn't surprised when the szorsa said, "The Raccoon for the risk you take."

Ren associated The Mask of Chaos with Mettore Indestor, the Caerulet who ought to have stood for law and justice, but instead sparked a riot on the Lower Bank. Ghiscolo now held his seat—and he'd used it to create the Ordo Apis, to target the Anduske, frame Vargo, and torture Grey. But that card, when in the "good" position in a nine-card spread, could also mean the necessity of stepping outside the system. Could that work here, or did it have to be interpreted according to its negative aspect?

The szorsa watched her with a knowing smile. "Try not to see too much for yourself. Only remember this: Not all may suffer the consequences they should. Sometimes the price for justice would be too high."

Only the central card remained. Ižranyi, Ažerais's youngest child, born without a twin. Paradoxically, it was Orin and Orasz: the twin moons sometimes said to be Ažerais's lovers, from whom she bore all her children. The card of duality.

"The Dreamweaver for the hub on which all else turns," the szorsa murmured. "You sit before me with a Seterin face and a

Vraszenian voice. But you are in Ažerais's Dream: Which of you can help your lost friend?"

For all that Tanaquis and Vargo called this the realm of mind, to Ren it was a profoundly Vraszenian place. It would not be Alta Renata who rescued Vargo, but Arenza Lenskaya.

She half expected to change on the spot. Her clothing remained Seterin, though, and her face felt no different. The szorsa didn't seem to be waiting for any shift; she swept up her cards and returned them to her deck, whispering the prayer of thanks.

Ren put two more coins in the bowl, one for the Face, one for the Mask. "Thank you—I know your name not."

The woman's hands tightened around her deck. Not looking up, she said, "I am called Zevriz."

It hit like a slap. Zevriz: the non-name given to those who were completely outcast, cut off forever from Vraszenian society. They weren't even supposed to receive food or drink from anyone. Remembering her offerings, Ren glanced at the bowl...and found it empty.

What did you do, *to be cursed like this?* But she couldn't voice that question. Instead she touched her heart and said, "I thank you. And..." What could she say to someone condemned to namelessness? "May you find peace."

The szorsa made no reply. Ren looked around, thinking of where she had dropped the medallion. Was that where she would find Vargo? A leap of faith: Maybe this was it. Upward, through the stone—

And the dream allowed her to leap.

The Great Amphitheatre, Ažerais's Dream

Chills wracked Vargo, an endless shiver he couldn't control. Shit fucking pisspot *hell.* Last time he'd taken ash, it plunged him into a plague street, leaving him swimming in dead and dying bodies leaking disease from every orifice. Like the house he'd been rescued from as a child, when yet another pestilence swept the Lower Bank. Vargo would have happily dived into the West Channel to get clean.

This time, the ash didn't fuck around. Vargo was sick. And that wasn't even the worst of his problems.

"Look—" He choked on the word, pressing fingers against the swelling nodes on either side of his neck as though that would relieve the pain. He imagined them popping, sending pus oozing down his throat. Another shiver coursed through him.

"Look," he tried again. "This is pointless. I'm not moving, and you're not getting in, so you might as well give up and go terrorize someone else."

The zlyzen circling the sloppy protective circle around him hissed, black tongues curling over serrated teeth and flicking against the invisible barrier of the numinat. Vargo shrank into an even tighter ball and wished for a red thread. Or even red chalk. The zlyzen were held back for now, but the hasty circle and overlapped triangles forming Sessat were too crude to last long, and he'd had to use Zavn for a focus because his bag had swallowed all of the more relevant chops.

"I'm not even sure you're real." He was sure. As real as the illness eating away at the edges of his composure. Ash made it real.

Just give them the fucking pendant. Its weight was heavy in his pocket. He curled his fist around it, sure beyond rationality that was what the zlyzen wanted. Unsure what they would do once they got it.

But he wasn't giving up yet. It would be pointless to go through all this nonsense *and* die without succeeding. His circle was shoddy, but it would hold a little while longer. Long enough for him to come up with a plan for how to get past the zlyzen to the foot of the path—if the sickness didn't kill him first.

The glowing fog around the wellspring swirled. Fucking Mettore Indestor, trying to destroy that thing. If he hadn't done that, Vargo never would have gotten shredded by the zlyzen, and Ren wouldn't have dropped the—

He mumbled a curse as the fog vomited out a new figure. "Great, another fucking nightmare."

But his vision of Ren wasn't some horror-twisted parody. She was herself—well, her fake Seterin self—and she recoiled at the sight of the zlyzen, who turned to face her in a shuddering wave.

Shit. She was *real*.

Vargo was on his feet before he knew it. Standing made his head spin and his stomach roil, but he managed to rasp, "Get out. I'll throw you the pendant and then try to draw them off." He was in no shape for a chase, but he might buy her a little time.

"And get torn to pieces?" Ren edged away from the prowling zlyzen, but her gaze was on him, and incredulous. "No. One friend already I have lost to these monsters. I will not lose another."

Friend. The word made his head swim and his body sway, closer to the edge of his protecting circle. The nearest creatures crouched, their bodies low and backward-bent limbs bunching like cats preparing to pounce.

She already blamed herself for Leato's death. Vargo was still hoping not to add to that weight, but— "I think getting the pendant out of here is a little more important, don't you?"

"No."

His question had been rhetorical. Her answer wasn't. Ren had told him many truths these past few weeks, some unpleasant, some outrageous...but none as honest as that.

She stared at him across the ravenous sea of zlyzen, and there was no uncertainty in her. She'd risked entering the dream to save him—not the medallion, but *him*.

He'd come all this way to right the balance between them, to make up for what he'd done. For sending her into the Night of Hells. Her coming to rescue *him* would only tip the scales back the other way.

In his mind, maybe. But not in hers. He saw that with the same preternatural clarity that told him the zlyzen wanted—

Vargo's mouth went dry. In a dead whisper, he said, "Ren—*run*."

She didn't move. "What?"

"The zlyzen..." They still held him trapped, but apart from the nearest few, their attention wasn't on him.

It was on her.

The whisper rose to a strangled yell. "It's you they want! They've been waiting—like they knew you'd come back!"

The zlyzen spread out, circling around Ren. Stalking, but not attacking, and she faced them with a courage he couldn't begin to understand. Her evasions brought her drifting toward Vargo, near enough for him to hear the murmur on her lips: "*Leap of faith.*"

"What?"

Ren pivoted to face him. "Vargo. Do you trust me?"

Trust is the thread that binds us . . . and the rope that hangs us.

"Yes," Vargo said.

She was close now. Ren held out her hand. He leapt from the safety of his numinat to take it—

And the dream changed around him.

The Labyrinth of Nadežra, Ažerais's Dream

The walls of Kaius Rex's amphitheatre crumbled to the ground, leaving fragments that reshaped themselves into pillars bearing sculpted, stylized heads. Not the painted clay shapes Ren was used to from her childhood, but beautiful works of art, some enameled, some gilt, others carved from rare and colorful woods. On one side of each pillar, jeweled eyes glimmered like stars; on the other side, the empty holes of a mask stared unblinking.

And across the ground spread a wide, inlaid path, the largest labyrinth Ren had ever seen.

She hadn't been sure what change to expect. For months the zlyzen had been haunting her nightmares, and she'd done everything she could to keep them out. When Vargo said it was her the zlyzen wanted...it made sense.

But only in part. She still didn't know *why*.

So she'd asked the dream to show her.

And it brought her here. Still atop the Point, but instead of the Tyrant's monument, what surrounded them was the ancient temple he had destroyed, the labyrinth built to honor the Wellspring of Ažerais.

"What does it mean?" she whispered.

Vargo's hand was still in hers, damp and trembling. He looked like absolute hell, his skin sallow, his eyes bloodshot, and his voice was a croak as he said, "Think it means I better wait to puke, or I might offend your goddess."

The zlyzen were still there. Not pressing close, though, like they'd been in the amphitheatre; instead they paced beneath the colonnade, outside the open courtyard of the labyrinth's path.

Some of the tension drained from her. But the distance still didn't solve anything: She'd walked the labyrinth to enter the dream. To leave, she suspected she had to do as a worshipper would and cut straight across the sinuous lines, leaving any ill fortune behind her.

Walking straight into the ill fortune that waited outside, charred and wrong-jointed and baring its teeth.

"Can you tell what they want?" she murmured to him. It might be a bad idea to ask him to call on the medallion's insights, but under the circumstances... "Beyond just 'me,' I mean."

The shake of his head was as much a shiver as a denial. "Don't even know how I know that. Pretty certain it's the fever talking. But they haven't tried to eat you."

No, they hadn't. Just like they hadn't eaten Gammer Lindworm, until Ren turned them against her.

When Ondrakja was dying from Ren's poison, she'd killed a zlyzen and drunk its blood. Ren hadn't done anything like that... but she had, after a fashion, bound herself to them. To their knot. The blasphemous mimicry of friendship Gammer Lindworm had created, that Ren swore herself into so she could turn around and betray Ondrakja again.

She might have turned on her leader, but her link to the zlyzen remained, mottled purple like an old bruise. And she only had to look as far as Vargo to know that connections made in Ažerais's Dream were as real as the cords of a knot bracelet.

Did it offend them, being tied to a traitor? Had they been haunting her dreams because they wanted her to sever the connection?

When she gave the thread an experimental tug, the dream lurched around them and the zlyzen yowled like they were in pain.

"My fever says they don't want whatever that was." Vargo rested his brow on her shoulder as though he couldn't keep his head up any longer.

Ren drew her hand back from the line. *I guess not. But what, then?*

A Vraszenian curse ghosted from her lips. After she'd strengthened her connection to Vargo... she'd begun to hear his conversations with Alsius.

Her stomach turned over. *No.* She'd spent months doing everything she could to keep the zlyzen away. The last thing she wanted was to bind herself to them more firmly.

But... she had to find out what *they* wanted. They didn't seem capable of speech or writing; on the other hand, Ren believed there was a feral intelligence there, something more than the mind of a simple beast. Gammer Lindworm had talked to them like she could understand them, and they her.

She was also insane.

Ren glanced over her shoulder and found not the wellspring, but a beautiful alabaster bowl, wider than her arms could span, filled with cool, clear water. She dipped the fingers of her free hand in it and touched them to her brow, praying briefly.

Then she laid those same fingers on the zlyzen thread and willed it to grow.

The Labyrinth of Nadežra, Ažerais's Dream

Vargo shivered, fear pinning him like a bug on a card, as the thread leashing Ren to the zlyzen pulsed into visibility beneath her hand.

"Don't," he moaned, but too late. Ren stood motionless, her eyes unfocusing, the zlyzen going still.

He tore his gaze off her to look around. The numinat he'd inscribed was gone; instead there were knee-high markers of carved wood, polished and oiled to withstand the elements, springing up from moss-covered ground like pegs on a guziek board. All were topped with carvings: spiders and foxes, ghost owls and rats, horses and raccoons and dreamweaver birds.

Could he drag her out while the zlyzen were distracted? Whatever strength the ash had lent him was fading, his connection to Alsius so attenuated that he feared a strong word would snap it. And with the sickness swirling through him, pulsing from his head down to his gut and back up again . . .

"They want to communicate."

Ren's whisper was nearly inaudible. Vargo snatched at it like a lifeline. "What?" he croaked.

The thread had faded, but her hand still hovered in midair. Fear trembled at the edge of her mouth. "They want me . . . to see."

Fuck this. Vargo reached for his bag—if he had to, he could re-create the numinat that brought them here—only to realize he'd dropped it at some point after inscribing his protective circle. It was as lost as they were.

Shoving his hand into his pocket, he was relieved to find the cause of all this trouble still there. He tightened his fist around the pendant—

—and felt a tug, an urge to follow that was too strong to be natural.

He'd let go of Ren. He caught her wrist just as something seized hold and dragged them out of the dream.

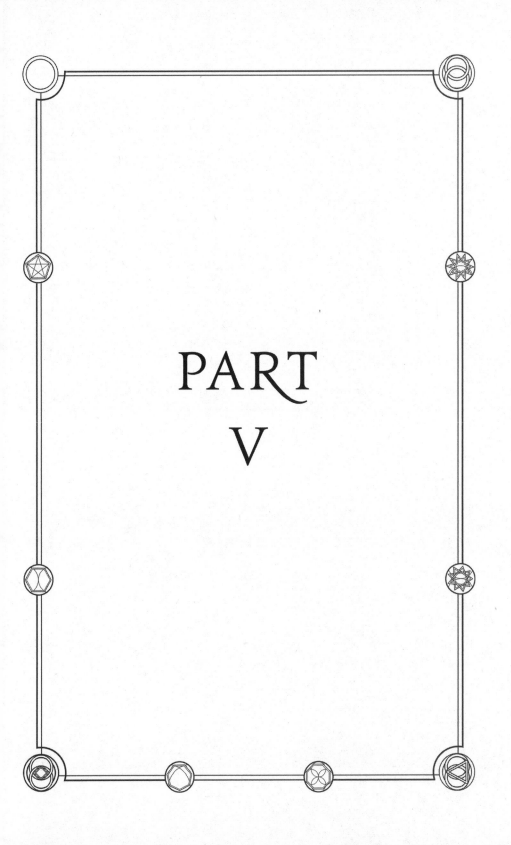

PART

V

21

The Mask of Nothing

Temple of the Illius Praeteri, Old Island: Canilun 15

::Be careful what you say—we aren't alone!::

Vargo staggered, Ren slamming into him hard enough they almost fell over. The numinat around them wasn't the one he and Tanaquis had inscribed. It was a simple Tricat, only large enough to hold the two of them, and underneath Vargo's feet was a plain focus of red glass.

A Praeteri numinat. And when he forced his gaze upward, he saw the worried countenance of Tanaquis...and the avid, delighted face of Diomen.

"It worked!" Tanaquis said, clapping her hands in relief and even cuffing Diomen on the shoulder. "Thank you, Pontifex."

::She brought him here to help—what Ren did ruined the numinat you used before—but I'm worried about what Tanaquis may have told him—::

Vargo swayed. He hadn't left the fever in the dream; he'd gone there in the flesh, and his flesh had carried that nightmare back with him. His head was spinning. Anytime he looked at Ren, his skull felt like a bell someone had just rung, and the disorientation of it made him lurch out of the numinat.

Alsius was easier to look at, as he scuttled up and hid in Vargo's coat. He only wanted Vargo to be safe. Diomen wanted to bring some grand plan to culmination. And Tanaquis...she wanted to reconcile the seemingly disparate parts of the cosmos, with a purity that was frankly daunting.

I know these things. How do I know these things? Like with the zlyzen. Vargo had just...looked. And known.

"Oh my. Did you repeat your zeal offering?" Tanaquis caught Vargo before he kissed the temple floor. His weight made them both stumble. "Come along. Let's get you home so you can call rest."

"This was foolish." Diomen's unblinking gaze was fixed on Ren. "Sister Renata, what could possibly possess you to take such a risk? People have been lost in the realm of mind before. I understand that a part of *you* was lost there, not long ago. Whatever you left behind at the time, it cannot be worth this peril."

She offered him an unsteady curtsy. When she spoke, it was in Renata's accent. "Pontifex, my apologies. I should not have attempted it."

Diomen bent to break the lines of the numinat, then stepped forward, looming over Ren. "You have not answered my question. Show me what was worth the risk to yourself. Show me, so that I may make it clear how little it matters, compared to you." His words sounded like a man in love; his tone held nothing that resembled affection.

Vargo wanted to cut out the man's tongue so he could never speak again. With Alsius nestled in his coat like a second heart, the thirst for long-delayed vengeance was nearly overwhelming. Ghiscolo might have been behind the attempt to murder Alsius, but Diomen had crafted that curse. Now here was the man himself. One strike with a knife and half their revenge would be complete. Vargo and Ren could figure out something to tell Tanaquis—*after* Diomen was dead.

::Vargo, don't. You're sick, and you're not thinking straight.::

Speaking felt like pushing words through a meat grinder, but he managed to rasp out, "Even if she wanted to, she can't. We were still trying to retrieve it when you pulled us out."

::You mean—all that for *nothing*?::

I'm lying, old man. Vargo kept his eyes on Ren. He wanted to scream. To run. To tear the clothes and then the flesh from his body, as if that would rid him of this fever. It was all he could do to hold himself together; selling the lie would be up to Ren.

She gazed steadily at Diomen. "Truly, Pontifex, I understand. I—I wanted to prove to myself that I was not afraid, after what I went through last year. Is that not the path of the Praeteri? We must master ourselves."

"The Gate of Fear is one of the Great Mysteries," he said in a forbidding voice. "You are not yet prepared for it."

Another curtsy. "As I have learned, Pontifex. In the future, I will seek your guidance before I try any such thing."

Somehow she turned that curtsy into a sidestep that got her past Diomen. Tanaquis said, "Right now, I think the only thing we should be seeking is a physician for Vargo. Renata, hopefully *your* report on your experiences will be more satisfactory than his tend to be."

If Diomen had tried to stop them, Vargo would have lost the internal battle not to kill him right there. But instead the Pontifex's gaze swept across the chamber, toward the numinat Vargo and Tanaquis had crafted. Lines that glittered like aža arced across it, tracing out the shape of a labyrinth.

"Go, then," he said, his expression unreadable. "I must clear that blasphemous mess away. And then, Sister Renata, you and I will speak again."

Old Island and Whitesail: Canilun 15

Renata waited until they were well away from the temple entrance and she was sure Diomen wasn't following before she said, "Tanaquis, please forgive us for lying, but the Pontifex..."

"Was behaving very strangely," Tanaquis agreed. "But if you were lying—does that mean you got your medallion back?"

Vargo gave a minute nod when Renata looked at him. His feverish gaze was full of questions, but Suncross wasn't the place to answer them.

"We did," Renata said. "And—forgive me—we need your help still. Vargo's the one who retrieved it. When he gives it back to me...I fear the same affliction that struck the whole Traementis register will strike him, too. Can you remove it, as you did for us?"

That brought them both stumbling to a halt. "The fuck?" Vargo rasped, while Tanaquis's mouth curved into a thoughtful frown.

Renata could almost see the gears spinning in triple time as Tanaquis thought. "Back to my house," Tanaquis said finally, with a decisive nod. "With a stop at an apothecary for some medicine."

There was no opportunity for conversation on the skiff ride to Whitesail. Vargo was too busy being sick over the rail, while Renata held on to make sure he didn't pitch over completely. Between retches, he mentally begged Alsius not to leave him alone, while Alsius perched on his shoulder, telling Vargo he wasn't going anywhere and not to be silly.

"Do you have your cards?" Tanaquis asked after they'd heaved Vargo over the threshold into her parlour. "Of course you do. Excellent. Draw—hmmm—three, while I see to this matter." She began tracing a numinat for the tonic she'd purchased on the way back.

The prayers were a calming litany in Ren's mind. Kiraly, Anoškin, Varadi, Dvornik, Meszaros, Stretsko, Ižranyi: all the Vraszenian ancestors invoked in the wheel that nameless szorsa had laid out. Who had that woman *been*?

When Tanaquis finished her work, Renata showed her the cards. "For where we stand, The Mask of Ashes—destruction. For our path, The Face of Balance, which is justice and order. And the destination is The Laughing Crow."

"Isn't that an ostretta?" Tanaquis said, frowning.

"It's the card of communication. I imagine the ostretta is named for it."

"Fascinating. I'll get to work."

Vargo had finished swallowing the contents of the tonic bottle. He lurched forward with a mumbled offer of help, but Tanaquis pushed him prone with minimal effort. "This is my third time—fitting, really. I'll go faster on my own."

Taking the three cards, Tanaquis disappeared up to her garret. Zlatsa appeared in her place; Renata scribbled a note on the back of some scrap paper Tanaquis had left in the parlour, then gave the maid instructions to take it to Traementis Manor, for Tess's hand only. Zlatsa mumbled some Vraszenian curses Renata could be presumed not to understand, wrapped herself in a shawl, and went out.

Leaving Ren alone with Vargo, whose eyes were now bright with stimulants as well as fever.

"Well, that plan went wrong at just about every stage." His voice sounded thin, as though he was fighting off a nervous laugh. Digging into his pocket, he pulled out the bronze medallion and set it on the table next to him with an ominous thunk. "Care to tell me what the fuck I blundered into?"

"You weren't supposed to," Ren said in a tired whisper, sinking down onto the floor next to him. Afternoon sunlight blazed through the windows; the whole morning had come and gone while they were in the dream. "That medallion... it used to belong to House Traementis. Letilia stole it when she left; it was among the jewels I took from her when Tess and I fled Ganllech. It's—well—cursed."

Alsius scuttled down Vargo's arm and was circling the medallion warily, rising and falling in sharp movements as though a fingerbreadth of extra height would give him better perspective. ::It makes no sense. I don't recognize this sigil at all. And... am I counting the number of sides correctly? *Eleven?*::

"There's a lot more that doesn't make sense. When I held it, I saw..." Vargo's hand hovered over the medallion, then withdrew. "You were going to take this curse on? Again?"

"Compared to letting it stay in the dream, or risking someone else being struck by it? Yes." She resisted the urge to wrap her arms around herself. It wouldn't help the chill inside, and it would only make Vargo wonder. *When I held it, I saw . . .* As Ren had seen, on the Night of Bells. Insights into the people around her, granted by the power of the medallion.

Before Vargo could say the obvious, she added, "I have no intention of keeping it. But destroying it will take some doing, and in the meanwhile, my own custody is the safest place for it."

::It's only bronze,:: Alsius said. ::Melting it shouldn't be difficult. Unless you're implying that whoever made it also imbued it for resilience?"

Vargo scowled at the medallion, with its odd, twisted triangles, joining up in ways that defied the normal logic of geometry. "What the hell is this thing? I feel as if it's operating like a Praeteri numinat, but it has a sigil. And why make something with eleven sides? Eleven's meaningless. Eleven is—"

She arrived there the same instant he did. "Beyond Illi."

Illius Praeteri.

Ren swallowed down a sick feeling. "I don't know how it was made, or where it came from. But that—that's a piece of Kaius Rex's chain of office."

The creaks of Tanaquis's footsteps above were the only sounds in the parlour. Carefully, Vargo scooped up Alsius and moved him away from the medallion.

"I didn't know when I lost it," Ren added, helplessly. "I thought it was an ordinary pendant. When I found out . . ."

"You started trying to get it back." Vargo dug around in his pockets until he found a handkerchief, then used it to mop the sweat from his face.

She didn't want to pile even more on him, and she didn't want to betray Grey's trust, either. But given their encounter with Diomen, their involvement with the Praeteri, and what Vargo had told her that day at the Charterhouse, there was one thing he *had* to know. "Ghiscolo has one as well. Or rather, I fear he has two now, Quinat and Sessat. What he did to you—he used a medallion to do it."

"I think this is the part where I say I'm going to be ill." Vargo meticulously folded his sweat-damp cloth. "But I've expelled everything there is to expel."

::Ghiscolo has one of these? *Two?*:: Alsius's mental voice was even more unsteady than Vargo's. ::Do you know how he came by it?::

Ren knew how to read the signs of lying on a human. She hadn't the faintest idea how to tell if Alsius already knew about this and was pretending otherwise. If he'd been his father's heir, in line to inherit the leadership of House Acrenix...

Then a tiny whisper of thought slipped out of him, as small and lost as a child's voice. ::Is this why my brother killed me?::

Vargo cradled Peabody to his chest, the other hand coming up to shield him as though that could protect Alsius from the realization. ::We don't know—::

::Quinat. Power. It makes sense. Nothing else ever did.::

Footsteps on the stairs warned of Tanaquis's return. Vargo's eyes flicked to the medallion sitting between them.

"It's my responsibility," Ren said softly. "I'll welcome your help in dealing with it, though."

Tanaquis entered before they could say more. "I'm all ready, except for one thing. Vargo, would you take off your shirt?"

"Not without an explanation or a drink," he said with a ghost of his usual dryness.

"The numinat on your chest that you showed me last year," Tanaquis said. "Renata told me it binds you to some kind of spirit. I need to study it to see if the effects of the medallion could bleed through to the spirit—and if so, whether it needs to be included in the cleansing."

Vargo didn't look in Renata's direction, but she heard Alsius sputtering. ::You told *Tanaquis* about me?::

::In fairness,:: Vargo thought back at him, ::I was Ren's enemy at the time.:: Out loud, he said, "I suspect it would be better to cleanse us both."

"Yes, but without a body—"

Sighing, Vargo extended his hand, Peabody balancing atop his palm. "His body is right here."

Tanaquis blinked. "Your spirit...is a spider."

"Something like that, yes. Can we get this done so I can go collapse in my own bed?"

She pursed her lips, then nodded. "But when you're feeling better, I have several questions I would *very* much like answered."

Don't we all, Ren thought, and followed them up the stairs.

Whitesail, Upper Bank: Canilun 15

With two previous rounds under her belt, Tanaquis went through the process even faster than Renata expected. The only variation was that she had Vargo place the medallion to serve as the focus, then had Renata remove it when everything was done.

For an instant before she picked it up, she wondered, *What if no one did?* At this moment, thanks to Tanaquis's work, nobody had a connection to the medallion. Could they simply get rid of it somehow?

Except that even moving it would mean someone touching it—she had no reason to think gloves or tongs would provide spiritual protection—and if it stayed on the floor of Tanaquis's workroom, it might end up in the hands of the maid, or a burglar, or it would default to Tanaquis's ownership by virtue of being in her house. Renata didn't understand the nature of the medallions enough to risk it.

Still, her hand trembled as she reclaimed it.

"May I see that?" Tanaquis asked as Renata's fingers closed around the bronze. "Only to see—I won't touch."

The Rook's caution twinged inside her. But with the medallion affecting her awareness, she knew that all Tanaquis wanted was to understand the harmony of the cosmic system. This was an unusual piece of it; of course she wanted to study it.

Tanaquis absently wiped chalk dust off onto her surcoat as she peered at the medallion, leaning from side to side to study the simple etching in the light. "Fascinating," she murmured, as Renata had known she would. "Are you aware of what this is?"

She could lie; Vargo, sitting on the floor with Alsius cradled in one hand, wouldn't call her on it. But the Rook hadn't succeeded yet in destroying any medallions. He might be right that he needed to start with Illi-zero, or that it would require the whole set...but it might also be that destruction required a greater understanding of numinatria than either of them had. "It's a piece from Kaius Rex's chain of office."

Tanaquis straightened abruptly. "That's a piece of Nadežran lore not many Seterins would know. Yes, you're right—see, there are marks on the sides, where it used to be joined to other pieces. I've read a great deal about his chain—or at least everything I believe has been written about it. But I meant the sigil in the center."

"I'm no inscriptor, and I never studied Enthaxn beyond what was required by my tutors," Renata said, in lieu of saying all she couldn't: that if Vargo and Alsius didn't recognize the sigil, she was hardly likely to; that if the Rook knew, he hadn't shared that knowledge.

Tanaquis dismissed her explanation. "That wouldn't have helped. This predates ancient Enthaxis and was anathema to its people. The faithful of the Ilumve were assiduous in destroying any records pertaining to it, casting that knowledge into the darkness to rot." At Renata's puzzled frown, she added, "Ilumve is the Enthaxn name for the Lumen."

::Ridiculous,:: Alsius muttered uneasily. ::She can't possibly mean that's—::

"Primordial." Vargo's voice caught on the word, and Renata didn't think it was due to any illness.

The Primordials: the nameless, demonic forces subdued by the gods, exiled to outside the bounds of reality. Their influence still bled through into the world, usually in small ways...but every so often, their power broke forth in stronger form.

Like when the entire Ižranyi clan died, leaving the city of Fiavla an empty, haunted ruin.

Oblivious to their reactions, Tanaquis kept talking, in her usual lecturing tone. "The eleven-sided figure gives it away. Eleven is the number of the Primordials, though whether that's literal or simply a way of saying 'beyond the gods we know' is a matter of some debate. There used to be sets of artifacts like these, channeling the power of a particular Primordial through the ten numina. The sigil marks this one as from a set dedicated to A'ash. They do have names, you know, even if they're mostly forgotten. A'ash is the Primordial of desire."

The medallion fell from Ren's hand.

Tanaquis glanced down at it, then up at Ren. *Renata. I have to be Renata.*

She clung to that thought like a rope. "It explains the curse," Tanaquis said, more slowly now, as if realizing that not everyone saw this as an exciting tidbit of history and mysticism. "A Primordial's power inevitably overwhelms anyone who draws upon it; artifacts of this sort were meant to limit that risk. Inasmuch as an uncontrollable, elemental force can be limited, that is. But even the artifacts carry their own risks. Lose one, and you'll eventually be destroyed by the same power you called on."

Warp and Weft. The question Ren had to ask herself. Was she ready for the consequences of joining herself to a Primordial artifact? She'd chosen without understanding... and now it was too late to take that decision back.

She could rid herself of it. Ask Tanaquis to remove the poison of the Primordial's influence a second time.

She wanted to, so badly that it felt like an unvoiced scream. This was the power she'd felt during the Night of Hells, the storm raging outside the Charterhouse. Not some twisted, Mask aspect of Ažerais. A *Primordial*. The thought of picking the medallion up off the floor again—tainting herself with the kind of power that had destroyed the Ižranyi, in Fiavla and throughout Vraszan—sinking herself into that mire, *knowing* what it was—

But her fears from before still stood. Who would have the medallion, if not Ren?

Her cards had promised there might be a chance to purge Nadežra of this poison at last. She had to trust that.

"—nata? *Ren.*" Vargo's hand on her shoulder startled her. He must have called her several times before resorting to hissing her real name. Tanaquis's expression was twisted into a familiar frown—the one she wore after someone made her realize a social misstep.

"I'm..." She touched his hand in thanks, but couldn't find it in herself to lie. She wasn't all right. She focused on Tanaquis instead, trying to contain her shaking. "If the records were destroyed, then how do you know about this?"

Tanaquis looked offended that someone would question her research. "The Lumen's light hasn't burned *all* writings on this topic. The Pontifex has an impressive collection."

"The *Pontifex*?" That burst from Renata and Vargo both.

The force of their reaction rocked Tanaquis back on her heels. "Yes, naturally. I assumed *you* at least knew, Vargo—you seemed familiar with eisar."

His fingers dug into Renata's shoulder, bruisingly hard. "What do you mean?"

"Eisar," she repeated, as if it were obvious. "That's why they affect the base emotions—desire, obsession, rage, and so forth. Because they're emanations of the Primordials. And what are Primordials, if not those emotions unchecked?"

Vargo's hand fell away, and Ren clapped her own to her mouth. *Every time I've been in a Praeteri numinat...*

She'd never seen Tanaquis look so disappointed. "I was afraid you would react like that. Honestly, people act as though the world will tear apart if you so much as *say* the word 'Primordial.' I'm not proposing to make their worship legal; that's far too dangerous. Only to understand what they are. They're a part of the cosmos, even if the gods have bound them beyond the Lumen. Yes, the raw power of a Primordial can be destructive—but that's why this research with the eisar is so promising! They bring just a tiny fragment of a Primordial's power through into the world, just as a focus brings a tiny bit of the Lumen's raw light. The Praeteri have been working with them for years with no ill effects."

No ill effects... except those Nadežra suffered. Ren felt even more sick.

Vargo echoed her thoughts. "No ill—" His shoulders jerked as though he was stopping himself from grabbing Tanaquis. "You have no idea what the other members have been using these foci for, do you?"

"I don't spend much time with the others outside of the rituals. Why waste my energies on petty numinatria when there are deeper mysteries to explore?"

He scraped his fingers through his hair as though he could dig the last few minutes out of his skull. "I am not *nearly* well enough to explain everything wrong with that question."

"You need to rest," Renata said. "And I—I need to think." It took all her will to bend down and pick up the bronze medallion, with its interlocking, twisted triangles. She'd touched it before and never felt anything; the crawling sense of *wrongness* she had now was entirely her imagination. It had to be.

When she straightened, some shred of her composure returned. Looking Tanaquis squarely in the eye, she said, "This must remain between us. Diomen can't be permitted to know that I have this medallion, nor any of the Praeteri."

::Especially my brother,:: Alsius added.

His reminder sparked another thought, dredged up from what felt like ten years ago. "And, Tanaquis—if you strike me from the Traementis register, will the others be cursed?"

"Strike? Why?"

Renata held up the medallion. "So this doesn't taint everyone else with its influence."

"That shouldn't be necessary," Tanaquis said crisply. "I can scribe a containment around your name."

Her certainty eased some of the tension—but not all of it. Nothing could remove the worm of doubt now crawling through Ren's mind. The medallion would fan her desires from sparks to flame. How could she trust herself? Was she trying to protect Giuna and the others because it was the right thing to do... or because Tricat was the numen of family?

It's the right thing to do. She had to cling to that.

Eastbridge, Upper Bank: Canilun 15

When Vargo arrived at his townhouse, Varuni took one look at him and flattened her lips. "I'll fetch your physician."

Grunting his thanks, Vargo dragged his ass upstairs and collapsed into bed.

::You should change,:: Alsius said. He'd slipped out of Vargo's collar and tucked himself into one of the gaps between the latticed joints of Vargo's headboard.

"Don't nag," Vargo groaned, but he obeyed, at least enough to shed boots, coat, waistcoat, and trousers and drape them over the back of his lounging couch. It wasn't until he was climbing back into bed that he realized Peabody had withdrawn far enough into his hole that not even his eyes could be seen.

I'm an ass.

::You're sick.::

Still an ass. Vargo had dealt with his panic by accepting the inevitability of his condition...but how could he expect Alsius to accept the revelations about Ghiscolo?

::It doesn't change anything. We knew he was behind the cursed cloak. Usurping my future as Eret Acrenix, taking this medallion—it's all the same.::

It wasn't the same. Alsius would readily have given up the heirship he never wanted; to him, that was a burden that only took time from his research.

The medallion would have been a different matter. Alsius believed in the radiance of the Lumen. If he'd known the nature of the medallion's power, he would have dedicated himself to destroying it—at least, Vargo *hoped* he would have. Perhaps that was why his father had never told him of its existence.

Vargo shivered. *Primordials.* He preferred to think about a mundane monster like Ghiscolo. That man might fuck up Nadežra with the Ordo Apis, but he couldn't annihilate thousands of people in the space of eleven days.

Except that Ghiscolo was also fucking up Nadežra with the Praeteri, and their eisar numinata.

Alsius had always told him eleven was a blasphemous number for inscriptors, though not why. Just tradition, superstition. That numinat in the Great Amphitheatre, the one for destroying the wellspring—had the figure enclosing it really been a decagon? Or if Vargo could have seen it from above, could have measured the angles, would it have come out to eleven sides instead?

His thoughts were weaving like a drunkard in the street. All Vargo wanted was to drown in the lethargy brought on by the medicines Tanaquis had poured into him. Instead he created a nest of bedding to prop himself at eye level with Alsius's hiding place. He was so still in his little cubby that Vargo wondered if the spider had fallen asleep. The ash-induced illness had to be affecting him, too. He hoped they'd both recover quickly, like they usually did.

Finally Alsius said, ::I suppose it doesn't matter.:: He edged forward far enough that the dim light caught the timid brushing of his forelimbs. ::Do you think my father was involved? With...my death?::

"No." That, at least, Vargo could be certain of. "He could have made Ghiscolo his heir at any time, or given him the medallion. Or both." Not without resistance from within the house, maybe— but if he could force people to do his bidding the way Ghiscolo had forced Vargo and Nikory, what resistance could stand against that?

Another shudder ran through Vargo. The worship of Primordials was banned everywhere he knew of, not because there was anything inherently wrong with fear or desire or pride, but because the power of those elemental forces inevitably overwhelmed whatever it touched. That was why the gods had bound the Primordials outside reality, to keep them from destroying the world. Only traces of that power seeped through, forming the impulses of the human heart.

And the fucking Praeteri were grabbing hold of those threads and *yanking*.

He had grabbed hold of those threads. Chasing after the secret of how to make eisar numinata. Crafting that focus with Sibiliat. Thinking that while the Praeteri might turn their knowledge to selfish, destructive ends, *he* could find a way to use them for good.

Closing his eyes, Vargo pulled the covers tighter against another bout of shivering.

::Do you think...do you think the taint kept his spirit from rejoining the Lumen?::

Vargo stifled a curse. He hated these sorts of esoteric questions at the best of times. For Alsius, numinatria was a spiritual practice as much as an intellectual one. For Vargo, it was just a tool.

But he couldn't leave Alsius without comfort. "Maybe your father had to take some extra time purifying his soul before passing to the next cycle, but... 'There is no shadow so deep, nor ignorance so embedded, nor sin so great that it cannot be revealed and redeemed in the Lumen's light.'"

A wan chuckle echoed through Vargo's head, and Peabody edged farther out of his hole. Black onyx eyes reflected the light like unshed tears. ::Listen to you, quoting Mirscellis at me.::

"You've quoted him to me often enough," Vargo grumbled. The dryness of his unbroken fever was making him uncomfortable in his skin. He sagged into his nest and twitched the covers into a hood, like a boy playing at being the Rook.

::I suppose I have.:: There was something wistful in Alsius's tone that Vargo preferred to leave packed away with all the rest of the thoughts he wasn't examining. After a moment, he said, ::You should rest until the physician comes. You look like hell.::

Feel like it, Vargo thought, sinking down farther and letting his eyes slide closed, but sleep had cocooned him tightly enough that he wasn't certain Alsius heard.

Kingfisher, Lower Bank: Canilun 15

After Cercel finally called quits to their drinking and bade Grey farewell, with a stern adjuration to visit her in the next few days, he made his slow and indirect way back to Kingfisher. The wind along the river ruffled his hair as he crossed the Sunset Bridge, standing it up in hanks. He reflexively thought that he'd need to get it cut soon—Vigil regulations—then remembered there was no point.

Dusk was settling over the city by the time he got home. Grey shut the door behind himself and stood for a time in the gloom. Enough of the beer had worn off for him to be paralyzed by the realization of what he'd done.

And the question of what he would do now. He couldn't make a living off his work as the Rook, much less support Alinka. Some of his predecessors had been thieves, seeing nothing wrong with stealing so long as it all came from the pockets and parlours of the nobility, but Grey couldn't bring himself to do that. He would need *some* kind of income, though. Cercel had, over his token objections, paid their joint tab; he'd walked over the bridge rather than taking a skiff, because the bridge didn't cost money. Even now, part of the reason he hadn't kindled a light was the awareness that all too soon, he'd have no coin for new candles or coal.

He made himself open the tinderbox and strike a light. Whatever his situation, sitting in the darkness wouldn't improve it.

I'll need to find some other occupation, he thought as he unbuckled his sword and laid it aside. That blade at least was his own—a gift from Ryvček, not Vigil issue—though after today he'd have no legal right to carry it. Unless his new occupation returned that right to him. The only skills he had were excellent swordsmanship, mediocre carpentry, and things that would get him arrested by his former comrades.

Not a mercenary company, though he suspected Cercel would arrange a place for him if he asked. That would just put him back under the command of someone who couldn't necessarily be trusted. Plenty of ex-hawks went on to manage prisons for Fulvet or work as private guards for noble houses, but the mere thought of the latter made his jaw tense with the Rook's rage. Even a house without a medallion, like Traementis, would still cause him too many problems.

That left being a duelist like Ryvček. At least there he could pick whom he fought for, maybe make a name for himself among the trade guilds and merchant families. Masks knew there were enough duels in Nadežra these days, though hopefully that would be less common once they managed to get Tricat out of the dream. His teacher would be only too happy to help.

He could even ask her tonight. Better that than sitting around in a house that felt far too empty.

Just as Grey went to blow out the candle, he heard a knock at the door.

A faint, uncertain one, as if the knuckles skittered across the wood rather than striking. He twitched the curtain aside to look out.

What is Renata *doing here?* Dressed in plain trousers and a skirted coat, but definitely made up as Seterin. Arenza was a common enough visitor, but never the Traementis alta. Grey drew himself into Captain Serrado's demeanor—*captain no more, though*—and opened the door. "Alta Renata. What brings you here at this hour? Not Traementis problems, I hope."

She came inside without a word. By the time he'd shut the door, the rigidity he'd glimpsed in her bearing had thrown off its cloak. Ren wasn't just tense; she was *terrified*.

"I looked for you at the Aerie," she said. In Renata's accent; then she shook her head, and the next words came out with Vraszenian pronunciation. "They took great pleasure in telling me you'd quit."

"Yes," Grey said cautiously. Was that what had her so on edge? No, it couldn't possibly be. "The stingers—" What point was there in keeping his own accent Nadežran? With Ren, he needed no masks. "But you came not for that. Ren, what happened?"

"I got Tricat back."

Grey steadied himself on the door frame as a flood of emotions—not all of them his own—threatened to knock him off his footing. Relief, worry, pride...but also anger and fear.

Fear like that which made Ren hug herself as if winter's bite was upon her. She had the Tricat medallion, with all the problems that went with it. He shoved down the Rook's suspicions—Why had she retrieved it without telling him? What did she want with it? Where was it now?—and searched for comforting words. He doubted she'd come to him for an interrogation.

"Will you sit?" he asked.

Like a badly manipulated puppet, Ren sat down in the chair he pulled out for her. Grey dragged his own close, but not quite touching. He couldn't tell whether it would be a comfort right now or not. The last time he'd seen her this badly rattled, it was when she'd laid his pattern and seen the darkness of his future. He'd risked touching her then, and it seemed to have helped. But her arms were still wrapped around her body, maybe just to hold herself together, maybe to ward him off.

She spoke without looking at him, her gaze fixed and blinking too rapidly. "We had a plan. Me, Tanaquis, Vargo. I was going to take ash and go into the dream after it."

Ash. Sickness rose in Grey's throat. For Ren to do that, after her experiences before—

But she'd said she was *going* to. "What happened?"

A brief sound rose from her. "Vargo went in before I could. To spare me from it. But he got stuck, so I went in, too—not with ash. There was a woman, a szorsa's szekani—" She shook her head. "We got it back from the zlyzen. Vargo did. Then he gave it to me."

The tight knot of unease unbound itself. But—zlyzen. Grey risked laying one hand on her arm. What he wanted to do was to fold her into his embrace, until his warmth drove away the cold shadows haunting her.

For a heartbeat Ren leaned into his touch; then she flinched away. "I'm sorry," Grey said, withdrawing.

The sound she made was nearly a cry. "I— Tanaquis had to uncurse Vargo, because he'd had the medallion. She saw Tricat. And she recognized..."

Her pupils were wide in the dim light, drowning in fear. "It's a Primordial. A'ash, the Primordial of desire. That's where the Tyrant's medallions get their power. What taints people—what taints *me*—it's—it's—"

Grey recoiled. Only the Rook's leash on his thoughts kept him from breaking as Ren was. A Primordial? If the zlyzen were a child's nightmare, then Primordials were the darkest fears of an entire people. Fiavla, the Ižranyi...A Primordial had consumed them both. At least Kaius Rex had been a man. Primordials were beyond understanding or control.

Except. If what Ren said was true, the two were intertwined through the medallions.

You're not tainted, Grey wanted to tell her. But he knew that for a lie, more than anyone save perhaps Ryvček. He had memories two centuries long of watching that taint spread and destroy. Fiavla had fallen in eleven nights of howling madness. Nadežra sank as slow and silent as a drowning man.

"We'll destroy it," he promised, his breathing uneven. "We'll figure out a way."

Her head jerked in an approximation of a nod. "We must. But— these things. They affect the mind. The emotions. You told me yourself, people who have medallions, by their own desires they are consumed. If that is true..." Sickness twisted her expression. "How can I trust myself? Circumstances brought me back to Nadežra, against my choice. But when we landed here, it seemed natural that I should take what I deserved—what I *wanted*—from this city. Get revenge for what it had done to me. Just like the Traementis used to seek revenge. And to do it, I infiltrated their family. Would I have done that, if I had not the Tricat medallion?"

Tears trembled along her lashes, on the verge of spilling as she looked at him. In a whisper, she said, "Even wanting you. Is what I feel for you real...or is even that desire poisoned by this thing?"

She'd flinched away from his offer of comfort; now he realized why. Ren saw lies everywhere she looked. Her many lives had been built on them. For her, truth was a thinner thread than the one he'd used to pull her out of Ažerais's Dream, during Veiled Waters.

Veiled Waters. When she'd lost the medallion.

They'd been dancing around this attraction for months, in all their various guises...but its start could be traced back to a fraught night in a kitchen cellar. *After* Tricat had been lost to the dream.

He leaned forward. "Felt you anything for me back when I investigated you? Or perhaps that has only begun this evening?" The shake of her head was small, but unhesitating. "Then how can it not be real?"

Grey offered his hand, another rope to lift her away from the nightmare. "If you cannot trust yourself, then trust me. My feelings for you go far beyond mere wanting...and I've never heard that love is a Primordial's domain."

Now the tears spilled. Ren looked at his hand—then at Grey—then flung herself at him hard enough that she almost overturned his chair.

He wrapped his arms around her, held her close, the way he'd wanted to for so long. Ren curled against his chest, shaking, as Grey drew her legs over his so he could cradle her in his lap. He stroked her hair and whispered soothing words in Vraszenian, the sound of that language flowing over them both like warm water, washing away the fear.

There was still plenty to be afraid of. But not what they felt for each other.

When Ren shifted, he let her stand. She yanked at her coat, opening the buttons, then stripped it off and hurled it into the corner; the muffled thunk as it landed told him why. The medallion must be in its pocket.

Dragging Grey to his feet, Ren cupped his face in her hands, her gaze searching his with a wordless question.

He answered it as best he could, lips brushing hers, catching the gasp as they parted. And then holding firm as she fell into the kiss.

For the first few heartbeats it was comforting. Soft, soothing, the two of them melting against one another. But the heat between them had been building for too long to stay banked. Somehow they made it past the chair without tripping; their blind journey up the stairs was more bumped elbows and hissed breaths than grace. Grey's arms got trapped between his back and the bedroom door, his wrists bound by coat sleeves. Ren's breath on his neck gave way to tongue, then teeth. Her legs parted around his thigh, and he managed to struggle free of his coat so he could pull her flush against him. The landing echoed with their shared moan.

"We are not doing this standing up," Grey whispered into her cheek.

"You're the one who stopped." Her breath dragged shivers in its wake.

"I'm trying to recall how doors work."

Her giggle remade him. He'd spoken of love earlier, but it was that soft sound curling between them that took root and twined the three parts of his soul into one certainty.

He was so lost in the warmth, the scent, the weight of her draped against him that they almost fell when she reached past and lifted the latch. Grey managed to guide their stagger across to the bed instead.

"Better?" Ren asked, propping up just far enough to meet his gaze, her own shadowed by the fall of her hair. He pushed it back so the moons peeking through the window limned her face. He saw no more fear there. Only the same question from before, and an echo of the heat blossoming through him—the reflection of his soul in her eyes.

"Yes," he said, to all of it, and lifted up to meet her kiss.

Three Hands Join

Kingfisher, Lower Bank: Canilun 16

Ren's first month in Traementis Manor, every morning had begun the same way: waking with the wary stillness of unfamiliar surroundings, until her mind caught up and reminded her. No such tension came now. Her first awareness was of a warm body next to hers; her first sight when she opened her eyes was Grey, asleep on his back, dark hair falling softly away from his brow.

She found herself smiling, without any reason to stop.

It wasn't as if her problems had vanished. The zlyzen hadn't haunted her sleep, and Diomen had pulled her from the dream before they could communicate anything across their strengthened bond...but she had no doubt that bill would come due. Tricat still lay in her coat downstairs; they still had no way to destroy it. The other medallions were still out there, and the Praeteri were still manipulating the city with Primordial-driven numinatria—a thought that sent a deep shiver through her.

But here, lying next to a sleeping Grey, she believed they would find a way to deal with those problems.

The night had been mild, and the sheet only half covered his body. She let her gaze roam, remembering the urgency of the night before, shared hunger finally confessed and made whole. Grey was right: She'd been attracted to him, body and heart, as Rook and as hawk, since well before she got the medallion back.

When her attention returned to his face, she found his eyes open.

He brushed his knuckles along her cheek, a touch softer than his smile. In the lazy moments before they drifted off, he'd found soap and cloth and washed her imbued cosmetics away. She'd given him a muzzy pout then, but now she was glad that the face he saw on waking was her own.

"You slept well," he said. Not a question. He'd woken her from nightmares before.

"Mmn." Snaking one arm across his chest, Ren burrowed her nose into the warm crook between shoulder and neck. "You're at least as useful as a kitten for that, and you wake me not at first sun demanding your breakfast."

His chuckle stirred her hair as he pressed kisses light as kitten paws across her brow. "If so early I woke you, it wouldn't be for breakfast."

"No, more likely it would be to break into some noble's manor."

That got a full laugh, his ribs shaking beneath her arm. "You have me there, Clever Natalya."

"So now I am the kitten. Or the feral cat, more like."

He kissed the tip of her nose. "It's all right. I like your claws."

"What does that make you?" She poked him in the side.

"You need to ask? Scampering across rooftops in a mask—could I *be* any more Kiraly?"

Her smile faltered, and Grey's amusement faded. "What is it? Something wrong?"

Ren traced one fingertip across his shoulder, not looking at him. So many lies to correct and truths to tell; they could spend a year untangling that snarl. "Only that I'm not Dvornik, as I claimed. The Tsverin aren't my kureč. All of that is made up. My mother never said who her people were." Her languorous relaxation faded, her throat tightening. "They cast her out. Because of me."

Grey stroked her hair, tipping his own head toward hers. "I love you not for being Dvornik, but for being Ren. And—well. I can cast no stones."

Unlike her, he had a kureč, the Szerado. But his given name…"I admit I've wondered, ever since Ryvček said you had another name."

Grey sank back against the pillow with a rueful sigh.

"Ah," Ren said. "I am guessing you like it not."

"I could have been Karoslav," he said meditatively, addressing the ceiling. "A nice, fine name. Or Zlagomir. Or something old-fashioned, like Piotr. But no."

She waited, lips pressed together where he couldn't see.

"Gruzdan," he muttered.

She'd braced herself, but she couldn't quite choke down her laugh. "Oh dear."

"Gruzdan Jakoski Szerado," he repeated, mouth twisting in a wry line. "I changed it as soon as we came to Nadežra."

"I see why." Now Ren raised herself up on her elbow, hooking her hair behind one ear. "Then—unless you have some burning desire to be called by that name—"

"I would rather be outed to the whole city as the Rook."

Laughter burst from her. "I'm sorry," she said, even though she could see him smiling. "I should not laugh. Normally I have better self-control."

"It's all right," Grey said, brushing an errant wisp of hair from her face. "You need not mask yourself for me."

There was more darkness there, Ren could tell. He never spoke of family other than Kolya; he didn't use his patronymic. But he showed no inclination to swim deeper into those waters right now, and she didn't press. She lost herself in another kiss instead.

Or tried to lose herself. Grey drew back and said, "Something troubles you still. My past?"

"Your future," Ren admitted. "The pattern I laid. I still know not why it is wrong." Nor how to fix it. She'd made offerings at the Seven Knots labyrinth on his behalf, but she doubted that was enough.

One hand rose to rub the back of his neck. "Ah, that. I…may have manipulated the cards a bit."

"You *what*?"

"You were able to pattern *the Rook!*" he said defensively. "I wished not to test what your gift would reveal when you patterned me. So when you looked away, I slid two cards from the bottom of the deck into the top."

Ren sat bolt upright. "Grey—"

He slid one hand down her arm. "I'm sorry for tricking you—"

"It isn't that. You *interfered with your pattern.* I've cold-decked clients, given them false shuffles, but never when trying to pattern them for real. With you, I meant it to be real." She pressed one hand to her stomach. "I think what I felt—that was you twisting your own fate."

Grey eased up to face her, sober but not afraid. "I won't tell you your trade. But everything that's happened—Beldipassi, the curse, sharing my secret..." His hand covered hers, warm and rough. "If a twisted fate led me here, I have no complaints."

Two cards slid in. Those were likely Lark Aloft and The Mask of Nothing, the two she hadn't been able to interpret. Without those...she would never know what the last two cards would have been. But Sleeping Waters would have been his good future. The right place at the right time. Instead, what he'd done had robbed him of that chance.

It could mean the death curse, but Ren wasn't at all sure. Horrific as the ambush that nearly killed him had been, she couldn't help but feel the pattern pointed at something else—and worse.

So your answer still stands. She had to mend it. Somehow.

Ren pressed another kiss to his lips, then reluctantly drew back. "More than a day I have been gone from the manor. I sent a message, but..."

"Duty calls." He held her a moment longer before letting her slip away.

Duty, and more than just the one she had to the Traementis. There was the medallion downstairs, the Praeteri's activities, all the questions Vargo had been too ill to ask. She might wish to cocoon herself in Grey's bed until the river ran dry, but neither of their lives allowed for such indolence.

Half her clothing was still downstairs, and with it, her portable cosmetics kit. Grey didn't have a very good mirror, but at this point she barely felt like she needed one. She was putting the finishing touches on Renata's mask when he came down, freshly shaved, and went to stare at her heaped coat. "It's in here?"

"Yes." She made herself pick the coat up, then fish the medallion out of its inner pocket so he could see.

Grey stiffened as though she had him at swordpoint. "Tanaquis recognized it, you said? Has she seen others?"

"The sigil only, I think. The Praeteri, they've also been drawing on Primordials. That's what the eisar are. Not just spirits that can touch the mind; emanations of the Primordials."

"So much for the Praeteri not being the Rook's business."

His response had the Rook's steel in it. Ren said, "Many symptoms of one disease, given that House Acrenix created the Praeteri. I know not what Ghiscolo aims for, but…"

"But?" he prompted.

"Vargo needs to know," Ren said softly, bracing herself. "Not that you are the Rook, but the rest of it. His pattern and yours tangle together. And mine."

Grey said nothing, but turned away, as though he couldn't bear the sight of the medallion any longer. Almost absently, he touched his chest. He'd donned a shirt, but last night her lips had trailed over skin still red and tight from the numinat that restarted his heart.

"You took me to Vargo that night, didn't you."

Before Ren could fall off the edge of the struggle between being honest with Grey and keeping her word to Vargo, he went on. "You don't have to tell me. It's the only thing that makes sense. Stopping a numinatrian curse would require an inscriptor. If it were Tanaquis, or anyone else, you'd have no reason to hide it. And not a day later you and Vargo were friends again." He laughed bitterly. "I'm mostly insulted he thinks I'm idiot enough not to guess."

Quietly, she said, "He helped you before he and I reconciled. And he knows not that you are the Rook, or that you know my secrets. He only asked that I not tell you."

Grey snorted. "Right. Because it lets him pat himself on the back for having helped me, without actually having to deal with me."

It means he will not buy your forgiveness with your life. Grey wasn't wrong; Vargo was dodging an uncomfortable conversation. But he was also refusing to take advantage of the good he'd done. Just like in Whitesail, if she hadn't been there to see.

They weren't hiding from each other like before; she could watch the bitter, conflicting emotions play across Grey's expression. "What explanation gave you for what happened to me?"

"None, and he hasn't asked. Though he…" She trailed off, uncertain if Grey guessing meant she was free of her promise to Vargo. But Grey had to know Ghiscolo had used the death curse before, and Vargo needed to know about the other medallions and the danger they posed.

Groaning, she tucked the medallion away and rubbed her face. "Djek. Between you two there are too many secrets, and me in the middle trying to untangle the threads of what I can say."

Grey pulled her hands away from her freshly made-up face and tugged her into a hug. "Then perhaps it's time Vargo and I talked."

Eastbridge, Upper Bank: Canilun 16

Vargo woke up once in the night to down the medicine left by his physician, but other than that, he slept like the dead. When he finally roused again in the morning, he felt improved enough that after dosing himself a third time, he scrubbed down with a rag, dragged on trousers and a robe, and tucked a still-snoozing Peabody into his pocket. Time to see what damage had been done to his businesses while he was having a staring contest with zlyzen.

He opened his door and found Varuni on the other side of it.

With his head still muzzy from a fading fever, he couldn't stop his instinctive recoil. How long had she been standing there? She might have heard his footsteps once he roused—but he didn't put it past her to have staked him out since dawn. Her expression was definitely that of a predator lying in wait.

And her words weren't much better. "You. Me. We're going to talk."

"Do we really have to have this conversation again?" he muttered, brushing past her and heading downstairs for tea to wash away the taste of the medicine, and tolatsy to fill a gut empty and sore from so much puking. "I'm sorry for wandering off on my own; it was necessary; nothing too terrible happened. I'm home. Your investment is safe. You want sweet porridge or savory?" With no live-in servants, Vargo usually made his own breakfast. Might as well make it as a peace offering for Varuni as well.

"We *aren't* having that conversation again," Varuni snapped as he activated the numinat for the stove. "I've memorized that script. I don't need you for it anymore."

The weary harshness of her response made him face her directly. "Then what conversation is this?"

"The one where I ask what the fuck is the point of me being here, if you don't actually want my help."

"There was nothing yesterday that you could have helped with. It was numinatria-related business."

That did nothing to mollify her. "There's been a lot of 'numinatria-related business' recently."

He hadn't told her about the Illius Praeteri. More out of habit than out of respect for the Praeteri's secrets, but also because he didn't see the point. It wasn't the sort of danger she could protect him from, and it had nothing to do with the agreements he'd made with the Isarnah. "None of it has been dangerous." At her scoff, he said, "You think you could have defended me from getting mind-controlled by Ghiscolo Acrenix? From getting sick?"

Dishes rattled as Varuni slammed a fist against the sideboard. "I think that if you don't give a shit about telling me what you're up to, then why should I give a shit what happens to you?"

"Maybe you shouldn't." Turning away, he opened the rice bin and measured it into the waiting pot. "You've got other grey market connections now. And with Era Destaelio ready to ease the tariffs on Isarnah imports, you don't really need me anymore."

"Right," Varuni spat. "Because that's all I am. An agent sent here to make sure my family's investment is safe. I've spent five years at your side without developing opinions of my own."

Vargo's shoulders hunched. Wasn't he carrying enough weight already? Alsius, the Lower Bank knots, the people of Nadežra—even if they didn't know it. And now Ren and Tanaquis, because fuck him if he was going to let them deal with the medallions alone. Varuni didn't need to add herself to the pile.

You asshole. He could hear her response without needing to provoke it. She wasn't asking him to do anything more than work *with* her, instead of around her.

And she was right. She wasn't tied into any of his knots; her bonds lay to the south, with her family. But that didn't mean she wasn't a loyal ally. One he'd been treating more and more like a burden he had to escape.

Jamming his finger into the rice to measure the water level, he asked, "Sweet or savory? While this cooks, you can tell me about these opinions, and I'll tell you what the fuck is going on."

It took a lot longer than the time necessary to cook the tolatsy. Vargo called a halt to the conversation long enough for him to doctor his porridge with honey and dried fruit and Varuni's with dried pepper; then they relocated to the morning room and kept going. Varuni did a lot less eating than he did, alternately talking and staring while he talked, because she had better manners than he did. Vargo shoveled the food down and spoke with his mouth full—and a good thing, too, because just as he was running his finger around the inside of the bowl to swipe up the last few grains, a knock came at the door.

Varuni went to answer it, still not blinking enough, and a moment later her call came from the foyer, with zero formality: "Renata's here!"

"You're looking better," Renata said when he came to greet her. "Good. There are matters you and I need to discuss."

A sidelong glance at Varuni showed her shaking her head; she'd apparently had enough of his revelations for one morning. "Let's go upstairs," Vargo said. The truth about Ren was *not* one of the things he'd told Varuni. That was hers to share if she wanted.

At the top of the stairs, he opened the study door. "I'm afraid I'm not at my be—"

Words died as he saw the shadow in his study, arms crossed, silhouetted against the grey sky outside his open window.

Vargo's pulse beat in his throat. But the Rook made no hostile movement, and Ren was clearly biting down on a smile.

He turned to shout down the stairs. "Varuni, the Rook's here. But he isn't trying to beat or kidnap me. Go ahead and enjoy your breakfast."

When he shut the door, he found Ren giving him a quizzical look. He shrugged. "Long story. Not as long as the one I'm about to hear, I suspect. If you two are planning to make me take my clothes off again, be warned, it won't be pretty. I've only managed a basin bath this morning."

He sprawled into one of his reading chairs, leaving the other for Ren. The Rook could stay sitting on the windowsill for all Vargo cared.

Or fall out of it. He'd be fine with that, too.

Ren offered Vargo an apologetic grimace. "Yes, we staged that business during the card game. But for good reason."

A little while later, Vargo was glad he was sitting. Not because what Ren said came as any surprise; if there were three of Kaius Rex's medallions floating around Nadežra, it stood to reason that there were more. And given the associations of Illi-zero, he couldn't fault the Rook's reasoning in thinking he might have it.

No, what would have toppled him over was the surge of disgust and anger. He'd thought Ghiscolo had proposed their original deal only because he was worried about Mettore Indestor, and because he wanted a Cinquerat seat. With the information Vargo had now...

"He used me to get Sessat." The words ground like rocks out

of his throat. "Because Acrenix holds the charter for storing and disposing of possessions confiscated from criminals." Had Ghiscolo used Quinat to push him toward Indestor, too? More subtly than the shove toward Sostira Novrus. Approaching Ghiscolo had been Vargo's idea, when he and Alsius found out Mettore had uncovered the Praeteri and was looking for an excuse to shut them down—but at the time, removing Mettore from his seat hadn't been in Vargo's plans.

All these years, Vargo had thought his mind a fortress. Now he didn't even have that.

::Just one more thing we'll make him regret.:: Alsius had woken during the briefing; he was crouched on Vargo's shoulder, ready to bolt for cover if the Rook made any move toward him. ::Now that we know about these medallions, I can start looking for them. I wager I'll have more success than some defenestrating lout.::

And I might do better at destroying them.

Vargo said that in the full knowledge that Ren would hear and the Rook wouldn't. Two hundred years, and the man—or whatever he was—had made no progress on that front?

Ren frowned at him. Vargo's next thought was directed to Alsius but intended for Ren. *Do you know who's under that hood? Just nod or stay still.*

For a moment he thought she was saying "no." But then her head moved in an infinitesimal nod.

Fine, he thought, keeping that one to himself. Ren trusted the Rook; Vargo trusted Ren. To the shadow on the sill, he said, "Tell me what you've tried so far with destroying the medallions."

The Rook's reply was admirably comprehensive, and gave Vargo some sense of the scale of the problem. "But I've never had a chance to try with Illi-zero," the Rook said at the end.

"Then that's where we start," Vargo said. "Do you trust Tanaquis enough to involve her? Normally my ego doesn't like admitting someone knows more than I do, but she's the best educated of us on the topic of Primordials." He almost got the word out without shuddering. Almost, but not quite.

The Rook exchanged a look with Ren, then gave the most reluctant nod Vargo had ever seen.

But it was easier to keep a secret if you knew everyone who held it. "How does Serrado fit into this? Why was he attacked?"

"I paid him a visit after the Essunta party," the Rook said, his tone as cold as an ocean-born wind. "I felt it was time we had an honest conversation."

"Serrado set up a meeting between Beldipassi and the Rook." Ren tilted her head toward the outlaw. "Ghiscolo found out somehow—we suspect Beldipassi's valet. Serrado took the curse meant for the Rook."

Ghiscolo. Vargo felt the weight of Ren's gaze. She'd started this conversation by saying she was tired of juggling secrets...but she was still holding some of Vargo's.

May I say it? he thought to Alsius.

::My brother—no, he is no brother of mine. Ghiscolo is a threat. I shudder to think who else he may have killed with that perversion of the Lumen's grace.::

Vargo let Alsius scuttle onto his hand and set him on the arm of his chair, then looked up at the Rook. "You've been sticking your hood in noble business for a while. Remember when Guebris Acrenix's heir was found dead in his home sixteen years ago? Failed numinatrian experiment?"

"I'm aware of it."

"It wasn't an experiment. It was the same death curse that was used on Serrado. And Alsius Acrenix didn't die—not exactly." Peabody lifted his colorful abdomen in salute. "We've been together since then. That's how I knew how to lift the curse."

Tracking the direction of the Rook's eyes was impossible, but the hood seemed fixed on the spider. Vargo added, "Not that you have any reason to believe me, but he never knew about the Acrenix medallion until last night. And if he'd known what it was—" Vargo shuddered. "He would have tried to destroy it."

"If he expects that to endear him to me," the Rook said, "tell him I like spiders about as much as I like nobles."

"Well, he doesn't like you, either. You threw him out a window."

Ren cleared her throat. "*The point is*, you have shared enemies. And my patterns say that your threads, joining together, might just make enough rope to hang our problems."

Vargo didn't share her confidence in pattern, but he wouldn't object to having the Rook on his side instead of being a thorn in it. In fact—"I understand you volunteered me to Utrinzi Simendis to take down the Praeteri."

"I understand that's been your goal all along. Though you've taken your time in going about it."

"Because I wanted to know how their numinatria worked. Now that I know more than I ever wanted to, it's long past time for them to go—and their leaders along with them." Vargo cracked his knuckles systematically, up one hand and down the other. "Let's talk about how to do that."

Isla Extaquium, Eastbridge: Canilun 17

Thunder rattled the sky as Renata's sedan chair arrived in the plaza in front of Extaquium Manor. But the storm wouldn't keep anyone from attending Sureggio's party; on the contrary, it was the reason for the occasion. There was an old Seterin tradition of writing poems inspired by the dance of the Lumen in the clouds.

Not that she expected many poems tonight. Sureggio's version was a drinking game, with guests downing spirits every time the lightning struck. She had no interest in this kind of event; she wouldn't have bothered to accept Parma's invitation were it not for one thing.

The Illius Praeteri were also holding a ritual, in a select gathering within the party itself.

Vargo couldn't strike against them in the hidden temple, not with it warded against intruders. It was possible to bring nonmembers of the Praeteri in—otherwise he and Ren couldn't have been brought in for their third initiation—but he'd studied the cult's register. That effect was created through the use of Tuat, which meant each member could bring only one guest. For a raid like Iridet wanted, capturing as many high-ranked cultists as possible, Vargo would need a lot more than that.

So instead they were targeting a ritual outside the temple. Renata wasn't far enough into their circle to receive an invitation; Tanaquis was, but unfortunately, Simendis had forbidden her to attend. He was still angry at her for not telling him the true nature of the Praeteri, and he'd refused to let her anywhere near Extaquium Manor, lest anyone connect his protégé to the cult. Which meant it was up to Renata and Vargo to find the secret gathering, bring in his force, and give Iridet the grounds he needed to prosecute their heresy.

Dampness hung heavy on the air. Despite the cleansing rain rolling in from the north, warmth and cloying scents blanketed the manor's front steps; inside, it was worse. The lights were all dimmed to a suggestive glow, shining off the bodies of the servants, who for the occasion had been painted with storm clouds and lightning bolts. The only fresh air came from the doors to the garden terrace. Beyond them, an awning of the thinnest net covered the scattering of divans and couches, each cluster supplied with its own water pipe for smoking. The numinat worked into the net would shield the partygoers from whatever fell from the sky: rain, hail, or even lightning, should the Lumen aim a strike at them.

Renata avoided the terrace. The haze of smoke out there would dull her wits even if she didn't partake directly, and the gardens didn't provide nearly enough space or privacy for a secret ritual. No, it would be somewhere in the house.

Moving through the party felt like her days in Lacewater, without the stinking canals. She had to revive every trick she knew to cut short unwanted suggestions and fend off wandering hands, even to the point of putting a discreet joint lock on one gentleman too drunk to recognize her as more than an attractive female body. She spotted Vargo in time to see him fumble a chilled drink into the lap of an aggressive suitor from House Cleoter. No sound or sign of Alsius; presumably the spider was off conducting his own search.

They needed to do the same. And what better way to search than to pretend to be seeking privacy?

Vargo shivered as she ran a hand up his spine to settle across his shoulders, like a cat that had been stroked backward. The midnight velvet nap of his coat was as soft as the pads of Clever Natalya's toes. Renata's chin came to rest on his opposite shoulder, and she greeted the surprised looks of the other guests with a satisfied smirk.

"You said you'd come find me." She let the whisper lick Vargo's ear, but made it loud enough for everyone to hear.

"I only just noticed your arrival." His hand found hers on his shoulder, and he toyed with the pearl closings of her gloves. "I didn't want to be rude and leave in the middle of a conversation."

"Then I'll be rude for you." Stepping back, she tugged him to his feet. To their audience, she said, "You don't mind, do you? I don't think any of us came here to *talk*."

As they made their way from the salon to the fresher air of the hallways, Vargo slid an arm around her waist and pulled her close. Under the guise of whispering something naughty, he said, "Well, that's a seed bun tossed to the snappers. I suppose this means we've officially reconciled?"

She giggled and swatted him before cupping her hand around his ear to whisper back, "It was the quickest way to get you away. I'd rather *not* still be here when the clothes start coming off. And it gives us an excuse to nose around."

"Indeed. If only we weren't burdened with such pressing concerns…"

Ren couldn't deny the way her skin tingled at the liquid warmth in his voice, the weight of his hand at the small of her back. But there was a difference between feeling it and wanting to follow through. "Vargo…I don't want you to take this the wrong way."

Her body remained pliant against his, but he was canny enough to separate mixed cues. The hand on her back lightened, leaving behind only the illusion of pressure. "You're not interested."

"More like not available."

It was a risk, saying even that much. Vargo knew almost all of her secrets now; it would take only one flash of insight to connect pieces she needed him to keep separate. But she couldn't take this too far—not when her relationship with Grey was still so new, and so fragile. Vargo might heat her blood, but Grey warmed her heart.

Vargo gave her a wry grin and a quick, impartial squeeze. "Don't tell Alsius. He'll be devastated. You're several cuts above what I usually drag to my bed."

He was masking something. Not the hurt of rejection; that, she'd seen on him before. Something else. "Vargo—"

"I'm happy you've found someone who can know all of you." His grin widened, and he winked. "I'll leave it to Sedge to make the appropriate threats."

Sedge would lose his mind when he found out she was sleeping with the Rook *and* a former hawk, all in one man. But that was very much a concern for later. "Shall we find ourselves some heretics?"

A bark of laughter drew several eyes in their direction. Vargo led her past them, leaving a storm of whispers in their wake. "Let's hope for heretics and not any of the other things we might stumble on here. I'm relying on you to preserve what innocence I have left."

His jest turned out to be not far off the mark. Ren thought herself worldly; it was a common saying that there were no children in the streets. Their tour through Extaquium Manor, however, made it clear to her that nobody could be as inventive as the bored and wealthy.

She was beginning to think they were never going to find what they were looking for when they came into a room that, according to bookshelves along the far wall, was supposed to be a library. "I didn't take Sureggio for much of a reader," Vargo scoffed. He kept his voice low even though the man passed out with his head in a large vase was unlikely to wake. "I suppose he just has these books for show."

"For show," Ren murmured, "or..."

The gaps weren't that hard to find, once she looked for them. Nor was the trigger, which Vargo located in the floor. Planting his bare hand against a marquetry circle, he twisted it, and the bookcase swung backward.

Beyond the low arch was a shaft, a metal staircase spiraling up into darkness, and a niche with a covered bowl of lightstones. Unfortunately, even setting a single foot on the first riser made the shaft echo with the creaking of the spiral. There would be no sneaking up these stairs.

Vargo drew back into the library. "I haven't seen Sureggio, Diomen, Ghiscolo, or any of the other important Praeteri down here. Do we gamble that this is it, and that they've gathered already?"

The storm had been building outside while they searched; now thunder echoed down the shaft. "It sounds like it's open to the outside, wherever it leads. But—" Ren leaned in to listen. In the wake of the thunder, something else came through. "I hear voices. I think this is it."

Though he wore the elegant clothing of a cuff, Vargo's smile was pure Lower Bank threat. "I'll signal my people. We're going to want to drive hard through the house. Can you wait here? Make certain nobody leaves... and nobody gets through to warn them?"

He barely waited for her nod before he was gone. Leaving Ren standing next to a secret door, wondering if she should close it, wondering if the man with his head in the vase was going to wake up, wondering—

Was that a scream?

The sound twined with the renewed thunder, and Ren risked a couple of steps up the stairs in order to hear better. It faded to agonized moans, but yes: Someone up there was in extreme pain.

She gripped the central post, fighting with herself. How long would it take Vargo to gather his people? And what exactly did she think she was going to do without them?

Those aren't the real questions. The real question was whether she could stand there listening to someone scream and not act.

Her mask was always with her, folded small and tucked into a well-hidden pocket. She drew it over her face, waited for the next roll of thunder, and flung herself up the stairs.

The boots of the Black Rose didn't fully muffle Ren's footsteps, but the sky and the screams gave her cover. At the top of the stairs was a small bedroom, unoccupied; it had double doors open to a terrace that must sit high on the manor's roof, sheltered from easy view.

A group of people stood on that terrace, beneath an intricate framework of numinata. Blue lightning danced along its rods, channeling downward to the tiles below, where a man lay naked and screaming. As the light faded, his distorted voice eased into something more recognizable. "Clay! Give me the clay!"

Sureggio Extaquium. Ren watched him swiftly mold the offered clay in his hands, and remembered what Vargo had told her about the making of Praeteri foci.

The fact that Extaquium was suffering for the creation of one did nothing to outweigh the suffering it would create elsewhere. *Who are you planning to use that on?*

A shadow suddenly eclipsed the door. Ren jerked back, but not fast enough; a hand caught her head, fingers digging into her braids so she couldn't slip free. It dragged her out onto the terrace and forced her to her knees.

"It seems our gathering isn't as private as you promised, Brother Sureggio." Diomen's rich voice rang out over the cultists, chanting in blasphemous praise to the Primordial of suffering.

They broke off and turned to face him. Ren's gaze swept over their ranks, cataloguing faces. Plenty of targets... but no Ghiscolo, not that she could see.

Sureggio lurched to his feet and shrugged on a robe. He approached with the halting steps of a man whose muscles weren't quite under his control, his flapping garment doing little to hide his nudity. The scent of scorched hair lingered on him; all that flesh on display was blasted smooth.

"It's that Rose person!" Ebrigotto Attravi exclaimed. "How remarkable."

Sureggio's words slurred as if he were drunk—which he probably was. "I can always make room for uninvited guests."

Their lack of concern eased the tension that had gripped the other Praeteri. Nervous laughter followed, chasing the rumble of a lightning strike. In the brief distraction, Ren twisted free of Diomen's hand, but Attravi's two strapping sons blocked her way with swords before she could get far.

I should have waited.

"There is no room for unbelievers in our gatherings," Diomen said, his voice as deep and uncompromising as the thunder. "And we must make certain the new focus works. Bring her."

Ren didn't fight as they pushed her across the terrace. With so many cultists around her, she didn't stand a chance; better to wait for an opening.

On the far side of the frame that had gathered and dissipated the lightning, a more traditional numinat was painted on the tiles. Heavy rain sheeted over it, stinging as it struck Ren's cheeks. At a wave of Diomen's hand, Ebrigotto Attravi came over to tie Ren's hands and feet.

When they shoved her into the numinat, she took care to roll so her back faced away from the Praeteri. Attravi didn't know the first thing about tying people up. He hadn't noticed Ren bracing her hands to gain slack, and his knot slipped as she worked her hands free. But she remained still as Diomen placed the new focus in the center of the numinat and retreated to safety.

As he bent to close the circle, she slapped her hands against the tiles and shoved her bound feet toward the focus.

For the briefest instant, agony unlike anything she'd felt before tore through her body—not just *pain*, she'd felt that before, but Primordial agony that seared her from her skin to the marrow of her bones—and she screamed.

But her feet slammed into the lump of clay and knocked it out of place. And with a flare of violet light, the numinat broke.

Isla Extaquium, Eastbridge: Canilun 17

Renata wasn't at the entrance to the stairwell shaft, because of course she wasn't. That woman dove toward danger like an osprey stooping for trout. Muttering a curse, Vargo surged ahead without waiting for his assembled knots, without waiting for Varuni and Sedge. He'd meant for them to lead the charge because *he* had a sense of self-preservation—but that was a few moments longer Ren might be in trouble.

We're going to chat with her later about the meaning of "wait here," he thought at the spider hidden in the collar of his coat. Alsius's silence was its own form of agreement.

The spiral staircase shook and groaned as Vargo bolted up as quickly as he dared. At the top he hurled himself out into the rain, where a crowd gathered at the edge of a complex framework of copper rods and wires.

He'd seen dogfights and bear-baitings often enough to recognize the same bloodlust in the cries of the cuffs. He let a lifetime of resentment at their hypocrisy power his voice as he shouted, "Members of the Illius Praeteri, stand down and surrender yourselves to Iridet's justice."

Inscribe under "words I never thought I'd say in my life."

But there was no time to savor the irony. Ripping one of the copper rods from the frame, Vargo surged forward and applied it to the back of the first set of knees in range. "In accordance with the"—his elbow smashed into Infassa Cleoter's nose—"Charter for the Purification"—a knee in Ebrigotto Attravi's groin—"of Heretical Numinatria."

The rod was a copper streak aimed at Sureggio Extaquium's head, but the man ducked before it connected. And in the space left behind, Vargo spotted Ren—no, *the Black Rose*—slumped in the center of a fried numinat, leather armor and hair slick from the rain and skin paler than usual.

Yelps and curses told him his people weren't far behind, and he heard the familiar metallic clink of Varuni's chain whip doing its work. As a punch came toward his face, he dropped to his knees and skidded across the tiles toward Ren, reaching for the rope that bound her ankles. If they'd killed her...

One black-gloved hand batted at him when he reached for the

rope. "I've got it," Ren said, even if the weak rasp of her words put that into question. "Catch the others. Ghiscolo's not here."

Sedge dropped to his knees next to Vargo, a flash of lightning illuminating a face bleached with fear. "I've got her. You—watch out!"

A boot crashed into Vargo's hip, sending a flare of pain up his back. He rolled and came to his feet—

And found himself facing Diomen.

You'll do, Vargo thought grimly. It looked like some of the Praeteri were escaping via another exit, but his people had corralled most of them. They'd be quick enough to sell each other out; street knots had ten times the loyalty of cuffs looking to save their own asses. And if Ghiscolo wasn't here, that meant Vargo didn't have to split his attention.

He palmed two knives. Iridet could just deal with not having the Pontifex alive to prosecute.

But he never got close. As he leapt, Diomen brought his hands together. Vargo had a heartbeat to see two semicircular pieces of a numinat in his grip, before they joined into a whole—and the world blew away.

Vargo was in midair, the rain frozen around him while everything else slid past. *That's odd*, he thought . . . before his perspective righted itself. The world wasn't moving, he was; Vargo was flying backward off the roof, and *fuck fuck fuck*—

He hit the tiles and slid toward the low railing that guarded the edge. Not low enough: His body went right under. His desperate snatch wrapped his fingers around one of the bars, but only for a moment; his weight was too much, the metal slicked by rain, and he couldn't hold on.

Vargo fell.

For half an instant, before he stopped with a sudden wrench of his shoulder. Another pained grunt overlaid his. Slitting his eyes against sheeting water that stung like ice, Vargo looked up . . . into a hood that held only shadows where a face should be.

The Rook.

Isla Extaquium, Eastbridge: Canilun 17

The Rook should have followed Vargo's people.

But he'd believed that up the side of Extaquium Manor would be faster than shoving through the party inside...and he'd been reluctant to follow along like another minion. Unfortunately, a renovation had removed the decrepit balcony he had planned to use as a waypoint, and by the time he found a new path to the roof, the chaos was in full blast.

Vargo's people fighting. Praeteri escaping. Ren curled on her side, and Sedge hunched over her.

He knew which of those places he needed to be—right up until the moment Vargo got blasted off the roof.

He stared down at the man he'd caught, dangling like a baited hook over the rain-flooded plaza several stories below. He'd lunged for Vargo on reflex. Now he had to make a choice.

It's possible the fall won't kill him.

Vargo's free hand wrapped around his rescuer's forearm, but the Rook's silk sleeve was too loose to provide a secure grip. And the lip of the rooftop jutted out too far to offer a foothold.

The shouting behind him didn't drown out the unsteadiness of Vargo's voice—nerves, fatigue, a breath of laughter at something that wasn't the least bit funny. "This is all very dramatic, but if that's the only reason you're not pulling me up..."

"I'm trying to find a reason I *should*."

For the first time in weeks, the Rook was nowhere in Grey's thoughts. It was only him, looking down at the man who'd...not murdered Kolya, not on purpose, but he'd *orchestrated* the explosion. The fact that Vargo had saved Grey's life didn't make up for that.

A cry lodged in his throat, all the things he'd lost because of this kinless bastard's greed and carelessness. The wound in his heart didn't fucking care if it was all to take down Indestor, the Praeteri, the same things Grey despised and the Rook fought against. It didn't care if Vargo hadn't intended for anyone to get hurt.

An accident: like Vargo slipping from the roof. He might not die. Let pattern and gravity decide his fate. In the absence of any adjustment, Grey's hold was slipping, his arm straining under the weight. Eyes wide with fear, Vargo tried to grab the rooftop edge with his free hand, only for his fine eelskin glove to slip like it was greased.

"The Rook doesn't kill." His whisper was almost lost in the fall of the rain.

"No," Grey said. "But if I remove this hood...I'm just a man." *One who's dreamed of this moment for far too long.*

The Rook would abandon him if he let Vargo fall. *Ren* would abandon him. Two new wounds in his heart, to replace the one he wanted so desperately to heal with the balm of revenge.

But that wouldn't heal anything. And as much as Grey would hate himself for not avenging Kolya...he would hate himself more if he did.

Grey caught Vargo's flailing hand, dragging the man high enough that he could hook one leg over the edge. Vargo hauled himself up to sprawl on his stomach as though embracing safety.

He expected to feel hollow inside. Bitter. He'd had his chance, and he'd given it up.

Instead he felt like he'd had his chance...and he'd taken it.

"That's for Serrado," he said, and left Vargo to wonder over what he meant. Turning away, he crossed the terrace in search of the Rose.

The chaos had ended. The man he assumed was the Pontifex was nowhere to be seen, but Vargo's people had the remainder well in hand, and Ren stood a little distance apart, watching him.

"I couldn't get to you in time," he said in a low voice as he drew near.

She touched his arm. The black lace of her mask didn't hide her mouth, and the trace of relief there. "It's all right. I'm fine...and you were where you needed to be."

Two Roads Cross

Eastbridge, Upper Bank: Canilun 18

Grey thought, when he headed across the river to Eastbridge with Beldipassi in tow, that the hardest part of this meeting would be facing Vargo.

Not because of any turmoil in his heart. That moment on the rooftop had brought him unexpected peace; he'd dreamed of Kolya last night, and for the first time since his brother's death, it hadn't hurt. No, he just didn't know how to *behave* around Vargo now. Whether to fake a rage that had faded, just to keep the man from wondering at its absence.

But when he walked into Vargo's study, the real challenge turned out to be not smiling at Ren like the new lover he was. They hadn't publicly met in these personas since the Traementis adoption ball, and so much had changed since then.

Letting the others see their newfound intimacy would spark noble gossip, though. Not to mention they didn't want Vargo thinking too hard about the partnership between Renata Viraudax and the recently ex-captain Grey Serrado. That man had an inconveniently sharp mind. So Grey gave Renata what he hoped looked like a sufficiently polite and distant nod...and then he gave another to the Rook.

There was something deeply peculiar about seeing the hood and those shadows from the outside, when he was so used to wearing them. As with Dockwall, though, the easiest way to convince someone there was no link between himself and the Rook was to put them both in view at the same time. And he hadn't needed to plead nearly as hard as he expected to convince Ryvček to join them. She said it was because she couldn't pass up the chance to see one of the medallions destroyed, even if all the hard work of making it happen was done by other people, and Grey had no doubt that was true.

But there was another truth they didn't voice. Ryvček was worried about him. And Grey couldn't say she was wrong.

At his side, Beldipassi bobbed an actual bow to the Rook, as if Nadežra's most notorious outlaw held a seat in the Cinquerat. Tanaquis was already there, apparently having erred regarding punctuality in the *other* direction for once. From her mutters, she was of two minds about trying to destroy an ancient numinatrian artifact, torn between outrage at the idea and curiosity as to how it could be done. The fact that the artifact called on a Primordial didn't seem to bother her at all.

It bothered Grey, more deeply than he wanted to think about. Even with Ryvček in the hood, he felt a skin-crawling mix of horror and rage as Beldipassi hesitantly took the silk-wrapped bundle from his pocket and unwrapped it to reveal the gold disc of Illi-zero.

"The Rook told me you could remove the Prim—The…influence…once it was destroyed?" Beldipassi's voice was as unsteady as his hand as his gaze flicked hopefully between Tanaquis and Vargo.

The look the two inscriptors traded was less than encouraging. "The curse, yes," Tanaquis said, bending over Beldipassi's hand like a courting suitor. Her nose was a breath away from brushing the medallion as she examined it, and Grey had to clamp his arms at his sides to keep from dragging her to a safer distance—as if there were such a thing. "But Vargo and I have been discussing what's known about Primordials, and his own experience with the effects. It likely isn't possible to remove the influence A'ash has had on your mind."

Only Grey's hand at Beldipassi's back kept him from fainting or fleeing. Tanaquis blinked at the medallion now fallen to the floorboards. Vargo groaned and rubbed at his face.

"What Tanaquis *means*," he said, shooting a glare at her, "is that we believe a Primordial's drive can only be increased, not removed, through the medallions. It isn't in the nature of Primordials to be what they are not. We can only wait for that influence to fade with time."

"But it *will* fade?"

Vargo stepped back to avoid Beldipassi grabbing his coat. "Yes. But it will take sincere effort on your part—you'll have to change your behavior. Given the medallion you have, that would mean seeing things through to the end rather than always launching new ventures."

Grey bit back an amused snort. He could understand leveraging any chance to make Beldipassi water his behavior down.

Tanaquis was taking the Rook's presence in stride to a surprising degree—or perhaps not so surprising, when one considered her utter lack of interest in politics, crime, or anything farther than a book and closer than the distant reaches of the cosmos. She didn't even look up as the Rook uncrossed his arms and said, "I've tried to destroy medallions in the past. With imbued chisels and hammers, with fire, with numinatria. But I suspect the sequence matters: What failed on, say, Quarat, might work on Illi-zero." The hood nodded down at the golden circle. "It turned aside my sword without so much as taking a scratch, though, so let's assume ordinary measures are a waste of time."

Ryvček was clearly doing her best to imitate Grey as the Rook, without her usual flamboyant poetry. He would catch hell for that later, his teacher complaining about how boring his approach was.

"Agreed." Vargo offered the hooded figure a polite, hesitant nod. Grey wondered if there had been a conversation before he arrived, and if so, what Ryvček had made of it. Probably not. Vargo didn't seem like the type to say, *Thank you for saving my life.* "Tanaquis and I have a few different ideas for how to do this. I don't have enough floor to try them all at once, so we'll have to go one by one. It might take a while."

It did take a while, as the first method failed. And the second. And the third.

Hours of chalking and erasing and more chalking, Beldipassi hovering close by to place the unaffected medallion where he was told and reclaim it as each effort came to nothing. The Rook remained an admirably motionless shadow in the corner; Grey suspected he was the only one who could read the tension thrumming there, the frustration of *seeing* a medallion and not being able to obliterate it. Vargo got more irritable as his theories died ignominious deaths, but Tanaquis only got more avid and determined. Vargo's spider jumped from shoulder to desk to shelves, and judging by Vargo's annoyed glares and Renata's occasional stifled grin, Grey assumed Alsius Acrenix had many opinions to offer.

Grey himself had nothing to offer. Anything useful that lay in the Rook's memories, Ryvček could provide—and more safely than Grey could, right now. He and Renata bled off their nervous tension by brewing tea and coffee and fetching whatever tools the inscriptors pointed at.

"I suppose it was too much to hope this would be easy," Grey muttered as Vargo and Tanaquis debated whether it would make any difference if they had access to the Ninat medallion instead. Vargo said yes; Tanaquis insisted that if anything they would want Illi-ten, until the Rook shot that one down on the basis of personal experience.

Maybe they needed both Illi medallions. Or his worst fear was right: They needed the whole set at once. If that was the case, this would never succeed.

Renata's hand twitched, as if she wanted to lay it on his arm. For an instant their eyes met, and Grey had the stupid urge to kiss her.

He coughed; she let a tiny flicker of a grin through. Grey said, "I'll...go fetch some fresh water." And hopefully cool his head.

He'd finished dumping the basin in the back canal and was looking for the communal pump when he heard a soft laugh. "We have drains, you know."

Varuni stood on the canal walk. Grey was surprised to see her; Vargo had indicated she'd be busy all day with Isarnah business. She hooked a thumb back at the kitchen door. "Pump, too, if you're looking for it."

"Oh." Out of habit, Grey glanced at her waist. No chain whips that he could see, which was a relief... until he looked up and caught her raised brow.

Djek. The whips were something the Rook would be concerned about, not Grey.

"Why are you here?" Varuni sauntered past him to stand in the doorway. Not quite an obstacle, but Grey suspected she would make herself one if she didn't like his answer.

It was a fair question. The last time she'd seen him, he'd been gut-punching her boss. "Eret Vargo is attempting some numinatria on behalf of Alta Renata."

"Again?" Turning her back on Grey with a muttered "asshole," Varuni stalked into the house. "He better not kill himself like last time. Restarting his heart is *not* what I'm here for."

The wet basin slipped in Grey's fingers and almost fell to the cobblestones.

He secured his grip and hurried after her into the dim shelter of the kitchen. He'd seen enough of Varuni, in both of his guises, to know she wasn't talkative. Maybe not an accomplished liar like some of the people gathered at Vargo's house today, but she kept secrets by keeping her mouth shut.

If she'd opened it now, it was for a reason.

Grey didn't try to catch her arm. He only asked, "What did you mean by that?"

She pivoted to face him and poked his chest, her finger unerringly finding the spot where he'd been burned. "You're a smart man. Put it together."

"I know he's the one who saved me. But why would Vargo's heart have stopped when—"

Varuni shrugged. "I'm not an inscriptor. But he did it on purpose. And he doesn't take any risks he doesn't think are necessary."

This time Grey didn't follow as she went upstairs. He stayed in the kitchen, holding the empty basin, trying to think.

He'd assumed the man had saved him as a favor to Ren. She'd told him about Vargo destroying the letter from Eret Viraudax, then defending her against Sostira Novrus in the Charterhouse. This might be more of the same. Buying forgiveness for his misdeeds with better ones later on.

But it didn't buy him anything if the beneficiary didn't know about it.

Whitesail, when he thought Ren wasn't there. Saving Grey, then asking her not to tell him.

And it was more than just a favor, a bit of emergency inscription on demand. Vargo had knowingly stopped his own heart. In order to save a man who wanted him dead.

Footsteps on the stairs; he knew it was Ren even before she appeared in the archway. "Is everything all right?" she asked.

Grey's thoughts were an absolute tangle—but this was neither the place nor the time to try and comb through them. Right now, what mattered wasn't Vargo; it was the medallions. "I'm guessing there's been no success."

"Tanaquis wants me to draw some cards," Renata said. "Pattern was useful in removing the curse, so she thinks it might also help with this."

"That's a good idea," he said reflexively. On consideration, though, he meant it: So far as he knew, the Rook had never attempted to use pattern for this purpose. Why should he? The medallions were ancient numinatria, not anything of Vraszan. But if the obvious things failed, maybe it was time to try the nonobvious.

Anything that gets this Primordial poison out of my city, he thought, following her up the stairs. *And out of Ren—before it's too late.*

Eastbridge and the Pearls: Canilun 18

"You're certain it isn't too..." Avaquis Fintenus plucked at the bodice of the muslin mockup, straining the basted seams with a held breath. If Tess took her measuring tape to the woman's throat now, she'd survive minutes on a breath that deep. "Too loose?"

Pasting on a friendly smile, Tess pinched at the material. Or tried to. She'd already taken in the cursed thing twice, but nothing short of casing herself like a sausage was going to please Avaquis. "Not without the buttons gaping," she explained, smoothing a hand over the pinned closure that was threatening to do just that. Even with bone reinforcing the lining, some things were impossible within the bounds of nature and imbuing.

It was a problem of Tess's own making. Renata had predicted last winter that her tailored cranberry wool coat would be in demand. As sure as one of Ren's patterns, Tess had been inundated with requests for such coats the moment the weather threatened to turn.

But half of being a good tailor, Tess was learning, was convincing clients that what looked fetching on one body was not meant for everybody. Tess had tried to sell Avaquis on a higher-waisted design that could have been the new trend of this year, but the woman was having none of it. "Couldn't you sew on more buttons?"

Tess's smile stretched near to breaking. *And some bodies look best floating facedown in the Dežera.* "Let me see what can be managed."

Far too many modifications later, Tess finally made her escape from Fintenus Manor with the mangled body of her mockup in her tailor's bag. The towers chiming the fourth bell of sixth sun chased her across the Pearls to Isla Traementis. Crone's crooked teeth, over three hours since she'd waved Renata off to Vargo's house? She was meant to meet Pavlin at seventh, and she still had to dump her bag and make herself pretty. Though at the moment, she'd settle for less frazzled and murderous.

"Best he get used to it," she muttered, making her way along the deserted walk that ran behind the manor house. "You'll always have cuffs making unreasonable demands." Not every client could be as malleable and cooperative as her sister.

Lost in thoughts of new designs she could stuff Ren into, and how to modify them when they were demanded by those without

Ren's shape, Tess failed to notice the sedan chair and bearers waiting in the back lane until she was almost upon them.

"You're late," one said, blocking her path. The other peeled away from the wall and shifted behind her before she could scarper.

"I'm sorry." The apology slipped out before Tess could think on it, and once it was loosed, she saw no reason not to follow it. "If I'd known two fine fellows were waiting for me, I'd have hurried my step."

While the men traded a grin at Tess's easy naivete, she slipped a hand into the bag at her side and closed it around her best scissors.

"En't no matter," the man blocking her way said, crowding her back against his associate. "Long as you come quiet with us now."

A glance into the empty kitchen yard told Tess there'd be no point in screaming. But that didn't mean she'd go quiet.

"Of course. Let me just—"

Whipping her bag at the man in front of her, Tess pulled out the scissors and plunged them into the one behind her. She must have struck something, if the grunt and warmth wetting her fingers were any indication. Before she could take advantage, though, her wrist was caught in a vise. The scissors dropped from numb fingers. Hauled off balance, she practically fell into the burlap sack bagged over her head. She choked on dust, darkness, and her own muffled shouts as the men bound her wrists and ankles and shoved her into the sedan chair.

Isla Traementis, the Pearls: Canilun 18

House Traementis's ruined finances had forced them to sell off their bay villa when Giuna was ten. By then their register had withered to just her mother, her brother, and four remaining cousins; Donaia's protective instincts were already strong. The notion of letting Giuna risk herself on the open water or in the fields around the city—or even in the city itself—was too much for her to bear, and so began years of Giuna near constantly mewed up in their Pearls manor.

Compared to that, even the Bay of Vraszan felt like a foreign land. Giuna had grown so accustomed to the ever-present scent of river mud that she didn't even notice it until it was gone, replaced by salt tang and clean rain. The low rocks of the bay islands were as exotic as mountains beneath her feet, and the flat, open expanse of water made her feel dizzy enough that she had to sit down. But it was a good dizziness, and she wished she could have spent more than a few days out there with her mother. She even found herself entertaining shameful thoughts about how long it would take House Traementis to recover enough to buy their old villa back from House Aldassare.

We have to find some way to thank Scaperto, Giuna thought as the Quientis yacht eased up to the Pearls river stair to let her off. Then an impish grin overtook her. *Though perhaps my mother's thanks will be enough.*

She climbed the stair and began wending her way through the islets toward Traementis Manor, with a Quientis servant carrying her small travel case. She couldn't remember a time when her family had paid for a splinter-boat or a sedan chair to carry them this last leg of the way, and even now that they could afford it, she didn't see the point.

"Please, visit the kitchen and take some refreshment before you go," Giuna said after the servant put down the case in the front hall. As Colbrin took her light cloak, she asked, "Who's at home?"

"No one, alta," Colbrin answered. "Altans Meppe and Idaglio are in Dockwall on business, and Alta Renata is out as well."

"Where did she go?"

The majordomo bowed in apology. "I'm afraid I don't know. Tess keeps Alta Renata's calendar, but she has also gone out."

Giuna pursed her lips. It was almost like dealing with Leato again—a thought that would always carry a sad sting. Renata didn't come home pretending to be drunk, and so far as Giuna knew she wasn't climbing through her bedroom window at night, but she was constantly out, often with no information on where she'd gone. *She's still not used to being part of a family.* A proper one, not whatever thin mockery Letilia had given her.

So it would be lunch alone. Giuna headed for the kitchen. In most noble households it was a scandal and a disturbance when one of the family showed up in that sacred precinct, but House Traementis had lost concern for such niceties when they dwindled. In every season but summer, the cook was used to making a tray for Giuna to eat while she read in the corner nearest the oven.

When she entered, though, she found a disturbance already underway. One of Captain Serrado's constables was there—the handsome one. Pavlin Ranieri, that was his name. He wore ordinary clothing and a look of utter distress.

"—outside and look; you'll see. Unless you sent one of your kitchen maids out there to slaughter a chicken?"

The bitter desperation in his voice brought Giuna alert. "What's going on here?"

The cook sighed. "My apologies, alta. This man is Tess's fellow, and he's distraught because she didn't meet him as promised—"

"And because there's *blood* outside!" Pavlin shouted. Then he dragged his voice down with visible effort. "Alta Giuna, may—may I speak with you privately?"

"Show me this blood," she said. "The rest of you stay here."

The back lane was foreign territory to her, but she immediately saw the rusted spatters on the stone. Not enough to be serious, thank the Lumen. "Yes, I see. What is it you wanted to say, Constable?"

He wrung his hands. "It's your maid, Suilis. Tess told me she'd been snooping around, asking lots of questions, poking in Renata's room—that sort of thing. She asked me to look into her. I mean Tess asked—"

Giuna laid a calming hand on his shoulder. "I understand. Did you find anything?"

"She's one of the Oyster Crackers," Pavlin said, then swallowed the rest of his explanation when Giuna's lips parted in recognition. "And—I'm so sorry for saying this, alta. But Suilis has worked more than once for Sibiliat Acrenix."

Giuna kicked the canal wall, and then had to sit down on it when pain shot up her leg. She'd hoped that Sibiliat might take her threat seriously—at least seriously enough to give her pause before she tangled with Renata. Again.

Instead, Giuna's public rejection might have driven Sibiliat to tangle harder.

But why Tess? Did Sibiliat think she could get at Renata's secrets that way? Tess might know them, but she would never spill them. The bond between those two went well past an alta and her maid.

Unless Sibiliat, in her frustration, took extreme measures to make Tess talk.

Giuna shot back to her feet. "Constable, I'd like to exercise my right as a noblewoman to request Vigil help."

Pavlin's expression crumpled like wet paper in rain. "I'm not a constable anymore. The captain and I—I mean, Grey and I, Master Serrado and I—we quit. A lot of people did, because of what's been going on there."

She'd heard bits of that from Nencoral. Not enough to put the whole picture together, but enough to realize that if the people she trusted were no longer hawks, she couldn't rely on the Vigil to help. Not if Suilis might be working for Sibiliat.

Besides, what if Tess didn't have that much time?

"You don't know where Renata is, do you?" she asked. Pavlin shook his head despairingly. "Then it's up to us."

Her determination was a facade over uncertainty and fear, but it had the effect of straightening Pavlin's spine. "I know where the Oyster Cracker base is," he said. "I don't know if Tess is there, but—we could try."

"I'll get Meatball. Suilis was always afraid of him. And—" Giuna stopped helplessly. Once they found Tess, whether among the Oyster Crackers or not, what then?

Pavlin hesitated, visibly biting down on an idea. Then he said, "Will you protect me, when this is all done?"

"Of course! Why?"

He headed for the kitchen door with ground-eating strides. "Because Tess was making me a coat."

Eastbridge, Upper Bank: Canilun 18

The bag over Tess's head left her eyes gritty and her nose stuffed with snot. The men dumped her in a corner of some building with only creaking floorboards and muffled conversations for company. And a temple clock, so close it made her own temples pound as it rang seventh sun and then the bells that followed. Leaving her to let fear soften her, Tess reckoned.

By the time someone saw fit to pull off the burlap sack, Tess's mouth tasted of sawdust and stewed fury. Scrunching her eyes shut against the grit, she spat to one side and coughed up the phlegm that had been building in her throat.

When her eyes cleared, she took in her dimly lit surroundings. She'd never seen the room before, but it was familiar nonetheless. Ondrakja had been fond of keeping luxuries she liked or that couldn't be fenced, and it seemed the Oyster Crackers were no different. The carpet covering most of the floor was as fine as anything Ommainit could produce, if you ignored the three conspicuous burns scorching the pattern. A teak bathing screen carved in the Isarnah style hid what was probably the closestool in the corner opposite Tess, while lightstones in lanterns of cut tin and colored glass limned the furnishings in an amber haze. At the far end of the room, stairs spiraled up toward what Tess assumed was the clock tower, and down toward what she hoped was escape.

She lifted her chin to glare at Suilis.

"Here's how it's going to be," Suilis said, straddling a stool just out of kicking range. The bright shell of her usual cheerful facade had cracked into a cynical half smile. "We're done playing around. You're going to tell me where your mistress hides her best jewelry. Not the usual stuff, but the things she *really* wants to protect. I'll keep you overnight, and if I find what I'm looking for, you'll walk out tomorrow morning with nothing worse than a night of lost sleep—and you'll forget we had this conversation. Understand?"

Tess dropped her gaze as though cowed. Jewelry? *That* was what this was about? No, Suilis was looking for something specific. Which meant Sibiliat was looking for something specific. Which meant that family heirloom she'd been asking after—the one Ren lost months ago.

Would Suilis believe the truth? If she'd gone to these lengths, it meant either she was lying about letting Tess go, or she'd given up returning to her role as a maid. This was the last act of a desperate woman.

Tess wasn't Ren, but she'd been a Finger long enough to know that desperation meant leverage. You just needed to show you were strong enough to use it.

"I've a counterproposal for you," Tess said, raising her head and straightening her shoulders. She couldn't look intimidating, but sometimes it was enough to show you weren't afraid. "You tell me what Sibiliat Acrenix wants with an old lump of bronze, and my alta will cut you free of whatever leash they're using to make you their dog."

She let that thread spool out long enough to catch Suilis's curiosity, then came in with her needle. "*And* I don't tell Vargo where the Oyster Crackers lodge these days. Seems to me he's always looking to catch another knot in his web."

Suilis recoiled so hard, her stool toppled with a clatter. "You don't know anything to tell."

"Isla Cospicho." Tess cocked her head as though listening. "Inside the Eastbridge Quaratium, sounds like. How does your knot sleep at night with these blasted bells going off all the time?"

"Wax in our ears," said a woman coming up the spiral stairs, followed by the two bullies that had jumped Tess. "Though we use our nights for things other than sleeping. I thought you said you'd take care of this?" That last was addressed to Suilis.

Suilis scowled. "I *am* taking care of it. I thought you said you'd leave me to it."

The woman shrugged one-shouldered and approached Tess. "Sounded like your harmless little maid has some fire in— *Tess?*"

What the room's shadows and eight years' time had obscured, the burn searing the woman's cheek and temple unveiled. Tess was still a pinkie when Ondrakja shoved a boy's face into the coals for cutting himself out of the knot, but it wasn't something any of the Fingers soon forgot.

"Es—" Tess swallowed the name, not certain it fit any longer.

"Esmierka now," the woman said with a wry smile.

"Esmierka." Tess let her own smile bloom into a laugh. "Maiden's knickers, Sedge never said you'd made it into the Oyster Crackers." Though it wasn't surprising. It was the dream of many Fingers, and Esmierka had a knack for breaking numinata.

"Little Sedge? He still kicking? What's he up to?"

"Fog Spiders, under Vargo. Finally grew into his shoulders, to hear *some* tell it." Tess shot a sidelong glance at Suilis.

Who scowled back before snapping at her knot-mate, "You know her?"

"Tied together in the Fingers." Esmierka righted Suilis's stool and took it for herself. It was too short for her long limbs, but she paid that little mind, folding up in sharp angles. "You the one who knifed Pito?" She jerked her head back at one of the men—the one bearing a bandaged forearm and a scowl.

Tess lifted her chin. Esmierka might seem friendly enough, but the Fingers were years in their past. Tess had shucked one of her fellow Oysters, and only one person could forgive that. "You the boss?"

A shake of Esmierka's head killed that hope. "The boss sent me to deal with this." Her unflinching gaze took in Suilis as well as Tess. "Been going on too long with nothing gained. Time to set it to rest."

"But my brother—" Suilis's voice cracked. She looked off at the Isarnah screen, but not before Tess caught sight of tears.

Sighing, Esmierka turned to Tess. "You know the piece the Acrenix are looking for?" At Tess's nod, she asked, "You know where it is so we can swipe it? Or maybe you can just swipe it for us?"

Tess hesitated. A lie would free her, but Suilis's desperation gave her pause. This wasn't a usual lift for the Oysters. "The Acrenix have your brother?" she asked Suilis.

For a heartbeat she thought Suilis wouldn't answer. Then, in a voice frayed almost to breaking, Suilis said, "He's being held in one of the prison hulks. Due to be sold in Ommainit. They said they'd get him freed if I get them what they want."

Tess's relieved giggle earned a glare. She would have waved it off if her hands weren't still tied. "Sorry, but that's easy as anything to take care of. My alta can do it better than the Acrenix can. And I'll see she does—*if* you let me go and tell me why Sibiliat wants that pendant so much."

"I don't know why."

"Then find out. You can—"

A pounding from below and a muffled shout of "Open for the Vigil!" made Tess groan. Everyone in the room went tense and wary.

"This is what the boss was afraid of," Esmierka hissed at Suilis.

"The Vigil answers to Caerulet. They can't—"

"Caerulet's already lost his patience. Isn't that why you bagged Tess? Come on." Esmierka drew a knife to cut Tess's bonds. "Lie for us, and I'll make sure you walk out of here."

Like Tess wanted to tell the truth to any hawks, after what happened with Pavlin and Captain Serrado. She nodded, and with Esmierka following, she went downstairs to the back entrance of the Quaratium.

When the door opened, it was hard to tell who was more surprised: herself, or Pavlin and Giuna. They gaped at her; she gaped at them; Esmierka stared at them all—and then got knocked against the wall as Pavlin charged forward.

"No, don't!" Tess grabbed him by the back of his coat. The coat she'd been sewing for him, and didn't *that* make sense; of course he'd pretend to still be a hawk in order to rescue her.

There'll be time for swooning later, she told herself sternly.

"Tess, you're all right!" Giuna almost let go of Meatball's leash, then clutched it tight again to keep him from charging into the fray Tess was trying to prevent. Over his barking, Giuna said, "We thought—"

Tess had missed her meeting with Pavlin. They must have found the signs of her struggle. "I know," Tess said. "It's all right, though. Well, it didn't start that way, but it is now. I was just about to make a deal with—" She caught herself short of saying Esmierka's name. Though whether that mattered, them having come to the Oyster Crackers' hideout and all, who knew.

Esmierka hesitated. Then she said, "Oh, Masks have mercy—we're not having this conversation on the doorstep. Come upstairs, the lot of you."

Suilis's confusion at the sight of them returning with a hawk and an alta in tow transformed into a recoil at the sight of Meatball. Apparently her fear of him hadn't been part of the act.

Esmierka continued their conversation as though there had been no interruption. "Suilis. Can you get the information Tess wants?"

From the way Suilis clenched her jaw, there were several answers she was holding in, but the one that made it out was a grudging "yes."

Esmierka faced Tess and her would-be rescuers. "Sorry, Tess, but your word isn't good enough. Alta Giuna: There's a man on a prison hulk waiting to be shipped off to Ommainit for wrecking Meda Nitarra's carriage. Can you get him free?"

Giuna shot a sidelong glance at Tess, who nodded encouragingly. She couldn't explain the whole story right then—maybe not ever, with it touching on so many of Ren's secrets—but she was sure this was worth it.

It didn't occur to Tess until after Giuna nodded back that the alta had looked to *her*, a common maid, for guidance.

"I can," Giuna said. "It'll take a little doing, because the prison hulks and the penal ships fall into an odd tangle between Fulvet, Caerulet, and Prasinet... but His Grace is a family friend, and we're on good terms with Her Charity as well. Yes, I give you my word."

"Then we give you ours that we'll deliver the information Tess has asked for within the next two days," Esmierka said. With a rakish grin, she spat in her palm and held it out.

Giuna quailed only for a moment. Then, with the brave air of a woman going into a duel, she removed her glove, spat in her own palm, and shook Esmierka's hand.

"Now get out of here," Esmierka said.

At least the other two waited until they were downstairs and outside before they let all their questions burst out. Tess brushed them off as best she could, while Pavlin brushed burlap debris from her curls. "I'm all right, really. Alta Giuna, I'm that sorry to say, but Suilis is working—"

"For Sibiliat. I know; Master Ranieri told me." Giuna's jaw firmed up. "I wish I could say I'm surprised, but—"

She wiped the rest of that sentence away with a sigh, and Tess let it lie.

"Are you sure you're all right?" Pavlin asked softly while Giuna flagged down a splinter-boat. His worried touch had descended from her hair, to her shoulders, to her arms. "I saw the blood in the lane, and you missed our meeting, and I thought—"

"I'm *fine*." Tess caught his hands to keep them from flitting about—and to steady herself. Now that the danger was past, the awareness of it was taking root. Pavlin's saucer-eyed worry would only feed her tremors, and she wanted none of that. She'd talked her way out of danger with a bravado worthy of Ren. What use did she have for fear?

She gave Pavlin a cheeky grin. "Only a mud-brain messes with me. I have scissors."

That got her a chuckle, and a smile that was all the encouragement she needed to rise on her toes and press her lips to his.

Eastbridge, Upper Bank: Canilun 19

Renata stood at the window, her gaze alternately on the street outside and the medallion in her hands. She tried more for the former than the latter, but all too often failed.

Because of the Tricat medallion, Tess had nearly gotten hurt.

Even a day later, her skin still thrummed with alarm at the memory. Tess coming into Vargo's house, bearing answers about Suilis and Sibiliat, and a story that made Ren want to gather Sedge and go show the Oyster Crackers some Lacewater justice. It wasn't a surprise that Sibiliat wanted Tricat; she'd admitted as much the previous winter, when she claimed it was an Acrenix heirloom. And Ren suspected that was the reason for her dizziness on the Night of Bells: the medallion showed her what Sibiliat wanted, and what Sibiliat wanted was the medallion. Resonance in a circle, building on itself.

But for someone to target *Tess*...

"That's how it goes," the Rook had said, with flat simplicity. "For two hundred years. Don't take this the wrong way, but you got off lightly."

Because in other situations, Tess might have been killed.

Thinking about *that* made Ren's hand tighten again on the medallion until the hard edges dug into her flesh. Tricat was the numen of family, and of justice. Spun against itself, the numen of revenge.

Those impulses had lived in her for a long time. It wouldn't take much to make them grow.

She pivoted away from the window and tucked the bronze disc into her pocket just as a knock came from downstairs. The Rook faded into the adjoining room—Grey this time, not Ryvček—and a moment later Suilis came in, as wary as a bird among cats.

Her gaze flicked over Vargo and Tanaquis before landing on Renata. "No Tess?"

"You'll deal with me," Renata said coolly. "What information do you have?"

"My brother—"

"Will be taken care of." The phrasing came out more ominous than she'd intended, and Renata forced herself to soften. "He won't be sold, I promise. We've already taken preliminary steps. You've brought something useful?"

Suilis wouldn't have come if she hadn't found anything to hold up her end of the bargain. Grudgingly, she reached into her pocket and drew out a folded piece of paper. "This is a copy, not the original, but I'm a fair hand at drafting."

Renata believed that. Rumor said the Oyster Crackers had accurate floor plans for every fine house in the Pearls. She took the paper and unfolded it—and then the paper rattled as her hand shook.

"May I?" Vargo rose and peered over her left shoulder, Peabody poking inquisitively out from under his collar. Tanaquis followed suit on the right, without asking.

Suilis hadn't brought her a letter or a notebook. She'd brought a diagram of a numinat. A numinat Ren had seen before . . . in the dream, on the floor of the Praeteri temple.

An echo of the past that is yet to be. That was what the nameless szorsa had called it.

"That means something to you," Suilis said, a note of eagerness coming into her voice. "It's valuable, right?"

Renata let Vargo take the paper. Her voice was steady, as her hand hadn't been. "You've done *very* well. Now you need do only one more thing."

Suilis's expression hardened. "I'm not doing anything for you until—"

Her words cut off as Renata drew out the medallion she'd been holding before.

"We could free your brother, as promised," Renata said. "But that might raise Sibiliat's ire. Simpler for you to take this to her, per your original deal—though if she reneges on her end, let us know, and we'll make certain your brother is safe."

One of Suilis's hands twitched toward the medallion; the other curled into a loose fist. "You're having me on."

"Not at all," Renata said. "I'm luring my enemy out by giving her what she wants." *Or giving her what she thinks is what she wants.*

If the situation with the medallions didn't make everyone so tense, it would almost have been funny. Five of them all had the same idea at once, when Tess showed up the day before—Ren, Vargo, Grey, the Rook, and Tess herself—and the only question had been which of their proposed jewelers to approach.

With the original to hand, making a forgery was easy.

Tanaquis assured them it took more than just the right sigil to call on a Primordial, but just for safety, they'd left a minute break in the lines, too small to see without a magnifying lens. Let Sibiliat have a fake Tricat, and see what she tried to do with it. Ren had every faith that Suilis would bolt with her brother at the first opportunity, before Sibiliat could test her new acquisition.

The medallion was gone so fast and so smoothly, it made Ren briefly mourn the days when her own touch was that practiced. "You won't see me again," Suilis said, already heading for the door.

"Good," Ren muttered.

Tanaquis and Vargo already had their heads bent over the paper, with cryptic, half-complete comments darting between them like dragonflies. The Rook emerged once more, and managed to rush to their side without looking like he was hurrying. Renata said, "What will that numinat do?"

They fell silent, though Alsius still nattered on about mathematical concepts that meant nothing to her.

Tanaquis looked troubled. "It's premature to draw conclusions without—"

"Not that premature. We can tell what Ghiscolo wants." Vargo's gaze slid past Renata and fell on the Rook. "He's trying to join them together again. To remake the Tyrant's chain of office."

Renata went still.

"Is that so." The Rook's voice was menace-soft. He leaned past Vargo to pluck the diagram from the table. "How does he propose to get them all in one place?"

Oblivious to the tension, Tanaquis crowded close to the Rook and traced her finger across the page in illustration. "There are two parts to the numinat. The first is meant to draw the medallions in, using a control effect. Those who hold them may be immune to the influence of other A'ash medallions, but not to the eisar of other Primordials. It will compel them to come—much like what the Pontifex and I used to pull Renata and Vargo out of the realm of mind, when they got caught. Then, once they're all in the figure, he'll only need to make the adjustments here, here, and here to begin the process of fusing them."

"He's depending on the resonance between the numina," Vargo added. "He has Quinat, which is enough to call Quarat to him. Sessat can bring Sebat, and if he springs Sureggio from prison, that gives him Noctat to get Ninat. It's not a bad plan." He leaned against the arm of the couch, a smug grin overtaking his wariness. "Too bad it's going to fail."

::Ah, of course. He can't call Tuat with a fake Tricat, and without those, he can't get the two Illi medallions,:: Alsius said, just as Tanaquis murmured the same thing.

You carry a great blessing. How many times had Diomen said that to her? That night in the temple, asking her what tool she had to hand to craft her vengeance . . . and the rage numinat had used amber, Tricat's stone. All his probing had never truly been about her; it was only about finding the Tricat piece of the set. Suspecting she had it wasn't enough; they needed the medallion itself.

Renata's sigh of relief went down to her toes. *He doesn't have what he needs.* Of course, Sibiliat would know soon that she hadn't gotten the real Tricat, and that would bring problems of its own; houses had fallen in the struggles over these medallions. But for now, at least, Ghiscolo couldn't—

At her indrawn breath, the Rook's hood tilted toward her. "You've thought of something."

Vargo's gaze sharpened. Of everyone in the room, he thought the most like Ren did, with the manipulative cunning of the streets.

"Fuck me," he whispered. "You want to let him go through with it."

Renata had the real Tricat with her, in a pocket imbued by Tess to be well-hidden. She drew it out now. "We discussed it when we failed to destroy Illi-zero. It may be that the only way to unmake these . . . is to have the whole set."

The Rook grabbed the wrist of her empty hand, his grip tight. "Are you certain that's what *you* want?"

"To destroy them? Yes." Ren met the shadows of his gaze squarely. "And that is nothing to do with Tricat."

"No, that's Ninat's domain," Tanaquis murmured. Plucking the diagram from the Rook, she examined it once more. "It would be an interesting challenge. Destruction as the apotheosis of creation. Yes, we could alter the alterations to achieve that end. Just reinscribe this Ninat figure as a tessellation rather than a concatenation..."

"Without boring you with details," Vargo said over her continuing ramble, "it's possible...if they had the real Tricat." He rubbed one hand over his face. "You're already thinking about ways to swap it in for the fake, aren't you."

Renata's gaze fell on the diagram. "Those squares placed all around—those are where the medallions will go, yes?" Tanaquis had drawn similar boxes for the pattern cards when she removed the curse. "I saw this numinat when I went after Vargo. In the dream—on the floor of the Praeteri temple. I think I was seeing what *would* be there, in the future."

"Tricat *is* time..." Tanaquis began, brightening.

Before she could start dancing down the path of theory, Renata kept going. "But the numinat was enormous, Tanaquis. Those squares were large enough for a person to stand in."

::It makes sense. If they're pulling the medallions through a control numinat, easier to leave everyone under that control until the whole ritual is complete. Lumen forbid Ghiscolo should risk *himself* to get what he wants.::

Vargo relayed the content of Alsius's observation, if not the discontent, and added, "He holds both Quinat and Sessat. He'd need someone else to stand in for one of those."

"Sibiliat," Renata said. "She's his heir, and she's been tied into this at every other step."

"With the Pontifex acting as Uniat while he inscribes the chain," Tanaquis said, sounding almost cheerful. "Very tidy. I mean, it will undoubtedly kill Diomen—you can't hope to achieve a binding like that without dying—but he's even more dedicated to the exploration of numinatria than I am. He understands quite well that death is the gateway to the infinite." For a moment her eyes shone.

The Rook was still as tense as a harp string. Renata said, "My question is: Knowing that, and from what you can see in the diagram... is it *feasible* to change the numinat's purpose to destruction? Or would it take so long that we'd have to subdue not only whatever muscle Ghiscolo has on hand, but also every other medallion holder?" She bent her head toward the Rook. "I have complete confidence in your fighting capabilities, but—forgive me—nine or more people at once might be a bit much."

"Oh, but nobody will be able to do anything once the ritual starts," Tanaquis said, as though that were obvious.

Since it wasn't, Vargo explained. "The focal numinata can't easily be broken into—or out of. I suspect the other medallion holders will take exception to being yanked into Ghiscolo's scheme, and he wouldn't want to deal with that. He might have a few guards, but unless he expects trouble, he won't spoil the secret of the temple—or the secret of what he's doing."

A chill went down Renata's back. "So either I hand over the real Tricat... or I go in there myself. And I won't be able to interfere if I do."

She knew they would argue about it. Tanaquis, with her usual dispassionate logic, had no objection to Renata risking herself, but both Vargo and the Rook felt differently—or rather, Grey did. She listened to several bells' worth of alternate and increasingly implausible suggestions until the others exhausted *if* she should go and moved on to *how*.

The plan they formulated was logical, and as watertight as they could make it. Still a gamble, no question—but for a chance at destroying the medallions and removing A'ash's poison from Nadežra, she would take that chance.

But as she left Vargo's house, she did wish there were a labyrinth on the Upper Bank, so she could pour offerings into the mouths of the Faces and the Masks. Instead she diverted down a quiet canal walk rather than heading directly to Traementis Manor. She rather suspected that soon she would have company.

It was Grey who caught up to her, not the Rook, but he pulled her under the shadow of a bridge with the Rook's caution. Their only audience was the raft of ducks paddling around the moored splinter-boats belonging to the nearby houses.

"I'm sorry. I know it's not..." He trailed off and pulled her close. His breath was soft as down against her brow. "I needed to see you without the shadows of the hood."

Because the Rook was torn between suspicion of her, as the holder of Tricat, and the chance to fulfill his mandate at last. Ren leaned into Grey, fighting the wary instinct that could never stop worrying about what would happen if someone saw. Her throat wanted to relax into her natural accent; she forced herself to remain Seterin. "I know. If this works, though..."

"I'm not telling you not to take the risk. No matter how much I'd like to." He pulled back enough to run a finger down her cheek. In his own clothes—neither Rook nor hawk—he wore no gloves. And she was Renata enough that even that small brush of skin against skin felt illicit. "Just promise me you won't risk everything. There will be other chances. There isn't another you."

She laughed, turning her face into his palm and allowing her accent to slip. "Have you mistaken me for someone else? Constant Ivan risks himself; Clever Natalya does not." *Except when she does.* It all depended on the story.

"This isn't a folktale." Grey pressed a kiss into her brow. "You make your own luck, Szeren. But don't press that too far."

Szeren. The handmaiden of Ir Entrelke Nedje, who distributed good and bad fortune to mortals. The name shattered what remained of Renata's mask, and she brought her lips to his.

24

The Mask of Bones

Isla Traementis, the Pearls: Canilun 20–22

It took three days for Ghiscolo to make his move.

Vargo set people to keep watch on the temple entrance, Acrenix Manor, and the other suspected medallion holders. The evening after the meeting with Suilis, they reported that Diomen had entered the abandoned shop in Suncross that hid the tunnel entrance, and he had not come out.

"Working on the inscription," Tanaquis said. "Which means they don't know yet about the fake—or else they're planning on kidnapping Renata."

Three days of waiting. Three days of Alta Renata canceling all her appointments and taking to her bed with an unspecified illness, which Giuna diagnosed as "overwork." Three days of trying not to let fear consume her, the way it had consumed the Ižranyi.

She laid a three-card line and got The Face of Stars, Ten Coins Sing, Pearl's Promise. Ren wholeheartedly believed they were starting from a place of good fortune; this was the best chance since the death of Kaius Rex to destroy the medallions. And Pearl's Promise suggested their labor might be rewarded. But how was generosity the path to their goals? The generosity of providing Ghiscolo with the real Tricat, perhaps.

Three days—and then word came. A group had left Acrenix Manor, heading for the Old Island. Ghiscolo was putting his plan into motion.

Temple of the Illius Praeteri, Old Island: Canilun 22

Thirteen people went in. Ghiscolo and Sibiliat and Fadrin; Sureggio Extaquium; Lud Kaineto and Mezzan with six others Ren recognized as stingers, two of whom were also Praeteri.

And Suilis.

Her brother had been freed, and Ren had assumed that meant Suilis was long gone. But she stumbled along between two stingers, clearly a prisoner. "Tell Vargo," Ren whispered to Alsius, who rode in her pocket like an eight-legged spy. She couldn't hear him, but he could convey messages. "They're using Suilis for the Tricat position." It made sense, she supposed; better that than flooding the Acrenix register with *three* unlinked medallions. And it explained why Ghiscolo hadn't discovered the fake—because the person carrying it didn't know what it was supposed to do.

Whether that would make things easier or harder for Ren's own plan depended on Suilis.

She and her allies couldn't bring many people into the temple, but that didn't mean others couldn't be useful outside. A little while after the Acrenix group vanished, Varuni and a quartet of Vargo's fists emerged, and Varuni signaled to Ren. They melted away into the alleys to watch out for any more trouble. Ren, going inside, found the two guards left behind now neatly bound and gagged in the back room where the fists had been lying in wait.

Hurrying through the tunnel, she heard voices and saw a light up ahead. Ren kept her footfalls silent until she neared the archway to the temple; then she shifted modes, storming in a perfect Seterin rage.

"Thief!" she shouted, pointing at Suilis. "You lying, false-faced thief!"

The stingers went for their swords, but they weren't prepared for her sudden arrival. Renata darted between them and grabbed Suilis, who was gaping at her in absolute confusion. "So this is where you've been hiding—with the Acrenix? Give me back my mother's medallion!"

No one made it into the Oyster Crackers without having quick wits. Suilis's expression hardened, and her hand twitched toward her neck, where a chain was just visible.

Renata seized that chain and yanked. As when she'd torn the knot charm from around Ondrakja's neck, the chain snapped, and the medallion clanked to the floor. She grabbed the fake and palmed it just before a stinger grabbed her.

Sibiliat's cold, clear laughter rang through the temple. "Oh, *Renata.* Your mother's medallion? Letilia was a thief long before Suilis was." She stepped up to where the stinger held Renata pinned— not very effectively, but Renata allowed his grip to remain. The whole point of this was *not* to escape with Tricat. "I told you, that's an Acrenix family heirloom."

"You're a liar," Renata spat. "This has belonged to the Traementis since the fall of the Tyrant."

One perfectly sculpted brow arched in reply. "So you *do* know the truth of them. You seemed so astonishingly ignorant, I thought otherwise. But family legend says our ancestor Carduin was Kaius Sifigno's bastard—so that makes it our heirloom, and your family the thieves." Sibiliat smirked. "Our claim is just a bit more distant than I led you to believe."

Ghiscolo appeared by his daughter's side. "Whether that's true or not hardly matters. These medallions belong to whoever is strong enough to take them. And of all those who have done so since Kaius Sifigno's demise, only *I* have found a way to link them once more."

He smiled at Renata—the same warm, personable smile that had made him the friend of so many in Nadežra. With Tricat in her possession, though, she could see past it, even though she tried not to. He wanted to finish what he saw as his lifelong purpose: the balancing of the medallions against one another, linked into harmony through a new chain.

Giving him the power Kaius Rex once had.

But that was Ren filling in the gaps: her medallion only showed her the Tricat aspects of his desires. She tried not to flinch as he leaned in, whispering in mock conspiracy. "But it's fitting that you should be the one to aid me. After all, you're the one who brought Tricat back to us."

His warmth fell away like a discarded glove when he glanced at Suilis, now in the grip of another stinger. "Lock her in one of the back rooms. She'll make a useful test subject afterward."

Renata did her best imitation of fighting as the stinger pushed her forward. She needed them not to question why she was here, not to suspect that there might be more planned. Just a fool walking into their net.

In the center of the chamber stood the numinat she'd seen in her dream, the numinat Diomen had spent the last three days inscribing. It made the figure from Veiled Waters look simple by comparison, with its web of interconnecting lines connecting Ninat to Noctat, Sebat to Sessat, and so on through the entire path of the Lumen.

Diomen smiled at her, too. But his was the smile of a zealot: someone so passionately dedicated to his cause, he would walk through fire for it. Or straight to his own death. "Sister Renata. Yes, it is right that it should be you—not that useless outsider. The blessing is yours, not hers. And now we will all be joined in the Lumen." He caught his own words and laughed. "Or should I say, beyond the Lumen?"

Chuckling, he went back to his work, but his phrasing twanged across her nerves as the stinger manhandled her into the Tricat position. *In the Lumen.* That was the kind of thing people said about the afterlife.

Beyond the Lumen was the domain of the Primordials.

Around the edges of the numinat, others were taking their places. Sureggio's unfocused gaze suggested he was on aža, and maybe some other things besides; his bony limbs barely seemed coordinated enough for him to walk when Sibiliat nudged him into place. But once that was done, she didn't move over to Quinat or Sessat, and Ghiscolo was settling into a comfortable chair.

Instead, Fadrin and Mezzan were taking up those positions. Alsius's grumbling from a few days before took on new, chilling dimensions. *Lumen forbid Ghiscolo should risk* himself *to get what he wants.*

Mezzan spat at Renata, earning himself a glare from Diomen, who wiped up the spittle with the hem of his robe. "You may have destroyed my house, bitch—but I found a new one."

Mezzan. Who was still cursed by A'ash, unless someone else had found a way to remove that curse. He would be consumed by his own Sessat-fueled desires…like the desire to belong to an institution greater than himself: House Acrenix.

Renata's heart was already beating fast, but now her whole body shook with fear. When she tried to step out of her square, something stopped her. Diomen had closed the line of Uniat and was now pacing along it with his hands folded and his head bent, chanting softly in Enthaxn. She prayed Alsius wasn't in her pocket anymore, that he'd leapt free during the scuffle with Suilis—and that he could get a message to Vargo.

They'd guessed wrong. The participants weren't who they'd thought. And she could think of only one reason why Ghiscolo wouldn't involve himself personally in his moment of triumph.

Suncross, Old Island: Canilun 22

Vargo had paid off the owner of the ostretta across the street from the temple entrance to close for the day; now he, Tanaquis, and the Rook watched from behind the curtained front window.

Alsius kept up a steady stream of narration through Renata's arrival, the scuffle with Suilis, the remaining stingers they'd have to watch out for, and Mezzan and Fadrin besides. He couldn't get close enough to take a good look at the numinat or listen in on Ghiscolo and Sibiliat's whispered conversation—not without being seen—but he notified Vargo as each of the medallion holders arrived and took their place.

They'd been correct on most of their guesses. Sostira Novrus, Cibrial Destaelio, and Utrinzi Simendis had already trailed into the storefront like sleepwalkers, along with Rimbon Beldipassi. The substitution of Fadrin and Mezzan for Quinat and Sessat was a surprise, but not an insurmountable one; in fact, Vargo looked forward to kicking Ghiscolo's teeth in *before* destroying the medallions. And while neither the Rook nor Tanaquis recognized the gentleman who followed—Alsius said the stranger took up the Ninat position, which answered the one truly open question—Vargo knew well the elderly woman who lurched up to the storefront like she was fighting the compulsion every step of the way.

There's Faella Coscanum to round out the set. We'll head in once she's through the tunnel, he told Alsius. To Tanaquis and the Rook, he said, "Get ready."

"But your man hasn't arrived with Serrado," Tanaquis said. Only Vargo's grip on the edge of the curtain restrained her from pulling it open far enough to reveal their presence. "Shouldn't we wait for them?"

If Sedge hadn't returned, there had to be a good reason; he wouldn't abandon Ren. Vargo had zlyzen scars striping his back to prove that. But whatever delayed them both, Vargo would have to worry about it later. "We can't wait for them. We don't know how much time we have to alter the numinat before the linking becomes irreversible."

"Agreed," the Rook said, the only word he'd spoken since his arrival. "We should go now."

"Give it just another moment for Faella to—"

::Vargo, there's a problem.::

Fuck. Of course there was. *What's happened?*

::Alta Faella just came through, but now Sibiliat is striking names from the temple register. You have to hurry, or you won't be able to get in at all.::

"*Move*," Vargo snarled, and suited action to word.

He rattled out an explanation as the other two followed him across to the abandoned shop. As he reached for the door, Alsius's voice came to him again—raw with sudden horror. ::Oh, Lumen, no.::

What now?

::Renata. She's trying to say something, and Ghiscolo just— Vargo, it's going to kill them! The numinat is going to drain—::

Then Alsius's voice cut off in a shriek.

Temple of the Illius Praeteri, Old Island: Canilun 22

The transformation of the numinat from calling to binding sent a wave of energy rippling through Ren, freezing her in place like a fly trapped in amber.

She couldn't speak. Couldn't move. Tricat held her immobile, pinned in place like an exotic butterfly in Beldipassi's cabinet of wonders. And time unfolded in front of her like the panels of a triptych— if the panels overlaid one another with perfect clarity.

It was like Ažerais's Dream, seeing the world in layers, except all of these were real. In the present, she stood in a ring of people: Rimbon Beldipassi, Sostira Novrus, Cibrial Destaelio, Fadrin Acrenix, Mezzan Acrenicis, Utrinzi Simendis, Sureggio Extaquium, a gentleman she didn't recognize, Faella Coscanum. And pacing an endless circuit around them, Diomen.

Overlapping that, she saw indistinct figures moving through the temple, spreading out along the walls. Hands rising and falling, chipping, hammering. Destroying the temple…or remaking it. Possible futures.

And underlying that…

Someone walked past Ren, close enough to touch if she could have lifted her arm. But this person wasn't the shifting mist of the future; she was the etched stone of the past. And familiar to Ren, with her double-buttoned blouse, her cascading crown of braids.

The szorsa she'd seen in the dream. The one who'd lost her name.

The Point, Old Island: Canilun 22

The Rook raced down the tunnel to Kaius's old temple, not caring if those trailing him could keep up. It would be his fault if the chain was remade, if Ren was sacrificed—his fault for not intervening sooner, for allowing them to gamble on this plan in the first place. And he couldn't say which he dreaded more. For the Rook, it was the chain.

For Grey, always Ren.

Necessity forced him to slow as he approached the open threshold that marked the temple proper. Alone, he wouldn't be able to cross it. Vargo was the first to catch up, and he grabbed the Rook's arm to drag him over the line—but his outstretched hand slapped air as solid as steel.

Vargo cursed. "We're too late."

The Rook turned to Tanaquis, stumbling up behind them. The run had slightly winded Vargo, but she was red-faced, bent over with one hand pressed into her side. "You're inscriptors," he snapped at them both. "*Fix this.*"

"Right, I can just reinscribe a register from out here." Vargo's biting sarcasm almost invited a similarly sharp response from the Rook—except he could see it was a thin mask over the fear beneath. "Tanaquis, any thoughts on how to break this?"

Tanaquis *always* had thoughts, and no reluctance about voicing them. Which made the sharp shake of her head all the more devastating. "I made an extensive study of the ward and the register when I first joined the Praeteri. It was an elegant workaround for the existing defense, but not one I could replicate from out here—it requires the register to be *within* the ward. And the Pontifex never shared with me how they managed to enter the temple in the first place."

The Rook slapped the invisible wall. "They did it somehow. Are you saying you're less clever than they are?"

Before Tanaquis could answer, Vargo said, "Alsius is inside. And he and I are connected. Could we use that?"

"He's not dead?" the Rook asked, ignoring Vargo's flinch. He'd caught fragments of something about Alsius amid the message of *they're all going to die* while he was running for the storefront.

"He's...somewhere dark. A bag, I'm guessing." Vargo swallowed, hand clenching in midair, pressed against the unseen barrier. "He can't see or hear anything. But he's still alive. And we're still connected."

"Connection or no, unless he's able to wiggle free and hold a pen, there's little he can do." Tanaquis traced the markings carved into the threshold stones. "This isn't like the numinatria we know, and it predates the Tyrant's conquest by a long time. I'd say it has more in common with...perhaps pattern might help? It's Vraszenian, after all. If only Renata were on this side..."

The Rook snarled. "It's no use wishing for what we don't have. There has to be a way. If the ward existed before the Illius Praeteri—"

Then it might be something *he* knew about. If he let himself reach for those memories.

He had no guarantee, and a lot to fear. Sinking himself into the Rook, in the hopes that some previous bearer had known how to get past this ward...if that got them into the temple, they might end the Rook's mission forever. Grey would never have to put the hood on again.

Assuming there was still a Grey left afterward.

But if saving Ren meant losing himself, so be it.

"Hold on." Dipping his head, he let his brow come to rest against the nothingness that blocked them. His hands curled inside their gloves, the leather creaking. A sound he'd used to intimidate people, more than once. Just like the shadows of his hood intimidated them, and the many shades of his voice: the mocking edge, the menacing purr, the whip crack of cold fury. He'd played the role so often, sometimes he forgot it *was* a role. Just like skilled crafters, lost in the intricate depths of their work, forgot the world around them. Forgot everything *but* the work.

And in so doing, they poured their spirits into it, imbuing what they made with power.

The timeworn stone of the passage floor blurred as his gaze lost focus on the present in favor of the past.

The Rook had traveled through the Depths and their linked upper passages many times. As Grey, trailing one cuff or another. As Oksana before that, when the Praeteri first rose, before the Rook decided—wrongly—that the cult had little to do with their mandate. He sifted back through time, through the various names that came and went, the faces hidden by his shadow. Memories of other lives, when he needed a place to hide and found his way here. Fleeing the hawks after he drove a supply wagon full of new weapons into the Dežera. Trysting with lovers who were drawn to the hood rather than the one wearing it. Crawling to a slow, bleeding death from a fatal gut wound, and later being picked up by his next bearer.

And before all that, the ghost of a memory so deep that it predated even the Rook. The woman who was the first, her voice rich even when lowered to a whisper, warm kisses traded under the weight of fear and in defiance of a tyrant. Hiding in the last place he would look, many grim faces joined in common cause. Tied together by purpose, by friendship, by oath.

Knots.

The Rook pulled up so sharply, he would have fallen if the other two hadn't caught him.

"The resistance," he murmured, rubbing at the memory of a charm knotted noose-tight around his wrist. Common in those days for everyone, not just for gangs; no one had given any notice to the ones worn by the dissidents who sheltered here.

Vargo and Tanaquis exchanged baffled looks, and the Rook said, "The ones who took down the Tyrant. This is where they hid. And they didn't use a register to get people in; their key was different. We need to find a charm seller."

"A charm—" Tanaquis bit off the end of her doubt. "I never even thought of that. Knots—they're geometric, after a fashion. Fascinating. You can't go out shopping, looking like that; tell us what to look for."

The Rook stifled a grim laugh. *Everything comes back to threes.* "A triple clover knot. Blue, if you can find it." He wasn't sure if the color mattered, but better not to test it.

Tanaquis wasted no time heading back down the tunnel. Vargo spared only one second to cast a desperate look toward the inaccessible temple before he followed. Then the Rook was alone, clenching his gloved hands.

So close. All the medallions lay on the other side of that invisible barrier. All those who had profited from their power, who had corrupted Nadežra with their unrestrained desires. Everything he'd fought against since his creation, in one place.

If he could get to it in time.

But even if he couldn't...He was protected against any single medallion's influence. Would that hold against the entire set, linked once more? It had never been tested. The chain had been broken before, though. Even if it was remade, he could break it again.

And this time, there would be no pack of dogs surviving to fight over the scraps of their master's power.

Pounding footsteps warned him of Vargo's return. There were spatters of blood on the man's face that hadn't been there before. "Stingers outside," Vargo said through his gasps, holding out a fistful of triple clover charms in every color imaginable. "Varuni's dealing with it. Tanaquis behind me. Coming as fast as she can."

The Rook wasn't going to wait for her. He pulled a blue charm from the tangle and let the rest fall.

Then he drew his sword and stalked through the ward, heading for the temple and the would-be Tyrant.

Temple of the Old Island: The Past

The nameless szorsa walked past Ren, her steps taking her in a curving path. She kept her hands folded and her head bent as if she were tracing a labyrinth—but her path wasn't like the one Ren knew.

Instead of moving in complex loops, now toward the center, now away, she arced back and forth across the floor of the temple, almost completing a circle each time before reversing direction.

But each circuit she walked brought her closer in toward the center.

Ren strained against Tricat's immobility, to no avail. She tried to speak—maybe she did speak—maybe she just imagined it, her voice ringing out in her head rather than in the air around her. "Who are you? What is this place? How came you to lose your name—what crime were you punished for?"

The szorsa stopped and looked up, but not at Ren. When her mouth opened, only shreds of her words came through, indistinct echoes fading in and out through the depths of time. She looked excited and awed, gesticulating at someone past the edge of Ren's vision. The muscles of Ren's neck ached as she fought and failed to turn, to look, to understand.

But she could see other things. The temple around her was different now—different *then*. Still the same shape, with the high, vaulted hall buried deep in the Point, but the carvings on the walls were nothing like the defaced numinatrian diagrams there in the present. She didn't even recognize their style. Nor could she move close enough to see what they depicted, apart from the general shape of human figures.

The szorsa moved again, across the path she'd walked before. By straining to her utmost, Ren could just make out lines chalked onto the floor. Something like a labyrinth, but simpler.

More like the thread labyrinths hung up as charms against bad dreams.

Movement again; the szorsa was back. And now she wasn't alone.

The young man she tugged in her wake was tall and strongly built, and likewise dressed in archaic clothing. In contrast to her braids, though, he had close-cropped blond hair, and his red doublet was northern in style. He cocked his head to one side and nodded thoughtfully as the szorsa gesticulated around her.

A northern man, here in Nadežra. Not unusual; the city had

been a port of trade since its founding, taking in ships from the Dežera's broad valley, from the coast, even from across the sea.

But Ren could think of only one northerner who might have been in this temple, centuries ago.

Kaius Sifigno.

Temple of the Illius Praeteri, Old Island: Canilun 22

The temple's main chamber was lit by a ring of braziers circling the numinat, red-burning coal and flickering fire instead of the pure, steady light of the Lumen.

Three stingers were waiting for Vargo and the others with swords drawn. No surprise; his little group had abandoned stealth for speed in the short run from the threshold barrier. The Rook met the stingers blade-to-blade while Vargo dodged past, more than happy to let the hood be the hero.

His sights were fixed on Ghiscolo, seated beside Sibiliat on the far side of Diomen's numinat. Two additional stingers flanked him, and he sipped from a cup of wine as though he were the audience at his favorite play.

A pleasant air that shattered at the sight of the new arrivals. "How did you get in here?" Ghiscolo demanded, rising to his feet as Vargo stalked up. His gesture stopped the remaining stingers before they could charge, but a nod to Sibiliat sent her circling around Vargo to waylay Tanaquis, staggering gasping into the room behind the rest of them.

Vargo could have stopped Sibiliat. But Tanaquis had her own defenses, and Vargo had someone who needed him much more badly.

"Where's my spider?" *Alsius?*

::Vargo?!::

I'm here. I'll get you to safety.

Ghiscolo chuckled. "I have so many questions. Or rather, I had questions when I first realized your spider *wanted* things—things more complicated than flies and a nice web. Things no spider would ever think about. But I suppose most of my questions have been answered by now, save one."

He reached under his chair and produced a thick bag embroidered with numinata. No wonder Alsius couldn't hear anything from inside there.

Ghiscolo dangled it between two fingers like a man taking kittens to the river. When Vargo would have lunged, guards be damned, Ghiscolo said, "No closer, or I'll crush him under my boot."

Memory made Vargo stutter to a halt. The day he'd learned what Alsius's initial plan to save himself had been—that Alsius meant to take *his* body, and only wound up in Peabody by accident—he'd made good on his threat to smoosh the chatty spider.

He'd lived through being crushed once. He didn't want to do that again.

Instead he forced himself to speak, gaze locked on the small lump weighing the bag down. The Rook had already dropped one of the other stingers; he couldn't see what was going on with Tanaquis and Sibiliat, but he would need allies before he could risk charging Ghiscolo. "Ask what you want."

Ghiscolo let the bag swing gently. "When exactly did you become my brother's keeper? And why did the Lumen see fit to reincarnate that useless fool as a *spider*, of all things?"

Alsius, he knows!

::Who? Knows what?::

Ghiscolo. He knows who you are.

While Alsius sputtered, while Vargo tried to think his way through to a solution, Ghiscolo shrugged. "Not that it matters. Only idle curiosity."

And he flung the bag into the nearest brazier.

A scream ripped out of Vargo as pain tore across his skin. His knees cracked against stone; he batted at flames that weren't there but burned him anyway, his thoughts reverberating with shrieks not his own. He tried to crawl toward the brazier—*Out, out, get him out!*—but now the stingers moved. A boot slammed into his shoulder; something inside cracked, the bone grinding against itself as he curled up against another kick. The hands in front of his face were unmarked, but in his head their bubbling surfaces burst, clear liquid seeping glossy across his skin and his thoughts a tangle of *Please, please stop not Alsius stop—*

A shadow like smoke shot past him, followed by a clatter and a blessed easing of the pain. The sharp ring of steel and a heavy thud; then Vargo's vision cleared enough to see the Rook, now down and wrestling with one of the stingers among a scatter of coals.

Before he could scramble across the floor to search for Alsius— he saw the charred remnants of the bag; Alsius had to be there—a pair of hands gloved in red-dyed kid wrapped around Vargo's throat. That grip, surprisingly strong, lifted him to meet Ghiscolo's furious glare.

Spittle hot as oil spattered Vargo's cheek as Ghiscolo snarled into his face. "I won't let you take what was meant for me." Darkness danced across Vargo's vision, Ghiscolo's thumbs pressing down in just the right spot. The world was fading, taking the pain with it. *I'm sorry, Alsius.* "Not my brother. Not you. Not anyone. Let's see what joke the Lumen decides to play on *you*—"

Ghiscolo's words shredded into a sudden scream. Then another one, and his grip spasmed open, letting Vargo fall. He slammed into the floor, gasping for air, head pounding with the renewed rush of blood.

Above him, Ghiscolo was dancing like a deranged marionette, his hands flailing at his own body. Then something detached itself from Ghiscolo, falling from the hem of his coat to the floor, something black and charred that *hurt* Vargo when it landed on the stone.

Alsius...and the excruciating venom of a king peacock's bite.

Vargo lurched up to his knees as Ghiscolo fell to his. Where were his knives? His muscles, still howling with the pain of Alsius's burns, couldn't muster the dexterity to find and draw them. Instead he lunged for the nearest thing to hand: the fallen brazier.

The grinding of bone in his collar, the searing heat on his palms and fingers—those were nothing next to what Alsius had suffered. Now and sixteen years ago, when his brother murdered him out of nothing more than the lust for power. Vargo brought the heated metal down on Ghiscolo's head, once, twice, three times, before it clattered back to the stone, next to the corpse of the man he'd sworn to bring down.

That swiftly, Ghiscolo didn't matter anymore. Vargo stumbled toward the charred lump twitching among the still ones. *Alsius? Alsius!*

::'M *fine*. No. Not fine. Enough, though. Bag protected me. And you. Stop fussing.::

Choking back a sob, Vargo scooped Alsius up with the hand that still had some semblance of use. *I'll stop fussing when you stop scolding.*

::We're both doomed,:: Alsius grumbled. Then, more quietly, ::That could have gone better...but at least it's done.::

The vengeance he'd pledged to get for Alsius. Vargo glanced at the blood leaking from Ghiscolo's skull, then at Diomen still pacing in an unseeing and inexorable circle, binding the medallions with his life. "Not yet."

Temple of the Old Island: The Past

Ren's heart was bleeding, her bones aching as she watched the nameless szorsa work with the man who would become Kaius Rex. He wasn't yet the Tyrant; he was young, unscarred, his clothing good but simple.

But he was here, in Nadežra, before the conquest. Why?

An echo of the past that is yet to be.

The "yet to be" part had sharpened into clarity when Suilis handed over the diagram for Ghiscolo's numinat. But the szorsa had also called it an echo of the past—and now, drowning in Tricat's power, Ren saw why.

The figure drawn by the szorsa and the northerner wasn't the same as the one Diomen had inscribed. It held the crisp circles and straight lines of numinatria, but also that looping, labyrinthine path. When it was done, the two of them circled the center of what they had created, laying down in their wake a series of all too familiar discs.

Gold. Silver. Bronze. Copper. Iron. Steel. Prismatium. Cinnabar. Lead. Gold. And in the man's hand, a medallion of dull tin. Uniat, before it became a chain.

This was how he'd linked them, joining the separate pieces into one unstoppable whole. Here—in Nadežra. In a hidden temple beneath the Point, with the help of a Vraszenian szorsa.

If she could have moved, Ren would have been sick.

"Did you know?" she screamed at the nameless szorsa. It was no use; the woman couldn't hear her. Maybe no one could. Maybe no one ever would. "Did you realize what those were—what he would use them for?"

Kaius Sifigno stood with his back to the szorsa, smiling down at what they had prepared. Was the fire of conquest already in his eyes? Or had that come later, after A'ash devoured him whole? What had he aimed for, when he made this power his own?

She had to watch. She had no choice, but she wouldn't have turned away if she could. Ren had to know what happened, how they'd transformed the separate medallions into a single interlinked chain, a man into a conquering Tyrant.

She had to know how Vraszan had fallen.

Temple of the Illius Praeteri, Old Island: Canilun 22

Kaineto was reaching for the Rook's hood when he collapsed from a kick to the back of his knee. Vargo staggered like a drunk, as though even that strike had been more than he had in him, but it gave the Rook the opening he needed.

Bone crunched as he slammed his head into the nose of the stinger holding him. Wresting the knife away, the Rook flipped it underhand. One slash to the fore, one to the back, and both stingers had bigger worries than who was inside the hood.

The answer to that question didn't matter now anyway.

He took particular pleasure—though no particular care—in binding Kaineto and rolling him out of the way, via a route that passed over the scattered coals of the toppled brazier. Vargo was no help anymore. He'd sprawled with his back to Ghiscolo's abandoned chair, one arm dangling limp at his side, working hand cupped around his spider.

The Rook turned to the one still on her feet. Tanaquis stood at the edge of the numinat, watching Diomen pace out his circle. She'd made short work of Sibiliat, dropping Ghiscolo's daughter with one of the Rook's sedative darts.

"What are you waiting for?" he demanded, gesturing at the circle of people. They all stood in a trance, their hands gripping the medallions, their eyes seeing things not of the here and now. All the vipers who filled Nadežra with their poison. "You said you could destroy them."

"I can." Tanaquis's grey eyes, normally so bright, were clouded with indecision. "I could. What I was going to do *will* work. But I think I ought to ask first whether I should."

He knew it. Or he *should* have known it, if the optimism of Grey Serrado hadn't veiled his eyes. Every time he thought he could trust a cuff, they showed him the truth.

The Rook stalked up to her, blade lifted to prod her past her hesitation. "So you mean to take them for yourself? Let's see you try."

"What?" She frowned at him, paying little mind to the steel ready to make her bleed. "No, not at all. What I mean is, given the price, is this still what you want?"

Vargo had managed to drag himself to his feet, and now he slipped between the Rook and Tanaquis. *Siding* with her. "What price?"

Eret Vargo. *Alta* Tanaquis. They both wanted power, in their individual ways. Money and control, or manipulation of the cosmos. "Does it matter?" the Rook snarled. "For two hundred years this city has paid a constant price. If we can end this, we *must*."

"Even if it means killing them?" Tanaquis gestured to the ring of nobles still caught in the numinat, and Diomen still walking his enclosing circle in an unbreakable trance. "If we let this continue, we can channel their sacrifice to either creation or destruction. Ghiscolo was willing to kill them to get what he wanted. If you feel the same way, then I can do this very quickly. But I did think I should ask first." She blinked, as if that hesitation surprised her.

Vargo swayed. "Are you seriously fucking asking if we should kill *Ren*?"

"No," Tanaquis said. "I'm asking if we should destroy the medallions."

"By killing Ren!" He tried to grab her arm and hissed when his hand touched the fabric. "Look, I don't give a shit in the river for people like Sostira Novrus or Sureggio Extaquium. And Masks know I've killed when I had to." Ghiscolo's crushed skull gave mute testimony to that. "But this—no. Fuck that. We can find another way."

A growl rose in the Rook's throat. "*Another way.* When doing anything requires bringing all ten medallions together—a thing that hasn't happened since the Tyrant's death? We should risk this continuing forever, because you don't have the stomach to seize this chance?"

"I thought you didn't kill," Vargo snapped.

He didn't. He never had. He'd fought, and he couldn't swear that no one had ever died from the wounds he'd given them, but he'd never struck with the intent to kill. He'd promised not to.

But he wasn't killing them now. Their own corruption had drawn them here, the insidious power of a Primordial winding around and through their souls like a strangling vine. They were tainted, every one of them, and they'd brought this death on themselves. With their greed, their lust, their vengeful ways.

Even Ren?

That thought rose up from the deep, a barely audible whisper of protest. What remained of Grey Serrado, buried beneath the weight and the fury of the Rook.

Yes, even Ren. Her intentions might have been good, but she was still corrupted. If her own choices damned her, then so be it.

No.

It was more than a whisper now. The Rook opened his mouth to tell Tanaquis to do it, but no sound came out. Something fought him.

No. A fire burned in the shadows. A fire the Rook remembered—because once *he* had felt it, no, not him, the woman who made him, the woman who loved and grieved and forged her pain into something more, in the hopes that others would not have to suffer as she had.

He fought against that fire. All the countless sacrifices that came before would be for nothing if they didn't make this sacrifice now.

No! If you're willing to sell out your own principles, then you stand for nothing! I will not let you do this—I will not do this!

It felt like tearing fabric, like the breaking of links in a chain. The threads that bound Grey Serrado to the Rook broke . . . leaving behind nothing more than a man in a hood.

"You're right." Grey's voice was rough, but it was *his* voice. He ducked his head, hiding behind fabric where before there had been shadow. Dragging his speech into the Rook's accent and intonation. "How do I break it?"

"Break what?" Tanaquis asked. "The medallions or—"

"The circle," Vargo said, handing Grey a cloth wetted down with wine from Ghiscolo's glass. "At the terminus of the spira aurea. Do it there, and everything else will unravel."

It wasn't far. Three quick strides took him to the numinat, and one swipe of his hand broke the line. The shock of it tore up his arm like lightning, but he welcomed the pain.

Diomen's momentum carried him face-first into the ground, and he lay without moving. The standing figures began to sway.

Grey had just enough time to leap to Ren's side before she collapsed.

25

The Mask of Worms

Temple of the Illius Praeteri, Old Island: Canilun 22

One moment, Ren was watching the nameless szorsa and Kaius Sifigno prepare to bind the medallions.

The next, the world shattered around her, and she fell.

All the layers of time collapsed into one: a time in which the Rook was holding her, his voice whispering, "Ren. Ren. Tell me you're all right."

Not the Rook. Grey. His hood still cast a deep shadow, but the face within it was recognizable as his own.

She opened her mouth to ask if it had worked, and stopped. Because she could see what Grey wanted: completion of what he'd set out to do, the destruction of the medallions. But only if it could be done with justice.

She could *see*. She'd never been able to see, when he was cloaked in the Rook.

And the medallion was still in her hands.

"What happened?" she whispered back.

Before he could answer, voices rose up in confused and angry cacophony. Ren got her feet under her in time to see the back of the man who'd been in the Ninat position vanishing down the tunnel;

Sostira Novrus wasted no time in following suit. Even Sureggio Extaquium was staggering out, babbling nonsense as he went.

There was no time for explanations. People still held the medallions, and they were getting away.

"Stop them!" She wasn't sure what accent that came out in, but it was loud and harsh enough to hide such details. Tanaquis went uncertainly to the archway, not fast enough to stop Sureggio, and she wouldn't be much of a barrier—but Vargo followed her, scooping up the sword from one of the fallen stingers. Even from a distance Ren could see the way his face twisted in pain as he touched the hilt; the other arm hung limply at his side. But whatever his state and his lack of skill, his grim expression made up for it. No one would want to challenge a man who looked like that.

Clearly nothing had gone according to plan—or almost nothing. Diomen was facedown and probably dead. Ghiscolo was unquestionably dead, lying in a pool of his own blood. Sibiliat seemed to still be breathing, but the dart sticking out of her neck said she wasn't a threat for now.

That left the remaining medallion holders. Six of them, not counting Ren herself.

The Rook—no, Grey; there were so many things she needed to ask about—stood close behind her. Using her as partial cover for his lost anonymity. In her ear, he murmured, "We weren't able to destroy them. I—" His voice cracked. "I don't know if we ever will."

We can. She didn't know how, and she'd been pulled out of her vision before she saw everything she needed to, but she'd learned one thing.

However the medallions had been bound together, it had involved pattern. Tanaquis was right: Taking them apart would require that, too. But not the ways they'd tried already. Something else.

She didn't have the faintest clue what that something else might be, though, nor the strength to do it right now. Grey at her back was helping prop her up. And Cibrial and Faella were demanding answers from her, from the Rook, from *anybody*.

So she would give them some.

"Listen to me!" she shouted over their voices. This time firmly in a Seterin accent, and with authority enough to quiet them briefly. "You all know why you're here—at least in part."

She held up the Tricat medallion, thrusting it toward them like an accusation. "Every one of you holds something like this."

"Not me," Fadrin blustered.

"Oh, *fuck off*," Vargo rasped. "If I have to come over there and strip you naked, I will. Everybody will see the only thing you've got to brag about is Quinat."

"You all have a medallion," Renata repeated. "Maybe it only came to you recently; maybe it's been in your family for generations. But do any of you know what it is?"

Beldipassi did, but he was too rattled to speak. The reply came from Utrinzi Simendis, in an unexpectedly calm voice. "A piece of Kaius Rex's chain of office. One that draws its power from A'ash."

Of them all, of course he would be the most likely to know. Not simply because he held the religious seat in the Cinquerat, but because he had a reputation as a scholar and a skilled inscriptor.

Nobody else understood. "What the hell is A'ash?" Cibrial snapped.

"The Primordial of desire," Renata said, and silence strangled the room.

She let that stretch out for a moment before she went on. "All of you, whether you've known it or not, whether you've *meant* to or not, have been drawing on the power of a Primordial. It's helped you see what other people want. Even get what you want." She pointed at Ghiscolo's unmoving body. "He used it to *control* what people want. And his goal—a goal Sibiliat was helping him with, and Fadrin, and Mezzan—was to remake the Tyrant's chain of office. So that he could have the Tyrant's power."

Now all the heads swiveled toward the two standing Acrenix. "I didn't know!" Fadrin said, and this time it had the desperate ring of truth. "Nobody tells me shit! Blame Sibiliat; she's in on everything her father's up to. He just said, 'Take these; go stand there.' It's their fault, not mine!"

Mezzan said nothing. He'd sagged to his knees, Sessat in hand, looking too broken to speak.

Faella's voice was cold. "I think there will be more than enough blame to go around."

"That's for later," Renata said, before Faella could start ripping into her enemies. "Right now, what matters is this: You're corrupted by A'ash. Just as I am. Every one of us has that poison in us—and we can't get rid of it. The Primordial's power will only grow as we give in to its urging. If you throw away your medallion, you'll just wind up cursed by the same power you drew on. And when I say 'cursed,' I mean this is what destroyed houses like Adrexa and Contorio. And very nearly Traementis. Not only you, but everyone in your register will be affected."

In her peripheral vision, she saw Vargo step on Tanaquis's foot. Good: He could see where she aimed. Now wasn't the time to tell people they had an escape. Now was the time to scare them so badly, they would do what she needed them to.

She gestured at Grey. "The Rook has been trying for centuries to save Nadežra from this poison. We're finally on the verge of success. But until that can be done, this is what you will do.

"You will hold on to your medallion. You won't give it to anyone else, or throw it away. And you won't use it. Hide it somewhere safe; never carry it on your person. Question every desire you have that relates to your numen. Because remember: You have a Primordial's rot inside you. Anytime you think about the power that might bring, the benefit you might gain from drawing on it, remember that a Primordial once obliterated an entire Vraszenian clan in eleven days and nights of terror. This could easily obliterate *you*."

Beldipassi was nodding his head so hard, it looked like it would come off. Mezzan had shaken off hopelessness and was staring at her with undiluted hate. Cibrial looked dubious and Faella unreadable—but Utrinzi Simendis bowed.

He said quietly, "This is the path I've followed for years. I wish nothing more than to keep this power contained." An ironic smile touched his thin mouth. "Which is, of course, A'ash's power work-ing within me. Sebat: the numen of purity and seclusion. I cannot escape that merely by being aware of it. But I will continue to do as you say."

Then he turned his gaze on the others. "As should you. By com-mand of Iridet, if you need more than a personal warning. How Alta Renata learned of all this, I do not know...but if any of you doubt her words, come speak with me. I will tell you all I know of Primordials—which will be more than you wish to hear."

"We'll see," Mezzan spat, getting to his feet and moving as though he intended to bull Vargo out of his path.

He was swordsman enough to easily bat away Vargo's blade and wrest it from his grip, but he stopped his charge when the Rook's rapier came level with his throat.

"Don't try me today," Grey said in a passable imitation of the Rook's voice. Ren could tell it for an imitation, but she doubted anyone else could. "I'm not feeling my usual reluctance to leave bodies."

Vargo shot him a worried look, quickly veiled behind a sardonic smile. "For once, we're in agreement. The rest of you can leave, but I think we need to have a longer conversation with Fadrin and Mezzan."

"I concur," Utrinzi said, and gestured at the detritus of the rit-ual: the broken numinat, Diomen's and Ghiscolo's bodies, the un-conscious Sibiliat. "By my authority as Iridet, I hereby arrest all members of House Acrenix who committed blasphemies in an at-tempt to take the lives of members of the Cinquerat."

Cibrial made a vicious noise of agreement. "I'll go fetch—No, not the Vigil. Perhaps some of Fulvet's skiffers. Come, Faella." She held out her hand to the old woman, and together with Beldipassi, they left.

In their wake, Tanaquis said, "We should remove one of the medallions from House Acrenix. I can mitigate the consequences of the loss, and clearly the effects of having two conflicting energies flowing through the same register are...not good."

Utrinzi nodded in agreement. "I would ask you to take one, Tanaquis, but now that you're in the Traementis register..."

The mental conversation between Vargo and Alsius was brief, but not so brief that Renata couldn't have stepped in with an alternative suggestion—if only she could think of one. Not Tess, and not Sedge; no sum of money could have persuaded her to risk them like this. The list of people she trusted enough was short, and pretty much only had two other names on it.

"I'll take one of them," Vargo said. "My register's as small as it gets. Fewer people to risk, if something goes wrong."

She expected Grey to object. He only said, "Quinat or Sessat?"

Vargo made a face like he was being asked whether he'd rather drink piss or eat shit. "I'd prefer Quinat... which is why I'll take Sessat."

With the Rook's sword at his throat, Mezzan had no choice but to hand it over. Vargo grimaced as his hand closed around the circle of steel—then twitched in surprise when the blade moved on to Fadrin.

Grey held out one black-gloved hand. "House Acrenix can't be trusted with any of this power. They've made that abundantly clear. And if I take this, no one else will be affected."

If Ren hadn't already suspected something had gone badly wrong with the Rook, that would have made it shriekingly obvious. There was no world in which the Rook would have taken a medallion, not for any reason. That was Grey's decision, alone.

What happened?

She couldn't ask, not right now. With Utrinzi and Tanaquis backing the Rook's demand, Fadrin grudgingly gave him the iron medallion of Quinat.

With Suilis's help, once Renata freed her from the side room, Utrinzi and Tanaquis were able to drag Sibiliat and the bound captives out of the temple. Vargo lingered, shooting a frown at the bodies of Diomen and Ghiscolo, at the remains of the numinat. And at the hooded figure standing at its edge.

He approached the latter, slow as a man wading upriver. "I

wanted to say...thank you. For..." Vargo's voice broke, and he touched the crook in his immobilized arm, where Peabody nestled in a sling made from the stingers' armbands. "For saving both of us. If it weren't for your help, we would have burned."

Ren cringed at the reference to fire, but there was no way she could have warned Vargo. The Rook's hood merely dipped in stiff acknowledgment.

With an awkward twitch of a bow, Vargo headed for the tunnel. "I'll come back with some people to dispose of the bodies and give this place a thorough scrub down. Not just the numinat. We should destroy anything else we find that's eisar-related. I'm not certain I trust Tanaquis not to keep something for experimentation."

Pulling Ren to the mouth of the tunnel, he shot another worried look in Grey's direction and dipped close enough to murmur in her ear. "Are you sure it's safe to leave you alone with him? He's...Something's off. He was willing to let you die to destroy the medallions."

Ren saw Grey tense. Vargo might have kept his concerns at a whisper, but the temple's echoing walls defeated that attempt at tact.

"I'll be fine," she said, not bothering to lower her voice. "I trust him."

Temple of the Illius Praeteri, Old Island: Canilun 22

Grey waited only long enough for the echoes of Vargo's footsteps down the tunnel to fade before ripping off the hood.

The Rook doesn't kill. No...but he would let people die. Including Ren.

The disguise poured off his body, leaving the fabric of the hood twisted in Grey's hands. The silence from it mocked him. The heat of the braziers didn't touch the cold inside as he approached the nearest one and wadded up the hood to rid the world of it forever.

Ren caught his arm before he could. "Grey. Tell me what happened."

"I made a choice. And now I'm making another." He pulled against her grip. Not hard. He didn't want to be stopped, but if she wanted to stop him...

She didn't let go. Turning, he let the hood fall to the ground and buried his face in Ren's shoulder. The horror of what had almost happened still didn't quite seem real. "I was willing to lose myself to the Rook forever, if that was what it took. To save the city, and to save you. But I couldn't... No mission is worth letting you die."

Her hand stroked his hair, and the temple echoed with whispered Vraszenian endearments. She didn't say the obvious: that he'd chosen her above the city. That he'd been selfish. That for the first time since Kolya died, he had someone who didn't believe he carried bad luck with him wherever he went, and he hadn't been willing to give that up.

"I ruin whatever I touch," he whispered into her skin. He'd even managed to break *the Rook*—something that had lasted two hundred years. Hot tears stung his eyes. "My grandmother was right."

Ren pulled back enough to look him in the eye, her hands not gripping his shoulders, but cradling them like fragile glass. "You ruin *nothing*. You have helped me glue the pieces of myself back together, to become stronger than I thought I could be. Grey, the cards I laid for you..."

She gestured around at the temple. The numinat chalked onto the floor, and the ceiling of stone that hid the Point, the wellspring, the site of the ancient labyrinth. "Sleeping Waters. The card of place. When I was in the numinat, I saw... pieces of the past. Kaius Sifigno came *here* to forge the medallions into a chain. Because of your decision, I live to tell you what I saw. Your good future, Labyrinth's Heart—it said you must remain still. It is the card of *not* acting. To avoid The Mask of Bones, the death of myself and all the others."

"But I poisoned my fate." Grey's throat tightened at the memory. "You said so yourself. By moving those cards—I saw how you reacted. Labyrinth's Heart is stagnation, too, missing the chance to end this at last. And something died anyway."

The hood lay at his feet, a mute accusation. They could see if the

Rook would still answer to Ryvček...but in his soul, Grey knew it wouldn't. He'd torn that fabric beyond repair.

Ren pressed her lips to his, a kiss of comfort rather than passion. "The threads go on," she said, fierce and sure. "We are not done. And I will never tell you that you made the wrong choice."

"No, not the wrong choice." He tried to find comfort in her kiss, despite the guilty weight of the medallion in his pocket. "But only because there was no right one."

Owl's Fields, Upper Bank: Canilun 23

Sostira Novrus had many places she might hide, but she hadn't counted on betrayal from within.

"What makes you think I still have that medallion?" she asked when Vargo and Iascat finally tracked her down to a cozy lovers' nest on the edge of Owl's Fields. Crickets chirped farewell to the last of autumn's warmth, the days grown short enough that when the bells of the nearby Ninatium rang first earth, it was to send off a sun balanced atop the horizon. That wash of orange fire gave her a glow of false warmth as she sat by the window, lounging in a pretense of unconcerned elegance. "Perhaps I threw it into the Dežera."

"And curse the entire Novrus register?" Vargo shook his head. "Not even you are that cold."

"Nor are you that stupid," Iascat said. "To give up the only thing of value you have in this negotiation."

He'd been surprised when Vargo showed up at his door, hands bandaged and arm in a sling, to suggest that now was an ideal time for that house coup...but his surprise had shrunk to insignificance next to the rest of it. When Iascat heard how Ghiscolo had used the Quinat medallion on Vargo, he'd promised to keep this meeting civil. The worst of that impulse might have faded when the medallion got used again on Serrado, but Vargo was still wary—enough so that he let Iascat be the one to stop Sostira when she would have darted for the door.

Iascat shoved her back and said, "Though you *are* stupid if you think I don't have house guards waiting outside in case you try to run. Sit down, Aunt Sostira."

"Why, so he can kill me like he did Ghiscolo?" she spat with a cutting gesture at Vargo. She let Iascat herd her, though, until she dropped onto a small tuffet by the cottage's hearth. "Kill me, take my medallion, curse my house, leave you weeping. I've seen what he wants—and what he doesn't. If you think he loves you, you're a fool. I told you before: He's using you."

Iascat didn't so much as blink at her words. "We're using each other. I once thought you and your wives were the same, but it was different for you, wasn't it? All this time, you've been looking for someone who loves *you* more than they want anything else. And then casting them aside when that inevitably changes."

It was an alien sentiment to Vargo; he couldn't understand people who needed someone else to be the center of their world like that. But judging by the way Sostira reeled, Iascat had struck right to her heart.

And he pressed his advantage. "Let me lay this out for you. I have the backing of the rest of the house and the Cinquerat to take the title, the seat, and the medallion. How we do that is up to you. You can retire gracefully and with the gratitude of the family, or...well. Let's discuss the apple before the worm."

"You don't know what you're letting yourself in for," she whispered. Something haunted her gaze. "There's more to it than anyone knows. When I stood in that numinat...I felt something. Not just the Primordial of desire—yes, I know where the medallion comes from. But there's something else there." One hand curled unconsciously into a claw. "I can't describe how I know. I just...know."

"Intuition," Vargo said. When both nephew and aunt looked at him, he shrugged. "Tuat. It seems all the medallion holders had visions during that ritual." Tanaquis had been devastated to hear that such cosmic knowledge had been there for the taking, and she'd missed it. She'd spent the last several days compiling detailed reports of everything everyone had seen. Everyone who was willing to share, at least.

"I think not knowing what I'm letting myself in for is going to be my general state for a while," Iascat said. "But until we're able to deal with this issue, isn't it better to keep the medallion safely between us? I understand that these things let you see what people want. What do I want, Aunt Sostira?"

Vargo bit down on the reminder that they weren't supposed to be using the medallions. What was one more spot of corruption on what had to be years of accumulated stain? But he still shifted with unease as Sostira fixed her gaze on Iascat.

Then, as if it had been a staring contest, she blinked. One hand dipped into the neck of her surcoat, and came out with a silver medallion on a chain.

Iascat took it without flinching. "Thank you, Aunt." He looped it around his own neck, then reached into a satchel at his side and pulled out a sheaf of papers and a portable writing kit. "If you'll sign these, I'll make sure they're appropriately filed with Fulvet's office."

Sostira's mouth soured like she'd bitten into an unripe plum, but she took the papers. Iascat cast a glance around the cottage while she signed. "I'll arrange for you to stay here. I'm afraid Benvanna's been adopted by the Acrenix—a choice she no doubt regrets now—but if any of your other prospective lovers are willing, they can join you here."

It was house arrest under a kinder name, but Sostira made no objection. She just handed over the papers in silence.

Varuni was waiting outside, leaning against a tree with her arms crossed. Vargo had offered his people as backup for this meeting, but Iascat had brought Novrus guards instead. Thanks to Sostira's increasingly erratic behavior, he had enough support from his house to make this coup work; now he had the authority of his new position as Eret Novrus. And soon, as Argentet.

When Iascat was done instructing the guards, he turned to Vargo. "I'll need to jump through all the hoops to transfer power as soon as possible, but I should be done with that by midnight. I don't suppose you're available?"

He truly had grown from the shy, stammering man who'd barely been able to admit what he wanted on the Night of Hells. Vargo wondered how much more he might change…and how much of that would be the influence of the Tuat medallion.

If that distinction even meant anything. That was the insidious terror of a Primordial: It fed what was already there, until your own impulses ate you alive.

"Crookleg Alley?" Vargo asked, testing. That was where he'd invited Iascat after the chaos of the Night of Hells. Whether Iascat met him there or summoned him to Novrus Manor like a hired courtesan would tell Vargo a great deal.

A smile flickered across Iascat's full mouth. "I believe you have a townhouse in Eastbridge, Eret Vargo. Unless you think I should be ashamed of our association?"

Relief washed through Vargo as he agreed. It lasted until Iascat left, and he and Varuni began their stroll back toward the city proper. A slow stroll; more of Vargo's energy was going into healing Alsius than he wanted anyone to realize, though he was pretty sure Varuni had guessed. The sky was clouding up, and a sharp breeze cut in from the ocean.

"I've got an appointment at midnight," Vargo said, wondering wryly what Iascat would think if he suggested taking a nap first. "But before then, I've got an errand to run. Want to come along?"

Varuni snorted. "For once you ask. Where's the errand?"

Three people had escaped Renata's speech in the temple. Sostira was taken care of; the holder of Ninat was a mystery they needed to chase down. That left one more loose end that Vargo was long past ready to trim off Nadežra's hem.

"Extaquium Manor." Vargo cracked his neck and checked his concealed knives. "We're going to have a chat with Sureggio."

Isla Traementis, the Pearls: Canilun 24

Once again the entry hall of Traementis Manor bustled with servants and luggage. Donaia had meant to remain at the Villa Quientis for a full month, but the upheavals in the city had brought her back early.

"As if I would sit out there while everything happens?" Donaia said with asperity when Giuna tried to apologize for something that wasn't her fault. "I'm not so old yet that you need to tuck me into a chair by the fire. Lumen's light—I had a letter from Cibrial asking if *I* want the Caerulet seat. If she thinks *that's* a good idea, then clearly someone needs to come talk sense into the Cinquerat."

Renata stifled a laugh. Even the truncated holiday had clearly done Donaia a world of good. She looked and sounded once more like the formidable woman who'd greeted her supposed niece what felt like a lifetime ago. Better, even: no longer the mistress of a fading house, struggling against the drowning tide of a curse.

I hope Tanaquis can protect them. She and Utrinzi had already uncursed every Acrenix bearing the name, while Ren strangled the vengeful instinct that wanted to see them suffer the full weight of Ghiscolo's actions. Letting a Primordial's curse rampage through an entire house wouldn't be good for anybody. But first, Tanaquis had edited the Traementis register to shield everyone else from Tricat's influence—at least in theory. Whether it worked remained to be seen.

The medallion wasn't in Renata's pocket, but it weighed on her all the same as she greeted Donaia. Family: something she would have to be wary of. She thanked the Faces and the Lumen both that she had years with Tess and Sedge before the medallion ever came into her life; it meant she had something to compare against, anytime she found herself questioning whether her behavior with them was out of the ordinary. But with the Traementis, she would have to be more careful.

A different weight burdened Grey, though he hid it well as he wrestled playfully with Yvieny. She'd charged full speed into the manor, shrieking for Meatball. When Grey finally disentangled himself from his niece, Alinka asked with a coy smile, "How is Arenza?"

Renata had practice—and imbued makeup—to hide her blushes.

Grey had no such protection, though he did manage to keep his glance from straying to her by dint of bumping noses with Jagyi.

Alinka would have none of that dissembling. "Oh! Is there a story there?" She poked his shoulder. "As I said, Era Traementis! His heart has been caught at last."

"By who?" Giuna asked, with all the sparkling-eyed curiosity of a girl in love with love. "Who's this Arenza? When do you even have *time*? You're always busy."

"Yes." Tess's dry tone could have emptied the Dežera, and the look she gave Ren could have sent it running backward. "I'm wondering that my own self."

A thump at the door would have offered escape, if Renata had any justification for going to help Sedge carry a traveling trunk into the hall. Since she didn't, she took far too much delight in blinking innocently at Grey. "You have a sweetheart, Master Serrado?"

His bland smile promised later retribution as he said, "I prefer to keep matters of the heart private. I'm certain Arenza would feel the same."

"Arenza what?" Sedge yelped, dropping the trunk just short of his toes. He shot Ren and Tess a panicked look.

Donaia frowned in confusion. "Who's Arenza?"

Fortunately, Colbrin led Meatball in just then, which set Yvieny off like a firework, and in the ensuing clamor the topic of Arenza fell by the wayside. After all the luggage was brought in, though, Sedge managed to shuffle over to Renata and mutter, "You getting that close to him? Is that safe?"

Because Sedge didn't know yet. Neither he nor Tess did.

She met Grey's eyes across the entry hall and twitched her fingers toward her siblings. He hesitated only a moment; then he nodded minutely.

It took a little while to extricate herself from the Traementis and to pass messages where they were needed. But within two bells, Renata and Tess were heading up to her room—"After all, you've been sick," Giuna said anxiously, waving her off—while Grey and Sedge took their leave.

After a quick change into loose trousers, Tess gave the tree outside the balcony a dubious look. "Are you sure about this? I haven't been climbing in some time."

"You go first," Ren said. "I'll be below to stop any fall."

There was no fall to stop. In a rustle of leaves, Tess scrambled up to the manor roof, with Ren behind her. There they found Grey and Sedge waiting, Sedge frowning at his scraped palms. "Just saying, you would have slipped, too, if I hadn't found that loose tile first," he grumbled.

"Probably."

Grey's agreeableness earned him a sidelong glare. "Don't say that just to make me feel better. You're too good at this for a hawk." Sedge turned to Tess and Ren. "He's too good at this. Admit it, you're Stretsko or something, en't you? That's what this is all about, you knowing Arenza and not being where you was supposed to be when I was sent to get you. I wasn't there to help Ren because of you!"

Brushing his hair out of his eyes, against a wind that was determined to fling it there, Grey said, "Kiraly, as it happens. But yes, that's what this is about." He hesitated only briefly before saying, "I'm the Rook."

Sedge gaped for a heartbeat—followed by a gale of laughter which was, in hindsight, completely predictable. It ebbed when Grey and Ren remained serious, and Tess drew in a long, slow breath of understanding.

"Well, that makes sense of a whole mess of things that didn't before," she said. Then she beat a fist against Ren's shoulder. "And you near tearing your hair out about liking them both. Ha!"

"Oh really," Grey said, grinning as though his retribution for Ren's earlier comment had come sooner than anticipated.

"Wait! Stop!" Sedge slammed his hands down, and immediately looked guilty at the rattle of tiles. They all fell silent, waiting for someone from below to call up asking who was tromping around on the Traementis rooftop.

Only after a minute of birdsong, canal splashes, and little else did

Sedge dare to whisper, "You're having me on. Right? En't no way a hawk's the Rook. Plus, you're too young. I saw the Rook, years ago."

"That was my predecessor. And I should probably tell you ... I'm not certain I'm the Rook any longer. I've set the hood aside. It's ... complicated."

Ren wasn't willing to let the admiration in Sedge's and Tess's eyes wither away. "The Rook was going to let me die to destroy the medallions. Grey refused."

"Or maybe not so complicated."

She shot him a fond smile, and got one in return. Sedge groaned. "You're gonna be goopy, en't you." Then he hunched his shoulders at Grey. "Well, I guess I can put up with it for the man who saved my sister's life. And you en't a hawk no more, so that's something."

Not a hawk. Not the Rook. But hers. Ren laid her hand over Grey's and held it tight.

"I think it's sweet," Tess said, laying her hand over their joined ones.

After a moment Sedge sighed and topped the pile with his own hand. "All right. If we're going the way of Fiavla, at least we'll be happy on the road."

Their hands below and above Ren's were a comforting warmth against that chill. A fabric could hold where a single thread would break. And if pattern had something to do with how Kaius had brought Nadežra low...

Then who better than a szorsa to unweave it.

~~Ninat~~

The story continues in . . .

Book Three of the
Rook & Rose trilogy

Keep reading for a sneak peek!

Acknowledgments

Usually, acknowledgments exist to thank all the friends and family members who kept the authors watered, fed, and comforted through the writing and publication process. But 2020 was an unusual year by anyone's standards, so we figured we'd break the usual format.

We're grateful to the doctors, nurses, and other medical and emergency personnel who kept the health system functional and beds open for the people who needed them, often at the cost of their own physical and mental health.

We're grateful to the essential workers who kept the rest of our society functioning—again, risking their own health and well-being.

We're grateful to the Black Lives Matter protesters and other activists who once again took to the streets and the halls of power to protest the systemic racism embedded in our policing and judicial institutions.

We're grateful to the officials who pushed for fair and free elections, working tirelessly against a tide of antidemocratic rhetoric and policy to make voting accessible and to see that every vote was counted.

We're grateful to the researchers who developed the vaccines that would let us return to something approaching normalcy, and to all the organizations that have been striving to make those vaccines accessible to the whole world.

In the smaller milieu of our social pod, we're grateful to Kyle Niedzwiecki and Adrienne Lipoma for letting us take over the den for most of the summer lockdown so we could escape into Nadežra, and particularly to Adrienne, who gave the authors' egos some badly needed pats on the head as we threaded our way through a complicated draft. Thank you also to the players of The Path to Power—Kyle, Adrienne, Emily Dare, and Wendy Shaffer—for being patient with the game going on hiatus when writing and the world became too much to deal with. Thanks to all the friends and family who supported us virtually, and especially to Carlie St. George and Conna Condon for their comments on the draft.

The teams at Orbit and Orbit UK have been amazing to work with. Thank you to our editor, Priyanka Krishnan, for wanting more flirting and banter and for giving us the room to let the relationships flourish. Thanks to Ellen Wright and Nazia Khatun for all your work bringing the Rook & Rose series to the eyes of enthusiastic readers. Thanks to Nikki Massoud, Thomas Mis, and the rest of the audiobook team for putting together a cracking good read. Thanks to Tim Paul for a lovely fantasy map of our city, and to Lauren Panepinto and Nekro for the absolutely beautiful book and cover design.

Last but not least, many thanks to our agents, Eddie Schneider and Paul Stevens, for taking care of business so we can focus on the writing.

And finally, to anyone else we ought to thank, we plead the amnesia of 2020. We are grateful to you all.

Glossary

advocate: An individual licensed to conduct business within the Charterhouse, usually on behalf of a noble house.

alta/altan: The titles used for nobility who are not the heads of houses.

Argentet: One of the five seats in the Cinquerat, addressed as "Your Elegance." Argentet oversees the cultural affairs of the city, including theatres, festivals, and censorship of written materials.

aža: A drug made from powdered seeds. Although it is commonly spoken of as a hallucinogen, Vraszenians believe that aža allows them to see into Ažerais's Dream.

Ažerais's Dream: This place, called "the realm of mind" by inscriptors, is a many-layered reflection of the waking world, both as it was in the past, and as it may be metaphorically expressed in the present.

Ča: A title used when addressing a Vraszenian.

Caerulet: One of the five seats in the Cinquerat, addressed as "Your Mercy." Caerulet oversees the military affairs of the city, including prisons, fortifications, and the Vigil.

Ceremony of the Accords: A ritual commemorating the signing of the peace agreement that ended the war between the city-states of Vraszan and Nadežra, leaving the latter in the control of its Liganti nobility. The ceremony involves the ziemetse and the members of the Cinquerat, and takes place each year during the Night of Bells.

Charterhouse: The seat of Nadežra's government, where the Cinquerat offices are located.

Cinquerat: The five-member council that has been the ruling body of Nadežra since the death of the Tyrant. Each seat has its own sphere of responsibility. See *Argentet, Fulvet, Prasinet, Caerulet,* and *Iridet.*

clan: Vraszenians are traditionally divided into seven clans: the Anoškin, the Dvornik, the Ižranyi, the Kiraly, the Meszaros, the Stretsko, and the Varadi. The Ižranyi have been extinct for centuries, following a supernatural calamity. Each clan consists of multiple kretse.

era/eret: The titles used for the heads of noble houses.

Faces and Masks: In Vraszenian religion, the divine duality common to many faiths is seen as being contained within single deities, each of which has a benevolent aspect (the Face) and a malevolent one (the Mask).

Festival of Veiled Waters: A yearly festival occurring during the springtime in Nadežra, when fog covers the city for approximately a week.

Fulvet: One of the five seats in the Cinquerat, addressed as "Your Grace." Fulvet oversees the civic affairs of the city, including land ownership, public works, and the judiciary.

The Great Dream: A sacred event for Vraszenians, during which the Wellspring of Ažerais manifests in the waking world. It occurs once every seven years, during the Festival of Veiled Waters.

Illi: The numen associated with both 0 and 10 in numinatria. It represents beginnings, endings, eternity, the soul, and the inscriptor's self.

imbuing: A form of craft-based magic that has the effect of making objects function more effectively: an imbued blade cuts better and doesn't dull or rust, while an imbued cloak may be warmer, more waterproof, or more concealing. It is also possible, though more difficult, to imbue a performance.

inscriptor: A practitioner of numinatria.

Iridet: One of the five seats in the Cinquerat, addressed as "Your Worship." Iridet oversees the religious affairs of the city, including temples, numinatria, and the pilgrimage of the Great Dream.

Kaius Sifigno / Kaius Rex: See *The Tyrant*.

kanina: The "ancestor dance" of the Vraszenians, used on special occasions such as births, marriages, and deaths. When performed well enough, it has the power to call up the spirits of the dancers' ancestors from Ažerais's Dream.

knot: A term derived from Vraszenian custom for a street gang in Nadežra. Members mark their allegiance with a knotwork charm, though they are not required to wear or display it openly.

koszenie: A Vraszenian shawl that records an individual's maternal and paternal ancestry in the pattern of its embroidery. It is usually worn only for special occasions, including when performing the kanina.

kretse: (sing. kureč) A Vraszenian lineage, a subdivision of a clan. The third part of a traditional Vraszenian name marks the kureč an individual belongs to.

lihoše: (sing. lihosz) The Vraszenian term for a person born female, but taking on a male role so as to be able to lead his people. Lihoše patronymics end in the plural and gender-neutral "-ske." Their counterparts are the rimaše, born male but taking on a female role so as to become szorsas.

meda/mede: The titles used for members of delta houses.

The Night of Bells: A yearly festival commemorating the death of the Tyrant. It includes the Ceremony of the Accords.

Ninat: The numen associated with 9 in numinatria. It represents death, release, completion, apotheosis, and the boundary between the mundane and the infinite.

Noctat: The numen associated with 8 in numinatria. It represents sensation, sexuality, procreation, honesty, salvation, and repentance.

numina: (sing. numen) The numina are a series of numbers, 0–10, that are used in numinatria to channel magical power. They consist of Illi (which is both 0 and 10), Uniat, Tuat, Tricat, Quarat, Quinat, Sessat, Sebat, Noctat, and Ninat. Each numen has its own particular resonance with concepts such as family or death, as well as associated gods, colors, metals, geometric figures, and so forth.

numinatria: A form of magic based on sacred geometry. A work of numinatria is called a numinat (pl. numinata). Numinatria works by channeling power from the ultimate godhead, the Lumen, which manifests in the numina. In order to function, a numinat must have a focus, through which it draws on the power of the Lumen; most foci feature the name of a god, written in the ancient Enthaxn script.

pattern: In Vraszenian culture, "pattern" is a term for fate and the interconnectedness of things. It is seen as a gift from the ancestral goddess Ažerais, and can be understood through the interpretation of a pattern deck.

pattern deck: A deck currently consisting of sixty cards in three suits, called threads. The spinning thread represents the "inner self" (the mind and spirit), the woven thread represents the "outer self" (social relationships), and the cut thread represents the "physical self" (the body and the material world). Each thread contains both unaligned and aspect cards, the latter of which allude to the most important Faces and Masks in Vraszenian religion.

Prasinet: One of the five seats in the Cinquerat, addressed as "Your Charity." Prasinet oversees the economic affairs of the city, including taxation, trade routes, and guilds.

prismatium: An iridescent metal created through the use of numinatria, and associated with Sebat.

Quarat: The numen associated with 4 in numinatria. It represents nature, nourishment, growth, wealth, and luck.

Quinat: The numen associated with 5 in numinatria. It represents power, excellence, leadership, healing, and renewal.

rimaše: (sing. rimasz) The Vraszenian term for a person born male, but taking on a female role to act as a szorsa. Rimaše patronymics end in the plural and gender-neutral "-ske." Their counterparts are the lihoše, born female but taking on male roles to lead their people.

Sebat: The numen associated with 7 in numinatria. It represents craftsmanship, purity, seclusion, transformation, and perfection in imperfection.

Sessat: The numen associated with 6 in numinatria. It represents order, stasis, institutions, simplicity, and friendship.

soul: In Vraszenian cosmology, the soul has three parts: the dlakani or "personal" soul, the szekani or "knotted" soul, and the čekani or "bodily" soul. After death, the dlakani goes to paradise or hell, the szekani lives on in Ažerais's Dream, and the čekani reincarnates. In Liganti cosmology, the soul ascends through the numina to the Lumen, then descends once more to reincarnate.

sun/earth: Contrasting terms used for many purposes in Liganti culture. The sun hours run from 6 a.m. to 6 p.m.; the earth hours run from 6 p.m. to 6 a.m. Sun-handed is right-handed, and earth-handed is left-handed. Sunwise and earthwise mean clockwise and counterclockwise, or when referring to people, a man born female or a woman born male.

szorsa: A reader of a pattern deck.

Tricat: The numen associated with 3 in numinatria. It represents stability, family, community, completion, rigidity, and reconciliation.

Tuat: The numen associated with 2 in numinatria. It represents the other, duality, communication, connection, opposition, and the inscriptor's edge.

The Tyrant: Kaius Sifigno, also called Kaius Rex. He was a Liganti commander who conquered all of Vraszan, but according to legend his further spread was stopped by him succumbing to his various desires. Reputed to be unkillable, the Tyrant was supposedly brought down by venereal disease. His death is celebrated on the Night of Bells.

Uniat: The numen associated with 1 in numinatria. It represents the body, self-awareness, enlightenment, containment, and the inscriptor's chalk.

The Vigil: The primary force of law and order within Nadežra, nicknamed "hawks" after their emblem. Separate from the city-state's army, the Vigil polices the city itself, under the leadership of a high commander who answers to Caerulet. Their headquarters is the Aerie.

Vraszan: The name of the region and loose confederation of city-states of which Nadežra was formerly a part.

Wellspring of Ažerais: The holy site around which the city of Nadežra was founded. The wellspring exists within Ažerais's Dream, and only manifests in the waking world during the Great Dream. Drinking its waters grants a true understanding of pattern.

ziemetse: (sing. ziemič) The leaders of the Vraszenian clans, also referred to as "clan elders." Each has a title taken from the name of their clan: the Anoškinič, Dvornič, Kiralič, Meszarič, Stretskojič, Varadič, and (formerly) Ižranjič.

extras

orbit

meet the author

Photo Credit: John Scalzi

M. A. CARRICK is the joint pen name of Marie Brennan (author of the Memoirs of Lady Trent) and Alyc Helms (author of the Adventures of Mr. Mystic). The two met in 2000 on an archaeological dig in Wales and Ireland—including a stint in the town of Carrickmacross—and have built their friendship through two decades of anthropology, writing, and gaming. They live in the San Francisco Bay Area.

Find out more about M. A. Carrick and other Orbit authors by registering for the free monthly newsletter at orbitbooks.net.

if you enjoyed

THE LIAR'S KNOT

look out for

BOOK THREE OF THE ROOK & ROSE TRILOGY

by

M. A. Carrick

extras

Ossiter's, Eastbridge

After so many years of desperation, misery, and loss, Donaia was hardly certain what to do with happiness.

Or, for that matter, with dancing. "Rusty" did not begin to describe her skills: In the middle of a set, she missed her cue to cast off and had to scramble out of the way of the pair of dancers hurtling up the set. Rather than try to find her place again, she ducked and dodged to the safety of the mingling crowd, chuckling at the thought of how Leato would tease her for abandoning her partner.

And she *could* laugh. Memories of her lost son were everywhere, always... but now she was trying to take joy in them instead of letting her heart remain mired in sorrow. Giuna had come of age; the guests had gathered at Ossiter's for a belated celebration of her natal day and her elevation to the position of heir to House Traementis.

Donaia let her gaze sweep the atrium, marveling at the crowd. Only five months since Renata's adoption, where the silence of the Tricatium had almost swallowed the bare scattering of people who attended; now that scattering had multiplied like silken scarves in the hands of a street performer. Even Octale Contorio, recently released from the Dockwall Prison, was there, regaling a small cluster of people with the poetry he'd written during his captivity. All the noble houses had sent guests, as had a triple handful of delta gentry families.

Almost all the noble houses, she amended. Not a single member of House Acrenix was present; Faella Coscanum had made it clear they were no longer welcome in polite society. Without a word of explanation as to why... But given that Ghiscolo Acrenix was dead, his putative heir Sibiliat was at the family's bay villa "for her health," and his adoptive mother Carinci had succeeded him as the head of their house, there was more than enough fodder for rumors. The most widespread one held that Sibiliat had murdered her father—but if that were true, wouldn't the Cinquerat have put her on trial?

Scaperto Quientis appeared in her view, one fluted glass in each hand. "I wasn't certain if you would need fortification or refreshment," he said, holding them both out.

Brushing flyaway wisps of hair from her face, Donaia waved off the wine and reached for the chilled lemon water. "No drinking for me tonight; I wouldn't want to put you through a repeat of our adoption ball. Nobody likes caring for a drunk."

"I didn't mind," Scaperto said, sipping the wine she'd refused.

Despite the cool glass in her hand, warmth spread through Donaia. At first she hadn't been sure how to interpret Scaperto's kindness: whether it was merely friendship for a grieving woman, or something more. But the days she spent at his villa had not only lessened the weight on her heart, they had cleared the fog from her eyes, too. While she wasn't quite ready yet for more than friendship, that shore was in sight. And she trusted that Scaperto would wait there until she arrived.

Renata swirled past in a rush of amethyst silk and embroidered cobalt dragonflies, light on her feet in the arms of Ucozzo Extaquium. Sureggio's recent suicide might have sent Parma Extaquium into mourning seclusion, but the rest of their house was happy to go on enjoying themselves as usual. Another thing for the rumormongers to chew on, given the close timing of Sureggio's death and Ghiscolo's.

Donaia savored the lemon water and tried to banish those thoughts. *You're looking for trouble where there is none. Can't you just be happy?*

Scaperto said, "I'm sure Faella knows."

To anyone else, it might have seemed like a non sequitur, but the two of them had been speculating for weeks. Despite Scaperto's seat in the Cinquerat, he knew no more about Ghiscolo's death than Donaia did. The lack galled him, and understandably so.

Sighing, Donaia said, "Of all the times for that gossiping old seagull to close her beak."

"Era!" Scaperto feigned shock at her rudeness, but clinked his glass against hers. "Every time I try to draw her out, she just turns her attention to the question of who will fill the empty seat. I know you refused it, but might a member of your house be willing? Nothing in the law says Cinquerat members *have* to be the heads of their houses."

As if he meant any old member, and not one in particular. A flash of amethyst caught her gaze; the dance was bringing her niece near again. Donaia could at least rescue the girl from Ucozzo's wandering hands. "Renata!"

Too late, she realized the pairs had shifted and Renata's partner was no longer Ucozzo. With a laugh and a courtly bow, Derossi Vargo led her off the floor. The two of them promenaded over to Donaia and Scaperto as if they were still dancing, and Renata dropped into a curtsy as she arrived. A year in Nadežra hadn't softened her crisp Seterin accent, but her tone was playful as she said, "You called?"

Donaia gestured with her lemon water. "Scaperto is considering tossing you into Ninat's maw. Do you want to refuse him yourself, or shall I do so for you?"

That set him sputtering. "I meant no such thing! I only thought—"

"That two Caerulets have died in the past year, so why not replace them with someone with incredible luck?"

The accusation carried an edge Donaia hadn't intended. But after losing so much to the curse on House Traementis, it didn't take much to make her worry. Renata was responsible for so much of the house's recovery; Donaia only wished she could repay her niece somehow.

But that would require her to know what Renata wanted. And that, in turn, might require *Renata* to know. For all her unshakable facade of confidence, sometimes it felt like the girl clung to her Traementis duties to give her purpose. She'd resisted Giuna's repeated suggestion that she could remain heir for a while longer, but in the absence of that guiding rudder, Donaia worried her niece might simply . . . drift away.

Renata's laugh carried an edge of its own. "I'm afraid I'd be very ill-suited for the Caerulet seat. I know nothing of military matters."

"Very few of us do," Donaia said. "Indestor had that seat for generations, and they granted very few charters outside their own control."

"House Coscanum holds one," Vargo mused.

Scaperto cleared his throat. "Yes, well. Naldebris doesn't want the seat. And I hope you won't take offense, Eret Vargo, that the Cinquerat is not considering you for it, either."

Donaia expected a sharp reply, but was surprised when Vargo looked like he was suppressing a full-body shudder. "That saves me having to find a polite way to say no."

Renata touched the watered silk of his sleeve, and Vargo flashed her a brief expression that was more grimace than smile. It seemed the cursed reputation that seat had acquired was enough to dampen even *his* ambition.

A small commotion at the door pulled Donaia's attention away from the conversation. She'd rented the entirety of Ossiter's for tonight—only her guests were permitted in—and one of the footmen was blocking a pair of people from entering.

"Excuse me," Donaia said, and hurried across the atrium.

Grey Serrado snapped her a very correct bow when she approached, as crisp as if he were still a captain of the Vigil. His sister-in-law, Alinka, stood in his shadow, half ready to retreat back out the door.

Donaia stepped around the footman and took Alinka's arm in her own. To the footman she said, "What do you think you're doing, interfering with my invited guests?"

The footman's bow was every bit as correct as Serrado's. "My apologies, era. It was a misunderstanding."

He wasn't bold enough to say to her face that he assumed any Vraszenians ought to be using the servants' door—even though Grey wore a fine coat of heather-grey wool, with a sword belted to his hip, and Alinka was in the pale blue surcoat and cream under-dress Donaia had gifted to her. "Come with me," Donaia said, dismissing the footman with a pointed sniff, and led the pair into the atrium.

Fortunately she spotted Renata's maid Tess, helping to re-pin Giuna's hair. Donaia had hardly seen her daughter all evening: With Sibiliat Acrenix and her dubious attentions removed from the field, quite a few prospective suitors were eager to parade themselves before the new heir.

But at heart, Giuna was still the girl who had spent most of her childhood mewed up in the manor of a dwindling family, with very few people to call friend. She had no compunctions about hugging Grey, exclaiming, "You came!"

He returned the hug, but then stepped back and bowed. "Of course, alta. We couldn't miss your celebration."

She swatted his arm. "Why so formal? If anybody takes offense at you skipping the courtesies, I'll just have you duel them."

Giving him a long-term contract as their house duelist had been Renata's idea. They didn't need one nearly as badly as they had in past years, when they couldn't afford to hire one in the first place, but it was a kindness after he quit the Vigil. Donaia only wished she'd thought of it first. She still remembered the starveling boy who'd shown up on her doorstep with his older brother, begging for work. A nearly familial friendship had grown between him and Leato, despite the differences in their stations, and she felt more than a little affection for him herself.

Grey said mildly, "I'd prefer not to mar the night with swords. Alta Renata."

Donaia hadn't noticed her niece approaching. Renata nodded to Grey, then turned and said, "Giuna, Orrucio Amananto was looking for you."

"Oh, *please* no," Giuna moaned. "Nothing against Orrucio—but if I don't rest, I'll collapse!"

"If the alta would like to sit," Tess said, gesturing at an empty chair set in front of one of the atrium's planters, "I could pretend there's something wrong with your hem. That should give you a moment to breathe."

Giuna plunked herself onto the chair with obvious relief. Alinka perched nervously on another one as Tess produced a needle and thread from somewhere, then knelt to work her magic.

Grey said, "Era, altas, would any of you like some wine?"

"Yes, please," Giuna said as the other two waved the offer away. He bowed and departed. In his absence—and with Derossi Vargo not there to make things awkward—Donaia nudged Renata and nodded toward the dance floor. "You've been nearly as busy tonight as Giuna. I don't suppose anyone has particularly caught your eye?"

Amused, Renata said, "Matchmaking, are you?"

"It's an old woman's privilege and duty to try and pair the young off well. While I may not be your mother, given Letilia's failings, how can I not try to make up the lack?" Donaia's former sister-in-law was still off in Seteris, enjoying life with some foreign nobleman, likely never giving a thought to her—

A strangled sound came from Renata, and then the high vault of the atrium rang with a voice that twenty-four years were not enough to scrub from Donaia's mind.

"My *darling* daughter! At last, we are reunited!"

Donaia went cold. *A nightmare. We've all been pulled into that dream realm again, and my worst nightmare is coming true.*

But no: She was awake. This was reality.

And that was Letilia Viraudacis—formerly Traementis—posed with arms wide in the grand entrance of Ossiter's.

Follow us:

f **/orbitbooksUS**

🐦 **/orbitbooks**

▶ **/orbitbooks**

Join our mailing list
to receive alerts on our
latest releases and deals.

orbitbooks.net

Enter our monthly
giveaway for the chance
to win some epic prizes.

orbitloot.com